Summer Never Comes

by
Gregory Sledd

© 2011 by Gregory Sledd
All rights reserved.
sleddwe4@sbcglobal.net

*Dedicated to
My Mom and Dad*

This book is fiction.
Similarities between the story,
real events and real people is coincidence.

Thanks to
Carol McFerris and Jose Villanueva
for their work on the front cover,
Aaron Polson for formatting

Chapter One

ON TIME for his meeting, Paul Roberts walked into the *Daily Illini's* basement offices. A decent number of students pecked at typewriters, talked on the phones or studied rolls of negatives tacked to the light box. He traded hellos with two staffers discussing the break-in at SOAP's, the Student Organization Advocating Peace, headquarters. Stan Laundry wasn't certain what was stolen, Ollie Harding mentioned smashed filing cabinets. In the background, wire service teletype machines click-clacked out the news.

"Come in," Editor-in-Chief Stef Tianen pointed to her desk. "Did you summer well?"

"I worked at a golf course until Labor Day," Paul matter-of-factly answered, "and came down last week."

"You should try Champaign-Urbana for the summer. With so few students, the feel's totally different from the school year; park a car anywhere, have the Quad to yourself, some bars are only open on weekends." She settled her heavy body into the wooden chair. "Of course, the heat and humidity are awful; the temperature hit ninety-six degrees four days straight in July. Believe it or not, I enrolled in a PE course, beginning tennis, afternoons one to three, fry city."

"I know you're into exercise, but that's over the top."

Stef bounced a racquet ball on her desk. "Can you realize we're seniors? Three years ago when our parents dumped us off, who'd have thought we'd go this far? Got any plans for after June in the real world?"

"I'll sign up for Commerce Placement Office interviews, but that's down the agenda." Paul shifted in his chair. Why discuss graduation in September, he worried.

"Well, with your grades snagging job offers from those big eight accounting firms will be a breeze, if that's your goal." She was complimentary, aware of Paul's serious study habits and high GPA. A staffer laughed and the teletype bell clanged.

"How about you?"

"Journalism grad school's a possibility," Stef switched to her businesslike voice. "But before graduation, we seniors have a newspaper to manage. One new project I've planned is a Saturday magazine: features on the Big U's uniquer aspects, more in-depth articles than what we write during the week, short fiction, poetry, commentary to make our fellow students think instead of drinking away reality until Mondays roll around."

"I've heard about this idea around the office, but is it sensible? Weekend disgustingness is what counts with us undergrads."

"Check the calendar, there are more activities than beers in the bars or booking in the Library. How many movies are shown on Saturday nights, or plays at the Krannert Center, Star Course concerts, religious services at the Newman Center?"

"Okay, I yield, intellectuality continues and the *Daily Illini* should report those events. What's your magazine's title?"

"That's undecided. Where you're involved is fact finding. Outline, structure, what we'll write instead of our last-minute, 'who-in-hell-knows what's in tomorrow's edition' confusion we stumble through. You know the kind of stuff I mean, right?" Irked by Paul's half-heartedness, the editor-in-chief handed him a piece of paper. "And you'll have chances for a byline; it's time you received some credit since our days are becoming short. Here're some subjects."

> A. How bad are the bars ripping off students with beer prices? Is 50¢ a glass outrageous? What about the 'plastic cups replacing glasses' rumor?
> B. Student fashions - Why have we punted on dressing up since the early '60s?
> C. The Slush Fund - Has the Athletic Association reformed, or is the scandal still hurting the university?
> D. Registering for the semester - Why must students run around to dozens of tables in the Armory to add or drop courses?
> E. The Big U and year-round Champaign-Urbana residents: love-hate or does everybody co-exist?

Summer Never Comes

From Paul's frown, Stef saw her list was a letdown. "Besides these, we can review any other suggestions the staff formulates."

"How about the school's budget, which curricula receive the most funding, and what happens if Springfield stops sending us the taxpayers' bucks? Or profile the black students, why are there so few?" Now Paul was creating. "Here's a better one. The anti-war groups, SOAP, RAW, SCRAP, DISGUST, whoever else—let's probe the demonstrators. What are the reasons there're so many; do they have parallel strategies? We could research their origins, I wonder if anyone remembers how the Champaign-Urbana peace movement started?"

"Where's a relevant story in that? All things have more than one; females, males, devils and saints, Republicans, Democrats. As for Vietnam, with Nixon in the White House, God knows there's plenty to protest."

Paul intuited his editor-in-chief's ambiguity. "Who's heading up the magazine?"

"Al Stojak, and coordinate with him after thinking through this format." The interview over, Stef stood. "But don't take long; we have a paper to publish."

Paul was disappointed. Not that he favored muckraking, he didn't. But features on beer prices or students' clothes sounded peripheral, too adolescent, too typically undergrad; he'd hoped for more substance. Regardless of the editor-in-chief stressing investigation, from experience Paul knew the magazine would wind up being shallow. Excepting anti-war editorials, Stef's *Daily Illini* avoided controversies.

Stef was satisfied that practical Paul would come around; confident he'd pitch in with his prudent, examine-every-detail approach. That was Paul, focusing on hum-drum specifics and number crunching. He'd accept the assignment, the *DI's* magazine would receive well-written copy, and the editor-in-chief would look smart.

Their ponderings and the office's calm were disrupted by the teletype's clack-clack-clack. Stef's newspaper instincts held her by the doorway as Stan and Ollie walked to the machines. Stan read the dispatches, tracing the words with one finger.

"Holy Jesus."

The teletype clinked a second bulletin and the editor-in-chief rushed over.

Summer Never Comes

Associated Press - Saigon - At 10:38 EST, United States Army Headquarters confirmed that a massive assault by United States and South Vietnamese troops has struck in the Laotian province of Muong Nong. One American regiment and four South Vietnamese battalions comprise the attacking forces. Army HQ describes 'encouraging progress being made toward the objectives.'

Reuters - Saigon - US Army Headquarters reports the primary objective of Operation Loading Dock was achieved with the capture of Ban Nabo. United States and ARVN forces are now advancing northwest toward the town of Sepone. Moderate Communist resistance is reported.

Stef stepped away, reviewed the press releases and, eying Paul, was hit with an 'editor-in-chief inspiration.'

"You were right, here's the assignment. Contact and follow up with the peace groups. Gauge their reactions, I'll bet my tennis racquet RAW, DISGUST and that guy Bernard Minerath will speak out. Like I said, it's time you moved out front for a change, shared in the glory." Wrapping an arm around Paul's shoulder, Stef's brain pulsed an uh-oh, what-have-I-done, I-should-have-thought-this-through alarm. But her friend spoke and the warning ebbed.

"I accept. Publicity for the anti-war groups makes sense, and who am I to question my boss?" Surprised by Stef's enthusiasm for a topic she'd dismissed twenty minutes earlier, Paul was more astonished at his own luck standing next to her when she reconsidered. This is worthwhile, he thought, an opportunity for the *Daily Illini* and a decent project for me for this year. But her remark, 'out front for a change,' what did that mean? When Stef removed her arm, Paul felt a twitch, whether physical or mental, he couldn't figure. I'll keep cautious, he thought.

CBS News - Saigon - The Pentagon reports a strong North Vietnamese counterattack underway in Muong Mong province, apparently intended to sever United States and ARVN troops from their South Vietnamese bases.

UPI - Radio Hanoi has denounced Operation Loading Dock as 'blatant Imperialist belligerence threatening to world peace. Once

Summer Never Comes

again, America demonstrates its fondness for aggression against freedom loving peoples. As always, America will receive what it deserves: reversal and defeat on the battlefield, omens of its losing the Indochina war.'

# # # #

An orange and blue frisbee flew in from Fraternity Park, bounced on the KIDs' patio and spun to the wall. Bill Lindner grabbed the plastic disc and tossed a perfect floater.

"Still got the ol' touch," a grinning Lindy twanged his guitar.

"See the sign on the bulletin board?"

"The one Caker posted about his New Student Week BYO party?"

"You mean BYOBB and D."

"Is Jethro Tull performing at the Big U this semester?"

"I heard a Moody Blues concert the beginning of November."

"No, Sly and the Family Stones."

"That'll be the day those frickin' bastards show. They've canceled on four gigs in the last two years. I was at Assembly Hall last time; must've been five thousand of us there that night and we must've waited three hours before giving up."

Members of Kappa Iota Delta fraternity, nicknamed KIDs two decades ago, relaxed outside their house. Twelve or fifteen upperclassmen lounged on the frat's metal furniture plus the boxy, brown couch they'd dragged from the living room. Moose Wozniak racked on the concrete by the double doors and his roommate, one-armed Dave 'Ozark' Pollard, slouched by him. All the brothers wore cut-offs and sandals but no shirts; even this late in the summer, working on their tans was basic. Half smoked cigarettes, a couple drank their day's first beers. Humid south winds rustled the trees, and Nemo's primo stereo with the eight inch woofers blasted 'Honky Tonk Woman' from the second floor.

In Frat Park, teams from two Greek houses practiced for the intramural football season; an impromptu volleyball game without a net went on near Chalmers Street; a trio of sunbathing, topless coeds laid on their stomachs on a blanket, and a biker cautiously maneuvered her ten-speed between the students and the trees.

Summer Never Comes

"Scooter and Lauren?"

"They're around; shackin' up in her apartment."

"What about Stu? Did he really flunk out?"

"Saw him a month ago at a White Sox game. He passed a summer school adolescent psych course with a B-minus, respectable enough to make it back to Champaign."

"What does BYOBB & D stand for?"

"Bring your own booze, broads and dope."

"How about Billy Powell?"

"I got a letter from him right before returnin' to Champaign," Lindy replied, "he bought the whole bunch of bananas, drafted a week after graduation. Billy wrote his ticket for 'Nam's stamped and copied in triplicate."

Ozark leaned on a door. "What'd he say about training camp?"

"Sucks worse than Computer Science 105. And it's boot camp, not training camp, he's in the Army, you know, not the Boy Scouts."

The breeze calmed, the brothers remembered their friend, and for five minutes there were no movements or noises from the trees in Frat Park or the KIDs.

A business major, Billy Powell had taken four years of finance, marketing and econ courses, accumulating a decent—though unremarkable—grade point average. He had an interest in accounting procedures for non-profit organizations, but not enough of one to concentrate in this field. Billy attended classes during the week, sometimes booked on weekends, and didn't belong to any clubs or extracurricular activities. After his two o'clocks he loved sitting in the Second Chance Bar with his girlfriend, Nancy Kissel. The pair drank beers, smoked Marlboros, listened to Three Dog Night records on the jukebox, and offhandedly joshed about marriage. During football season, Billy cheered for the Fighting Illini on Saturdays and watched Butkus and the Chicago Bears on Sunday afternoon. He roomed with Lindy one semester, who nicknamed him 'Rot,' a contraction for 'Carrot Top,' on account of Billy's red, curly hair. As a sophomore, the year the KIDs nearly upset Delta Tau Delta for the intramural football championship, Billy started at linebacker and broke up a pass in the title game's first half to save a touchdown. He sat out his junior and senior years, though, due to sore ankles and the fact that Tim

Summer Never Comes

O'Toole was quicker at the position. Billy's most memorable U of I moment had come two springs ago, during the Amazing Streaking Craze when, wearing only white socks and black tennis shoes, he'd led a dozen brothers across Frat Park to troop through the Phi Sigma Delta house. Hustling back in the rain, Billy tripped and tumbled into a gigantic mud puddle next to the patio.

In short, Billy Powell was one of many laid-back KIDs, racking until noon, digging happy hours in the bars with his buddies, doing laundry maybe once a month, and rolling in the sheets with Nancy. He was content with college, at ease in Champaign-Urbana, unconcerned about tomorrow.

Vietnam and the new draft law derailed Billy's and thousands more teenagers' futures.

Seven years of fire fights in the jungles, napalming and carpet bombing by the Air Force, raiding the Ho Chi Minh trail, ambushes in Cambodia and Laos, suicides by Buddhist priests, coup d'état in Saigon. POWs and MIAs, fifty-three thousand casualties, flag-covered coffins, murder, massacre, used-up lives—all had slipped by but none was enough to take the United States out of the war. Hundreds of millions of dollars wasted, fears, frustrations, dissent, draft-dodgers burning their draft cards, and conscientious objectors running to Canada. Riots and near-rebellion broadcast on television, a tragic national election, hypocrisy and lies by two-faced politicians, the pigheaded stubbornness of hawks and doves. Bogged down, fed up with 'Nam, exhausted, unnerved, an America rarely yielding to sanity.

One concession was reforming the Selective Service System.

Early in Nixon's administration the biased, arcane, hometown-run draft boards were abolished, replaced with a national lottery for all eighteen-year-olds—a scheme exposing everyone to the same risk of Army conscription. The first drawing was a televised event using a mammoth glass bowl filled with 366 ping pong ball-like capsules, each with a date inside, and a big piece of paper on the wall with lines numbered from one to 366. The balls were pulled from the bowl and the dates were written on the sheet beginning at line one. Low numbers, up to 122, were sure to be drafted while the highest third, above 245, were gratefully, gleefully safe. The middle birthdays, between 123 and 244, remained in doubt—a twilight zone, dependent on the war's successes and setbacks, and the manpower the Army demanded to fight it. All males gambled with their numbers in the draft pool for twelve

Summer Never Comes

months, endured at age nineteen or delayed for countless reasons, college deferments the most popular. Once out of school, graduates, like everyone else, went into the pool.

In the first lottery a winter ago, Billy Powell's birthday, April twenty-fourth, was drawn from the big jar in front of the camera as number two. No hopes, no appeals, no luck. With graduation, what waited was basic training and a year's tour of duty in Vietnam.

On that December evening, with hundreds of fellow University of Illinois students having low numbers and abruptly bleak futures, Billy headed to the Red Lion Inn to get wildly, heinously, the furthest-edge-of-hell drunk. Dozens of buddies from KIDs, his business major friends, hangers-on sniffing a party and Nancy accompanied him—his girlfriend hugging his arm the whole night, smiling, outwardly as blasé as usual, but in her heart deathly worried for Billy. The whole crowd was pushed along to disgustingness by the Lion's bartenders, who decided these hose-jobbed, not-a-prayer, gonna-be-drafted bastards deserved all the freebie pitchers they could knock back. No one recalled a gathering so bizarre—so much socializing and drinking without celebration or fun. After hundreds of chugged beers, clouds of cigarette smoke, hours of arguing politics with pals and strangers, lousy music from the band on stage and a brawl around the pinball machines nobody understood why, after years of miseries and regrets, the country was still in a war in Asia. "We should say the whole thing's a mistake, enough Americans have died, we're finished, we're leaving." The logic seemed a no-brainer to the KIDs, but they knew it would never happen. The United States—at least the cabal controlling the government—wasn't so rational.

At last call, when the evening ended, the hundreds of inebriates in the Lion staggered past Billy to shake his hand, everybody cussing, saying what a goddamned shame it was he'd been so screwed. Billy Powell promised the KIDs and Nancy he'd return for Homecoming someday.

# # # #

Lindy and Paul Roberts, roommates and brothers in Kappa Iota Delta, walked down Gregory Hall's marble steps and into the thousands of fellow students experiencing Quad Day.

Summer Never Comes

The Quad was the campus' central mall, a grassy park running south to north, a fourth of a mile long by a football field wide, surrounded on all four sides by low, horizontal university buildings. Lincoln Hall and Noyes Lab were aged, from the turn of the century. The Tudor-style English Building was the prettiest, the Administration the boxiest, the old Auditorium dilapidated, the Foreign Languages Building the most modern, looking mistakenly erected upside down. The Illini Union occupied the north end, the original half dating from the 1940s and funded by New Deal money.

For Quad Day, booths, tents and tables lined the criss-crossing walkways, occupied by campus and community organizations marketing their messages to students. This year's groups included Star Course, Students for McGovern, the Ag Club, WPGU-FM, Atius-Sachem, the Mathematics Library, Willard Airport, Undergraduates for Muskie, the antiwar group DISGUST—Disengage International Suicidal Gestures under Student Terms—McKinley Hospital and the Wheelchair Illini. In addition to milling undergrads checking the displays, hundreds more relaxed in the glaring sunshine in the Quad's middle—alone or in circles, drinking beers, smoking dope and skateboarding through the crowds. Upperclassmen, with their carefree, we've-already-taken-this-stuff-in approach, meandered about, indifferent to the advertising but definitely attracted to students of the other sex.

Close to Lincoln Hall, the two KIDs listened to screaming extremists from RAW, Radicals Against War, and watched them prop up their decrepit, tilting-to-one-side, card table.

"Out of Vietnam, now! We should've never been in!"

"Nuke DC, not Hanoi!"

"Stick it into Tricky Dick, he's humped our asses for years!"

"Draft beer, not teenagers!"

"One, two, three, four, we don't want this goddamned war!"

"Think we'll make the Union?"

"I hope so, Lindy," Paul replied, "I need a meal."

"Good being back down here, isn't it, Robby, part of the ol' student body again? Bless 'em all, eh?" Unlike the universal 'Lindy,' the nickname 'Robby' was only used by Paul's close friends in KIDs.

"Yes, only I wish most of these students were somewhere else so I could eat lunch." They stopped, unable to walk because of the mob surrounding the 'Truths about Marijuana' display neighboring the Pom Pom Squad exhibition.

"Hold your horses, buddy, we'll get there. God, look at these women, I love it." Lindy's right hand patted his roommate's shoulder while the other cradled his acoustic guitar. "Tell me, is this the second year we've held a Quad Day?"

"Third; when we were freshman was the only time there wasn't one." The two broke into the clear at the next booth, the Independent Campus Republicans for Nixon-Agnew.

"Figures. How'd we survive that first semester without this?"

"Which was why the deal was begun, because we barely didn't." Laughing, the friends passed SOAP's presentation, their leader, Laurie Allman, distributing her latest twenty-four page pamphlet entitled *Physio-Psychotic Uncertainties of Wars and Conflicts on Indigenous East Central Asian Peoples*. Paul took a copy.

"Could be right. Of course, you probably had this entire place eyeballed the first day you showed up. Like the corn and soybeans surrounding our campus, you've always had your feet planted on the ground."

"What a line, you know I couldn't stand Champaign three years ago." The roommates were next to the English Building, halfway between the old Auditorium and the Illini Union.

"What about Urbana? That actually is the town we're strollin' in," Lindy grinned.

"Smart ass."

"Well, you lived in a dormitory back then, what'd you expect?"

"The trouble wasn't the dorms." Paul stared toward a lonely student standing on the English Building's second floor.

His mind thought back to freshman year, to the Thursday of that New Student Week when he'd moved into Peabody Hall. Through his window, Paul had watched weather totally different than today's—overcast and rainy with the temperature chilly enough that he wished the heat was working or he could ask someone to turn it on. Paul wanted to change out of his cut-offs and into a pair of jeans but, since he hadn't unpacked and hung his clothes in the closet, couldn't find his long pants. Cold down here, Paul recalled thinking. The wind blew through the window panes making the room freezing. The showers started again and nobody was outside on the sidewalks. Paul had come down to the University of Illinois from his parents' home in Hazelcrest by himself; he didn't have friends or recognize anyone, and didn't know the roommate assigned by the Student Housing Service. Tom Bordenkircher was from Quincy; he was tall, hulking, and weighed twice as much as Paul. Tom was around campus buying books and Paul had locked the door when he left to keep strangers out. Even with the light on, the dorm room was dark. With a sore throat and aching back, he didn't feel well. No friends, chilly, sick, missing his long pants, Paul sniffled.

"We both handled life back then and here we are now, seniors; we navigated the course all the way—take the money and run." Interrupting Paul's memories with a second shoulder slap, Lindy shook his head, his long, blonde hair sweeping in the wind. "You know, they should arrange an affair like this for us after we graduate, a get-to-know-the-real-world-before-you-get-out-there event. Yeah, that's the ticket."

"Who would come to it?"

"Lots of people, my mother for one." Lindy spotted a gorgeous coed. Giggling, he gestured to the girl, pointing out Paul with his guitar. "Oh, Robby, that one there, the braless babe wearin' the paisley shorts, she's yours. Hey, hey, hold on, I think she's checkin' you out."

"You're insane. Besides, June afternoons are too hot to spend wandering around whatever kind of 'Real World Day' you're imagining."

"No worse than in September." The pair weaved through more undergrad mobs, Lindy leading and Paul following. "And that could change; the weather's known to turn cold down here."

Cold down here. Paul was so lonely that first New Student Week, and his freshman year that he'd wanted to quit—thought real hard about leaving school, though he never talked to anyone about it, not his roommate or his parents. Paul was afraid being in college away from home, but more frightened to confess and give up. Nowhere to run, he was stuck.

But because Champaign-Urbana with its thirty-three thousand students is a curious sanctuary with a motivating, laid-back, hippie culture—an earnest, hilarious, intense, frivolous experience—and because Paul had to attend classes, study in the libraries, stand in cafeteria lines, use the laundry room, wash up in the john and buy stuff in Campustown, he made friends. In spite of his timid, drawn-into-himself personality, somehow college came together—the pluses and disappointments, good times and letdowns.

Summer Never Comes

Fighting Illini football was his earliest stepping out. Paul had never been to a huge place like Memorial Stadium with crowds of forty thousand people, orange and blue, the Marching Illini and cheerleaders, tailgating and school spirit for a bad team. Hanging with the guys from Peabody Hall was okay too, though after the games they headed straight to the bars—too awkward for Paul because in his freshman year he was still learning to drink beer.

Another pastime his first semester was the Newspaper Library, a collection of thousands of editions of papers and periodicals dating back a century or more. Located off the underground hallway between the Main Library Building and the Undergrad, Paul had accidentally discovered this place one night when hunting for a bathroom. Returning, he read about the British general election of 1874 in an oversized volume of the *London Times*, and the next week glanced through 1963 copies of the *Champaign News-Gazette*. Though an accounting major, Paul was intrigued with studying the past and had enrolled in three history courses as electives. He also found a friend, Anne Marie Curry, a *Daily Illini* reporter using the Newspaper Library to research her stories. An outgoing Annie coaxed Paul into joining the *DI's* staff, where he met another freshman, Stephanie Tianen.

At the paper he was the gofer for routine assignments. In his sophomore year he was a photographer covering intramurals, mainly football. His best picture was a shot of two players, a receiver and a defender at the goal line jumping in the air, grabbing for the ball. A split-second before the catch, with the football between and above their heads and arms, Paul snapped the shutter, his timing so on the mark that from this photo either player could have caught the ball—a really great picture lauded by the *Daily Illini's* reporters. But this job didn't last. Some hotshot freshman with a car trunk full of equipment, who'd taken photography courses at a Catholic high school in Chicago, joined the paper and pushed him out. Paul stayed on as a researcher, assisting others with their articles. He had minimal interest in being a feature writer—going out on his own, finding a story and following through.

"Like I said, no steamier than September. And my mom would come to the 'Get to Know the Real World Expo.'" Lindy again waved to the braless coed.

Summer Never Comes

"Now it's an expo?" Paul shoved back. "And what would your girlfriend say if she saw you gawking at these women; what if Emily were somewhere out here right now? You'd be in trouble without even realizing."

"Just joshin', havin' a bit of frolic." Squeezing his guitar with both arms, Lindy checked out the World Heritage Museum Volunteers display. "Em's my true love, I wouldn't commit any sin to upset her; she's too gentle a person for any hijinks."

"And too sweet for you," Paul kidded.

"No doubt, Robby. Where in the heck is this World Heritage Museum, anyway?"

"Fourth floor of Lincoln Hall," Paul pointed toward the building. "When you organize your 'Senior Day Expo,' or whatever you're naming it, one thing you should have is an all-the-places-on-this-campus-students-never-visited-but-should-have map."

"Not bad, I'll position it right next to the 'all-the-facts-we-need-about-the-real-world' kiosk."

"The what?"

"The spot containin' the info about what to expect when we're finished with the Big U."

"That's one table I'll pass on; I'm waiting as long as I can before learning that stuff. We've got another whole school year to get through first." Paul's mood returned to the lonely student in the English Building and his Peabody Hall window. "And who says we'll make it? We might fail one or two courses and have to repeat a semester."

"No way, buddy, both of us have sack schedules this autumn. Anyway, your grade point's so high you'd have to sleep in the whole year to flunk out. Why do that?"

"Because we have plenty going for us here. Why give up and leave? There's no sense wanting school over with."

"It's not quitting, Robby, but this all ends in June."

"How come?"

"First, we're gettin' older, life changes—we don't stay the same; people become involved in different things. You may be an accountant but you've had a history course or two, right? The world, countries, societies develop as years and decades pass. Progress goes on all the time, everywhere, for everyone, whether it's decent or dreadful." For security, Lindy gripped his guitar, hoping he wasn't panicking his roommate.

"Second, there's the 'our generation' thing. Look at us, we're enrolled in college but how did we get here? My grandparents—yours too—were immigrants who shipped over from Europe in a steamboat, hoping for brighter futures for themselves and their families. Those old-timers slaved in the factories, tended to their houses, scraped to pay the bills, and booted their children through high school. The next generation, our parents, did the same, worked, kept up the home, and planned for us to attend college because they, for whatever causes, couldn't. Our parents made sure we enrolled here so that when we're adults we won't have to struggle and scratch like they did. They want an easier life for us, with fairer opportunities, than they had themselves. At least that's what my mom told me my dad said all the time before he died. We've received a lot in our lives because our families pushed us. Maybe our generation's got some responsibility to move onward, progress. Young people are supposed to risk. And when us baby boomers do this for ourselves—improve our lives—we should help others at the same time, make sure no one's left behind."

"How can college kids accomplish stuff like that? I haven't seen many Gene McCarthys or Bobby Kennedys marching around this campus lately. What are you talking about, saving the world with your guitar?"

"Maybe this idea is a stretch," Lindy replied, "but we gotta do good for others—buy a stranger a cup of coffee, help a lady across the street, lend someone a dollar when they're down. And after the day-to-day favors, we see what else is out in the wide world; jump on that sled, slip down the hill. Maybe there's challenges for us we don't know about."

"I know about responsibilities, but that's for when we're grown-ups. We have enough here in school, in Champaign and Urbana. It's foolish wishing college finished; our time is right now, on this beautiful campus, with plenty of possibilities."

"Beautiful campus?" Lindy laughed. "Now who's over the top? Remember where you're at, the University of Illinois, smack in the middle of our flat farm fields, not some surfer's beach on the California coast."

"You understand my meaning. Our generation's young, we should stay where we are."

Summer Never Comes

"But we're not adolescents forever. When I was a freshman, I never thought I'd reach my senior year, or need to consider graduation or what's next. It has been a pile of quick semesters down here. I'm no sociology major or expert on life, but I think if we come back for Homecoming in thirty-five or forty years we might say the same thing. 'Those decades, where've they vanished; what have I achieved in my time?' If that's the case, we should start to make a life for ourselves."

"That's all you talk about. Move forward, travel the roads, find the future. What about the present?"

"Today is only a second long, then click, it's over, here's the next moment, June, tomorrow."

"No," Paul was obstinate.

"We'll both leave, Robby." Lindy gazed at a sweating, fully-uniformed—including pads—University Hockey Club skater and turned ridiculous, "That's why we should invent that 'Seniors Day.' No, a 'Quad Day for the Seniors,' that's the ticket."

He swung a hand in the air, outlining an imaginary, oversized poster, then saw his buddy's head drooping down, his mood glum. At the Union's south patio, Lindy grabbed Paul's arm.

"What did you say?" Paul snapped, his interest in generations and challenges ended.

"You're right, big year ahead," he shepherded his roommate up the steps, "we're gonna have a hell of a time on this picturesque campus of ours."

Two dozen undergrads faced the patio's corner where Bernard Minerath lectured, denouncing Nixon and the government. For as long as students recalled, Bernard—no one ever called him Bernie or another nickname—had been a part of the campus anti-war crusades. In the last semesters he'd labored as leader of SCRAP—the Student Committee Requiring an Adequate Peace—picketing university buildings, letter writing to the *Daily Illini*, coordinating with fellow peace groups, preparing for the right moments, Operation Loading Dock the most recent. At the edge of SCRAP's cadre, a *DI* photographer snapped a roll of film, knowing one or two photos would be printed in tomorrow's edition.

# # # #

Summer Never Comes

Packs of students wandered the Wright Street sidewalks in front of the Illini Union Bookstore. With the fall semester starting Monday, thirty-three thousand students needing textbooks, and this building one of only two places in Champaign-Urbana to buy them—practically every U of I student jammed through this bottleneck to snag what he or she needed. Most pushed into the single entrance while a luckier number pulled themselves out the same door, hands over their heads clutching too-small white and black paper bags filled with oversized, too-big texts and tomes. A score sat at the curbs, paging through the hardcovers and paperbacks, awed at the axioms, elements, formulae, philosophies, proofs, and theorems they read. "I will never, ever learn this stuff," a few regretted, "why am I enrolling in this class?"

One KID patronizing the bookstore was junior Dale Kinsey. Shoving in and squirming through mobbed aisles to the Law College section, he grabbed ten of the heaviest, costliest volumes, muscled to the cash register and paid the $236.36 bill with a blank check his father had given him when he left home last week. Two hours later, in the exchange and returns line, a mischievous Dale explained he'd mistakenly bought books for his spring courses, not this semester's, and received a cash refund. Dale planned to spend $194.17 the next morning for a brand new set of Gemini speakers at York Radio in Champaign.

# # # #

On Thursday night, all eighty-nine members of Kappa Iota Delta went drinking. Observing tradition, the party was in Stan's Tavern's basement, a cigarette-clouded, poorly-lit room with dark wooden benches around the walls, wobbly chairs and tables in the middle and—due to thousands of gallons of spillage—a grimy, tacky floor. A seedy Campustown pit, the place was a favorite of hard-core, beer-loving Champaign-Urbana students. At the evening's start, around 9:30, house treasurer Mark Mickey signed a check for $87.50, enough for fifty pitchers of fire-brewed Stroh's. This was hastily drunk, and by eleven o'clock the brothers were buying their own.

"Here's to Hodnik, he's true blue, he's a mother through and through. He won't let us dance, and he won't let us sing, and he won't let us do a goddamned thing! So drink, chug-a-lug, chug-a-lug, chug-a-lug."

Summer Never Comes

The fraternity's pledge class was called to chug, then the seniors, juniors, any women present, any "E" KIDs—those living in East Dubuque, Edwardsville, Effingham, Elgin or Evanston—and KIDs with hometown honeys. Moose demanded to guzzle as many beers as Ozark, but their buddies lost count. When Stan's closed, many had problems returning to the house—most doing more stumbling than walking. One total inebriate was freshman Tommy Quarters, for a whole block hopping over automobiles parked on Second Street, hurtling his body from trunk to hood to trunk to hood, never touching any streets or sidewalks.

All the KIDs were home by two a.m., though few racked out. Nemo's stereo blasted Jefferson Airplane, Chuck Pastron led a discussion in the stairwell on the Fighting Illini football team's prospects, Denny Parenti and Beebo Butkus ordered Garcia's pizza for the third floor, and young Tommy Quarters passed out in Frat Park.

"Hoo-wee, Robby, what a night." A bushed Lindy lay in their room's bottom bunk. "Looks like everyone appreciates your new popcorn maker."

"Really, a decent birthday present from my parents." Kernels were scattered over their floor, remnants of five batches Paul had popped for the brothers.

"That's right, twenty-one years old," Lindy sighed, "damn, you're legal."

"We're the same age, no big deal."

"Oh, I don't know about that, Robby, I can't picture you as a..." He was nearly asleep and 'White Rabbit' thumped through the walls.

"Lindy, that stuff on the Quad."

"Yeah, the coed I was wavin' to…keep it between us, don't tell Em, okay?"

"No, the generation talk. Were you serious; going out, taking chances and making sure no one's left behind?" Paul peered over the side of his top bunk. Still awake, Lindy smirked.

"Sounded admirable, but I think I had too many beers before spoutin' off."

"We weren't drinking this afternoon."

"Nailed me there," Lindy yawned. "Who knows, the world's a hard place to handle; reformin' it could be worse. And that's a safe thing with holin' up in college, we are protected with only miniature hassles, we can ignore reality. But not forever. Sooner or later ol' buddy, sooner or later ol' roommate, we're gonna catch our chance, that gate's gonna swing, the scales will tilt, our number'll…come up…"

"…Like Billy Powell," Paul finished the sentence.

"Poor Billy.… Hopefully we won't get drafted, God almighty I pray not, but we'll face something in our lives, good breaks, dilemmas, a fantastic opportunity we'll only collect once. Maybe how we handle the test is nearer the point, not goin' out in the real world to find what's comin'…how we manage…to survive the situation.…"

"Lindy, how long have we roomed together?"

His friend didn't answer. The only noise on the second floor was the volume jacked on Nemo's stereo, its needle circling and scratching a record over and over.

# # # #

"The *Daily Illini* condemns the on-going American offensive in Laos," Stef Tianen wrote in her editorial. "It is a tremendous tragedy carrying the Indochinese conflict into another long-suffering country. Widening the war will not, as the Nixon administration believes, bring peace to Southeast Asia, but simply prolong the anguish and add to the numbers of victims.

"This latest, blatant Imperialist belligerence once again highlights the hypocrisy foisted on the people by the Washington government. We are, we are told, seeing 'light at the end of the tunnel,' disengaging from the conflict, succeeding with 'Vietnamization,' and promised the total withdrawal of the half-million Americans from Southeast Asia.

"This week, we witness the shocking reversal: the Army's onslaught against a people whose single crime is living at a crossroads, occupying a parcel of land where opponents want to fight.

"Our leaders say we are moving toward peace, that we should have patience. Our leaders say we are moving toward peace, yet resort to unjustifiable military assaults and deceptions. Our leaders say we are moving toward peace, but continue to drop bombs, conscript teenagers and entangle our generation in other peoples' troubles.

"Our conscience believes that we, the people, have listened to lies long enough; that there is another way.

Summer Never Comes

Sit-ins, marches, demonstrations, walkouts, strikes, moratoriums. Our protests question, increase, influence, hit home, cause change. To every military misadventure, we object. To every politician's skeptical scheme, we dissent. Against every right-wing lie, we speak the truth. As time passes, our convictions strengthen, firm in resolve, certain of righteousness, determined we will remake our country.

"The call of war is loud, the absence of peace profound. We must never give up."

Chapter Two

THE RAIN the first day of classes—the twenty-seventh out of twenty-nine years, as Paul informed his friends at dinner—ended after midnight. By dawn a cold front moved through central Illinois, making Tuesday the pleasantest day in Champaign-Urbana since the student body's return.

That morning, Lindy read the *Daily Illini* articles about Operation Loading Dock; joined a discussion with Bobby Sox, Stu and Nemo in the KIDs' dining room, and agreed with Bobby's rant:

"Why in hell are we in such a goddamned candy-assed country like Laos? I say get the Christ out before we blow up the freakin' whole world!"

Emily Ritter, Lindy's girlfriend, overheard like conversations in Blaisdell Hall. Unconcerned about Vietnam or politics, she shut the matters from her mind. In the afternoon, the pair met in the Union for a Coke, then strolled out to the Quad, passing a clipboard-carrying SOAP activist at the door.

"Sign the petition to end the draft! Send a message to the right-wing warlords we're not fighting anymore! We can make it happen!" A handful of students paused to add their names.

"What do you think of these, Em?" Lindy strummed a half-dozen chords on his guitar. The pair rested on the grass, one of several couples enjoying the late summer day.

"That's nice, Will, does it have a title?" she inquired in her soft voice.

"Nope, just improvisin' what's in my head, the sweetest part of performing," his voice was affectionate, how he loved chatting with his girlfriend. "You should take up an instrument, Em, it's a sound hobby."

"I don't think so; music consumes so much time, I couldn't practice as much as you."

"Few do, except Clapton and Harrison."

"Yes, Will, and a trait to be proud of, I'm sure." Emily's voice was curt.

Summer Never Comes

"But I'll always salt time away for you, dear; you're my queen of hearts hiding up my sleeve." Lindy laid his guitar down. "Settlin' in to your classes okay?"

"Well enough. There's plenty of reading in my Shakespeare course, but that's what English major do."

"Which'll be your favorite, do you suppose?"

"Biology 100."

"Never enrolled in that one myself, though I've heard the material's so down-to-earth even business majors can comprehend it. Peculiar, a hardcore liberal arts person fancying science." Lindy gazed toward Noyes Lab. "What makes you say that, anyway?"

"Bio 100 is something fresh. Concentrating on so different a subject twice a week will shift my mind away from plays and sonnets."

"A fish out of water. That's the reason I love you so much, Em, level-headed answers. Say, 'Fresh Somethings,' there's a title for this melody." Lindy looked in her eyes, "Robby says hello."

"How is Paul, did he have a pleasant summer?"

"You know ol' Robby and his peaks and valleys, he left here last June, sidled through vacation on the south side and couldn't wait to return to Champaign. He said he went to a few White Sox games and took a trip with his parents to Michigan—to some town called Frumpehlport—that's all she wrote for my roommate. Actually, he's doin' something like you are, enrolling in another history class this semester; his fourth so far. My two best friends acting eccentric, the broth thickens."

"You're taking a philosophy class, aren't you? Students studying subjects outside their majors is common and opens more doors. I thought stepping through doorways is an idea you're fond of."

"I know, only it's weird a die-hard accountant dialed into havin' his pencils sharpened and fifty-two cards in his deck gets a kick out of grays." Lindy became serious. "But I'm worried, I think Robby's having a tough time adjusting to the fact he's a senior, and when we leave this June, he's not comin' back."

"I don't understand, Paul normally knows his way." Two dogs scampered by, chasing an orange frisbee.

"When it's numbers for his bean countin' courses or *Daily Illini* newspaper research, no one's an abler seaman at rowin' with oars. What I mean is my roommate and I are outta here—burnt toast in nine months—and Robby's unprepared. He's had such a super time these last years he's trapped, thinking the Big U should be his whole life for a lot longer. And graduation, there's a subject he absolutely refuses to thrash through; I'll wager this worsens the nearer we navigate to June. Robby's such a mood machine when he wants to be."

"Liking our school isn't a shame, Champaign-Urbana is an excellent place, people grow up here and Paul is one of them. I think he's changed since I've known him."

"Well, there's a difference between those notions, and I'd say Robby's light on the growin' side."

"You're the expert on maturity, are you now?" Emily used her hold-her-boyfriend-honest tone. "I'm skeptical any of us in college truly comprehend responsibility."

"That's another of your traits, Em, tuggin' me back to reality, like a dependable woman should with her man—first and foremost," Lindy shook his head, his blonde hair swirling around his ears, hoping Emily appreciated the joke. A skateboarder raced by, arms outstretched and shirt tails flying.

"And you, Will, are you happy being a senior?"

"Love every minute, finally scrambled to the top, a step down the windin', long road. Three years knocked off, one left on the game board."

"And leaving the university?" she asked apprehensively.

"That's what generally happens when an undergraduate graduates."

"I know, but…" Emily's voice trailed off and she turned away.

"Crocodile tears because you're not graduating with me, correct?"

"That's right; I'm a year behind, I'll stay in school and where will you end up?"

"Don't worry, Em, whatever that place is, I won't be far from Cham-Bana or you. If it's our fate, we're destined to be together. Who can say?" Lindy held her hand, "Maybe I'll start a rock 'n' roll band and light out for California."

"You and your music. Sometimes I feel you value that guitar more than me."

"What a line! Actually, the scales are about even between the Les Paul and you. But you trump my ol' Gibson, my dear. Yep, I love you way more, I'm certain."

Summer Never Comes

"You make me so mad at times, William."

"Another oldie! I have a strolling soap opera for a girlfriend, topple me over with a feather!" Lindy smacked his forehead with his open palm, tumbled on the ground and cajoled Emily into laughing.

"We have to discuss this. We've been seeing each other for almost a year, that's a big part of our lives, especially since I beat out your Gibson."

"I know, Em, and we shall. Say, I just imagined an inspiration—that horse of a different color. When I set up my band," stroking her leg, Lindy noticed her frown, "what if you travel to California with me? We'd shack up out there, you could finish school, earn your degree and find a teaching job. I'd come home every night from the recording studio and play the latest, hottest, top-of-the-charts songs I composed for you."

Emily's mouth curved upward, "That would be wonderful, Will."

"Okay, we'll hammer out the details." Lindy grabbed Emily's shoulders and maneuvered her so she was lying on her back on the grass, his face above hers. "But not today, because the weather's too nice, you're too beautiful and we've got all the time in the world."

"If you put it that way," she wrapped both arms around her boyfriend's head.

Hardly any students noticed Emily and Lindy making out. One undergrad trooping past and caring the least was a bearded RAW radical, hauling along his bundle of orange and black leaflets, handing the papers to anybody grabbing for one.

"Down with the war! Stop the fighting in Asia! Impeach the politicians! Impeach the government! Impeach society!"

# # # #

When Emily was a sophomore and Lindy a junior, both had taken Math 112; she enrolling in the course with three of her friends. The instructor habitually arrived five minutes late, and many students gossiped while waiting. Before a class in October, Lindy—one of the sociable-est students in the room—boasted over the parties the KIDs tossed to celebrate Homecoming, recounting so many tales that he ended up inviting all the algebra students to the dance.

Summer Never Comes

Emily and her girlfriends were the quietest in the class, and considered Lindy a colossal braggart. But with no plans that Saturday night, the coeds walked from Urbana to KIDs' house at the corner of Third and Armory. The boisterous mobs of undergrads in- and outside the fraternity; the beer barrels and wine jugs; the blasting stereo and the jammed, shaking, quaking dance floor were shockers to Emily and Nicole Liftuss, her roommate, these two girls more accustomed to spending weekends sitting in their dormitory, watching television and sipping hot tea. After one drink, the girls shuffled toward the door to leave, but were blockaded by a pack surrounding the kegs.

"Well, well, well, looky who's showed!" Lindy, with a few of his buddies and a brew in each hand, sidled next to the coeds. "Glad you made an appearance, ladies."

"Hello yourself," Emily replied. "Fascinating fraternity you belong to, is the music always so piercing?"

"Only for festivities like this," Lindy tapped his toes in time with the Kinks' 'Lola.' "Been here a while?"

The group's conversation—more like shouting over the racket—continued for twenty minutes covering the basic undergraduate topics: hometowns, majors, where everyone lived on campus, how much everybody studied, who booked on weekends. One by one, Emily's girlfriends stepped away for a beer or paired-up with other KIDs. When Nicole walked off with Bill Wick, Emily and Lindy were alone—excepting the thirty or forty squeezed and squashed revelers around the liquor.

"Here we are, at last alone on this deserted desert isle," Lindy beamed.

"That doesn't describe the spot we're in."

"Spoken like a proper English major, if I read between the lines."

"Actually, I am."

"Because of our class in Altgeld Hall I figured you for math, you're so no-nonsense, writing pages and pages of notes."

"The course is an elective for me. How about you, are you a math major?"

"Okay, honesty's the best policy," Lindy raised his eyebrows, "I'm not one neither."

"More clichés?" Emily smiled.

"I like arranging my ducks in rows."

Summer Never Comes

"Do you always talk this way?"

"Practice makes perfect."

"Enough, already!" Emily was giggling, because of Lindy's idioms and his boogying in rhythm with the music.

"Damn the torpedoes, don't abandon ship!" They tapped the keg, strolled to the patio, where the temperature was cooler and the tunes not as earsplitting, and chatted for a long, long time.

Emily enjoyed knitting and owned baskets and boxes of yarns; Lindy played hockey but not skillfully. She was a Methodist and attended services nearly every Sunday; he a baptized Catholic and once- or twice-a-semester churchgoer. Lindy was an only child, and his dad had died when he was in third grade. Emily's parents lived in Deerfield and was the second oldest of three sisters, but her uncle had passed away five years ago, leaving Aunt Joanna to raise her two cousins. Lindy enjoyed college from his first hours in Champaign-Urbana, "bright and carly, safe and sound," he pronounced. Even after her freshman year, Emily confessed to missing her family and barely tolerating the University of Illinois. Lindy loved music, extremely dug playing any of his three guitars; Emily read books. He never missed Fighting Illini football in Memorial Stadium or a home basketball game at Assembly Hall. Emily's cousin, Tony Ornatek, played second string center with the Illini, but she'd only watched one football game, and never understood why anyone would want to do anything athletic and get dirty and sweaty. Like the majority of KIDs, Lindy could be the hard-core drinker; Emily preferred a half glass of wine over beer.

In the rain later that night, with Lindy escorting Emily to a second party and then to her dorm, the pair seemed opposites. Lindy was a backslapping, hell-raising compadre, thrilled whooping it up at keggers with the stereo humongously cranked, or content rapping with bunches of near and dear friends in his room at three in the morning. Shy Emily was uncomfortable with the unavoidable college crowds. She went to classes, was satisfied to study alone in the Library, planned to be a teacher—hopefully high school English in the Chicago suburbs—and meticulously prepared for her career. The Champaign-Urbana social life, happy hours in the bars, football weekend bashes, smoking dope and the drug scene, seemed senseless; an engaging novel or pleasant conversation with one girlfriend was enough for her.

Summer Never Comes

Yet, after their Homecoming evening and morning, Lindy and Emily were attracted to each other, realized they complemented the other, filled voids, highlighted topics neither would consider on their own. The quirky fate and fortune of couples. Emily and Lindy helped each other grow, not mature as adults because these two—along with thousands of U of I undergrads—were much too adolescent for accountability. But the pair could, as Lindy said, "read between the lines, bare one's hand to the cold light of reason."

Lindy took her on a second date and a third, dinner at the Round Barn. They spent Fridays and Saturdays together, and saw each other during the week. Emily asked to go to a presentation of *Richard II* at the Krannent Center for the Performing Arts. Lindy bundled her to the season's last home football game, versus Northwestern, the weather so frigid she didn't enjoy herself, but stayed to be with him. Emily discussed John Wesley; Lindy recounted the Fab Four's sway on American society. She went to a hockey game, Lindy a performance of *The Pirates of Penzance*. Lindy escorted Emily to the Red Lion Inn—the most heinous and despotic of campus bars—and the next weekend they sampled Earl Grey tea in her dormitory's lounge. Emily and Lindy saw each other so often that by Thanksgiving they considered, and their friends totally agreed, that they were going steady. She started calling him Will, the only person besides his mother to use that nickname. Over Christmas vacation, Lindy drove from his mom's house on the south side to Deerfield to meet Emily's family and talk with the cousins who had no dad. In the spring semester the pair settled into a delightful friendship—studying at the Library Wednesday and Thursday nights, dating on the weekends, and regularly relying on Paul or Nicole to clear out so they could sleep together.

Like all relationships, theirs was a work in progress. Lindy enjoyed the carousing college undergrads instigated just this side of dodging trouble. The introverted Emily did her best to curb Lindy, to keep him to herself, and half the time this was fine, Lindy grateful for breaks from the juvenile mayhem habitually overwhelming the KIDs' house. But he hugely appreciated Paul, Bobby, Stu and all his buddies, and Emily learned to share her boyfriend with his fraternity brothers. For her part, she was a sulker, acting like a child, not talking to others, freezing them out until securing what she wanted. Emily had done this to Lindy. The first silent treatment

Summer Never Comes

he'd taken badly, but laughed off the second so unceremoniously that after one day Emily saw how harsh she treated him and came to care for Will the more.

There was also his music. Lindy never tired talking about rock 'n' roll and his heroes, Eric Clapton and George Harrison. He endlessly practiced guitar to the point of aggravating his tolerant friends, had dreams of one day working in the music business, a vision of touring the country with an all-star band, and the fantasy of striking it rich as the next McCartney. Emily was fairly convinced, as she'd observed on the Quad, that her Will needed to deliberate before declaring the sweetheart of his life—her or his Les Paul.

And a problem, perhaps a catastrophe, was present. As honest, broadminded and kind, as eager to act the goof in screwball adventures with his pals, all could be negated by Lindy's furious temper. Never the quietest person in a room, he was considered a gentleman. But in the infrequent, despondent moments Lindy would plunge into rages consuming his energy and thinking. Lindy had once argued with Bobby Sox in the laundry room over who could use a clothes dryer first. Bobby famously short-fused himself, the two cussed away for ten minutes, so nasty that KIDs on the third and fourth floors hurried to the basement to watch the expected fist fight. There had been more tantrums, mostly against buddies, rarely at strangers, and Lindy came to appreciate the adage that a person always hurts most those that are closest. Following a tirade, after reconsidering for a day, an apologetic Lindy made the point of returning to whomever his explosion clobbered to fix the wreckage. This was what he did with Bobby Sox in the laundry room for two hours. Lindy repaired most relationships, but accepted that each time he launched into his frenzies he lost a piece of his companions' respect. Even acquaintances not victims learned to remain wary, to hold back a bit and not entirely trust him.

Emily heard about her boyfriend's failing from Paul and other KIDs. Their warnings scared her because she'd never witnessed a violent temper, been the prey of such abuse, and couldn't know what her reaction would be if and when it happened. She talked with Lindy about how she would feel if he attacked her. He'd try his best not to, he claimed, announced, felt he could be different with her and hoped, as they grew intimate, there'd be no reason for an explosion to destroy them. But a truthful Lindy stopped short of the unqualified guarantee Emily wished to hear.

Summer Never Comes

"This is bigger than both of us and better left unsaid."

By the summer before Lindy's senior year the two were a sweetheart couple. Emily offhandedly joked about weddings, with Lindy absentmindedly ignoring the asides or mocking them with a yarn. He took to memorizing clichés for Emily, a cloak and dagger code recapping their dialogues and many times making her laugh.

"The honest truth is a thing of beauty is a joy forever."

In a nutshell, their relationship.

# # # #

"This is the pits," Bobby Sox was agitated, "first week of classes and I'm headin' out bookin'."

"Bobby, someday when you reflect," Stu Cummings mimicked his parents, "you'll thank the university for the opportunity."

"Correct-o," Lindy joked, "be grateful for what we have, this repository of higher education if there ever was one."

"A great frickin' semester shapin' up, I can see that now."

For the first time this school year Bobby, Lindy, Stu and Paul were on their way to the Library. The previous evenings all four had studied in the fraternity, no problem if a body wasn't bothered listening to six or eight stereos blasting rock 'n' roll at disgustingly earsplitting volumes. But serious booking was done in calmer, quieter surroundings, away from KIDs' childishness.

"See what I have to put up with?" Stu chided his roommate. "He is always complaining. Bitch, bitch, bitch."

"Yeah, but you love it," Lindy said. "If you didn't, you'd have roomed with someone else the last two years."

"If I don't live with Bobby, who'd put up with his ratty-ass, smelly feet?"

"Think your deal's crappy?" an eyes wide-open Lindy smirked. "At least you're finished with him in June when we graduate. Then the turn's poor Jeannie's, she'll be layin' by Bobby's paws and own them forever. Talk about cuttin' mustard."

"If Bobby's lucky," Stu added. Walking east on Armory Avenue, the KIDs crossed Fourth Street.

Summer Never Comes

"Wait a minute, what's this, hassle-me-semester?" Lagging a few steps behind his friends, the thin-skinned Bobby Sox turned defensive over his steady girl. "Beat me, freakin' a-holes."

"Okay," Stu waited for his roommate, "we've dumped enough garbage on you tonight."

"That's right, this is a long year." Lindy also backed up, leaving Paul by himself in front of the Ice Rink's stairs. "Say, Robby, what's the latest on Operation Loading Dock?"

"The battles are continuing, American troops have total control of those two towns in Laos and are heading straight north from there."

"What about the South Vietnamese? I thought they were taggin' along."

"Only to make it respectable for the television cameras while the Americans do the fighting."

"Why is the Army advancin' north? Weren't they supposed to halt after capturing those villages?" Bobby was curious.

"Right now, the troops are thirty miles from the border," Paul answered. "The strategy could be to airlift enough soldiers in that area, stockpile supplies, then go forward."

"You mean invade North Vietnam? The Army ever done that before?"

"We've dropped millions of pounds of bombs on them but never have marched into their country, except for raids to rescue shot-down pilots."

"I wonder how far that bastard Nixon will go?"

"And if Billy Powell's with this Operation Loading Dock?" The KIDs sadly remembered their fraternity brother and his unreal, horrendous luck dumping him in the war.

"I'll betcha Billy's nowhere near Laos," Lindy remarked, "he's sharp enough to steer clear from that kinda crap."

"I hear a demonstration protesting this Vietnam garbage is planned for next week." Bobby kicked a stone.

"Yes, the campus' four peace groups are organizing an all-day affair on Wednesday on the Quad," Paul summarized the facts, "part of a nationwide 'Moratorium on Business as Usual.' The *Daily Illini*'s running a story tomorrow."

"All those peace groups, I never understood why there're so many. What would be wrong with a singleton? There's only one war."

Summer Never Comes

"Maybe it's so wall-to-wall because, like Billy, the peaceniks have low numbers and want publicity to protect themselves from bein' drafted." Lindy and the others passed Fifth Street and the Alpha Phi Sorority.

"What's in the *DI* tomorrow?" Stu stared at the sorority house.

"The rally and the moratorium," Paul answered.

"Okay, and what's the deal with Saturday night?"

"The famous 'Welcome Back Everybody' party, can't wait." The friends were half a block from the Library.

"Should be a rowdy one, been a while—four or five days—since we've done any real drinkin' together. I hope Shaky Jake's act is together for his first fling as social chairman. What about you, Bobby, stickin' around?"

"Nope, headin' north on I-57 to Chi-town tomorrow."

"Tomorrow's only Thursday."

"A shame," Stu cheerily volunteered, "A knock-down party, my roommate leaves a day early so his mommy can wash his dirty laundry, and I get my room to myself for the whole weekend."

"See my consideration? I'm around Monday through Friday, then blow out of town so you guys can have this campus to yourselves. 'Course it looks in pretty ratty frickin' ass shape when I return on Sunday nights."

"Good egg, Bobby," Lindy said, "doubtless your pals immensely appreciate the kindness."

Entering the Library, Bobby, Paul and Stu climbed the stairs to the lonely, spartan Reference Room. Lindy headed to the Commerce Library to photocopy reserved reading material and meet a guitar-playing buddy, Franky Konkel.

All evening at the corner of Armory and Wright Streets, members of SOAP, protesters from DISGUST, and RAW's and SCRAP's revolutionaries elbowed and argued for sidewalk space and students' attention. RAW's display, a plywood plank diagramming troop movements in Vietnam, was kicked by SCRAP and toppled over; while a bicycle rider swerved to miss SOAP's petition holder, scaring the coed and scattering her papers into the street. DISGUST's stuffed effigy of a dark-haired, moustached South Vietnamese generalissimo failed to light when the anarchists struck a match to the mannequin.

"Finish the fighting. It's cooked beans so far."

Summer Never Comes

"North Vietnam's the wrong place to bomb, blast the Pentagon instead!"

"Peace through peace is the true alternative. Better than peace through war."

"Ignore the rest, find peace and tranquility with DISGUST."

The majority of passing undergrads ignored this vaudeville.

"How are you, Paul?"

"What's up, Rander-roo? Calling it a night?" Paul and his friend exited the Library around eleven o'clock.

"Yeah, too soon for serious booking," Randy Miller answered. "By yourself?"

"I walked here with Lindy, Bobby and Stu. My roommate met a buddy then went to Second Chance for a beer, the other two bolted early to hit the Snack Bar."

"Is Stu on probation this semester?"

"Correct, but he enrolled in summer school and came to the Library tonight. Promising signs." The two passed by St. John's Catholic Church. The large doors opened and an elderly priest ambled down the steps.

"How's the *Daily Illini* starting the school year?"

"Fitting in freshman staff always makes September hectic, more so this semester with installing new telephones and covering next week's rally."

"Should be exciting, our first chance to confront the politicians. We'll show everybody where we stand on this 'Nam bullshit."

"Which peace group do you belong to, Randy?"

"SCRAP," he proudly answered, "the ones with the answers to cleaning up this mess."

"Bernard Minerath's crowd. Tell me, why all these different anti-war groups? What's the sense having more than one on our campus?"

"Different reactions to deteriorating circumstances. SOAP was founded early on, about the time Lyndon Johnson tricked us into Vietnam. The war wasn't overwhelmingly terrible back in '65 and the protesting was wishy-washy, which is why SOAP's people are so low-key. Laurie Allman, their leader, is the nicest person you'll meet—the kid sister you'd want in your family. She detests the war along with the rest of us, but works against it in a subdued style—which was protesting's earliest approach. But a year goes by, the government ships tens of thousands more soldiers to Asia, the military's

Summer Never Comes

escalation sinks down the toilet, demonstrating turns zealous, and DISGUST and RAW are organized. They're the ones instigating the student voter registration drives in Champaign County to control local governments, novel strategies but a failed movement. Then comes '68, the Democrats' Chicago convention and Tricky Dick's election. He wins the White House with his secret plan to end the war, which was only more deceit and fighting, like this week's happenings in Laos. SCRAP was created last year to really bury these warmongers and their disasters. Whatever we have to do to end this damned war—that's SCRAP's mission—it's the only sensible option we see."

"Couldn't 'whatevers' lead to extremes?"

"We won't break windows or pitch bottles at the police, not this time at least." Randy joked. "Next week's rally is an illustration. We'll be the source for as much information as possible about what's destroying our country, aim for more focus than entertaining undergrads for an afternoon. We want everybody carrying away a motivated, activist, let's-end-this-thing-once-and-for-all attitude."

"Are all the other groups in sync for this?"

"Yes, with their own responsibilities. SCRAP's is handling the stage and arranging for speakers, SOAP will organize the information booths, RAW's is advertising and DISGUST will marshal the Quad, seeing that the audiences behaves. But everyone's main mission is turning out as many students as we can, proving we hate this war and the government should withdraw today."

"Sounds thought-through," distracted from his fraternity brother, Paul's eyes followed a coed in sweatpants into the Armory.

"Whatever dissent to send the message, that's our duty. This war is so horrible we have to work like hell until we pull out of Vietnam and bring our friends home. Too many have been murdered in Asia, and more will be massacred tomorrow if we don't finish it off—if America doesn't quit." Randy made a fist with his left hand. "But you know what's the evilest crime? The way those goddamned Washington politicians exploit the war in spite of what the people say. Whichever gang's elected, whoever's in power in the White House or the Capitol, there's no difference. The same policies are manipulated, rationalized, but never changed. The right-wingers draft our generation, train us to fire guns, order us to Asia to fight and get us slaughtered. For what? I don't see the sense in anything we're told about why we're there. Stop Communism? Save Vietnam? Save it for what? For more chances to be killed and waste our lives? That's why the war's got to end, before our whole generation's sent to 'Nam. Look at Billy Powell."

"Yes, it's terrible when an easygoing, decent guy like Billy is absolutely screwed and forced into the Army," the two walked by the Phi Mu sorority, the KIDs' neighbors. "But don't you think some people believe defending Vietnam is righteous?"

"That's a hell of an explanation for what's gone down in 'Nam or this country the last seven years. There's nothing honorable in murdering people while at the same time lying about it. There's nothing moral if you're a politician witnessing the anti-war riots—hear the protesters and ignore the people. Nobody with a conscience, who hasn't been brainwashed, could consent to that.

"What did they offer Billy, except issue him a helmet, boots, a backpack, a rifle, and shove him into an infantry squad? Who gains from the thousands of our generation killed and missing in action? Do their families think their deaths are meaningful? What about our friends that'll be drafted today and butchered tomorrow? What if you and me ship over to Vietnam? I don't want to get ambushed by a sniper in the jungle and no one else should, either. That's why I say the time for puny, pint-sized protests against the war has passed. We've got to move the country. We, the people have to take over the government to stop the fighting. Peace now, Paul, peace now."

# # # #

Paul lay in his room. The windows were open and a car screeched past on Third Street.

Intriguing, people's responses to events. Walking to the Library tonight, Lindy, Bobby and Stu regarded Vietnam like some minor topic, an exam essay question, a football game or a weird, wild-assed rumor about a fraternity brother. Only Billy Powell's name elicited emotions. Randy Miller however, a solid student, affable, with many friends in KIDs, was total passion over 'Nam—wholly committed to peace, if not revolution. Two approaches for his article. Maybe Lindy would have more, Paul was sure of this, his roommate forever primed for speculating. Maybe he's received a letter from Billy, that's another angle. I'll stay awake until he gets back so I can ask him.

Around 2:15 the door creaked.

"You awake?" Lindy didn't wait for an answer. "Fine, I'll turn on the lamp."

"Where've you been? Bobby was worried about you," Paul sat up.

"I'll bet, his only bothering is haulin' butt back to Chi-town and makin' out with his hometown honey. Robby, you'll never guess, you won't believe…you just…just won't, I can't figure myself, it's so awesome. I'm in a band, an honest-to-goodness, alive-and-breathing, love-my-mother rock 'n' roll band!" Lindy let out a whoop. "Far freakin' out!"

"Quiet; somebody in this house is racking."

"Oops." He sat at the desk.

"How did it happen?"

"Well, I hit the Commerce Library to photocopy the advertising articles and buy some sheet music from Franky Konkel. Instead, Franky starts rappin' about these guys he's jammed with over the summer. There were four: drums, bass and two on axes, occupyin' a real decent studio set up west of First Street here in Champaign until one, a dude named Abruzzo, wanders off and marries some woman. Can you believe it? Bolts from a bunch of hippie musicians for a wife! Now they're searchin' for a replacement guitar player."

"And you recommended yourself."

"Didn't need to, Franky said he had me in mind from that barbecue and monster jam session we hosted the first warm weekend last March. Remember? The fifteen or twenty groups in Frat Park all playin' different sets, and Franky and his maniac drummer friend were in one of them. That night he was impressed with my rendition of 'My Sweet Lord.' Today he offered me the open spot in his band, and I accepted."

"How long did you deliberate?"

"Oh, about a tenth of a second. Think I'd even need that much?"

"Surprised you took three years to hook up with a group. When's your first gig?"

"Not for a while, first there's a few weeks of rehearsing. Franky's a hard-core perfectionist, definitely wants to sound mellower than these other fair, fat and forty bar bands."

Summer Never Comes

"I thought the idea was finding a stage to make music and money."

"Yes and no, Robby. If the deal was only bucks, I'd agree, but where's the sense in performin' before you're ready to max out? I've spectated the scene before when guys step out to play and audiences can tell there's no practice behind them. The band misses cues, harmonies are atrocious and someone forgets the lyrics to what they're singin', a complete case of eating humble pie. There's no compensation in embarrassment."

"How often is practice?"

"Every night for three or four hours, starting next week. We gotta know what we're doin' and be professional. Our cost of doing business."

"Well, congratulations, I know you want this," Paul was indifferent.

"Thanks, buddy. Say, remember what we talked over on the Quad, about latchin' into the real world and improving things? Maybe this fills the bill, this could be my chance."

"You're saving the planet with a rock and roll band instead of your guitar?"

"Not bail out the world, though that's a reasonable vibe, but now's my time to grab for the brass ring, trek that extra mile, game plan my life. A man's gotta do what a man's gotta do."

Sitting on the bed, Paul considered seguing to his *Daily Illini* story. But studying Lindy, distracted by his new band's probabilities, he balked. A breeze blew the curtains away from the window and neither spoke for three or four minutes, a lengthy silence for the roommates. They'd been best pals long enough, knew the other's moods, that both understood Lindy was the one to restart a conversation, and the fact he didn't hit them as odd.

Paul was wary. Rooming with Lindy these semesters had provided a close friend to hang with, someone he was comfortable talking to anytime about anything. Pets, cars, movies (both liked *Kelly's Heroes* and *The Candidate)*, nicknames, idiosyncrasies, disgusting habits, sports, vacations, checking accounts. Woodstock and the Chicago Cubs' choke in '69, the Apollo moon missions and *Let It Be* in 1970. Favorite foods, furniture, grade school, geography, shoes and sandals, moms and dads, fears and hopes, aspirations and apparitions. In two years there was no subject the pair neglected. He wished they'd be roommates forever, so many topics remained. Now change—Lindy was finding new adventure, stepping toward a future Paul would not be in. He'd be by himself, like his freshman year.

Summer Never Comes

But aware performing with a band Lindy's dream, and thinking it fair his roommate gaining a shot, Paul checked his pessimism. "What's your group called?"

"We're Frogfeet."

"Come again?"

"Frogfeet."

Paul mulled over the word and snickered. His chuckling growing to a guffaw, he held his stomach with both arms.

"And what is so funny with the name?" Lindy was relieved seeing his roommate not totally depressed.

"I'm imagining you on stage, 'Frogfeet, featuring Lindy Lindner and his size eleven, high-top tennies.'"

"Why don't you go to hell," he pitched a pillow at Paul.

"What's Emily going to say?"

"Yes, Em." Lindy stared at the *All Things Must Pass* poster taped to the door. "The next time we're seein' each other is Saturday's party, that's when I'll inform her. Better face-to-face, in the king's English."

"Think she'll be pleased for you and this band?"

"By the way, Robby, so far you're the only one I've told, so camouflage this under your hat until I break the bulletin to her, okay?"

"No problem; but what about her reaction?"

"Even if you run into her around the campus in the next few days."

"And an answer to my question?"

"Straightforwardly, I doubt Em will appreciate it one, tiny bit, not one iota. She'll see hookin' up with Frogfeet as me pullin' away from her, like our whole world will crumble because I want to play my guitar on a stage. Em'll consider this as an insult to our relationship, sort of like what you're thinkin' right now."

"Am I such an open book?"

"Laying smack dab in the center of a coffee table." Lindy grinned at his roommate. "Don't worry, the ball's gonna keep rollin', it'll work out."

# # # #

"North Vietnamese and Vietcong troops," the *Champaign News-Gazette* reported, "have heavily counterattacked along the Laotian-South

Summer Never Comes

Vietnamese border. The apparent Communist strategy is to isolate the entire allied force from their bases. Radio Hanoi, previously denouncing the advance into Laos as 'blatant and disgusting Imperialist aggression,' has guaranteed the invading forces will be 'thoroughly, mercilessly annihilated.' US Army command reports American casualties of 85 killed, 169 wounded and 13 missing in action. Communist losses are estimated at 650 killed. To date, the fiercest fighting has occurred two miles north of Ban Nabo.

"The Champaign Police Department is investigating a break-in last night at the offices of the student group Radicals Against War," the *News-Gazette* also printed. "The break-in occurred between two and four a.m. Nothing of value was reported stolen. Damage was confined to the contents of three filing cabinets emptied out over the floor. RAW's offices are located at 618 Green Street.

"The State Department has confirmed the November visit of Undersecretary of State for Southeast Asian Affairs James R. Camp to the Urbana campus. Mr. Camp is a 1938 graduate of the university."

Chapter Three

"SHAKY JAKE, your premier party as social chairman's a success!"

"Really. I'm glad the dozen Alpha Gams who promised to show put in an appearance." Amidst the mobs, an unflappable, chuckling Kenny Jacobsen wound the tapper into a fresh keg, the evening's fourth.

"Let's go, you brewin' the Budweiser right here on Third Street?" Moose Wozniak bellowed.

Tim Malito set his empty plastic cup under the spigot, "Somebody hand me another glass, this kegger's still foamin'."

"Hustle your ass, Timmer, I'm thirsty."

"Chill, Mooser, the party's one long night, you don't want to peak too soon," Jake held two glasses for his girl, Kay Reising, and himself.

The famed 'Welcome Back Everybody' party kicked off after nine o'clock. Brothers and their dates, KIDs' Armory Avenue neighbors, a few relatives and total strangers—more bodies than anyone ever recalled, packed into the foyer and shoved through the patio doors. Navigating near the kegs and wine jugs was slow, and as the house filled the temperature became muggier. The deafening stereo volume made conversation difficult, except between records. Empty cups laid on the floor, and the living room already smelled syrupy-sweet and smoky from spilled beers and cigarettes. The KIDs were ecstatic seeing this many women in their fraternity on a Saturday night, but mostly the brothers killed time with their beers, working up the nerve to ask a babe out to the dance floor.

"Been to Big Joe's yet?" Ozark stepped to the barrel to fill his thirty-ounce porcelain mug.

"What's that?"

Summer Never Comes

"A barbecue joint north of Barnett's Liquors, cooks the spiciest ribs I've tasted this side of 147th and Western Avenue. Serves plenty to eat, with fries, coleslaw and home-baked rolls."

"Paul, how are you?" Surrendering to the blasting music, Stu Cummings tugged his girlfriend and Paul toward the living room. "Joyce Belker, this is Paul Roberts, after Bobby Sox, my roommate, one of my best buddies. Joyce is an Alpha Phi."

"Do you know Arlene Byster? We were in Accounting 341 last spring," Paul was congenial. "She knew her stuff, aced all three hourly exams. Don't know about finals but I can't imagine Arlene doing worse than another A."

"That's my problem," Stu said, "geniuses for acquaintances."

Searching the living room, Joyce settled on the far wall, "Why is the fireplace cold?"

"We only light it for intimate get-togethers," Stu answered, "not blowout bashes like this, too tempting to fry somebody when there's hundreds of people and a dozen kegs around."

"I imagine a midnight fire is romantic when nobody's here."

"Maybe the brothers will scoot early and we'll find out," Stu took her hand. "Come on, Joyce, let's dance."

"Nice meeting you." Leaning against the wall, Paul watched the twenty or thirty boogying couples on the carpet.

"Look out, keg number five's hauling through."

"We need to spin Rod Stewart's *Every Picture Tells a Story* on the turntable."

"Honestly, the Student Record Service is selling albums for $3.19 apiece."

"But the best deal's at Foremost Liquors, 99-cent six packs of Old Milwaukee."

Ron Gimbel and Barb Douglas, his blind date, sat in two chairs, Ronny cradling a beer cup between his legs. Friends for an hour, they'd had a polite chat walking from Allen Hall to KIDs. Inside the fraternity, though, their brief relationship turned awkward, Ronny wanting to hang with his buddies but obliged to remain with an apprehensive Barb. Her first time at KIDs, she didn't recognize anyone. By eleven p.m., the pair ran out of conversation, tough anyway because of the earsplitting music. So they silently sat, with Ronny occasionally heading to the keg for refills.

Summer Never Comes

Freshman Tommy Quarters reeled in the middle of the floor, maintaining his streak of dancing every tune with a different woman. Scooter Petersen and his steady girlfriend, Lauren Rose, lingered on the crowd's fringe, barely moving, staring in the other's eyes, on their own faraway campus. Tim Malito boogied with a girl Paul recognized as Cindy Klippel, down from Aurora for the weekend visiting her brother.

Wearing a royal blue silk shirt, a twenty dollar pair of dress pants and leather shoes with two inch heels, Dale Kinsey stuck out from the sports shirts, tank-tops and Illini football jerseys in the room. He deliberately arrived late, traipsing down the stairs so as to be noticed by the partying crowds. Sipping beer, Dale snaked among the hordes, nodding to only those brothers saying hello first. He was stalking for a broad he could chat up, dance a song with, then lure to his rack. Since dozens of the women in the room were strangers, Dale cockily calculated a quick hunt.

"What'd you think of Mary Lou's dinner tonight?"

"Wanna hit the midnight skin flicks at the old Auditorium?"

"Come on, honey, I use that line a lot, and it always worked before."

"Did you know the Marching Illini are going coed? Until this season the football band's been all male, we're the first Big Ten school adding women."

"On that bulletin, I need another brew," Del Hansen strolled off, leaving Paul by the trophy case. He looked at Scooter and Lauren, Jake and Kay, Stu and Joyce, Tim and Cindy, and Tommy plus Pick-a-Name boogying to the Beach Boys, excellent KIDs dancing music. Eddie-Bob McMahon clomped by wearing his Sigma Alpha Mu jersey.

"Wall, how ahr yo', boy?"

"Kentucky, you old confederate, where the hell've you been?" Paul straightened up.

"You hav-in' a good time t'night?" Swirling a half-full cup and waving to numerous acquaintances, Kentucky's baritone voice was as hearable as the stereo. "Doin' aneh dancin'?"

"No, only drinking and talking to the brothers. That's what these gatherings are for, right?"

"Imbibin' an' jaw-in'." He tugged his wide-brimmed hat. "They is foh you t' step out an' meet people, not t' stand heah by th' side o' th' wall."

Summer Never Comes

"I've moseyed around, honestly. Ten minutes ago I was over at the kegs with Stu and his date."

"Wall, thet's a beginnin', Ah reckon, but not much o' one. Lordy, Ah don' know about you, Robbeh."

"Hopeless?" Paul indecisively nodded, playing along to Kentucky's act and half-agreeing with his friend's reasoning.

"Check this scene out, hockey fans."

"Lind-eh, mah ol' hayshaker."

"Emily, good seeing you," Paul was thankful for a reprieve from reprimands.

"Miss Em'leh, yohr servant, ma'am." Kentucky removed his hat and bowed. His long, brown hair was parted in the middle, completely covering his ears.

"Hello to both of you," with the crowd's bedlam and booming music, Emily's soft voice was nearly inaudible.

"Ken-tuck, from the doorway it appeared you were dolin' out a hefty homily to our buddy," Lindy grinned.

"Ah wuz ex-plainin' th' purpose foh relaxation an' parties, simple as thet."

"No doubt he needs it. I've done my best teaching him the ropes these semesters, don't know what he'll do at graduation when we march over the hill."

"Now, Will," Emily admonished him, "putting down your best friend is impolite."

"Just kiddin' a tad. No harm, no foul, right, Robby?"

"Miss Em'leh, how wuz yohr summer?"

"Relaxing and pleasant, thank you, I enjoyed being away from classes after last spring."

"You carried eighteen hours that semester, didn't you, Em?" Lindy massaged her neck.

"Yes, the majority in English literature."

"Which means plenty o' time spent readin' prose, sonnets an' Shakespeare, if Ah am cor-rect." Again Kentucky bowed and Emily blushed.

The stereo quit midway through 'People Got to be Free,' the dancers groaned and dozens of joking, reveling, ecstatic-for Saturday-night KIDs clogged through the living room towards the barrels.

Summer Never Comes

"Thank goodness we can hear."

"But not for long, I'm afraid," Lindy scoped out the packs heading for the bar. "Tell you guys what, if you escort Em out to the patio, I'll battle the brothers for an extra round of brewskies."

"Sounds like a deal to me," Paul stepped to Emily's side.

"Ah will beg t' be ex-cused, Ah must pay mah respects t' th' otheh beaut-iful ladies heah t'night. If'n you'll pardon me, Miss Em-leh." He bent over. "Agin, yohr servant, ma'am."

"It was wonderful seeing you, Kentucky," Emily's tone was gentle.

"Thanks for the advice," Paul said.

"Locate you later, pal." As Lindy disappeared into the keg mobs, Emily and Paul watched Kentucky sashay towards three coeds huddled near the fireplace. The southerner doffed his hat and in seconds the trio was beaming, thoroughly at ease. What's his secret? Paul speculated, as he threaded Emily through the crowds to the screen door.

"We were at the Undergrad Library until 10:30."

"Scooter and Lauren look serious out there."

"And been that way since they were in school together."

"Which was kindergarten. Hey, I need a brew."

Dale Kinsey captured his woman. As garishly dressed as Dale, she wore tight-tight corduroy bellbottoms, a loose-fitting, hot pink blouse unbuttoned below her humongous boobs, no bra and too much rouge. Smoking, she carried a crushed pack of Lucky Strikes in one hand and her face flaunted a 'who cares, so why bother' expression. Nodding as they rapped, she apathetically scoffed when Dale poked his fingers down her inner thigh. When the music started, the girl fizzled her cigarette in a beer cup and followed Dale to the dance floor where the pair stalled, rubbing bodies. She bit Dale's ear and her palms patted his ass. After a single tune, they wandered upstairs to his room.

"We'll tailgate again this year for Dad's Day."

"Honest, my roommate went home for the weekend."

"The secret to acing Geography 103 is the discussion sections—show up and ask questions. Concentrate on the TA recognizing your face, which comes in handy when it's time for passing out grades."

"At least it's cooler here." Paul guided Emily away from a dozen fellow partiers also outside for a break. "Did you have a busy summer?"

Summer Never Comes

"I attended three family weddings in July and August," Emily spoke softly but focused on the screen doors. "At the second, my cousin's, I was a bridesmaid. The dress colors were turquoise and pink."

"Did Lindy travel to them with you?"

"Only the first two. The third was in Toledo, and my parents, sisters and I flew there. How are your classes this semester?"

"Reasonable, I'm enrolled in my usual business courses, Philosophy 393 with Lindy, plus a history seminar. And yours?"

"Another full load for being on track for my education degree, but no classes scheduled on Wednesday and Friday afternoons. When Will and I are finished on those two days we'll spend time together." She glanced at the house. The music was more deafening than when they'd exited. "I wonder where he is?"

"It's tough moving around with all the bodies. Haven't you two been dating for almost a year?"

"Eleven months," she corrected, "our anniversary is in four weeks."

"Right, the rainy Homecoming weekend."

The music died and the dancers shrieked, followed by a scraping needle dropping in a record groove and 'Big Girls Don't Cry.' Cheers roared, with a score more couples jamming the floor. Also rolling out was Lindy, theatrically tripping through the doorway, hobbling towards his friends, hyping the performance by intentionally splashing beer from the cups between his hands.

"What an Oskee-Wow-Wow journey inside there, an absolutely commingling crowd." Feigning panting, he offered one glass to Emily, a second to his roommate. "Robby, from the house you two looked like a contented couple. If I didn't reckon the eternal verities, I'd surmise Em your girlfriend and not mine."

"You do know better, Will," she mildly scolded.

"Tell him," Paul parodied Emily's tone, "what took so long?"

"Well, first the keg went dry, so Moose and me had to tap a replacement," Lindy wiped his forehead and winked. "Then I ran into Killer and sparred with him for two or three rounds."

Puzzled by his roommate's gesture, Paul chugged the half-glass of suds. "Empty, think I'll fight the mobs for more beer."

Summer Never Comes

"Hey, I didn't intend breakin' up your confab," Lindy grabbed Emily's waist, an affection she complemented by sliding to his side.

"Not a problem, we just finished discussing the weddings Emily traveled to this summer."

"Marriage? Eek!" Lindy pretended shock. "Smarter that stays under lock and key."

"Oh, Will!"

The pair watched Paul wedge into the crowds. Lindy gulped his beer and eyed his girlfriend. At six foot two, he was a solid eight inches taller. She wore a freshly-ironed green blouse, new bellbottoms and her hair was wound in a ponytail. Lindy's wrinkled rugby shirt had a hole in the left sleeve.

"I was teasin' about the wedding thing, Em. Keeps Robby guessing. Come on, let's stroll." Lindy held her hand as the two stepped to the sidewalk bordering Frat Park.

"Paul was cheerier than you described him when we sat on the Quad."

"He hasn't been in one of his grumpy, kiss-it-goodbye phases lately."

"Paul is Paul, your friend relying on your support." She gazed at the stars.

"Em, a couple of guys have invited me to come into a group with them, a rock 'n' roll band that goes on stage and performs in the bars." He optimistically hyped the idea, "Potentially the hippest novelty since plaid Bermuda shorts."

"I'm surprised, when did this happen?"

"A buddy laid the offer on me last Wednesday. Four guys played together all summer here in Champaign, then one bolted for his wedding, slam-bam, Katie bar the door sudden." Instantly Lindy realized mentioning marriage was a blunder. "I jammed with two of them for a bit last year, you remember me talkin' about Franky Konkel, don't you, the perfectionist freak?"

"They considered you for the replacement?" an irritated Emily looked at her boyfriend.

"And I grabbed it. This is my first chance with guys intending to regularly perform onstage. The other times were one night stands, nothing more than huge, ol' screw off sessions, I don't think I was ever paid for any of the gigs. This opportunity is hard-core, put in the hours, really stretch-it-out effort. It was simple sayin' OK, to see if an average Joe like me can handle it."

Emily shook her head, "Easy agreeing because of the extra time and work?"

"Let me put it this way. I was watching a *Star Trek* rerun during New Student Week. In the episode, one of the female characters is an old-timer talking about the planets she's explored. One day while warpin' around in a far out galaxy she came to grasp her age, the decades addin' up and, as she depicted it, 'there were more years behind than ahead.' In a fashion, that's my feeling, time is short, no sense wasting any, and beam me up, Scotty."

"You upset me with this talk. You're only twenty-one, you and the rest of us will live for many more years."

"I'm sorry scaring you, Em, and no, I don't think I'll get cut short before my time, unless after graduation I'm drafted." Now Lindy was uneasy, this conversation not following his outline. "It's what you and Robby and me have discussed. I'm in my senior year and after this June life changes. Like everyone else, for the first time I'll have to grow up, make real decisions. With these musicians, these next months may be my sole shot to prove to I've got enough guts and grit to work for the dreams I want."

The pair leaned against a parked car on Chalmers Street a half block from KIDs, the booming music echoing to them. Lindy studied a brooding Emily. "Aren't you curious how the *Star Trek* episode concluded?"

"Did they have other guitar players in mind?"

"According to Franky, they figured I'd be interested and asked me first. I wanted in and said yes."

Arms folded, Emily's lips were tight together, "When is your first performance?"

"To begin with, there's practicin' to plow through. We figure on a month of rehearsals for puttin' a song list in shape before hittin' the bars." Lindy's tone returned to buoyant explaining the band.

"How often will you rehearse?" she matter-of-factly asked.

"Four or five nights a week. I haven't even met two of the guys."

"And after that you'll perform in bars around the campus?"

"Yeah, plus other college towns: Eastern Illinois in Charleston, Illinois State in Bloomington. Heck, The Guild even plays way down south at Carbondale."

Summer Never Comes

"How many performances a week will you schedule?"

"Good question, maybe two or three."

"Then it's only for this first month you'll be working hard, that won't be too awful."

"I see where you're headin', and it's not how you think. There's rehearsing after we start linin' up gigs. Practice never ends, no rest for the wicked."

"We are a couple, Will, you could have talked to me first, I should have a say and you should hear my opinion." An auto raced toward the Quad, the radio drowning out KIDs' stereo. "What does this mean for us?"

"I imagine not as much time together as last year. But I don't think we'll practice both evenings on the weekends, so we can see each other then. And we'll hook up during the week, I promise."

"This will be different," Emily was disappointed, "we were so close, getting along so well, and now this…this group."

"We'll see each other, Em, I just said that, I'm not throwing you away and never plan to. I'm takin' on a boatload: classes, booking, practicin', performing, it won't be simple for either of us. But please appreciate my side. Music's my life, dear to me, you've known that for a long time. If I don't take this risk, grab the wheel and captain my own boat, I'll never discover my talent; there might never be another chance, or if there is, it may come years from now. Who can tell, some day we might marry, and after raising our children, buying a house and fixin' it up, payin' each and every bill, how much energy will remain? When will my break arrive, if not now? Like the man said, posing questions, don't you think?"

"At least you place me in your future." Emily's hip slipped nearer to Lindy's body.

"We've dated for a year, that's a long time for me seeing one person. There's been a lot that's been fantastic and I like to think we're for each other, we need each other. You'll always be there, I promise."

"Oh, Will, what if it doesn't work out and bad things happen? What if there aren't enough days for everything, including me?"

"Worst-case scenario is the band flops, one of those here-today-gone-tomorrows. If the group does bite the bullet, at least we'll see each other more by Thanksgiving."

Summer Never Comes

Emily rested her head on his shoulder. Lindy rubbed her arm and the two heard the Rascals' 'Baby I'm Blue' rumbling from KIDs.

# # # #

"Keg number eight's tapped."

"Where'd Ozark and Eddie-Bob disappear to?"

"Come on, honey, I'm offerin' you your last chance."

"Not a keeper, definitely a two-bagger, I'm glad I dumped her."

"Bolted for the skin flicks at the Auditorium."

"What a horse's ass, all he talked about was football, I'm glad I dumped him."

Past midnight and the house was loaded, a fair part of the crowd packing around the kegs. With the barrels in a corner, partiers pushed from three directions, confusing the traffic and drinking patterns. Paul followed the mob, inching forward for a refill, fretting over Lindy's wink. Unexpectedly, he was jabbed in the ribs, so hard his empty cup almost dropped out of his hand.

"What's shakin', buddy?" The boisterous, boasting, pompous voice only belonged to one KID.

"Killer, how's it going?" Paul adopted the carefree tone. "Wild party?"

"Passable. I've eyed more broads in one place but this is acceptable; I've tasted frostier brews in my time but this is adequate." Killer rocked on his heels. "Tell me, where's Lindy vamoosed to?"

"Twenty minutes ago he was on the patio with Emily."

"And about when I was talkin' to him. Had a really factual dialogue developin', telling him about the far-out stuff I experienced over the summer, the swank box seats I snagged at Wrigley Field for the Cubs games and roughin' it one night camping in northern Wisconsin." Killer predictably sounded overexcited. "Then I asked a question about this pop orchestra he's hooked up with, and next thing I know Lindy's vanished—adios, took a powder."

"You've heard about Frogfeet?"

"So that's the name, is it? I didn't even have an opening for learning that. Strange, I'll tell you, like he didn't want to converse with me. And that's not Lindy's way, he generally sketches in details." Killer's shrieking was

Summer Never Comes

easily hearable over the music. "Say, Pauly, have you noticed a dazzling, blonde chiquita from Peoria trottin' around here? I chanced on her in my finance class and told her to stop by if she wanted to feel some hard rock goodies. You know, rack and roll, ménages à trois, breakfasts in bed."

"Can't say I have." Paul yelled into his ear. "What's her name?"

"Beverly." He looked around the jammed-in crowd, shaking his head.

"I'm sure she'll show, who'd pass on an invitation like that?"

"True, true," Killer was upbeat. Ahead of Paul in the mob, he reached the keg and filled his cup. "Well, I'm cruisin' and seein' if old Bev's put in an appearance. Good night, Pauly."

"Later," laughing as his fraternity brother stepped away, Paul leaned over and pumped the tapper a dozen times.

"Your friend is eccentric."

Paul turned. The voice belonged to a blonde-haired coed. He peered at his glass, uncertain how to answer. "He's not so bad, only occasionally obnoxious, like everybody else."

"A charitable response."

"Can I fill yours?" Paul handed his full cup to the girl, grabbed her empty and noticed her foot tapping on the foyer's slate floor. Finished at the spigot, he followed the coed through the crowd. "You're not the Peoria woman Killer is searching out, are you?"

"Oh, no, my hair color's coincidence, I've never seen him before tonight." She was three inches shorter than Paul's six feet, with a slim, perfect body, her bellbottoms' beltline riding low on her hips. "Is his name Killer?"

"It's Gary Groth. A year ago, Gary and the rest of the freshmen were holding football practices in Frat Park preparing for the intramural pledge league."

"How did their team do?" She interrupted.

"No talent, they stunk up the season with a 0–6 record. But a gung-ho Gary designated himself a defensive lineman plus cheerleader. During practices, he roamed the field, yelling, slapping his classmates' backs, instructing teammates on how the game is played, and by personal example doing his damnedest to show them. From what you saw, Gary being a pass rusher is no simple assignment since he's six foot two and maybe weighs a hundred forty pounds."

Summer Never Comes

"I figured as much." She held the plastic cup to her lips, biting the rim.

"Back to last autumn: every play Gary's in he does his best to sack the quarterback, only getting knocked down flat. He must have made fifteen or twenty attempts. But on one scrimmage, rushing against Moose Wozniak, Gary catches his break."

"Another classical nickname?"

"Of course. Moose tips the scales at two-seventy and is the house team's starting center. Nobody ever hustles by him and to the quarterback." A more confident Paul smiled, enjoying the conversation. "The night before this particular practice, Moose had put down a few beers at Stan's, more likely five or six pitchers. On the first hike, Gary plows straight into the Mooser and somehow, someway, nobody still comprehends how except that Moose was hung over, Gary knocks him flat on his ass, pardon my language. The entire park is silent and for once even Gary can't find words."

Still nibbling the cup, the girl relaxed on the wall.

"Finally, with the Mooser stretched on the ground, Frank Byers runs up and screams 'Ladies and gentlemen, the new cham-peen of Fraternity Park! THE KILLER!'"

"I love it." She touched Paul's arm.

"Honest to God true story," he crossed his heart with his fingers and grinned again, "so descriptive a label it's hard remembering his actual name."

"Mine's Sharon Taylor." She moved her hand around Paul's back and hugged him.

"Paul Roberts, Sharon, glad meeting you."

"Where did you learn telling tales like that?"

"I'm not talented at stories. For this one, I was an eyewitness the day Killer flattened Moose."

"Describing the scene is easier when you're an observer, the inner eye dissembling details."

"Spoken like a philosophy major."

"No," she smiled shaking her head," I've never enrolled in a phil course in three and a half years."

"You're a senior?"

"Yes, how about you?"

Nodding, Paul and gulped his beer.

Summer Never Comes

"Finished in June?"

"I suppose so," he sounded flat, "and yourself?"

"Graduating, but hopefully staying. I'm applying to the College of Veterinary Medicine, which, if I'm lucky, means four more years of the U of I"

"A female vet? I didn't think women tried for those jobs. Taking care of animals seems too grueling for a girl, like a female carpenter—not many of those around." Paul ruefully realized he'd insulted the only woman who'd talked to him all night.

"What am I hearing? We're in the '70s, not the 1950s. Do you think women should be stereotyped, are only qualified for menial jobs, like secretaries or bank tellers? Society's evolving, discrimination was yesterday, civil rights and equality is our present. Requirements for careers aren't outdated labels, but aspirations, aptitude and training to succeed." Sharon did not sound snubbed, but confident in her beliefs. "Don't you think girls know how to pound a hammer?"

"Let me backtrack, I apologize for my sarcasm and don't want you categorizing me as a sexist. Life's about everybody having the same prospects. The female carpenter phrase wasn't out of line, however."

"Yes, plenty of women look ridiculous in bib overalls. But I'm aggravated when my gender is put down. Women have the rougher route if we want more than stay-at-home existences, we deserve realistic opportunities to establish ourselves. It's time to acknowledge women are as qualified as men for every career."

"How'd you come by this attitude, if you don't mind me asking?" Paul loosened up, thankful he hadn't blown his chance with Sharon.

"Three years experiencing the University of Illinois. There's so much knowledge and potential here if we baby boomers are intelligent enough to appreciate it."

"You get this from Champaign?"

"And the six girls I live with in Urbana, all with the same outlook. We spend nights and days working out how the world should be run, that today's the moment for parity for both sexes, and how women should exploit these breakthroughs."

"Whoa, will you let men in?"

"To our ideal, progressive world? Of course, there's plenty of room."

Summer Never Comes

"I mean your house in Urbana, can us men hike over and visit?" KIDs and their dates, chuggers and strangers, post-laid undergrads and a few sadly shut down, passed by Sharon and Paul. "I didn't realize vet school was a four year program."

"And as intense as medical school. All life needs protecting." They watched Killer rapping to a brunette. "What's your major?"

"I'm in the business school, accounting."

"That puts you in David Kinley Hall and the Comm West Building, with debits on the blackboard, assets in textbooks and liabilities on paper. Here's a question, is the name accounting or accountancy? I never knew which."

"Accountancy is the formal title of the four year program."

"Which means when you're finished in June you find a job?"

"That's the intent," Paul dryly answered, "time to head into the real world."

Sharon studied his face. "There are worse scenarios, you could graduate and stay unemployed for six months; or when you leave school you're drafted."

"A buddy is over in 'Nam now, receiving his extra credit at Saigon University. Billy Powell had a real low number and no hopes of avoiding the Army."

"What's yours?"

"359. The only way the government snags me is if North Vietnam invades Rantoul. But seven or eight seniors aren't so fortunate, for them the Army after graduation is a genuine horror." He sounded downcast.

Intuiting Paul's mood, Sharon nudged his elbow. "I'm sorry spoiling your Saturday night."

The stereo blasted 'Little Deuce Coupe' for the third time since midnight. Around the room, couples hopped up and boogied. Tommy Quarters grabbed Barb Douglas, Ron Gimbel's blind date, and darted to the floor. Seeing Sharon tapping her foot again, Paul debated asking her to dance. He chugged his leftover beer, set the cup on the floor, but before he spoke a totally inebriated, enjoying herself coed tumbled toward the pair, pretzeling around Sharon's neck.

Summer Never Comes

"Hey kid-doo, how's my-old roomie, havin' a-nice time?" she slurred and Sharon struggled to prevent them from falling. Her frizzy hair hid Sharon's face.

"Paul, this Mary O'Donnell, a housemate and best buddy. She loves beer, too." Sharon stabilized her friend. "Mary, you're drunk, how did this happen?"

"I think-you're correct, kid-doo," Mary yelled as she steadied on Sharon, "though I'm thrilled reaching here."

"Looks like you're done in." She chuckled. "Sorry, Paul, I better see her home to bed."

"Where's your house?"

"On California Avenue, just east of Busey."

"That's a mile away, I could walk with you to help with your friend."

"A sweet offer, but we drove in my car. I liked the tale and conversation. Do it again?" Sharon navigated the tipsy Mary through the crowds.

"Sure, glad to, fine with me, anytime, absolutely, positively, my pleasure," Paul gasped for phrases, recalling Kentucky's earlier lecturing.

"See you later."

"Travel safe." Paul looked at his watch, 1:45, then his beer cup on the floor. He'd had plenty to drink but picked up the glass and headed to the keg.

# # # #

"Your friends loved the party," Kay Reising said.

"Super bunch of guys, a great evening." On a mattress on the floor in his room, an ecstatic Shaky Jake squeezed a satisfied Kay in his arms. Falling asleep, he stroked his thumb up and down her back. The pair listened to the house stereo playing three floors below.

Nude except for the gold chain around his neck, Dale Kinsey sprawled on his bed. The broad straddled his legs, face on his pot belly, one of her nipples pointing toward the wall. Naked too, she ran her fingertips through Dale's hair. When she paused, he wiggled his knees to start her scratching again. Dale gripped a wine glass in his right hand, a lit cigarette in his left, and decided this bimbo wasn't as gorgeous as he'd supposed four hours ago.

Summer Never Comes

Drooping his head against the backboard, he gawked at the ceiling. The Temptations' 'I Wish It Would Rain' spun on his turntable, and two wet rubbers laid on the carpet.

On the patio outside Dale's window, Dicky Lyston, Joey Panky, Billy Cherwinkie and the heavily loaded Eddie-Bob McMahon sat in a circle, passing around a joint, the mini-butt held in a pair of pliers.

"I survived the sway in Section K."

# # # #

Paul was wide awake in his top bunk. The door opened and Lindy, carrying two beer cups, stepped through and slumped into a chair.

"What's up, Robby?"

"I'm enjoying the peace and quiet of Saturday night."

"Well, nothin' criminal with that," Lindy chugged one glass. "How was the rest of the party?"

"Pretty decent, the stoners lost control of the stereo around midnight, and instead of their acid trip we played respectable dancing music."

"Did you have a good time?" Lindy flipped on his desk lamp.

"Can't complain, I drank enough and almost made it to the dance floor."

"That a fact?" Lindy sat up. "A good lookin' babe, no doubt?"

"She was cute, but had to leave before I asked her. And you, how'd the conversation with Emily go?"

"Not so agreeable, been through simpler times. I told Em about my band earlier than I planned because everyone inside the house had found out."

"Is that what Killer was rapping on?"

"You ran into him too? When I left Em and you for refills, I ended up next to Killer in the mobs at the keg."

"Which is where I saw him."

"There's something about him and crowds, he's always knotted up in one. Any rate, in front of everybody Killer starts congratulatin' me about Frogfeet, how it's gonna be super havin' a celebrity in the house, how I'll be able to snag free beers for the brothers at the bars we play at plus backstage passes for everyone when we go on road trips. And you know Killer, he's never heard of a whisper, the numb-nutted dumbass. After his broadcasting, the whole bunch at the barrels starts slappin' me on the back and I knew I was in trouble up to my big toe. Thank goodness you two were on the patio. I figured the best course was to find you, get Em alone and right away let her know." Lindy chugged the second beer.

"How'd she take it?"

"Upset right from the first sentence, then the mopey Sister Sally act. Part of her complaint was me failin' to sound her out before informing Franky Konkel I'd join Frogfeet. Her sentiment is we should discuss significant stuff before a decision, not after. Em's also worried I'll perform so much I'll disappear this semester and won't see her anymore."

"And?" Paul leaned on one arm.

"I told her even though there's so much goin' down I'll fit everything in, whatever happens I'll always have time for her. But you know Em, so uncertain, I hope she believes me."

"You were honest, weren't you?"

"That's a hell of a comment. Of course." Lindy slouched in his chair. "We spent the evening talking and walkin' around Frat Park, then the Quad. I can't count how many times we passed the Union, me tamping down her worries. And that's the truth, totally is. Why would I jeopardize what I've got with Em? She's the sincerest, most wonderful woman I've ever met, keeps me on a path and away from the weird-ass stuff we KIDs get away with. More so than you or Bobby or Stu have ever stopped me."

"Complimenting or complaining?"

"Take your pick," Lindy weakly smiled. "What I'm sayin' is even with this band flyin', I don't want to screw up with Em, there's a balance and I need to succeed at both."

"Sounds as if you're in a corner."

"If my girlfriend were around I'd call it the horns of a dilemma. Everything's gonna be fine. This semester'll be a ball-buster for yours truly, but with a little fortitude I'll handle it, and so will Em. She's a good kid, she'll understand this is something I've got to pull off. Funny, we spent a whole evening together and she never asked me for the band's name." Lindy stood and turned off the light. "I need another beer."

# # # #

Summer Never Comes

Alone in her dorm room, a melancholy Emily lay on her bed, gazing at the ceiling. It wasn't right for Will to play with this band, wrong for him to take his time and waste it on a ridiculous, childish adventure. What was there to gain? Go out and see if he's competent, follow a dream, take a chance before it's too late? What kinds of excuses are those? None making sense to her. Why would he do this when his life was so full, abandon her to a foolish, inane, absurd fantasy, some scheme that won't succeed? How long should she wait for him to realize the mistake he's making? What should she do?

A miserable Emily pounded the mattress. In love so much, she couldn't conjure anything but waiting for Will to understand how she cared for him, and to return to her.

Chapter Four

"Thanks for meeting with me."

"This is a pleasure, history grad students from Charleston, Illinois aren't often interviewed by *DI* reporters."

"I'm enrolled in a history course this semester, with Professor Arnstein."

"He's the department's expert on Victorian England," Laurie Allman answered in a calm voice, "and wrote the text book used in History 132."

Early Tuesday morning, Paul sat drinking coffee with Laurie in the Illini Union's basement Cafeteria. "Eastern Illinois University is in Charleston, isn't it?"

"Yes, my family's farm is located in Ashmore, ten miles from the campus, on land we've worked for eighty years." Laurie smiled as fellow students passed their table for the breakfast line, "Tell me, why are we talking?"

"The *Daily Illini* is researching a story on the U of I's peace movement, the beginnings, today's activities and goals. A fraternity brother of mine in another anti-war group mentioned you, as a longtime activist, being a good source."

"SOAP's story starts with Lyndon Johnson duping America into Vietnam. In August of 1964, according to Pentagon accounts, North Vietnamese gunboats attacked two American naval vessels in international waters. LBJ described the incident as 'deliberate aggression on the high seas,' and ordered the military to retaliate. Congress almost unanimously approved the Tonkin Gulf Resolution, and away America went to war."

"Didn't two senators vote no?" Paul asked.

"Wayne Morse of Oregon and Alaska's Ernest Gruening, the first doves. Remember, this is happening with Johnson campaigning for the presidency against Barry Goldwater, the country's original 'nuke 'em first, ask questions later' politician. Back then only a few, namely male college students worried about the draft, argued for peace and felt the hawks should be challenged. In Champaign, SOAP was organized to alert students to the deceitful way the war began, the costs if Vietnam continues and continues, and the consequences for anyone close to conscription. We supply information and justifications to help end the war."

"What are examples?"

"The historical record, for one. Evidence shows Johnson lied in '64, the tale didn't make sense that our seven hundred-ship navy could be endangered by a few Communist gunboats. Secondly, we document the dozens of Pentagon research projects the University of Illinois oversees and the school's compensation. Millions of dollars squandered on the strangest schemes; the funds the military complex doles out to manipulate people are mind-blowing. And, as I said, we provide draft-threatened students channels for avoiding the Army: sympathetic doctors to consult for medical examinations, for one."

"Looks tasty, don't you think?" at the next table an undergrad was enjoying the Cafeteria's unofficial breakfast specialty, a pecan cinnamon roll.

"Which fraternity are you in, Paul?"

"Kappa Iota Delta."

"KIDs on Third Street, across from the Phi Mu sorority," Laurie chuckled. "You guys have wild parties, I heard last Saturday's spilled into Frat Park."

"That's our reputation. I wish we were known around campus for being scholars rather than drinkers. Were you there?"

"I was invited but that's not my style, I'm not a bars scene fan." Laurie relaxed in the chair, "Who's your friend mentioning my name?"

"Randy Miller, from SCRAP."

"That mob."

"Why call them that?"

"Because they're a gang of thugs, Professor Arnstein would label them rapscallions."

"My friend's an OK guy."

"Likely one of the few in SCRAP that is," Laurie replied. "Whenever the anti-war groups get together, every time there are protest activities,

Summer Never Comes

SCRAP insists on center stage, takes control and always extorts advantages. If someone else has more appealing displays or pamphlets, they'll steal the flyers and reword the ideas as their own. If someone occupies a more prominent place, they'll shove their way to where they expect to be. Look at what happened with the Quad Day site assignments."

"How's that?" Paul wrote in his three ring binder.

"As we were instructed, DISGUST, RAW and SOAP followed the university's registration procedures for permits and located our booths in the assigned areas along the sidewalks. Did you spot SCRAP's position? The steps right outside the Union. Of all the campus organizations they were the only ones situated where everyone could notice them. And because they were in the open on the patio, SCRAP was the only group photographed by your paper."

"Now that you mention it, SCRAP was on the *Daily Illini's* front page. Which is my editor's choice—publicizing peace protesting makes her feel the *DI's* doing our part." Paul made a note to check with Stef Tianen about pictures when he saw her this afternoon. "But I walked around that day, past SOAP's and SCRAP's locations. From what I saw, SCRAP didn't attract any more students than anybody else."

"Which emphasizes the campus' indifference in ending the war, why so few care about an issue with the potential to inflict whole worlds of hurt. Consider this: thirty thousand spectators come to Memorial Stadium to watch mediocre Fighting Illini football teams win three or four games a season. Last Thursday, at our SOAP meeting, there were twelve undergrads. Tens of thousands killed in Vietnam in the years since Tonkin Gulf, God knows how many maimed or missing, and a mere dozen attend a gathering for stopping the murdering and dishonesty that triggered it. How sad."

"Student apathy: I am neither for nor against," Paul said. "Why stay all these years? Why care about the anti-war movement if so many concede and quit?"

"Necessity. Even if undergrads presume we're protected or too out-of-touch to be bothered, our generation must protest until the country's bad guys are replaced and policies change. Eventually Americans will recognize the war for the mistake it is: a gigantic, wasteful blunder the government shouldn't have started in the first place. With enough evidence and arguing we'll reach that point; slowly the country will awaken." Laurie searched the

Cafeteria, watching one student refill his coffee cup for free from the huge metal urn next to a pillar. "Or some appalling disaster might happen. Then people will say enough is enough and the politicians will stop the war. Until then, someone has to hold the issues in front of U of I students. That's what I've done for the past five years and why I'll carry on."

"Are you wanting a tragedy full of hurt and victims, then be the one to claim 'I told you so, why didn't you listen to me years ago?'"

"No, like the bars, that's not what I'm into," Laurie relaxed in her chair, "I'm not a narcissist."

"What about RAW, DISGUST and SCRAP and their intentions?"

"I'd say the other groups are mostly sincere with ending the war, except for that outrageous SCRAP crew. I think they're devious, like their leader."

"You've talk to Bernard Minerath?"

"Four years ago when I was a sophomore we were in classes together, including History 152. Bernard knew the material, prepared for discussions and always asked curious questions—the ones prompting professors to interrupt reciting lecture notes and explain a topic."

"Is Bernard a history major?"

"I'm unsure, he might have been in political science. And he was older than me, maybe a junior or a senior. Back then I remember him as a nice guy, not gregarious, but amicable. After classes, along with our fellow '152 students, we'd stop in Stan's for beers—our personal discussion section over a pitcher of Stroh's. Bernard liked to kick back, even go dancing at Chances R. He was a different person four years ago."

"Doesn't sound so bad, a guy in a bar rapping and drinking," Paul scanned his notes. "But you say he's not to be trusted."

"After three classes together we stopped seeing each other, which is common with Champaign-Urbana's thousands of students. I didn't meet him again until three semesters later, at the last election, after SCRAP had organized with Bernard as its leader—which I thought was a positive. That year, SOAP supported Joe Pisciotte, a university professor campaigning for state senator, and I contacted Bernard inquiring whether SCRAP would help at a rally. What a makeover from our old history course days! No hellos, reminiscing or closeness. He was somber, nearly rude. Bernard held to his own ideas about backing candidates—the single issue was Vietnam, community problems were taboos. If the anti-war movement wasn't foremost, SCRAP's assistance was unattainable."

"Refresh my memory on that election."

"The Oakley Dam Project was one controversy. The Army Corps of Engineers proposed constructing a levee on the Sangamon River to create a reservoir out of a thousand acres in Allerton Park. Some said the objective, flood prevention, was beneficial, others thought the dam would harm the region's ecology and fauna. When I discussed this with Bernard, he said no to it and every other local matter, except the war. His is the only way. He composes the script, the followers obey orders."

"A disappointment?"

"Definitely. I know I'm the one maintaining the war should be constantly, sincerely advocated, and I'll admit my SOAP is not the most forceful campus group for achieving that. But Bernard's stance is too extreme."

"Give me illustrations." More students walked to the urn for free coffee, one filling his whole thermos.

"The break-ins the last two weeks at SOAP's, RAW's and DISGUST's offices."

"I've only heard of the first two."

"Kevin Connors, DISGUST's chairman, phoned me last night, and his account matches a pattern. At all three offices there were scavenged-through filing cabinets and one wooden desk splintered into pieces, neatly piled in the middle of the floor—not scattered around. As if the intruders announced, 'See what we've done to you and how we did it.'"

"Deliberate?"

"Yes."

"Not our fellow college students out for a disorderly Saturday night?"

"Their modus operandi marking their determination." Laurie was explicit.

"Who are you claiming is responsible?"

"A guess would be SCRAP, because they haven't been vandalized and their leader, Bernard, is the guy with the nerve for these tactics."

"What would be a motive?"

# # # #

Summer Never Comes

Associated Press - Saigon - United States Army Headquarters confirms North Vietnamese troops have recaptured the town of Huong Hoa and cut off United States forces from their bases in the south. Allied units are being supplied by irregular air drops, reportedly near the Se Bang Fal River. As a result of this deteriorating logistical situation, Operation Loading Dock has slowed. Heavy fighting is reported, with Marine reinforcements being airlifted to the Huong Hoa area.

UPI - Saigon - United States Army Headquarters reports that reinforcements from Hué have joined the battle in Huong Hoa and are 'engaging and pressing Communist forces' in an effort to recapture the strategic South Vietnamese region. Control of Huong Hoa is 'considered vital' by the Army's command in order to reestablish secure supply lines with the United States and ARVN forces in Laos, and continuing Operation Loading Dock and the Se Bang Fal offensive.

# # # #

"Saturday was another total blow-out KIDs party. How many kegs floated?"

"Twelve, plus ten jugs of wine. The empties are sitting on our patio waiting to go back to Barnett's." Paul laughed, "This is the second conversation today with my fraternity's drinking reputation mentioned. Since when have you taken an interest in our weekends? I thought *DI* social reporting was out since the 'Campus Scout' was revamped."

"I hear things." Stef Tianen shifted to her all-business tone, "I want to talk over the new project."

"The weekend magazine, have you named it?"

"Al Stojak and I settled on *Spectrum*. Runners up were *Weekender* and *DownTime*, but both sounded too trivial, we wanted a title connoting substance." The editor-in-chief slid a pair of handball gloves across her desk. "I'm wondering if your peace movement story might be too ambitious an undertaking. With the numbers of campus protesters the entire assignment—researching backgrounds, scheduling interviews and returning to double check sources—means plenty of chasing, especially for someone with your detail-minded habits."

"I'll grant it's complicated. With five peace groups, including one ad hoc collection of LAS instructors, investigating everyone's origins and how often they meet and plan will take time. Discovering who's in charge of each will be a deal."

"Exactly my thoughts. We're looking at three or four months' work, at the earliest finishing next spring. Which is too late. If I were a hundred-percent sharper, last summer I would have detailed a reporter to dig into the peace movement's history. As I say, now we couldn't complete it until March or April, when we're coasting toward graduation."

"Are you switching this story to someone else? Don't you think I can handle it?" This afternoon, as at other times, Paul was wary of Stef.

"Ability isn't a question. Your writing for the paper has always been well-composed. And I haven't discussed this proposal with anyone else on the staff. The issue is not leaving loose ends for the next editor-in-chief, that's sloppy planning." Stef relaxed in her wooden chair, as ever positive she could persuade Paul. "For replacements, what about the topics we reviewed two weeks ago? A few will honestly make worthy stories, don't you think?"

Paul felt slighted. The conversation with Laurie had piqued his curiosity in the anti-war groups, he wanted to stay with the project. For once in his college years, he stood firm. "Since we're being honest, the others were crap. The more I think about my article, I'm convinced it's worthwhile. These latest battles prove Vietnam is a huge mess for America, that the war isn't ending anytime soon. Connect the campus' reaction with the peace groups' demonstrating and we offer Champaign-Urbana more to deliberate, we get our generation involved. Isn't that journalism's mission? Research the facts and write stories compelling enough to prod readers? That's why you're calling the magazine *Spectrum* instead of the puffier alternatives, right? As far as this being too much work, maybe yes, maybe no, I'll assess that as my research progresses, and if I need help I'll say so. I won't bog down or miss the deadline, I also don't want to leave anything undone come June."

Contemplating this logic, mindful of his reluctance over graduation, the editor-in-chief smiled at Paul's last sentence.

Summer Never Comes

"I've already started. I spent the morning with Laurie Allman of SOAP, the other person nailing me on KIDs' drinking. We began with Johnson's two-faced Tonkin Gulf Resolution. What a bastard, LBJ, escalating a few gunshots in the middle of the ocean into a Communist invasion of the whole world."

"He's not the first president to deceive us into a war and won't be the last."

"So true. SOAP is in a comfort zone of only presenting facts. Their approach is unpretentious, like Laurie. She's a bookish sort of undergrad, not someone you'd imagine committing five years to the anti-war movement. My sense is their 'only the details' method bogs them down. Laurie brought up the *Daily Illini's* picture policy—why some groups' photographs are printed and others aren't."

"Oh?" Stef bounced a tennis ball. "How'd you respond?"

"Editor's discretion, with no particular groups favored. That's the answer, right?"

"As my predecessors, I look for fairness, with the understanding that photographs underscore a story or entertain readers. Why the questions, do you want your old photo assignment back?"

"Confirmation of what I told Laurie." Paul opened his notebook, satisfied with Stef's response. "Here's a sidebar: Laurie knows Bernard Minerath, or once did is more accurate. Both took the same history courses when she was an undergrad, one with the Civil War professor, Robert Johannsen. After classes they'd sit in the bars drinking together. I got the feeling Laurie was close to Bernard back then, enjoyed hanging around with him. Then they lost contact, not like a couple splitting—just the way friendships fizzle out in the Cham-Bana crowds. They didn't meet again until the last election, when Laurie requested SCRAP's help for a local candidate's campaign. She claimed Bernard was changed from their history class days—totally business, no friendship or warmth. She called him rude."

"Could be a long time ago Bernard Minerath was a hound dog for the ladies and Laurie Allman a jilted love, a one night stand. Student romances quash many of us. If years ago they were companions or something more intimate, her present opinion of him may be biased."

"I doubt her intention is payback. Laurie may dislike Bernard today, but she's dedicated enough to recuse her emotions. Remember the years she's worked for SOAP, that's loyalty to a cause."

"Emotions hinder judgment, especially when we're young. But melodramatic as it appears, I'm uncertain how Bernard's personality plays into your article." Stef was back in her editor-in-chief role, "Or even if there will be one for you to compose and for me to publish."

"You want to cancel it?"

"I have doubts."

"We should continue because we have the responsibility, we're the witnesses. Vietnam, Laos, Operation Loading Dock, the anti-war groups, next week's peace rally are on our watch. Our job is reporting what we see and laying out the facts for our fellow students. If we don't chronicle these years, who will? It goes back to what I said earlier about journalism: purpose, conscience, substance. And I'm surprised I'm debating this instead of you. I'm the staff researcher; you're the editor, the one expected to maintain the *Daily Illini*'s mission, determine how our record will read, how tomorrow's students will understand our time."

"I've never heard you talk this way, why with this story?"

"You didn't think I had it in me, is that what you're saying?" Paul conceded Stef was correct, his speaking out was odd. Why a spark today? Something about the peace movement's issues, the foolishness the latest American offensive in Laos illustrated? Curiosity in Laurie and Bernard's friendship? Did the war now mean more to him because his friend, Billy Powell, was in 'Nam? Stef supposing him too untalented to write the piece? At last, finally, acknowledging he was a senior and had to contribute?

The doubting editor-in-chief sat in her chair. Informing readers, as Paul asserted, was journalism. Even the student-managed, only-published-five-days-a-week *Daily Illini's* purpose was chronicling crucial events like Vietnam and the country's reaction. But hadn't thousands of reports, explanations straight from Saigon, boots on the ground narratives, editorials and exposés already been filed? From every possible perspective and prejudice? Weren't readers as bored with articles about Vietnam as they were embittered by the war itself? What was the benefit of another story? Yet, what Paul argued was the reporting Stef wished for her newspaper. Credibly researched and written articles—reality regardless of effect. He made sense, and his appeal to conscience won Stef over. The qualms from a few weeks ago, however, after she'd impulsively assigned him this story, bothered her. What if he stumbled on unanticipated somethings? What if Paul-the-bookworm matured into Paul Roberts, investigator, and he closed on the truth? But the editor-in-chief was confident she could cope. Plans could be adjusted, reporters and stories throttled, rewritten or ignored.

Paul had framed his strongest case, then thought to back down. Maybe he didn't mean it. His analysis was sensible from the academic standpoint, not in the real world. What did he know about responsibility, anyway? Decisiveness was suddenly feeling awfully scary.

Stef tossed the tennis ball at the wall and peered at her friend. "Okay, the story's still yours."

# # # #

"Where are you guys heading?" Randy Miller asked.

"The Undergrad." Paul lifted his book bag.

"Third week of classes, time for seriousness about school," Bobby Sox added as they left KIDs. The evening was sultry and the three wore cut-offs, t-shirts and sandals. "How about you, Randy, no books tonight?"

"I'm attending a moratorium planning meeting."

"Where's it at?"

"The Union, this is our fourth night in a row; all the campus peace groups will be there." Randy sounded self-important.

"A who's who of peace?"

"Funny line, Bobby, but there's work involved preparing for Thursday afternoon to be a success."

"Like what, Randy?"

"The basics: the rally's starting time; where do we locate on the Quad; who applies for permits from the university; who sets up the stage, lectern and chairs? Where do we rent a sound system? Advertising the event, who finds and schedules the speakers? Who picks up the garbage after the rally's over? And booths will be arranged around the Quad for campus organizations to man for peace—who marshals them? Remember, no business as usual, support the moratorium."

Summer Never Comes

"Yeah, yeah, yeah," Bobby shook his head, "tell that to my finance professor, he's handing us a quiz Thursday morning."

"Then turn out for the afternoon rally. If the entire student body joins in, we'll send a message, the politicians will have to listen to the people, not the right-wingers propping up Vietnam so monopolists can rip off more money. That's the only way to finish off this damned war. If we sit on our asses, it'll continue forever."

"You argue like a *DI* editorial." The five foot three Bobby hurried to keep pace with his taller fraternity brothers. "Hold on, there are two things happenin' Thursday?"

"The Moratorium on Business as Usual is a day-long strike, no student's supposed to participate in any normal activities, and wouldn't it be something if the whole campus joined in? The second part's the peace rally."

"What's one rally gonna mean? A couple hundred U of I students cutting classes and hangin' outside catching rays doesn't sound like a huge protest. How much of a difference is that, who'll notice?"

"If only undergrads at Illinois, no one. But the protesting isn't limited to Champaign-Urbana, campuses across the country are involved. The louder the dissent, the profounder the impact."

"Seems like somebody's makin' a lot of calls to orchestrate this scheme. As I said, I wish you peace freaks would phone my fin professor and negotiate a moratorium on that quiz."

"First things first, Bobby. We finish off the war, then do away with exams."

"Randy," Paul interrupted, "since you're familiar with the groups, how about getting together for a question and answer session on an article I'm researching for the *Daily Illini*?"

"Super idea, publicity is a plus. Come with me to this meeting, we'll talk on the way and you'll see first hand how the rally's developing."

"Thanks for the invitation, but Bobby and I are heading to the Undergrad."

"Booking, always sensible. By the way, where are your roommates?" Randy inquired. "You four generally convoy together."

"Lindy's practicing with his band again, and Stu's already in the Reference Room with his new girlfriend; she has him hitting the books. We're meeting later at Second Chance for a sociable brew."

Summer Never Comes

"Maybe I'll stop by myself when the meeting's finished; we'll talk then." Past the Ice Rink, Randy headed toward the Union.

Entering the hectic Undergrad, Paul and Bobby walked down to the lower level. The long tables were packed, the oversized lounge chairs near the windows filled, students stood in cliques telling jokes, and there was a low buzz of many yakking voices. Because of the noises, Paul avoided midweek booking in this place. Tonight he was with Bobby because his friend needed to check out a pamphlet from the Reserved Reading Area. With Stu on his own, Bobby, detesting loneliness, wanted a buddy with him.

# # # #

Emily sat alone in her dorm room studying Biology 100's textbook, *The Biosphere*.

"All life on the Earth is of course ultimately powered by the sun, and accordingly it is strongly affected by variations of the incoming solar radiation over the globe. This can be caused by the annual changes in the distance of the Earth's orbit and by solar storms emanating from the sun's surface.

"Averaged over the globe, about 30% of the sun's radiation is either scattered by the constituents of the atmosphere or directly reflected by clouds or the Earth's surface. Scientific investigation has demonstrated that this percentage has remained constant for millions of years."

Last spring, the second half of her sophomore year, Lindy and Emily booked together every Tuesday evening. The two met at 6:45 in the English Library where, by mutual agreement, they studied for three hours. None of Will's under-the-table pokes or clichés, no dour looks from Emily, only concentration and serious work. At evening's end, the two relaxed in the Undergrad tunnel, ate a slice of pizza at Garcia's on Sixth Street, or returned to Blaisdell Hall and chatted about nothings particular. As all her time with Will, Emily cherished these English Library dates.

"Happy as a lark, the golden age of fleas on a dog."

Sadly, not this semester. Will was rehearsing with the band every evening. How much time, Emily wondered, would she be by herself and what other pieces of their friendship lost?

Summer Never Comes

When she was a new freshman, Emily had few friends. There were the girls sitting around the lounge, gossiping, watching television, and sometimes they'd take in a movie at the YMCA or attend church. But there was no soulmate to share with, and Emily went home to her family nine weekends that year—a three hour car trip to Deerfield and another three hours returning to the campus on Sundays. Sophomore year started the same isolated, depressing way until the weekend Nicole and the others convinced her to take in the KIDs' Homecoming dance. What fabulous luck! She found Will, her decent, amiable, always-looking-after-her boyfriend. Emily's life widened, she became perkier and more confident— happy not needing to dawdle in the dorm lounge with the other coeds.

Then, at KIDs' 'Welcome Back Everybody' party, Will told her about joining the band. From the first sentence Emily wished he wouldn't, argued to persuade him to reconsider. Will tried making her understand and Emily conceded he presented a believable case, but she refused to bend. During the walk from KIDs to Blaisdell, when she realized he wouldn't be talked out of his plans, a pouting Emily quit speaking to him. Will was wrong, period.

The quarrel continued when Will telephoned the next day. Though pleased her boyfriend was thoughtful enough to talk again, a still-upset Emily hadn't forgotten Saturday night. The call was short and unpleasant. Afterwards, when she calmed down, Emily selfishly allowed she was angry because they would not be together as much as last year, she wanted to cling to her time with Will.

Apart from her boyfriend, abandoned in her dorm room again, Emily was frightened. What to do this semester, how to handle this danger? Plead to return to the way they were? Hand him an ultimatum, her or the band? Break off their relationship?

Maybe she should phone to say hello, find out what Will was doing tonight and discuss their quandary. No, in eleven months, Emily called only when absolutely needed. He was the man and telephoned her, that was their arrangement. Emily would wait.

# # # #

Summer Never Comes

"Okay, good, right on time." Franky Konkel kicked an empty beer can, "'Mad,' less snare at the outro."

"Gotcha," 'Mad' Johnny Wilson, Frogfeet's drummer, beat his crash cymbal.

"Lindy, I liked your humming there at the chorus, but softer next time, will you?" Franky adjusted his Stratocaster's strap. "Let's sing it again."

"Okey dokey."

"We think we're goin' back, to a place where…" Franky and Andy Arthur harmonized.

Rhythm guitar for this tune, Lindy stood to the left with Donny 'Woofer' Raasch. Andy and his keyboard were on the basement's opposite side and 'Mad' and his drum set sat ten feet away. Half concentrating, Lindy yawned, not caring for the Byrds' melody or lyrics.

This was Frogfeet's third session with all five together. Last summer, Franky, Woofer and 'Mad' had jammed in a band named Harold Coolidge. Andy and Lindy were the rookies, capable musicians but showing different styles, and Lindy decided fitting in would take tons more rehearsing. He had trouble following Woofer, the bass player skipping a beat about every ten bars. Vocals needed work too, Franky's the only decent-sounding voice. A so-so crooner, Lindy contributed little more that background.

"Okay. Enough with that one." Franky ordered. "Let's shove on to 'Tend My Garden.' Lindy, you take us out."

"One of my favorites," Woofer yelled.

The five knew the tune, having repeated the arrangement six or eight times last night. 'Mad' liked singing, even though he didn't have a part, and Lindy enjoyed playing lead on his Gibson—it forced him to concentrate. The song sounded a tad livelier tonight.

Frogfeet worked until 11:30, a four hour grind, with Franky giving the group a couple ten-minute breaks.

"That's a wrap. We'll call it and reload again tomorrow," Franky wiped his Strat and placed it in its case.

"Far out!" Dropping his sticks on the floor, 'Mad' stood for the first time all night. Five feet nine, dark red hair covered both ears and his shaggy beard needed trimming. "Who's in for a frosty?"

"Boogying to the Red Lion sounds super."

"I'm there," Woofer volunteered.

"Yep," Andy pounded a b-flat.

"I'll pass, guys," Lindy finished cleaning his guitar, "I gotta be up early tomorrow for my eight o'clock."

"You sure? You can always cut the class."

"Convinced, I'm fagged."

"Can we drop you off on our way to the Lion?" Franky picked up a soda can from the floor.

"No thanks, I'll hoof it."

The group rehearsed in the basement of a house at the corner of Locust and John Streets, a half mile from KIDs. Needing to book before racking, Lindy preferred walking back to wake up and not allow his fellow band members second chances to hijack him to the bars. With the muggy air and sleepier than he figured, Lindy was yawning before reaching First Street. God, what a dump truck of headaches I've bought myself. Franky and Woofer were lucky, graduated last year and working part time to pay bills. 'Mad' was a physiology major, but not panicked over school. And Andy, the affable-est of the group? Lindy wanted to get to know him better.

Five guys in a basement, jamming and practicing songs every Cham-Bana student has heard hundreds of times, nothing original or creative, just copy. Where's the rush, is this the break I prayed for? Will Frogfeet ever escape from the basement? If we don't, will anybody search for us? I hope, because it reeks down there. But at least ol' Lindy's in a band, my first, legitimate, lawful chance to hop on that stage. Well, not much of a band and probably the platform won't be anything special, so long as it doesn't tumble over. Maybe the future shuffles in small steps. What cliché was written on a wall in a Lincoln Hall john? 'The best is yet to be.' What about that second bon mot? 'Don't give up your day job.'

He'd handle whatever to make Frogfeet a success, as he told Robby, Em and all his friends. Lindy truthfully believed this his best shot, the last hurrah before graduation and turning into an adult. It's gonna be draining, but he had to grab for the brass ring. Strange, not finished with college, yet worrying over the finale, I sound like my roommate. What choices to make? How far to go? Hand Frogfeet the priority with everything else shoveled aside, cut back on booking, blow off school, snub my pals? Absolutely go hard-core and drop out of the Big U? No, too late for that, too far off the ledge, I'd lose the semester's $181.00 tuition and be in massive trouble with my mom. Besides school and homework, I'll have to make more time for everything else.

What about Em and Robby? His girlfriend had let Lindy know what she thought, there was no way she appreciated the band. After Sunday's phone call he wasn't sure Em fancied him much, either. Lindy would have to apologize, prove he loved her, forever loved her because he truly did.

Robby was Robby. Wary, afraid to step out, but a fair and foul weather buddy. He'll understand if I'm AWOL, bust ass and follow Frogfeet to the extreme end. I'll make it up to him, too, like I will to Em, I can't let them down. Oh, man, I haven't seen Robby since Sunday, wonder what he's been into this week?

Walking across Frat Park to KIDs, Lindy saw most of the house's lights were on. The old college life, 1:30 in the morning and everyone's wide awake. He wondered if Robby was in their room, then hoped he was asleep or at the Snack Bar or anywhere else. Lindy didn't have time tonight to sit around and rap with his roommate. He had to study for tomorrow's classes.

# # # #

Stef Tianen wrote Wednesday's editorial.

"America has fought in Vietnam since 1964: raiding, bombing and killing, accruing years of sorrowfulness and denial. Operation Loading Dock and the Se Bang Fal offensive are today's examples of this wayward national policy falling farther from universal brotherhood, and evermore toward bloodshed and death.

"The Washington warmongers accountable for this destruction of the peaceful world order must be forced to listen to the people's voice. Now is the moment to demonstrate our disagreement with the criminal course the government is pursuing in Southeast Asia. We must rise up as one.

"The theme of tomorrow's nation-wide protest is a 'Moratorium on Business as Usual.' In order to make our plea for peace heard, everyone opposing the government's policy in Asia is urged to abstain from all or some normal daily activities. A rally sponsored by the campus' activists and peace groups begins at two o'clock on the Quad. The *Daily Illini* urges the entire Champaign-Urbana community, every citizen concerned for America's future, to participate.

Summer Never Comes

"Stop the killing before there are none left to murder, before everyone is dead."

"We must end the war."

# # # #

Peace rally Thursday, the hottest day in Champaign-Urbana since New Student Week. At nine, the temperature reached eighty-five degrees, by 11:30, ninety-two. The organizing committee picked the easiest weekday for protesting, Thursdays typically light on classes. With many professors against the war, scores of lectures, labs and discussion sections were canceled or attendance declared optional. And, opportunely, the university's physical plant embraced the Moratorium's mood when air conditioners all over campus puzzlingly stopped operating in mid-morning.

Exiting the Union, Paul was among the thousands of students stuffing the Quad. Near the old Auditorium he saw the scaffolding Randy Miller had mentioned, a banner draped over the stage's middle and large public address speakers at either side. Two hundred yards away, Paul could not guesstimate the numbers of people standing on the platform.

"Wall, Robbeh, come t' ob-serve th' cir-cus?" Kentucky, thin and dyspeptic, wearing his wide-brimmed hat, sauntered toward him.

"I don't think many would appreciate you calling this rally a circus," he grinned.

"That's all this assemby is. It sure-leh is not a de-mon-stra-shun for aneh serious pur-pose, no suh!"

"Why say that? I'm certain more students than you think worry about the war and want to work against it."

"Ah do not de-ny thet thar ah some out he-ah thet care about bringin' ouh boys home. But foh ev'ry one oh' those, ah'd wager there ahr five with no in-clination whut thes is all about, they could not find Vi-et-Nam on a map if awarded four hints an' five chances. If'n th' wind shifted, th' sky clouded up an' th' rain began t' fall, they'd all be anxious about not gittin' wet, thet's whut they'd be frettin' about, their own be-hinds."

"Settle down, Kentucky, no sense reconstructing the War Between the States."

Summer Never Comes

"Ah reckon you-ahr right on thet one. There all-readeh is enough combat in th' world." He surveyed the Quad. "Say, whar is Lindeh? Ah reckoned he'd be out heah with all th' otheh lib-rals."

"Sleeping," Paul replied.

"On a beaut-iful day like thes?"

"Since he started practicing with Frogfeet, Lindy hasn't been back to our room before one or two in the morning, and I haven't talked to him since Sunday."

"Ah'm proud thet he's followin' hes dream, but Ah hope thet boy knows whut he's doin'. Wall, Ah'll be movin' on, now. Ah've witnessed enough of thes spectacle."

"Not staying for the speeches?"

"S'long, Robbeh," Kentucky loped toward the Union.

Dale Kinsey and Tommy Quarters skulked through the student throngs. Dale was dressed as an archetypical college revolutionary: sandals; faded, patched Levi's; a rumpled, untucked denim work shirt; and a just-purchased red bandanna wrapping his forehead. Mumbling "Peace now," he occasionally lifted a fist in the air. Tommy tagged along, in cut-offs and a tank top, wide-open eyes ogling from side to side. Not since the Chicago Bears game his father had taken him to last autumn had Tommy seen so many bodies in such close surroundings. Undergrads socialized; musicians played bongo drums, banjos and one flute; scores chugged beers; dozens more smoked joints. One couple mostly hid under their blanket, the coed resting on the grass on her back, squeezing a partner around his neck, an anticipating-a-rush-and-climax-any-moment grin on her face. The boy mounted his girlfriend, their torsos plunging and pulling up and down, up and down, the cover humping in the air. Except for the peeping Tommy, none of their blasé neighbors bothered the lovers.

Earlier this week, Dale had discovered Tommy's family resided in a north shore, wealthy, conceited, short-on-scruples Chicago suburb. Growing up in a 'money buys anything, especially extravagances and excuses' enclave, Tommy was clever at blowing through tons of cash for his pleasures, excesses and vices—with never, ever worrying over consequences. Spotting this, Dale unashamedly mutated into the freshman's friend, conjuring ways to show him some rollicking times, hoping to leech a few months' freebie ride. His scheming included introducing Tommy to 'Loops,' the legendary

Summer Never Comes

Urbana pusher; patronizing north Champaign's whorehouses; wasting a weekend at the strip joints near Chanute Air Force Base; hitting on a few unsuspecting high school girls in Rantoul, then shelling out for quickies in back seat of Tommy's car. This afternoon Dale escorted him to the Quad, promising they'd jump on a pair of broads, chug pitchers at Whitt's End, snag a motel room and "pump 'em all night." The idea sounded decent to young Tommy as he waited for his new pal to snare two attractive victims.

Paul shuffled his way down the sidewalk and through the crowds. With herds of students heading in different directions, he was constantly shoved away from where he wanted to go. Thousands more mingling and jabbering undergrads were out this afternoon than for Quad Day, but the amused, hassle-free mood was the same. Booths lined the walkways under the trees, Paul wondering how the structures weren't trampled by these packs. The Campus Democrats, with typically more volunteers than required, handed out campaign literature for upcoming elections. Paul observed these politicians, even ones running for Champaign County coroner and recorder of deeds, somehow melded the peace movement into their candidacies.

Caught in a knot of people near SOAP's display charting the progress, procedures, wrongness and absurdities of conscription, one coed grabbed his waist, smooched his cheeks and wondered if "he was ready for a hand of free lovin'." Taken aback, the shy Paul shook his head and sidled past the Coalition of Afrikan People. This campus minority brooded behind an empty table, ignoring their fellow students, not bothering with flyers or shouting a message, their sullen stares daring any honkies to approach to inquire about their causes or complaints.

Always imaginative, DISGUST draped four bed sheets shaped as ghostly effigies from a tree limb. Skulls were drawn on their heads and each spirit held one sign:

"DEATH"
"TO"
"ALL"
"WARMONGERS!"

"Here's the group that's really concerned about peace," RAW yelled.

"We are for an honorable disagreement," the SOAP supporters argued.

"Don't listen to those wimps, RAW stands for absolutely no more wars—never!"

Summer Never Comes

"But we've got to be logical."

"Why don't you pud-knockers go play with yourselves. Down with reason and down with 'Nam."

The mobs tugged Paul from the Administration Building, the booths and sidewalk. Trapped in another flow, he elbowed toward the Quad's center, into bright sun and closer to the old Auditorium.

On stage, Randy Miller and his fellow workers for peace were meticulously busy. Randy's responsibility was logistics: positioning the podium, straightening the chairs and plugging in the PA system. Untangling cables and testing speaker hookups, Randy walked to the lectern and gazed toward the Union, over the thousands of undergrads lounging below him. He tapped the microphone with his fingers and a loud "THUD" echoed the Quad. The loafing Illini cheered, Randy waved and stepped to the side. Other, more prominent participants climbed the scaffolding stairs, past him and onto the platform.

"All these people, Scooter, I've never seen so many here before."

"You're right, Lauren, big happenings today."

"I wish the weather wasn't so hot, cooler would be pleasanter." They rested on the grass near Lincoln Hall. Undergrads around the two, anxious for the rally, began clapping. As Scooter joined in, Lauren poked his ribs. "Look, Nick and Sue!"

Standing, the two weaved through the mobs, careful not to step on any fellow students.

"How're you doin'?" Scooter energetically shook Nick Aspen's arm. "Haven't seen you two since your wedding. Where you been, what've you been up to?"

"Hanging in Urbana." Nick fondled his wife's shoulder. "We drove down with our furniture two weeks before classes started and settled in at the apartment. We had the campus to ourselves, sort of our second honeymoon. Takes time, this married thing."

"I'll bet," Scooter retorted.

"Enjoying life as newlyweds?" Lauren asked Sue.

"More privacy than when we were engaged, simpler than sneaking around their fraternity every weekend searching for a mattress in an empty room."

Summer Never Comes

"And the Orchard Downs apartment," Lauren domestically inquired, "enough space?"

"Not much for closets, and the living room is undersized, particularly with our ten speeds parked by the wall."

The methodic applause built over the Quad.

"You guys missed a super party last Saturday."

"Fourteen kegs, right?"

"Floated 'em all. Then, like the old days when we were roommates, had a third floor hallway party." Scooter squinted into the sunlight. "Speaking of drinking, what if we blow off this rally and head for a round of brewskies at Second Chance?"

Nick looked to his wife for approval. "Fine by me."

"Let's hurry," Lauren said, "it's so humid out here."

As the women led the foursome away from the stage, unhurried, rhythmic clapping was taken up by the whole Quad.

"Chairs, where are more chairs?" an aggravated Randy asked the RAW radical.

"Hey, man, I supposed seats was your job."

"No, that was decided at our meeting two days ago, you guys were told to line up tables and chairs."

"Geez, man, slap us, guess we blew it."

Students, professors, do-gooders, activists, crusaders, SOAP, RAW, DISGUST, SCRAP, True Believers, hard-core radicals, Leninists and anarchists mingled on the stage. Bernard Minerath, a vice-chancellor and three harsh-faced students stood at the stairway, listening to the applause. After five minutes, an emcee approached the podium, raising both arms to quiet the crowd.

"Fellow peace protesters." The students noisily cheered and the smiling emcee waited for the enthusiasm to abate.

"Thank you for attending this rally to stop the war in Vietnam. For too many years, the government has requisitioned our fellow citizens to battle in Asia for their mistaken, misguided adventure. They have notified us, the draftees fighting the war, of its justness and necessity, the moral imperatives of combating Communism, what an historic responsibility we have to save the world. Today, on the Quad, across Illinois and throughout the country we hurl back their edicts, declaring to the government how unreasonable we consider them to be, how ruinous to the nation their intolerant, warmongering leadership has been, and that we have had enough."

The mobs whooped.

"This afternoon, we have assembled representatives of the student body, the university administration and the Champaign-Urbana community to demonstrate our solidarity in opposing the war. Without added delay, I introduce our first speaker, the founder and dedicated leader of the Student Organization Advocating Peace, Laurie Allman."

Standing behind the podium, Laurie launched into her evaluation of the campus peace movement, SOAP's role as the oldest organized anti-war group and her area of expertise—the consequences and costs of jungle defoliation on Southeast Asian history. The focal parts of her speech included descriptions of the eight most indigenous species of palm trees in Vietnamese forests and the devastation nine separate grades of napalm inflicted on this vegetation. At the pace she lectured, Paul calculated, the war might conclude before Laurie's discourse. He daydreamed, losing interest in her data and statistics.

"Storytelling today?"

"Sharon, what are you doing here?"

"Hanging, like everyone else."

"Yes, naturally, of course, good seeing you." A nervous Paul dragged his feet. "Did you get your roommate home last Saturday?"

"Mary was okay in my car, but after we parked she bolted to the bathroom and lost her cookies in the pot."

"We've all been there."

"So true." Sharon wore white tennis shorts and a long sleeve shirt, the tails knotted underneath her chest. "How's the rally?"

"Just beginning. The first speaker is lecturing about chemicals and perishing plant life. Hopefully the next ones will be more motivating or these guys will lose the students."

Near the pair, six undergrads handed a joint around their circle.

"The war is such a mess—the whole country is against it." Sharon pushed her blonde hair off her face. "Plus, here's our whole generation, willing to join in for potential trouble as long as the hassle is nominal. And look at this weather, perfect for being outside. With this combination, the real conspirators, the string pullers, will always count on us students to support their causes. As long as we're not expected to give too much."

"Twenty minutes ago I talked to a friend of mine with the identical outlook. An unkind assessment of our generation."

"We've received so many more benefits in our lives than we deserve. When you're handed everything, especially without paying for any of it, you expect more. Why work if you don't have to? We'll get by, someone will save us with another gravy train, if it's not scheduled for today, we can wait until tomorrow, we've got time."

"Until something better comes along," Paul answered absentmindedly.

"Another freebie or the next problem."

"Maybe we could start a 'cause of the month' club—rent an office in the Union, print announcements in the *Daily Illini*."

"And hold our own rally to protest the other campus issues." Sharon warped to Paul's fantasy.

"Have the President of the United States say he is neither for nor against causes."

In the crowds, undergrads tossed frisbees, finding the game more appealing than the lackluster words and phrases from the public address system.

"You never answered my first question. What about another tale?" Sharon held his arm.

"Life's boring at KIDs lately, no thrills on Third Street in Champaign."

"Well, to break the tedium," she grinned, "how about dating an Urbana resident?"

"Never thought about it," Paul was preoccupied counting bodies on the stage, "but I don't know many girls."

"What about yours truly?"

"Is this an invitation?" he watched a doper rolling a second joint. *Here's your opportunity, Robby, don't blow it.* "Busy this weekend, Sharon?"

"By chance, I'm free both nights."

On stage, the discoursers following Laurie Allman droned into limited, narrow topics—orating but not rousing, parsing the constitutional contradictions of Congress' approval of the war instead of lighting emotional, sensational scenes of suffering and death, dissecting casualty lists and statistics rather than advocating proposals for putting an end to it all.

Summer Never Comes

Following Kentucky's and Sharon's predictions, as their attention span for protest slipped, the drifting Illini zoned out on the Quad.

Around 3:30, after Professor Dale Widmayer's dissertation, complete with bibliographic references, on the physiological similarities of English Lord Protector Oliver Cromwell, Austro Hungarian Emperor Franz Jozef, and South Vietnamese Vice President Nguyen Cao Ky, the emcee stepped forward. As she surveyed the gathering, few looked back at her. Lounging students worked on their tans, ate munchies, chugged more beers, tried picking up dates, played backgammon, sang tunes or read magazines. The crowds' edges shrank as dozens and dozens ambled away. White clouds puffed above Altgeld Hall, the first in three days.

"Comrades, the next speaker is known as a leader since the earliest days of campus protesting, identified with the peace movement prior to Tonkin Gulf and the troop buildups, before the bombing campaigns and the bombing halts, before peace conferences and their failure, one of the first voices in Champaign-Urbana challenging the war, the founder and chairman of the Student Committee Requiring an Adequate Peace. Comrades, Bernard Minerath."

The True Believers applauded as Bernard stood at the lectern, his only movement his head unhurriedly turning left and right. He was six feet tall, his body characteristically sFerris for a student but with well-built shoulders, a result of hours of weightlifting. He wore dark-brown corduroy Levi's too long at his shoes and, even on this muggy afternoon, a dress shirt, sleeves rolled up to the elbows. Bernard's black hair was parted in the center, covering his ears. In any breeze the absolutely straight locks flew around and sideways. He had the habit of flipping his head back and combing a hand over his scalp to neaten the part. His facial expression was a perpetual, no-nonsense scowl, a caution of his austere, don't-screw-with-me character.

Bernard stayed stationary for five minutes. Some students, figuring out the past two hours' chatter from the loudspeakers had been interrupted, turned from their beers, boyfriends or books and focused on Bernard. Gradually, the crowd's buzzing quieted. By the steps, Randy Miller approved.

"Fellow students.

"Every summer in the town where I grew up, in the backyard next to ours, a child played in her sandbox. A bucket and shovel, a hose for water, a few plastic dolls, sand tramped into her parents' house. This little girl was happy in her sandbox in her yard because, though very young, she understood she was sheltered in our neighborhood and protected by her family. Security was a foundation of this girl's life, as it is for us, as it should be for everyone in our country, and all peoples of the Earth.

"Sadly, this is not so. In our present, the world is the opposite of the neighborhoods of our youths—dangerous and perilous, full of fears, fright and uncertainty—with suffering among us and struggles splitting us. One division is the conflict in Vietnam, certainly a country where innocent children do not have safe havens for play.

"The war has been fought for many years, wasted untold resources and slaughtered countless lives, with none of its consequences worthwhile, with only confusion, pain and brutality for the people in Asia. Vietnamese, Cambodians, Laotians and Thais have watched their lands devastated, acquaintances and families viciously murdered and, most dreadful of all, their futures destroyed.

"And our country, though not a battle zone, has also been corrupted. Fair housing, anti-poverty programs, aid to education, civil rights and environmental initiatives fail for lack of support—their funding seized for the Pentagon. Cities and college campuses riot, our friends are drafted and forced to fight and die. Narrow-minded leaders, regardless of political party, have made the United States the world's aggressor instead of the highest hope for fellowship and peace.

"What should we do? Do we acquiesce and let the politicians deceive us into more war?"

"No!" the True Believers sitting near the stage answered.

"Do we permit the murders of more innocent peoples in Asia?"

"No!" more students joined in.

"Do we waste our time, waiting for the army to conscript us?"

"NO!"

"Do we watch while the world is destroyed?"

"NO! NO! NO!"

"Do we stand up, protest and fight back?"

"YES! YES! YES!" the suddenly-psyched Illini, the whole Quad, the entire mob, the beer drinkers, pot smokers and lovers snuggling in their blankets, rose and cheered.

Summer Never Comes

"That is what we must do. Battle against the establishment because this country should not fight pointless, pitiless wars, not manipulate other countries and cultures, not immorally plot havoc, misery and disaster, not kill. We must end the war!

"Other governments call on the United States to stop the bloodletting and madness. These nations have been disregarded. The press and media publish editorials urging the killing cease. The killing continues. Popular leaders in our own country argue for a halt to the suffering and a return of our nation's policymaking into the people's hands. They are denounced, discounted, discredited and, in two criminal episodes, assassinated. On promises of an end to the war, new leaders are elected to Washington. They ignore their voters, lie and prolong failed policies.

"We must reverse the course. The time is now to show our opposition to the sinful path the government pursues in Southeast Asia, a wayward national policy moving farther from universal brotherhood and ever more toward violence and death. It is left to our generation, those made to carry the terrible, costly burden of fighting this war. It is left to our generation, one voice but thousands strong, to ensure that our future—and the future of all the little children playing in their sandboxes in their backyards—is peaceful and secure." Bernard raised one arm from the lectern and pointed toward the crowds. "Let us begin now. United we must end the war."

The whole Quad was up and applauding, some students somber, unsmiling, others hooraying and leaping in the air.

"Let us continue the protests, our pursuit of proletarian justice, begun this afternoon. Tomorrow we will demonstrate again, not only on our campus but throughout the state and across the nation. Our resolve is firm, our ambitions honorable.

"United we must end the war."

As Bernard walked to the stairway, the waving, rooting, stomping, hugging-someone-next-to-you and the goddamn-it-hell-yessing went on, rowdy, raucous and noisier. Randy Miller excitedly patted his shoulder, but Bernard ignored him and hurried past.

"Clean up's not our job, I know that for certain." DISGUST objected.

"Don't try skating out, that was the deal," one of RAW's hippies corrected, "you're the trash crew."

Summer Never Comes

"Ain't what I remember, don't even got a broom to push." At the stairs, as Bernard and his True Believers marched by, the peace activists shoved a large garbage can back and forth between them.

Roaming the Quad, Tommy Quarters and Dale Kinsey snatched two coeds in cut-offs and halters. With smarmy introductions, Dale easily connived the Bromley Hall roommates into leaving the rally and heading for Whitt's End. More sweet talk by Dale and six rounds of brews bought with Tommy's bucks persuaded the women to shack up with the KIDs in the Century Twentyone Hotel on Third Street. Tommy signed for a room with double beds and a jumbo bathtub, and the foursome wasted the afternoon guzzling Jack Daniels, smoking dope and screwing. First Tommy did one coed while Dale and the other girl watched, next Kinsey and his bimbo in the tub, both couples in their beds, then all four again on the same mattress. (Crap, what was the tall one's name, Lucy?) Young Tommy, gaily fagged, dreamt this his Garden of Raunch. Dale wished the room's stereo had a deeper base so he could listen to Hendrix or Cream, and the women took home twenty bucks a piece for their time.

# # # #

Lindy woke from his nap at four o'clock. Few of the brothers were around and KIDs was too quiet for late afternoon. He walked to the kitchen hoping to connive an early supper out of the fraternity's cooks. Lindy needed a few hours' booking at the 'Brary before heading to Frogfeet's nightly jam session.

"Shoot, Lind-eh," she screamed in her down-home drawl, "you don' look too wide-eyed. Whut you bin doin' wid yo-self?"

"Not much, Mary Lou, precious little. But can you feed me, please?"

"Shoot, that's all you thinks we's good for in thes kich'n. Feed me, feed me, feed me. Shoot, don' you know this ain't no all-night diner?"

# # # #

Thunderstorms flooded the campus the day after the Moratorium. As a cold front plowed through central Illinois the temperature dropped to fifty degrees, and the protesting Bernard and his anti-war schemers feverishly

Summer Never Comes

arranged flopped. The stage by the old Auditorium stood unused, the booths lining the sidewalks tipped over in the gusting winds, no carefree Illini tossed frisbees and no couples cuddled under their blankets. The only activity outdoors was picketing around the Administration Building by chilly, totally soaked True Believers. As Kentucky and Sharon calculated, with bad weather and lacking entertainment, students lost interest in something so basic as ending war.

Early Friday morning, Bobby Sox declared for peace by cutting his classes and driving home to Chicago.

Chapter Five

SATURDAY NIGHT in the Union, the 'Is McCartney Dead Club' held the semester's first meeting.

"Okay, so far what's our proof?"

"There's the *Abbey Road* album with all four Beatles walking in a straight file. First John, an angel, leads the funeral procession; Ringo's next, a preacher in black; Paul, may he rest in peace, follows shoeless—that's how corpses are buried—and George is last, the gravedigger wearing work clothes."

"Don't forget the license plates: '28-IF.' Twenty-eight if Paul had lived," Steve Ferris eagerly added, "and he's the only one without a beard."

"Also on that cover, right above Paul's head there's a trinity, three people dressed in white, the father, the son and the holy ghost."

"The stuff in *Magical Mystery Tour*. In a picture of the four, Paul's the only one with no shoes. In another, a black corsage is pinned on his lapel while John, Ringo and George have red flowers. And the blatant-est clue is the picture of Paul behind a sign on a desk saying 'I Was.'"

"The *Hey Jude* cover, McCartney's beardless, wearing a white shirt, nobody else is. And in the photo on the top of the door three of the four are looking towards the sky."

"On *Sgt. Pepper's* back side George, John and Ringo face the camera but Paul is turned away. On the front, there's the hand over Paul's head, a death omen, plus the left-handed guitar flower arrangement."

"What does that mean?" Mike Klippel asked.

"Flower arrangements honor the stiffs at wakes and Paul's left-handed."

"On the inside flap, he's the only one with his knees visible, as if he were squished into a coffin."

"The lyrics in one song, what's the title?"

"'A Day in the Life!'" Bob Testin screamed, and the Beatles freaks merrily recited the lyrics:

> I read the news today oh boy,
> About a lucky man who made the grade.
> And though the news was very sad,
> Well I just had to laugh.
> I saw the photograph,
> He blew his mind out in a car.
> He didn't notice that the light had changed.

Finishing the verse, the zealous Beatlemania victims clapped and the meeting, stuck in a groove, spun past midnight.

"What if we're wrong, this is a prank and Paul's the one who'll live the longest?"

# # # #

"Em, how are you?" Clothes wet from walking in the rain, Lindy beamed his sincerest smile and the two kissed. "What miserable weather, not fit for animal or vegetable, it's a wiser night to shelter and study."

"You look fatigued, Will," grateful for the affection, Emily was concerned with her boyfriend's appearance.

"Thanks for the worry. I'll confess this schedule I'm holding—jammin', classes, schoolwork—requires serious adaptation and many, many late hours. But I'm in fine fettle now, ready to hit those books, joyful being with the woman I love." Lindy shook his head to dry his long, blond hair and, aping Tarzan, slapped his fists on his chest.

"How is practice?" Emily sat at her dorm room desk as Lindy unlaced his shoes and plopped on the bed.

"Tolerable, but I'll admit more toil than I imagined. Five guys practicin' together to sound decent in so few days is a wicked nut to crack. Our voices are poles apart, we must come up with at least seven rhythms when we rehearse each tune."

"Oh?" she was mildly elated.

Summer Never Comes

"But we'll reach the top, just more rehearsals to sing through, that's all. You know a short-order chef's recipe, crack three eggs to fry one omelet."

"Oh," a crestfallen Emily responded, "when is your first performance?"

"In a month or six weeks, which should allow plenty of time for playin' halfway respectably." Lindy was keen to recount his last few days but sensed Emily's melancholy. "How's your week been?"

"I've studied by myself, a few nights here in my room and the last three in the English Library. I started of one my term papers for this semester, on Samuel Johnson's *Rasselas*."

Lindy looked at his girlfriend, sitting erect, gripping the chair arms. He stood, put Emily's hands in his own and guided her to the bed. "How about Thursday, Em, did you grab a protest sign and march with everybody else until the rains came?"

"I was at the rally for a while with Nicole and Madeline. The mood was similar to New Student Week's Quad Day with the crowds and booths around the sidewalks. Students sat on the grass close to the old Auditorium where the stage was set up, a usual college scene—idle undergrads not very attracted to what they're there for."

"The ol' student apathy grievance everyone tags on our generation, involved so long as it's a piece of cake."

"Were you at the rally, Will?"

"Nope, I shot hoops in Huff Gym Thursday afternoon," Lindy hesitated, framing a lie, "with Bobby and Stu."

"Ten or fifteen protesters spoke, but most were boring and many students left before the speakers finished. The last one stirred the crowd with a speech including a cute anecdote about keeping the world safe for little children to play in. Students should have stayed to listen to him." Emily's eyes brightened, "You won't guess what else I saw. Paul was on the Quad with a girl, a blonde. I didn't recognize her but they stayed together for half an hour."

"Fantastic!" Lindy was hugely thankful he hadn't fibbed with Robby's name. "My roomie steppin' out, that's wonderful."

"Has Paul mentioned this girl to you?"

"Aw, you know Robby, plays the sphinx of silence when he's determined to." Lindy covered up again, unwilling to confess, because of

Frogfeet's rehearsals, he hadn't talked to him all week. "Geez, maybe he's on a date tonight, I'll have to check this out tomorrow."

"Paul's sensitive, a considerate person and deserves a girlfriend."

"Every male enrolled at the Big U merits at least one sweetheart, my sweetest."

"I hope Bobby, Stu and you don't hassle him."

"Us KIDs? We won't rag on him too much, likely it'll be way overboard. Can't fan on an opportunity, all part of the service."

"Remember, Paul's your best friend and friends should support each other."

"I'm aboard one hundred percent." Lindy reckoned he had an inventory of surplus clichés. "How about us, are you still angry or has our horse left the barn?"

Emily grinned, welcoming his banter. "After last weekend's party, Will, I was upset. One day we're enjoying the afternoon, joking about moving to California, then a week later, because of your band, I'm informed our time together is on hold and we'll be apart for a whole month. There was too much to grasp in one night, especially at your fraternity's party with hundreds of people crowded around us."

"Can't dispute the point. Frogfeet and what it means to me, to us, is a puddle to jump, I wished I'd figured a more considerate way to explain. I realize what I did to your feelings and faith in me, damaged both. I know our opinions vary and believe me when I say I won't try convincin' you to absolutely agree the band's my right move. I want to continue discussing our relationship 'til you're satisfied I'm serious about smoothing out the rough patches, which was my aim last Sunday, too. I hope that's enough."

"Sunday's call wasn't a success because I wouldn't pay attention. Sometimes I don't listen, that's my fault. You're right, talk and we'll be fine."

"I'm glad, I want to hold on to our friendship."

"We're fine," Emily repeated, relieved Will was bothered enough to mend their differences, "and watch out for Paul, too."

"That's right, my roomie and his mystery date, there'll be wigs on the green for him." Looking around the room, Lindy fixed on a photo of them at last spring's KIDs' formal. "By the bye, there's another date on the calendar, in three weeks exactly one year for us."

Summer Never Comes

"Saturday of Homecoming weekend, our anniversary. Oh, Will, I'm so delighted you remembered."

"God, how could I forget our experiences that night. The bash at KIDs, the rainstorms and the apartment party I dragged you to, the heat in that room with sixty or seventy bodies. We boogied in the corner and could barely breathe, the dancing went on 'til four or five in the morning." A laughing Lindy sidled closer to Emily.

"A long evening and early morning."

"But unforgettable." Lindy swung an arm around his girlfriend and kissed her. "If I didn't fall in love with you that first night, it surely headed me in that direction. Say, isn't Homecoming the same weekend in October this year?"

Emily did not reply, preferring smooching instead of conversation.

"I think so. Let's celebrate the occasion. We'll go to the Illini game, eat dinner at a nice restaurant, twirl the dance floor at KIDs' blowout party, then return here for the rest of the night."

"Splendid." Eyes closed, Emily made mental note to talk to Nicole to save the dorm room for Will and her.

"Then it's arranged, you, me and Homecoming, 365 days later. I love you, you're mine."

Lindy switched off the light and the pair scrunched on Emily's narrow mattress, fondling the other's body. Winding down, yielding to his exhaustion, Lindy slept. Emily was content lying next to her slumbering boyfriend, glad they'd talked over the band, pleased he'd brought up their first date and settled plans for Homecoming. With patience, the semester and their love would undoubtedly, gratefully, turn out right. Emily shut her eyes, her arms around Will's neck.

# # # #

Walking to Sharon's house, wind was more the hassle for Paul than rain. In the stiff breeze umbrellas were useless and he rolled his up while crossing the Quad. Sharon had offered to drive into Champaign to meet him but he declined, considering it improper for a girl to pick up the man on their first date. Besides, living in Champaign all his semesters, this was a chance for exploring unfamiliar Urbana streets.

Summer Never Comes

Paul thought tonight's date a fluke. Pleasant conversation at KIDs' party with a girl like Sharon, so cute and level-headed, was a fantastic break, an only-twice-before in his college years happening. Meeting at the peace rally was luckier. If they hadn't run into each other on the Quad, Paul admitted, no way he'd have phoned. As Kentucky opined, he lacked the nerve to abandon his cocoon. *Lord, don't let me screw up or bore this woman, please don't let this be the last time I see her.*

Sharon's house on California Avenue was a two-story, clapboard structure built in the 1920s, the front yard more dirt than grass, gutters sagging from the eaves, one downspout missing and four bicycles chained together on the long, roofed porch. Sharon waited in the parlor. The room's three couches were arranged around the burning fireplace and pillows covered the floor. Simon and Garfunkel played on a second floor stereo.

"Hello, Paul, how are you?" she came toward him.

"This is a big place, must be plenty of bedrooms upstairs. How many live here?"

"Seven, counting me. Last year we squeezed in eight, but that was overcrowded. This semester everybody has their own room."

"That would be nice. With eighty-nine in KIDs we're packed like sardines, everybody's doubled and tripled up and there's always too many lined up for the johns."

"Here, I'll introduce you. Angie Sperry, Karen Gasper, Julie, Maureen, Audrey, this is Paul Roberts. And you know Mary."

"Enjoy Saturday's party?" he asked. "I was in the crowd around the kegs talking to Sharon when you pushed through and wrapped your arms around her."

"God, how many more are gonna claim they saw me totally wasted?" Mary O'Donnell slumped into a sofa as her housemates giggled, "Okay, I don't remember your face or body but I'll believe it if you say so."

"Where are you heading?" Angie inquired.

"To the old Auditorium to take in *Casablanca*—Bergman and Bogie." Sharon zipped her jacket, adjusted her floppy hat and turned from her housemates.

"Good meeting you," Paul waved and they walked out the door.

Summer Never Comes

"Sure is an awful night." The drizzle had stopped but leftover raindrops from the tree branches pelted the pair. "Might be the end of the warm weather."

"About time, hourlies begin in two weeks, cold helps us study," Paul spoke over the howling wind.

"Do you book a lot?"

"I imagine as much as everyone else. I like quiet, out-of-the-way places."

"Unusual, most undergrads prefer rooms with people. Where's your favorite?"

"The History Library on the Main Library's fourth floor is ideal—peaceful, warm in the winter, with big wooden tables for spreading out papers."

"Never been up there. The highest I've gotten is the English Library on the third floor." Sharon looked at Paul from under her hat, her blonde hair tucked inside the coat collar.

"Get high on the English Library. Clever play on words, could be a substitute for the university's 'Learning and Labor.'"

"The motto for the '70s," she rolled her eyes with a gosh-how-corny face. The pair hurried, hoping to reach the old Auditorium before another shower. "So, you study alone?"

"People don't bother me, as long as the room's under control and I can concentrate," he sounded defensive. "How about you?"

"I generally book in our house. The seven of us are enrolled in the same classes and for convenience work as a California Avenue study group."

"Hold on, why do you think I book alone?"

"You said it and that's what I hear, what my cousin's told me."

"Who is…?"

"Your friend, Kentucky."

"He's family? You sure don't talk like you're from the south."

"I grew up in Lake Bluff, a town north of Chicago; my parents still live there. Cousin James is on my mom's side of the family."

Paul realized this was the only time this year he'd heard Kentucky's first name spoken out loud and needed a moment recalling his last. "What else did he mention about me?"

"James regards you highly, though he feels you should 'Move out and meet more people.'"

"Is tonight his way of helping—hooking us up?"

"No, James didn't arrange our date. I came to your fraternity's party at his invitation but we met on our own. Chance, not conspiracy. Thursday's peace rally was more happenstance, I recognized you in the Union and followed to say hello." She touched his arm. "Naturally, James and I get together, we met yesterday for breakfast, but you weren't in the conversation."

"Kentucky is baffling, you never know where you'll run into him or what he's up to. He's actually a closer pal of my roommate, Lindy."

Next to the Foreign Languages Building, Sharon saw a short line waiting at the old Auditorium. "I agonized over admitting this, I didn't want to wreck our first date."

"Funny, I had the same feeling walking up to your door. I want this to be a decent evening, step off on the right foot and not mess up. How am I so far?"

"We're doing okay."

Compared to Sharon's living room and fireplace, the half-filled Auditorium was chilly. The two discovered each liked sitting on the balcony's left side with their feet hanging over the rail. Before the film, the audience cheered as a crew of Engineering College students launched Space Age paper airplanes from the back of the balcony, hoping the gliders floated to the stage.

"This was my first time watching *Casablanca*. The best scene was the crowd in the bar singing 'Les Marseilles' to drown out the German soldiers." After the movie, the wind was still strong but the sidewalks dry as they returned to Urbana.

"I love the finish when the plane flies off in the fog but always feel sorry for Rick Blaine. Tell me," Sharon asked as they arrived at Treno's, "were you offended when I told you about James?"

"Not mad, but deception bothers me." A pitcher and two beer glasses sat on the table between them.

"This isn't a trick. You believe me, don't you?"

Paul studied Sharon, hair tousled from the hat, eyes focusing on him, her manner outgoing, charming, unworried, her smile affectionate. In an instant he comprehended, concluded, she was entirely, straightforwardly honest. "Yes, I do."

A pleased Sharon sipped her beer. "How did you decide on your major?"

"My cousin, Bob, is six years older than me and received his accounting degree from the U of I. After graduation he landed a job with Arthur Andersen Accountants in Chicago. My dad wants the same career for me because math's always been easy for me, as it is for my cousin and my dad. Debits and credits are organized, columns add up and if they don't, glitches are simple to work through." Paul shrugged. "Someone has to pin down details."

"Do you enjoy matching digits to integers?"

"I suppose, since it's my major, since I've studied accounting for three years and this is my dad's plan for my life. I guess so because, as I say, everything's black and white, comes together at the bottom line, there's satisfaction in tabulating the answers."

"Do you think that's what an accountant's career will be when you graduate?"

"Numbers are numbers, whether in a business class in Champaign or a corporate office in Chicago, St. Louis or wherever. Hold on, we're in Urbana right now, aren't we?"

"There's a black and white distinction." Sharon grinned. "Here's another: do employees affect the business equation?"

"Of course, they're responsible for the company's operations, but profit is the objective."

"What if individuals interfere?"

"I don't see how. A firm's staff understands the purpose is earning more money. Their assignment is showing up, working efficiently every day and improving procedures where possible. These modern mainframe computers are examples—plug them in and watch numbers get crunched. With these room-sized machines' processing capacities, people matter less and more revenue shifts to profit. An employee's job will be typing data on key punch cards, sorting the piles and waiting twenty minutes for the answer. The computer calculates without a person. Amazing, imagining the future."

Sharon munched a pretzel. "Isn't there more than dollars and debits?"

Summer Never Comes

What did she mean, Paul wondered. Did accounting confuse her, was she asking for fuller explanations of financial theories or computers? Was Sharon swinging the conversation from business and his major to personal stuff? He would trust.

"I've enrolled in four history courses in my U of I semesters."

"That's a different direction," Sharon said happily. "Is it also black and white?"

"Pieces are. History is a collection of names, dates and happenings. Thomas Jefferson was the second Vice President, Benjamin Disraeli served twice as British Prime Minister, William McKinley was assassinated in 1901. The fascination is connecting today to earlier events, how the past produces our present. If not for long ago, there wouldn't be a current. The British constitution is a case in point."

"I didn't know the English have one." Sharon ate another pretzel and watched Paul's face, more animated than ten minutes ago.

"They don't, not a document of rules written in black and white document," he smiled. "Theirs is established on precedents dating to the Magna Carta. Anyone studying English history understands their political system's roots extend from the thirteenth century. The Tudors, the Stuarts, the house of Hanover, Parliament, the monarchy's weakening, dominance of the cabinet and prime ministers, the Labor Party and welfare state, seven hundred fifty years flowing together. Tides of history, to use one of my roommate's clichés."

"And the relevance of these old-days?"

"History matters—studying the past guides the future—today's mistakes are avoidable if we're aware of what went wrong decades ago."

"Well said," she leaned back in the chair and finished her beer. "How'd a number cruncher develop this curiosity with the past?"

"When I was twelve, my Aunt Jeannette gave me a set of books about the Civil War written by Bruce Catton. His research included conversations with Union veterans when he was growing up in Michigan—yesterday reaching toward today. I've read them three or four times."

"Sounds to me like you're addicted."

"The subject is an absorbing hobby. But as my dad says," his mood morphed from enthusiastic to sober, "you can't make any money or pay the bills with it."

Summer Never Comes

"Why not?"

"What's the value of a history diploma, where can I go with it? Stay in school and earn a master's or PhD, then teach in the same high school for thirty or forty years?"

"Is that so dreadful?" Sharon looked around the bar. "You could make a career as an historian, research and write your own books in this library of ours. Wouldn't that be worthwhile?"

"Frustrating, because it would take too long—a lifetime."

"I thought you wanted to play it safe and stay in school."

Paul was puzzled. He'd always lacked a response to this quandary, his future, a stymie in his mind. Paul gambled she would let him shift the conversation. "What about you, why veterinary medicine?"

Sharon guessed the segue. "A motivating career, a way to usefulness. Vets heal animals and people, one physically, the other emotionally."

"How'd you choose it? Do your parents own a farm or keep animals around your house?"

"The only pet my family's ever had is a tabby kitten, and my mom barely tolerates the cat hair. What drew me was a summer job at an animal hospital. Plus I enjoy science, particularly biology, so this is a practical application for my U of I education. If for some reason I'm not admitted into a Vet Med College there are other outlets for my degree, teaching high school for one." Sharon smirked over her beer glass. "But I'm confident if I work hard, caring for animals is the career for me, a meaningful future."

"You sound like my roommate. We talk about the future a lot and he's anticipating it, as you say you are."

"Nothing wrong with that, right?"

Paul rested his chin on his fist. "It's a scary place, so many uncertainties we'll confront and need to solve, too many answers that will wind up wrong. Delay is securer."

"Anomalies, yes, but don't regard the future as a dilemma. College students should meet challenges—where to live after graduation, the choices of jobs and companions, how to aid others and promote good. Progress means driving forward, not hesitating. Retreating from tomorrow is no way to push ahead. If plans don't work at the start, remember someone like you, an accountant, will have your debits and credits to total when you get there." Sharon saw Paul's grimace, "I hope you took that as the joke I intended."

Summer Never Comes

"The last time Lindy and I talked over the future we almost argued. He is so much for walking through doors and down paths he can't wait to jump, the worst case I've ever seen. He's got these ideas not only for himself but for our whole generation, it's in his head that we baby boomers take on this mission to better our world for everybody."

"Sounds noble."

"How can immature college students show the way for everyone else? What do we know? Who says we have the solutions?"

"Maybe not today but we might tomorrow. Remember, we're young, with decades ahead of us. We've been given so much—more money, education and opportunities than any earlier generations. Some—all of us—should accept the responsibility to dream and perfect our world."

"Lindy, word-for-word," Paul smiled.

"Because Lindy's not the only individual thinking this way. Repaying what we've received is a conviction many of us have."

"I agree helping others is the right thing to do, but claiming our generation should set off on some…" Paul searched for a word, "…crusade, is over the top. The movement's never been tried before and won't work now."

"Precisely why it's novel. You said crusade. How better off will society be thirty-five or forty years from now if we decide for decency?

"It would be moral, turning the world around, but I see another problem. What if our generation comes together and says 'Follow us to the promised land, we're certain we know, our strategy is foolproof, this is the path to the pot of gold!' And what if it turns out we don't? What if we mess up, our ideals are unworkable, selfish and criminal? What if we're not so smart?"

"Our generation confesses, mends the mistakes and tries again. We have the time."

Paul relaxed in his chair, "Just like Lindy."

"What's your roommate's real name?"

"Bill Lindner, but like your cousin, everyone uses his nickname. We've roomed together for four semesters and he's my best pal here in school."

"Relying on buddies is priceless." A contemplative Sharon nodded her head.

Summer Never Comes

"That's what my dad told me when I began college. Whatever I did, to make sure my friends are decent and care."

"And Bill—Lindy—is one?"

"No doubt, he's always upbeat, ready to help and more mature than me." Paul refilled both glasses.

"How did you meet?"

"In our freshman year we both signed up for PE 107, Beginning Swimming for students who can't float or open their eyes underwater. Our lockers in Men's Old Gym were next to each other and we'd talk when classes were over. One afternoon we stopped at Second Chance for a beer and Lindy told to me about his fraternity, Kappa Iota Delta. I liked what he said and pledged that spring."

"Isn't the Old Men's Gym's pool real shallow?"

Paul laughed at Sharon's contorting the gym's name, a common Big U quip. "About four feet deep at one end."

"Do you have any brothers or sisters?"

"A sister, she's sixteen."

"So Lindy is the big brother you never had?"

"Except for a neighbor when I was in high school, but he left."

"And this semester, are you two still close?"

"I suppose, though I haven't seen Lindy much the last few weeks." Paul circled the beer glass' rim with his finger, "He's jamming every night with a band called Frogfeet."

"Never heard of them," Sharon drank her fresh beer.

"Neither has the rest of the campus. They haven't played at any bars yet, only practice every night until one or two in the morning."

"He must like music to work so much."

"A passion. Lindy would make it his career if he could."

"Which doesn't mesh with your earlier portrayal. You implied he's aimlessly bouncing around but Lindy is aware of what he's doing."

"He may know what he wants but not the route to get there. He's spread too thin—Frogfeet; studying for classes; our fraternity brothers; and his girlfriend, Emily Ritter, who's especially upset over his tangent."

"And his roommate. Miss him?"

"I do. We've always hung around together, been involved in the same stuff, now he's gone and there's a hole."

Summer Never Comes

"Few of us are continually constant. Lindy must believe in his band to invest so much."

"But we're seniors. After graduation and finding our nine-to-five jobs there's plenty of time for him to make it his hobby." The door to Treno's opened and closed with arriving students, half standing in line to order food and munchies, the rest searching for friends or empty tables.

"Besides booking and hanging with Lindy when he's available, what else do you do with your time?"

"I'm a researcher for the *Daily Illini*. This semester I'm writing articles for a new weekend magazine the paper's introducing."

"What kinds of stories?"

"One is reviewing the Athletic Association Slush Fund scandal. The most intriguing is the anti-war groups. Why are there so many in Champaign-Urbana, what do they stand for, do they cooperate, are they successful?"

"What will you to write?"

"I'm beginning with a chronology. There are four campus anti-war groups, the first dating to 1965 and the rest organized since then. The oldest two, SOAP and DISGUST, believe logical, moderate methods are safer, while RAW and SCRAP moralize the ends justifies the means, with SCRAP the most fanatic."

"Nothing wrong with differences if they collaborate to stop the war, as long as what they do isn't criminal. Of course, broken windows in Campustown wouldn't be a shocker, vandalism's struck before." Sharon poured a half glass of beer for herself. "Other than timelines, what else will you give *Daily Illini* readers? Shouldn't there be a hook to keep students reading to your article's conclusion?"

"I don't know if it's a hook, but the offices of three of the four peace groups have been looted—one during New Student Week and the second and third were ransacked the weekend before the rally."

"Which one was spared?"

"SCRAP."

"The most radical, while the do-gooders were raided. Our fellow students out for kicks, maybe fraternity pranks, but not yours, not KIDs," Sharon joked. "However, J. Edgar Hoover and the FBI could have moles surveilling the central Illinois peace protesters and their ultra-secret, socialist-anarchist cadres. The government right-wingers could be waiting for us to declare revolution so the G-men can storm through and arrest all of us hippies. Bureaucratic fascists scheme that way. Then again, a left-wing conspiracy is possible, those radicals in SCRAP you mentioned could be behind the lootings. If they accept the 'anything goes' mantra, maybe they're spying on their rivals and plotting further break-ins. Maybe the FBI and the SCRAP fanatics are coordinating strategies."

Admiring his date, Paul enjoyed Sharon's grasp of his peace movement story—her nonchalant mockery, not disparaging, but a way to have fun. Paul wondered why he didn't have this conversation with Stef Tianen. Laughter came from a table of students wearing University of Wisconsin football jerseys.

"Laurie Allman offered the same opinion."

"Who?"

"SOAP's leader, the first speaker at Thursday's peace rally. We met for breakfast earlier this week."

"The tedious one wearing on and on about American-made chemicals defoliating Southeast Asian palm trees?"

"Boring on stage but an interesting individual. Laurie's worked in the campus peace movement since their beginnings in '65 and takes her anti-war crusading to heart. She hypothesized SCRAP was behind the break-ins."

"And her reasoning?"

"SCRAP's the only anti-war group left alone by the burglars. Plus, she knows their leader, Bernard Minerath, and is convinced he's a bad person—devious enough to cause trouble."

"Does she have proof—fingerprints, a photograph or the plot's outline written out on paper? And why would this 'Mind-Warp' commit a felony? What's his motive?" Sharon smiled at her intentional gaffe with Bernard's name.

"No evidence, merely suspicions. But there's a quality about her. Once in a while you come across a person so genuine you're certain they can't lie." Paul paused, apprehending how Laurie and Sharon shared this trait, "There's a thing—the look in their faces, mannerisms, the way they talk—you believe whatever they say, that they'll always speak the truth. I only met with Laurie for an hour but she's that kind of person. If her instinct is Bernard and SCRAP are involved, the lead is plausible enough to follow."

Summer Never Comes

"To where is my *Daily Illini* reporter with the two first names traveling?" Sharon teased again. "Some cloak and dagger, midwestern anti-war conspiracy encampment?"

"That's the third time you've used that word tonight."

"Conspiracy?" She smiled and shook her head, "A figure of speech, you're welcome to it for your story."

"When I write about the peace groups it won't include conspiracies because I'm uncertain there is one. As candid as Laurie is, in spite of all she believes she knows, corroboration, not speculation, is needed to confirm theory. I'm sticking to facts."

"Yet, copying facts on paper is so…"

"Boring? Like me?"

"…Black and white."

"Thank you for that. But my article is for the unbiased record. The 'hook,' as you said before, is piecing together the story so students understand we need to work to end the war. If I do it right, logic validates my argument." Paul counted the red Wisconsin jerseys. "Of course, the break-ins are attention-grabbing. Laurie said the looters left a warning at SOAP, one smashed desk in a neat pile in the middle of the floor. I checked with the Champaign and Urbana police departments and RAW's and DISGUST's offices had the same deliberate damage. Bad guys on campus terrorizing the peace movement."

"Isn't that a jump, students threatening students. Why bully the peace movement, they're the good guys. Of course, this is only October, as the school year moves on there could be more destruction." Sharon watched Paul smile and knew her questioning reached him. "Anything else?"

"Stef Tianen, the *DI's* editor-in-chief, did her best to talk me out of the story a week after assigning it to me. That seemed strange."

"Is that a plus or a negative, is your editor a good guy or a bad guy?"

"Stef's strong-willed about the *Daily Illini* operating by her agenda—nowhere as guileless as Laurie Allman—but not a bad guy. Her intent is to ensure the paper prints credible, readable stories. Even if Stef doubts I'll write the story the right way, I'd rely on her ninety percent of the time."

Sharon and Paul watched the Wisconsin football jerseys leave Treno's.

Summer Never Comes

"We got beat by the Badgers this afternoon, the score was 31-7, Lonnie Perrin scored our only touchdown." He emptied the pitcher into both beer mugs. "I still say you remind me of Lindy."

"How so?"

"The blonde hair, but yours is styled cuter. Other similarities are your candor and tendency to lead a conversation."

"Okay, let's switch, you interrogate and I'll respond." Sharon batted her eyelashes, "Ask me ten questions."

Paul grinned at her theatrics, "All right. Do you enjoy college?"

"Yes," she responded swiftly.

"Do you like studying alone?"

"No, never, I hate it," Sharon snickered.

"How about booking with another person?"

"Yes, very much so, thank you, but I'd need space for concentration."

"Do you date a lot?"

She paused, "I go out with my share of male college students, but I'm choosy."

"Glad to hear that. Do you enjoy sitting and drinking in bars?"

"Yes. What type of query is that?"

"Hey, I'm the inquisitioner."

"Pardon me, I forgot my place," she grinned.

"Do you like," Paul needed courage, "sitting in a bar and drinking with me?"

"Only on our first date."

"Does that mean you agree to go out on a second?"

"If asked properly."

"What would you prefer doing if I invited you out again?"

"We'll worry about it later." Her hands remained folded, "That's eight."

"How about next weekend?"

"Yes."

"Super!" a beaming Paul finished his beer.

"You have one more."

"I'll hold it for later."

"See?" Sharon held her glass with both hands. "I can restrain myself for five minutes."

"But you should be careful, you might be accused of tediousness like me."

"We've been in this bar for an hour, talking over I don't know how many topics and not once, Paul, have I considered you boring. I honestly wouldn't spend time with you if I did. Remember, I'm choosy."

Leaving Treno's, the pair walked back to Sharon's house. None of her housemates were in the living room and embers smoldered in the fireplace. Paul piled four logs in the hearth and the two lay on the floor near the fire, sharing a pillow. When he left, rain was falling again.

Upstairs, Sharon met Mary O'Donnell and the friends stepped into her bedroom.

"How was your date with the frat rat?"

Sharon undressed next to the closet. "I wouldn't call him that. Paul has interesting sides to him, he's a nice guy."

"You'll never land any action from a Mister Nice Guy is what I say. You're the one girl in our house who's onto that."

"Action." Sharon was philosophical. "The time comes when you search for more than a body in bed."

# # # #

With a note pad, Stef Tianen sat on her apartment's worn sofa, feet propped on the coffee table. Her Schwinn ten-speed leaned against the couch's back, a wet bathing suit draped over the handle bars. Wearing a corduroy bathrobe, she sipped wine and stared out the window at the drizzle, reasoning through her article for Tuesday's newspaper. The only noises came from the bedroom where her evening's date, some stud she'd met in the IMPE Building, rolled over on her mattress. He was high as well as horny, but Stef worked at the story before putting out what he wanted.

"Unending War and Continuing Protests."

"Twelve days ago, United States and South Vietnamese forces invaded the territory of neutral Laos. Operation Loading Dock's stated purpose was the disruption of the Ho Chi Minh Trail, the alleged primary route for supplies coming from North Vietnam to Communist and Vietcong forces in the south."

Summer Never Comes

Stef substituted "raided" for "invaded," and erased "the territory of" and "primary."

"The advancing armies initially made quick gains, occupying the Laotian villages of Ban Nabo and Sepone, and claiming the seizure of considerable quantities of material."

Reviewing her notes, the editor-in-chief double-checked the names' spellings, wondering how many people lived in the towns and how many had died.

"After their capture, American forces maneuvered toward the Se Bang Fal River and the border of North Vietnam. During the offensive's second phase, American and ARVN forces encountered strong resistance, with the advance failing to reach the river objective."

Stef gazed outside at the mist. If Laos were neutral, what were Communist troops doing in the country and why had American troops invaded? She didn't deliberate long, however, knowing few of her readers would ponder this question.

"Displaying the aggressiveness which has marked them as a courageous fighting force, Vietcong units counterattacked, recapturing Muong Nong, cutting off supplies and causing severe logistical problems to the American and ARVN forces in Laos."

"Let's go," the boyfriend yelled, "partyin' time."

"As in the past, military activities in Southeast Asia aroused the anti-war movement and protests throughout the United States. On college campuses, rallies were organized denouncing the invasion and the Nixon administration. The 6000 student sit-in at Cornell University gained the attention of the national press, and the around-the-clock vigil at the Selective Service System's headquarters in Washington, DC was taken to heart by the draft's opponents and American people discouraged by the war."

Finishing her wine, Stef added "again" to the first sentence.

"On Thursday, the Champaign-Urbana community participated in the 'National Moratorium on Business as Usual.' Reliable sources have estimated 60% of the student body boycotted classes, signaling their disagreement with war policies. The *Daily Illini*, also declining to conduct business as usual, published the Thursday edition with an entirely blank front page."

Summer Never Comes

"I'm playing with myself, waiting for you to squat on my face."

"The protest's highlight came at the afternoon demonstration on the Quad attended by an estimated 4000 students, faculty and staff members. The rally was capped with a thoughtful speech by Bernard Minerath of the Student Committee Requiring and Adequate Peace. Developing an analogy of unsafe children living in a dangerous world, comrade Minerath qualifies himself as a current and future leader in this campus' struggle for peace."

Stef erased "thoughtful," added "electrifying and moving," and replaced "a" with "the" before "current and future leader" in the paragraph's last line.

"In Southeast Asia, the United States airlifted reinforcements from the Hué military base, secured Munog Nong and established communications with the troops in Laos. The invading forces were withdrawn from their advanced positions in the face of strong Communist resistance."

Stef deleted "Communist" from the text.

"American casualties were reported as 125 dead, 300 wounded and 15 missing in action. The Pentagon stated that the campaign's objectives had been met, although conceding the withdrawal was 'deliberate and grueling.'"

The editor-in-chief scribbled the date at the article's bottom. In the kitchen she filled her wine glass and a second for her boyfriend, then walked into the bedroom where he straddled the mattress. Placing the glasses on the floor, Stef stripped off her bathrobe and slipped under the blankets beside a naked Dale Kinsey.

Chapter Six

"WAKE UP, you lazy son of a bitch, no sense wastin' a whole day in the rack."

"Bill Lindner, I thought you'd dropped out of the University of Illinois." A drowsy Paul leaned over the bunk to snatch his roommate's pillow, but lost his balance and tumbled to the floor, blanket trailing. He crawled towards the desks and covered himself with his sheets. "This is Sunday morning, we should be sleeping."

Lindy glanced at the Big Ben alarm clock. "God, you're right, only 10:30. How you been, Robby?"

"Hanging in with the basic student stuff, classes, researching papers at the Library, cramming for hourly exams. And you?"

"Busy, busy, busy."

"I've noticed, practiced five nights in a row this week?"

"Along with yesterday's early-bird morning session." Lindy added.

"Making progress with the band?"

"Well, it's only been a fortnight, and you know it takes any decent musicians a couple days to plug the axes into the amplifiers. And the percussion's gotta be spotted in absolutely the perfect place, rushing would be the acme of absurdity, or at least a different drummer."

"How's the music sounding?"

"Plus, until Thursday we were short extension cords for Andy Arthur's keyboard, and Franky forgot to buy blank sheet music so we couldn't copy out our arrangements, that almost mailed us back to the post office."

"For someone with a tell-it-straight reputation, you've turned crazily evasive."

"Shiftiness, I noticed myself, sorta beggars descriptions," Lindy propped his head on his hand. "After all these rehearsals something's missin', Frogfeet's sounding rough, not playin' any sharper than at the start. We can handle our instruments and love jammin', but padlock us in our basement and tell us to harmonize and it's uncommon languages, crystal clear as mud. Maybe more time will deliver us from our fate."

"Second thoughts?"

"Disappointments might be the description. I really hoped the five of us would feed on each other, blast off, but for a while we'll have to live with lowered expectations. Maybe the glass-half-full approach is it's only been a couple weeks—what we've worked on so far isn't bad and our launch is just around the corner. Like a jigsaw puzzle, you wait 'til the pieces are in place to recognize the picture."

"What's the brake holding you back?"

"Might be different techniques as performers. Or inspiration. If it's the first case, us five will have to sit down and decide which style's best. Like any other relationship, sometimes people gotta compromise."

"If it's a spark, can Frogfeet locate one?"

"You mean stumble over it? Yeah, probably, possibly, or one day we come clean and call it quits."

"Abandon the dream?"

"Would be rough, Robby. But we aren't near that extreme, not by a long shot. I've read some bands need months or years before singin' the high notes." Lindy switched to positive, "Remember The Beatles in their Liverpool nightclubs. As I said, it's only been days for us, there's still highways to walk."

"Roads again," Paul smiled, "ever wear them out?"

"Every home should have at least a two-laner, you only need an extra pair of shoes to go with 'em."

"Are you sleeping enough?"

"Not sure. Last night I passed out at Em's, dead in the water. If I'd had the energy I woulda been totally embarrassed."

"What did she say?" The room was chilly and Paul pulled the blanket to his chin.

"Nothing, Em snoozed away right next to me. I think she was satisfied havin' me there—awake or unconscious, God bless her. As of next month, Em and I have been datin' a whole year. We talked about it, how I invited everyone from our algebra class, the party after the KIDs' bash, and the stuff we did together gettin' to know each other—especially that seven hour Chi-town to Champaign train ride her and I endured at Christmas. Em's a gentle soul and definitely cares about me. This Homecoming we're celebrating our anniversary—we'll attend the game, eat a cozy, peaceful meal someplace, then hit the dance here at KIDs."

"Where will you find a relaxing dinner on a night every restaurant is packed?"

"You romantic a-hole, we'll snag a spot. It doesn't have to be fancy, just an evening with a table, a flower and showing I care." Lindy threw a pillow at his roommate. "Speakin' of scorchers, I heard about your hot one."

"What do you mean?" Paul innocently said.

"Don't toss me that line. Em saw you with a girl out at the Quad on Thursday, a blonde of all things, and I knew you had something on last night. Two plus two. What's her name?"

"Sharon Taylor."

"Cute?"

"Definitely, about five feet eight, slim body, blue eyes, wears her hair in a ponytail, real nice eyes."

"When'd you meet?"

"At the 'Welcome Back Everybody' party. While we were in line for a beer I recounted the 'how Killer earned his nickname' tale, then we found each other at the peace rally. Sharon asked me out is more the truth."

"Well, as I say, capture 'em any way you can. What'd you do last night?"

"Took in *Casablanca* at the old Auditorium, then sat in Treno's for a couple of hours. Sharon's good talking to, doesn't agree with everything I say, makes me reason—more than I want."

"The sincerest type of woman, someone who calls you on the carpet, leans on you to pick up your u-trow from the floor after they've been yanked off."

"Lindy!" Paul was embarrassed.

"Okay, okay, you couldn't reach that far inside Treno's, just ruminatin' for the future. Seein' her again?"

"For sure. And she's Kentucky's cousin."

"Holy moly. Always figured Ken-tuck for an original."

"Sharon's different, not eccentric or sardonic, determined but not bossy. And she's sweet."

"Well, however it turns out, I hope the liaison succeeds. A girlfriend's an experience, prevents you from gettin' set in your ways." Lindy brushed his hair behind an ear. "I did something brainless with Em last night. As we were talking about the happenings on the Quad, she asked if I went to the peace rally. I said no, Thursday afternoon I played hoops at Huff Gym with Stu and Bobby. I told her that instead of confessing I'd racked out. I almost used your name, too, which woulda been a huge faux pas since she spotted you with Sharon. That's the first time I've ever lied to Em, guess I couldn't admit I was so wiped out I needed sleep in the middle of the day."

"Doesn't seem like a big deal, an afternoon nap."

"It's not, isn't, shouldn't."

"Then…"

"Why? Pigheadedness, not owning up I'm snowed under with the extra work because of Frogfeet, and givin' Em any ammunition for saying 'I told you so.'"

The roommates were silent, Lindy embarrassed by his behavior but relieved he'd acknowledged his mistake. *Why'd he fib in the first place, would he come clean?* Em definitely deserved the truth. But concealing his nap was a small, white lie, no big thing as Robby commented, and not calamitous if he didn't explain to her.

Paul was happy having one of their decent conversations, the first in two weeks. The old Lindy, candid about himself, his plans and Emily, a sounding board. Paul could work through ideas, not retreat or clam up. With these good times, Sharon last night, Lindy this morning, life was worthwhile.

"How about breakfast at the Union?" Lindy stepped to the window.

"Still raining?"

"A drizzle, but doesn't appear too windy." He kicked the blanket away from Paul, "Hurry up your ass. Bacon, eggs, toast, then to the 'Brary for booking."

"Study on a Sunday afternoon? It's not even finals week and the Bears-Lions game is on the tube."

"I know," Lindy pulled on his dark brown sweater, "but I got another practice tonight with Frogfeet."

Summer Never Comes

"Oh," Paul said listlessly.

Lindy missed the switch in his roommate's tone as he grabbed his towel and toothbrush and walked to the john. Paul rose and opened his closet. At least he'd have breakfast with his friend.

# # # #

The Digital Computer Laboratory's basement was always overcrowded on evenings before programs were due. Tonight, CS 105 students crammed the place, undergrads enrolled in this introductory course sitting on the floors and stairwell—with books, handouts, slide rules and cheat sheets—in bunches or alone, conferring or concentrating on FORTRAN, subroutines, do loops and glitches; brooding over their personal programming fiascoes and obsessed by one goal: writing a program for enough points to end up on the right slope of the frickin' freakin' famous bell-shaped curve, as Bobby Sox ragged, and dodging a crappy grade. Then they could head to their dorms for sleep, IMPE to exercise or the bars to drink, anywhere but this hated building.

Dale Kinsey walked into DCL behind schedule. In forty-five minutes, he and one of the coeds from the peace rally, the real tall one with the red toenails, were meeting at Whitt's End for a beer. To keep this date, Dale needed to hastily complete the '105 assignment. Circling the basement, he recognized his discussion section classmates struggling to decipher the problem, then snickered watching a half-dozen desperate students scavenging the huge trash bins, searching for usable enough printouts to copy. Dale decided both approaches were a waste, his scheme was stealing a for-sure passing grade.

After twenty minutes' scouting, he spotted one naïve-looking undergrad. This hacker had paperbacks, programs and keypunch cards scattered around the hallway—proof of hours of scholarly effort. His gut instinct to hang, Dale dropped on the steps and lit a cigarette.

The lonesome freshman, oblivious to the crowds and confusion, unaware he was being stalked, focused only on finishing the assignment. After five minutes, he rubbed his eyes, grabbed into his pants pocket for a dime, stood and strolled to the soda machine. As the freshman stepped away, Dale hustled towards the piles. Faking lacing his tennis shoes, he snatched a printout and a bundle of keypunch cards, straightened up and slipped into the mobs before his victim bought a Coke. Returning to his spot, the freshman realized his work was missing, checked the other stressing students, then caught on he'd been robbed.

Dale's luck was in, the pilfered program returning a hook on the curve. Decenter, he made it to Whitt's in time for his rendezvous. By midnight, Dale and Lucy—God, she had long legs—were locked in her Bromley Hall room, drunk and making out on the carpet.

# # # #

Hourly exams began two weeks before Homecoming. Mechanical Engineering 270, Mechanical Design, took their test on Wednesday.

1. A magnesium tube is 5 in. OD and has a wall thickness of ½ in. The tubing is used as a pressure vessel to hold at an internal pressure of 4 kpsi. Calculate the radial-and-tangential-stress and the three principal normal strains at the outer and inner radii.
2. A cylinder is 300 mm OD by 200 mm ID and is subjected to external pressure of 140 MPa. The longitudinal stress is zero. What is the maximum shear stress and at what radii does it occur?
3. A Euler column with one end fixed and one end free is to be made of an aluminum alloy. The cross-sectional area of the column is to be 600 mm^2 and is to have a length of 2.5 m. Determine the column buckling load corresponding to the following shapes: a solid bar; a round tube with a 50 mm OD; a 50 mm square tube; a square bar.
4. A bolt circle has holes of ten ½ in. bolts of which eight are coarse-pitch and two are fine-pitch. If the fine-pitch bolts are to be opposite each other, how many ways can the bolts be inserted?

# # # #

"The first of a series of meetings," the *Daily Illini* announcement read, "will be held for those graduating seniors planning to utilize the resources of the Commerce Placement Office for next spring's job search. Their purpose will be to familiarize students with the office's services and procedures for signing up for on-campus interviewing. Thursday, 4 p.m. Location: 141 Comm West. Dean Lars Johnson presiding."

# # # #

In the afternoon Paul walked away from KIDs, through the Snack Bar, past Memorial Stadium and Assembly Hall, across St. Mary's Road, and sat by a farm field fence. He peered at a barn fifty yards away, a long building with a spire on the roof and a lean-to shed in the yard. A dozen cattle stood in a muddy patch, bending their heads into a trough, gnawing hay.

The damned job interviews notice, why'd I have to see it in the *DI*? I could've turned the page, ignored it for a while longer and wouldn't be in this cornfield, low-down, running out of alternatives, like three years ago.

Enrolled in Accounting 101, Paul had listened to lectures explaining t-accounts, cost of goods sold and actual versus accrued; studied chapters about owner's equity, prepaid expenses, depreciation, capital gains and profit margins; and copied notes on lifo, fifo, price-earnings ratio, par and present value. "Whereas management accounting is concerned with accounting information that is useful to the organization," and "financial accounting has the primary objective of providing information to parties outside the business...the terms are not precise descriptions of the activities they comprise."

And he didn't get the subject, a confused Paul had trouble understanding generally accepted accounting principles. Why write the same number twice in different columns since the amount will only be subtracted once from a checking account? Why worry over using the calendar or designating a fiscal year? Why obsess about consistency, conservatism and materiality when, as he'd told Sharon, what's essential is the bottom line. A freshman beginning college, a despondent Paul fell behind and feared flunking out. This was when he scouted the Library's third and fourth floors for the quietest, remotest, to him the best places, to study.

Paul pulled mediocre midterm grades: three C's and a D. Frustrated, he quit hanging around with the guys in Peabody Hall, struggled by himself in the History Library, and only met up with Lindy at Men's Old Gym for their swimming class. All he did was book for hours and hours—afternoons and evenings, stumbling and failing.

By Thanksgiving, Paul needed help.

Marty Barr was a teaching assistant. Organized and accustomed to rescuing lost freshmen, Marty tutored him through December to final exams in January, clarifying what baffled Paul. With morning sessions on weekends, he learned Accounting 101. No sidestepping or slick tricks, but reading, re-checking and memorizing, tackling case problems until ledgers backed up income statements, retained earnings transferred to the balance sheet and the AICPA's *Opinions of the Accounting Principles Board* made sense. Paul pulled a 4.0, a B average for the semester, decided he could handle the university, and the following years his GPA climbed. Booking became, as Lindy posited, no wolf in sheep's clothing.

But Paul was still lonely. He watched the tube in the dorm lounge and joined in rap sessions on his floor, but never made friends—he detached himself from other students. This included his first roommate, Tom Bordenkircher, the huge guy from Quincy. The two were enrolled in mismatched schedules, never ate together in the cafeteria, and Tom partied with his own buddies. The second semester, with another Housing Services assigned roommate, was worse. Stanley Olekczynski was moodier than Paul, dressed weird, stopped shaving and ended up with a peach fuzz chin, played folk songs on his guitar but was tone deaf, and habitually spoke Spanish rather than English. Humorless, he was aloof to others' opinions. They were never friends because in the ascetic Olek Paul recognized himself, a castaway on the outside.

Paul saw Lindy, but not often because their swimming class was finished and he wouldn't pledge the KIDs fraternity until the end of the year. He worked in the *Daily Illini's* office, helping with the paper's bookkeeping and researching for his friend, Annie Marie Curry. Through the balmy spring weather when happy-go-lucky undergrads wasted afternoons outdoors, Paul studied accounting, read old periodicals in the Newspaper Library and sought out solitary campus hiding places.

After three years with the Big U's thousands of students, and two years in the crowded KIDs, Paul still finds excuses for isolation, a friend's aside, the Commerce Placement Office announcement. Then he drifts, to a secluded table in the Reference Room on a Saturday morning, an empty classroom in Greg Hall during finals week, brooding by a post at the South Farms. Not what he wishes, but how he is.

Yet there are sparks when Paul steps up, contributes, grows. Hiking with the guys to football games his freshman year, hooking in with Marty Barr, joining KIDs, arguing over the peace movement article with Stef, dating Sharon, deliberating with her and Lindy over a future of accomplishing good. If Paul is tentative, intimidated, backsliding, he is glad he now and then gambles.

But what about roadblocks? How do I recognize uncertain, too-much situations? Which ways do I go? Shelter or move, hang on or change, tackle the future, or regret and be sorry?

Questions.

# # # #

"Okay, okay, okay guys," Franky Konkel tapped his Strat. "'Mad,' choke the cymbals at the intro. Lindy, you missed your break."

The drummer pushed back his long hair. "We hit the middle eight, sorta a Wilson Pickett in 'Sugar, Sugar,' but also almost sound like the Flyin' Nun durin' her crash landings. Let's go."

Twenty sessions in eighteen days and, as Lindy confessed to Paul, little to show. When he hooked up with Frogfeet, Lindy figured their rehearsals would be intense, glorified jam sessions. The five would have at it an hour or two each evening, play and rap and play, experiment with melodies, find what sounded decent and stuck to the wall, zero-in on favorites, then tweak, fine tune and pat themselves on their backs. This was how natural musicians performed.

"Such are the stuff of dreams."

Not a chance. As Lindy learned, rehearsing was a chore, each of them handed assignments from Franky, the hard-assed boss monitoring the confusion and slip-ups. Eight nights ago, Franky decided someone's guitar wasn't tuned, so he, Wooter and Lindy riffed chords for ten minutes figuring out who was off-key. Seven nights ago, Franky obsessed over their play list. Wednesday, Woofer and Franky mixed it up over lyrics while 'Mad' and Andy Arthur begged off. On Thursday, the five listened to REO Speedwagon records about two dozen times to mimic their harmonizing.

Summer Never Comes

Three nights ago it was positioning the amps and microphones for the clearest feedback. Then 'Mad' arrived late, claiming he overslept. Yesterday, Woofer didn't show at all, ticking off Franky, Lindy and Andy, but Franky kept them in the basement the whole evening rearranging their original songs, a labor because even when the guys wrote melodies or lyrics, the finished pieces were nothing to crow over. The nearest to respectable was Andy's ballad, 'Mediocre Music,' but so weepy and woeful Franky ignored it most nights.

The outcome? A submerged tenth, misfortunes of war. One middling tune, the next two awful, even the same song sounded shoddier the third or fourth run-throughs. The five were exhausted from standing on their feet all evening and mentally wiped from focusing on melding into a group.

"Vocals need the work, somebody's flat in 'Ride, Captain Ride.' At least the verses aren't bad," Andy summarized the band's shortcomings. Franky's voice was fair, Woofer sang passable background and 'Mad,' like most drummers, couldn't hold a note.

"Enough talk. Let's run through 'Free the People,' but this time, Lindy, find your break, okay?"

> Free the people, from the fire,
> Pull the boat out of the raging sea.
> Tell the devil, he's a liar,
> Come and save the likes of me.

"Why do we have to rehearse so much Delaney and Bonnie? They suck and anyway that's not what the bars crowds want to hear. We need heavy metal we can jam ten or fifteen minutes straight through without restin'—something to rip at." Woofer toweled off his forehead, "Blood, Sweat and Tears; James Gang; or even the 'Stones is what students listen to—that's rock's future."

"Man's got a point, heard duplicate arguments on 'PGU radio this morning," 'Mad' slapped his cymbals.

"Is this rock and roll music or a manifesto? Do students want to mellow out or rebel? If they want tranquility, the songs should be pretty and sweet. If they want to deliberate society, then musicians should lead, help 'em see the light."

Summer Never Comes

"Right on, especially Champaign undergrads. There's so much crap hittin' the fan, we need to get involved, point the way."

"Exactly, I say we set trends with our music, jump it forward into the new decade, the '70s," Woofer argued. "There's too much goody-goo-goo folk music around. I think our first set should kick off with 'Funk 49.' Then if you ask me, following that…"

"Who did?" Franky interrupted.

"Hey, I'm a part of this band, doin' my bit, I got a voice."

"But not much of one," Lindy added.

"Listen, you shriveled turd, who in hell do you think you are, with your frickin' pansy Beatles haircut? Just stick to keepin' up with me on that moldy Gibson. And why don't you try tunin' that axe, since it's about all you can handle around here even on your best days?"

"That's a whole lotta crap from one little half-assed bass crasher," Lindy unclipped his guitar and elbowed toward Woofer.

"Come and get me, you noisy fart."

As 'Mad' rapped a drum roll, Woofer lunged forward. Franky meant to move between the two but was blocked when his guitar whacked the microphone.

> We're lost in the room, we're lost out at sea,
> How do we get back, by God don't ask me,
> It seems that our fate, will be far away,
> We'll always be lost, in a sad, sad day.
> That's all we can sing, whatever we think,
> Because it's our mediocre music.

Andy's melancholy thwarted the face-off. Lindy re-strapped his guitar and strummed some chords while 'Mad' knocked out a beat on his bass. Their squabbling shelved, the five returned to jamming, though Lindy used up most of an hour to calm down and follow Woofer's beat.

"Midnight. That's plenty, no sense hearin' all these high notes in one session." Nobody laughed as Franky laid his axe on the floor.

"Lindy, I was joshing when I insulted your haircut, OK?"

"I'm cool, Woofer, sorry about the crack over your voice, it's not so outta key."

Summer Never Comes

"Oh, man, what a night," 'Mad' dropped his sticks on the floor. Of all the 'Feet, he cared the least for his instruments. "Franky, you press us too hard; who are you impersonating, Keith Richards?"

"This rehearsing's all about being ready for the stage—our debut, that first gig." The musicians got a rise from those two words, a magical, miraculous phrase equal to scoping the campus' most gorgeous girl in Whitt's End, and knowing you were the only guy in the joint.

"When do you think that's gonna happen?"

"Not for a while, boys." Franky shut his guitar case, "Never have enough practice, y'know."

"What does the agent say?" Woofer unplugged his Grenadier amp.

"Talked to Gary Anderson two days ago. He says there's work in the bars and at frat parties, especially with Homecoming next week. But I told him we need more time, you've gotta agree we could use a month more in this basement before we're smooth enough for the public."

"Wish I could meet Gary someday, only know him by reputation and those big, horn-rimmed glasses he wears."

"I'll bring him around. He's a man who knows his stuff; been doin' the job for years, handled the gigs for my old band, Hard Spots, and books acts for bars in Bloomington and Decatur. If he agrees we should rehearse more, we're sure as hell gonna do the work."

"How's Gary convinced we hafta keep at it if he's never been down here listenin' to us?"

"As I said, he's looped the whole eighteen. Loosen up guys, with enough practice, we'll arrive. How about more band talk over some beers at the Red Lion?"

"Super idea, Franky," 'Mad' agreed.

Woofer raised an arm, "Come on, Lindy, you in? I owe you a brew."

"I don't know fellas, remember, I'm still a student."

"Don't pass us such crap, we've heard that line for weeks. You're either with us or you're not, part of this band or not, drink with us or you don't. We gotta create camaraderie in this cellar when we jam."

"And hittin' the Lion gets it done?"

"Sure as hell won't hurt. Friendship starts with warm hearts and cold beers."

"I really shouldn't, I'm facin' bookin' for two hourlies next week, one's in macroecon, which blows my mind even when I'm sober."

"Who mentioned inebriation? One or two pitchers won't flunk you out of the Big U, will it?" Franky stepped to the light switch.

"Right on," Lindy conceded.

"The band drinking together makes music together." Andy Arthur hugged his shoulder as the 'Feet climbed from the basement, "Lindy, this is the beginning of a marvelous friendship."

# # # #

Paul laid in his bunk with the light on, 2:45 in the morning and his roommate wasn't back from rehearsal. He wanted to talk to Lindy about the Placement Office announcement and the crappy mood hitting him at the South Farms. With his band's practices, Lindy might not have seen or thought about it, so he was unsure of his reaction to job interviewing. But Paul was positive of what he'd say about sulking with cows: What a waste, sitting in a hay field, get off your dead ass and face what's coming, time's movin', don't fence yourself in. If diggin' up real jobs is what's called for, let's get on with it. A smiling Paul stared at the Big Ben clock, speculating on his roommate's exact words.

What a difference with his band. Last semester, after an evening's booking, Lindy and Paul hung with Stu, Bobby Sox and the rest of the KIDs. The roommates went to bed at the same time, usually talking themselves to sleep with "no question so silly, or wall left standing." Now Paul was by himself most nights, Lindy not returning to the room before 1:30, after he was in the rack. Twice the last two weeks Paul faked sleeping when he walked in, and last Tuesday Lindy seemed to realize but didn't say hello. Paul presumed his roommate so burned out he didn't have time for him, which was OK but not OK. Tonight, Paul hoped Lindy was talkative.

His arm banging the door, Lindy wobbled into the room, not noticing the light, "Robby, did I wake you?"

"I'm not asleep yet."

"Well, that's a shame," he tumbled towards a chair. "Everybody should grab his share of shuteye, especially this time of night. That's what I'll be doin' after sittin' here a minute havin' a shot at soberin' up."

Summer Never Comes

"How was practice?"

"Not high or low, not either nor neither. Some songs sang fair or didn't, some melodies won a door prize, others the trap door. I guess you'd say mediocre music, that's what Andy Arthur's namin' it. He thought up lyrics tonight to fit some of Franky's chords just as Woofer Raasch and I were set to square off."

"A fight between you and someone in Frogfeet?"

"Can ya believe it? After an hour of practice we got to arguin' over I-don't-know-what, his voice, my blonde hair, orange and blue or blue and orange, total irrelevances, except smart-ass me, I shot my mouth off. Coulda been a sight to see, a couple hippie musicians with our dukes up. We were still holdin' our guitars when we went at each other, coulda used 'em as clubs. The axes were plugged in, so we'd a probably electrocuted ourselves, which might've fine-tuned our dispositions. But Franky shoved between us and stopped the tussle before we hadda chance to trigger any damages." A yawning Lindy gazed at the ceiling.

"I'm glad someone with common sense straightened it out. You've been practicing all this time, from 7:30 until now? Sounds like a long session."

"Not that protracted, we hit the Red Lion to chug down some beers."

Paul studied Lindy's bloodshot eyes, "Have your share?"

"That's ol' Robby, monsieur observant, mister busybody, can't put anything past my ol' roommate. And we had luck. Rudy and the Jerg were workin' and passed us our share of freebies when Tyke, the owner, was over at the hard liquor bar. I'd say we snagged a pitcher a man, maybe two or three. Us 'Feet—that's what we've dubbed ourselves, us 'Feet—decided it was a good night t' improve our band camaraderie, that's the phrase Franky employed."

"In the Lion?"

"Why the hell not?" Lindy grabbed a textbook.

"No particular reason, except I thought you always came straight home from rehearsing."

"Robby, I can watch over myself." He slammed the book to the desk. "I don't need you checkin' on me all the time."

"I didn't mean anything by it, just with your nine o'clock advertising class tomorrow morning you might need to sleep."

Summer Never Comes

"There you go, pushy, pushy, pushy. I can handle life, I managed fine before we were roommates, so put a frickin' sock in it, will you?" Lindy yelled and straightened in his chair.

"Okay, sorry. I'm just watching out for you, to make sure you're all right. Don't you think you're exaggerating?"

"Y'know, you're like everyone else around this place, tellin' me how I should think, where I should go. Goddamn-it!" Lindy's temper snapped. "Do this, remember the other thing, don't blow that off, study for the finance quiz, make sure you show up on time for class, write that philosophy paper, don't forget practice tomorrow, and to buy frickin' fuses for the freakin' amplifier on the way frickin' over. Hey, haven't seen you all week, let's make a rap session in the hallway to discuss whatever or who-in-the-hell-cares. Take me out on a date this weekend because we haven't hugged since Wednesday. Hit that note, be freakin' polite to your fraternity brothers, don't forget to do the frickin' wash, and don't forget to fold the shirts. Goddamn-it!"

"Now, Lindy…"

"Don't 'now Lindy' me, you wimpy pain in the ass, I'm sick and tired of this crap. I'm bustin' ass, and everyone else up to and including you, my chummy, buddy roommate, sits around with no cares in the wide world, no hassles at his ankles. I'll bet you studied your nuts off all evening and you're caught up for the hourly exams. Hell, I'll bet you're ahead, I'll bet all your books are highlighted, your notes written out, your phil paper's frickin' typed. You're not like ol' poor Lindy who's behind everywhere in everything, son of a bitch." He slid a stapler across his desk, knocking over an empty pizza box.

In his bunk, Paul rolled toward the wall, tugged the blanket over his head and shut his eyes. Listening to his inebriated roommate, he wished he hadn't left the light on.

"You're mister mechanical booker, you wouldn't know what to do if you were behind because it's been years since you were in a jam, since you've taken any goddamned chances. Jesus Christ, now you've even got a girlfriend, that's how far life's danglin' at the edge." Lindy's tone sank from irate to nursery rhyme satire, "Robby's got a girlfriend, Robby's got a girlfriend, la-ti-da-ti-da-da, maybe we'll write a so-ong, la-ti-da-ti-da-da, Robby's got a girlfriend. When ya gonna jump in the sack and pump her, huh? Tell me the date for that thrill. Bet you haven't got a clue, not one hint. There's something I've still got on you, I know how to drop my pants when there's a woman naked in the room. If I had any time. What a frickin' mess, Christ almighty, what a frickin' mess!"

# # # #

Drying his pots and pans, Randy Miller rushed through his meal job in Sigma Alpha Mu's kitchen, annoyed with the extra tubs the cook, Mrs. Georgi, had dirtied during dinner. By 6:45, Randy finished, sprinted across Armory Avenue to KIDs, took a fast shower to scrub off the grease and smell, and in fifteen minutes was out the door, jogging to the Illini Union.

This was the night for the all-university-all-peace-groups meeting for bipartisanship and cooperation. Since the Moratorium three weeks ago, and before, many, numerous anti-war activists had grasped that a half-dozen disconnected factions was a flawed approach to protesting. At the rally, when minimal planning would have enhanced the campus' peace cause, neglecting assignments showed the movement as inept. Organization on the Quad had been so slipshod that at the event's finish every protester left the stage, walking off to eat dinner, with no one staying to break down the platform, pack away the public address equipment or collect garbage. Forty-eight hours later, in the cold rain, the university's janitors arrived to clean up the mess. An associate dean in the chancellor's office wanted to charge someone for this work but was uncertain where to mail an invoice. A Stef Tianen editorial calling for "level headedness not immaturity, support instead of antagonism" derailed the billing threat, though in the same piece Stef portrayed the peace effort as "a league of declining intentions and diminishing results." The commentary rankled Bernard Minerath and his followers, sponsors of tonight's 'coordination conference.'

Sprinting to the Union's patio, Randy heard the Altgeld Hall bells strike 7:30, chiming the cast iron version of 'Hail to the Orange.' He anticipated this meeting, a new alliance between SOAP, RAW, DISGUST and SCRAP, and had his own suggestions, particularly about picketing during Undersecretary Camp's visit next month. Inside the Union, he bumped into the post-dinner crowd climbing the stairs from the Cafeteria and students strolling toward the lounges to study.

Summer Never Comes

"Damn, forgot my humanities notes, I should have brought them so I could book here." Randy rushed upstairs to Rooms 269-273. Scampering in the hallway, he saw the doors still open. Reaching the closest entrance Randy braked, not wanting to charge in.

"If it is so agreed by those present," Bernard announced, "the motion is carried and this meeting adjourned."

Come again? He was only five minutes late. Grinning undergrads, a pair of handshaking professors and two *Daily Illini* reporters exited the room.

"All over, Sween?"

"Yeah, we're finished," Mike Sweeney, a fellow member of SCRAP, paused. "Definitely a thrilling night."

"What happened?" As people filed past, Randy turned his head. "Paul, hello. Sween, this is Paul Roberts from the *DI*'s staff and a frat brother."

"Writing for tomorrow's edition?"

"No, that's the other reporters' assignment." He waved to Stan Laundry and Ollie Harding. "I'm here researching for another of the paper's projects, and it looks like I'm late like you, Randy."

"I was just asking Sween what went down."

"Like our regular SCRAP sessions, Bernard started this one right on time. Up at the front table with him were DISGUST's chairman, Kevin Connors, Chuck Rigali, the head of RAW and another guy representing SOAP."

"A guy? Laurie Allman wasn't there?"

"She was a no-show."

"Wonder why Laurie would miss this meeting?"

"Well, she did." Mike Sweeney looked toward Randy, "After everybody sat, Bernard began talking about the need—necessity was his word—for more control over the Champaign-Urbana peace groups. He listed our screw-ups, especially the peace rally gaffes three weeks ago."

"Did he mention the garbage?" Randy asked.

"Yes. With the Big U's thousands of genius students, Bernard remarked, having hassles collecting trash was idiotic. He also knocked the way the Moratorium fizzled after the rally and nothing went down the next day."

"Because of the rain," Paul interrupted.

Summer Never Comes

"But Bernard argued even with weather hang-ups in Vietnam the Washington government manages to carry on a war. He said we should be as capable and stick with our protesting for longer than twenty-four hours. He stressed commitment, and pretty quick the crowd comprehended where he was leading. Bernard being Bernard, we realized he had a plan."

"He's that kind of person," Randy proudly agreed, "why he's in charge of SCRAP. What did Bernard say next?"

"'The never-ending danger to the world is the war. This demands a shared solution, submission of egos and goals to the common struggle facing us.' Then he talked about the girl in the sandbox again and gave us the 'one voice one thousand strong' passage. After three or four minutes' of preliminaries, Bernard came to the meeting's purpose. He proposed abolishing the existing groups and establishing one whole-campus peace committee. Connors of DISGUST and RAW's Rigali endorsed the initiative. Both were enthusiastic, especially Rigali—he's such a chatterbox."

"Was anyone against this 'whole committee?'"

"Nobody disputed his logic, not even RAW's silly bastards loafing at the rear of the room. This is way more logical than negotiating from now until June over who does what and when. A motion was proposed for the separate groups to disband and join together to create this movement with Bernard as chairman. One DISGUST guy seconded and the room unanimously voted aye."

"And the others are out of business?"

"Not yet. But both Connors and Rigali agreed to shut down no later than this weekend and join Bernard."

"And SOAP, what did their people say about Laurie Allman's plans? Will she go along with everybody else?" Paul asked.

"That's strange," Mike answered. "Only two or three from SOAP attended and were real quiet. They've never been big talkers, tonight even less, basically invisible. Without Laurie there was no one saying what SOAP would do. But, like RAW and DISGUST, I gotta believe they'll come out and support the new committee, it makes the most sense."

"What's the new group's name?"

"University Network Involved to End Destruction. UNITED."

Summer Never Comes

Before Randy asked another question, Bernard and his comrades marched through the doorway. Mike reached to slap his shoulder, but Bernard did not pause. He and his True Believers paced down the hall.

"Must have another appointment," Randy rationalized as Mike and he stepped toward the staircase.

"UNITED will bring the students together."

"No doubt."

Outside, Mike Sweeney headed toward Campustown, a frustrated for forgetting his books Randy returned to KIDs, and Paul walked to the History Library to study and think.

# # # #

"356-1285"

"Hello?"

"I'd like to speak to Laurie, please."

"Excuse me?"

"I'm looking for Laurie Allman."

"Who are you?" the voice on the telephone was curt.

"My name is Paul Roberts, I'm a reporter with the *Daily Illini*."

"Why is everybody bothering her?"

"I ate breakfast with Laurie a few weeks ago and we discussed her peace movement work. I apologize for intruding, but I have some questions about the new group and would like to talk to her again."

"Laurie told me. You're the accountant enrolled in one of Professor Arnstein's history courses. Laurie said you're a courteous, quiet person, and doesn't understand how you became a newspaper reporter." Her tone was politer, "Well, she's not here."

"Do you know when she will be back?"

"No."

"Will it be later today?"

"Nope."

"Do you know where she is right now? I'll walk and find her."

"Sorry."

"Can I leave her a message?"

"You may, but I don't know when she'll receive it," The voice returned to brusque.

"Are you her roommate?"

"Yes."

"Can you take a message from me and leave it around your apartment so Laurie will see it when she returns?"

"As I said, I don't know when that'll be."

"Is she okay, is Laurie sick or did she have an accident?"

"She's fine, just gone."

"This is Wednesday, the middle of the week, halfway through a semester. Laurie doesn't seem the type of person to travel or blow things off."

"Who mentioned leaving town?"

"Doesn't Laurie have classes to teach?"

"I'm sorry, Paul, all I'm saying is she left, she's not here; I'm not telling where she's at and I wish everyone would quit hassling her."

After this phone call, Paul walked to Greg Hall and the History Department's third floor office.

"May I help?" the secretary sat at the desk nearest the door.

"I was wondering if you could tell me where I'd find a teaching assistant, Laurie Allman."

"Are you another one of her discussion section students?" The secretary shook her head. "Her office is upstairs in Room 424, but I can tell you she's unavailable. Yesterday we received a call from Laurie, she's requested a personal leave of absence."

"What exactly does that mean?"

"I wasn't the one to talk to her and don't know her reasons, but Laurie has apparently withdrawn from the university for the balance of this semester."

"Wow, that's bad," Paul knew his surprise showed to the secretary. "Isn't quitting halfway through unusual?"

"Though not unheard of. Before permission is granted, the department chair considers the circumstances as well as a student's record. In Laurie's case she was afforded the benefit of the doubt."

"Do you know how I can contact her?"

Summer Never Comes

"I'm sorry, but our policy is not to disclose personal information. If you're in Laurie's History 111 discussion section, the new TA is Mike Lyngaas. His office is also on the fourth floor and I believe he's available this afternoon."

"Appreciate your help," he left the office.

What's the meaning, Paul wondered, why did Laurie quit the university the same week UNITED was founded? If anyone would join a renewed anti-war coalition, that person was Laurie. She's been against Vietnam for so long, it's sensible her remaining involved. Could it be, as SOAP's leader for so many years, she couldn't watch her organization close down? Did Laurie dislike Bernard so much she refused to cooperate, even with the cause unfinished? No, he concluded, her nature is undertaking the worthwhile. What was Bernard's phrase, a 'shared solution?' Sounds tailored for Laurie—a message she'd endorse and a way for her to get back together with Bernard. That's not the reason she's gone.

# # # #

"Thanks for coming to the office so soon. I was an alternate for a weekend racquetball tournament and received a call earlier this morning that I've qualified. Now I'm rushing around packing my gear and leaving town in forty-five minutes." Stef Tianen set her duffle bag, draped with tennis shoes, on the desk. "Those protesters, wasn't Tuesday's meeting super? In twenty-four hours a new group's established. Long time coming, I'd say. Were you there, Paul?"

"Meant to, but arrived late, I didn't expect that brief a session. I had some luck, though, and was filled in by one of UNITED's members. I saw you had Stan and Ollie covering it."

"They did a competent job reporting the facts, I gave the pair a byline in yesterday's edition. About your peace story for *Spectrum*... Now's the time for a big push, to go at it one hundred percent, maximum effort, you know what I mean." All business, Stef squinted her blue eyes, "I admit I've been skeptical about your article. With the half-dozen campus anti-war groups, the project looked too complicated, a dissertation on organization or disorganization, take your pick."

"Especially with me writing?"

"That wasn't my inference. I suspected our approach—rehashing bunches of details—was too obscure. Circumstances are different now, UNITED adds definition. Bernard Minerath's straightened up the radicals and the peace movement can aim at their objective."

"Which is?" Paul was surprised, expecting more arguments against his article.

"Pitch in, shake the campus, end this damned war. And that's where the *Daily Illini* assists. The rest of this year we profile UNITED's achievements, showing students stepping up to change their country."

"Aren't you ahead of yourself? UNITED has yet to accomplish anything significant enough to report. We should wait."

"Caution, from someone two weeks ago self-righteously lecturing me about the newspaper's role in society? What happened, swallow more of those carefulness pills you carry around?" Zipping her duffle bag, Stef saw the taunt upset her friend..

"Prudence and restraint are also reporters' assets."

"I agree. But the peace movement's acquiring momentum, not lobbing around the confusion the old factions loved so much. Take a look at this," she handed a sheet of gray paper to Paul. The letterhead read 'UNITED TO END THE WAR,' with a drawing of a baby girl playing in a sandbox on the left margin. A press release was typed on the page announcing UNITED's formation, along with a summary of the group's goals.

"Clever art work, when did it come out?"

"Bernard sent me a copy this morning. The point is a swing in direction's coming, the anti-war crowd's moving ahead and I want the *Daily Illini*—as you lectured me—participating, not observing. So we're positioning the paper behind UNITED. I want to muster every effort we can." Stef looked at the clock on her office wall.

"Am I dropped from this story?"

"Where'd that come from? You thought up the assignment and stay on it. Whatever help you need—researchers, reporters to work with—is yours." She reached for her bag, "When it comes to composing the piece, however, you and I will work together. I want in on the writing, not banging the typewriter keys, more developing the theme."

"You're editor-in-chief," Paul was unenthusiastic.

Summer Never Comes

"Tell me, Tuesday night at the meeting, did you pick up any rumors, hear anything unexpected?"

"No more than Stan and Ollie reported, except Laurie Allman was absent."

"That's not a huge deal." Duffle bag on a shoulder, Stef walked towards the doorway, "Now that those old peace groups are out, she's finished, too. From what I hear, this was her time to move on. Mine, too."

"By the way, where's your racquetball tournament?"

"Eastern Illinois University, in Charleston."

# # # #

"What happened?" Emily sipped her soda.

"In a thimble, a muddled mess, I lost my temper with Robby."

Early Friday afternoon, Lindy and Emily sat in Second Chance's back room, nearly by themselves. With the Fighting Illini playing football in East Lansing and no parties this weekend, many undergrads had left campus and headed home. Of course, there was a basic, die-hard crowd, including Moose, Ozark and Tim Malito, around the pinball machines, and Credence Clearwater Revival playing and replaying on the jukebox.

"The band had crummy practices all week. During the most frustrating session Woofer Raasch and me got into it over some crazy thing and had to be yanked apart by the others, we were that close to dukin' it out. After rehearsal was over, the five of us walked for some brewskies, hit the Lion around midnight and made up for lost drinking time. I rolled into KIDs about 2:30, with Robby wide-awake. I was dead-tired drunk but he wanted to talk. He made a remark I took as people—including him—pokin' their noses into running my life, and I laid into him with both barrels. Right between the eyes for my poor roommate."

"How mean were you?"

"Remember me describing the shoutin' match with Bobby Sox in the laundry room, when we chucked dirty underwear at each other, even pairs not belongin' to us? Subtract the u-trow and this was a parallel episode. I ranted at him for being a goody two-shoes student, and even insulted his new girlfriend."

"Did Paul say something to set you off?"

"Robby reminded me I had to be up for a nine o'clock class the next morning, the most innocent comment a body can make. He was lookin' out for me and I chewed his butt." Lindy shook his head, "Four days later, I'm still ashamed of myself."

"Was there anything in his tone that was annoying, did he act like a wise guy?"

"My roommate was nothing less than a totally considerate buddy. After I dumped on him he didn't say anything, only rolled over and pretended to fall asleep. But I know his feelings were hurt." Chugging his beer, Lindy watched two coeds flipping the 'Nine Ball' machine, three games for a quarter. "I'll tell you, Em, I sit here, confess blowin' up is wrong and wish tantrums weren't in my personality. Then socko, bammo, my life stumbles and I hit the warpath. The cruel part is many times, like this one with Robby, the person I dump on has no role in what's got me upset—just happens being in the room when my mind cracks. When life is easy and workin' out, you know I'm everyone's best pal. But have the frustrations really pile on, like rehearsals this week, I explode—I won't cope with my problems and I blame others."

"You have to discover a better way, Will, a resolve within yourself."

"Sounds simple, but now's not the right time for repairing my psyche. There's too much occurrin', other tribulations to toil through."

"Is the band one of them?" Emily hopefully lifted her eyebrows, as she did when expecting encouraging news.

"We're stuck in neutral, an accident waitin' to happen. We run through practices, do everything we should, but our rehearsing's not earning results. We're baffled we can't find ourselves. Arguments, like the one between Woofer and me, point out the frustrations. And there's other parts of my life heatin' up, too. With midterms nearing, I could use more booking, but darned if I know where to find it." Another CCR record blasted through Second Chance.

"What are your next steps?" Concerned over her boyfriend's problems, Emily did not mind Lindy skipping over her. *Please,* she prayed, *please say what I want to hear.*

"Continue practicing, sharpen our music, try soundin' professional." Lindy sensed Em would be happiest if he'd confess the band a mistake. But even to his dearest, most intimate acquaintance, he'd hold back, only disclose his doubts to a point, because with more work for sure the band would improve, his dream would happen.

"Have you and Paul talked again?" Emily masked her disappointment.

"The next day I apologized five or six times and Robby said he understood, so I suppose we're back bein' pals, we will be buddies." Lindy filled his beer mug, "but as every other time, I feel I'm a jerk."

"You must try harder with your friends."

> Someone told me long ago,
> There's a calm before the storm,
> I know, it's been comin' for some time.
> When it's over so they say,
> It'll rain a sunny day,
> I know, shinin' down like water.
> I wanna know, have you ever seen the rain,
> I wanna know, have you ever seen the rain,
> Comin' down, on a sunny day.

"So, Em, Homecoming's around the corner," Lindy slapped his hands. "Ready to party hard, to play the happy couple?"

"Very prepared. I'm anticipating next weekend so much," Emily brightened, "as long as you're certain you'll have the time."

"Reserved and booked, my sweets, with my cares dropped at the door. Hourly exams will be finished, and I made Franky promise on a tall stack of Beatles albums the band's on hiatus. No bookin', no rehearsals, equipment repairs or music, no outbursts or excuses." Lindy reached for his girlfriend's hand, "Just us two setting things back on track."

"That will be marvelous."

"By the way, did you happen to talk to Nicole about the you-know-what for the you-know-when for the you-know-whos?" He feigned shyness.

"Sometimes, Will, you take for granted that my girlfriends are prudes. Yes, all arranged. Next Saturday night Nicole is staying across the hall in Elaine's room."

"Into the wide open spaces, out to dreamland."

Summer Never Comes

Long as I remember, the rain been comin' down,
Clouds of mystery pourin', confusion on the ground.
Goodness through the ages, tryin' to find the sun,
And I wonder, still I wonder, who'll stop the rain?

After his regular dollar's worth of quarters but no free games, Tim Malito bought a second beer, found a table and listened to CCR.

"Excuse me, what's the time?" the voice belonged to a gorgeous, grinning, red-haired coed. She wore an olive green army fatigue coat with the corporal's stripes ripped off the sleeves.

"3:45."

"Fine, still early. My name's Katy Karas."

"Tim."

"Cold weather outside; think there's any chance for improvement?"

"I hope so, at least in time for Homecoming next weekend. Spectating Memorial Stadium football in sunshine is a great way wasting the afternoon."

"I've got another idea for unwinding," Katy sat at his table. "Want to hop in bed with me?"

Tim nearly dumped his beer mug.

"I live in Illini Tower, we could walk there in five minutes. There's a bottle of wine in my refrigerator and I just bought a record album by a new singer named Harry Chapin."

"I know where IT is, I pass it every day."

"IT means something else, inner thigh, and right now mine's ready for you."

"You're picking me up?"

Katy shoved his hand below the table. "I own a double mattress and the sheets are halfway clean."

Tim didn't care for fondling her, but couldn't prevent Katy from pulling his hand towards her panties.

"I'm not a hooker, only I've been celibate for five days now and want some wild man to grab me and screw me. And baby, that's you."

"It's not even dinner time and tonight I'm booking at the Library." The pinball machine 'clapped' as Moose matched again.

Summer Never Comes

"My roommate's gone all weekend, I keep packages of Trojans in my cabinet for turn-ons like this," she snuggled to Tim's side, "and I love French kisses."

"If we were loaded and this was eleven or twelve at night, no problem, I'm there for you. But before dinner? *Star Trek* reruns are on Channel 3 in an hour."

"I'm not a virgin, I've made it before, plenty. Right now I'm psyched and hot." Katy clutched both his legs between hers. She crept her fingers underneath Tim's shirt sleeve, rubbing his wrist. "I'm stimulating, fantasmic, anyway, anyhow you want."

Tim chuckled at her proposition and ego as they hurried toward the door.

# # # #

"Tonight's the first time since last winter I'm taking in The Guild, hope they're as good as I recall." Hurrying north on First Street to Chances R, Sharon stayed close to Paul's side and out of the wind.

"They are. I heard them during New Student Week, the same six with the same sound."

"And who was your date that night?"

"Lindy and a dozen of the brothers." The two waited for a gap in the traffic before crossing Green Street. "Lindy's a real Guild freak, appreciates them as much as The Beatles."

"They're a copy band. From your portrayal of him as a true musician, I'd think your roommate would prefer a group singing their own material."

"Lindy thinks it's a shame The Guild only performs two or three original tunes, but their vocals, along with the trombone and sax, light him up."

"How's his band progressing?"

"Frogfeet's practiced a ton in the last month—five or six nights each week—but he says it'll be a while before landing their first gig."

"And their repertoire?"

"Couldn't say, it isn't mentioned much."

The pair passed Barnett's Liquors. In the jammed parking lot, two students loaded a half-barrel in a Buick's trunk. On their lift, one toter lost his grip, dropping the keg on his toes. As he hopped on his uninjured foot, the barrel rolled down the pavement, past the other cars and out to Green Street. The beer's owners chased the runaway, one skipping, both cussing. Laughing along with the parking lot crowd, Sharon glanced at Paul, his head drooped down, unaware of the comedy.

"Hello, are you still with me?"

"Sorry, I was preoccupied with Lindy."

"He's not vanished to California, has he?"

"For all we get together these days, he might as well be there. Lindy's so far away it's as if we're not roommates anymore. Lately we only talk once in a while, not every night. And the conversations can be congenial or crappy."

"What language," she kidded.

"What I mean is we sit in our room and both speak, but aren't connecting when it comes to really deep discussions. Do you remember seeing the spring job interview notice in the *Daily Illini*?"

"No," Sharon was honest.

"The announcement informed Commerce College seniors about future prep sessions, the companies coming to recruit, kinds of questions to ask, our answers, how to dress and salaries to expect. For me the start of leaving the University of Illinois."

"Only you, no one else?" she teased her boyfriend again.

"Okay, at least those without graduate school plans. It bothered me so much—about what college means to me—that I spent an afternoon out at the South Farms, agonizing over my future."

"You with the grazing cattle?"

Paul smiled at his unpretentious girlfriend. "That night, I waited for Lindy to return to KIDs because I wanted to lean on someone for five minutes. But he didn't come home until 2:45 in the morning and was in bad shape, totally inebriated from drinking at the Red Lion. I tried telling him how confused I felt, didn't know what to do over job interviews and wasn't ready for them, but I ended up nowhere. Lindy didn't care a bit and let me have it. I reminded him he had to be up for his nine o'clock advertising class and Lindy lit into me again. He chewed on me and lost his temper, like he once in a while does. I gave up reasoning with him, turned over and faked falling asleep. If Lindy wasn't my best friend, I'd look for another roommate."

"Are you two still on the outs or have you reconciled?"

"That's his up-front side, Lindy smooths over the troubles his tantrums trigger. He's sincere when apologizing and, like every other time, means it when he pledges he'll never lose it again."

"Did you ever chat about job interviewing?"

"The next day Lindy spent forty-five minutes coaxing me to open up, but I didn't bother. He was amiable only because he felt sorry for me or himself, I'm unsure which. Right now his mind is on Frogfeet's rehearsals every night and other matters don't register. He's away so much that his friends in the house see he has no time for us, he doesn't care."

"What are the problems here, Lindy moving on with his band, or you depressed for yourself?" On Water Street, with students ahead and behind them, the two neared Chances R. "Isn't it selfish, wanting your friend the way he was because you're insecure?"

Paul appreciated Sharon expressing in words what he was frightened admitting. "I'm a puzzle, don't know where to go. Lindy's my friend, I hate sitting in our room, watching him obsess on a fantasy and discounting everything else."

"Toward the career he wants to succeed in," she was direct.

"You talk like the Placement Office. Later on there's time for that stuff—professions and vocations. Now is now, we should enjoy college."

"We're not meant to dream while we're in school?"

"Our university days are for studying for good grades, not spinning off on whims, straying away from everything. Lindy's wasting so much time practicing, other parts of his life are affected the wrong way. He's missing out on what we used to do, like watching The Guild perform."

"What about me?" Sharon asked. "I'm going with you to Chances R and have listened to you since we left Urbana."

He squeezed her hand. "And I'm grateful."

"You talk, Paul Roberts, as if the whole world owes you, should coddle you."

"Is it wrong keeping friends?"

"Of course not, depending on people is natural. But over time we, and what we want, change."

Summer Never Comes

"Some things are too perfect and should stay status quo. Why veer off a hundred eighty degrees?"

Sharon peered into Paul's eyes, exasperated with his denying logic. "Is that what Lindy's doing? Appears to me he's deliberated this rock and roll band idea plenty and now is following through."

"But reshaping his life."

"His or yours? Remember, there are no certainties for Lindy, you or I."

"We're discussing friendship. And I apologize if this is immature, but after three years as buddies I miss having Lindy around, relying on him. That's my hang-up." The pair were on Chester Street and, typical for a performance of The Guild performance, saw a long line of students at Chances R's door.

"Wall, howdeh, cousin."

"James, out for the evening, I see."

"Ah am look-in' forward t' some spirited tunes t'night, cousin, yes, Ah do." Kentucky raised his hat to the pair, "How ahr you, Robbeh?"

"Fine."

Seeing Kentucky, Paul's mood improved. Reaching the door they paid the two dollar cover charges.

The Guild packed Chances R, crowds jamming to the stage, the main floor's tables and the three balconies, Sharon and Paul sitting next to the upstairs bar. The band performed their always-superb, psych-up-the-audience show, with the students dancing and singing along, from 'Soul Shake' and 'Heavy Church' to the old rock 'n' roll favorites.

> Here's my story, it's sad but true,
> About a girl that I once knew,
> She took my love and ran around,
> With every other guy in town.
>
> Take out the papers and the trash,
> Or you don't get no spendin' cash,
> If you don't scrub that greasy floor,
> You ain't gonna rock 'n' roll no more.
> Yakety-yak. Don't talk back.

Summer Never Comes

"Do you think Lindy will ever play on this stage?" Sharon shouted after 'Blue Moon.'

The second set kicked off with 'Only You Know and I Know,' 'Lowdown,' Paul's favorite, and 'Why Do Fools Fall in Love.' In The Beach Boys' medley, the crowds roared through 'Fun, Fun, Fun' and quieted during 'Good Vibrations.' The Guild trumpeted 'Something in the Air,' and one guitar player shot off his toy cap gun in the finale, the 'William Tell Overture.' Five minutes of clapping, stomping and rowdiness by wall-to-wall undergrads, bartenders and waitresses earned an encore.

Leaving Chances R, most students trooped back to campus on foot. Eight or ten zigzagged on the sidewalk, hung on each other and serenaded First Street with a verse of 'I Get Around.' Sharon and Paul never saw Kentucky after their hello at the bar's entrance.

"Great show, those guys always hit their notes."

"The brass is the topper, more rousing than only guitars." Paul slid Sharon's hand into his pocket. "Last year, Lindy and I heard The Guild the night they auditioned a demo tape for a Los Angeles studio. At the end of the performance, Lindy skipped down from the balcony, skated to the stage, falling over he's laughing so hard, and had a stab at stealing the tape. What a crazy night."

"How close did he come?"

"Not very, there were too many elbowing students, and one girl with really big boobs blockaded Lindy, nearly knocking him over. If we'd snatched the recording I don't have a clue what we would have done with it—none of our friends own a tape machine." They walked south as a single car turned on Stoughton Street. "I must've sounded brainless on our way here tonight. Remember our first date in Treno's and me mentioning my old neighbor?"

"You never told me his name," Sharon laid her head on his shoulder.

"Larry Rhodes, we were great friends in grade school and high school. He's eighteen months older than me and a big brother I never had. In the summers before we were old enough to work part-time jobs, Larry let me hang with his pals, made sure I got picked on his baseball teams and saw I didn't get hurt. I remember the two of us always tossing around a football. Larry threw perfect spirals and I was learning to catch them. We used to play catch and talk, like Lindy and me here in Champaign. Once we had a conversation about *Rowan and Martin's Laugh-In*. I asked Larry what he thought about Arte Johnson's jokes, and he came back with a totally sophisticated answer. Or I thought it was pretty complex since I was fourteen or fifteen. One day, five years ago, he left for college. We shook hands before he got in his parents' car and I watched him drive away. I was miserable. The next time I saw him was Christmas break. The first morning he was back I ran over to his house with a football to say hello and show him I could catch spirals. Larry opened the door and his appearance was how we look now, like college students. His hair was long, way down his neck, he hadn't shaved in three weeks and his eyes had the glassy, I-smoked-dope-all-night gaze." Paul shuddered and Sharon chuckled at his reaction.

"I asked Larry if he wanted to throw the football and he said no. How about later? He was busy. In the afternoon? All he did was scratch his stomach. After two more sentences, Larry said he had to go, not a goodbye or see you around, only that he had to go. He shut the door and left me out on the porch by myself. I never saw him again that Christmas and haven't said any more than hello to him in two years.

"I make pals then lose them—first Larry, now Lindy. So, I'm truly grateful having you for my girlfriend, I hope we stay together and I won't disappoint you with the way I am."

The wind blew from the north, knocking leaves off the trees and pushing Sharon's hair over one shoulder. "What's Emily's view of Lindy playing with Frogfeet?"

"She's in love with him and wishes someday they'll marry. Emily realizes a wedding's a few years off, but is willing to give Lindy the chances he's taking, wait for him to finish with Frogfeet and return full time to her."

"And Lindy's feelings for her?"

"What you'd suppose. They're a sweetheart couple, everybody in KIDs recognizes that. He likes her, actually loves Emily, possibly may marry her. But in Lindy's life, at this moment, on this campus, his band comes first."

The neon sign in Abe's Red Hots' tiny window blinked to a deserted sidewalk.

"Just think, if my car wasn't in the garage with a cracked radiator we wouldn't be hiking to Urbana. We could hop in and gas up for a road trip to grab breakfast."

"Where'd we drive at two o'clock in the morning?"

Summer Never Comes

"How about south on Route 45? It's thirty or forty miles to Charleston and Eastern Illinois University, that's where we'd eat."

"Then what, visit friends?"

"Yes, pull over, knock on a front door and say, 'hello, we're from Urbana and Champaign, and can we use your bathroom?'" Sharon joked. "Do you know anyone down there?"

A wide-eyed Paul gawked at his girlfriend, dumbfounded he'd missed the link. "I do, of course, certainly, a student I met three weeks ago, who I want to talk to again. When do you get your Camaro back?"

"The mechanic has ordered parts, so about the Tuesday after Homecoming. Want to borrow it?"

Paul explained as the two arrived at her front door, Sharon shocked by her boyfriend's reversal, changing from dejected to focused.

Both were delighted discovering the living room empty, her housemates already upstairs. The pair sat on a couch, Sharon enticing her boyfriend to spend the night, but he balked—too many people around. They napped on the sofa, woke at four, and Paul went home to KIDs.

Chapter Seven

"Homecoming!" A howling Lindy pounded the bunk, "Hail to the Orange."

"What is the deal, can't I sleep in anymore on Saturdays and Sundays? Is it toking some wicked weed, or has practicing in that basement corroded your brain?"

"Maybe so, Robby, maybe so. Only I know this weekend I'm not playing my ol' Gibson; I can sit around chewin' straw and eatin' off the fat of the land."

"Is this William Kendall Lindner speaking?"

"Sure as hell is. Frogfeet's on a two-day breather, unwinding and re-stringin' the axes. I'm celebrating Homecoming and spending time with Em. God bless everybody and may God bless the Fighting Illini."

"I don't understand you," a half-awake Paul enjoyed his roommate's dialogue.

"Neither do I, except to say it's a vacation from music and school. Somehow I finished my booking, did okay on my hourlies and managed not to exasperate any buddies. It's behind me, Robby, I feel like I'm starting over."

"Well, if you are, welcome back."

"Thanks. I admit bein' a pain in the rear to a lot of people the last month and feel like the old line, 'when Greek meets Greek, then was the tug of war.' Maybe I can turn a new page." Lindy fell out of bed and sat at his desk. "How'd the house decorating go?"

"We painted the sign last night, didn't you notice when you came home?"

"Not really, the brews we had after rehearsal sort of blurred my vision."

"Check it out. You'll dig our slogan, 'Huck the Fawkeyes.'"

Summer Never Comes

"Who originated that peach?"

"Shaky Jake."

"A-h-h-yes-s-s, a t-t-true s-s-scholar." Lindy mimicked W. C. Fields while dressing. Hearing knocking, with one leg in his pants and the other out, he hop-scotched to the door. "Nemo, haven't seen you in a while, how you doin'?"

"Yeah, where you been? You got a telephone call."

"Not around much, I guess." Lindy stepped into the hallway with his jeans half-on. "Em probably checkin' on me."

# # # #

Band members arrived at the Armory in mid-morning. Horns tuned, drummers assembled beneath a basketball hoop, the Illinettes rested on the green tartan turf, one flag carrier practiced by herself, and the ROTC color guard stood at ease. Beyond the oval track, next to the walls, moms and dads of the Marching Illini snapped photos, gossiped with fellow parents and admired their children. Joggers and passersby unfamiliar with game day preparations paused to spectate. This being Homecoming, the quasi-formal, thoroughly-psyched alumni band organized opposite the Marching Illini. Wearing orange windbreakers and blue hats, these old-timers jubilantly anticipated a day of performing for Champaign-Urbana's football crowds. At noon, Director Everett Kisinger whistled both bands to attention. Stepping through the Armory's oversized doors, the musicians tramped south on Fourth Street, playing and singing the 'Illinois March.'

On the walkways surrounding Memorial Stadium, UNITED volunteers, including Randy Miller and Mike Sweeney, handed out leaflets and barked to the crowds entering the gates.

"Remember the war, remember peace more."

"UNITED will stop the killing!"

"USA out of Vietnam. Bring the troops home to the States now."

"UNITED is a synonym for peace."

Fans and tailgaters ignored the True Believers, with no one grabbing their brochures. Homecoming buttons, football programs, orange flags with blue 'I's, kegs, coolers, barbecues, fold-out tables piled with munchies and fond memories were more prized.

Summer Never Comes

"Stop the war, our protests will do it. The fighting must end!" Randy shouted.

"REMEMBER THOSE WHO WILL NEVER COME HOME," a hand-painted sign requested.

As kickoff approached, the parking lot partiers filed to the stadium. Randy and Mike hauled their box of leftover flyers into Gate 11. At 1:30, right before game time, the forty-three thousand people in Memorial Stadium were called on to stand for a moment of silence for alumni lost in the country's past and present wars. A Marching Illini bugler played 'Taps,' and Paul, Bobby Sox, Stu and every KID thought of Billy Powell.

# # # #

Dale Kinsey blasted Percy Sledge through his earphones. He wasn't attending the game, never had in three years at the U of I, though he wished the Fighting Illini had more victories. Competitive teams boosted his scalping business.

For two hours this morning, along with Tommy Quarters, he'd circled Memorial Stadium haggling, buying and reselling tickets. As the crowds cheered the opening plays Dale retreated to KIDs to total his profits, shred unsold tickets, and wonder why so many stupid students and foolish alums paid to watch a dumb game. Around three o'clock, two men, not undergrads, walked in and cased his room. North Champaign despoes, Dale was certain. One kept both hands in his coat pockets, the second carried a brown paper package under his arm. Yanking off the earphones, Dale opened a drawer, grabbed an envelope with the money he'd cleared this afternoon, and handed the wad to the first stranger.

"All there, dude?"

"Two hundred dollars, as agreed." Dale meant to sound adult, but over-emoted in his snotty my-shit-don't-reek tone.

The stranger counted the bills as his accomplice dropped the package on the desk. "Ex-cel-lent."

Untying the string, a smirking Dale examined the plastic bags of white powder. "Yeah, how's the quality?"

"Just pure enough, dude, for the high for the honky dope heads you service."

Summer Never Comes

"No hassles, I'm cool, this college is such a bunch of pansy-asses."
"Obliged for the business, hope you make a decent profit."
"Say hello to Loops."

# # # #

Another KID missing from Memorial Stadium was Lindy—this morning's phone calls settling and wrecking his plans for the afternoon, evening and coming weeks. As half time neared, along with Franky, Woofer, 'Mad' and Andy, he practiced in their basement for tonight's scheduled-at-the-last-minute gig. Plucking his guitar, partly listening to Franky's solo, waiting for his cue, a hyper, nervous, shamefaced Lindy brooded over his conversation with Emily four hours ago.

"Hi, how are you?" He'd stood at the hallway pay phone. "Have a sound night's sleep?"

"Will, sweet of you to telephone, thank you. I didn't expect this, thank you."

"My pleasure." *Boy, Em's perky, why am I dumping on her?*

"The weather's sunny and cool, perfect for watching a football game, isn't it?"

"I've already been outside and you're right, the temperature's in the fifties but with a north wind." *Come on, you putz, why are you putting this off?*

"That's fine, I'm planning on wearing my big blue hat with a scarf and bringing a pair of gloves. I also borrowed an extra woolen blanket from Nicole for us to sit on, so we should be warm. What time do you want me at KIDs for the luncheon buffet?"

"Well, Em, there's news," Lindy shuffled his feet on the carpet. *Okay, here it goes, the end of the line for me.* "Frogfeet's landed a gig."

"The practicing has paid off. Congratulations, Will, I'm sincerely delighted you accomplished what you set out to do. I realize the last few weeks I haven't been supportive, but I'm glad for you now. Have you told Paul, Stu, Kentucky and Bobby? What's their reaction?"

"You don't quite understand. A gig's a job for us, we've been hired to play for money." Lindy rubbed his eyes. *God, Em's in such high spirits and sounds genuinely happy, she has no clue what's coming.* "Franky Konkel called me right after I got outta bed this morning. Phi Alpha Theta, a fraternity the block over from KIDs, had the band for their Homecoming dance cancel out, something about the flu or the trots. Their social chairman phoned our agent, who lined us up for tonight, a real in-the-nick-of-time situation. We're bein' the good guys and stickin' our foot in the door to boot."

"The band is performing tonight?"

"Right, our debut." *Please, Lord, don't let this be as unholy as I imagine.*

"That's fortunate for them," Emily hesitated, "but a shame for you, isn't it? You'll miss performing because our day and evening are arranged. I suppose I'm glad but also sorry for you at the same time."

"No, I'm the one apologizing. I'm with Frogfeet, I'm playin' at that fraternity tonight." Lindy pictured Em holding the phone, sitting on her bed, maybe in her bathrobe, with the clothes she intended wearing laid out over her dresser. *Gosh, I've fashioned some failures in my life, but how could I drop a load like this on my girlfriend?*

"Will, everything's ready, the plans are made, our dinner at the Round Barn, the dance and sleeping together tonight here in my room. We talked this over, it's all settled."

"I realize, Em. I can't tell you how shaken I am. We're gonna have to cancel for this evening. I'm sorry, absolutely regretful, but I'll make it up to you, I promise." Lindy listened to sniffles. *However miserable my voice sounds over the phone, if she only knew how rotten I consider this whole disaster. This is not a pretty picture.*

"Aren't there five in your band? Can't they go on without you, can't one of the other guitar players cover for you?"

"Not really, the music wouldn't sound mellow missing my rhythm guitar."

"What about hiring a substitute?"

"I don't think so, the gig's only a few hours from now and it was a trick for Phi Alpha Theta scrounging us up on such short notice. Findin' one replacement musician would be practically impossible." *Please, my dear, just a speck of understanding is what I'm pleading for.*

"There must be a hundred guitar players in Champaign-Urbana, tracking one down to take your place should be feasible."

"But not the same, I've rehearsed all the songs, I'm a part of the band, no one can fill my shoes, no way. This is my moment and spotlight, my claim to fame." *Did those words sound that egotistical? If they are, I'm definitely in sad shape.* Lindy heard more sniffles.

"But your group wasn't working this weekend. Saturday and Sunday are a break for you, aren't they? A holiday for us."

"You're right, the band's supposed to be off and I was stayin' away from my guitar. But this is our chance to finally jump on the stage, launch the rocket, the long and windin' road. Remember?" *I should be wiser, humoring my girlfriend right now is the supreme blunder.*

"We won't see each other tonight?"

"Right, the Homecoming dance here at KIDs is off." *At least she's not crying. I wonder if any of her girlfriends are around Blaisdell; would that be helpful or an embarrassment?*

"We're watching football this afternoon, aren't we? We can still do that, it would be our date."

"I'm afraid the game's out, too. Real pronto, Frogfeet needs to fine-tune our sets, compact what we have into three hours." *God, there must be something positive I can say.* "But you can still attend KIDs' party. Robby, Stu, Bobby and everyone else will be here. Robby said he's bringin' his brand new girlfriend, her name's Sharon, you can meet her." *How feeble. If that's my offering, I'm toast.*

"They'll all be there, Will, enjoying the evening, except you."

"And I'm honestly sorry. I know I come across as the heel, but this is the leg up I've pushed for my whole life, I've got to see it through. I'll fix this mess, I promise." *What possible repair is there? Whatever Em says, whatever people think of me for stiffing my girlfriend, I deserve it.* "How do you feel?"

"Disappointed, disillusioned."

"I know you are, and I can comprehend, relate." *This is pretty pathetic, too, I'm reaching down to the bottom.*

"Truly, Will? Do you believe yourself?"

Back in the basement, Lindy focused on 'Black Magic Woman,' figuring the melody a decent dancing tune. Franky Konkel wanted a perkier opening.

"Our first gig," Andy Arthur calmly announced as the five finished the song.

"Far out." 'Mad' crashed the cymbals.

"We need more practice." Franky was relieved they'd gotten together this afternoon.

Summer Never Comes

# # # #

On their last down in the first half Iowa's quarterback lobbed a bomb into Illinois' end zone. The Illini defense intercepted for a touchback and with two seconds on the clock the ball was spotted on their twenty-yard line. At the snap, tailback Lonnie Perrin took the handoff up the middle and sprinted eighty yards for a touchdown. All the KIDs in the east balcony—Paul and Sharon, Scooter and Lauren, Moose, Ozark, Hod, Killer, Shaky Jake and Kay, Tim Malito and Katy Karas, Ronny Gimbel, Jerry Dudek, Orion Nelson and Eddie-Bob McMahon—celebrated as Lonnie trotted over the Hawkeye's goal line, making the score 28–0. Paul kissed Sharon, emotion noticed by Stu and Joyce Belker. The crowd hooted as both football teams ran to their locker rooms and the Marching Illini began the half time show.

"Chief!"

With a boda slung on a shoulder, Bobby Sox sat one row in front of Paul and Sharon. Keeping to his ritual of toasting each Illini touchdown, extra point and field goal with a chug of root beer schnapps, Bobby was as intoxicated as his wineskin empty.

"Didn't you say he drove home to Chicago for weekends?" Sharon watched the drunken KID swing in rhythm with the band's music.

"Nine out of ten, but every year Bobby stays in Champaign for Homecoming and gets as wasted as he looks now. Tomorrow he'll telephone Jeannie to confess." Paul stared at his fraternity brother and hugged his girlfriend.

Playing a second Sousa march, the Marching Illini stomped into a routine featuring the Illinettes. In formation near the sidelines, the alumni band maneuvered on the field.

"Chief!"

"Whadya think, the Illini gonna hold the lead?"

"Looks reasonable, at least better than poor Bobby," Stu answered.

"Chief!"

Facing the stadium's home side, the Marching Illini finished a rendition of 'Got to Get You into My Life,' not sounding rock 'n' roll-ish with mellosaphones, saxophones and tenor drums.

"Chief!"

Summer Never Comes

"I think this is it."

On top of a ladder, Director Kisinger blew his whistle and slashed his baton through the air. In cadence with the drums the Marching Illini paraded into a square, played the opening bars of 'Mister Touchdown,' then sang.

> We are marching for dear, old Illini,
> For the men who are fighting for you.
> Here's a cheer for our dear Alma Mater,
> May our love for her ever be true.
> While we're marching along life's pathways,
> May the spirit of old Illinois,
> Keep us marching and singing, with true Illini spirit,
> For our dear, old Illinois.

The applauding fans watched the band tramp northward, still in their square. As the musicians crossed the goal line, someone, a student, an Eagle Scout, clad in Indian headdress and buckskin regalia, arms folded, head high, strode from the sideline and slipped into the band's formation.

"Where'd he go? Where'd he go?"

The band piled into the end zone, marching in place. Chief Illiniwek crouched and zigzagged through the maze of musicians, hiding from the crowd.

"Where'd he go?"

On the exact note, as he'd carried on for forty-six years, the Chief sprinted into the open and war-danced down the field. Tootling the 'Three in One,' the Marching Illini followed, spelling I-L-L-I-N-I. The rhythmic applause and howling by the students in the balcony were so deafening that Paul couldn't hear the music. The Chief danced into the south end zone with his traditional leap into the air, hands touching his bare feet, as the boisterous crowd bellowed and whooped. Arms horizontal at his chest, he paced toward the east grandstands and at the fifty yard line raised his hands above his headdress. The crowds quieted, the band crooned 'Hail to the Orange,' a voice in the balcony hollered "now everybody sing," and the assembled loyal Illini joined in.

Summer Never Comes

Hail to the orange, hail to the blue,
Hail Alma Mater, ever so true.
We love no other, so let out motto be,
Victory, Illinois, varsity.

The Marching Illini played their trombones, sousaphones and piccolos, and the Chief stepped and danced, speeding up as the music quickened. Like every half time, the crowd clapped, haphazard at first, then in tempo with the bass drums and faster and rowdier. At the dance's end, after his grandest jump, Chief Illiniwek left the field, arms folded, head and war-bonnet high. The jovial students hurrahed, forever proud to cheer their hero of the University of Illinois.

Half time celebrations ended, the bands trooped to the sidelines, both teams returned to the field and the murmuring crowds settled in their seats, chatting with buddies, speculating on the second half, eating hot dogs and checking their bodas and flasks.

"All right, another tradition." Ozark shaded his eyes.

In the clear sky, one hot air balloon, a giant, blue ball with an orange basket dangling from the bottom, drifted toward Memorial Stadium. The football fans and KIDs supposed the airship belonged to Garcia's Pan Pizza, the Flying Tomato Brothers frequently floating over Zuppke Field on game days to advertise their restaurants.

Depending on a day's breezes, balloons traveled toward the stadium from various directions, pilots flying fairly near the field and ordinarily higher than this blimp. This afternoon's maneuvers were atypical. As Paul and the bewildered Illini watched, the dirigible glided with the north winds, over Bromley Hall, the Six Pack dorms, the IMPE Building and toward the stadium, perfectly centered between the east and west balconies. At the ten yard line, the balloon rapidly, dangerously, shockingly lost altitude, sinking three or four hundred feet—a descent so abrupt the crowds screeched, terrified the airship was crashing. During the plunge, however, the pilot ignited the gas burners and the basket leveled off at the balconies' railings. The co-pilot sliced a rope, unfurling an orange and black banner from the gondola's bottom.

"UNITED TO END THE WAR."

Summer Never Comes

The students applauded, Paul uncertain their reaction relief at not witnessing a catastrophe or support for UNITED's slogan. Cuddling his boda, a startled Bobby Sox, fantasizing an alien, indigo blob invading from outer space, practically crapped in his pants. The balloonists waved as the airship gained altitude and floated toward Savoy.

"What a stunt!"

"Close call!"

"I never saw a blimp sail so near Zuppke Field. Think there's a city ordinance about that?"

"Brave thing to do."

"Takes balls!"

"I'd heard a rumor about this operation but never imagined the flight would be so successful. Bernard pulled off a coup," Randy Miller was totally thrilled.

"Wonder what a balloon trip costs?" Stu speculated to Paul.

On the second half kickoff, Mike Gow caught the ball and sped for another touchdown. 35–0!

"Blowout! Blowout!"

In the student section, the crowds devoted less attention to the gridiron and more to partying. The KIDs abetted the fraternity in front of them, the Fijis, passing a coed from row to row above their heads, shoving her to the balcony's top. The alcohol bootlegged into the stadium inside pockets and underneath coats was finished off, a reprieve for the inebriates, including Bobby. On his politest behavior, Stu did his darnedest to make Joyce welcome. Recent graduates Mike Ryan, Ken Jurek and Roger Shook bragged over earning real money in the real world, reminisced about the old days and secretly wished they could return to school for longer than a weekend. The unofficial kazoo band tramped around the grandstands, serenading the fans. French kissing, Tim and Katy left early. And on the field with every touchdown, the cheerleaders pumped push-ups equal to the Illini's points on the scoreboard, a humongous task in the fourth quarter.

"Boy, is your roommate drunk!" Paul shouted.

"No," Stu screamed back and leaned toward Bobby, "disgusting!"

"Show some sympathy," a laughing Sharon scolded, "your poor friend's wasted and you're razzing him. Someday this might be you."

"Don't worry, we'll haul him back to the house."

Summer Never Comes

Eyes closed, Bobby flip-flopped over the bench, his shoulders swaying. He wobbled through the third and fourth quarters, in no danger of hurting himself but oblivious to when he'd see that blue balloon again.

"Unbelievable," Paul scanned the sidelines with Stu's binoculars, "Kentucky's standing next to the head coach."

"Didn't you know? Bob Blackman and cousin James' family go back years," Sharon answered. "The coach and my uncle were college roommates at USC and worked together at Dartmouth."

"Which explains why Kentucky never sits with us during the games."

Sharon stared past Paul, watching the Illini cheerleaders cross to Iowa's sideline to kidnap Herky the Hawkeye. "I wanted to be a cheerleader, I imagined it would be fun."

"What happened?" Paul asked.

The final score was 50–0, with Coach Blackman carried off the field, Kentucky's shoulder supporting a leg. Paul and Sharon hugged, Paul aware she was holding him really tight. Taking turns propping up his body, Stu, Joyce, Sharon and Paul guided Bobby Sox out of Memorial Stadium.

"Grease the Hawkeyes." He mumbled.

# # # #

"Chuck Panther, welcome back to the old frat."

"Man, far out, yeah, I mean, thanks."

"Can you believe that balloon? I thought it was all she wrote and she was gonna nose dive to the ground."

"We blew 'em out, most points scored by the Illini since Grabowski."

"Gotta say, UNITED produces publicity, only around a few weeks but has the whole campus talkin' about them."

"They were lucky, without a north wind the stunt would've failed."

"Found a great job with an awning manufacturer in Aurora, never thought I'd have one paying seventeen thousand dollars a year."

"Leaving the stadium I grabbed one of UNITED's fliers. Protesting the war makes sense."

"I'll bet Bobby sleeps off his hangover and puts in an appearance at tonight's dance." Paul passed Sharon a cup of beer. "What a load maneuvering upstairs; how can anyone so short be so hard to handle?"

Summer Never Comes

"Bobby reminds me of Mary O'Donnell at last month's party, but hard figuring which one was in worse shape. It's me; I must attract drunks."

"Wall, if'n you-all ain't a sore sight," Kentucky ambled towards the two, raising his hat to Sharon. "Cousin, do yohr parents know you ahr seein' thes Yan-kee?"

"Now, James, you'll embarrass us."

"Mah dear, Ah haven't bin able t' do thet in two yeahs t' thes boy, no ma'am."

"How'd you like the game?" a grinning Paul shifted Kentucky to other subjects.

"A right-fine per-for-mance. Ah think th' grid-iron eleven ahr learnin' th' play book."

"And Coach Blackman, James?"

"A decent an' up-standin' gentleman of th' Ivy League."

"He should have more victories," Paul added, "today only makes our record 3–3."

"We-all will win mohr games thes yeah, mark mah wurds," Kentucky gazed around the living room, spotting Scooter and Lauren near the fireplace. "Say, Rob-beh, why don' you-all at th' *Daileh E-li-ni* do a story about air traf-fic at football games."

"Beg your pardon?"

"Thet damned fool in th' balloon buzzin' th' stadium like he wuz a seagull. Ah sympathize with th' cause, but theah coulda bin a calamity if'n he'd sunk aneh furtheh'."

"The pilot knew his work, planned flying low to stun the crowd with UNITED's banner," Sharon said. "And did, listen to everyone in this room talking about it."

"Wall, Ah be-lieve Ah best be movin' on. Plenty o' people t' pay respects to." Again Kentucky removed his hat and bowed. "Cousin, as usual mah felicitations t' yohr momma an' daddeh."

"We'll find you at the dance, James."

"Look out, make way for the toters!" As the KIDS, their dates and the alums applauded, Jake and Orion Nelson hauled a fresh keg through the packed room.

"Whenever James and you get together, Paul, you laugh. Do all your friends affect you that way?"

Summer Never Comes

"Don't think so," he glumly answered.

"What's wrong?"

"I'm thinking of Lindy."

"Will he be back for dinner?"

"No, Frogfeet is practicing as long as possible before driving to Phi Alpha Theta."

"We can walk to watch them later, if you like," Sharon said.

"Maybe," Paul was noncommittal.

"And Emily, will she attends tonight's dance?"

"Lindy invited her."

Moose and Ozark edged around the mobs, the Mooser balancing six beer cups above his head, while an alum dressed in orange Levi's, blue gym shoes, an orange rugby shirt and blue suspenders, with a golf club and a half-dozen balls, hurried to Frat Park. "Once more for the old days."

"What's your opinion of Lindy's decision?" Sharon asked.

"Pitiful."

"Why? This is his chance, the break Frogfeet needs for their future."

"No way I'm buying that logic. Homecoming is Emily's and Lindy's anniversary. They arranged today three weeks ago, dinner at the Round Barn, the dance, the two of them alone back in her room. Now, at the last second, their date's canceled and Emily's abandoned. Worse, Lindy gave her the news over the telephone, not in person."

"Your roommate will make up with her, won't he?"

"If Emily accepts whatever apology he offers. But what will equal what she's lost? Affection and patience cover only so much hurt."

"I agree, Emily won't care for Lindy's behavior. After she reasons it through, perhaps she'll understand Frogfeet's opportunity as Lindy does—his one big moment in history."

"That's a peculiar phrase, something Lindy and I hashed over." As frequently, fortunately occurred, talking with Sharon brightened Paul's mood.

"How'd he describe it?"

"With The Beatles, what else? On side two of *Abbey Road*, Ringo solos a few bars before the four sing 'Carry that Weight.' Lindy said Ringo's drumming is a hard-to-equal effort, some of music's best-ever moments, a pinnacle. We went on to reason how some events or ideas turn out being more inspirational than others. A minister's Christmas Eve sermon, a well-composed paragraph in a novel, an aunt's or uncle's story about surviving hard times when they were young. Another illustration is John Kennedy's inaugural address, where he imagined 'a more fruitful life for all mankind…with a good conscience our only sure reward,' JFK challenged our generation to move forward."

"Do you agree with what you just said?"

"I admit there are times when circumstances intrude and people must act. But Lindy's band—his watching out for himself and trashing Emily—is a mistake. How many shots at ruining relationships is someone allowed? You don't renege on promises to the person you love. He's guilty of that a lot lately, discounting friends. He's screwing up his life, not holding what he has, blowing off what means the most."

"Like the rest of us, Lindy is searching." Sharon leaned on the trophy case, "Often the timing is wrong for finding the future, but it's got to be done. The world is a strange place, destiny happens anytime. If we don't explore on our own terms, tomorrow and what follows materializes when we're unsuspecting."

"Fate is irrelevant. Lindy's on a narrow path, deserting his girlfriend, turning self-absorbed. How can dumping on people be justified with whims about tomorrow? If this is progress in life, it's wrong and validates that change is bad. The present is better—it's sheltered, you know your limit and don't fool with it."

"So much for JFK's New Frontier."

KIDs left the post-game kegger to clean up and change for the party. Only Paul, Sharon, four aging alums and the despoes remained in the living room.

"This is too deep for Homecoming weekend."

"You're right, party time. Go Illini." Setting her cup on a table, Sharon blushed. "I had a sprained ankle."

"Come again?"

"The summer before my sophomore year in high school I was thrown riding a horse. I was sore for six weeks, missed cheerleading tryouts and never got picked. I would've had fun."

Staying for dinner, Sharon had left a blouse and skirt in Paul's room prior to the game, saving a trip back to Urbana. She dressed as he waited in

Summer Never Comes

the hallway. Women roamed all over the fraternity on this hard-drinking, hard-core, blow-out weekend.

As the brothers, their dates and alums sat down to supper, Bobby Sox laid unconscious on the floor in his room. A barf bucket stood next to his body, left by Stu in case his roommate lost his cookies. Still drunk, Bobby instinctively rolled on his side, reaching for an imaginary blanket.

# # # #

Lindy and the 'Feet arrived an hour early for their gig. Finished setting up, the five impatiently sat on the stage, toying with their instruments, staring at an empty room. Franky Konkel mentally reviewed their sets, scratching and tacking on songs.

"What the hell, let's play," Woofer jumped to his feet.

"Ignition, blast off!" a boisterous 'Mad' pounded his cymbals as they grabbed their guitars.

"Good evening, Phi Alpha Theta," Franky nervously announced. "We are Frogfeet, this is Homecoming, and for the next hours we're gonna sing you a good time."

'Mad' bashed his tom-tom and the band was sailing.

> Miles from nowhere, guess I'll take my time,
> Oh, yeah, to reach there.
> Look up at the mountain I have to climb,
> Oh, yeah, to reach there.
> Lord my body has been a good friend,
> But I won't need it when I reach the end.
> Miles from nowhere, guess I'll take my time,
> Oh, yeah, to reach there.

A half-dozen students strolled toward the stage but didn't applaud when the Cat Stevens tune wrapped up.

"Hope the crowd gets keyed." An apprehensive Andy Arthur whispered.

Summer Never Comes

"Hope we have a crowd," Lindy jauntily answered, finally on his stage, performing, in the spotlight, "and don't hurl them out along with the bath water."

> Baby I'm-a want you, baby I'm-a need you.
> You're the only one I care enough to hurt about.
> Maybe I'm-a crazy, but I just can't live without
> Your lovin' and affection, givin' me direction,
> Like a guiding light to help me through my darkest hour,
> Lately I'm a-prayin' that you'll always be beside me.

One girl and a guy danced, but most stood there, wandering away after listening for a song or two. The room wasn't a third full, a sight no singer relished. After half a set, with weepy music, stretched out gaps between tunes, a busted amp and snapped strings on Woofer's bass, the 'Feet confused the audience and lost their enthusiasm.

"Whadya think?" Andy muttered.

"Not too decent."

"We're wound up, gotta settle down." The 'Feet slid into 'One Man Band,' except for 'Mad' who for the first six bars pounded the beat to 'Try a Little Tenderness.'

# # # #

After dinner, many KIDs stepped out to the patio.

"A little chilly." Sharon wore the corsage Paul had given her.

"Do you want to go back in?"

"We should walk, with the crowds the house will be stuffy."

"How about my sport coat?" He draped his jacket over Sharon's shoulders.

"At supper I noticed most of the brothers were dressed like you, coat, dress shirt, a tie," she shook her head, "and blue jeans."

"What can I say, the Big U style. Of course, these pants are a different pair from the ones I wore to the game, my newest Levi's, and they're clean, mostly."

Summer Never Comes

"For Homecoming, I would hope," Sharon dramatically declared. Circling Frat Park, the pair turned the corner at Armory Avenue and her boyfriend watched the party in Lambda Chi Alpha's front yard. "If Emily had been at dinner she could have sat with us."

"And if Lindy were here, she'd be happy. I'll repeat, I can't comprehend my roommate dumping Emily and our friends, and leaving behind security."

"It's his life, he obviously believes the decision worthwhile. Don't you think your moment will come?"

"To join a band?" Paul joked.

"Leap, choose, risk."

"A person can't ignore uncertainties forever, all I ask is delaying a while longer."

She punched his arm. "You are exasperating. First rational, then burying yourself in a cave, writing off everything except this university of ours and what we have today. How can someone so brainy be so thick?"

As always, a temperamental Paul welcomed Sharon pressing him to think. Cheers exploded from the partiers in Lamb Chop's yard.

# # # #

"Jake, what's tonight's turnout, how many kegs?"

"Hundreds, humongous, sixteen."

"How y'all doin'? Mighteh fine t' see y'all he-ah."

"Hey, buddy! Great party, definitely super. No doubt in my mind you're KIDs' premier social chairman ever."

"I appreciate that, Killer. How's the beer pouring?"

"What's the band's name?"

"UNITED's balloon was as exciting as the game."

"Think she'll show?"

"Knickerwooks."

"Did you invite her?"

"There's no reason the Illini shouldn't have blown out Iowa, we're a helluva better team than they are, right, Donny?"

Summer Never Comes

On top of the house's kegs and wine, Moose and Ozark had purchased a case of Mogen David blackberry brandy, selling half the MD 20/20 pints before dinner, mostly to freshmen, and the remainder by the band's first set.

Knickerwooks blared Led Zeppelin's 'Whole Lotta Love' and 'Stairway to Heaven.' The partiers jammed the dance floor for their rendition of 'Teen Angel' and stayed out there the entire evening.

"Say…man…know what Kinsey's pushin'?"

"Yeah…some real good shit."

"The first set's pretty fair, I hear they're playing Hendrix in the next one."

"I'll check out UNITED and see what they're about."

"I love you, Lauren, and have for all these years. Will you marry me?"

"Oh, Scooter!"

His elbow whacking the barf bucket, Bobby Sox heard music from two floors below. "Christ, what happened, how did I end up in my room? Holy hell, what was that frickin' blue spot in the sky?" With a case of the munchies, Bobby recalled the game, his afternoon's drinking and reckoned he was still living. He combed his hair, grabbed a clean shirt from the closet and headed to the party.

Paul and Sharon danced the whole second set, the twist, the jerk, one polka, the mashed potato and two waltzes, then climbed the stairs to the living room.

"Fantastic times," she merrily said, "I've never boogied so much."

"Every Saturday should be Homecoming." Paul hugged his girlfriend and spotted Stef Tianen in the mobs. Reaching the kegger they ran into Emily. "Hello, I'll introduce you two. Emily Ritter, this is Sharon Taylor."

"Nice to meet you," Emily avoided looking directly at them, searching the room instead. "My dorm was deserted tonight, the emptiest I've ever seen, so I wanted to get out and be around people."

Students sidled around the three, towards the kegs, away from the bar, out to the patio, into the ladies' powder room and up to the second floor. The living room was packed, with no empty space anywhere. Yet, in middle of the jolliness and racket, Emily was heartbroken.

"Tell you what, I'll tap us some beers," Paul left the women and was sucked into the throngs.

"Which dorm you live in?" Sharon asked.

Summer Never Comes

"Blaisdell Hall on Pennsylvania Avenue. And you?"

"I roomed in Hopkins three years ago, but now six friends and I rent a house in Urbana."

"Moving out is an option I haven't come to," Emily scanned the foyer and living room again, "I'm satisfied where I am."

"I imagine you're not pleased with Paul's roommate. I'm sorry he isn't here for you."

"It's awful to be stood up, especially on our anniversary. I truly believed Will wouldn't act this way, abandoning me with so little warning. Now he and everything is uncertain. Did this ever happen to you?"

"Once, early in high school. But I wasn't bothered because it was a blind date," Sharon joked, "and a month later I learned the guy was a nerd."

"I know he seldom shows it, but Will is a romantic. This Homecoming was one of those times. We had a wonderful weekend arranged, our first two days in a row together all semester. Then this morning after a phone call, not even face-to-face, the plans collapsed and I'm alone. Will has never done anything like this to me. He is such a decent person, I know he'll always be there, I don't understand why he deserted me."

Two KIDs marched by lugging another fresh kegger, with Ozark running interference.

"I'm certain Lindy considers tonight's performance worthwhile. Isn't it admirable achieving an ambition you've always dreamt about?"

"What Will is doing is a job, nothing else. They didn't have to start their career tonight—it's not as if this is their only or last opportunity playing for an audience—there are other parties besides Homecoming. And what about me? Don't I merit Will's consideration? As his girlfriend, I should count. On the biggest weekend of the semester, everyone is in such a wonderful mood, enjoying themselves, and here I am, by myself."

"I'm certain he's thinking about you, that's what Paul says, you mean so much to Lindy. But all of us live by priorities."

"If that's true, where is my boyfriend and how high am I on his list?" Emily surveyed the room again.

"If this is his first chance to play with his band, isn't that significant, perhaps not necessary, but vital to him?"

"What I said about Will's reliability was truer when we started going out than today. I'd always counted on him as my rock, but this semester Will has changed so much that he's dishonest with me." Emily glimpsed at Sharon with a just-between-us-girls-look, "Two days after the peace rally we were talking in my room, the first night we'd seen each other in a week. Between school work and his band, Will admitted not having time for extras. I asked if he'd gone to the protest and he said no, he'd played basketball with Bobby Sox and Stu. But that Thursday I saw Stu on the Quad with the same girl he's dating tonight. They spent that afternoon sitting near the stage listening to the speeches."

"Paul mentioned this, Lindy's lie being a split second choice, and how he, your Will, was disappointed with himself. Did you tell him you knew the truth?"

"I had put it out of my head, a small detail. But with what's happened between us the past few weeks, and especially this morning, that was his first step toward the riddle he is, not the dear, dependable companion he was."

Sharon yielded, unable to support Lindy any longer. How much her personality is like Paul's, she thought.

"It wouldn't have been so bad if…"

Four giggling, carefree, wild-for-Homecoming-weekend coeds exited the ladies' powder room, with Katy Karas the perkiest. "Tim's a dreamboat, a darling, affectionate, and his hands never stop when we're in bed. I'm keeping his kinky body."

Knickerwooks started their third set, couples hurrying down the stairway to dance. With ratcheted music, conversations turned gruesome, the entire room shouting and competing with the band.

"Old buddy, how you doin'?" Killer slapped Bobby Sox's shoulder as they stood in the partying mobs by the kegs.

"Having a good time?" Bobby half-smiled.

"Sure am." As usual, Killer howled louder than everyone else. "Say, you feelin' sprightlier and normal-er than during the game? If you ask me, by the third quarter you looked dead. Naturally, it happens to all of us sooner or later, just a matter of time and space and barf for you, pal."

"Bobby," Paul careened through the crowds, "glad seeing you're awake. Back to human?"

"Killer and I are discussing that."

"Well, you appear resurrected. Say, do you remember the same thing happened to 'Stein last year on one of those derelict White Horse Inn quarter-beer-n-dime-hotdog Fridays? After stumblin' back to the frat after two or three hours' drinking he passes out asleep under the hallway water cooler, but thought he'd been toted outdoors to Fraternity Park." Killer so mischievously snickered his fraternity brothers knew he was faking. "'Stein was absolutely pissed before he regained his bearings."

"Emily Ritter's showed, Bobby, she's by the stairs talking with Sharon. Why don't you come over to say hello?" Paul juggled three beer cups and the two seniors started for the stairway, leaving a hee-hawing Killer to himself.

"How much is Kinsey chargin' for the stuff?"

"Yes, Scooter. Marriage is what I've wanted all along."

"Randy, who organized the balloon idea?"

"My ass the Illini have a chance beating Michigan next week."

"Finish off your Mad Dog?"

"Where'd all these people come from?"

"When will they leave?"

"I had a chance with that last broad, but she blew me off when Killer barged in."

# # # #

Not a hard-core house, Phi Alpha Theta's Homecoming dance struggled through Saturday night. At eleven o'clock, the fraternity's members still wore their coats and neckties and tapped beer out of their quarter barrel. Some had left the house, searching out livelier parties. Frogfeet's performance was no help. The band's selections were dreary, Lindy and Andy swapped grimaces each time one of the five's voices dropped a note, and every missed beat got a reprimanding stare from Franky Konkel. But Lindy, as conscious as his band mates of the gaffes, smiled and smiled, glorying in his first gig.

> Words, a simple song
> A minstrel sings.
> A way of life in his eyes,
> Hear the morning call of waking birds

Summer Never Comes

When they are singing, bringing
Love—love.

# # # #

Dale Kinsey killed the evening chugging beers with the despoes and threading through the house sniffing for women. He danced with one coed, but was shut down when he unsnapped her bra. Not his kind of lay, Dale rationalized. At midnight, he hung out at the kegs, back against a wall, a cigarette drooping from his mouth.

"I hear your shipment showed," Stef Tianen moved next to him.

"Word travels," Dale shoved her hand down into his pants.

"What's the price?" she kissed an ear, ready for the come on.

Kinsey stepped away from the wall, starting them for the stairs and his room. "For you, honey, if you're extremely hot, there's a special deal."

Even with Paul, Sharon and Bobby as companions, Emily had a tough time not sobbing. Her only pleasant moments were dancing with Bobby and hearing about his dream of a monstrous, blue moon smothering his face. Understandably she obsessed on her Will, all the unfairness, and how abandoned she felt. Emily knew that the more despondent she acted, the harsher Will's friends would look on him. If not intending to ruin his credibility, she did nothing to let the KIDs think otherwise.

While Emily and Bobby were on the dance floor, Knickerwooks and the crowds collaborated on weaving a 'snake.' Sixty or seventy partiers lurched to the stairway, twisted through the living room, out to the patio, back in the front door and to the second floor. The tail broke off, straggled into Tim Malito's room and a mini celebration sprouted. Around 1:30, a bemused Tim and an incredibly horny Katy discovered a dozen of the brothers and their dates occupying the chairs, the carpet and his bed. Postponing screwing, they restarted drinking. Emily and Bobby went downstairs for one more beer, then Bobby escorted her back to Blaisdell Hall.

Most of the brothers who'd purchased their Mad Dog were satisfied with a pint, but Tommy Quarters bought two. Completely inebriated for the nineteenth or twentieth night this semester, clutching the empties, he crawled to the basement boiler room and passed out.

Summer Never Comes

"What number keg is this, Jake?"

"Thirteen."

"Too bad Knickerwooks only played four encores."

"Sue, that's right, Scooter proposed to me just as the dance started, over by the fireplace!"

"Oh, congratulations."

"Is the party still on in Malito's room?"

"Who won the room raffle?"

"Wall, it rightleh wuz a pleasure t' make yohr acquaintance thes eve-nin' mah dear. Ah do hope t' see you soon."

"Lauren and Scooter are getting married."

# # # #

"I feel so sorry for Emily." Paul carried his girlfriend's extra clothes.

"Stood up is a huge downer." The two crossed the Quad and Sharon gazed at the old Auditorium. "She needed nerve coming to the dance, I'd have done anything besides partying with my boyfriend's pals."

"Outside of Lindy and her roommate, Emily only has a few close acquaintances. KIDs might have been her only option, except staying by herself in the dorm, which would have been misery. At least she was around people to take her mind off Lindy."

"I didn't know what to say to her when you went to the keg, I wanted to chat, not wordlessly stand there."

"You two looked fine when I returned with Bobby."

Sharon squeezed Paul's hand. "Emily mentioned the peace rally and Lindy's fib, saying it was only a little detail. But as we talked, Emily became convinced Lindy was wrong for lying three weeks ago and deserting her tonight. The poor kid."

"Are you amending your opinion? That my roommate, and everybody else, shouldn't renege on promises?"

"I understand Emily's feelings, people hurt when friendship fails. But I still maintain if your roommate thought tonight was his big gamble, he did the right thing."

Summer Never Comes

"For himself." Paul lifted the garment bag to his shoulder. "To lie is bad, but ditching your girlfriend isn't. The reasoning confuses me. Did Lindy make the correct decision today? Yes or no to the question."

"He found himself in a dilemma: chase ambition or play safe for his girlfriend. There's no simple answer, each alternative is flawed because no one is happy and everyone takes a loss. I feel sorry for both. Sometimes going forward is confusing. Lindy has to live with what he's done, that may be the harshest consequence."

The pair were silent the rest of the walk back to Sharon's house. Inside, Angie, Julie, Karen and their boyfriends sat by the fireplace. Paul and Sharon joined the couples, Paul taking the job of keeping the logs burning.

# # # #

The drained and disappointed 'Feet, anxious to call it a night, pack up, get paid and skate, staggered to the end of their last set with another Moody Blues tune and a near-empty room.

Lindy stepped to the center for his evening's lone solo. As dissatisfied as the other four, he'd loved the experience. He'd stick around and play longer if anyone clapped for an encore, but knew that was a Hobson's choice—nobody wanted one. Lindy adjusted the microphone, lifted his foot on a wooden chair, twanged for his key and remembered Emily. The few fans in the room quieted and Andy Arthur leaned on a speaker.

> You sheltered me from harm,
> Kept me warm…kept me warm.
> You gave my life to me,
> Set me free…set me free.
> The finest years I ever knew,
> Were all the years I had with you.
> I would give anything I own,
> Give up my life…my heart…my home.
> I would give everything I own,
> Just to have you back again.

CHAPTER EIGHT

"PRAIRIE WINDS BALLOONING, this is Brad speaking, may I help?"

"The last few football games my buddies and I have watched your balloons float over Memorial Stadium. We're interested in renting one and flying for an afternoon. Can you fill me in on specifics?" Paul sat alone in Bobby Sox's room, talking on his friend's telephone and paging through *Playboy's* October issue.

"Right. We're located on Route 45 in Savoy, near the golf course, and open every day except Mondays. We operate four balloons, all newer than five years. Any can be rigged with one of two different sized burners that inflate the balloons, the hotter one lifting a balloon higher. Flights take off from the fields next to our warehouse, and we depart around nine in the morning or right after lunch. Air time is approximately two hours, but most passengers arrive early to watch us blow up the balloon. If customers want to traverse a certain area, and depending on a day's winds, we'll truck our equipment to an estimated starting spot. There's an extra fee for setting up away from our warehouse. We sail ten or fifteen miles at an altitude between one and two thousand feet. If you add an hour to return after landing, the whole trip takes half a day. Rates are thirty to forty dollars per person, depending on the distance you want to fly."

"What's the gas keeping these balloons airborne?"

"Not a gas, hot air," Brad authoritatively answered." Propane heaters warm the air blown into the envelope, creating an artificial atmosphere more buoyant than normal air, allowing the balloon to ascend. After lifting off, we maintain altitude by firing the burners and forcing more heat into the envelope."

"As the burners combust, why doesn't a balloon continue rising higher and higher, never coming down?"

"Every balloon has a hole at the top called a parachute vent, controlled by a rope attached to the basket. Opening the vent releases hot air, cooling the envelope's interior and causing the balloon to descend."

"What's the inside's temperature?"

"Up to 120 degrees, but generally no more than 100."

"Can the fabric burn?"

"Balloons are nylon, which melts at 230 degrees, so they're safe."

"How many people travel on a trip?"

"Baskets hold three or four passengers, in addition to the heaters and propane tanks."

"How do you know where to retrieve a balloon when the flight's finished?" Paul looked up from Bobby's *Playboy*, more inquisitive about flying than he guessed.

"Pilots communicate by radio with a ground crew trailing the airship. We reach the landing site as quick as possible."

"Do you come down in unusual spots?"

"Better believe it. Only the winds maneuver balloons, so once or twice each year we drop in an unappreciative farmer's field," Brad sounded proud.

"Can someone fly by themselves?"

"Our pilots crew the airships ninety-five percent of the time, though we have customers we allow to solo after authenticating their licenses. We also teach classes for rookies."

Paul turned a page in the *Playboy*. "Are reservations needed?"

"Yes, especially for weekends. Right now Saturdays and Sundays are booked out a month. When Big U students came back in September, the wait was longer."

"Why's that?"

"Warmer weather, undergrads paying for thrills, football weekends. People get a high flying past Memorial Stadium checking out the game day crowds."

"Like the Iowa game last weekend when that blue balloon floated over, what a freakish event."

"Closer to a horror story we're catchin' hell for," Brad was agitated. "Losing altitude and dropping directly over the field was way too perilous a

Summer Never Comes

stunt. My boss had fifteen or twenty phone calls bitching about what those nimrods did. Television stations, the police, I never realized telephones rang so much. The National Guard's even threatened us with an FAA investigation. Of course, in a weird-ass way we're admiring how the flight was handled. With the variables, amazing they traveled right over the field at the half time's finale. If the pilots hadn't had great instincts calculating their speed and perigee, the balloon would have definitely crashed."

"Was your pilot on board?" Paul closed the *Playboy*.

"No way, any one of us would have been fired before landing. We rented the balloon to a woman claiming to be qualified and recommended by one of our regulars. The lady paying the bill was a university professor and gave us a cash bonus."

"What's she teach?"

"My boss asked that question when we retrieved our balloon—English history—which is baffling. Any highbrow PhD should be smarter than engineering such a stupid stunt."

Over the phone, Paul heard a car engine, a door open and close, then footsteps.

"Anyway, you and your buddies want to fly?" Brad's voice was more business-like.

"We'll discuss the deal and call you back," Paul searched for another magazine. "What was the cost?"

"Thirty to forty dollars per person."

"Thanks for the info."

# # # #

On Tuesday, Paul and Sharon picked up her Camaro and took the trip they'd planned the night of The Guild's performance. Arriving in Charleston, the pair drove east on Route 16 toward Ashmore, easily locating the farm he was looking for, a white house, two silos and a dark red barn.

"This is so sparse, totally opposite my home town, the nearest neighbors must be a half mile away."

"Picture perfect. College students should leave the campus oftener to appreciate Illinois' prairies." Sharon parked in the barnyard. The sun warmed the morning and both heard a revving tractor motor in the soybean fields.

"I felt you would find me." Laurie Allman led Paul away from the Camaro and towards a haystack.

"I should have been cleverer. Last week I had two conversations with Charleston mentioned before remembering you lived around here, one with the *Daily Illini's* editor, the second with Sharon."

"Who owns a decent-looking car. Have you been friends long?"

"We met at a party a month ago."

"Is she the only one who knows about this visit? And do you trust her?"

Paul was puzzled. "I'd say as much as you rely on your roommate."

"Lindsey is a dear. We're both History Department teaching assistants and have roomed together for two years."

"A friend for sure, she volunteered nothing when I phoned."

"Which was my doing, I asked Lindsey to screen my whereabouts. That's my upbringing, I come from a private family."

"And the reason I'm here—why are you on a farm ten miles from Charleston instead of Champaign?"

"I couldn't stay on the campus because I wasn't safe. Someone's intimidating me." Laurie was apprehensive, not the laid-back, bookwormish girl he'd eaten breakfast with in the Union. "I have office hours for my students twice a week in the TAs' lounge on Greg Hall's fourth floor. The Wednesday after the peace rally I arrived at eleven in the morning, my usual time. Ten minutes later I received a phone call. A man's voice said a new regime was coming and I would be wise to be on board. The call was short, less than thirty seconds, without hellos or goodbyes. Two days later, the same message—a warning to agree with the approaching consolidation, the new day of all toiling as one. There were a third and fourth calls after that."

"Did you recognize the voices?"

"No, although I'm convinced it was the same person each time. By themselves, the messages were creepy, but more disturbing by the third one I figured out each call occurred precisely ten minutes after I entered my office."

Summer Never Comes

"Did you show up the same time each day?" Paul looked toward Sharon, next to her car reading a book, and realized this was the only time in his life he'd heard someone describe this scary an episode.

"My arrivals varied by fifteen or twenty minutes, but the phone always rang ten minutes after I walked into the lounge. Somebody tailed me, there was a spy in Gregory Hall. Or more than one, because I never entered the same door twice in a row, I used different ones each day."

"Did you always go directly up to the fourth floor?"

"Except one morning when I detoured to the History Department's office to pick up a discussion section's exam booklets. But when I reached the lounge, ten minutes later the telephone rang. Unnerving, considering the fourth floor's lonesomeness—so few people around and doors are always closed, even with professors or instructors in their offices. Today I wouldn't go into the bathroom up there by myself."

"Did you discuss the phone messages with anyone?"

"After the third threat I met with the department's chair, Professor Hill. She contacted the Campus Police, and the officers replied they'd investigate. But what can the police do? I doubt they'll guard my Greg Hall office. This is the '70s, campus security has never been an issue. We're on our own."

The flat fields surrounding the farmhouse stressed Laurie's vulnerability. Besides Sharon by her Camaro, the only person Paul saw was a farmer halfway to the horizon, operating his combine, harvesting crops.

"Does our discussion bother you, do you want to stop answering questions?"

"We can talk. But if we continue, my remarks must stay out of your paper and, if possible, not discussed with Sharon."

"Returning to the messages, what did they say?"

"They spelled out the coming re-order, the indoctrination, an organized party, the unification."

"UNITED. They wanted to ensure you went along, or kept out of their way. But you've been involved with the peace movement for so long and worked as much as anyone else. I'd think you'd be the first agreeing to merging the separate groups. Why would you be harassed?"

"Perhaps I wasn't the only one bullied, perhaps students in RAW and DISGUST and SCRAP received similar threats. The someones behind these tactics want absolute certainty that their schemes evolve as projected."

"Did you contact other anti-war groups and ask if they were," he hesitated choosing a word, "approached?"

"I meant to but ran out of time. I left Champaign in a hurry."

"Were the phone calls the only reasons?"

"There was another incident." Laurie moved closer to Paul, as for protection. "Lindsey and I have a cat named Diesel, a black male we adopted a year ago. He was generally an indoors animal, occasionally escaping, but never outside of our apartment for long. About the time the telephone calls started Diesel ran off and we didn't see him for four of five days. Not worrisome because cats are cats. The day of the fourth call, at about 8:30 in the evening, I walked home from campus on my normal route, north on Fifth Street to Springfield Avenue. A block from our apartment a man, a student wearing a long, green army coat, got out of a parked car and stepped in front of me. He grinned, opened his coat, reached in and handed me a grocery bag. Diesel was stuffed inside, bloody, legs twisted, barely alive. This person smirked again, called 'keep the peace, see you around,' and strutted to his car. When I got to my apartment, the phone was ringing and one of them threatened me again, saying to watch behind me when I crossed the Boneyard Creek. That was enough, I phoned my dad the same night, he drove to Champaign and brought me back to our farm."

"What about Lindsey? Is she afraid living by herself in your apartment?"

"My roommate's not involved with war protesting or SOAP. And Eric, her boyfriend, is a two hundred fifty-pound starting defensive lineman for the Fighting Illini. He and his football buddies have Lindsey well guarded."

"I'm sorry about your cat," a sympathetic Paul hugged Laurie. "What do you think the bad guys are after?"

"Exactly what occurred at Bernard Minerath's meeting, the disbanding of the separate campus peace groups, replaced by a single, umbrella organization for all future anti-war activities, one voice, united, for whatever conspiracies they will connive. Now you understand my wanting anonymity. This is a dangerous, scheming mob. I want seclusion and maybe you should, too."

Paul got the warning, his congenital caution contemplating retreat, to leave Laurie's farm and dump his peace movement story. But conscience counseled continuing. "Are you returning to school?"

"I don't feel safe this semester. They know who I am and for whatever rationale have me marked."

"Who do you think is responsible?" Paul noticed Sharon had quit reading and rested on her Camaro's trunk, watching the farmer riding his tractor.

"There's one suspect with the mind for this, and if my memory is reliable, never appreciated cats." Laurie watched Sharon walk toward them. "When I asked earlier if you could trust your girlfriend, I didn't intend insulting her or you. Maybe people we've known longer are the ones we shouldn't trust."

"No offense taken; experiencing what you have, I'd act the same way. Some last questions. Besides Walter Arnstein, how many professors teach English history courses?"

"There's David Long, Megan Rogers and Antoinette Gulley."

"Which one, do you imagine, would pilot a hot air balloon?"

Laurie laughed for the first time this morning. "With his thick glasses no way Arnstein files away in one, and I doubt Professor Long, being sixty years old and near retirement, would either. That leaves the women, Rogers and Gulley."

# # # #

"The temperature certainly has dropped, must be ten degrees chillier than Saturday." Outside the north wind swirled the branches, in the Illini Union the sun illuminated the South Lounge's high, wood ceilings. Looking at the carpet to avoid the bright light, Lindy sounded as friendly as feasible, "I'm glad we could get together, Em. Robby told me you made an appearance at the Homecoming dance."

"I arrived around 9:30, as Kenny Jacobsen was introducing the band." *I hate that word so much,* Emily brooded, *anything referring to music, and promised myself I would never say it again.*

"Well, at least you didn't lay low in your dorm. Was it an enjoyable evening?"

"Isn't that an absurd question, following your behavior? On Saturday morning I was so happy, anticipating our weekend. Then, after you phoned, I was aghast being handled like a leftover, and frankly thought better of you.

Summer Never Comes

After we said goodbye, when I knew our day was gone away, I sat heartbroken on my bed for an hour, staring out the window. So many of my friends went to the game Blaisdell Hall was completely empty. At the dance that night, even with Paul, Bobby, Stu and Paul's girlfriend, I felt so awkward I felt like a stranger. A houseful of partiers in KIDs, everyone dancing, talking about the game, the balloon and the banner, with me by myself, just the way you abandoned me." *Brokenhearted,* she concluded, *does not express my emotions. Appalled a person as considerate and loving as you would be so cruel. My goodness, I wonder if Will is as drained as he looks.*

"I'm sorry, Em. I know you were hurt. If there'd been any way to maneuver around what I did and not upset the apple cart, I'd have. Honestly, even after I phoned to cancel our date, I didn't know what the right decision was. I was so miserable wreckin' our plans I nearly ditched the gig, it was that close." Lindy raised a hand, holding his thumb an eighth-inch apart from his index finger. "The whole afternoon I was bummed, glum, so down I couldn't concentrate on the tunes we were rehearsing. And during the performance I had you on my mind, especially singin' solo for our last song."

"But you did play, chose them and deserted me. Those musicians of yours mean more than the girlfriend you've dated for a year. I looked forward to last Saturday as a caprice, an idyll, our first time this semester we would have spent a whole day and night together. Homecoming would have been so much fun, the football game, dinner, the dance. I even sewed new pillow cases for us for that night, blue for you and pink for me." An angry Emily sat at the corner of the couch, scrutinizing her boyfriend. *Even if Will appears exhausted, I won't be lenient. You deserve to be berated for hanging around with those guitar hooligans; you like them so much, go spend all your time with them, you seem to anyway. But the pillows on my bed, we didn't use them, they're still clean and fresh. And, yes, even if I'm upset right now, I want you, crave you, every day and night and forever. Our time has always been so wonderful, whatever we do, chatting, dinner, studying in my room, in bed. Even if I'm not physical or sensual, I adore sleeping with you, our bodies close, touching and playing, giving and having our delightful, erotic moments. Is it that way for you, Will, do you love lying next to me all night? You always seem to. Or am I only another ho-hum, nothing-so-special encounter you may or may not remember after graduation and we break up?*

Summer Never Comes

"I looked forward to the weekend, too, Em, I would've loved space from Frogfeet before we hit the road. That's what I told Robby that morning, dubbed it a two-day vacation. And the way the gig worked out, we sounded so off-key and caught with our pants down, we would've been smarter not listening to our own sound equipment."

Emily ignored the joke.

"What you said is true, there's no excuses. But the practices we've worked through should go toward something, so playin' with the band last weekend was a responsibility. I'm embarrassed I'm an immature bum and disappointed you, and wouldn't disagree if you told me to go to hell. But I hope you don't, I think we still have a bond." Hiding a yawn, Lindy wondered if he should move closer to Em. "I suppose we've got to settle on what's next."

"Doesn't tomorrow depend on you, our friendship continues if you want it?"

"What kind of response is that? I'm the guilty party, the guy dumping on you."

"You're the one with a fantasy, the egotist driven by these ambitions." *There, I didn't want to, but I said it. I hope you're not angry with me. You have your flaws, everyone does, no one is perfect. Working through them, overcoming, is what counts in life.*

"My only idea is playin' music and doing right by you."

A room for relaxing, the South Lounge was typically quiet this morning. Students with time between classes occupied the Queen Anne armchairs and leather sofas, some booking, a few reading the *Daily Illini*, but the majority spacing out.

"I can't blame you if you chewed on my rear end for another hour. Lord knows I deserve it," Lindy masked a second yawn.

"Is that what you want? Would it satisfy you listening to my complaining about how mean you behaved, grumble over how much I feel let down? Say that behind your silly clichés and I'm-a-friend-to-everyone mask of yours I think you're nothing but a phony who can't rationalize beyond your own vanity? Would that be penance for your sins?" *Oh my, that was too theatric, I didn't want to call you conceited, that was unfair. I'm just so mad and feel so forgotten.*

Summer Never Comes

"I want us to remain companions, Em, but after last weekend I know it won't be simple. This month no doubt looks like a disaster from your point of view. All I can say is I'll do better, the next few weeks will be an improvement. Maybe you don't believe me, maybe my word isn't worth the paper it's inked on, but I'd like to work things out."

Your clichés aren't silly, Emily told herself, *they're sweet, as you're cute. I love you, Will, truly do. I'm convinced you can be so decent, caring and concerned for me, and we can rebuild our love. I remember the cozy days, the relaxing September afternoon on the Quad when we laid on the grass and kissed and wondered about living in California. Those are my fondest memories, I pray for there to be more. I'm here for you, want us in each other's future, it can be so simple. But you have to resolve your life, choose the valuable and worthwhile. Please understand, my darling.*

The wind rattled the tall window panes, a few students sat on the floor, and a janitor strolled through emptying garbage cans into his cart. The South Lounge's calm ended, however, when one of Bernard Minerath's True Believers trooped in holding a handful of leaflets above her head.

"Organize for peace, end the war!" she loudly declared. "Let's take it to the Washington fascists."

"When is your next practice?"

"Tonight." Lindy timidly replied.

\# \# \# \#

Messages were tacked on the KIDs' bulletin board.

"House Meeting, Monday, 7:30."

"Sign up for Hound Dog Hockey. Six intramural games scheduled this season at the Ice Rink. All welcome for this house team. No hockey, skating or athletic ability necessary. Find O'D."

"Looking for bodies to man the roll call line for Carole King concert tickets, especially needed for midnight to 8 a.m. shift. Location, Union Vending Machine Room. See Dudz."

"Urgent! Desperate for History 111 term paper by 8 o'clock Friday morning, any subject. Frnk Gardner."

\# \# \# \#

Summer Never Comes

"Snatch!"

In his room, Tommy Quarters scraped a chair toward the window. The lights were off and the drapes opened to the night sky. A toilet paper roll with a half inch of sheets wrapped around the cardboard center stood on the sill, and jammed on this makeshift stand were binoculars aimed across Third Street toward the Phi Mu sorority. Tommy re-focused his glasses on the second floor, watching one woman strut around in her orange bra and blue panties. When the coed stripped off her underwear, he asininely chuckled and hopped his chair nearer to the window.

"Hell yes, honey, if you want I'll pop over to jack off between your boobies."

Tommy was one of dozens of KIDs nightly scoping the Mus. As with his other mania, he obsessively overdid himself. Of all the brothers living on the fraternity's east side, Tommy spent the most hours hankering for quickie shows.

"Snatch!"

# # # #

"You finally proposed to Lauren, you son of a bitch, way to go!" After midnight, Stu, Paul and Bobby unwound in Scooter Petersen's room, devouring batches of popcorn, two Garcia's extra large pizzas and a six-pack of Pabst Blue Ribbon beer.

"It had to come sooner or later," Scooter beamed.

"When're you tying the knot?"

"Not for a while, fellas, I'd guess ten or twelve months from now, the end of next summer, around Labor Day. My mom's a believer in extended engagements and fanatically arranged weddings, from tuxedos and menus to guest lists and toasts."

"Frickin' lucky bastard," Bobby Sox laid on the floor between the empty pizza boxes, "your girlfriend's down here where you can make out with her every night. And you usually do."

"June isn't far away," Stu consoled his roommate, "then your nuts'll be grabbed three or four times a week, too."

"Except until then I'm trapped in Champaign-Urbana."

Summer Never Comes

"Don't sulk over losing one weekend with Jeannie. Staying turned into a good deed, you had a chance to hang at the dance with Emily Ritter and cheer her up, at least make her less sad."

"It was the decent thing to do, especially with the rest of you off gettin' laid. Someone had to protect her from our fraternity's despoes. Emily looked so low, she didn't deserve attending the Homecoming party by herself." For a moment, Bobby showed his thoughtfulness. "And what, Paul, is wrong with your brainless roommate? What the hell kind of golf club is rammed up his ass, stranding his girlfriend on a Saturday night?"

"We've only talked once since the weekend, so I don't have a clue what he's thinking."

"That's Lindy's problem, never around anymore. No hangin' with the brothers or hoops at Huff Gym, no hearts games in the living room. When was the last time we boogied to the bars to drink? All he knows is his band, letting everything else slip, including his girlfriend. He should be careful before Emily loses interest and runs off."

"Lindy'll straighten out, he's not stupid." Paul closed Bobby's November *Playboy*. "I know he met with Emily this afternoon to apologize."

"She sounded totally offended on Saturday. Lindy better shape up and bend both knees when he pleads for forgiveness." Bobby walked to the bunk beds. "Of course, ol' Robby, he looked decent at the dance with his new babe, never saw this boy enjoy life so much. And did you check him on the dance floor? None of us knew he owned those shake and bake moves. Hell, the way things are progressin', there'll be a lot more, including Mister Roberts, goin' down before I do."

"Tell us, how was your hot one?"

"Fine, real fine," Paul awkwardly grinned.

"That's it? Open up, give us more."

"Yeah, particulars," Scooter repeated, "like what's the color of her sheets, is her bedroom wallpapered, or didn't you survey that far away from her body?"

Paul raised himself from the bed, "You know, it's really quiet around here."

"Don't switch subjects."

Stu shut a pizza box. "Robby's right, there's not one stereo blasting tonight."

"What do you expect, freshmen mostly live on this floor." Scooter curled his legs into his desk chair.

"Even pledges spin records. With Scooter's engagement announced, wouldn't it be a prank if…"

SPLAM!!!

The door kicked open and fifteen swearing, on-a-suicide-mission freshmen jumped through, grappling for Scooter.

"Shower, grab him, shower his bony ass."

"Freakin' a-holes, not without a goddamned fight!" Bobby screeched.

Scooter bolted underneath his desk, wedging into the tiny space against the wall. Stu, Paul and Bobby leaped for the doorway to block the hordes from hijacking their friend and carrying him to the bathroom.

"Where the hell'd he go?"

"Watch out for my legs."

"The desk, below the goddamned desk. Go for his 'nads."

"Crap, there's more of us than them! Get psyched!"

The three defenders brawled like maniacs, the small room to their advantage, elbowing, swearing and shoving to jam the attackers back through the door. But heavily outnumbered, Stu, Bobby and Paul couldn't battle for long. The seniors were bulldozed against the bunks, and two pledges fell to the floor yanking Scooter from his hiding place. All he wore was a pair of faded blue pajama bottoms.

"Way to go, pledge class solidarity!"

"Pick him up, drag this son of a bitch outta the door."

The freshmen seized Scooter's arms and legs and started for the hallway, but needed a few seconds reversing their momentum to exit the room. And their uproar alerted the rest of the house. What seniors on hand, Orion, Moose, Chuck Pastron, Nemo and Tim O'Toole, blasted down the hallway, throwing themselves into the mobs, blockading the room. The pledges owned Scooter, but were stuck.

"Hold on, pal, we'll save you."

"Let's waste these bastards."

"Who the hell these mini-dicks think they are?" The two hundred fifty pound Moose reeled in one pledge and plopped him on the top bunk.

The dozens of sweating KIDs cussed, tackled, muscled and laughed as they manhandled Scooter and mauled each other. Showering a fraternity tradition for decades, both sides respected the rules: no individual contests, no punches, kicking, biting or fists in the nuts, with the outnumbered seniors realizing they were the eventual losers.

"We gotta blow the Christ outta here." With numbers and surrounding Scooter, the pledges mounted one humongous lunge for the hallway.

"Okay!" Tommy Quarters howled, "One…Two…THREE!"

The freshman class burst past the doorway, and the seniors, with tons more groaning and swearing, gave ground. The mobs wrestled closer to the john. Somebody turned on the water and steam rolled into the hallway.

"Keep moving, we've got him now!"

"Goddamned pledges!"

"Let's go…let's go!"

By the john door, the beaten-down seniors scraped together a last stand—Stu, Bobby, Paul, Mooser, Beebo and Hod mulishly determined to hold Scooter and the herds out of the bathroom.

"No way you bastards are blowin' through us."

"Keep pushing, hold 'em, keep pushing!"

"For God's sake, don't twist my arm!"

"Holy sweet mother-in-law of Jesus," Tim Mailto yelled to fellow spectator Eddie-Bob McMahon, "this'll go all night!"

The melee at the bathroom entrance stalemated, neither side dislodging their opponent. Hands grabbed for the squirming Scooter and everyone—opponents and observers—screamed profanities disgustingly, crappily obnoxious even for Kappa Iota Delta.

Finally, the lucky break. The heaving, lunging, grasping and grabbing were too much for Scooter's thin pajamas, the seams ripped and the shredded fabric was yanked away by Tommy Quarters. Bare-assed among a groping mob, he quit resisting. With this less to fight, the freshmen wrestled the seniors out of the way and delivered their naked victim to the showers. Both sides hoorayed and sang the fraternity's 'Sweetheart Song' when Scooter, along with eight or ten KIDs, went under the water.

> The moon is a big, golden yellow,
> With thousands of stars shining bright,
> Something wonderful really has happened,
> To make this a perfect night.

Summer Never Comes

Twenty minutes later, the seniors relaxed in Scooter's room recounting the riot. The place was pitted out, with the pizza boxes crumpled and papers strewn around the floor, the bunks toppled, a raggedy Blood, Sweat and Tears poster drooping from the wall, tomato paste smeared on the curtains, the place stinking worse than the IMPE locker rooms. One smashed-to-pieces chair laid in the corner, some moron had shoved a PBR can through the closet door and Bobby's *Playboy* was missing. As Scooter scrounged a pair of u-trow, his roommate, Ron Gimbel, strolled in. An aeronautical engineering major and humorlessly conscientious booker, he had studied in the Reference Room all night.

"You missed a goddamned decent showering, Ronny, could've used you."

"We held those frickin' freshmen for half an hour."

"You shoulda seen Scooter's bare cheeks trottin' down the hall."

Ron stood in the middle of the room, gazing at the floor and the trash. Shuffling his feet through heaps of papers, ripped Garcia's boxes, balled-up blankets and torn towels, he grabbed some sheets that earlier in the evening were pages in a loose leaf binder. Now the orange cover was slashed in half, this wet garbage stained with green peppers and reeking from beer. Looking at his classmates, Ron dropped the papers to the carpet.

"These were my Chem 356 notes."

# # # #

After his two o'clock, Kentucky exited Lincoln Hall, yanking his coat collar up and hat brim down. As customary on Tuesdays, he bided time waiting for Paul and the walk to back KIDs. This afternoon, cold, westerly winds blew from the prairies, strong enough to tip garbage cans along Wright Street and, for the first day this semester, make bike riding hopeless.

"Robbeh, how wuz yohr business class?"

"Microeconomics never thrills me—nothing but oxymorons—the longer I sit in that room the less I learn. Today we discussed behavioral science essays about maximization of utility."

"Wall, jes' re-mem-ber, th' semester is half over." Crossing the Wright Street bike path, the pair spotted a waving Randy Miller.

"Hell-o thar, Randeh, how y'all?"

"Afternoon, Kentucky. Going back to the house?"

"Yup. Thes is not th' type o' day t' be out-doors, no suh."

"The more November, the frostier the weather."

"Ah haven't seen y'all around much, late-leh. Whut y'all bin up to?"

"Peace," Randy answered.

"Ex-cuse me?"

"UNITED, the newest protest group, I'm working for them since my SCRAP disbanded."

"Ah see," Kentucky nodded as the threesome hurried west on Chalmers, passing the YMCA Building. "An' in thes gang, whut is it exactly y'all do?"

"I'm assigned to public relations and the membership drive. Right now both of those activities are connected."

"Y'mean advertisin', like th' balloon an' banner durin' th' football game? Did you plan thet?"

"No, the flight was Bernard Minerath's last-minute project, organized forty-eight hours before Homecoming. Most of us were as astounded as the fans. It for sure caught the student's attention, there's as much talk about the balloon on the campus as about the Fighting Illini's win. Since Saturday we've taken hundreds of calls at UNITED's headquarters."

"It wuz a cheap trick thet jus' happened t' wurk."

"The wind undoubtedly was fortunate, but who'll quarrel with luck? I say anything aiding the anti-war effort and slamming the right-wingers is fair."

"Fair or foul, from th' field, it looked like a riskeh prank. Anutheh fifty feet east or west, then whut?"

"Kentucky makes a point, the balloon could have rammed the balconies, become a disaster marking students as irresponsible juveniles." The breezes pushed back Paul's brown hair, uncovering his forehead.

"Well, it didn't fail and we're celebrities. Besides, the balloon's pilots weren't students."

"Who wuz in theah?"

Hearing Kentucky's puzzling, Paul switched subjects, "Did you say you're on the membership drive?"

"Yes, we've begun our 'stand around' campaign to persuade students to join UNITED. Especially good places are the Union, the Library and Green

Street in Campustown. After Christmas, we're planning a direct mail canvass to the entire student body."

"That's a lot of postcards."

"Our goal is enlisting at least half the undergrads," Randy answered.

"Who ex'ctly ahr you-all tryin' t' show it to, t' impress?"

"The task is mobilizing the people. When the Washington politicians are struck by the huge numbers opposing their policies they'll realize what a mistake the war has been, from the fraud five years ago that connived us into Vietnam to the hundreds of soldiers killed each month. They'll have to pull us out."

"Now Randeh, Ah'm tru-leh not tryin' t' in-sult your move-ment," he tugged his hat lower, "an' Ah und-ehstand yohr sincerity. But d'you realleh expect thet confused crowd in th' Capitol t' react to whut trans-pires in Cham-paign-Urban-na?"

"Not only here, Kentucky. What if peace protests spring up at dozens of universities around the country?" Randy motioned with his hand not holding his books. "What if our demonstrations are vaster and more radical than ever before? What if, in four or five months, there are hundreds of campuses with thousands of students signed up in a real effort to get us the hell out of Vietnam? If college students band together, if we finally, completely organize ourselves, we'll kick off a movement to haul the country with us, unifying everybody against this war. I'll admit this sounds idealistic, but isn't this our mission in life, rejecting yesterday's status quo, working for a cause, struggling for a difference? We were raised as our country's smartest generation, we should act like it."

"Isn't thet whut's happ'ned foh th' last few yeahs?" The three crossed Sixth Street. "Protestin' an' dissent a-gainst the wahr?"

"With unfinished results. The anti-war movement dumped LBJ in '68, but now Nixon's in the White House, the crazy lunatic, and just as two-faced. Remember what he did in Cambodia in '70 and Laos two months ago—crossed the borders to attack whoever he wanted. Does anybody believe he gives a rat's ass about withdrawing from 'Nam? Not without being told he won't, not without being pushed."

"An' thes is whut U-NITED is wurkin' for now, t' sign up students to make thes heah statement?"

"Want to join?" Randy grinned. "You'll be my first recruit."

Summer Never Comes

"Ah ap-preciate yohr offeh, but respectfully decline."

Opposite the Tri-Delt house, the KIDs approached the campus' most turbulent wind tunnel, Chalmers Street between Illini Tower and the thirteen-story Sherman Hall, two of Cham-Bana's highest buildings. Gusts shoved the KIDs backwards and Randy, knocked off-balance by the gales, dropped a textbook from the pile under his arm. Leaning into the breeze, Paul retrieved *Ideology and Revolution in the Soviet Union*, brushed off the dirt, and handed the paperback to his fraternity brother.

"Thanks."

"You're describing a master plan for us and the country," Paul yelled over the wind.

"Bernard might call it that, I wouldn't. But if we end the war, our generation will achieve while we're still young, comprehend we make a difference, set the mold for the rest of our lives, give us confidence to stay involved instead of growing up second-rate and lazy." The three struggled to Fourth Street, where the breezes lessened. "Take your roommate for example, Lindy and his music. He's stepping out."

"Solely, exclusively for himself," Paul was abrupt.

With Frogfeet mentioned, Kentucky intuited Paul's irritation. "Thes heah Bernard. He runs yohr group?"

"He's the chairman of UNITED."

"A good ol' boy? Knows whut he's doi-in'?"

"Bernard's smart and has been around a while."

"Wall, Ah hope you-all ahr successful in bringin' peace to thes country of ouhs, e-nuf have bin killed in Asia, we sure-leh do not need mohr dead."

# # # #

"Okay, guys, we're stickin' with this. If Andy devoted the time to write the song, the least we can do is play it respectably. Once more."

"Once more, Franky, takes it to the sixth time."

> The walls are closed and empty,
> Waiting for Peggy to come.
> The room is just not happy,
> Peggy, bring along some sun.

Summer Never Comes

> Night time is always for losers,
> People who can't have some fun.
> I won't spend my time that way,
> Peggy, bring along some sun.

I really do appreciate Andy's songwriting efforts, Lindy mused, because he's my best buddy in the band and I can't string three words together myself. I enjoy his poetry, but this melody, like his other original pieces and the rest of our music, is too melancholy. Slow, slow, slow, two months of the same, sorry slow. We should forget the Middle Ages and innovate, create. Upbeat songs are what we need to perform, lively music exciting a crowd. But Andy doesn't compose those kinds of verses and the other 'Feet wouldn't want to play them, they're comfortable singin' the tunes every last one of the other campus bands perform. Sticks in the mud, bumps on the log, dull on our legs. Is this how to light a fire? Maybe we should purloin a page from The Guild's book, rework oldies, like 'So Long, It's Been Good to Know You,' or 'The Daring Young Man on the Flying Trapeze," adopt them as our signature, quirky pieces; that would set us apart. Of course, if I mention this brainstorm to Franky, Woofer and 'Mad', like always I'll take home the brush off.

"Okay, that was close to the beat. How about the Badfinger numbers next, the ones we blew through last night?"

Franky was right deciding we're playin' no more gigs until our music improves. That Homecoming performance was a stinker, one night we'll forget faster than a cat licks up milk, I was almost mortified accepting the money; we can't say we earned it. So he's got us here, back in this basement, sterner than our first weeks, runnin' us like dogs until we sound like musicians. Man, the others look awfully tired with all this practice.

"Good, we held tempo that go around. Lindy, your voice was weak, give it some strength."

"I'm with the program."

"Let's go again, then another after that. Again."

Franky lays it on with a trowel. When he declares 'again, again, again' I want to copy what I heard Bobby Sox did on Homecoming, toss my cookies. I must admit, though, in these last two months I have improved with my axe, even if the band's sound hasn't. The way Franky shovels, there's only a matter of time before we escape this basement and turn respectable. Another yawn, what time was it? I never expected bein' bored playing my guitar, probably this monotonous, dull music, not my idea of a holiday inn. Maybe I should argue tonight with everyone for those eccentric songs. No, what's the use bein' shut down? I'll start with Andy and talk to him.

"That was real harmonious, a few more reps, then we'll break."

# # # #

Paul, Bobby Sox, Stu and three hundred fellow seniors shuffled into 141 Comm West.

"Good afternoon, it is a pleasure seeing so many of you here today," Dean Johnson stood at the lectern. "In the next hour, we are conducting a sample job interview for you to observe and learn from."

"A real flash there, already frickin' knew that," Bobby complained.

"Shut up," Stu scolded his roommate, "this is the adult world."

"Miss Linda Greene, an aspiring CPA candidate, has consented to act as the ersatz applicant. The interviewer is Thomas Gading, an alumnus and partner with the Chicago office of Boyle-Moran Consultants. Mister Gading is a veteran of campus recruiting, his firm having hired approximately five dozen University of Illinois accountancy graduates over the past ten years. He is familiar with the questions asked and the qualities looked for in applicants. In sum, Mister Gading has guaranteed to make this as realistic as possible. No doubt you will find this informative, I recommend you pay attention."

The crowd quieted as the mock session began. Many seniors edged forward in their seats, some scribbled in their tablets, one audience member pointed his tape recorder microphone toward the stage, and even Bobby concentrated on the actors. Paul listened to Linda Greene's answers, so rote he assumed Commerce College seniors could find basic job interviewing manuals in the Undergrad and memorize responses identical to hers. Paul visualized preparing for his interviews, revising, tweaking, repeating the routines. We'll all face this, want this, need to be hired for some job by any kind of company in a miscellaneous industry producing monotonous, everyday stuff, promoting bland, boring, mostly-legitimate services. Any occupation, with any ambiguous business, maybe JKL Enterprises, or the MNO Corporation, as long as you land one after graduation and take home some money. Is this college's reward? Four years' studying narrowed to a chair in some cubicle mumbling clichés you hope interests some humdrum, dreary conglomerate? That's it? No more?

The session ended, the seniors applauded and left the room.

"I'm glad that wasn't me," Stu walked out the door.

"It will be, buddy," Bobby Sox followed his roommate, "it's freakin' gonna be all of us."

"At least we won't have three or four hundred eyes squinting at us."

"Just you and one guy in the interview room. Those are still stiff odds, maybe worse," Bobby zipped his coat. "What do you say, Robby?"

"I suppose you're right."

# # # #

A week after his conversation with Brad at Prairie Winds Ballooning, Paul walked into Greg Hall to track down the English history professors. Professor Rogers was out, her only office hour 3:30 to 4:30, Friday afternoons. Professor Gulley's office was on the fourth floor, located, he realized, near Laurie Allman's TA lounge.

"Back in twenty minutes," a card read on her opened door. Slipping inside, Paul saw a desk cluttered with stacks of typed term papers. A window was cut into the wall, and to the right of the hazy panes hung a huge color poster of a hot air balloon sailing in a blue sky. The picture's caption announced "Floaters Always Get It Up," with Prairie Winds' address and telephone number printed at the bottom. A bookcase tilted against the opposite wall, the shelves holding dozens of volumes including *Tudor Prose*, *The Government of Elizabethan England* and *Social Change and Revolution in England: 1540–1640*. Forty or fifty editions of *Blackwood's Edinburgh Magazine* lay on another, mimeographed copies of *Punch* cartoons dating from the 1860s on a third, and on the bottom shelf, by itself, a copy of *Ideology and Revolution in the Soviet Union* by Howell L. Meade. From Paul's inspection, this was the sole book in Professor Gulley's office not a history of Great Britain and, he recalled, the same title Randy Miller had dropped in the wind storm at Illini Tower.

Summer Never Comes

# # # #

"The weeks preceding Thanksgiving," Stef Tianen wrote for the editorial page, "is a more serious time on our campus. Dwindling football weekends, shorter, colder days and a semester half-over turns the student body towards academics. Our focus dwarfs to our classes, final exams and satisfactory grades. This is the university's gist, the stuff of youth, dwelling on, looking into ourselves, preparing for our lives.

"Yet introspection, however meaningful, is shortsighted. We live in a world with responsibilities. Friends, family, our community and society call. Questions of consequence in September are no less significant in November and cannot be forgotten.

"One such obligation is Vietnam. Though the maneuvers and assaults of Operation Loading Dock are finished, the same cannot be said of the war. The fighting and suffering continue, as does the politicians' determination to belligerently, myopically stay the course in Southeast Asia. The war, by its own, will not vanish into history.

"Ever present, drawn out, unceasing, the meanings of these adjectives are alike. They are characteristics of a war that has stayed too long, as well as the definition of our commitment to bring it to a close. Our duty is clear, our efforts must never cease.

"From its inception, University Network Involved to End Destruction has fixed our community's attention to this mission. The organization's membership drive is an ongoing reminder that self-centeredness should not take hold in us, that participation in our world is required.

"The *Daily Illini* applauds UNITED's efforts, we urge all to support and join their call."

# # # #

"Shoot. Why do you boys all-ways eat early? I don' unnerstan' it, I sureleh don't."

"I can't figure either, Mary Lou," Paul shrugged, "but could you feed me, please?"

"Why cain't you eat whens youse s'pose to?" Mary Lou complained and dished up his dinner: roast beef, mashed potatoes and gravy, mixed vegetables, all double portions. She handed Paul the plateful of food and smiled, showing the missing teeth in her mouth. "Here you are, chile. Anotther ear'ly bird is Bill Lindneh. He'll be down here soon, askin' an' pesterin' an' botherin'."

"Thank you." He quickly ate, finishing before the waiters started setting up the KIDs' dining room for supper or Lindy arrived in the kitchen.

Hurrying to the Library, and prior to meeting Sharon for their study date, Paul wanted to locate *Ideology and Revolution in the Soviet Union*. The main card catalogue listed the university's copies held in the Undergrad's Reserved Reading Area, these texts required assignments for specific classes. The Reserved Reading's index inventoried books by the course calling for them, and guessing Meade's a title for a political science class, Paul flipped through the poli sci cards. Not there. Next he scanned the history section. Success. *Ideology and Revolution in the Soviet Union* was reserved for History 333. Paul found fifteen copies on the shelf, checked one out and went to a study carrel to read.

"Persistent struggle against entrenched power and authority requires a party apparatus forged through struggle, capable of influencing the masses and coercing opinion."

"Socialism will develop into Communism when people become accustomed to observing the elementary conditions of social life without violence and without subordination."

"As Comrade Stalin declared, 'No ruling class has ever existed without its own intelligentsia.' However, the intelligentsia's discontent as a component within revolution is evident."

"It would be a mistake to give free reign to phrase mongerers who allow themselves to be carried away by the dazzling revolutionary spirit, but who are incapable of thoughtful and deliberate revolutionary work."

"In all societies, political culture is an amalgam of traditional, often subconscious influences, and deliberate indoctrination by dominant institutions."

"Bourgeois profiteering relationships, continuing onward on their capitalist, oppressive trajectory, annihilate the individual and the working class society. At that ideological moment, the party's revolutionary momentum moves forward to claim primacy."

"Lenin's democratic centralism means leaders chosen by the rank and file. After selection, the party leaders are supreme, and any effort to agitate or combine against their decisions is treason to the party."

"Bolsheviks, Mensheviks, Leninists, Socialist Revolutionaries, Kadets, Decembrists, all factions, regardless of their parochialisms, adhere to the doctrine of Communist domination."

What subject did 333 cover? Paul found a course catalog at the Undergrad's circulation desk.

"History 333: Tudor and Stuart England, 1485–1660. Professor Antoinette Gulley."

# # # #

"This is where you spend your evenings." Sharon walked into the History Library with Paul.

Four long, wooden tables were packed into the room's open space. On two, many-paged Webster's dictionaries rested atop lecterns. Unlike the unfilled Undergrad, here crammed bookshelves butted against the tables. Paint peeled off the ceiling, steam heat made the small room stuffy, and patrons staring out the windows saw a nearby brick wall.

Sharon laid her bag by her boyfriend's and drifted into the shelves. She returned with a dusty volume, *A Social History of the French Revolution* by Norman Hampson, and skimmed the pages for a quarter hour. While Paul worked an accounting problem set, Sharon re-checked lab results and occasionally, purposely, poked her boyfriend's leg, breaking his concentration. When Paul glared back, she guiltlessly grinned.

"Have a productive time studying?"

"When not disturbed by a female comic."

"Lighten up." Sharon said. The pair left the Library and returned to her house and her living room.

"Where is everybody else?"

"The evening's early and you know us bio majors, forever learning."

"I've noticed, booking unless badgering."

"Since we are alone, what deep, dark subjects and secrets should we delve? Confidence, qualms? Hope, despair? Desires, sorrows?" On the couch, she moved close to her boyfriend and, as Paul expected, toyed with his shirt buttons. "Or Lindy's and Emily's labels, check possibly mate?"

"Those two are such a mess," he sagged into the cushions. "Lindy for certain will stick with his band because with them he's found the opening for his music. But I doubt he'll break with Emily, because even if he's abandoned her this semester, my roommate has a conscience and is still in love. Emily, without other real friends, will wait, hoping for her best scenario, for Frogfeet to fail. And her inaction is OK, since I'm sure after enough time they'll reconcile. Even if the two are opposites, there's an attraction."

"Continuation, indecision. Endurance, irresolution. Depart, return."

"How do science majors become wordsmiths?"

"This is a university, other people besides *Daily Illini* reporters own a thesaurus," Sharon fondled his shirt, "and speaking of reporting, you never filled me in on your talk with Laurie Allman. In fact, during the return trip from Charleston, this whole week and tonight, even for a Paul Roberts, you're more than taciturn. Progress, stillness?"

"What Laurie disclosed—her rationale for leaving Champaign, why the decision was so quick—I'm obliged to keep confidential. Looking back, I'm surprised she opened up at all. What I will admit is my peace movement story's not following the expected direction." Paul held her hand. "Remember our first date, sitting in Treno's, joking about good guys, villains and the real conspiracy?"

"An enlightening discussion, a pitcher of beer to resolve the country's problems. Hoover, the FBI, the Midwest hippie cadre and cabal. Is that's where it's at?" Sharon mocked herself as she coaxed Paul off the sofa. "Bingo, I love it. Let's call J. Edgar right now and nail the bad guys, toss them in jail, bury the key."

"Slow down, what I'm uncovering isn't next month's plot for overthrowing the government, more a string of coincidences."

"Such as?"

A wary Paul was uncertain what to tell Sharon, yet he greatly wanted to review the facts to determine a perspective. Who better to assist than his practical, perceptive, with-it girlfriend? Fine, but remember your pledge to Laurie. "The balloon pilot who flew over Memorial Stadium last Saturday is a professor teaching a sixteenth century English history course. She obviously has a link with UNITED, along with an interest, a curiosity, some kind of connection with Communism."

"There's nothing peculiar about people exploring unrelated subjects. Examination is college's purpose. Look at yourself—an accountant, piqued by history, working for a newspaper."

"The peace movement plus Communism combination is too coincidental. What if this history professor and other activists have aims beyond protesting the war? Now that the separate groups are gone, so are the movement's quirks. UNITED's goals will be the ones followed."

"Their objective, which Bernard Minerath has promoted this semester, is to end Vietnam. Rally on the Quad, light some candles, bring our troops home and let's have peace. And whatever happened to honest dissent? Presuming anti-war protesters are Communists makes half our country followers of Lenin."

"According to Laurie, there's more. Today's anti-war movement is less naïve than three years ago, the newer recruits are more cynical and brutal. That's what Laurie's coped with, she's seen, suffered, their other side. But now I'm coming near the information I'm to keep to myself."

"The story will have holes if you withhold evidence, even for well-meant intentions." Sharon was realistic. "You're washed out before beginning."

"Unless Laurie's information is a starting point. More clues have to be around our campus, a few weeks' investigating could lead to corroboration. With luck, I'll verify what I need without implicating her."

"You're an authentic reporter talking this way." Her boyfriend's objectivity pleased Sharon. "So what's the fundamental question?"

"To develop the story, because at this point there are still unknowns and one problem. Before leaving school, Laurie confronted a crisis and warned me to be cautious, make certain of the people I trust." Paul peered at the unlit fireplace, wondering about the time.

"Heed as in only take care, or yield and give up? You couldn't quit, now that you're in the middle and finding the truth."

"Who mentioned looking for truth? I'm on assignment for the *Daily Illini*, not searching for any holy grail. We're in a college town with bunches of students and protesters, many not knowing what's happening, some playing with conspiracy, who may or may not end up doing the right thing, who may or may not want to hurt people. Who am I to be caught in that? The safe play may be avoiding the whole mess."

"You are already involved." The front door opened and the pair heard voices in the hallway.

"Who's in the living room in the dark?" Karen Gasper demanded.

"I hear heavy breathing," Julie Feely mocked.

"Where have you two been?"

"Sharon? And that must be Paul." Karen walked toward the fireplace. "Book your buns off tonight?"

"Had a great time in the History Library," he replied.

"And now, still enjoying the company?" Julie guided Karen to the stairs. "Let's leave them alone. I want to ask you about the last three episodes of *All My Children*."

"How did you hook up with your housemates?" Paul asked.

"We were lab partners our freshman semesters and mutated to each other. Where were we?"

"Verging on disagreeing."

"How about a neutral subject? It's almost Thanksgiving; are you going home to the south suburbs?"

"I suppose, nothing else on the calendar." He sighed and his body drooped.

"Blasé about long holiday weekends?"

"I don't mind visiting my parents, but for me four days is too long. On Thanksgiving the only ones at dinner are my mom, dad, my sister and me; we eat early in the afternoon then wash dishes. It's so boring, my father doesn't even like watching football games on television. How about you?"

"I'll be in Lake Bluff. With our relatives in town, there're people all over the place, too many and too hectic for one meal. The crowd's always so big I can never relax and talk to my cousins." Sharon turned toward her sulking boyfriend. "I have a thought. Why don't we come back together to Champaign-Urbana the day after Thanksgiving? I'll pick you up in Hazelcrest on Friday morning, we'll drive down and have the campus to ourselves for two days."

"You, showing up at my parents' house in your Camaro?"

"Yes, I can meet them."

"That's a wrong idea, my ride for returning to school is lined up with Tim Malito, I wouldn't want to renege." Paul was embarrassed. "Honestly, I haven't told my parents about you."

Neither astonished nor hurt, Sharon tickled his stomach. "As an alternative, you can ride the Illinois Central on Friday and we'll meet after the train arrives."

"How do we eat? Are any restaurants open when the Big U's shut down?"

"Incidental details," she laughed, "I'll cook."

"What about your roommates, will they be around?"

"Someone usually is, but this is a big campus. If we want, we can get lost."

"Feed me and it's a deal."

# # # #

Alone in his room, Paul re-read passages from Howell Meade's book.

"The principle of socialism must be 'from each according to his ability to each according to his work.'"

"Defense of the fatherland means recognizing the legitimacy and justice of war. Legitimacy and justice from what point of view? Only from the perspective of the socialist proletariat and its struggle for emancipation."

"An obligation of the central committee is the necessary disciplining of party comrades judged deviationist, of two minds or dangerous."

"The liquidation of the capitalist system is the crucial question concerning the development of society. Khrushchev once declared, 'we will bury the enemies of the revolution,' but also asked 'who will prevail, the working class or the bourgeoisie?'"

"There are no absolute rules of conduct, either in war or peace, everything depends on circumstance. The dictatorship of the Communist Party is maintained by recourse to every form of violence."

"In the final analysis, the ultimate development of the Soviet system may be decided, therefore, by the kind of world order its critics and opponents create."

Summer Never Comes

Bored by political doctrines, Paul doodled in the back of his notebook, sketching fantasy maps with imaginary rivers, pretend mountains, made-up streets and unreal railroads.

He'd wanted to explain more to Sharon, talk about Laurie Allman's threatening phone calls, her confronting the fanatics and mutilated cat. But Paul was relieved he held back, not only because of his promise to Laurie but to protect Sharon as well. If Laurie was right, someone wanted her out of the way. Investigating the anti-war protesters and UNITED was risky. Maybe the people who pursued her in Greg Hall were stalking the farm in Charleston, perhaps they'd spotted Sharon's very conspicuous red Camaro. Maybe the bad guys were outside on Third Street tonight, and some bully would hassle him tomorrow. How would he react? Be brave, or crumble and chicken out? Do the right thing or fold? Is this worth it, the headaches I'm taking on? Who can I ask for advice?

Paul sat at his desk, scribbling his maps. Around 1:30, the door opened.

"Hey, what's happenin'?" Lindy slumped into his chair.

"Long time, no see."

"Yeah, the sometime student, the partial roommate, the incomplete undergrad, the here but missing," Lindy chuckled. "How's classes?"

"Econ hourly next Tuesday, that's it until Thanksgiving. And you?"

"Things to do, Robby, a swamp, a morass, life's not slowin' down. Say, what's the latest with your sweetie?"

"We studied in the History Library, then walked to her house and discussed my newspaper story. Hard to believe, we've been dating for almost two months. I'll have to introduce you two someday," Paul grinned but Lindy didn't notice. "How's Frogfeet this week?"

"Practice, rehearse, drill, strum those chords, beat the drums, sing those verses. But we're movin' along, I hope."

"When's the next gig?"

"Don't know, Franky and Gary Anderson haven't lined any up."

"I read an interesting book tonight at the Undergrad."

"Yeah," his voice was emotionless.

"Did you ever hear of the title *Ideology and Revolution in the Soviet Union*?"

"Can't say I did," Lindy absentmindedly answered, "and can't admit I care."

"It explains Communism."

Summer Never Comes

"No foolin'? Well, Robby, that's not a subject to interest me. Just bunches of words from a crowd of guys standin' on a tall wall wearin' weird-ass hats on real frigid days, a lot of oration from a country that'll never bother me." Lindy took off his coat, shirt and pants and flopped into his bunk. "I've got enough problems without worryin' over the Russians or Commies or reds. Put another way, I don't give a crap."

As his roommate slept, Paul returned to his doodling, still wishing to talk to someone.

Chapter Nine

"THE MEETING will come to order." All the chairs in Rooms 269–273 were filled, with True Believers in the front rows and Paul one of two dozen students standing at the back.

"On Wednesday, James R. Camp will visit Champaign-Urbana." A third of the crowd hissed as Bernard Minerath studied his papers on the lectern. "On that day UNITED will picket at each location Mister Camp appears. An itinerary is currently unavailable, but when it is published you will be informed of UNITED's activities. Everyone wishing to participate will sign the sheet on the desk when the meeting is concluded.

"For those unfamiliar with his background, Secretary Camp is a 1938 graduate of the University of Illinois, was an operative for the Office of Strategic Services during World War II, and since 1947 has worked in four presidential administrations. As Undersecretary of State for Southeast Asian Affairs, he is one of the half-dozen government officers most responsible for prosecution of the Vietnam War. Mr. Camp is visiting Champaign-Urbana to accept the President's Council Award in recognition of his financial contributions to the school."

"He's also a total son of a bitch," Mike Sweeney whispered to Randy Miller, "the first politician in Washington to say we should nuke 'Nam out of the universe, even before the strategy became popular in the Pentagon. He opposed the constitutional amendment lowering the voting age to eighteen, is against student draft deferments, thinks every teenager should go into the Army right out of high school and wants conscientious objectors locked in jail. Camp takes for granted a chunk of his government job is traveling around the country insulting the anti-war groups. He's the type of bastard who picks fights with peace protesters during his speeches to come across as an ultra-super-patriot and a martyr for television cameras."

"If he's coming here looking for trouble, we'll accommodate him." Randy said. "We can stick Vietnam up his ass and snatch national publicity."

"The second order of business is the campus membership drive." Bernard glanced from his notes, robotically combing a hand through his straight, black hair. "Thus far, UNITED has enrolled two hundred sixty supporters. This is satisfactory but much work remains. Starting today, the target is seventy-five new members each week. Based on other schools our size, this is attainable."

"On the membership drive, I have a suggestion," Randy interrupted. "I think we should locate volunteers around the Quad's buildings at the ten-minute breaks between classes. We can have boxes of literature and enrollments forms at every building, and the person in charge of staffing them can work out a schedule so the rest of us know when it's our turn to help. I think the English Building, Davenport Hall and the Library should be the first sites. UNITED members with classes in them could be the leaders."

"Sounds sensible," a student next to Paul remarked, "we've got enough members to cover the Wright Street buildings, even Harker Hall and the Chem Annex. We could work in pairs, one getting people's attention, the second soliciting students that stop."

"Better than us parading around the Quad every afternoon," Mike Sweeney murmured, "preaching to anybody happening to stroll by."

"If we don't have enough bodies for all day," a girl behind Randy and Mike added, "what about mid-morning and early afternoon times—eleven until three—when most students are around campus? With this colder weather, eight or nine in the morning is too early."

"Plausible," Bernard sounded impartial. "Further comments?"

The room was silent and Randy hopeful his proposal would be supported by many meeting attendees.

"Very well." Bernard tapped the podium. "What UNITED shall do is run a series of advertisements in the *Daily Illini* outlining our organization's objectives and the students' roles. These ads will commence after the Thanksgiving vacation. Our current afternoon endeavors on the Quad—parading as someone described it—will continue."

A disappointed Randy sat back in his seat.

Summer Never Comes

"The third subject concerns UNITED's leadership. A central committee has been appointed. The members are Gordon Josef, Mike Walters, Leander Valent and myself. The central committee will be responsible for effecting and enacting UNITED's day-to-day activities. If at any time anyone has issues or queries, please contact one of us. Questions?"

There were none.

"Number four. All pre-UNITED protest groups have integrated into our organization. As of this week, we are the only ones in Champaign-Urbana responsible for effecting change."

"Does that mean the others have merged with us, including SOAP?"

"Either ceased to exist or assimilated into UNITED, the result is the same. We are the sole instrument of dissent."

The meeting continued until 9:30, with Bernard covering and controlling eighteen topics, setting objectives, outlining plans for achieving them. Everyone—True Believers, members from the disbanded groups, new recruits and those hanging in back—paid attention, occasionally asking a question, but not disagreeing or challenging Bernard and the cause.

"Randeroo, good meeting?"

"I'd say so, Paul." The KIDs were in the second floor hallway as UNITED members exited the room.

"Is Bernard always so businesslike?"

"Every meeting he chairs is methodical, like a train schedule, with a fixed number of issues covered each night, and always ending at the same time."

"What if the audience wants to argue a controversial topic? Does Bernard permit debate?"

"The membership drive discussion I started is the most we've rapped."

"Which wasn't a lot."

"Correct. Because Bernard is meticulously prepared and his plans are so logical, what he presents to us is crystal clear. There's no sense re-hashing subjects that have been thoroughly thought through."

"In other words, decided before the meeting is called to order."

"Though not always," Randy said. "I remember a few issues last year with the old group, before UNITED, when Bernard allowed a vote."

"How often did that happen?"

"At least twice. He's not a dictator, we're closer to democratic centralism. Bernard determines the collective opinion, then strategizes the mission."

"That's not my conclusion from tonight. There was no majority rule, everyone accepted his fiat." Paul and Randy stood outside Rooms 269–273. The only ones inside were Bernard and his True Believers.

"He's the boss," a defensive Randy shrugged, "a no-nonsense authority, with his mind on the one job in front of him. Remember what's at stake: Bernard and comrades like him are struggling to change an entrenched government policy in place for ten years, organizing a movement to end the damned war and find us some peace. They're taking us beyond the point of a bunch of goody-goody folk singers strumming 'Blowing in the Wind' on our guitars. They're looking out for us so we don't do a Billy Powell: drafted and shipped to Vietnam."

"I'm not disputing the objective, though it's bizarre college students would wholly fall in line with one person instead of spawning their own ideas."

"I apologize, too, Paul, for preaching. The main point is the damned war, failure still followed. Vietnam is so bad, the stupidity that got us in, the despair, so many people killed and wasted. Saying we're opposed isn't noble or courageous enough. We've got to get involved and must accept assignments made by the leadership to end it."

"Conviction is a worthy trait, a component of change." The two walked toward the stairway. "One more question. Last week in the windstorm you dropped a book, *Ideology and Revolution in the Soviet Union*. Is that for a class?"

"No, UNITED suggested reading. A couple of meetings ago Bernard declared it would be worthwhile for everyone to study it."

"Why a book about Communist government?"

"Comparisons, contradictions to our own." Randy buttoned his jacket. "Remember, the toilers of the proletariat are to be as informed as the intelligentsia."

"Where'd you find a copy?"

"Reserved Reading in the Undergrad. Bernard told us they'd be there."

"Reserved books can only be borrowed for two hours. How did you sneak one out from the Library?"

Summer Never Comes

"I was so into it after reading the first chapter I bought my own copy at Follett's."

# # # #

"Paul?"

"What brings you to the Union tonight, Stef?" The pair stood by the Check Cashing Window.

"Wasting time. I was meeting a friend at the Library but decided to pass. I didn't want to sit in my apartment, so thought I'd buy a Coke and play a couple games of billiards. Want to join me?"

"No, thanks, I'm on my way back to KIDs for a late night pizza."

"Basic college food." Stef Tianen carried a zippered case holding her cue stick. "I talked to Al Stojak this afternoon."

"I think *Spectrum's* first issues were excellent, especially the article detailing university finances. After Stoj's explanations of the weird ways the administration budgets money, the school will have a tougher time levying another tuition increase." Paul hoped his compliments would derail the editor-in-chief.

"Stoj says you haven't talked to him about the UNITED story. With Thanksgiving and Christmas vacations coming up, we've got to block out column inches in the magazine for your article."

"I'm not ignoring him, Stef, but after seven weeks, I'm only in the middle of my research, with plenty remaining. Which is where I've been tonight, upstairs at UNITED's meeting. When the three of us meet, I want my facts organized, not sloppy."

"As I expect professional work. I also want the *Daily Illini* stepping up our support of UNITED, but can't until we publish the story. Which is why, if you're bogged down, the offer of help stands. What staffers would you want to work with? How about Stan and Ollie; you get along with them, right?"

"I appreciate the gesture, but bunches of reporters running around the campus will confuse the investigation, clues could get missed or misinterpreted. One person following the details is the way to go."

"Extra bodies will hurry along the story. Many times alternate opinions are sharper motivators than one lonesome person sitting in a room eying the ceiling." The editor-in-chief realized her remark was too callous. "Of course, I'm sure you're on top of the story, all Stoj and I want is to stay informed."

"Here's a concession. Next week this right-wing State Department official is visiting Champaign-Urbana, with UNITED organizing a day-long protest. Some members are predicting a confrontation and major embarrassments for the Washington government. Let's watch what happens. If it's denouement, this could be the time to write the story. If the protest fizzles, like the Moratorium went bust last month, I'll update you on my work but keep investigating for evidence."

"Sounds like middle ground."

"A deal." Paul lifted his bag and stepped away. "I'll continue as a one-man job, but ask if I need help. After the Camp visit, us three will sit down and I'll explain my story."

"Well, if that's the compromise we can make. Remember, we want to promote UNITED."

# # # #

"Can I see your ID?" An attendant sat behind the counter at the Stacks' entrance. Her job was allowing admission only to faculty, graduate students and library employees with correct identification; and confirming patrons signed for books before carrying them out. "Hold on, open it up, I need to check that bag."

The Stacks, the primary storehouse of printed material owned by the University of Illinois, was a cubed structure built onto the Main Library's west side. Unadorned, dimly lit, isolated and damp, expanded section-by-section over three decades, the building held millions of books, periodicals and reference volumes, level upon level, aisle after aisle, shelf atop metal shelf. Because of its restricted access, most U of I students had never gone in and many, though hiking by every day, probably never wondered what was inside the humongous, brick box.

And Dale Kinsey, with no scholarly need for the Stacks, shouldn't have been able to enter. When the attendant asked for his ID, he hustled past while she concentrated on the next student through her gate. Moseying down the center aisle, Dale passed six or seven rows, reached a metal stairway and climbed the shallow steps. After browsing for five minutes and concluding he was the only person on the ninth level, Dale grabbed two volumes: *New York City Police Department Report, 1885-1889* and *Index to the Testimony and Proceedings before the Lexow Committee Investigating the New York Police Department*, and returned down the aisle looking for a bathroom.

Dale had intended bringing a broad along for some kinky, deviant, his-buddies-couldn't-figure-how-or-why library sex. This afternoon he'd chatted up Stef Tianen, promising to screw her in a place she'd never imagine. Always ready for a physical workout, Stef said yes, then revolted by a rendezvous in a ladies' john, reneged. Next he invited funky, tall Lucy, his Bromley Hall honey, but she was disgusted as well and told him to go play with himself.

"Excuse me." The voice belonged to a coed. Fence-rail thin with black hair, she wore a dirty Army fatigue coat and her extra-wide bellbottoms were frazzled at her shoes. "Sorry bumping into you. This place is so lonely, I didn't expect meeting anyone else."

"No problem," Dale sounded smarmily charming. "I'm feeling a little isolated myself. Say, maybe you can help me find another book or two."

"I don't think so, this is my first time in the Stacks." Smiling, she stepped closer to him.

"What a coincidence, mine too. The bars are usually where I spend most of my time." What the hell, Dale thought, might as well try to salvage my night. "Say, what's your favorite one for relaxing in?"

"The Red Lion, of course."

"Damn, another fluke, mine too, again. How 'bout your favorite drinks?"

"Beer, wine, screwdrvivers, I'm not particular. And you?"

"Hard core all the way." He boasted.

"I've been known to stay until last call, myself."

"Well, there's plenty of evening left. Whadya say if we see who can out-drink who?" He dropped the two books on a shelf, grabbed the girl and kissed her forehead. Better making out with anyone else besides yourself. "My name's Dale."

"I'm Robin Ferris."

Summer Never Comes

# # # #

UPI – Saigon – United States Army command reports uncovering evidence of an apparent Vietcong massacre of the civilian population of Loc Mo. According to the spokesman, 117 peasants were murdered. In the past, this village had been described as 'a model of support for the Saigon government.' The Army has offered to transport representatives of any interested news organization to the area for a firsthand view and photograph opportunities.

# # # #

"Thus far this semester, we have spent our time studying the historical perspectives and dynamics between good and evil. As everyone is cognizant, these two sides of the moral spectrum affect how we live our everyday lives. Decisions we make must take right and wrong into account. And, as we have discussed, the boundary between the two concepts, good and evil, can be blurred, with differences rationalized. The latter may be required to abet the former. Extemporized, is evil action sometimes necessary and justifiable to accomplish good? Or does the committing of evils debase the doer to that level? Let us discuss an example."

Professor Jadin Hudson steered his wheelchair around Room 219, Gregory Hall. Paul and Lindy, two of his thirty Philosophy 393 students, sat in back. Attendance had been high all semester, indication of how intriguing undergrads judged the subject matter. Even Lindy showed and, like everyone, found the class most captivating when listening to Professor Hudson instead of taking notes. Paul was an exception, writing in his tablet but also doodling on the pages' margins.

"It is Saturday night and you are in your car driving down Sixth Street, as we all know, a one-way road, rushing to meet your friends for a drink at one of the local taverns. Speeding, you pass an empty parking space, but cannot stop quickly enough to back into the spot. You brake seven or eight car lengths away from the space and consider your options. What should you do?"

Summer Never Comes

"Tool around the block and snag it on the next go 'round," a student volunteered.

"A possibility," Professor Hudson turned his wheelchair, "but in the rearview mirror you see a car pulling up. This vehicle might take the parking spot away from you in the five minutes needed to circumnavigate the block."

"Put your car in reverse and back into it."

"Yes, but you are thirty yards ahead and might crash into the auto driving toward you."

"Make a u-turn and beat the other cars to the spot."

"The third option, breaking the law. Of the three, circling around, backing up, and a u-turn on a one-way street, the first is reasonable, another dangerous and the last illegal. But in various sets of circumstances, any would be acceptable to an individual. If you were late for a date, on a rainy day with absolutely no traffic on Sixth Street, the u-turn, though against the law, would be a tolerable expedient. Does this mark the driver a criminal?" The professor observed agreeing nods around the room. "Yes, but there is no big deal about it. There are no witnesses, no Champaign police are patrolling to hand out tickets, and there are no other cars on the street to worry about crashing into. The u-turn is made, the car parked, you buy your beer and no one except yourself knows it occurred."

Students relaxed, with scant concentration necessary ten minutes into the class. Lindy peered out the windows.

"A second illustration. You are finished drinking for the evening and return to your apartment. Your roommate has gone home for the weekend, leaving you alone. It has been a long, dragging day and you go to bed. During the night, peculiar noises waken you, glass breaks, a light is switched on in the hallway and you hear footsteps coming closer, toward your bedroom. For protection, you reach to the floor and grab a baseball bat hidden under your mattress. The footsteps approach the doorway. It opens and a person, a stranger, is holding a pistol. He points the weapon at your face with the intention to shoot, but he is silhouetted by the hallway light, and you have the better angle and a fraction of a second to react first. What do you do?"

"Hammer his brains out," the undergrad next to Paul unhesitatingly answered. "Save yourself first and ask questions second."

"Again, the probable, logical solution. Would anyone feel remorse after beating and possibly killing the intruder?"

About a fifth of the class' students raised their hands.

"And the rest, no guilt?"

"If I knew the guy was in my apartment to mug me," the same student said, "it's justifiable defending myself."

"Under the law you have the legal right. However, is not assaulting and killing a person immoral? Is it still evil, or not?" Professor Hudson wheeled to the desk in front of the room. "Additional comments?"

"If it's self-defense, no court would say or convict otherwise," a coed retorted.

"That's right, acceptable."

"Therefore, evil is acceptable," Professor Hudson concluded.

"But you're talkin' about your own life," Lindy spoke out, "and can't let that guy shoot you."

"Is it illegal or wrong for someone to wound or kill you?" the professor asked Lindy.

"Yes."

"Then is it not as evil for you to fire on someone, regardless of motive?"

"Well…" Lindy wavered, "sure it's wrong, but motive is the difference."

"As you might perceive, I do not disagree with your feelings. Almost everyone would plausibly concur there is nothing criminal with self-defense. Survival is basic and necessary. But there is a further consideration." Professor Hudson maneuvered his wheelchair to the class room's middle. "Conscience. After the incident, when the police have come and gone, the burglar has been taken away, your adrenaline subsides and you are alone, what then? If you did kill this marauder, what is your subsequent reaction? Relief it is over, superseded by absolute knowledge you did the right thing? Or is it replaced by remorse, the thought that, yes, even though I saved myself and at that moment did the right thing, I wish I hadn't been put in that spot because in other situations my actions would be wrong. Is gratitude for surviving replaced by shame? Does evil rationalize itself into your equation? Can you live with yourself for the rest of your life? Will you not be so sure tomorrow?"

Summer Never Comes

\# \# \# \#

"Dear Kentucky,

"Hello from Saigon!

"I was checking the calendar the other day and saw it must be about the Big U's Homecoming. With the football game, the partying and drinking that was always my favorite fall weekend, and I hope you have a blowout time this year. Due to my prior commitment with Uncle Sam, I am sorry I'll miss the festivities. Tell Shaky Jake to keep those kegs iced.

"'Nam sucks big time, a real hellhole of a country for a shit-load of reasons, one being the weather, hot and humid, worse than Champaign in August, and when the monsoons come, you're up to your balls in rain. What I wouldn't give for a decent air conditioner and a cold wind from Wisconsin.

"The censor tells me I can't say where I'm stationed, but whatever the location, it is the pits. Duty or drill every day, crappy scenery, constant noise, horrendous food. We're generally restricted to base and when we get leave there's not many places to party. There's no decent bars like Whitt's End or Murph's and we never know if the bartender working in a joint is friendly or Charlie.

"I found some buddies in basic training and have made good friends in my squad. In some ways the Army's like our fraternity, a bunch of guys hanging together, watching out for each other. The difference is you never get away, it's impossible to go off to hide by yourself. You chow, rack, drink and crap with your platoon, but they're there when you need them. As far as why everyone thinks America's over here, we're all over the map, from the obnoxious, gung ho, right-wing volunteers who want to kill off the whole country to a few old doped-up hippie draftees hating everything and who won't talk to anyone. Mostly everybody can't stand, detests and loathes this rat hole, just wants to serve their year, get short and return to the world.

"I haven't experienced much of the war. My unit has been lucky and pulled guard duty around our airport. There's rumors of us shipping north to a fire base close to the DMZ but I'm praying that's a long way off. I honest to God don't know how I'll handle being pinned down in some swampy, flooded rice paddy or under fire in the jungle. But when it comes, I hope I'm brave enough and don't let my buddies down.

Summer Never Comes

"How's Champaign this year? I heard the Illini have won a few football games and bet that makes Sleezy Parisi ecstatic.

"What about Stu? Did he make it back to school, is he still on probation, is he doing better grade-wise this year? I hope so. Tell him for me he sure as hell better haul his sorry ass to the Library and camp out there and pull decent grades. I'd hate like Christ to see him march off a transport here in 'Nam.

"Nancy has written me countless letters. There are two or three every mail call and whenever I read one I think back to our time together at the Big U. Now that I'm here in 'Nam and haven't seen her in months, I understand how sweet she was to me and how there were days I could have been nicer to her. Believe me, when I'm back stateside I'll be the politest, kindest, good-mannered, not-one-problem boyfriend any woman will ever have. No more hanging and drinking in the bars thinking I'm so cool, and no more non-stop-nothing-but-rack-and-football on Saturdays and Sundays. Being gone makes you realize what means the most and what is good.

"Well, lights out in five minutes, got to close this letter. Say hello to Moose, Ozark, O'D, O'T, Tim, Scooter, Ragman, 'Stein, Skworch, Byers and all the other KIDs, have a great rest of the semester. I trust you think of me once in a while.

"Your friend,
"Billy Powell

"P.S. Hoa Binh"

# # # #

"What's it like up there, performing in front of us students?"

"Man, the sunnier clime, you feel you're in the thick of the action, a different view from sittin' with the other Toms, Dicks and Harrys around the tables."

"Wall, Ah'd imagine so." Wasting time before their one o'clock classes, Shaky Jake, Lindy and Kentucky loafed in KIDs' living room.

"The Red Lion's stage looks so small, bands never seem to have enough room for their equipment, especially the night Kay and I watched you play."

Summer Never Comes

"It is a crowded space, and with Andy's keyboard we've got to be careful to not boogie back and forth too much. But far as I'm concerned, even if it were the size of a phone booth, I'm jubilant playin' there."

"You like it?"

"Something I've wanted my whole life, Jake. If I live to be fifty-five, I don't know if I'll ever have awesomer fun or vaster thrills."

"How many times has Frogfeet performed?"

"Homecoming weekend and twice at the Lion."

"Now thet Ah think on it, Lind-eh, Ah re-call thet yohr band was not goin' t' play until you practiced up t' be th' finest orchestra on campus."

"I reckoned that was the way it was goin' down, too, Ken-tuck, but history's tides washed over. Our agent, Gary Anderson, is a close friend of Tyke, the Red Lion's owner. After us 'Feet agreed performin' two nights for free, Gary persuaded Tyke to give us a chance on Tuesdays. The hard part was convincin' Franky Konkel, our band's head honcho, to let us play for an audience. Franky was real reluctant, but Gary and the rest of us argued we could jam in our basement until the Fighting Illini football team beat Ohio State and we still wouldn't sound as quality as he wants us. Franky finally said yes, and now the Lion on Tuesdays is our regular gig, sweet as a peach, our hub in the universe." Lindy rested his feet on the coffee table.

"Now there's two reasons for spending time in that bar, Lindy's music and the freebie beers Rudy and the Jerg pass out when Tyke's missing." Jake glanced at the *Daily Illini*. "Do you think you'll get as professional as other musicians that have performed at the Lion?"

"A question between two stools. Class acts like Bonnie Koloc, Head East and REO Speedwagon are tough comparisons. Forgfeet'll have to hustle some to catch them."

"How's the money?"

"Not as profitable as you'd think, twenty-five a man a gig."

"Ahr you-all gonna play at aneh ot-heh taverns in thes town?"

"For now I hope not, one weeknight's plenty. But if Tyke needs us for performin' in his Bloomington bar, we might drive there."

"Is Frogfeet writing any original material?"

"We're workin' on a few tunes, but only one of us has enough patience for composing. Bein' original is more effort than you think. It'll be some time before we sing them on stage." A yawning Lindy slumped in his chair.

"Your own material would set Frogfeet apart."

"A step at a time, Jake, it'll be just as valuable building a following and having students turn out when we play."

"Will you practice as much from now on?"

"There's a saving grace, Franky promised we'll thankfully cut back our rehearsals as we play gigs. I need time for the rest of my life, there's other fish to fry."

"Here's the big question. You're starting slow and want to do things right, you've had your first gigs and earned some bucks. Now in November there's potential. Say by graduation Frogfeet is a success. Would you stick around Champaign to continue performing or head off to find a regular job?"

Other KIDs exited the house for their one o'clocks, including Dale Kinsey and Tommy Quarters.

"The ol' cart in front of the horse. Come June that would be a sweet problem, but right now I don't see that likelihood, we're just a ho-hum, run of the mill bar band."

"Don't write it off, reality's a comedian." Shaky Jake stood and walked away from his friends. "Time for my lit class. Lindy, I'll look forward to listening to you again at the Lion."

"He is sure-leh happy about yohr band."

"All us rock 'n' roll stars are popular nowadays, comes with the terrain."

"Shee-it." Kentucky rubbed his beard. "Say, Ah did not see Robbeh at lunch."

"You're right, not like that boy passin' on a meal, especially his favorite, grilled cheese sandwiches and Mary Lou's chili."

"D'you know whut he is doin' t'day?"

"With Robby dating Sharon as much as he has and me occupied with Frogfeet, our orbits don't intersect, I haven't seen enough of him to say what he's up to. I guess I'm more of a phantom than a roommate."

"Thet has bin com-mented on, yohr absence from us."

"I hear what you're sayin', my life is so up in the air. When I started with Frogfeet I never fathomed we'd practice as much and I'd spend so much time with them. It was all the worse when we sounded crappy at Homecoming. Now, with Franky's okay to perform and our gigs at the

Summer Never Comes

Lion, we're doin' what I enlisted for, appearin' on a stage in front of audiences. Like I told Jake, the few hours a night we perform is so much fun it's a rush, happy days are here. But while we're up there, ol' Mister Conscience is pestering me, too, I know I've left behind my friends and other things I used to enjoy. Remember the Hound Dog hockey notice on the bulletin board? I read that and for a moment wanted to lace up the skates and play like I have the last two winters. But with the band, there's no way I have time. I wish I could, I need the exercise and camaraderie, but I can't."

"Whut up-sets you is thet there is not enough time fohr a hockey game?" Kentucky was skeptical.

"The team's only the tip of the iceberg. What's worse is walking so far away from Em, Robby and everyone else. I know this paints me as selfish, wantin' a baked cake and eatin' it too. But I'm convinced I'm onto something with my band, an opportunity which may never come again. With only six months of college left, I've got to do this now."

"An thet is th' reason foh not spendin' time with friends, buddies thet will be gone in half a year, jes like you ahr, who you may not see agin?"

"Maybe not a rational explanation, however an excuse." Lindy rested in his chair, feet still plopped on the table, and peered outside to Frat Park. Since the weekend the weather had warmed, with many undergrads in shirt sleeves. "It's a dilemma, Kentucky. If the band's successful, I'm elated with my thrills on stage. But the happier I feel playin' my guitar, the more I dump on my friends."

"Does it have t' be thet way?"

"The joy I take from music equaling the piles I crap on my buddies, a zero sum game? It no doubt looks that way to everyone and how it's working out. If there were extra time, if I were more concerned for my friends, I might balance everything."

"Ah think you ciphered it right theah, Lind-eh."

"Sounds simple, but I'm discovering reality isn't painless. Look how I've chewed Robby's ass a couple times the last three weeks, how I'm snubbing Em, one of the gentlest, most considerate girls I've ever known, throwing away our year of friendship."

"And?"

Summer Never Comes

"What should I do? Tell the 'Feet I'm takin' a week off to get my head straight, use the time to be more responsible and a better friend to her and Robby, I know that."

"An' theyh you have it. D'you think seven days is long enough?"

"Considering how far I've flown off the radar screen, no. But it could be a way to salvage their respect." Lindy shut his eyes. "It's time I became dependable and a more reliable boyfriend."

"By th' way, boy, don' you have a class at one o'clock?"

"I do, but this afternoon I believe I'll stay irresponsible and rack."

"Oh, Lord-eh."

# # # #

When Undersecretary of State for Asian Affairs James R. Camp flew into Willard Airport, UNITED rallied to meet him. The undersecretary spotted the protesters in the cornfields and at the fence when his airplane landed, and waved to another assemblage of fifty or sixty True Believers as the aircraft taxied on the runway. Over one hundred UNITED picketers congregated inside the terminal when he, his aides and Secret Service detail marched through to his limousine. These students, as the ones outside, stood deadpan, murmuring among themselves, not yelling or shouting. Reporters and photographers from the *Daily Illini*, the *Champaign News-Gazette* and the *St. Louis Post-Dispatch* were also in the concourse, ready for the day's skirmishes between the hard line, war party government official and the college do-gooders, the hawks and the doves, the wrongs and the rights. The press was disappointed, though, when the only indication of confrontation was a single sign held by one student.

"PEACE"

"Good morning, nice to be back." Secretary Camp congenially remarked.

UNITED's members lined up on the east side of Route 45 when the motorcade drove toward the campus. For four miles, from Savoy to Kirby Avenue in Champaign, small cliques of a half-dozen protesters stood at hundred-foot intervals. No one chanted or shouted, jumped or leapt, acted like maniacs, defiantly raised a fist or lobbed anything at the passing cars. Only the students' signs and posters broadcast their message.

Summer Never Comes

"END THE WAR"
"UNITED FOR PEACE"
"THE KILLING MUST STOP IN VIETNAM"
"SOUTHEAST ASIA – AMERICA'S DISGRACE"
"QUIT THE WAR – AND NEVER AGAIN!"

At noon, Mister Camp was the guest of honor at the chancellor's reception in the Illini Union. The undersecretary received the President's Council Award and delivered a short talk on the school's improving national reputation. The speechless pickets stood in the hallways, holding their placards. When he walked to Altgeld Hall to address the Political Science Department faculty, UNITED waited at the doors with orange and black banners.

"AMERICANS SHOULD HAVE PEACE!"
"THE UNITED STATES OF DESTRUCTION!"

"Good afternoon." The undersecretary called.

"It's only a matter of time before one side erupts," the newspaper reporters huddled, "then we'll write our headlines."

Camp's final appearance was a speech to students in the Lincoln Hall Theater. Due to pleasant weather or a compulsion to challenge the doves, the undersecretary and his entourage altered the announced itinerary, strolling down the Quad instead of driving their limousines through Campustown. UNITED was prepared and bunches of pickets met the politicians the whole way, mute except for their signs.

"ONE-TWO-THREE-FOUR, WE DON'T WANT ANYMORE WAR!"

"HEY JIMMY – TRY BROTHERHOOD"

"END THIS SAD, SORRY, BLOOD-DRENCHED ADMINISTRATION!"

In the weak November sunshine, the crowds mushroomed to hundreds and, confronted by his voiceless rivals, the undersecretary's mood shifted from relaxed to no-nonsense, "Jimmy's game face," one reporter pronounced. His assistants also switched, becoming as expressionless as their boss. The excursion's ambience ended, the friendly chatter swung to gruff instructions and pouts.

Paul stood in the big lecture hall's rear with the *News-Gazette*, the *Chicago Daily News*, the *Saluki Times* and a late arrival, the *Pantagraph* of

Bloomington-Normal. As Camp and his followers were ushered through a side door, a handful in the six hundred-odd audience, likely instructors and university staff, clapped. The ovation ended, however, as the applauders realized their small numbers. The undersecretary, standing on the stage with his hangers on and Secret Service guards, brusquely nodded.

"This is his kind of crowd, a gang of students hating his guts," the *Post-Dispatch* declared, "they'll enjoy chewing on each other."

"Ladies and gentlemen," Professor Charles Pearlman of the Nuclear Engineering Department announced, "I have the honor to introduce today's speaker, an alumnus of our school, a dedicated public official, a participant in the international arena, the Undersecretary of State for Southeast Asian Affairs, the honorable James R. Camp."

"JOHNSON-NIXON-CAMP: AMERICA'S KILLERS"

"UNITED FOR PEACE"

"THE WHOLE WORLD IS WATCHING!"

"THE WHOLE WORLD IS WATCHING!"

"Students, faculty and fellow loyal Illini. As always, I am pleased to return to the University of Illinois, my alma mater, the school I entered as an adolescent, the place I grew and matured, and a college I have always believed one of the truly great institutions of our nation's higher educational system." His compliments received no acknowledgement, and more posters were raised.

"BAN THE WAR"

"RELENT AND REPENT!"

"LET'S HAVE PEACE IN OUR TIME, JIMMY!"

"Though our land grant school is not as old as colleges of the eastern establishment, when coming back to Champaign-Urbana I am always reminded of our noteworthy history and meaningful achievements. John Milton Gregory, the first regent of the Illinois Industrial University, as we were named a century ago, the *Daily Illini*, one of the half dozen oldest college daily papers in the country and first to join the *Associated Press*, the nation's first Architectural Engineering Department launched in 1893, the adoption of the school colors in 1894, Thomas Arkle Clark's appointment in 1901 as first Dean of Men at any university, the inauguration of the Homecoming tradition in 1910, a library of six million volumes, pioneering work in the field of computers, and the continually developing physical plant, with one recent addition being our new Assembly Hall. These accomplishments and more are groundwork to build on.

"As the current residents of this campus, you profit from your predecessors' legacy. A spinoff of this largesse, an understandable inclination, might be to relax and enjoy your years here, taking what is provided and, as is youth's nature, working only as little as required. A university such as ours, located on the Midwest's prairie, insulated from the world's unrest, makes this all the easier. There are many diversions in college, amusements, celebrations and parties to attend, pastimes, I must admit, I chased in my years here." The theater's crowd was silent, and the undersecretary realized his gambit at humor had failed. "Yet, to live only for the moment, to not give back and repay is misguided, to be unconscious of the trust we hold is amiss. Being part of a community such as this, in times like ours, carries obligations."

"WHY BATTLE? MAKE PEACE INSTEAD!"
"FIGHT NO MORE – END THE WAR!"
"MY GOD – SEE THE LIGHT!"

"Obligations. The first is to your parents and families, those who have sacrificed for your opportunity to attend the University of Illinois. Not only have they borne the monetary costs, but the everyday, emotional ones as well, the years of preparing you for the moment you leave their homes and are ready to stand alone in the world. Their leap of faith should always be cherished.

"The second is to the university. With its libraries and laboratories, professors and researchers, this distinguished institution holds a century's accumulation of knowledge, know-how, experience and expertise; wisdom for us to utilize, but also a stockpile for us to foster and grow. Thousands of graduates lead better lives because of their years in Champaign-Urbana. Many tens of thousands more will enjoy this privilege in years to come because we must, we will nurture this school, and support and strengthen our alma mater."

"WE SHALL OVERCOME"
"HO CHI MINH FOR PRESIDENT"
"DOWN WITH THE GOVERNMENT – UP WITH PEACE"

"It's going to come soon, he can't bottle it up forever," the *Daily News* muttered.

Summer Never Comes

"The third responsibility is to yourselves. You must push, you must find the motivation and mettle within that will mold your lives, prepare you for tomorrow, consign to you meaning. Your future begins in these premises, but continues on in the world at large. It is for you, in attendance today, to release your potential." Tightening his grip on the podium, Camp rushed his speech, reading his notes instead of glimpsing at the audience and the posters.

"And after this preparation, when you have acquired the knowledge and learning, after you have chosen your careers, it is time to leave these secluded surroundings and enter the real world, to contribute your share toward solving society's problems. Teaching, medicine, the business world, physical sciences, social services are all worthy occupations. But there is another undertaking that is the more important, a cause most urgent, a danger we must confront, a crusade in which we must not fail: our country's fight against those global forces dedicated to destroying our nation and bringing down our way of life, the decades-long battle against Communism and the current war in Vietnam."

"Here we go," the *Pantagraph* whispered, "what this crowd's waiting for."

"A donnybrook between Jimmy and the hecklers," the *Saluki Times* concurred.

Camp peered at the audience, waiting for his last paragraph to push the students to finally, disruptively break out screaming. What he received was silence and what he saw were extra signs lifted up, more posters than bodies and heads. The theater looked like an art class.

"HANG IT UP ON THE WAR!"
"GET AMERICA OUT OF THE DAMNED PLACE!"
"LE DUC THO FOR VICE PRESIDENT!"
"NO MORE WAR – LOVE INSTEAD!"
"PLUTO FOR UNDERSECRETARY!"

"No one likes war. Numerous civilized societies are not good at it, government officials hope to avoid it, presidents promise to protect us from it, citizens oppose it and dodge it. Such is the case today.

"Our conflict in Southeast Asia is not popular, nor have the years of fighting in Vietnam, Laos and Cambodia made support for it fashionable. It is out of step in numerous segments of our country's population, detested by many I have met. Countless citizens have been called to duty, with their families facing the sadness of their sacrifices. But unpopularity does not mean disgrace, disapproval does not equate to discredit, and a hard task is a responsibility that must be met, and will be faced by our government. This administration, our nation's leaders, will not shrink from what must be done. We will not, as has been suggested by anti-war, peace-at-any-price liberals, give ground or retreat. We will not, as some cadres in the United States say, admit the work is too difficult, we have forfeited enough, we must recognize our mistakes and it is time to surrender. Such talk is not a sign of strength nor a firm national policy, and will not protect America. Only through seeking out and fighting our enemies on the battlefield will we defeat those determined to destroy us. Only through rigid resolve will we achieve the victory over those who hate us. Only through true grit will we succeed. And that, I am happy to say, is what your government will do, not abandon our allies, not listen to doubters and doomsayers, not quit. Regardless of the expenditures and the costs, in spite of obstacles in Asia and obstructionists at home, we will continue the war in Vietnam. We will win the military victory."

"HEY JIMMY – LESS TALK, MORE COMMON SENSE!"

"WHO WILL YOU DESTROY? THEM OR US?"

"He really nailed the hippies that time," the *Post-Dispatch* said.

"They've got to let him have it," the *Tribune* agreed.

Camp sipped a water glass, pausing for the anticipated boos and outcries that crowds, particularly college students, hurled at him when he upheld his government's war policies. But there was no racket or rioting, just dozens more of those goddamned signs. A master dueling with the hecklers and subversives the undersecretary encountered in America, the sounds of silence confused him.

"Camp always delivers a real stem winder for a finish," the *News-Gazette's* John Barrett offered. "He'll let them have it in another minute."

On stage, the undersecretary surveyed the quiet crowd, then frowned, Jimmy's game face again. The reticent students stared back, a few score using their crayons to draw new signs.

"RETREAT ISN'T SO BAD!"

"WHAT, HOW, WHEN, DO THE DEAD THINK ABOUT VICTORY?"

Summer Never Comes

"This address' subject is responsibilities and I will end with a discussion of one more. Free speech, the right to be heard. Dialogue and discussion are basic to our country, the first amendment to the Constitution guarantees it, and without this privilege our nation is nothing. A visitor to this campus is entitled to talk, orate, advocate and be allowed to express his opinions without interference. When conspiring, scheming, radical, revolutionary mobs inhibit any citizen, including myself, from speaking his mind, it is a sad day for the republic." Camp pounded the podium and raised his voice. "Unprovoked protest whose sole aim is to destroy dialogue in America cannot be countenanced. Those caught up in such malicious behaviors are themselves ill-mannered, ignorant, illiterate, boorish snobs, unfit to be citizens, undeserving to attend a school such as this university. And they should know better."

Clutching his notes, the undersecretary stomped away from the podium, stepping on Professor Pearlman's foot in his haste to leave.

"That was over the top, don't you think?" the *Pantagraph* scribbled on his pad.

"Just what the doctor ordered," the *Post-Dispatch* said.

"Frustrated and Irate James Camp Blasts Peaceful Student Statement," the *Daily Illini* headlines read, "Upset Undersecretary Denounces Diligent Dissent."

# # # #

"Come in. Your name is…"

"Paul Roberts."

"Yes, the person that called for an appointment." Young for an assistant professor, affable and smiling, Antoinette Gulley wore her hair down to her collar, curly and very full. A paisley blouse clashed with her long print dress and tennis shoes. "What can I do for you?"

Paul sat in a wooden chair. The term papers piled on the desk two weeks ago were gone, and *Ideology and Revolution in the Soviet Union* was missing from the bookshelf. "Two friends in my fraternity are enrolled in your History 333 class and have talked about your lectures. The course sounds like one I'd like to take as an elective."

Summer Never Comes

"I'm happy students speak favorably about me. 333 is one of a series of upper-level courses structured to provide graduate students, history majors and undergraduates with an in-depth knowledge of pre-industrial England. In the three years I have taught it, my focus has been sixteenth and seventeenth century social and cultural aspects versus political developments. The next time I plan to concentrate on Stuart authors. What is your specific interest?"

"Actually, I'm an accounting major, but I've had four history courses and have already reviewed the books for the course."

"Is there any one period that stands out?"

"Cromwell, the Civil War and the Restoration." Paul was relieved Professor Gulley didn't consider it strange that a non-history major was interested in her class.

"A defining time. During the Interregnum the English could have fallen into anarchy, but instead chose the rule of law and continued their development into a world empire."

"One question I have concerns the reading. Will the same textbooks be required?"

"I contemplate no changes, and believe the current list explains the subject and appropriately complements the lectures."

"What about the supplemental books in the Reserved Reading section?"

"Optional readings depend on future, updated articles being available and published in journals."

"One paperback I spotted in the Library surprised me." Paul glanced at his notes. *"Ideology and Revolution in the Soviet Union,* by Howell Meade."

"The book shouldn't be in my section, its inclusion was an oversight by the library staff, I never put it there to begin with." Professor Gulley shook her head. "I've intended to walk over to the Undergraduate Library to have it removed, but haven't had time."

"The Meade text is unrelated to History 333 and I won't have to read it next semester?"

"Precisely, a volume whose subject is twentieth century Russia is unconnected to my course. But are you assuming 333 will be offered in the spring?"

"Yes."

215

Summer Never Comes

"I'm sorry, I'm teaching History 334 next semester."

"What years does that one cover?" Paul feigned disappointment, having already checked the spring course catalogue.

"England from 1660 to 1815."

"A shame, I was looking forward to Cromwell and the Civil War, I'll have to think about the other one."

"Take this." The professor reached over to her shelves. "A course outline for 334 may convince you to enroll. Why don't you review it and come back if you have any questions."

"Thanks, I appreciate the information." Paul looked at the Prairie Winds Ballooning poster next to the window. "That's a neat picture. Do you fly in them?"

"I do, as a matter of fact. I started when I was in college," Professor Gulley grinned.

"Sounds like an extraordinary hobby, gliding without engines or noises, seeing human beings on the ground as the size of ants."

"Different strokes."

"I suppose so. Again, thanks for your time, I'll get back to you." Paul walked out of Greg Hall and to the Undergrad Library's lower level.

"Hi," he laid his notebook on the counter.

"Can I help?"

"Could I see a listing of the titles held in the Reserved Reading Area for History 333?"

"Why don't you use the card catalogue? The books are inventoried in the drawers." The attendant looked old enough to be a grad student and wore a faded blue plaid shirt.

"What I really want is a full list I can photocopy instead of spending twenty or thirty minutes writing them down."

"We don't have that available."

"Are you sure? There must be ten or fifteen different books for that course and I'm sort of in a hurry."

The grad student adjusted her wire-rimmed glasses. "We do have the instructors' request forms on file, those list the reserved books."

"That's outstanding, I can't count how many index cards and titles I've accumulated for this research paper." An embarrassed Paul was relieved his lie was plausible.

Summer Never Comes

"I'll relate, last summer I wrote a fifty-page thesis for Behavioral Social Psych." She opened a cabinet and handed the sheet to him.

"Okay if I take this to the Xerox machine?"

"Not a problem, as long as I get the document back."

Paul stepped away from the counter. Eleven titles, including call numbers and authors, were typed on the page, the last being *Ideology and Revolution in the Soviet Union*. On the 'requesting instructor' line, Professor Antoinette Gulley had signed her name.

# # # #

"Robby, how you doin'?" Lindy turned toward the doorway.

"I didn't expect seeing you this early. No practice?" Paul entered their room.

"We low-keyed tonight, talked through a few new songs, rapped with Gary Anderson, never fired up an amp. But here's a scoop, we got the word that starting after Thanksgiving we're performin' two nights every week at the Red Lion."

"I thought your band was only the Tuesday act, why a bump?"

"Gary negotiated this deal with Tyke. The band gets paid one hundred twenty-five dollars the first night and a hundred for the second."

"Discount music?"

"The cost of doin' business, how you gotta break the ice to make a name."

"Which nights are yours?"

"Tuesdays and Wednesdays, at least through Christmas."

"Why not weekends?"

"We aren't professional enough to pack in room-filling audiences."

"Not respectable for the Lion on Fridays and Saturdays, and cut rate music during the week," Paul chuckled. "For a band working towards being a class act, Frogfeet is stepping out."

"No one's as flummoxed as me with Franky Konkel's change of heart. But I'm not complainin' because the money will come in handy."

"What's better, practice or playing?"

"On stage, absolutely. If we were gonna stay in that basement, I'd go animal crackers and so would Andy Arthur. Performin' live is tons more fun, when we're up there we feed off the audience, learn by doin', see what's a success and what bombs. Of course, playin' has problems of its own, loadin' up, traveling and unpackin'; and if the crowds don't like us, hostility makes for long evenings."

"You're really on that road you've talked about."

"Wherever Frogfeet's travelin', it is moving my life at warp-speed. This autumn has been a quick couple months."

"Worth it?"

"I've learned a lot about the music business' ropes, which will be helpful when I get outta school. Nothing in this experience tells me I should dodge it as a career." Lindy stood at the opened window. A warm wind, uncommon for November, blew in. "But do I regret the time it's cost me? The answer is yes, I feel bad walkin' away from you, Bobby, Stu and Kentucky; missing the night Scooter got showered. And I really feel crappy over how I've treated Em. But life is a game and the band is my gamble in this inning."

"Playing on stage justifies the other stuff you've ignored?" Paul sat at the second desk. "Weird, you sound exactly like Sharon. She thinks you're doing the right thing, pretty much used the same words about opportunities."

"Damn, I have got to make this woman's acquaintance." Lindy smiled, "You can't break away from people like us, hey, Robby?"

"I don't understand you is closer."

"This is gonna work out, I know it will, I only regret bein' such a half-assed friend. What do think about this extra mile I'm goin'?"

"It's your choice, I have no problem with your reaching for success. So far the band is doing well and I'm happy for you."

"What do you have a problem with? I'm lookin' for an honest opinion about Frogfeet." Spending time with Paul to atone for his bad behavior, Lindy was also sincerely interested in his roommate's judgment.

"As I said, your decisions."

"That's all? No little lectures over how I've ignored you and everyone else, blown off school, selfishly run away?"

"If you're interested in someone's attitude, start with Emily and her feelings, make things right with her. She's a wonderful person and you owe it to both yourselves to keep her happy."

Summer Never Comes

"Em has always been my sweetheart, the one I hurt the most because she's depended on me and I let her down. If my last two months were quick, no doubt they've been an eternity for her. I still haven't forgotten how I dumped on her on Homecoming. I told Em how I went back and forth that night, how tough a decision playin' with the band was, but I'm uncertain she believes me." A stereo down the hallway spun Big Brother and the Holding Company. "All the people I've harmed. But I want to come clean. What are the words to pick up the threads?"

I have a hard time, Paul thought, comprehending my roommate, seeing Lindy disconnect from our friends, only considering himself, dismissing opportunities to settle problems, shutting me out. He has been self-centered. I'm sorry for both of us, Lindy because he's given so much away, myself because I've waited so long for my roommate to repair his screw-ups. Lindy should have treated everyone better, should have had this conversation with me earlier. How can I explain this and not sound like a crybaby?

"Come on, I'm lookin' for pearls of wisdom from my buddy."

All right, Paul decided, *here it goes.*

"Do you think a five-minute chat will set things right, what you say in one night compensates for two months of disrespecting people? You once said we're too young to be experts in life, but I remember another cliché: talk is cheap and always will be. Friendship is more than a hint or a promise, what makes it are the small things, the kindnesses, going out of your way to do a favor, willpower backing the words."

"I'm not blind to the last months, Robby, they have been painful, and yes, I know I've walked away. But there's so much on my plate and so little time. I've come so far with the band I've got to stick with them and can't quit. Everything else I can squeeze in if I just try a little more."

"That's your problem. This whole semester has circled around you with everything else a maybe, a perhaps, an I'll catch up with you next week, somehow it'll work through, I'll figure fitting it in tomorrow. But, but, but. You can't be a conditional friend. We're all tired of Lindy, the fly-by-night rock 'n' roller, we'd like to see the old, dependable, the-good-guy Lindy. You should start acting like it again."

"You're goin' too far. I am sitting here talking with you to settle up; maybe I haven't done much of this lately but I'm attempting right now.

Summer Never Comes

Okay, so I've slacked off, but I don't think I should be tossed over the side. I'm not the first guy off following his own course. And if I have, so what? What if I want to do what I think is right, if I'm selfish? There's plenty of time this year to settle accounts. I can still do it."

"Listen to yourself. Are you talking friends or balancing a ledger?"

"Friendship should always win."

"And needs the effort to achieve."

# # # #

"Joyce, take a look."

"Papers taped to a big wall." Returning from a coffee break, the two stood in front of the Undergrad's floor to ceiling bulletin board.

"This announcement right here." Stu pointed to a yellow, letter-sized sheet about waist high. "'Law School Admissions Test. Application and fee must be submitted by December 1. Examination offered the third Saturday in January.' I'm signing up."

"You're interested in law school?"

"Why not? I've always done well on big tests, I may get a break. I've got to do something after graduation, and a bachelor's degree in political science doesn't open many job possibilities in the real world."

"Lucky with a test score is only the first part, studying law is a commitment. I'm doubtful a Thursday-night snap decision is the adult way to select a future. And being practical, you're on academic probation, do you think you can be admitted?"

"My grade point's improving this semester, I'm earning at least straight B's—the influences of our booking in the Library. As far as getting accepted, there's always the case of Bucky Sanford. He was a senior in KIDs last year, the laziest of lazy asses, sat around talking sports, never studied and nobody actually knew his major. Last winter he scored super high on the LSAT, something like a 720 out of a possible 800, and was accepted to four schools. This year he's enrolled at John Marshall. My idea may be spur of the moment, but it's possible."

"All I'll say is good luck and hope you're not disappointed." She kissed Stu as they walked away from the bulletin board.

Summer Never Comes

# # # #

"Good of you to call, Will," Emily was happy talking to him, even if by telephone.

"Enjoyin' the pleasant weather?"

"Not wearing a winter coat this week has been nice."

"For sure, I saw frisbee tossers out on the Quad yesterday, plus a couple of cuties in bikinis catchin' rays."

"That is a bit too far."

"A fool's paradise preceding the winter snows." Lindy stood in KIDs' second floor hallway. "How's that Bio 100 class coming along?"

"The topics have been interesting, but listening to lectures through earphones in the lab for an hour every week is growing old. I'll be glad when the course is finished."

"All you have to do is pull yourself through to the end of the semester. Look at it this way, it's more convenient than sittin' in a class room with a boring professor and avoiding fallin' asleep. Heck, you could get hurt dropping from some of the chairs on this campus."

"Oh, Will," Emily giggled, enjoying the tease, "you're right and I shouldn't complain, I've enrolled in worse courses. And Thanksgiving is nearing, the campus seems to be already winding down."

"Em, about this weekend."

"Yes?" she interrupted, anticipating, longing for their date.

"About these next two days, I'm outta commission."

"I'm sorry, you do sound a little down, are you not feeling well? That would be a shame with the weather looking nice for Saturday's football game. If you are ill, I could walk over to visit, bring a hotpot and tea and we could sit in your room and talk."

"Sick isn't the explanation, it's Frogfeet. We've scheduled gigs in Decatur on Friday and Saturday payin' thirty dollars a night per man. We're leaving tomorrow afternoon and comin' back Sunday."

"Like before," her friendly tone ended.

"But I want to see you when I return, there's things to discuss, it's time to clear the air and make more amends. What if we get together for a while Monday night to study?"

"That's fine," her voice was apathetic.

"Sounds good, it'll be relaxin' finally going out on a date, we'll even grab a slice of Garcia's pizza. You know, Robby's still seein' Sharon. Hard to believe, that boy with a steady. I never thought he'd step to the counter and pay his money."

"I'm glad for him."

"I hear she's got a real spiffy car, a red Camaro. Can you picture Robby drivin' around campus in one of those? Strange as it sounds, I haven't met her yet, they've dated for two months but our paths don't overlap. That should change in December, though, with all the Christmas parties I'm sure we'll hook up. Maybe the four of us can set aside an evening for dinner. From what Robby tells me, Sharon and I see the world through the same lens."

"That seems about right."

"Say, you sound tired."

"I have two reading assignments to finish tonight, and an eight o'clock class tomorrow morning."

"Okay, I won't keep you. Don't forget about Monday night, I'll look forward to it and give you a call when I get back on Sunday."

"Whatever you say."

"Have a good weekend, Em. I hope you get your work done, and stay with that Bio 100 class."

# # # #

The warm autumn weather held the next seven days. This was a bonus for football fans watching the Illini play Northwestern University for the Sweet Sioux Tomahawk Trophy, these die-hards glad for a reprieve from the season finale's typical winter clothing: hats, scarves, boots and blackberry brandy.

The game was one event holding students around campus, and on Sunday the Thanksgiving departures began, with Bobby Sox the first. Early in the morning he loaded his Pontiac, pulled his riders out of the rack a half hour earlier than scheduled and drove to Chicago. One of his passengers was Emily, deciding to abandon school after her conversation with Lindy. On Interstate 57, Bobby raced the engine to eighty and arrived home in time for lunch.

Summer Never Comes

The KIDs' living room was emptier, newspapers and letters were piled in the foyer, not to be opened for a week, and fewer stereos blasted—a certain sign of absent students. The exceptions were the fourth floor despoes, this crowd hanging out, blowing their speakers and toking until late Wednesday afternoon.

Chapter Ten

Paul enjoyed riding the Illinois Central Railroad back to campus on days like the Friday after Thanksgiving. Returning early meant fewer passengers, a window seat and space to stretch. The trains on Sunday and Monday would be overcrowded with students standing in the aisles or sitting on suitcases for the three-hour trip.

The *City of New Orleans* arrived at the Champaign station at eleven a.m., twenty minutes behind schedule. Paul stepped down from the coach and, with sunny weather and one bag to carry, planned on walking to KIDs.

"Honey, want a ride?"

Spotting his girlfriend, Paul's face brightened. "What are you doing here? I thought you were driving in this afternoon."

"Change of schedule, I woke up with my parents this morning and hit the road when they left for work." Sharon strolled toward Paul to kiss him. "When I exited the expressway I came right here to meet your train."

The two passed through the depot and crossed Chestnut Street, where four or five cabs waited. Sharon's Camaro was parked adjacent to the *Champaign News-Gazette's* office. They drove through the empty campus, some blocks with no parked cars along the curbs. Moose's Buick was the only auto in the KIDs' lot when they pulled in.

"Here's a suggestion for saving time," Sharon said as they reached the door, "why not grab your clothes and hang at my place for the weekend?"

"I thought I'd stay at KIDs and meet you around campus each day."

"My house is large enough and none of my roommates will be back until Sunday, you can sleep in any room."

"Guess it makes sense." The fraternity was cold, Paul remembering the KIDs dialed the heat down over vacations. Upstairs, he repacked his suitcase, carrying two accounting textbooks with him.

Summer Never Comes

"This is an eerie town with no students."

"Even the Library is closed today, but the bars are open. Shows what's essential in the Twin Cities."

Driving into Urbana, Sharon parked on her house's gravel driveway under the oak trees. Hundreds of acorns lay on the ground, hiding the yard's dirt.

"Hungry? How about Campbell's soup and a salami sandwich?"

"Sounds tasty." The two set their bags by the front door.

"How should we spend the weekend?" She licked mayonnaise off her fingers.

"I have two hourlies next week, but know the material and don't have to hard-core study for either. What's your idea?"

"Tomorrow, if the weather stays warm, we could drive to Allerton Park for a long hike in the woods—experience nature and outdoors."

"I've never seen Monticello—the mansion, gardens and statues are supposed to be picturesque. Too bad the season's so late and the trees are bare."

"A date?" Sharon handed him a soup bowl.

"They're your wheels." As the pair ate lunch, Paul picked up a copy of Tuesday's *Daily Illini*.

"The New Approach: Non-Violence versus In-Your-Face.

"The expected responses to James R. Camp's Champaign-Urbana trip would have been the simplest. The undersecretary's visit could have been disrupted by rowdy, caustic demonstrators shouting him down his entire time on campus. With his well-deserved reputation for exploiting antagonistic audiences, the hypothetical headlines from such protesting would have been predictable: 'Radical Students Disrupt Determined Government Official's Speech,' and 'Immature College Intelligentsia Refuse to Listen to Other Side.'

"But UNITED, the campus's newest peace coalition, did not choose this course. Illustrating intelligent, regimented tactics, this anti-war organization demonstrated the student body's sincerity for the cause of peace. UNITED's 2700 members cooperated in Gandhi-like activities emphasizing our commitment to ending the war. The undersecretary, confronting resolute but unanticipated civil disobedience, retreated to in-your-face histrionics wholly unsuited to the situation he found himself.

Summer Never Comes

Instead of dialogue, he scolded; discarding discourse, he reproached; not interested in discussion, he reprimanded. The actual stories written that day point this out: a frustrated administration official castigating citizens exercising their Bill of Rights-guaranteed freedom of expression. A new day's level-headedness overcame reactionary, intolerant intransigence.

"UNITED deserves our ongoing support for leading the crusade toward a world with no wars."

Paul placed the paper on the table. "The *DI* claims twenty-seven hundred protesters were in the streets for Camp's visit."

"From what I heard, that was the size of the crowds needed to rally everywhere he spoke. A lot of student bodies were required to picket cleverly enough so Camp would blow his top. UNITED bettered their Homecoming balloon episode, first drama in the sky, then sandals on the ground. I was impressed and so were my friends. Protesting is having a winning month."

"I'm not disputing the figure, the numbers could be low. Undergrads were out in force at Willard Airport, Route 45 from Savoy, the Quad, and all 663 chairs in Lincoln Hall Theater were filled."

"How do you know the exact number?"

"I counted them last week." Paul sipped tomato soup. "The point is I thought UNITED has fewer members."

"Newspapers' penchant is exaggeration." Seeing his distant expression, Sharon back-tracked, "Of course, not your *Daily Illini*, your reporters never embellish."

Paul absentmindedly scratched his hair, long after half a semester without a trim. "At their meeting three days before Camp came to the Big U, Bernard Minerath said their membership was 260 and set the next months' enrollment target at seventy-five per week."

"More students could have come forward to help out, or UNITED managed a quickie recruiting drive. A 'de-camping Camp campaign.'"

"Yes, speedy volunteering. But I didn't read any announcements in the *DI* or hear about other advertising."

"It's possible, those protesters—along with the buses for shuttling them between the airport and the Quad—were no mirage."

"Which is another incongruity. Seventy-two hours before Camp's trip Bernard claimed his schedule was unknown. In addition to enrolling thousands of students in three days, at the last minute UNITED had to coordinate Camp's itinerary with positioning the pickets, including the impromptu, just-for-the-kicks-of-it stroll to Lincoln Hall. However parsed, the day was consummate organization, total luck, or some spy snatched inside information."

"What else bothers you?" Grasping her boyfriend's deductions, Sharon finished the sandwich.

"There's the Russian government textbook catalogued under History 333 in the Reserved Reading area. Professor Gulley told me she never authorized it for her course, but the Undergrad Library has a request form signed by her."

"Maybe she forgot."

"Or lied, because here's another inconsistency: Randy Miller, a UNITED member and a fraternity brother, bought this book at Follett's. When I checked there and at the Illini Union Bookstore, copies were on the shelves in both places, inventoried under Gulley's course. Eighty-nine were purchased from both stores. *Ideology and Revolution in the Soviet Union* wouldn't have been stocked by either if Gulley hadn't arranged it. Here's an instruction manual for socialism and insurrection, explaining how Communism can infiltrate and overthrow a country, and UNITED's people are encouraged—obliged—to read it. These facts, plus her Homecoming weekend balloon flight over Memorial Stadium, connects Gulley with UNITED."

"Maybe she's a concerned citizen doing her part to end the war, working to fix one of our country's crises. Goodness knows there are problems galore needing an overhaul." Sharon peered into the pot for leftover soup. "Democracy's mission, people making a difference."

"Why conceal putting the book on reserve? Other alibis besides blaming the library staff would be more credible."

"You're back at the start of the circle."

"Right, the likeliest probability—a citizen doing her part. Along with some fiction for last week's quickie thousands of volunteers." A dubious Paul shook his head. "What about Laurie Allman's mutilated cat and her being scared off campus? If they wanted Laurie's cooperation, why not debate with her in the open, candidly, minus the exploitation? There's no sense to their tactics, except the bad guys plotting to neuter the opposition."

Summer Never Comes

Unable to scrape up more soup, Sharon settled for munching saltines. "I thought you were an accountant and researcher for the *DI*. Here you are involved—deciphering clues and chasing villains."

"I enjoy connecting dots. But UNITED is too suspicious, maybe it's their objective I haven't fathomed." Trolling the spoon around his bowl, Paul recalled their talk on their first date at Treno's. "And I feel crummy about lying to the History Department's secretary, the snow jobs I handed Gulley, the Reserved Reading clerk and Brad at Prairie Winds Ballooning."

"Does that bother you?"

"Honesty is important, without it, peoples' lives have less worth. Upfront with others earns a clear conscience."

Sharon ate a third cracker, delighted with her boyfriend's ethics. "What about these scheming bad guys, whoever they are? If their intrigue is succeeding, to keep our campus safe, they need to be exposed. Maybe one hundred percent integrity isn't the course to follow; to discover what they're after you've got to be shrewd, employ discretion and tact."

"Put another way, cut corners."

"How about energetic and aggressive? Don't forget scrappy."

The pair talked away the afternoon, discussing the war, the university, Nixon, Muskie, McGovern, McCarthy and McCloskey, the noisiest bars in Champaign, the cheesiest pizza in Urbana, the coldest beer anywhere in central Illinois, why a house as big as Sharon's was built with only one john, Laurie Allman and Diesel a second time, Paul's hairline, Sharon's bra size, and if either of them would ever land a job paying really decent money—thirty thousand dollars a year. The November sun set and the two sat in the kitchen's wooden chairs. After a half hour in darkness, Sharon suggested building a fire and rolling the television next to the hearth. They lay on the floor, watching the flames and the Marx Brothers' *Duck Soup* on Channel 3. When the movies finished at 1:30, the station signed off with the national anthem and a test pattern.

"This is our longest time together all semester, an agreeable way to waste a weekend."

"Not squander," Sharon leaned over to kiss him, "contented, intimate down-time sounds dreamier; exploring each other's thoughts, dissecting our psyche—learning, considering, feeling."

"Killing time, shooting the breeze." Paul poked the smoldering logs. "How many bedrooms did you say are upstairs?"

"Seven, including mine."

"A suspicious person might speculate everything you've done today, drive back to campus, collect me at the train station, suggest I stay in your house, the food, the fire, is to maneuver me into a compromising position."

"I hope you're not complaining," Sharon whispered, her face four inches from Paul's, her hands pawing his shirt.

"Not a bit, but this is my job."

"Take over anytime."

As embers flickered, Paul pulled Sharon toward him. "Which room did you say was yours?"

Soon they laid naked between the sheets in her bed, finding each other, Paul a little anxious, Sharon assured. She smooched him on the lips, cheeks and forehead—really moist ones—then she shoved his head down to her stomach. He'd never kissed or caressed a girl's tummy before, and the moments he laid there, feeling Sharon's lungs inhaling, exhaling, were so special, so stimulating. Paul felt he should come up with and whisper a witty aside, then figured this was a spot way beyond conversation. Sharon slid underneath his torso and clutched his shoulder blades with one arm, massaging his back. After some minutes, she quit kneading and Paul felt her tightly grab his body, her legs wrapping around him. She rocked as her hands pressed on the back of his neck. A turned-on Paul placed his head next to hers, felt her fingernails dig into his skin, and went off, with anticipation banging into bliss. Their rocking slowed and Sharon relaxed, dropping into the mattress.

"Sex is so sweet."

He glanced at her, seeing perspiration beads underneath her chin. When Sharon loosened her hug, a contented, panting Paul slid off, snuggling next to her.

"Remember earlier this evening, your remarks about compromising positions?"

"What did I say? Don't pay any attention, only my suspicious nature."

"It's true. Except for *Duck Soup*, which was our bonus, this whole day was a set-up, why I met your train this morning, to have plenty of time this weekend to get us in bed. I even convinced Mary to stay away until Sunday so we'd be alone."

So laid-back, so peaceful, Paul wasn't at all bothered and cared less. "Didn't you think I'd figure out...get around to...jumping in the sack with you?"

She brushed the hair off his forehead.

"Does this change our relationship?" Paul focused. "Suddenly we're more than friends sitting around discovering the way the other's mind is put together. Now there's this physical thing, we know how to turn each other on, a crutch we can retreat to."

"For my money, Paul Roberts, you're a considerate, kindhearted person I want to get to know, I'd like spending more time with." A wind gust or rain rattled the window panes, Sharon couldn't tell. "In a way you're right, if two people stay horny and blasé, sex masks their problems. Companionship is many things: familiarity, indifference, intimacy, detachment. We won't reach those complications if we remain sincere. In short, enjoy the moment, ease off and let's analyze ourselves in the morning."

"Did you know that November is the second cloudiest month of the year?"

"My God, I'm sleeping with a meteorologist!" Sharon turned and her fist pounded the pillow, enough that their blanket slipped, exposing her breasts.

"I love you."

Her slapping over, she spoke with much affection, "My emotion as well, dear, I truly do. What's the first cloudiest month?"

Paul rolled on his stomach, laid his head on her chest, and both slept.

Sharon's bedroom measured twice as large as Paul's at KIDs. Pillows lay against the walls, the double mattress and box spring sat on the floor, and concrete blocks substituted for a night stand. Her room was on the east side of her house, meaning waking with the sunrise. But on Saturday morning, looking through the drapes Sharon saw an overcast sky with a misty rain falling.

"December is first." Paul rubbed his face. "This is a great bed you have here."

"Especially with two. Do you know the time's almost 10:30?"

"Are we driving to Allerton?" A yawning Paul held her waist.

Summer Never Comes

"The weather's drizzly, which makes for a soggy walk. The statues won't go anywhere if we don't show to check them out. What will we do all day?"

"We could pull a John and Yoko and stay in the rack, give peace a chance."

"I'm Catholic. The Virgin Mary wouldn't be benevolent to me if we did."

"What I said about sex as a crutch, when other parts of our relationship aren't working, I hope you don't think I'm ashamed over last night."

"Don't be silly," she sounded practical, "there's not a guy at this university frightened of taking a woman to bed."

"How do you figure that—a personal survey of campus males' lovemaking?"

"I enrolled in Health Ed 205 last year—the sex course—attended every lecture and read the book. Men's urge is satisfying and releasing anxieties, you love loving, can't have enough."

A bemused Paul listened to the howling wind.

"You've probably figured I'm basically a shy person, especially with women. I'm not the most romantic man around, haven't dated much in college and I'm stunned we're in your bedroom. I never had much chance with girls in high school either, my only dates were the junior and senior proms and both of those were set up by friends. In KIDs, there's always somebody to hang with, we always do things in groups and I've buddied around with Lindy. When you and I started going out, it was an eye-opening, idyllic experience. These two wonderful months are the longest I've dated a girl, I hope the next ones are as amazing."

A serene Sharon, cozy under the blankets, charmed listening to Paul's self-scrutiny, nudged nearer her boyfriend's body. "I'm positive the future will."

"You say the weather's rotten?"

"Yes, the hike at Allerton is out. Why not call your friend, Laurie, and drive to Charleston?"

"There are questions I could ask, particularly concerning Professor Gulley. But why travel forty miles in the rain, we could stay on the campus and study."

Summer Never Comes

"If you want an afternoon booking session, I can work on my Vet Med admissions forms."

"How's that progressing?"

"All I've done so far is line up people for letters of recommendation. But the application's seven or eight pages long—not a document to fill out at the last minute."

"When's the deadline?"

"Middle of January."

"Are you applying anywhere else besides the U of I?"

"Out of state is problematic. There are only two dozen vet colleges in the country and most, being state-subsidized like Illinois, give priority to their own residents. Champaign is my most realistic choice."

"What are your odds?"

"Three or four hundred apply each year, with sixty to seventy accepted."

"Stiff competition, but I have faith in you." Paul lifted his head off the pillow and concentrated on the clock, eleven a.m. "Time to say hello to the Big U."

"The University of Illinois is shut down today, out to lunch. What if we screw one more time?" Sharon scratched his back.

"Stop, I'm ticklish."

"Pauly is ticklish, Pauly is ticklish," she childishly repeated.

"Okay, retaliation time." He dove below the cover and bounced his girlfriend. The two wrestled, with Paul eventually surrendering and plopping to the mattress.

.

# # # #

Lindy's train ride was as uncrowded as Paul's the day before, but took forever traveling from Chicago and pulled into in Champaign three hours late. Even with the rain, he decided to hoof to KIDs instead of taking a taxi. He hurried through the streets, hop-scotching a puddle under the University Avenue viaduct. Crossing a footbridge, Lindy watched the eddies in the Boneyard Creek.

Summer Never Comes

Knowing how lonely the campus would be, he wished Em was with him. Lindy was flabbergasted she had left the campus with Bobby Sox last Sunday instead of marking time until their Monday night date. He really wanted to sit down to discuss the long and short of their relationship. Lindy had tried calling from his mom's home in Chicago but couldn't get Em on the phone and, admitting his neglecting her, accepted the snub.

Could he have avoided this mess, was he jumping over the side with Frogfeet? Kentucky and Robby hit on it before Thanksgiving. Shunting himself away he wasn't 'Lindy the good guy' anymore. What a shame. Before these last weeks, life had been a bed of roses with his friends in KIDs and especially Em. We were so, so close three months ago, now it's flying off and what's left is an empty, eggless nest. Was his behavior evidence for Professor Hudson's 'acceptable evil' theory? Can a bunch of wrongs make a right? Did this mean his band was bad?

From Lindy's viewpoint, there were excellent explanations for committing so much time to the group. As he told Paul, music was his career, just as soon start now. Performing onstage was valuable experience, that premier line on his résumé when he searched for jobs after graduation. And, not to sharpen the point too finely, the 'Feet needed all the jamming the five could manage. A doubting Thomas had only to check with Franky Konkel to know the importance of practice to a rock 'n' roll band.

"One more time, again, sharper, let's get it right."

Yet Lindy realized other parts of his life, friendships, reputation and scruples, were hurting, he was toying with fire working so much. Em and he were two ships passing in the night, talking but never listening, suspecting not solving, worrying not mending, and because of these missteps their love was wrecked. If he could only make her appreciate what the band meant, how big it was, ask her to wait a little longer, convince Em he wished to patch things up, return to the way there were. Why couldn't he do this? He didn't want to keep her at arm's length, he missed Em as badly as she pined for him. He only needed the time until the 'Feet were on their feet with a decent sound.

Reaching Frat Park, Lindy spied the KIDs house two blocks away. The ground was too muddy to cross and he stayed on the sidewalks.

That wasn't the story's only side. The days at home with his mom were two of only a few this semester he'd had enough sleep and plenty to eat. He didn't like living on four or five hours' rack time in Champaign, grumpy and hung over when waking up, he'd become a glutton for punishment. And he was falling behind, way back, with his booking. Finals were approaching and he had to play his cards right for a full hand of good grades.

Lindy had come down this Saturday to study. With a deserted campus tonight and tomorrow morning, he could write that finance class term paper and review those advertising articles. As he planned the booking to finish between now and Monday Lindy turned optimistic, deciding he could maneuver out of his pickle. If he was on an evil course, the riddle was evading the devil—no dead men's shoes for him.

Lindy neared KIDs. The only car in the lot was Moose's '68 Skylark which, due to a leaky water pump, hadn't moved since Columbus Day. The house was very cold, the only signs of activity the letters and newspapers on the floor underneath the mail chute, and he imagined he was the first one back. After unpacking, he dialed Franky's number on the hallway pay phone. Prior to Thanksgiving Lindy promised to check on the latest gig situation when he returned to Champaign, but had made the 'Feet's leader absolutely swear to no rehearsals, performances or rap sessions until the band's regular Tuesday night Red Lion appearance.

"Franky, what's tricks?… Yeah, real nice time at home, chowed like a horse, how 'bout you?… Yeah, yeah…I watched the Bears and Lions too, Butkus is such an animal, someone should clamp him in chains… So, the latest scoop?… What?… No, I really can't, I've got bookin' to tackle, all the crap that's piled on since September, including two term papers, honest… That's easy for you to say, you're not a student anymore… Repeat that number, how much money? Everyone's at your place right now? …But I thought we were off this week… I don't know, it could be tough, there's not much time left in the semester… I'm the only one draggin' my feet?… Well…why the hell not… Yeah, yeah, yeah, okay… Be there in forty-five minutes… Say hello to Andy."

# # # #

Following extra sex, Paul and Sharon rolled out of bed around two o'clock. At his girlfriend's prodding, Paul phoned Laurie Allman but talked to her father, who said Laurie and her mom had driven to Charleston and would be away until evening. After the call, the two walked to campus. The rain had stopped and was replaced by fog.

"The Library really is closed until Monday."

"The Union's always open, we can take over a lounge." They stood at the Undergrad's doors and Sharon sniffled in the chilly air. "I'm thinking about your story's anomalies. Laurie, a balloon, Professor Gulley, a book, UNITED orchestrating Camp's visit and too many student bodies. What if you searched for the connections between UNITED and this professor, something more than the 'concerned citizen' hypothesis?"

"That's my idea, but how to probe without raising suspicious?"

"You could tail Gulley and bug her office, find out her schedule and where she lives, see who she hangs around with and how she spends her free time. But there's only one of you, not the web of stalkers that shadowed Laurie. You'd spend your days following her, nights too, and we wouldn't get any sleep or other mattress stuff." The overcast covered the treetops with the sky so dark that, passing Davenport Hall, the two could not see the Administration Building across the Quad.

"Which would be a shame." Paul squeezed Sharon's hand. "But I want my investigation on a different level. Chasing Gulley assumes a plot and she's a suspect, which may or may not be the circumstance. Of course, I could check her History Department biography. Gulley's pretty young, I could get lucky and uncover a link—a thesis or articles she's written, where she lived during graduate school and other hobbies besides ballooning. Another person to investigate is Bernard Minerath. I wonder if his university records corroborate he's been in school as long as Laurie claims."

"Why that route, why not talk to him straight away?"

"I'll get there. Sensible journalism is preparation before interviewing, especially with someone so dogmatic as Bernard."

"I'm impressed." Sharon was pleased with their parallel reasoning.

"But this is uncomfortable. Digging for information is a job I've usually handled by spending time at the Library or the Urbana County Courthouse, paging through old records or newspaper files. Ferreting out conspiracies—and doing it fabricating my own deceptions—is unnerving.

"I feel like Stef Tianen. When Annie Curry convinced me to join the *Daily Illini's* staff, Stef was already there. From the first, everyone realized she was gung-ho, wanted to cover the sensational stories and, if there was any way to finagle it, have her byline on page one. For three years Stef worked more Saturdays and Sundays, wrote more exposés than any other reporter because she was determined to be named editor-in-chief. But besides her complete-the-mission willpower, there's the other side. If she had to, Stef would rationalize to herself and others her reasoning for grabbing assignments, claiming qualifications later turning out untrue. She'd sneak around campus for her stories; never landing in major trouble but should have a few times."

"Didn't the Illini Publishing Company make out her agenda?"

"This wasn't the first instance an egotistical student's promoted herself to win that job. Thinking it over, Stef was a smart choice. She's talented and the *Daily Illini's* a more organized, improved paper with her in charge. *Spectrum*, the weekend magazine, is an example." Paul paused on the south patio's steps. The fog was thicker, hiding Altgeld Hall. "But she succeeded the wrong way, by duping people; that's what's bothering. When uncertain, be truthful."

"Which is what you're working for this semester, resolving your questions about UNITED, searching for facts, accuracy, the greater good. And your motivation is different, you're following your conscience, the responsible path."

"Now you sound like Lindy's road metaphors."

"Is that helpful or bad?"

"Probably for the good. Nothing like morals walking the campus with you."

"An angel on your Illini sweatshirt."

"There's another concern, Stef's prodding me for updates. So far I've blown her off, but promised after the Camp visit we'd meet with Al Stojak, *Spectrum's* editor, to review my research. The appointment is this week."

"What will you tell her?"

"Caution says submit my work, see what the editor-in-chief judges significant, and wait for her to tell me what's next."

"Stef could say continue your investigating, wherever it leads. That's what a realistic—as you claim she is—newspaper person would do."

"What if Stef tells me to finish the story right now, even if I know there are loose ends? What if she reviews what I have and decides the premise is faulty, my investigation's full of mistakes and orders me to quit wasting time? Or if she takes my work and writes her own story? Any of these options is bad."

The two went inside to the Union's President's Lounge. The lighting was dim, some lamps—due to university economizing—without bulbs screwed in their sockets. A yawning Paul sat on a couch, shoes off, feet on a cushion. Sharon spread her Vet Med application on a corner table and, as beat as her boyfriend, propped her head on one arm. After an hour, she strolled toward Paul.

"Where've you been, stranger?" Sharon sat down and tickled his socks.

"Behave, this is the Union."

"We're the only ones here and not taking our clothes off," she raised her eyebrows, "yet."

"Do you always pay so much attention to your boyfriends?"

"Only those I downright care for." She ran a hand inside Paul's bellbottoms and massaged his shin.

"Now that booking's finished, what do we do with our evening?"

"Flick?"

"Everybody does that."

"Food?"

"We had a super late breakfast."

"How can I forget." Sharon poked Paul's ribs. "Bars?"

"Too early."

"Bed?"

He blushed.

"Goodness, we are choosy." She glanced at her wristwatch, 4:45, and grabbed his hand. "Which leaves the last option. On your feet, Paul Roberts, we'll travel a few blocks for something we both need."

Tying his shoes, he collected his books and followed his girlfriend. Walking south on Wright Street, Paul supposed Sharon might be taking him to the YMCA, but they passed that building. A second destination was the Library, but that was closed. At Armory Avenue they turned west, mingling with other students and faculty-looking types. Sharon was escorting him to St. John's Church for mass.

"You don't mind spiritual assistance, do you?"

"This will be the smallest congregation I've ever seen in this place."

Summer Never Comes

Entering the middle doors, Paul wished to sit underneath the choir loft in the last pew on the left, the corner the KIDs normally occupied. Sharon guided him up the center aisle, however, halfway to the sacristy. He knelt and concentrated on the crucifix. What a weekend—an abandoned campus, hanging with Sharon at her house—now religion.

Thank You, Lord, for this. I understand You won't appreciate me saying I'm grateful spending time with this girl, that You judge what we did last night wrong. But please consider my view. She's my cherished, intimate friend, and when I'm with her I feel lucky, not lonely, which to me is worth the world. As I said, I know You don't look kindly toward Sharon and me sleeping together, and I apologize. But is it really bad to make love with the one you love? All I know is this is wonderful, we are close, and I care for my girlfriend, I want to be with her. If our relationship's meant to be, Lord, please help it along. Amen.

"Ex-cuse me. Move oveh, please."

"Kentucky," Paul grinned, "unbelievable."

"An' why not?" He sat in the pew and looked past Paul to Sharon. "How-deh, cousin."

"Hello, James."

"Good evening," the priest announced, "let us prepare for the coming of our Lord God to us tonight."

Since the regular student choir members were gone this weekend, there was no music and Mass quickly moved along.

"The gospel is from Matthew.

"'For it is like a man going abroad on a journey, who called his servants and handed over his goods to them. To one he gave five talents, to another two, and to another one, each according to his particular ability. And he who had received the five talents went and traded them, and gained five more. In like manner, he who received the two gained two more. But he who had received the one dug in the earth and hid his master's money.

"'After a long time the master of those servants returned and settled accounts with them. He who had received the five talents came and brought five other talents, saying, "Master, thou didst hand over to me five talents; behold, I have gained five others in addition." His master said to him, "Well done, good and faithful servant; because thou hast been faithful over a few things, I will set thee over many; enter into the joy of thy master." And he who had received the two talents came and said, "Master, thou didst hand over to me two talents; behold, I have gained two more." His master said to him, "Well done, good and faithful servant; because thou hast been faithful over a few things, I will set thee over many."

"'But he who had received the one talent came and said, "Master, I know that thou art a stern man; thou reapest where thou hast not sown and gathered where thou hast not winnowed; and as I was afraid, I went away and hid thy talent in the earth; behold, thou hast what is thine." His master said to him, "Wicked and slothful servant! Thou didst know that I reap where I do not sow and gather where I have not winnowed? Thou shouldst therefore have entrusted my money to the bankers, and on my return I should get back my own with interest. Take away therefore the talent from him, and give it to him who has ten talents. For to everyone who has shall be given, and he shall have abundance; but from him who does not have, even that which he seems to have shall be taken away. But for the unprofitable servant, cast him forth into the darkness outside, where there will be weeping and gnashing of teeth."'

"This is the gospel of our Lord."

Sharon, Paul and Kentucky exited St. John's together.

"Wall, a hap-peh Thanksgiving t' you both."

"Likewise. When did you come back to Champaign?"

"Thes afteh-noon. Had a right-fine time back home, even if thes is a Yankee holiday. Mah mommeh and daddeh ask t' be remembered t' you, cousin."

"They are well?"

"Ver-eh much so. How long have you two bin on campus?"

"Since yesterday," Paul nervously answered, envisioning Kentucky gossiping over his staying with Sharon this weekend.

"What are you doing for supper, James?"

"Ah did reckon on headin' t' th' Steak 'n Shake on Green Street, thet may be one o' th' few places open to-night."

"Why don't you join us?" Sharon held Paul's arm. "We're cooking at my house."

Paul fretted and shifted on his legs.

"Thet is a right-generous invite, cousin, an' thank you, but Ah imagine Ah'll mosey-on mah way. An' Ah'll see you to-morrow, Robbeh." The southerner strolled toward Sixth Street as Paul and Sharon walked in the opposite direction.

"A shame James didn't accept our invitation, sometimes he is stubborn. You wanted him to eat with us, didn't you?"

"Of course, he's a fraternity brother," Paul sounded annoyed.

"I don't believe you."

"Truthfully, I'm glad he passed. Nothing against your cousin, Kentucky is my good friend too, but after tonight everybody returns to the campus, we won't be alone and I won't have you to myself."

Sharon studied his lost-puppy face. "I agree, I invited James because he's family and would have been insulted if I hadn't. He's realist enough to understand our relationship; I was fairly certain he'd decline."

Paul was relieved. His gamble with a candid answer had succeeded. For dinner, Sharon fried hamburgers, boiled macaroni, and mixed in American cheese—a basic student meal—remarking her cousin likely ate better at the Steak 'n Shake. The dishes in the sink, the pair laid by the fireplace with their wine.

"What did you think tonight's gospel meant?" He peered at the jumping flames through his glass.

Eyes shut, feet close to the hearth, Sharon's head rested on Paul's stomach. "The guys with the talents? Do your best in life."

"Did you notice the reading's tone? As if God were saying you better make certain you work with what you've got, or there'll be 'gnashing of teeth' for a person not busting some ass."

Sharon laughed at his interpretation of Matthew. "And accurate; an individual should strive to improve. Hiding is wasting ability."

"In this parable, the two servants that did right by their master were awarded with more responsibility. 'Good job, don't stop now, do it again, no time off.' There is such a thing as accomplishing too much and going too far with duty. What's the logic in receiving extra tasks if you've already finished your share? After a while, when you've proved yourself, worked hard enough for other people or earned enough profit, the reward should be to kick back, enjoy a vacation, have a good time. But the gospel lectures you must continue and never quit."

"Explore that theory for a moment." Sharon sipped her wine. "You begin with certain abilities. After a time you increase them to a higher step, your new norm. To improve again you must pass this second level, reaching a third, a fourth and so on, or you're not using what you previously developed. If you let down, you've copped out."

"There must be a threshold when you've achieved enough, where you don't have to put out anymore and get a break."

"I'm curious, what's yours?"

"I don't think I've reached it."

She kissed Paul. "When you do, dear, let me know."

# # # #

Tim Malito had enjoyed his three days at home. His mom fixed his favorite foods, he racked out until noon, played basketball with his younger brothers, and hooked up with Katy Karas one night in Chicago. On Sunday when Tim's parents drove him and Ron Gimbel back to Champaign, they ate dinner at the Boar's Head Restaurant, his Dad's treat. This was curious, since his parents typically dropped him off at KIDs' door and right away departed.

By the evening, all the KIDs had returned, the heat was dialed up and stereos blasted. Nobody bothered studying, so the night dissolved into partying and rapping in somebody else's room. Feet propped on his desk, listening to the Doobie Brothers through his headphones, Stu gazed out the window, daydreaming about Joyce. Without warning, the volume jumped to ten and he tore off the headset.

"Son of a bitch, why'd you do that?"

"You looked too restful, and don't call me names." Bobby Sox stood in the doorway with his duffle bag. "Anyone else around?"

"Haven't seen Lindy or Paul, but Scooter blew through twenty minutes ago on his way to Lauren's apartment for his nightly shack up. How was your weekend?"

"Great, as always," Bobby cockily responded.

"Get a kiss from Jeannie?"

"At least."

"Glad hearing that. Who was in your car on the way down?"

"My only passenger was Emily." Bobby shook his head. "She's one puzzled girl, Lindy providing the confusing. I heard the entire lowdown, how in September Emily looked forward to school, a lot more than her freshman and sophomore years because she and Lindy would be together, and how happy she was the first weeks when they were hanging out. Back then, Emily talked about wishing Lindy would take their friendship up a notch."

"As in engagement or marriage?"

"Sounds off the wall for Lindy, but that was Emily's hope."

"Mister Roberts, welcome back," Stu raised his arms.

"Thank you, thank you." A smiling Paul dropped his suitcase next to Bobby's bag.

"How was the old holiday?"

"Weekend's been outstanding, unbeatable," Paul sounded surprisingly animated to his friends.

"Sure are a lot of people around here bragging about their great weekends."

"Don't worry," Bobby consoled his roommate, "your time's comin'."

"I had a typical vacation, just not fantastic."

"When's Lindy supposed to show?"

"Don't know," Paul answered, "I didn't talk to him before we left on Wednesday. Did you bring Emily back with you, Bobby?"

"As I was sayin', she's totally ticked at your roommate. Emily said her good times ended when Lindy found Frogfeet, and described the autumn as downhill from that day, dumped in a hole with no out. Emily told me about the canceled dates, Lindy's alibis, the promises he's broken, the peace rally and basketball game lie, how she knows his ego is somewhere else when he's with her. After every screw-up he apologizes and guarantees to repent, but runs away as soon as the band phones. He better be careful or it'll be all she wrote between them."

"I only knew about his Homecoming no show."

"That was the first and worst, but not the only. He's stuck it to her for two months, which is why Emily drove home with me last Sunday. Lindy rescheduled their date last weekend when he bolted with Frogfeet to play in Decatur."

"Sounds how he's acting with us. Lindy hasn't been himself since September, so wrapped up in his music. He's never here, never sits and chews the rag, when he is in the house he's half-asleep."

Summer Never Comes

"But Emily's not ready to quit on him, "Bobby added, "she still hopes Lindy breaks out of his one-track mind. If Emily felt she could trust him, she'd take him back in a second."

Stu replaced albums and dropped the needle on Bread's 'The Guitar Man.'

"Poor Lindy, I hope he sets himself straight."

"I don't feel sorry for him," Stu put on his earphones, "he probably had a great weekend, too, whatever he did."

# # # #

"Welcome back," Nicole Liftuss sat their dorm room.

"How was your vacation?" Emily laid her luggage next to the closet.

"As fair a time as possible for four days in Springfield."

"And the brothers and sisters?"

"All still at home." The oldest from a family of eight children, Nicole considered college an escape from Sangamon County.

"Have I had any calls?"

"None. Did you expect he might?"

"It would have been nice, maybe he'll still phone tonight."

"Perhaps, Emily, but it seems Lindy's been 'maybe calling' for the last few months."

"Maybe a maybe is better than a never."

"You have a lot of patience, more than I would have if Lindy were my boyfriend. All this maybe stuff would make me insane. How do you do it?"

"Maybe I do, maybe I don't."

> What thou seest when thou dost wake,
> Do it for thy true-love take,
> Love and languish for his sake.

Chapter Eleven

On Monday the temperature dropped to freezing, with the weekend's drizzle becoming sleet. By noontime steps, sidewalks, and the Alma Mater Statue were sheathed in ice. Even with walking and driving dangerous, students still biked on their ten-speeds around campus.

"Whoa, this is a terrifying trip," Mary O'Donnell yelled, "classes should be canceled for days like this."

"Unlikely, weather never shuts the university down." With her body rigid, Sharon made short steps as the housemates warily hiked to the Chem Annex and their physiology lecture.

Mary gripped her friend's shoulder. "How was your Thanksgiving weekend?"

"I drove back Friday morning and met Paul at the Illinois Central station. We were the only ones around, though we ran into my cousin on Saturday. I appreciate you and everyone else staying away as long as you did."

"Did the scheme work, did he move in for two nights?" Mary slipped again.

"He enjoyed not traveling between Urbana and Champaign."

"What about the sexy love affair? Did you shack up in your room, or is your boyfriend as bashful as we assumed?"

"Paul is self-conscious, wants a fun time but holds back, perceptive but prefers the middle of the crowd." Sharon shifted to the grass and the bumpier ice. "I'm not talking about this weekend because the evenings turned out nicely physical and stimulating, thank you very much. The old Taylor charm is opening him up."

"I never thought you'd hit on the quiet type, sitting around watching the tube and meditating with a wall flower." Mary skated on the sidewalk.

Summer Never Comes

"You exaggerate so. Like the rest of us girls, I'm mellowing. We've had our chaos, now it's time for peace. Paul's low key, has a sense of good and bad, that's his best quality."

"What's the meaning of good? To talk with, hold your hand, wet, slobbering, kisses, yanking your clothes off, lighting you up on the mattress?"

"Mary, we've known each other long enough to be straight on that subject." She ducked her head to miss a low-with-ice tree limb.

"A good man is a catch, even if it doesn't fit your image." The two stepped to the street, which was slushy but easier walking.

# # # #

Sharon's hometown, Lake Bluff, on Lake Michigan's shore line, with backyards and blocks of tall trees, was comfortable, congenial and overlooked. A dozen shops occupied the one-street business district, and the junior high was near enough to her parents' house on Evanston Avenue that the four Taylor sisters walked to school every day. The village's big event was the annual Fourth of July parade, bringing in fire trucks and marching bands from neighboring cities along with squads of sailors stationed at the Great Lakes Naval Training Center in North Chicago.

For twenty-two years her dad had worked as an information systems manager for a Loop advertising agency, wore a suit, rode the North Shore Railway and, like his daughters, walked to the station. Her mom cleaned, cooked, contributed to these and those charities, chatted with friends in the afternoons and, when Sharon's younger sisters started first grade, found a part-time job. This upset the girls because they were devoted to their mom and not having her home all the time would be strange.

Lake Bluff was too small for a high school so Sharon, like her older sister, Michelle, started as a freshman at Lake Forest High School. She rode the bus, which was different, studied more, which was fine, liked her classes, especially biology, and met new friends, all of whose families seemed to have more money and lived a notch grander than the Lake Bluff kids. But most of her classmates weren't snotty and Sharon fit in. She was happy with her family and school, assured in her young life.

Summer Never Comes

And she found a boyfriend. Johnny Olson lived in Lake Forest. Sharon's age, dark-haired with sideburns, ordinarily serious and restrained, the two were in the same freshman classes. His family owned a fish canning business in Chicago where Johnny worked on weekends and summers. He played, according to his buddies, not a bad game of golf and drove a knockout car, an orange Oldsmobile Cutlass convertible. Sharon's family, especially her dad, got along with Johnny when he came for supper. Generous, well-mannered, informed on many subjects, he never controlled a conversation. Johnny joked with her siblings and found them dates; liked movies with twisting plots, Italian restaurants, cold beer, rock concerts, and hunted for unique places to take Sharon. Lake Geneva, Wisconsin, was their favorite. The two went steady from their sophomore year, and by the junior prom, the first night they slept together, Sharon imagined marrying Johnny, settling in pleasant Lake Bluff or fancier, richer Lake Forest and continuing the cozy life she'd known so far.

But things happened.

Her mom came down with a chest cold which turned into pneumonia, so sick she quit her part-time secretary job at the car dealership, dire enough that after a week of lying around the house she spent five days in a hospital. Their dad came home on earlier trains, the family ate more TV dinners and pot pies, everyone took turns washing clothes, and their Aunt Frances, cousin James' mother, drove from Kentucky to help. The four sisters were frightened their mom might die, greatly relieved when she recovered, and through the emergency Sharon learned she could act like an adult—do her part, be responsible.

Next, Johnny disappeared for a week early in the summer, skipped town, and none of his golfing pals had a clue where he went. It wasn't as if he'd stood up Sharon or broken dates because they hadn't made any for the time he went missing. Johnny schemed to keep those days blank, she later figured. Towards the end of the week, when Sharon was genuinely worried, she decided to phone his family to find out if he was all right. But Johnny called before Sharon, saying he was home and would she like to go for a ride? He arrived in Lake Bluff fifteen minutes later, convertible top down, and they drove off. Johnny apologized for being gone but never told Sharon where he'd been or what he did, and guessed—anticipated—she wouldn't ask. He restarted their friendship right where he'd left it, considerate when they went out, talked over their future, and spent a whole afternoon playing Chinese checkers with her recuperating mom. For the rest of the summer, Sharon's boyfriend was as affable as before the mystery.

Sharon went along for a while, accepting Johnny's return, mainly because he was the same gentleman as always, didn't do more goofy stuff and none of their high school friends knew more about his lost week than she. By the Fourth of July parade, however, an epiphany struck. First Mom, next Johnny. Reality lobbed curves, the world wasn't the steadfast place she supposed, there wasn't a predictable refuge, a forever cocoon. Life was challenging, with unknowns, hard times, and to meet it she resolved to grow up.

Instead of living at home after high school graduation and, as her parents advised, enrolling in secretary and stenography courses at a local junior college, Sharon decided to go away, be the first of the Taylor sisters to attend a four-year university, find a career, aim for independence. This shocked the family. Even her dad, considered by everyone a very intelligent man, had not earned a degree before starting his job. They argued with Sharon that leaving was a major step, maybe delaying and working for a year would be more sensible than applying to schools hundreds of miles away or in a different state. Sharon listened but didn't back down. She dearly loved her family, no doubt would miss her mom, dad and sisters, and the whimsy of a wealthy husband like Johnny was appealing. But like many adolescents, she wanted to take in the college scene, find her way, contribute and see if there was more.

When Sharon talked with Johnny, he ran through the predictable rationales to persuade her to remain in Lake Bluff: the two of them were close and should stay together, there were plenty of fun times ahead, he'd always spend money on her, and was sorry if anything he'd done caused her to leave. But Sharon sensed the insincerity, Johnny acted a not-so-convincing performance. Which confirmed her intuition, breaking up and going away to college was okay.

At the University of Illinois she majored in biology and became tight, true friends with six girls in her science classes. As sophomores, Sharon, Julie, Angie, Maureen Danaher, Karen, Audrey and Mary O'Donnell rented the California Avenue house and stayed together through their senior year. The women were supportive, scrupulously hardworking, hard-core, kindhearted, occasionally outrageous, certain college was a trip and believed life in the new decade, the '70s, was a phenomenon to hit on, not wait for. The housemates copied out notes, prepped for quizzes, researched term papers, dissected guinea pigs, crammed for hourlies and nailed down excellent grades. When classes were done, however, after the girls finished for the night or week, they had an awfully rowdy, helluva time. Multi-course dinners, all-night keggers, lava lamps and scented candles, bongs carved from Idaho potatoes, marijuana on the porch, weeks without wearing bras, men in and out of the house. Julie exercised so they jogged and played handball in Huff Gym, Maureen loved writing poetry and the seven consumed nights and bottles of wine critiquing her sonnets, Angie found a sweetheart and the girls plotted to hurry the engagement. They biked to Rantoul, collected old clothes for a north Champaign Baptist church, were weekend regulars at Barnett's Liquors, and helped clean up a neighbor's yard when she was sick in bed for a fortnight. Two or three times they roguishly played to some guy's ego, luring him to thinking he was the center of the universe, the darling of one housemate's life, then playfully, pitilessly trashed his self-esteem. As juniors, and coordinating with The International Female's Union for Freedom through Peace, the seven arranged a two-day seminar on gender issues which was attended by two hundred fifty students and faculty, earning an admiring article in the *Daily Illini* and a letter of appreciation from the chancellor's office. Once a year the girls hosted a weekend get-together for their families, scrubbed the john, hid the liquor, wore dresses and cooked a gourmet meal. Part-time jobs, lovers to swap and compare, White Lightning punch to concoct, volunteering at local charities, taboos to ignore, figuring class schedules and typing lab results, chugging through happy hours, nude sunbathing in the backyard, final exams to ace; everything was experienced, tackled, accomplished, with Sharon as realistic, idealistic and wild as her housemates.

 And she absolutely adored, utterly dug sex. After the humdrum, unadventurous but I want to hump Johnny Olson, Sharon found her hippie, screwball, free love generation arousing, amusing, satisfying, affectionate; physical, often reckless, sometimes shameful; randy and once scandalous. She didn't have a new lover every night, but for three years she wasn't shy about meeting friend of a friend and hauling him back to the house, or picking up guys in the bars who couldn't remember her name the next morning. Maureen mused that she topped the charts, Karen was envious and Audrey sorted through the leftovers. But Sharon didn't throw herself at men or consider herself a whore. Sex reached, no connected with, what her friends did, enjoy life.

These were Sharon's Illinois years. With her girlfriends, she maxed out work and pleasures, pulled a 4.60 grade point, ate up Cham-Bana's frolicking and reckoned she didn't miss much of college. Thanks to the Camaro her dad bought her, she drove to Lake Bluff often enough to keep up with family gossip. Her healthy-again mom returned to the part-time job; Michelle married Marty, her teenage sweetheart, worked as a secretary and saved to buy a house; her twin sisters graduated from eighth grade; and Johnny Olson got engaged to the blonde bombshell from their high school class, the babe with the biggest boobs. All these hometown happenings upheld her earlier decision to move away. As much as she loved her family, Sharon was glad living somewhere else, doing her own thing.

By spring of junior year, Sharon and her housemates recognized change was coming: the heavy rap sessions, the all-night booking, quarter-beer and dime-hot dog happy hours, sex with whoever whenever wouldn't last—none of them would stay twenty-one. She wasn't bored, blasé or beat down, only aware moving on was closing in. As in high school, even with applying to veterinary school, the moment was now for decisions, the next steps, the future. This time reassessing was easier because her dearest friends were in the same spot, what to do with your life? In others ways it was tougher because the consequences cost more, were long-term or unknown. There were fewer wild parties and more girls-only discussions by the fireplace, less drinking and more reflection, as much loving but also laying in bed at three in the morning, contemplating graduation with a Bachelor of Science degree.

Sharon had no regrets. If only ninety-eight percent proud of her undergrad days, the victories and earned self-esteem, the havoc the housemates instigated, her sensible, bantering, promiscuous persona, she was certainly satisfied Champaign-Urbana had been rollicking—a blast—semester after semester of not-to-miss partying, episodes and affairs to retell and never forget, enriching, heartwarming. Trusted friendships, self-confidence, a half-dozen disappointments but no shame, and time to move on again.

Summer Never Comes

# # # #

Associated Press – Saigon – Unnamed State Department sources confirm four cabinet members of President Nguyen Van Thieu's government have pled guilty to embezzling United States foreign aid monies into their private bank accounts. These South Vietnamese officials have resigned their posts, and with their families, have been allowed to emigrate to the United States. The disclosures culminate a six-month investigation by two American news organizations.

# # # #

Sleet stopped falling by dinnertime, the clouds cleared and the temperature dropped to the twenties. The slushy puddles froze solid and travel was as hazardous in the evening as during the day.

"Do you figure, buddy, we'll be on time?" Killer asked as he and Randy Miller skated on Fifth Street.

"Bernard's meetings always begin at 7:30; if we hurry, we should make it with five minutes to spare."

"Well, let's get a move on!" Killer declared in his half-conversational, semi-screaming voice.

"I think you'll get into this, UNITED's taking off since Camp's humiliation two weeks ago." Missing a foothold in the ice, Randy bent both his knees to keep from tumbling.

"That's what opened my eyes, yessir, it's time everybody proceeded to throw in their share. Yep, 'tis the season." Killer slapped his hands together.

"Glad hearing you say so, only the moment's way overdue. All of us should have recognized years ago how the Washington warmongers were scheming to continue on in Vietnam as long as they could. We should have known and stopped them. This isn't the first time politicians duped the country into a worthless war and it won't be the last. But if we come together, really raise total hell and show the reactionaries they can't trick us citizens all the time, we'll make it a lot harder for them to screw us again."

"That's the spirit!" Killed shouted.

Summer Never Comes

The Union's hallways were uncommonly jammed, Randy assuming films playing in the ballrooms or an ice cream special in the Cafeteria. The two KIDs and dozens of students climbed the stairs, with just as many descending. In the corridor he spotted a crowd around Rooms 269–273, UNITED's usual meeting place. A note taped to the door read "Tonight's Scheduled Session Moved to Illini Room B." Five minutes later, with Mike Sweeney, they entered the brightly-lit ballroom with its ornate ceiling, parquet floor and rows of chairs facing a long banquet table.

"There must be three or four hundred people in here," Killer complained, "and what the crap, every seat's taken."

"This is great, the best attendance ever." Randy watched Bernard and a knot of True Believers standing in the front.

"You know, pal, these aren't all undergrads, there's old farts in here."

"I'd say they more resemble professors and instructors, Killer."

Bernard stepped to the lectern exactly at half past seven. Tacked to the wall behind him was a brand-new, orange banner the size of a bed sheet with 'UNITED' printed in black letters in the middle. As scores more students boisterously crowded in, Bernard stared at the latecomers, remaining silent until the gathering quieted. One of the last to show was Paul, who stood by the door.

"Good evening. The advertisements discussed at the last meeting have been placed with the *Daily Illini* and will commence running this weekend. The announcements will stress UNITED's achievements this semester and explain our upcoming plans. The main focus of the ads is the membership drive. The objective is to reach all on the campus and to recruit them to the cause. By the numbers present tonight, it is apparent this message is coming across. We must continue these efforts. Beginning this week, a program will be instituted in which our organization's members will go out in teams to all," Bernard emphasized the adjective, "all dormitories, fraternities, sororities and sundry housing units to explain UNITED's mission and enroll more comrades."

Randy saw a raised arm near the front, which Bernard disregarded.

"There will be six members in each cadre. Our Board of Directors will supervise the groups and be the primary speakers, others will handle question-and-answer sessions and the enlistment paperwork. Each conscription meeting will have a quota. Current UNITED members will be contacted to schedule sessions for your residences." Bernard drew a line on his paper. "Second. The daily membership drive will continue and expand to all the Quad's classroom buildings with designated recruiting teams for each. This has yielded acceptable results, which optimistically can be increased."

This idea sounded familiar to Randy—basically the one he'd proposed three weeks ago. Again, he saw questioning hands ignored by Bernard.

"UNITED will also institute a faculty recruitment program. Some professors have come forward to work on this aspect of the membership drive. It is expected that current UNITED members will volunteer the needed assistance."

Randy interpreted the murmurs as approving of these new efforts. He glanced at a vigorously nodding Killer and a curious Paul studying Bernard.

"The next topic is December's major project, a food drive to benefit the people of Vietnam. Beginning one week from today, UNITED will locate collection stations around the campus to accept donations of canned and packaged foods which will be shipped to Saigon prior to the university's Christmas vacation. The drive's purpose will be highlighting the fact that the Vietnamese population's well-being can be affected in positive, humane ways—a counterbalance to Air Force bombing sorties and Marine search-and-destroy missions. There are sign-up sheets at the front of the room for those wanting to volunteer. Though not mandatory, it is expected everyone will contribute time to this project."

The meeting continued with Bernard covering eight additional issues. Five or six attendees Randy recognized as regulars raised their hands and one or two in the crowd stood to interrupt for questions. They were ignored, hushed up or pulled down to their seats by the True Believers.

"In closing," Bernard announced at 9:30, "I remind you the plans outlined tonight are not uncomplicated. They will require time and the forfeit of activities and diversions we appreciate and enjoy. But our goal is the noblest our generation will ever attempt, the worthiest challenge we may confront. To end a war criminally brought on by the Washington government. To end a war which, in the last decade, has torn this country apart. To end a corrupting war that has claimed tens of thousands of lives in Southeast Asia, and has wounded us so much. This is our mission, one we shall complete by any measures required. And when this insurrection is over, we shall have peace. Peace in Vietnam, Cambodia, Laos and Thailand—

regions knowing only fighting for thirty-odd years. And peace in our country and the world, so that the new order of reason, understanding, cooperation and centralism may rule. This is our task. We labor for its achievement."

The Illini Room B crowd applauded. A few UNITED members walked toward Bernard for questions or to shake his hand. They were stopped by the board of directors stepping between him and the crowd. The directors pointed the students toward the long table with sign-up sheets for the membership campaign and the food drive. The True Believers dutifully wrote in their names. An unsmiling Bernard remained behind the podium, surveying the scene.

"Paul," Randy shouted over the growing clapping, "glad you made it."

"Interesting evening, sounds like the coming weeks are set for Champaign and Urbana." They were amidst the students filing out the exit.

"We keep making our mark. There's plenty of work, but when it's finished we'll be better off."

"I'm uncertain about that." He was slapped on the back.

"My old pal, Pauly Roberts. How ya doin', amigo?"

"What's up, Killer?"

"Well, I'm in UNITED, yep, registered and received my membership card. Got to end the war, you know."

"And joining UNITED helps?" Paul sounded skeptical.

"If everyone does," Randy replied. "Involvement is what's needed. If the entire student body mobilized, we'd really shake up the country. That's the only way the war will end—when the government grasps we're against them and Vietnam."

The three KIDs followed the crowd into the hallway, pausing at the Check Cashing Window.

"No doubt about it, we've got to do our part." Killer raised a fist in the air.

"You were right about Bernard, he's totally business, never smiled all night," Paul said to Randy. "What about those guys up in front with him? They looked like bodyguards."

"You mean the board of directors. Bernard can't run UNITED by himself, especially as we enlist more recruits."

"I was surprised by the numbers that showed."

Summer Never Comes

"There's passion for finally finishing with Vietnam."

"Come on, peace!" Killer yelled, attracting the attention of passersby in the hallway.

"Come on, peace," the students repeated, as if the whole Union was chanting.

"Come-on-PEACE."

"Come-ON-PEACE."

"COME-ON-PEACE!" the mantra roared over and over.

"The masses are speaking," an excited Randy declared, "the campus is staying involved."

"With one voice," a cynical Paul commented.

Killer left his fraternity brothers to join an impromptu parade through the Union. Four UNITED members grabbed the meeting's orange and black banner and carried the flag in the procession.

Paul watched the hundreds of long-haired, bellbottomed students troop around with the standard. They weaved into the South Lounge, waking the nappers, passed the administrative offices, the distinguished alumni's portraits and the Vending Machine Room in the east corridor, wound by the north entrance, interrupting work at the Reception Desk, turned the corner and stomped toward the Check Cashing Window. The demonstration made two more circuits, attracting loafing undergrads, with Killer and Randy marching near the banner. Also in the crowd were UNITED's directors, the True Believers, and one person Paul hoped he would spot tonight. Professor Antoinette Gulley tramped around, talking to other faculty, hair pulled back, wearing her gym shoes.

Peace was popular in the Union.

Paul slid down Wright Street returning to KIDs. The night sky was moonlit and the sidewalks totally slick. A biker zipped by on the icy path.

\# \# \# \#

Common for winter and university buildings, cold weather meant stuffier, uncomfortable temperatures in Illini Hall's basement. *Daily Illini* reporters opened windows, typed their stories in short-sleeve shirts and clamped fans on their desks to circulate air. Stef Tianen's office, with two steam radiators, was the warmest room of all.

Summer Never Comes

"Ready for our leader?" A cigarette smoking Al Stojak propped his feet on the desk.

Paul sat in a second chair, holding a manila folder full of photocopied newspaper articles and scribbled notes. "Here's what I've got on the anti-war movement. I hope it makes sense."

"I'm sure there's enough for *Spectrum*." Regarded as the most laid-back *DI* staffer, Stoj was exceedingly caring of fellow reporters, forever offering favors, and always meeting deadlines. His obsessions were intramural athletics and U of I varsity basketball, with an absolute recall of team records since the Fighting Illini started playing collegiate sports. How these traits earned him the weekend magazine editor's assignment was a mystery to the paper's staff. "Stef told me you've been on this since September."

"The project's complex; like many investigations, my digging was more tangled than I suspected."

"Newspaper work isn't a straight line, I know, especially with different sources and figuring the truth." Stoj shifted his feet, shunting aside a pair of swimming goggles. "But now that you're finished, we can organize your material for the magazine. That's what we're here for, right?"

"I don't catch your meaning."

"Stef told me this is a wrap session, to decide on a publishing date, and estimate the space to give it in *Spectrum*."

Paul fretted. When the editor-in-chief called to schedule this meeting she'd mentioned nothing about writing the article. Stoj's comment indicated as much: that his assignment was over—the fear Paul had discussed with Sharon last weekend. Maybe ending right now is shrewder, he mused, the inconsistencies I've uncovered will open eyes if Stef lets me compose the piece that way—contradictory. But I'm certain there's more to UNITED. Should I acquiesce—argue for extra time or stymie as I did two weeks ago in the Union?

"What's in your research, Paul? Over the phone Stef wouldn't talk specifics, as if she didn't know herself." Stoj puffed smoke rings into the air.

"That's my fault, Stef's repeatedly asked about my investigation the last two months, but I've kept this to myself."

"Strange, our editor-in-chief operating that way, she's normally hands-on with the paper's business." For the first time this conversation, Stoj sounded engaged instead of indifferent.

Summer Never Comes

Should I brief him, Paul brooded, on UNITED's peculiarities and my suspicions? Where would I begin? Maybe I can use Stoj as an ally. Arguing with Stef the two of us can wear her down, convince her to give me more time if I want it. Would Stoj go along?

"Sorry I'm late, guys." Wearing sweats and panting, Stef rushed into the office. "I'm in a handball tournament at the IMPE Building. My match took six tie-breakers to win and I'm scheduled for the semi-finals in thirty minutes. So what have we got here? Have you finally come clean, Paul, and covered your story with Stoj? What's your opinion, is it what we want, sound reporting but sympathetic to the peace crowd? Settle on a title and length? I hope you have because time's tight this afternoon, we've got to hurry this along."

"Just getting into it." Stoj yanked his feet from the desk.

"Super, because anything you've received from our Mr. Roberts is more than I've learned the last few weeks." Stef wiped her forehead with a towel. "What do you think?"

Straightening up, Stoj's cigarette fell to the floor. Before answering, he bent over to salvage the butt. A resigned Paul squirmed in his chair, opting to yield.

"Actually, content doesn't matter, I'm sure whatever Paul's pulled together so far is fine. Bottom line is I'm postponing his UNITED piece in *Spectrum*—now's not the favorable moment." She dried her forehead again.

Neither Stoj nor Paul fathomed how Stef could reverse her mind on a subject both considered settled. Stoj took it in stride, happy concurring with his boss, unbothered she was supervising his magazine. Paul was totally relieved. By some rationale his story was saved.

"When will the article run?"

"I'm thinking after semester break—February or March—to allow events time to develop. That's what I assume you want; correct, Paul?" She grabbed her duffle bag and started for the door. "I'm really sorry we can't sit here but I've got to hustle back to my tournament. If you want, why don't you two stay and assess Paul's work, see what the *DI's* treading into, and leave me a heads up. Later."

Stoj and Paul stared at each other.

"If that's what Stef thinks, who am I to disagree?"

Summer Never Comes

\# \# \# \#

"Long time, no see, lover." Sharon stooped over and kissed a sprawled-on-the-floor Paul.

"Seventy-two hours, don't know if I could survive another twenty-four."

"Flattery will carry you everywhere, dear." She dropped her books and sat by her boyfriend. "Anything new in life?"

"Not much, except falling on my buns four or five times sliding around our campus."

"Who didn't, this much ice is dangerous stuff." Sharon rubbed his knees. "Yesterday coming back from classes Mary dumped into a puddle outside our house. She was irate."

"The smartest thing I saw was a guy tramping through the slush in a pair of golf shoes."

"With the tiny metal spikes on the bottoms? Wonder what he did when he entered a building." Sharon grabbed her book bag. "Shall we hit them?"

"Not yet, it's early," Paul apologetically held her back, "besides, I haven't talked to you in three days."

"If you insist." Sharon relaxed. "How is your roommate?"

"Lindy returned to Champaign on Saturday. Ironic, he and I were on campus early and neither knew the other's whereabouts."

"We were here Friday, what's the big deal? If we'd have seen him in church along with my cousin, then you'd have bizarre."

"There was no chance of that. After arriving, Lindy learned Frogfeet had a gig lined up in Bloomington-Normal. The band drove off, performed, and that night on the return trip their equipment van had a flat tire. They didn't make it back to the U of I until late Sunday. He was supposed to book for two days to catch up but now is farther behind."

"Tough break with the mechanical problem, but your roommate can always study. This is only early December, finals are a month away." Sharon shoved her feet into the hallway.

"Lindy's not some genius coasting for the rest of the year. He's an average student who's sloughed off since September with plenty of school work left to complete. For him it's not 'finals are still a month off,' more like 'they're not far away.'"

Summer Never Comes

"My point is, the semester's salvageable. If Lindy's as insightful as you maintain, he'll buckle down and raise his grades to where he needs them. Until then, I'm crediting him for sticking with his music. Persistence is commendable."

"Perhaps you're right, Lindy will work it out." Avoiding quarreling, Paul brushed her blonde hair. "Next Wednesday we're having a party for Frogfeet at the Red Lion, Shaky Jake is corralling everybody to lend Lindy's band some support. Want to come?"

"Say again? One second you're complaining Lindy's blowing off booking, the next you're inviting me to the bars on a school night for his band."

"I'll concede the thin consistency, but the fraternity's aiding a brother, a 'Students for Frogfeet' movement."

"I doubt that phrase will rival UNITED for the undergrad's sympathies."

"As do I, but this is a total college idea, good times drinking with the KIDs party mongers." Paul became serious, "I went to another UNITED meeting two nights ago."

"Did you enlist?" she joked.

"No, but I saw Professor Gulley."

"The concerned citizen." Sharon looked at her preoccupied boyfriend. "What's the problem? Did she wiggle out from under her rock and speak and implicate herself, or worse, argue against radicalism and the peace movement?"

"Gulley's involvement was carrying a sign in the crowd. She didn't talk; no one spoke, as a matter of fact, except Bernard Minerath."

"Is that unusual? He's UNITED's leader."

"Here's a ballroom in the Union, packed with hundreds of college students educated by the Big U to examine, research and scrutinize, and one guy is the sole speaker: formulates the ideas, does the commanding. Some students interrupted but Bernard didn't recognize them; towards the end no one even raised their hands. Imagine, people who'd deliberate the diameter of a safety pin permitting one guy to give them orders. It could be a study in social psychology: a group following the person with the most nerve and intelligence to dominate."

Summer Never Comes

"Any more astute observations, Professor Roberts?" Sharon rested her hand on his leg, as relaxed as possible on a concrete floor.

"I had my meeting with Stef Tianen and Al Stojak, *Spectrum's* editor."

"And the results?"

"Stef ran in between handball matches, only staying long enough to say she's holding my story and publishing it sometime after semester break."

"You were saved by handball?"

"Stef's always liked sports, but not so much to interfere with managing the *Daily Illini*. There's another explanation for the delay."

"Tomorrow why don't you confront her, say 'what's the deal here, Miss Editor-in-Chief, why have you blown me off? What I'm researching is worrisome, we need to pay attention.'"

Paul smiled at his girlfriend, silly and straightforward at the same time. "I won't waste my luck offering Stef chances to reconsider. If she's preoccupied and I slipped through, I'll accept the break but watch for hidden motives."

Sharon stood, pulling Paul to his feet. He grabbed his book bag and followed her into the History Library.

# # # #

Since the fraternity's founding in 1951, Kappa Iota Delta prided itself on above-average records in athletics. Markedly talented in sixteen-inch softball and golf, the house won its share of games and competed for an occasional championship, last year taking first place in intramural bowling. Many brothers worked as IM referees, and the PE Department's sportsmanship award was named for alumnus Terry Cabay.

Talent and adolescent macho, however, were missing from the Hound Dogs, the house's hockey team. Conceived in the era of brothers Tente, Pfordresher, Capadona and Stachon, by the '70s, the squad was a vaudeville, the roster consisting of two or three decent high school players, guys with borrowed equipment out on the ice for laughs, and KIDs who couldn't stand on skates.

"Think we got a chance?" Shaky Jake entered the Ice Rink for the game.

"None," Stu declared, "no way in hell we're watchin' a win."

Summer Never Comes

"Suppose you're right, why spoil a perfect record."

"Zero and twenty-eight the last five seasons." Paul volunteered.

"Who's in the net today?"

"My roommate."

"Bobby?" Jake was shocked. "The shortest guy in the house and he's goalie?"

"The dumb son-of-a-bitch wanted to play, figured he couldn't be any worse than K-Mow's performance last week."

"K-Mow was stoned."

The Hound Dog's starting line was Moose at center, Killer and Tim Malito at forwards, and Joey Panky and Dale Kinsey as defensemen. On the face-off their opponent, the Faculty Establishment, controlled the puck and scored in fifteen seconds. At the second tip-off, Moose kicked the puck with his blade, slapping it the length of the rink for an icing call.

"Okay, smart offense. Bobby, stay alert out there," Stu yelled as his roommate lifted his stick.

"Hey, Robby, what's up?"

"Lindy, didn't expect seeing you here, thought you booked in the afternoons."

"I was in the Undergrad reviewin' for the Phil 393 hourly but fell asleep. When I woke, I figured I might as well catch the game." He stood next to Paul.

"How you doing, Lindy?" Stu patted his back, "Don't see you too often in daylight."

"All right, a guy's surely dealt a quickie reputation."

"Deserved, I'd say." Stu returned to the game. "Oh, crap, the rush is on."

The Faculty Establishment whacked the puck from their zone, zooming through KIDs' front line in a four on one breakaway. Awkwardly skating backwards, Dale Kinsey tripped and fell on his knees, struggled to stand, but stumbled and crawled to the boards. The Establishment scored again, Bobby never dropping his stick.

"That's okay, stay with it, you'll save one yet!" Stu encouraged his roommate. Both teams changed lines and Tommy Quarters lugged himself over the side to the ice, ashamedly clutching the railing until Rudy shoved him toward the neutral zone.

Summer Never Comes

"Seen Emily lately?" Paul asked.

"We talked on the phone last night. She sounded glum, like her heels were dug in over something. As if I didn't know what."

"Did you hear Bobby drove her back and forth to Chicago at Thanksgiving?"

"Yeah, he filled me in on their tête-à-tête—amazing the nine or ten topics those two covered in three hours. The way she and Bobby listed my screw-ups, I don't merit due process as much as ineffable contempt. Bobby's convinced Em's patience is dead and gone, and she's ready to toss me away." Playing center, Scooter tripped one of the Establishment with his stick, drawing a two-minute penalty but saving a goal. The KIDs' crowds hoorayed.

"With your record, can you blame her? You shouldn't have postponed that date before Thanksgiving." Distracted watching the game, Paul's conversation turned tactless. "Or canceled those others this semester. You've got to smarten up, reneging even once is horse's ass stuff. Another girl wouldn't tolerate half the nonsense you've forced Emily to endure. How you can continually cold shoulder a sweetheart like her is a mystery."

Lindy wished he was still napping in the 'Brary, forgotten the hockey game or hadn't stood next to his roommate. He'd known for some time—the months since Frogfeet's start—the heartache he was provoking. *How couldn't I, my conscience is as cogent as everyone else's. What does Robby and everyone think—I'm some thick-headed chunk of rock? I don't need this abuse right now.* Insulted, Lindy rationalized himself the victim and, even around thirty or forty KIDs, came close to flipping out right here in the Ice Rink—grabbing Robby's shoulder, screaming at him to mind his own business and go screw himself. He hustled to the edge, grappling with words, to hell with consequences. But his second impulse was wiser, because acting the fool wouldn't resolve any dilemmas, only cost more goodwill. His roommate's rebuke was right on; quit denying, accept the guilt and rebuild.

"I'm for sure gonna see her tomorrow afternoon, honest. Maybe Em and I can fix this mess." Lindy pounded the boards to psych up the Hound Dogs.

"About time you did what's decent. Emily's too respectable a woman to let slip away."

Summer Never Comes

"What about me?" Again Lindy was offended by his preoccupied roommate's comment, then answered his own question. "Yeah, my back's to the wall, but that doesn't mean I can't haul my meat out of the fire, I can get straight with Em."

"Oh, no." Stu turned away from the rink. Bobby had skated out from the goal to stop another breakaway, but tumbled flat on his stomach as the Establishment scored into an open net.

"Seen Sharon this week?"

"A couple of nights ago at the Library." Paul grinned.

"You two are becomin' quite the campus number, according to Kentucky."

"What did he say?"

"That he attended church last Saturday with you and the sweetie." Lindy mimicked an I-know-something-you-don't-know tone.

The first half ended with the score six to zero. As their fans applauded the KIDs skated to their bench. Bobby ripped off his gloves and mask, heaving them at the wall.

"My roomie's pissed, better see if I can calm him down." Stu hurried away.

"So I came back to the campus early."

"I'm not raggin' over it, Robby, I'm glad for you, it's cool your havin' a honey." A chilly Lindy raised his coat collar. "The rake's progress. In September, I'm the one with a steady girl and bliss. Now in December, you're the toast of the town, long weekends with your main squeeze; and me, the floodwater's rising to my nose."

"Every person's future is unwritten; you can influence the way your life unfolds."

"And starting tomorrow that's what I'm doin' with Em—elect new joys and delights."

In the second half, Moose controlled the face-off, but slipped over the blue line and lost the puck. The Faculty Establishment skated, passed, checked and tallied again and again while Hound Dog only managed two shots on goal, twice their first half's effort. When the clock ran out with the score 11–0, the whole team, excepting Vic Extensionelli, doubled over from too little conditioning, too much exertion, and too many beers and smokes.

"Boy, we were frickin' turds." A growling Bobby Sox hauled his equipment back to the house.

"Cheer up," Stu mugged his roommate, "at least you didn't lose any teeth."

"That's right," Paul added, "this wasn't Hound Dog's worst loss."

"There's a relief knowin' someone sucks more than me. What's the record?"

"Fifteen-zip, two years ago."

Bobby shuddered. "Who was the crappy-ass goalie in that disaster?"

"Billy Powell."

# # # #

"Here you go, Em, precisely what we need on a raw, frosty afternoon." Lindy sat opposite his girlfriend in the booth. "Isn't this place a treat, two in the afternoon and undergrads are buyin' burgers like thirsty alums snaggin' beers on football weekends. Someone's a whiz kid, building a McDonald's in Campustown."

"It would be nice operating a business like this, the owners must make a reasonable salary." Emily sipped her cocoa.

"An authentic gold mine but boring—flippin' all-beef patties and saltin' french fries for a living," Lindy watched the counter, crowded with customers queued six deep, "too near a nine-to-five routine."

"And not as exciting as playing second guitar in a college rock 'n' roll band," Emily ended his thought.

"You're a mind reader."

"Analyzing you these days is simple." She stared past Lindy. All of Mac's tables were occupied—in-a-hurry undergrads ate standing and more carried their bags and drinks out the doors. Two booths away, ignoring the commotion, an Arab sat with his slide rule, keypunch cards and computer print-outs.

"What else do you spot in me?"

"An enigma, someone I care for and imagine loved me, a companion who in the past I could chat with, plan a future and dream with, rely on." Emily's tone was unemotional. "Now this person is different and doesn't consider me or others, only focuses on the side of his life he judges indispensible."

"Doesn't sound rosy, Em. I recognize my selfishness the last few months, cutting people off and bein' a shallow, fair-weather friend. Robby lit into me over this yesterday, telling me I should straighten out." Lindy swirled a marshmallow in his hot chocolate. "As a defense, I could list the apologies you've already heard, rationales I accept as true and you don't. After these months, another rehash would mean I'm not clever explainin' myself or my case is weak. But that's dwelling on yesterdays and I want to be upbeat, go forward, recapture our closeness. And I know what you're thinkin'—with my track record of reversals this semester, how's this gonna happen, what magic will yank a rabbit outta my hat, do I have the common sense? I think yes. The unfortunate fact, though, is our friendship can't match a few months ago or last year's, and I won't maintain it will. Life is different now, we have to bend. But the adjustments don't have to topple to the worst because there's hope. With Frogfeet playin' regular gigs, we've finally cut back our practices. Weekends are a no-go because we're booked on Saturdays and Sundays, but there's weeknights—that could be our time. Just as last year when we started dating, the two of us with so little in common, neither knew if we'd work out, it was a gamble but it succeeded. And we can go again."

"Words are not enough, I've listened to too many for too long, actions are more honest. Tell me, these last months, do you think the risk was worth it?"

"What's your question, Frogfeet or us?" His girlfriend's grimace answered. *Oh, God, what a blunder I just made.* "Sorry, Em. Of course our year was worthwhile, we've had wonderful times and I enjoy being with you. Despite everyone considerin' me thoughtless, I know I've disappointed you. I hoped the outcomes would be better but the band's troubles didn't make it so. The next months, we can recoup."

"How can we repair our relationship? What is different, how will you change?"

Emily's bluntness was unexpected, Lindy imagining her as his reserved girlfriend from September. Okay, time to step up. "For starters there's weekdays—the Mondays, Tuesdays, Wednesdays and Thursdays we're gonna have for ourselves. We can pack a ton into them, bookin' for one, sitting around and catching up for another, that dreamin' you mentioned. And, not that I'm flush, but I am earnin' extra money now, we can step out, splurge in a couple of those restaurants we ate at last year, including your favorite, the one with no corners, what's the name?"

"The Round Barn." Emily credited him for remembering this much. "The remainder, together on weekdays, we could do that?"

"Not a shadow of misgivings it can't happen, the next best thing to the original." Lindy's confidence wavered, ruing his earlier error and certain his next sentence would be another. "Except next Wednesday, that night's reserved, Shaky Jake's planned a party at the Red Lion to boost my band."

Confounding, Emily sadly concluded. *Is Will that insincere, does he consider me appallingly naïve, a milquetoast?* She peered at her hot chocolate, the cup two thirds full. The Arab with the computer cards strolled by their booth, and the crowd at the counter were still buying cheeseburgers.

"Poor, darling Will, how many concessions, how long can you compromise? You want to do right, but not five minutes elapse and already another broken promise. What should my reaction be? As other times stay silent, hoping you'll accept my affection and acknowledge we're in love? What has that brought me the last two months besides nights alone, delaying my life?" Emily reached for his hand. "Maybe I haven't spoken enough or at all, but I want nothing more than to be with you the way we were last year—before your band, when we drank tea in my room, attended parties at KIDs, and talked and talked and talked. I care for you and want to be with you, let's retreat to the way we were."

"What you say sounds idyllic. I wish my days were as painless as the baseball and apple pie you allude to, because parts of life are dear relationships. But I can't go that far, Em, not right now. On top of you, school work and KIDs, I'm obligated to the band." He sneezed and wiped his nose with a handkerchief. "This crazy weather could lay low anyone."

"Must you be, does your music mean so much? There is much more in life we can search for together. Remember that afternoon on the Quad? We mused over traveling to California on your winding road to live our lives. We can do that, it's possible."

"There are times, Em, I don't sleep enough or haven't studied for a class, when I genuinely agonize over what I'm doin', days I'm depressed about my situation. But the scale's opposite side is Frogfeet and that fantasy of mine, the boon, my vocation finally matching my ambitions. We're not the best campus band, heck, I'm unsure if we're competent at all; maybe we'll never climb from the basement. But the 'Feet is something I've started and must see through."

"Commitment." Emily was very sad.

"Yeah, and responsibility, too. In a goofy way this is teaching me how to mature. I know people around here, especially this semester, don't use those words to describe me and that's not how I'd portray myself. But my obligation is sticking with Frogfeet to the end."

"And us, Will, isn't there a connection?"

"This sounds bad, my music and band buddies more valuable than my girlfriend. I'm sorry and don't want to lie, I love you enough to be upfront. Once, maybe there was this solid, unbreakable bond between us, I'm certain of that. Now, with me in a new chapter, our affection's been set on a shelf, a called time-out. But there's always tomorrow to bring us back."

Emily cried walking back to Blaisdell Hall. She'd been truthful with Will, more than ever before, admitting she loved him. However, they'd had two dissimilar, disappointing conversations, she wanting to sustain their relationship, with Will abandoning their happiness. He was swinging out on his own and Emily hoped he succeeded in his adventure. Where did that leave her? She was not in his life anymore. Would she be a few weeks or months from now, should she wait? Perhaps Nicole was right, Emily fastened too much faith to maybes.

Lindy skated the ice returning to KIDs. Once and for all he'd wanted to clear away misunderstandings, to head in an encouraging direction with Em. He reasoned he'd been halfway compromising, offering her two or three nights during the week. Anything extra was hypocritical, no sense being more of that than he already was. This weekday friendship would work, too—more scheduled than the old days, but with plusses. They'd see each other regularly, do things, like dinner at the Round Barn, and Em could help him catch up with his studying. Zounds, a flock of birds shot with one arrow! The rest of the conversation, priorities and seeing Frogfeet through, he was honest. Where was the logic giving your word one minute then conceding the next? Em had nailed him on plenty of those already. He regretted there was so much negotiation in life, wished there were more days in the week so he could satisfy Em, the 'Feet, Robby, his pals and his conscience. But there wasn't, isn't and never would be. Lindy would survive for himself.

# # # #

"The war continues in Vietnam. In time, the conflict will again engulf Laos and Cambodia, the balance of Southeast Asia, all of Asia and the world.

"There is a way to combat this futile, catastrophic course. University Network Involved to End Destruction encourages the entire campus community to enlist to promote peace. Only through the involvement of all individuals and people, conscientious citizens and comrades, will the failed course of aggression be ended.

"Enroll now!

"UNITED to end the war!"

"Join the Food Drive for Peace!

"UNITED is now collecting canned goods and foodstuffs. These items will be shipped to our agents in Saigon to aid the innocent victims of America's brutal war and cruel oppression.

"All donations will be accepted!

"Contribute food!

"Contribute to Peace!

"UNITED to end the war!"

Advertising in the *Daily Illini* did the job. The 'Food Collective Stations,' as Bernard designated them, were filled past his expectations. Bags of sugar, cans of Campbell's soups, Spam, Rice-a-Roni, tins of King Oscar sardines, Kraft Macaroni and Cheese, boxes of Girl Scout cookies. Saltine crackers, Aunt Jemima pancake batter, bags of popcorn, Eight O'Clock coffee, Kool-Aid, an entire skid of Green Giant canned vegetables donated by the Interfraternity Council, crates of hot dogs and boxes of frozen hamburger patties likely stolen from the university food service, all amassed in UNITED's rented pickups, galvanizing the whole campus. Every day the packed trucks drove the foodstuffs to a railroad car waiting in Champaign.

Summer Never Comes

Stef Tianen assigned a reporter to document the drive's progress, with pictures showing students, faculty and even year-round-looking residents carrying boxes and bags to the trucks, with smiling UNITED volunteers dressed in orange and black shirts accepting the contributions.

The membership campaign also satisfied Bernard. Teams spoke at dorms and the Greek houses, introducing UNITED, canvassing for new recruits. Students signed up, happy to pledge their time and money. Walking the university or hanging in the bars, an undergrad was likely to be approached by an orange and black-clad protester asking if he'd heard of UNITED, inquiring if she'd joined, wanting to know if they'd do so today.

"Come on, peace!" The True Believers shouted over the Lion's music or Second Chance's pinball machines.

\# \# \# \#

"The *Daily Illini* wholeheartedly supports the growing efforts of UNITED to organize our campus in the cause of peace. The time has long passed for resolution of the Vietnam War. Thousands of University of Illinois students have started and concluded their years under this conflict's threatening shadow, hundreds of alumni have crossed the ocean to fight, and many have not returned.

"Now there is hope, a chance for our community to raise one voice, to demand a cessation to the hostilities.

"With UNITED we can work for the new day of peace."

\# \# \# \#

The *Champaign News-Gazette's* afternoon edition reviewed the ongoing peace activities.

"The United States is witnessing a widening conflict in Vietnam. What was once a minor police action with Americans in the roles of advisors has become an escalating war with thousands of casualties and no solution in sight.

"As the fighting spreads, so do protests. Citizens disagreeing with our government's policy have done everything imaginable to express their feelings. This is the guaranteed right of Americans.

Summer Never Comes

"College students have led in these rallies. As the ones drafted to fight in Southeast Asia, this generation's profound concern with Vietnam is explicable. Spontaneous, rowdy, unruly, at times lawless, the fiercely anti-war demonstrations have emphasized college students' sincere hopes for peace.

"An increasing number of University of Illinois students, however, are choosing another route, having thrown in with the recently-created University Network Involved to End Destruction, UNITED. This organization came into existence by allying, some have claimed eradicating, the former campus peace groups, and now is recruiting the student body with the apparent purpose of establishing itself as the lone, monolithic, campus anti-war force.

"By itself, one more peace group in Champaign-Urbana would be a minor development. It is their focus that is disturbing. Having accomplished its goal of consolidation, of being the self-acknowledged sole authority, one wonders how UNITED and the students will be employed or misused."

The next morning, pressroom foreman Wally Byam drove into the *News-Gazette's* lot on Market Street, as usual early for his shift. Parking his Pontiac, Wally straightaway spotted a problem with the paper's Chevy pickup. The truck was lower to the ground and tilted to one side. Stepping over, Wally noticed all four tires were flat.

"Son of a bitch." He kicked the rear bumper.

Wally walked to the office for his morning coffee and to phone the Shell gas station to borrow an air compressor. For the hell of it, he thought to check the Ford delivery van in the loading dock. Wedging his body between the brick wall and the vehicle, Wally stooped to examine the wheels on the passenger side. Flat.

"Now, how in Christ?"

# # # #

For two nights in the Library's remotest alcove, with not even Sharon for company, Paul struggled on the project. He edited four different drafts, checking, correcting, agonizing over words, obsessing on content, worrying how the page will look—his résumé, the record of three and a half years in college, a summary of his experiences at the University of Illinois, the document corporate recruiters would scrutinize next semester. The page

Summer Never Comes

needed to present ability, aptitude and maturity, with no misspelling or dangling participles, no logic out of sequence, no ifs, questions or controversies. Paul realized this one sheet signaled the finish of his present. Composing the résumé, he unwillingly acknowledged graduation was approaching, his time to prepare for tomorrow. God, he hated this.

Dawdling on his way to the Quik Print Copy Shop, Paul detoured through Gregory Hall and the History Department to check Professor Gulley's biography.

Antoinette Burton Gulley, Bachelor of Arts degree, Michigan State University, MA and PhD, Dartmouth College, was thirty-six years old, unmarried, and for the last three years an assistant professor in Champaign-Urbana. Widely traveled, she'd spent summers in Britain, Romania, Yugoslavia and the Soviet Union. Her doctoral thesis was titled *Insurgencies in Tudor and Elizabethan England, with Their Correspondence to Revolutionary Movements in the Twentieth Century*, the biography noting that a majority of her thesis was researched in Moscow. Professor Gulley's teaching responsibilities at the University of Illinois included History 131, England to 1688, three upper-level courses and one graduate seminar.

Paul was disappointed in the professor's unremarkable background, with no suggestions—except her thesis' theme—of sedition. Who knows, Paul reasoned, perhaps she's only observing UNITED, preparing other dissertations on historical and modern-day rebellions. As Sharon commented, maybe this woman is merely a concerned citizen.

Paul continued on to the Quik Print, ordered one hundred copies of his résumé, then headed to Second Chance for a beer, a quarter's worth of pinball and to forget this errand.

# # # #

Bobby Sox used the afternoon to shop for Jeannie's Christmas card, checking McBride's Drugstore, The Loft, and the Five & Ten. At Follett's, he found the most touching. A collection of animals, an elephant, crocodile, rabbit and monkey were drawn on the front, the menagerie looking in various directions, searching the starry night sky. Inside, the message read: "Don't worry—He always shows up."

Summer Never Comes

Bobby liked it. The card proffered a holiday sentiment, but was also meaningful for Jeannie and himself.

"Dearest," he wrote, "At this holiday so full of feeling and joy and Love, I send you this card with my whole, glad Heart. This is the sixth Christmas we've been Together and also the last one we will be apart. This Promise, that the Future will be Ours, is the best Christmas Present for both of Us. All my Love, Bobby."

# # # #

"There is a theoretical large city in the United States. A minority of the population has been outraged by affronts it considers against its interests. This minority ceases to respect the law, turns to rioting, and announces plans to march into neighboring areas, up to now controlled by the majority, to plunder and spread the insurrection.

"This is life or death for this metropolis.

"You are a member of the majority, charged with defending the city and authorized to use whatever necessary force.

"Identify the issues. What would you do?"

Paul looked at his wristwatch, fifteen minutes to answer the Phil 393 hourly's final question.

"The issue is what is more important, the majority's security for the only reason that they are the larger part of society, or the protection of citizens' rights. Prior to ordering out the troops, the question to be asked is, does the minority have a valid argument? Are there grievances which demand attention?

"History teaches that most segments of society have never rebelled or rioted without reasons, justifications they think are compelling. Examples in America are the southern states prior to the Civil War, the labor movement in the late nineteenth and early twentieth centuries, and the civil rights protests of the last two decades. History also shows that after violence begins, differences are more difficult to decide. Too few times have talks or negotiations taken place first to try to head off a conflict. And because factions many times fail to negotiate, the results are not what they should or could have been. One or both sides lose more through fighting than they could gain through discussion.

Summer Never Comes

"Therefore, the first option is to parley.

"However, if the majority bargains in good faith but talks fail, and assuming I am in full agreement with the majority's position versus the minority's, the course of action is self-defense. This would take the form of what is necessary, but should not be overwhelming. The point is not to totally destroy a faction or subjugate them to the level where there are ruinous feelings or hatreds for years and years to come. Rather, the force used to salvage the situation should be only that amount which holds off, limits it from getting any worse than it might, and saves lives in both the minority and majority. In other words, the present common good should be preserved as much as possible while also safeguarding future options for tolerable relations between them. Force, a physical presence and/or overwhelming, should only be necessary to defend the city from the minority as a last, last result."

Paul re-read his answer, crossing out the second "necessary" in the last paragraph and substituting "required." With five minutes in the period, Paul did something rare for college: leave an hourly exam early. He stood and smiled at his worried roommate.

Lindy reached the last question later than Paul.

"The issue here seems to be whether to use violence to stop violence. It is better to resort to the means of the other side in order to preserve oneself? If the issue is society's survival, or at least one's own part of society, then violence must be used if it is necessary. This brings up the argument of whether or not that part of society which defended itself is any better off morally for using these means. If it survives, it is better off than if it would have been destroyed. The question of whether or not it is still moral is a moot point. Survival is the objective."

The bell rang and class ended.

"Please finish up your exams," Professor Hudson instructed.

# # # #

"Here it is, a Wednesday night and Miss Taylor is fancying herself up. What do you have in mind?" Mary O'Donnell leaned on the half-opened door.

"A date." Sharon stood in her room brushing on eye shade.

Summer Never Comes

"Well, la-ti-da, Miss Pretty Pink Panties, must be special."

"If you insist on knowing, I'm going with Paul to the Red Lion."

"All this dolling to drink in that dump?"

"I'd hardly call clean Levi's and an ironed blouse dressed up." Sharon combed her hair.

"For a Wednesday, I would. The way you're decked out, I'd have imagined at least a Friday afternoon happy hour. Taking your car?"

"I'm driving to KIDs, from there we'll walk to the Lion."

"Then it's smart I put a dollar of gas in the tank this morning. Why is Mr. Meek-and-Quiet taking you out on a weeknight?"

"His roommate's band is performing. Paul said most of the KIDs are attending to support him." She checked herself in the mirror.

"Beautiful, Sharon, gorgeous, stunning." The friends walked out of the bedroom. "Don't forget, if you find any worthwhile guys, you're still hunting for me."

# # # #

"Is Lindy nervous?"

"A tad, this is his first time playing for the brothers," Paul answered.

"Have you ever heard him sing with Frogfeet?"

"Never, Lindy got going with them right at the time we started dating. Not that I'm using you as an excuse for blowing off my roommate's music."

"I understand, I've always collected undivided devotion from my lovers," Sharon mocked her boyfriend. Hiking on Third Street with the other KIDs, they passed the Sigma Alpha Epsilon house, the two golden lion statues sitting on the porch wearing red Santa Claus hats.

"Who are those celebrities up there?"

Sharon and Paul glanced back.

"Bobby, stepping out to the Lion?"

"Yep, wouldn't miss Frogfeet." He hurried to catch the pair. "How you doin', Sharon, haven't seen you since Homecoming."

"Where's Stu?"

"Booking. This semester he's serious about staying in the Big U. Did Stu tell you he's registering for the LSAT? Imagine, a year ago my roommate was so wasted he couldn't find the Library with a map, now he's applying to law schools. Joyce's influence is succeeding."

Summer Never Comes

"Girlfriends have positive effects," Sharon poked Paul in the ribs, "right?"

"Absolutely." Paul faked a grimace, then lunged for Sharon, pulling her face next to his.

"Please, you two, this is a public place, not so much emotion." Bobby pretended surprise seeing the normally uptight Paul goof with Sharon. At the Red Lion's door, eight or ten undergrads stood ahead of the trio as the bouncer checked student IDs.

The low-ceilinged Lion was cramped, shadowy and smoky. Bernie Wysocki, Augie Tonne and Terry Skworch occupied one table, and Ron Gimbel, Tim Malito and Katy Karas relaxed in a corner, their heads against the wall. Paul, Sharon and Bobby passed the main bar, weaving through the crowds to a table in the middle. Dale Kinsey and Tommy Quarters sat nearer the dance floor with two girls wearing so much makeup the KIDs reckoned they were hookers.

"Are we drinking beer?"

"There's my share for a pitcher." Bobby handed Paul a dollar.

"Got it." Paul rested one hand on his girlfriend's shoulder, then snaked through the mob to the bar.

On stage, the 'Feet positioned their equipment. Lindy tuned his Gibson and searched the tables, easily spying his loitering, drinking fraternity brothers. Like Robby, this was the first occasion most would hear him play.

"Go, Lindy!" a voice cheered.

"You got pals here tonight?" Franky Konkel strapped on his Fender. "Then we better make the music listenable."

Returning to the table with the third pitcher of wine he'd bought tonight, Tommy Quarters discovered Dale fondling the redhead, the broad Tommy supposed his evening's date. Dale whispered in one ear, his tongue licking her lobe.

"Tell me, Tommy," the blonde asked, "did you say your parents live around Chicago?"

"Highland Park, on the north shore."

"Are they rich?" She nudged closer, angling her fingers for his lap, counting on getting laid and a profitable evening. Tommy let her bite his chin, then, a first for this semester, felt embarrassed.

Summer Never Comes

Eddie McMahon stood at the Deuces Wild pinball machine. Downing screwdrivers and feeding quarters into the slot, Eddie-Bob hadn't won a game in forty-five minutes but matched once.

"We snagged a break," Paul set the pitcher on their table, "the Jerg's tending bar, the beer only cost fifty cents."

"Hell, yes, this is gonna be a super night. You got my money?" The forever cheap Bobby filled the glass mugs. "I'll pop for the next one."

The house lights dimmed and Franky played the opening song, an Andy Arthur composition.

> Frogfeet, Frogfeet, this is our name.
> We play the tunes, that is our game.
> Don't worry if you don't get
> The madness on this stage,
> We know the score
> And we all came to play.

"I like their sound. Sharon, check the drummer."

'Mad,' psyched sooner than usual, his long, red hair shooting sideways, slapped the beat, breaking a stick halfway through the song.

"They play loud."

"What band doesn't?"

Frogfeet finished, the partisan KIDs crowds roared, and Lindy raised his fist.

"Thanks for the applause. It's super havin' supporters, groupies and strangers rollin' in off the streets. I understand there's lots of Lindy's buddies here, which we appreciate," Franky shouted into his microphone. Howling erupted and Lindy beamed. "So sit back, hope you dig our music and buy some brews."

Lindy stepped to center stage for the next song, another Andy original.

> Our friends are all around us,
> All we do is reach out.
> Don't be afraid to miss them,
> That's what pals are about.

Summer Never Comes

With the drawn out rhythm and only occasionally banging the bass, 'Mad' chilled behind his drums. Around the Lion, KIDs turned from the stage and chatted.

Paul studied his roommate. Dressed in a faded orange and blue Illini t-shirt, too-short Levi's, and black high-top tennis shoes, nervously shuffling his big feet to burn energy, the clownish Lindy strummed his guitar and crooned the chorus, showing off years of practice, weeks of hard-core rehearsals with Frogfeet, and downright enchantment with performing on stage, the spot he loved over every other. *My roommate and Sharon have it right, people need to go their own way to find their lives.* Tonight justifies Lindy's last three months—a decent performance and sound, with his buddies enjoying the show. I was selfish wanting Lindy out of the band, staying around the fraternity so I could hang with him as much as we used to. And foolish me? *I should push myself, all I need is courage.*

"Wall, looky heah. Cousin, whut ahr you doin' with thes bunch?"

"Hello, James, pull up a chair. Come to listen to the music?"

"Ah reckon thet's why ah'm in attendence." Kentucky glanced toward Paul. "How is Lind-eh soundin'?"

"Decent. Did you hear his solo?"

"Jus' th' end. Wuz thet an original song?"

"Believe so." As Paul answered, Frogfeet played a GrassRoots medley, Franky on lead vocals, Lindy and Woofer singing melody. Their next arrangement was a waltz-like Chicago ballad. "Care to boogie?"

"Excuse us." Sharon and Paul stepped toward the stage as Kentucky courteously rose and Bobby guzzled his beer. Reaching the dance floor, Paul waved to Lindy, his roommate lifting the neck of his guitar.

"This is only the second time we've danced together." He slid his arms around Sharon.

"What about the night at Chances R watching The Guild?"

"No, we sat in the balcony and never made it downstairs."

Sharon whispered in his ear. "Remember, your third dance with a Taylor girl is a sign of eternal affection and devotion."

"Then what happens?"

"Make it to three, dear, to find out." She kissed his chin.

With an empty pitcher, Bobby Sox headed to the bar. "Jerg, how about a refill?"

"Sure thing." He set the pitcher under the tap. "Lindy's not bad tonight, I'd say one of Frogfeet's better."

"How many times you heard them?"

"A half dozen. Gimme a buck and wait." Hitting the cash register keys, the Jerg dropped the dollar in, picked out four quarters and placed the coins in his fraternity brother's hand.

"Thanks." Bobby spun away from the bar. "Scooter, Lauren what's up?"

"Where are you sitting?" Scooter held his fiancé's hand.

"In the center, I think we can scrounge a couple more chairs." The three zigzagged through the Lion's audience. "How're the wedding arrangements coming along?"

"We haven't settled much," Lauren answered, "but will when we go home for Christmas and talk to our families."

"Planning a big reception?"

"It would be nice inviting all our friends to a blow out party, but the numbers depend on our parents' say-so. Scooter's mother is terribly particular."

"How about the date?"

"Labor Day or October has been discussed."

"Make sure it doesn't interfere with next fall's Fighting Illini football schedule."

Kentucky chivalrously removed his hat for Lauren as Bobby and Scooter slipped two tables together. Sharon and Paul were dancing, hip-hopping to an old rock 'n' roll song, and standing still when Lindy performed 'Here, There and Everywhere.'

"He sings that tune well."

"Lindy should, he's worn out every Beatles record he owns. And mine, too."

Dale Kinsey put his moves on the hookers. He chatted up the blonde, grabbed the redhead's inner thigh, and offered both of them ten bucks each for service later that night. Kinsey in a three-way, Tommy Quarters fumed. The redhead unbuckled Dale's belt as he loosened the blonde's blouse. An upset Tommy stayed at their table for another minute, then conceded and beelined to the hard drinks bar.

Summer Never Comes

Sipping their wine mugs, an empty-minded Lee Mulberry and the vacant Joey Panky leaned on the bar's wood post. Each wore a green Army fatigue coat with circular 'peace' patches sewn on the sleeves. With their fourth floor despo pals they'd passed a joint around at KIDs before rolling to the Lion, Lee especially digging drinking after toking. Unshaved for a month, they stared at the stage, rarely turning their heads. Joey Panky smoked a Lucky Strike, the butt drooping from his mouth.

After Frogfeet's first set, Paul and Sharon returned to their friends. In addition to Bobby, Kentucky, Scooter and Lauren, Ronny Gimbel, Tim, and Katy had moved from the corner. The group squeezed around three tables.

"Good crowd," Paul commented.

"We could have a house meeting."

"No officers."

"Who needs them?"

"We haf t' ob-serve th' formalities."

"How about marrying Scooter and Lauren?" Bobby teased as she blushed.

"No minister."

"You two looked might-eh fine out thar."

"I have a marvelous partner," Sharon nodded.

"How maneh times have you danced?"

"This is the second, James."

"Ah see," Kentucky drawled, "th' approachin' Taylor girl tradition."

"Wait, I'm in a set-up, right?" Paul stared at the grinning Sharon.

"The superstar." Bobby clapped as Paul, Sharon and Kentucky turned to see Lindy saunter toward them. The KIDs in the Lion cheered.

Lindy blushed. "All right, guys, that's enough, save the ovations for later."

"Good first set." Tim patted his back.

"Yes-sir, right fine."

"Appreciate it." Lindy borrowed Bobby's mug. "There's a ton of the brothers here."

"I counted fifty."

"Compliments of the Lion." The Jerg delivered two pitchers and tousled Lindy's hair.

Summer Never Comes

"You're all really great, comin' out tonight," Lindy mocked his pals, "especially when I know you're swamped with booking."

"Frogfeet sounds better than you've let on. What's up for the next set?"

"Two more originals, then a ride into Three Dog Night."

"What about 'Tell Laura I Love Her?'"

"Come on," Lindy put down another beer, "that's Chances R material, we'd be tossed from here."

All the laughing, bantering KIDs enjoyed the happy times.

"Here's to Terry, he's true blue, he's a drunkard through and through!" Bernie Wysocki screamed, stood and pointed to brother Skworch as the KIDs joined in. Terry rose, lifted a full beer pitcher to his mouth, and the KIDs howled louder. "He won't let us dance and he won't let us sing and he won't let us do a goddamned thing. So drink, chug-a-lug, chug-a-lug, chug-a-lug, chug-a-lug…"

A gulping Terry held the pitcher with both hands, every few seconds raising it higher, tipping his head back, unhurriedly swallowing the suds. The KIDs, including Lindy, urged him on.

"That's right, pace."

"Slow, Terry, slow, you're halfway there," Lindy inspected his chin, "no spillage yet."

Past horizontal, Terry chugged and guzzled, with only a few drops splashing his lips.

"Almost there, Terry," Lindy focused on his mouth, "a couple more ounces and you've bled her dry."

Terry lifted one arm into the air, with the pitcher at vertical and foam left.

"Go, go, go, go."

Terry yanked the pitcher from his mouth and collapsed to a chair, beer dripping down his t-shirt. The KIDs and dozens of Lion customers whooped.

"What a spectacle, only the second time I've seen an entire one drained." Lindy turned to Kentucky and Paul, theatrically wiping his forehead with the back of his hand.

Paul remembered the 'Welcome Back Everybody' party, the identical way Lindy had dried his brow. Tonight, as in September, his roommate joked with their fellow KIDs, enjoying the crowds—the most relaxed and self-assured Paul had seen him since that first party. Pouring another beer for himself, an animated Lindy raised his mug to a no doubt wise-ass comment from Bobby Sox.

Lindy and Sharon are right, risks succeed. I should, will, I handle my life.

Elbowed by the mobs, Tommy Quarters skulked in the dark passageway between the two bars. He sneered at Dale Kinsey, unashamedly mauling the hookers' blouses. At least Dale'll have to use his own money to pay for the trick. Tommy watched the KIDs surrounding Lindy and considered sitting with the brothers. Wonder what most of them think of me? Behind him, Eddie McMahon was still wasting quarters and flipping hard, with Joey Panky spectating. What losers, thank God I haven't skidded that low. Finally, Tommy checked out one girl standing in the passageway, decided he liked her body, and sidestepped closer.

"Drinking anything tonight?"

"Wine, thank you," the girl softly replied. Tommy bought a glass for her and a beer for himself.

"This is the smokiest bar on campus, our clothes will stink from tobacco tomorrow."

"Yes, I could do without the smell. Cigarettes are so unhealthy."

"Do you come here often?"

"No," she said, "like you, I don't care for the smoke. Tonight is different, I'm curious about this band."

"Frogfeet sounds like the rest of the Cham-Bana groups, down and out and hung over. They'll never amount to any more than they already are." He shifted his mug from his right to left hand. "My name's Tommy, what's yours?"

"Emily Ritter."

"Wanna go somewhere else?"

"That would be nice."

Thanking his buddies one last time for their bravado, Lindy returned to the stage. "I'll see if I can get the others to play 'Tell Laura I Love Her.'"

"Go, Lindy go! Go Lindy go!"

Brother Lindner, swimming the high tide, so exultant he could walk on the moon, so ecstatic his shirt buttons would pop if he had any, waved and trooped across the dance floor. "Far out, what a great night to be alive."

Summer Never Comes

An oblivious Eddie-Bob worked the flippers, unaware the jukebox had shut down and Frogfeet was singing. For the evening, his score was zero in the games won column.

Chapter Twelve

NOT STICKING around for an after-supper cup of coffee, Stu left the KID's dining room and hurried upstairs.

"Going to the Illini b-ball game Saturday?" Tim Malito yelled.

"Is that a three o'clock tip-off?"

"Yeah, what do you think of our chances against Butler?"

"Dunno, too early in the season for predictions." Stu slowed at the doorway. "Hey, I'd love to rap but I gotta get goin'."

"Sure, are you attending the game?"

"Don't think so." He waved and rushed on.

Bobby Sox laid on his bunk, reading the back cover of Procol Harum's *A Salty Dog* while Paul sat at a desk listening to the record. "Watching football on the tube? Packers and Bears at Soldiers' Field with a kegger, remember?"

"No, booking at the 'Brary, tonight I'm reviewing my psych notes." He stuffed a notepad in his book bag. "Later."

"Never thought I'd see the day ol' Stu would fan on the Bears and beers, then boogie by himself to the Undergrad."

"Finals are close." Paul paged through Bobby's December *Playboy*. "Maybe he's serious this semester because Joyce has him into booking."

"Whatever it is, it's not our old Stu," Tim stood by the door, "he barely slowed down when I mentioned the basketball game."

"Which is encouraging," Bobby answered, "he can't flunk out, without chances to graduate, the LSAT, law school or whatever he's frickin' plannin' on doin'."

"June isn't far off," Tim folded his arms, "you seniors are worrying over that stuff."

Summer Never Comes

"Ah, graduation, the end, no more school, leaving, what beautiful words," Bobby Sox looked content.

"Maybe that's the catch-22, fail a course," Paul stared at his friends.

"You a-hole, that's the dumbest damned thing I've heard since Thanksgiving," Bobby scolded. "No one purposely eagles down here."

"Yes, it's too blatant, someone would need a sneakier scheme to stay for more than four years."

"Is he serious?" Tim pointed a finger at Paul.

"Might be, Mr. Roberts is a strange desperado."

In the windy night, Stu hurried to the Undergrad, waving at Alpha Phi. Being Monday, Joyce and her sorority sisters were holding a house meeting which, he knew, would last the evening. Reaching the Undergrad's doors with dozens of fellow students, Stu headed through the turnstiles to the lower level, passed the armchairs by the windows and the bookshelves, and laid his book bag in a carrel.

Education, college's mission. Intramurals, concerts, the bars, midnight movies, 2:30 in the morning pizzas, pranks and pinball are comical time wasters but no way, no how, no where the equal of learning what the University of Illinois teaches. To justify four, five or six and a half years in Champaign-Urbana, students must earn a diploma. With a degree there are prospects for motivating jobs, first class careers and meaning from life; without one, the drudgery of uninspiring, tedious work, an occupation not a vocation, employment not a profession, ennui instead of fine art. Stu's uncle Joe, a carpenter for forty years, had called a college education "the greatest, damnedest union card you kids can apprentice for."

Studying, booking, cracking them open, hard-core cramming, weekends in the 'Brary, pulling a nighter. Many teenagers make capable students. If courses require four hours a night plus the odd Saturday evenings, that's what they'll devote for good grades. A few lucky ones, the brains, have to study very little, their minds so keen that the only necessaries for 'acing' hourlies are reading the chapters and listening to lectures. Opposite these 'A' students, the five-pointers, are the strugglers—too lazy to put in any time or not intelligent enough for college, satisfied with 'hooks' and an occasional 'B.' Four years will pass and these undergrads, with a 3.00 or 3.25, won't get into graduate school or land decent jobs.

Summer Never Comes

As college years goes by, though, some students change, grasping that pitchers, partying, and tailgating are only enjoyed once papers are written, lab results logged and hourlies handled. Realizing the wasted earlier semesters, they bust ass in the remaining ones to recoup the poor grades. When questioned about their grade point averages, they'll typically respond "a 3.75 (or whatever), but that's with 3.0s my first two semesters."

This is Stu, unconcerned about booking as a freshman, supposed college would never end as a sophomore, nearly flunking out as a junior, in his senior year on the rebound, inching up his GPA, the Big U's benchmark. So, tonight, two weeks before Christmas, earlier than his friends, here he is in the Undergrad preparing for finals, determined to excel this semester.

Stu peered at the opened books on the desk, read a dozen pages and reviewed lecture notes, concentrating on the words, connecting facts with the logic the professor stressed in class. His work is more manageable these days.

# # # #

"How are you this evening, ma'am? I was wondering if I could talk to the people who live here."

"My housemates are out, what can I do for you?"

"All right, my name's Gary Groth. We're sort of neighbors, I reside in that four-story building, the fraternity over there." He pointed across Third Street. "And I'm walkin' around tonight talkin' to students about UNITED. No doubt you've heard of us."

Holding a coffee cup, the girl stood in her doorway, peering past his shoulder. "You live in KIDs? I've been to five of your parties, you sure don't skimp on kegs."

"Thanks for the compliment, ma'am, and I'll pass it on to our social chairman. Returning to why I'm on this frosty porch of yours."

"You say you're with UNITED? Those are the peace people all of a sudden popping up on campus, right?"

"Yep. We are the premier, sole student organization representing the Champaign-Urbana anti-war movement in central Illinois," Killer recited verbatim from the UNITED facts sheet. "Our efforts are designed to make the optimal use of the student's feelings about the war, amalgamating our energies to the most effectual action."

"And?" The girl sipped her coffee.

"That's why I'm here, my assignment is soliciting the small-ish student housing units, lettin' everyone know about our activities and asking you to join us to fight the war."

"You must be desperate visiting our little place, with only three of us you won't add many recruits for your time. You'd be more productive canvassing where there's plenty of students, our neighbors in the Phi Mu sorority, Bromley Hall in the next block or your own KIDs."

"We're handlin' them also, ma'am. But my task is concentrating on the off-the-path residences. No stone unturned, yessiree, that's my motto. We want to contact everyone in Cham-Bana, tap all the students, get them involved."

"In what?"

"Like I said, ma'am, UNITED. Even if it's already December, we're turnin' everyone on to us. The more members we get the dynamic-er the message we send."

"To who?"

"The people runnin' the war, the politicians callin' the shots in Washington, the warlords of the Pentagon with their fingers on the button, the jokesters who dumped us into Vietnam but can't flush us out."

"How will you contact them? March there, mail a letter?" The girl cupped her ear with a hand. "Or call them on the phone and say, 'Hey, Mr. Powerful Four-Star General, listen up, there's bunches of us at the University of Illinois upset over the way you're waging war in Asia, we can't comprehend any progress, so stop right now and get us the heck out of Saigon.'"

"Not exactly, ma'am." Killer enjoyed the give and take with this girl, stayed focused and didn't laugh. Why in hell, he wondered, can't I ever date a bambino like this? "The plan is doing it with numbers, democracy in action at dozens and hundreds of campuses, and thousands and tens of thousands of students, our parents back at home with everyone else in their towns, all the country's citizens coming together in the cause. If we enlist the masses of demonstrators we hope for, the hype itself will send a message."

"That's your plan, protesters and publicity, like the stories I've read in the *Daily Illini* the last few weeks?"

"Affirmative. Once we line up the newspapers behind us, we'll really make an impact."

"The two-bit *DI* and someone like you tramping around on a winter night knocking on the doors of dinky houses like mine? That'll warrant the congressmen's attention?"

"Well…" For an instant, Killer doubted his mission.

"I think that phone call to Washington might be the shrewder tactic. Or a telegram; that way they'll receive your statement on paper, read it and keep it."

"All right, ma'am, come off your high horse. I'm doing my damnedest offerin' you the hard, cold facts about UNITED and you're not cooperating one, tiny bit. Are you jaggin' me around or are you always such a hard ass?"

"Both." Smiling, she set her coffee cup on the floor. "I know about you guys, how can anyone in Champaign-Urbana not? Your orange and black shirts show up everywhere on campus, and three or four times a week your advertisements are printed in the *Daily Illini*. You're doing a first-rate job promoting and explaining. But I'm not the political one, my housemates are more into the process."

"Can you get them? I'd be glad chatting with anyone for ten minutes about UNITED's plans for the school year."

"They're gone tonight, studying."

"Well, I could give you the info to pass along. Here, there's plenty." Killer reached into his backpack for a half-dozen brochures. "My favorite's the piece debunking the government's propaganda for starting the war in 1964, along with Johnson's cover up of his '65 troop escalations. Hypocrisy up the yin-yang, duplicity exposed. And speaking of overexposure, it's definitely chilly standin' on your porch. Could I hit you up for a mug of that coffee?"

"That's the wisest thing you've said. Why don't you come in?"

"Yes, ma'am."

# # # #

Summer Never Comes

Minus his roommate, Paul walked into Room 219. Professor Hudson was by the blackboard. Since the first day, when the professor was late and struggled rolling his wheelchair through the door in front of gawking students, he had always been inside the room before everyone else.

"Good afternoon. I will distribute the results of last week's hourly." The professor handed the stack of test booklets to the nearest student, who shuffled through the pile until she found hers and passed on the rest. As the exams moved across the room, Paul's apprehension increased. With the professor a scrupulous grader, the university's unwritten 'at least a B for upper-level classes' dictum was inapposite for Phil 393. Decent grades were earned.

"All right!" a student exclaimed melodramatically, flaunting his exam, obviously scoring higher than expected.

"On the whole, the results were encouraging, and I am pleased to observe most are grasping the principles we have discussed the past few months." Professor Hudson pivoted his chair toward the class. "It is apparent you are capably applying these ideas in reasonable, logical formulations, not simply regurgitating words on paper."

The lone student in the back row, Paul received the now-thin stack, his blue book underneath the top one.

"This is a very good/superior exam," the professor commented, "you show the ability to argue a premise, especially in question 1. As supplemental postulation for your claims in question 3, refer to Colin Strang's essay 'What If Everyone Did That,' in *Ethics*, Thomson and Dworkin editors. A-"

Fine, Paul calculated, my five point's a possibility. He laid his booklet on an empty desk and hunted for Lindy's.

"A relatively average attempt, you need to expand on your thoughts in a more ordered manner. C-."

Poor Lindy, another hook, so typical this semester. Opening his notebook, Paul doodled as Professor Hudson began his lecture.

# # # #

"Hi, Emily."

"Good evening, how was your day?"

Summer Never Comes

"Your typical weekend, racked until 11:30, ate lunch, then watched the Fighting Illini game on the tube. We blew away Butler by twenty points. Were you busy?"

"Nicole and I walked to Lincoln Square to Christmas shop. I bought my dad a wool sweater and my mom a cookbook."

"The weather's too cold for that long a hike. If you'd phoned I'd have driven you two, maybe bought you something nice to wear for tonight." Leaving Blaisdell Hall's lobby, Tommy Quarters held Emily's arm.

"We were gone by ten this morning, you were asleep."

"I'd have gotten up. Besides, after seeing you five straight nights I'd be glad taking in a morning as well."

The pair reached Tommy's Monte Carlo. He politely opened the door for Emily and, behind the wheel, inquired if the car's radio was too loud and what station she preferred. What a difference, Emily reflected. Will had quit being so courteous last summer and wouldn't have asked at all about her day, even if they were going out. Tom, on the other hand, cared enough to offer to drive her shopping.

"Where are we heading?"

"I made our reservations at the Round Barn."

"That's nice, I haven't been there since…" she hesitated.

Tommy dialed down the volume. "Sorry, missed your answer."

"…In May, when seven of us girls celebrated finishing the semester," Emily lied, her previous dinner there was with Will for her birthday in April.

"This'll be a first for me. I hear there's no corners in the place, only curved walls." Tommy turned onto Green Street.

Gazing through the windshield at the Union, Emily wished her new boyfriend had taken a different road, fretting that one of Will's friends, or worse, Will, would spot her in Tom's white car.

"Can I ask a question? Since you're a junior and I'm a freshman, is it awkward dating someone two years younger? Not that there're age barriers at the Big U, but I don't think this happens often."

"I'm not uncomfortable in the least, Tom, we seem compatible. If I went out with another freshman, the experience would be strange because he might be too juvenile, which you're not."

"Fine, I'd hate thinking you unhappy." He waited for the traffic light at Fourth and Green, aware this was the first time anyone in Champaign-

Urbana had called him Tom instead of Tommy. "It would be a waste of a Saturday night only drivin' around for some food, and not as two people working on a decent relationship."

"That's considerate. Our conversations this last week have been beneficial. I see I'd fallen in a rut, shutting myself away, presuming good things instead of acting for myself. This isn't insulting my Blaisdell friends or anyone else, cloistering was my omission. You've been the catalyst, brought me out and moved me along. You're an unselfish person for providing the chance."

"Thanks."

They drove to the Round Barn, arriving precisely at eight o'clock and were seated by the curved wall, as private as possible in a circular room. Self-assuredly instructing the waiter, Tommy ordered a German white wine and appetizers. Emily was impressed with Tom's well-bred manners, a rarity among adolescent Champaign-Urbana undergrads and acquired, she assumed, from his family's country club membership. If Will had sat across the table he'd squirm in his chair, fidget with the plates and silverware, razz the waiter—suggesting he chill, check if the chef was awake, and did they need any help back in the kitchen washing up dishes. Then he'd order a Budweiser. Emily was too accustomed to his routine.

And the dollars Tom spent, his parents must be wealthy. All week the two had eaten at swankier restaurants, not the normal campus hangouts, and attended movies and shows average students could only afford once a semester. Awed by money was unbecoming, Emily conceded, but after two years as a poor undergrad and dating a forever-broke boyfriend, sudden indulgence was captivating.

Tom reviewed the entrees, inquiring as to Emily's tastes, and when the waiter returned, ordered dinner for both; she never opening a menu. Such high society luxury. Emily glanced around the dining room, hoping no one recognized her.

Drinking wine, the pair discussed topics weighty and inconsequential, grown-up and ridiculous, ambiguous and intimate, Tom allowing her to steer the dialogue, agreeing to mostly everything she said, with only occasional questions or off-the-wall opinions. Emily was suspicious their first few dates, wary of Tom's fawning and motives. But he'd been a gentleman the entire week, avoiding allusions to his former raucous self, other lowlife KIDs or sex. Emily was relieved for relaxed conversation, thrilled to be liberated from Will's obstinacy. During dinner, Tom excused himself and left the table, laying his napkin on the chair, etiquette-wise the proper way to act. Will likely would have flipped it to Emily, asking her to guard the rag while he hit the john. When the waiter arrived with the check, Tom pulled enough money from his wallet to pay the bill, advising him to keep the change. He did not, as Lindy and fellow college students would have, miserly estimate a five percent tip.

"Thank you for a delicious, delightful meal, Mr. Quarters," Emily respectfully said.

"Next time we eat here I'll remember to ask for fresher lettuce in my salad. And my name's Tommy or Tom." He creased his napkin into a taut square. "Do you know the first things I noticed about you last week in the Lion? Your body and voice. You weren't wearing a coat, your red turtleneck sweater was tucked inside your jeans, and even with the racket, you spoke as sedately as if the bar was a library. You stayed in character, modest and lovable."

Emily was unsure of Tom's implications. "That was all you saw?"

"Hell, you had the shapeliest waist in the joint," Tommy switched to a thoughtful tone, "but out of place with the other women, the ones you know are sniffin' around for freebie beers. In a crowd like that, you stand out—genuine, well-intentioned—the kind of woman I really appreciate for putting up with me. A lot of people don't consider me the nicest or most honest guy on campus. I know Orion Nelson, Tim Malito, Lindy, Stu Cummings and most of the upperclassmen think that way—that I don't merit membership in a fraternity based on trust."

Emily stared at Tom, seeing sincerity, a trait she'd missed this semester. This was the first time all week Will's name had been spoken aloud.

"And I'd say the reputation was deserved. Since New Student Week I've been in the middle of so much disgusting junk, cheating, gambling, drunkenness, tricks I've snatched in bedrooms, downers I wouldn't discuss with ladies. I dropped so far into the deep end I couldn't resurface. Now, being with you, I see there's a basis to everyone's opinion of me; I'm a fool." Tommy grinned. "Maybe I've grown up a bit the last seven days. I wanna say thanks."

Summer Never Comes

The clichés, ones Will might recite, touched her heart. Tom had scruples.

"I don't think you're a shamed person. This has also been a revealing week for me. I'm uncertain how friendly you are with Will, Paul and the other seniors, or how frequently you talk with them, but these last months were a trial. Until this semester, Will, or Lindy, and I were girlfriend and boyfriend, close to an understanding." Maybe that's an overstatement, Emily conceded to herself. "Then he joined that band and his darker side showed. Immediately his priorities reversed, music was his only concern, he only considered himself. I was forgotten, not knowing where I stand or if I counted, even after I waited, talked with him, argued, hoped and waited longer."

"Have you opened up to anyone else, the girls in the dorm? How about Lindy's buddies?"

"Yes, particularly Bobby Sox, who is a sweetheart for letting me share my troubles. But Bobby has his own girlfriend he's wrapped up with, driving to Chicago almost every weekend to see her. You, Tom, since you're unattached, have time for me. You let me deliberate, wander through topics, I'm my own person. These last days have been my pleasantest since September. Thank you for giving them to me."

"Well, I'm happy we're both thankful." Tommy reached for her hand. "Can we continue dating?"

"Of course."

A waiter balancing a trayful of dishes marched by. The rest of the restaurant's tables were empty.

"There's a last subject. Lindy. You say you still like him and that's fine, I'll take my chances, just like you're risking with me. What about his pals? So far this week we've been lucky, no one in KIDs is aware we're dating. Eventually, someone—everybody—will learn the secret. When they do, so will Lindy. There could be hell to pay."

"I've waited three months, Will and I had our opportunities but failed." Emily unhappily responded. "When we're discovered, his friends will realize that, too."

# # # #

Summer Never Comes

Saturday was the fifth straight night Frogfeet played the Lion, not a basic way Champaign bars booked live entertainment. Too many repeat performances by a band was bad business because bored-with-the-same-songs customers stopped buying beers. But the rowdy ovations Frogfeet collected the night the KIDs crowded the joint impressed Tyke. When his regular Thursday booking, Yellow Ocher Red, canceled due to raspy voices, he scheduled the 'Feet and stuck with them when Cold Press, the Friday and Saturday night band, was stranded in Danville with a cracked engine block.

> We've got the word, to keep on movin'.
> The life of a singer is tough,
> Drivin' the country, singin' our songs,
> This is the way we live and love.

"That was exactly on time, 'Lost Love' is next." Franky Konkel slapped his guitar. Even though the 'Feet's sets never varied, their leader chattered between every song.

Playing his usual rhythm accompaniment, a relaxed Lindy winked at a girl near the stage, the same woman that showed last evening, the evening before and the evening before that. He strummed a b-major chord and guiltily thought of Emily, reckoning he hadn't talked to her in over a week, definitely his own fault, a Sword of Damocles. But with so many gigs, his only other optional activity was sleep. The sometime-student was now a no-show, cutting most classes and appreciating Robby picking up his Phil 393 exam for him. With the hook minus, though, his roommate shouldn't have wasted the shoe leather.

> People say I spend all my time
> Chasin' a dream that won't be mine.
> The dream's the girl I now sing of,
> But the woman's gone, a lost love.
>
> We had the good times we all want,
> Afternoons together we spent,
> Kept away from life's push and shove,
> But that's over, a long lost love.

Summer Never Comes

Through the smoke, Lindy gazed at the middling-sized weekend crowd. We're holding our fans, that's an assist, they're satisfied and so's Tyke. And our music's progressing, with fewer screw-ups, verging on professional. He glanced around again, spotted the babe and waved. Boy, she's cute, a real ripe tomato. Total it up, rock 'n' roll music is great.

"Okay, guys, respectable set, let's break for fifteen." Franky shook Woofer's hand, jumped off the stage and beelined for the bar.

"Andy, what about refreshing 'Lost Love's' lyrics?" Lindy looked behind him. "We should add verses for each band member."

"Yeah, group lyrics, a group trip, group love." 'Mad' beat his snare.

"A group freak." Andy Arthur chuckled, and with his fellow 'Feet steered through the tables.

"I will be elated when tonight's over, I love performin,' but so many gigs in a row is a trek. 'Gig Trek,' get it?"

"Could be worse," Andy put an arm around Lindy's shoulder, "might be five straight nights in five strange central Illinois towns with us driving through sleet and snow."

"I suppose there's a sunnier side." Lindy leaned on the bar. "Whatever happened to the rehearsin' we were plannin'?"

"This is the real world, buddy, life is practice, practice is life and work means money. Anyway, I thought playing on a stage was your dream."

"I'm not complaining, but it would be super wedgin' in time off, like Franky promised a couple weeks ago, two or three performances then a break to retool our stock songs, or escape and snatch some sleep."

"I hear you, Frogfeet's a travelin' band of late," Andy chugged his beer, "but the experience is a gas."

"Premium ethyl. On stage is such a rush, checkin' out the couples dancin' or the envious roadies peerin' back at us. You know, when I spot someone at a table starin' back toward me I think, 'Ha, ha, ha to you, pal, eat your heart out. I didn't sit back, waiting for this opening to come to me, I'm up here because I hustled to my dream to make it happen.' That's terrifically neat."

"Music's our karma, you and I are lifers. Gotta hit the john, see you on stage."

Summer Never Comes

A contented Lindy contemplated his beer mug. Damn it, I should've talked to Andy about smoothin' the chorus in 'Bristol and Vellum.' I'll catch him after he zips his fly.

"Hi."

"Hello to you." The cute babe stepped next to him. Fence-rail thin, she wasn't dressed as neat as Em. Her blouse had a hole on the collar, the extra-wide bellbottoms were frazzled at her shoes, and her Army fatigue coat was dirty. "We finally meet, my name's Lindy."

"I'm Robin Ferris."

"You must be keen on our music, spectatin' this weekend like you have."

"Longer than that, I've listened plenty of days and to enough performances to know you guys are an okay sounding band, improving and mellower, more confident and cool."

"Thanks, no sense sittin' on the ol' laurels only anticipatin' hatchlings." Lindy was positive his face had a huge 'oh, gee whiz, that was goofy' expression. "You a student?"

"Yes, I live in Scott Hall."

"Really! We're basically neighbors, I'm at Third and Armory, in KIDs."

"I've made a few parties this semester."

"Just about the whole campus has crashed our bashes."

"Funny, I haven't seen you at any of them." Robin smiled.

"I've been travelin' with Frogfeet these last months. Socializin', among other activities, has been tough."

"Let's go, buddy, time to make more music." Andy walked toward the pair.

"Will you guys play until one a.m.?"

"That's this madness' method."

"I'll wait if you want to talk." Robin hopefully said.

"Sounds like a deal."

# # # #

Another advertisement was printed in Tuesday's *Daily Illini*.

"War is not the solution to world crises. Throughout history, armed conflicts have been the tools of aggressors, the desperate alternatives of failing societies bankrupt of original ideas, the road for those unwilling to search out the logical but taxing courses. War is the easy way out.

"The path of peace is the harder to accept, requiring conscience, courage to say 'enough is enough,' and a willingness to turn the other cheek.

"It is simple reacting in anger, difficult to deliberate, mediate and fairly, equitably solve peoples' problems.

"UNITED believes the United States should cease relying on the easy way and return to the ideals of decency and brotherhood.

"UNITED to end the war."

# # # #

Late meeting Sharon, Paul carried a popcorn box in one hand, his book bag with the other, and at the Psych Building's doors had to lay the bag down to turn the handle. Entering the atrium, he found his girlfriend sitting on the low brick wall bordering the trees, flowers and rocks.

"I forgot napkins." Paul opened the greasy box.

"Did you ever consider the strange ways the university's designing space these days?" Sharon stared at the skylights eight stories above. "Look at this place. The building has offices facing the outside and into this courtyard, which is cubic feet pretty much wasted. You'd think architects would've filled the void with extra rooms rather than these bushes and boulders. And there's the Foreign Languages Building, starts out small and narrow on the first floor then widens as it rises. Weird, as if the Big U warped into confusion for ten years."

"Some say architecture parallels society's psyche." Paul wiped his buttery fingers on his white socks. "Wonder what the future will think about us."

"Plus the silly underground Undergrad Library, not exploiting any acreage at all." A chuckling Sharon peered at Paul. "You think my elevator's not climbing to the top, don't you?"

"Booking too much?"

"Or not enough. Finals pretty soon."

"But first Christmas."

"Ho, ho, ho, Santa," Sharon mimicked an elf's soprano voice.

Paul licked his fingers. "Seriously, don't forget the party Saturday."

Summer Never Comes

"Since when are KIDs' parties anything but fun?"

"Major, significant drinking?"

"That's about it, making sure you guys drain every keg. You're coming to dinner at my place before your fraternity's bash, right?"

"Of course, your roommates have chatted up this 'traditional' Christmas dinner for weeks."

"Remember, wear a coat and tie." The sun emerged through the clouds, brightening the atrium. "Maybe why I'm loopy is I delivered my Vet Med College application today, beating my before-the-holidays deadline."

"Good luck, kiddo, I'm certain you'll be admitted." Paul gazed at the office windows cut into the high walls. A pipe-smoking, bow-tied professor-type waved.

Sharon grabbed a handful of popcorn. "A kernel for your thoughts?"

"The reason I'm late is I was waiting in line at the Quick Print for my résumé."

"How many copies did you order?"

"A hundred, they'll sit on my shelf until interviews in the spring. No sense buying stamps until I'm forced to."

"Delay, delay, delay. What else have you been up to?" She was uninterested in re-arguing Paul's future.

"I've tried contacting Bernard Minerath for an interview but can't locate him. He's not in UNITED's headquarters in the Union, doesn't answer his phone and I'm fairly sure he hasn't lived in his apartment all week."

"How do you figure that?" A preoccupied Sharon shook the box, loosening seeds stuck in the butter.

"I've walked past his building the last five days. Letters and magazines are stuffed in his mailbox, the drapes are closed and there're no footprints in the snow at the door."

"Maybe he's human after all, rendezvous-ing with his underground girlfriend in some hush-hush hotel."

"Atypical, however. Bernard's not the type to shack up for a whole week."

"The guy is someplace, if not in Champaign or Urbana, somewhere else."

Summer Never Comes

"Why leave for so long when the semester's closing toward finals? He must have classes to attend."

"Maybe he's not a student." Sharon stared into the box.

# # # #

"Dear Billy,

"I was glad you wrote us. We passed around the letter to the upperclassmen and all your old buddies, I mean every one, say hello.

"We are having a normal fall semester. As predicted, the Fighting Illini football team finished with a 4-6 record. The highlight was Homecoming when we blew Iowa out of Memorial Stadium, 50–0, what a thrill. Just as exciting that weekend was watching Bobby Sox. He was so drunk in the east balcony that Stu and Robby had to carry him back to the house where he slept off his liquor for four hours prior to the dance. But Bobby made an appearance and had the common sense to avoid the Mad Dog the Mooser was selling that night.

"Scooter Petersen has finally asked Lauren Rose to marry him, which also occurred at Homecoming. They plan to marry next autumn. Hopefully, you will be back in the country and able to attend the wedding with us. As you might guess, the pledges tossed him in the showers after a half-hour skirmish with the senior class. Unfortunately, I was out of the house that evening and not a participant in the conflagration.

"The house football team reached the intramural playoffs this year, finishing 4-1 in the regular season. We defeated Acacia in the first round but were trounced in the quarterfinals by Theta Chi. I am embarrassed to report that the score was 34-6.

"The KIDs' b-ball squad looks promising. We have two pledges, Baro and Tracy, who are both six foot four and quick. We also have three very weak houses in our league.

"Lindy has found his band. The maniac has played at the Red Lion every night for the last two weeks, which means he is not around our fraternity very much. Robby and the rest of us are more than a bit concerned. He seems to be putting too much of himself into his music and letting everything else slide. But you know old Lindy: 'Beatles forever!'

Summer Never Comes

"You will be interested hearing that our campus' peace groups have become very structured. And controlled. The newest one, named UNITED, has assumed an umbrella function as the leader of anti-war activities, with some impressive ideas to keep the war in front of us. This month, they are concentrating on a food drive for the people in Vietnam. If protesting can help end the mindless, inane fighting you're in, I feel this will be the year.

"That is all for this letter, time for Mary Lou's spaghetti dinner.

"Merry Christmas and all the good luck in the world to you and your Army friends. We are always thinking about you.

"Kindest personal regards,
"Kentucky"

# # # #

Besides New Student Week registration, the Armory was busiest during the ten-minute breaks between classes when hundreds of undergrads shortcut through the building. The rest of the day, the two-block long structure was empty—the reason many joggers, including Tim Malito, ran laps on the tartan track. Six and a fraction circles made a mile, with his typical time eight forty-five to nine and a half minutes. This afternoon Tim ran a brisker pace, needing to go back to the house to book. His hydraulic fluids exam was scheduled for the first day of finals, and he wanted to sort through his notes before taking them home at Christmas. Tim weaved through the few pedestrians crossing the Armory's floor, walked one lap to cool down, and grabbed his coat from the bleachers.

Outside, he spotted a UNITED food drive van parked on Fourth Street. Six orange and black-clad True Believers manned the truck's rear while extra 'peace-trekkies,' as the student body had named them, paced the sidewalk distributing leaflets.

"The Vietnamese have to eat, too, donate for their well-being," the True Believers preached. "Help us atone for the government's blunders, give some food."

"Contribute the cans you can."

Students strolled toward the van carrying bags, sacks and cartons. A few dropped coins in a box a trekkie held out to passersby.

"Thanks, man." He rattled the money jar. "UNITED to end the war."

Summer Never Comes

How many spots had Tim noticed these vans around campus? At least twelve. He guessed UNITED didn't own a dozen trucks, they were driven to new campus locations each day. However, UNITED magically appearing everywhere was impressive.

Entering KIDs' living room, Tim saw Shaky Jake and the brothers setting up the house Christmas tree, this afternoon's task clamping the Scotch pine into the stand. After supper, the little sisters would help to decorate with lights, tinsel, ornaments, and peppermint schnapps-laced hot chocolate.

"Nice looking evergreen you bought."

"Thanks," Jake rested his arm on Tim's shoulder, "It's fuller than last year's stick. Comin' to the tree-trimming?"

"Don't think so, time for hard-core booking."

# # # #

That evening, Paul, Sharon and thirty-odd KIDs decorated the tree, Paul delighted seeing Lindy making a late appearance. His roommate dodged hanging tinsel but tipped a few cups of hot cocoa and schnapps. After Sharon drove back to her house, the roommates went upstairs.

"Things fine with you two, Robby?" Lindy plopped on his bed.

"Awesomer than I imagined. If I'd realized Scooter, Bobby and the other heavy daters were enjoying so much fun, and women's perspectives were so contrasting to men's, I'd have jumped into this girlfriend routine sooner than my senior year."

"Relationships are great, no doubt, occasionally baffling, but absolutely worth their weight in gold. The key to the door is chancing on the right girl, the one who sees your soul. When you connect, friendship, maybe even intimacy, comes naturally, genuinely." The schnapps caused Lindy to yawn. "Sharon's a senior too, right?"

"Graduates in June and plans to study veterinary medicine here in Champaign."

"Yeah, you've told me, lately my memory's such a basket case. Has she been admitted?"

"Sharon delivered her application yesterday." Paul gazed out the window. "One hurdle is the interview, which is scheduled after semester break. But with her nearly straight-A grades and interest in animals, she'll be accepted."

"What'll happen to you two if your honey stays down here? Come June, all of us, probably even me, ship back to Chi-town and your basic Monday-through-Friday jobs. But your sweetheart returns to grad school in September. Of course, you can drive down on weekends. That would be a trip, football games with money in your pockets, walkin' the campus not bothered about heading to the Undergrad to book. Maybe that's what I'll do, too, spend my weekends playin' at the bars, a new definition of the alumni band. Imagine, you can come and see me over at the Lion."

"What a shame, I finally meet a girl interested in me and we'll only spend eight months together. Sometimes life sucks because I can't picture moving back to Hazelcrest, living in my parents' house and seeing Sharon for only a few hours on the weekends."

"Don't worry, brother Roberts, sooner or later every rat finds the maze's escape hatch." Lindy sat on his bunk, wishing he'd fanned on the third schnapps and cocoa. "Did I tell you about my soirée at the Lion last weekend? There was this girl hangin' around both nights—a thin, scrawny thing not with anybody—watchin' us play. Saturday between sets, Andy and I are havin' a beer and she walks up to rap. Turns out she's attended tons of Frogfeet's gigs, remembered when we started out, where most of our performances were, our play lists, and knew something, a whim or a nervous habit, about each one of us 'Feet. She must be our most dedicated, die-hard fan to gather that info. And we hit it off. After packin' away the equipment, her and I, her name's Robin, sat in the Steak 'n Shake drinkin' coffee. Honestly, I think she's after me."

"How do you figure? Is she a groupie chasing your blonde hair and black tennis shoes?"

"Robin just about came out and confessed, said there's never been anyone as cute as me onstage."

"Way to go, McCartney. What happened after the boyish charms and good looks compliments?"

"I was awed. That's the first time a woman's hit on me since performin' with the 'Feet. But I had to hold Robin and myself back. Right now, involved with another girl is insanity. How many complications do I need? The band, classes, finals. And Em, she's the main reason—I've treated her so shabbily I couldn't do this to her, another woman would be the end. Hell, I want to square things with Em, not close down the relationship."

"I'm glad you're talking common sense, but it's not the first time I've heard this claim."

"Don't disagree, hell's highway is paved with admirable intentions. But there's time for contrition, still more chances to make rights."

# # # #

Paul crossed the Quad, on his way to Sharon's for another tree trimming. The only students out on this cold, sunny afternoon were seven or eight undergrads wearing orange and black warm-up jackets. These UNITED members hustled around the Senior Bench of the Class of 1912, handing out leaflets to students, pleading with and persuading them to sign the papers clamped on their clipboards. From the way the hopscotching True Believers blew on their fingers, Paul guessed the protesters had been toiling for quite a while.

"Yo, here's the destination! Register for peace, join the movement! How about it, buddy; have you enlisted yet?"

"Excuse me, join what?" Paul innocently asked.

"UNITED!" the trekkie shouted, astounded someone on campus didn't get the cause. "This is your chance to make a statement, do your thing, fight the war!"

"Why the belligerent phrase?"

"That's what we're about. Some people, the unluckies, army draftees for example, are forced to fight, kill and be the victims, with no choices but to suffer and endure. Others, like us fortunates in UNITED, are following our mission to reform the world, highlight the hypocrisies and push for reason. We battle to end the fighting."

"How?"

"I'm outside in this winter weather, talking to students, telling everyone how bad Vietnam is and how we can stop the murdering." The True Believer's tone was calmer than when he'd first approached Paul.

"Fighting is odd rationalization for a peace group, it doesn't sound pacifist."

Summer Never Comes

"An idiom to gain students' attention. UNITED's approach is deliberating with common sense, building support to bring the people together. We're not out here marching on the Administration Building or burning down the Armory."

"Valid point," Paul acknowledged. "Say you convince Big U students to sign your forms, join up, volunteer a few hours a week and donate money—we're all a little involved—then what do you do with us?"

"That itself is an accomplishment, correct? One hundred percent of the students here and across the country, in the same cause, fused together, cohesive."

"Here and in the rest of the country? I didn't know UNITED was all around America."

"The Illini UNITED are local, but organizations like us are on plenty other campuses, pushing the same activities we are."

"How many schools, is there a count, do you know the locations?"

"One concentration's in New England, most of the Ivy League, plus colleges in New Jersey and Pennsylvania." The trekkie stomped his feet for warmth. "As I said, enrolling with us will make a statement to Washington. No more wars."

"Can't disagree, but I don't think I'm interested." Paul stepped toward the Urbana side of the Quad.

"Why not?" The activist held his arms out. "People are dying in Vietnam every week, every day, every hour, slaughtered by American soldiers. What's more vital than stopping murder and bringing the peace?"

"For me, no time, a hectic schedule," Paul shook his head, "happy hours, Christmas parties and a few finals."

"You don't actually need to attend meetings or volunteer for many activities, only give us your name. If you did, you'd have a lot of company, you'd help."

"Afraid I can't do that, either, but when the chips are down, I'll contribute, I promise." Paul walked back toward the trekkie. "Tell me, how successful have you been enrolling students?"

"Last I heard, we're at four thousand," his spirits lifted as Paul moved closer.

"That's a huge increase since Thanksgiving."

Summer Never Comes

"Peace is popular," the activist proffered his clipboard and a ballpoint pen, "how about it?"

"Sorry, but I'll grab a leaflet." He stuffed the pamphlet in a notebook. "Thanks for the conversation."

"It's what we're fighting for." The True Believer turned away, searching out more pedestrians. As the sun set behind the Administration Building, Paul hurried toward Davenport Hall, deciding to file the flyer with the dozens of other pieces he'd collected.

\# \# \# \#

Scooter Petersen neared the Sixth Street Campus Barber Shop. As most of his friends, he'd shunned haircuts since September, with curls now covering his ears, neck and shirt collar. He liked it long as did Lauren. However his mom, the family enforcer, preferred a trimmed, clean-cut style. Thanksgiving break hadn't been too awkward, Scooter only hanging around the Petersen household on the holiday, but Christmas vacation was different. He'd be home for two weeks, an awful long time to listen to his parents' complaints. So Scooter walked in, waited forty-five minutes for an open chair and missed the first half of the afternoon's *Star Trek* episode.

\# \# \# \#

"How's UNITED progressing, Randy?"

"Positively energizing, I hear our membership campaign's enlisted five hundred this week, bringing us to forty-eight hundred."

"Those numbers must satisfy Bernard," Paul said.

"I agree, but our objective's still a ways off, thousands more have to sign up for peace. Interested in joining?"

"Thinking on it. A few days ago I was stopped by a peace trekkie at Lincoln Hall. We had a ten-minute discussion, with him pressing the arguments I've read in the *Daily Illini*."

"We aim for thoroughness. Bernard and the directors have outlined a recruiters' presentation; with research showing sticking to this script gets us a new enrollee sixty-five percent of the time. We're also plotting a campus map in our office, with dots marking where each new member is enrolled.

Summer Never Comes

We know the Quad's the prime recruiting area, with the sidewalk between the Administration Building and Greg Hall the densest."

"Innovative, how long has UNITED maintained it?" Paul's cheeks shifted on the toilet. He and his fraternity brother occupied adjoining stalls in the KIDs' second floor john.

"For the last month," Randy's voice was strained, but not from conversation.

"Was the chart Bernard's brainchild?"

"The idea came from a director who's a marketing major, the one drafting the recruiting scripts. I don't know if Bernard's aware of it because I haven't seen him lately."

"Are you in the office often?"

"I staff the phones on Monday and Wednesday afternoons, which are handy times for hearing updates."

"Stories about Bernard have been missing from the *DI* the last couple of weeks, as if he's gone quiet."

"Someone said Bernard's out on a trip to the East Coast."

"What about his classes?" Paul ripped a half-dozen sheets of toilet paper from the roll sitting on the floor.

"Got any TP over there? This stall's out."

"What's it worth?" Paul laughed and slid his roll underneath the partition. "Do you know where Bernard's gone?"

"New York, New Jersey or Delaware, I understand he travels to those states every month or six weeks, oftener last summer."

Paul heard Randy's toilet flush. Doing the same, he stood, unlatched the door, walked to the bathroom sinks and turned on the faucet.

"Ah, yes, the pause that refreshes, hey, gentlemen?" His yelling echoing off the ceramic tiles, Killer rambled into a stall, sat and sighed. "It's great being alive."

Drying their hands, Paul and Randy saw Shaky Jake sneak into the john. Raising a finger to his lips for quiet, Jake held the door open as Stu, the Jerg and Nemo—as stealthy as their leader—tiptoed in, holding cups and plastic pitchers. Stu also carried a metal bucket Paul recognized from the basement maintenance room.

"Killer, got a date for Saturday?" Randy loudly asked. Jake flashed a thumbs up.

Summer Never Comes

"As a matter of fact, the weirdest episode occurred three nights ago. I was hustling the sidewalks, fulfilling my volunteer stint for UNITED," he groaned, "starting at the little two-story house across Third Street next to Phi Mu—the one with the old porch and crappy front yard. A good-lookin' honey answered the door and I pitched the standard UNITED promotion. She—her name's Chris—was somewhat of a smart aleck but receptive. I got asked in for a cup of coffee, we hit it off, and I invited her to the Christmas dance."

"That's encouraging, Killer, does she have any housemates?"

"Two, Connie and Gracie. Want me to set you up?"

Jake and the Jerg filled their pitchers at the faucet, with Paul grabbing the extra. Stu and Nemo stood in the utility closet, pouring water into the bucket. Randy stepped toward the stall to rap and muffle their noise.

"Is Chris a good looker?"

"A knockout," Killer spoke with his typical over-sensationalism. "Dark hair, always smiling, real outgoing, knows how to keep up a conversation."

"Where's she from?" Randy looked at his friends and snickered.

"Somewhere north of Rockford."

Bobby Sox skulked into the john carrying one of Ozark's thirty-ounce beer cups, raised the glass over his head, pantomimed a scream, then scooted to the sinks.

"Say, boys, is there anybody else out there with you two?" Killer sounded concerned.

"It's me, Jake, washing my popcorn popper."

"I'm helping," Bobby added.

"I'm soaking my socks," Stu shouted from the closet. Paul and the Jerg chuckled again.

"Oh?" Killer's tone was definitely suspicious.

The faucets off, every KID with a pitcher, bucket or cup surrounded Killer's stall.

"Where'd you say Chris was from?"

"I think the town is Rockton. Randy, who exactly is out there?"

"How you doin', Killer?"

"Nemo, is that you, ol' chum?"

"Yep, it's me, old buddy," Nemo aped his sassiness.

Summer Never Comes

"All right, lemme hear you, now!" Jake's yelling imitated baseball announcer Harry Caray's seventh inning stretch routine. "A one, a two, a three!"

"Take, me out to the ball game. Take, me out to the crowd," the Mooser hurried through the door, guffawing and singing along.

"Buy me some pea-nuts and crack-er jacks. I don't care if I ev-er get back." The water carriers raised their cups and pails above the metal partition. Stu stepped up on a toilet with his bucket.

"For it's root, root-root for the Il-li-ni. If they don't win it's a shame. And it's one, two, three strikes you're out…"

They dumped on Killer.

"…At the old ball-game. Hey!"

"You sons of bitches!" Killer bellowed, shriller than anyone had heard him howl before. "Bastards! Assholes!"

The conspirators whooped. More KIDs rushed in, wondering what the hell'd happened, Jake and Stu shook hands, Moose doubled over, and a laughing Paul leaned against one sink, dropping his pitcher. The stall door opened and a drenched Killer, not bothering to pull up his u-trow, plodded out.

"Rotten sons of bitches."

# # # #

"God, Robby, I wish I coulda seen Killer catch his 'nads last night. It's always decent watching him chopped down three notches."

"Moose laughed the loudest, so hard he dropped his beer bottle."

"The only thing I'll say is after Killer finishes raggin' for a week and a half, I'm sure he'll find a way to settle scores."

"As long as it's water, the revenge won't be bad." On their way to the Library after lunch, the roommates waited for the traffic light at Armory Avenue and Sixth Street "By the way, will you be at the Christmas dance Saturday?"

"Afraid not, Frogfeet's playin' at the Bloomington Red Lion."

"You guys are pushing in tight with them," Paul said.

"It's Tyke, the owner. I think he's listened to us too much, we're fryin' his brain."

"Which is a positive, right? Steady work for Frogfeet."

"I suppose," Lindy half agreed, "but life would be more exciting performin' somewhere besides his two bars."

"Can't your band find other places?"

"Franky Konkel and Gary Anderson cut a deal with Tyke. He guarantees us so many gigs a week, and we show up for the money."

"Maybe you should change your name to the Lion's Feet." The pair and hundreds of impatient fellow students crossed the street against the red light.

"How about Lionspaws? Or Lion's Pause?"

"There you go." Paul glanced toward St. John's church. "Once more about this weekend, you're missing the dance?"

"I may not return to the house Saturday night, we've discussed shackin' up in Bloomington and for a change travelin' on Sunday in sunlight."

"If that's the case, do you mind me reserving our room?" Paul shyly inquired. "Hopefully I'll get Sharon back to her house, but if the party turns wild, we may…"

"Robby! Naturally, it's yours, be my guest, I owe you bunches from last year, I'll make certain we stay away." Lindy patted Paul's back. "I recall the oldie days when you'd be totally embarrassed bringing a woman to KIDs and enduring the razzin' from the brothers. How we change. Take me, Lord, I've heard it all."

The roommates, along with the mobs of pedestrians, jaywalked toward the Main Library, crisscrossing Armory Avenue in no particular pattern, bicyclers dangerously zigzagging and drivers in their cars haphazardly turning on Wright Street.

"Talk to Emily lately?"

"I'll tell ya," Lindy's mind swapped Paul's girlfriend for his own, "that woman is one tough nut to locate. I've phoned every day this week, twice on Monday, but only get through to Nicole."

"Does she call back?"

"No, and that's bizarre. Em's never been one for contacting me, but until this month, I can't remember a time she hasn't returned my messages."

"Pardon the bluntness, maybe three months is her limit, maybe Emily's teaching you a lesson."

Summer Never Comes

"That's Em's character, having her own way regardless of how much time. I should take the bait, let her think she's punishing me with the penance I deserve. But Em deserves better than me actin' out a farce."

The pair walked into the Library, Lindy heading upstairs to the Reference Room to study, his roommate through the corridor to Gregory Drive and his class in David Kinley Hall.

Behind in everything, Lindy had tons of booking to tackle. In a couple courses, the predicament was dire because he'd cut half the classes and now, as the semester moved to the last weeks, didn't have any clue about what his professors were emphasizing. This afternoon, Lindy had skipped his one o'clock to research his Ad 225 project. After reading United States Census Bureau reports and Chamber of Commerce pamphlets, he planned writing the paper, then finding somebody in KIDs to type it for him; remembering Bill Wick charged fifty cents a page. Lindy spread his index cards and notes on the long, wooden table.

So many loose strands, where'd, how'd three months vanish, why am I so foolish? Lindy only needed one moment for an answer. Frogfeet chewed up countless hours, long nights and numerous, copious weekends. Music, his obsession, was fun but squeezed a price tag. Each rehearsal, Red Lion appearance, road trip and rapping-drinking session was a lost evening of studying. This hadn't been calamitous in September and October, Lindy never owning the reputation as a hard-core booker. But in previous semesters, as finals neared Lindy always turned earnest, caught up, and the homework devil received his due.

How will I pull it off this time? In the next months Frogfeet would play more, not less and, as their reputation preceded, there'd be extra, stretched out travelings. Recognition, prominence, a fame game? *Aw, hold your horses. Holy moly, there's my résumé to get printed, another chore, and next semester job interviews, what a trick fitting those in. At least spring, his college swan song, would mean less studying. Maybe there'd be no job interviews. Andy's lyrics could improve and some night, somewhere, some big shot might hear them play and the big break would arrive. Frogfeet could take off.*

Get your head outta your ass, Lindy, concentrate on this term paper, figure the direction Phil 393's headin', fine-tune that résumé, eat dinner, and get in touch with your girlfriend.

Summer Never Comes

Why is Em last on the list? A tenth inning? A ribbon on the package, frosting on a cupcake? Cute logic but feeble clichés. Right now she wasn't his urgent-est problem, nearer a marginal detail. Em a negative, how terrible, what was happening? Was Robin scudding his head through the clouds? Had he removed Em from his life because she cold-shouldered the most meaningful part, his music? Lindy certainly leaned that way. Could he repair his relationship with Em as he'd squared himself with Robby? His conversation last month with ol' Kentucky turned that trick, made him realize he had friends in KIDs. Lindy could do the same with his girlfriend. Em at least, no, that's wrong, definitely deserved twice the effort, she means that much to me. Yes, of course, forget Robin and any other women and their distractions.

Lindy tugged the cap off his Bic pen. Why didn't Em call him back? In the past, she'd always had time to listen to how his days went, his oddball ramblings, tomorrow's dreamings and nearly-heartfelt apologies. Now silence. Em was reinforcing a point, she was mad and wanted Lindy to prove himself with some ironclad affirmation. That's the answer, once and for all, hat in hand, hand on the torch, hands across the sea, holding hands, express his love. But how, if he couldn't reach her?

Eureka! Lindy would hike to Blaisdell Hall and find her, that's the solution. Face-to-face, person-to-person. He wouldn't telephone he was coming over; just appear, a babe on the doorstep. When? Lindy remembered Em was free this afternoon. Should he chance she was around Blaisdell right now? Detour to the Campus Florist on Green Street for a bouquet? Might be hokey, but a shocker. He stared at the index cards and notebooks, then packed up his research. Screw the term paper, it'll wait. Lindy was determined to show Em she was tops on the chart, and prove this to himself.

# # # #

In Paul's finance course, boring Professor Joyce rambled through his tedious, notorious-in-the-Commerce College close-of-semester review. Too near retirement to research and update his material, the sixty-four-year-old instructor always exhausted the subject a month before the class' last weeks; this scheme his way of covering the shortfall.

Summer Never Comes

Paul spent the period doodling and analyzing everything but fin. One more term paper, not a problem to write. Sharon, buy a corsage for Saturday night. His roommate and Emily, hope they make up. Christmas vacation, a humdrum two weeks with my parents. UNITED and Bernard, ambiguity. If Bernard was absent from the campus, as the peace trekkie and Randy supposed, was Professor Gulley also missing? Were they together? Would it be coincidence or proof of a plot? As finance class droned to the bell, Paul remembered Gulley kept office hours this afternoon.

Twenty minutes later, he climbed Greg Hall's steps, feeling the fourth floor's warmer temperatures; the university's steam heating system working well this winter. The long hallway was abandoned as he approached the professor's door. Locked. He headed for the History Department.

"Could you tell me if Professor Gulley is available today?" Paul asked the secretary.

"Are you another of her students? The professor is out of town, she left five days ago, and we expect her back next Monday." She spoke in a monotone, as if she'd repeated the sentences ten or fifteen times.

"Do you know where she can be reached?" Paul lied, "it's important I contact her by this weekend."

"I understand the professor has traveled to Denver. We have no forwarding address or phone number, but if you like you may leave a note in her mailbox."

"Thanks." Paul opened his notebook and scribbled on his fin class doodle page. Tearing out the sheet, Paul walked to the faculty boxes and found Professor Gulley's stuffed. He jammed his paper in and strolled away.

No Bernard, a gone Professor Gulley—two who should be in Champaign-Urbana but weren't; Paul decided to follow up another suspicion.

Inside Room 361, Lincoln Hall, the first in the Political Science Department's office labyrinth, there were more mailboxes, a coffee urn with styrafoam cups on a corner table, and a sign by the sugar bowl reading '10¢ per cup.' He passed through the little lounge and into the receptionist's room.

"Excuse me?"

"Goodness, Paul Roberts, it has been months!" Annie Marie Curry walked around her desk. "How are all my old friends at the *Daily Illini?*"

"Just fine, somehow surviving without you."

"Always believed the paper would, I never was much of a contributor." She hugged Paul.

"That's untrue, your tenure as interim sports editor is still talked about."

"Ninety-eight hours; I counted after being fired. The first female reporter to sneak into the visiting team's locker room in Memorial Stadium, that was me. I still remember the disciplinary meeting with the Illini Publishing Company's board."

"How's grad school?"

"The right decision, staying in Champaign-Urbana instead of hunting for a real world job. What's Stef Tianen up to these days?"

"Making like Miss Perry White. Efficient, officious, maneuvering; still playing every intramural she can sign up for."

"Athletics always were Stef's release." She sat on her gray metal desk. "What brings you to this bastion of liberal arts?"

"A favor. There's a poli-sci major I'd like to check on, his name is Bernard Minerath."

"UNITED's boss is in political science?"

"What I'm told by my contacts in Admissions and Records. I'd like to know the classes he's taken the last seven semesters."

"That's a tricky request. University policy is to withhold that information from anyone except the student or parents. But what the heck, because it's you asking, hold on a minute."

Annie touched Paul's shoulder and walked to the next room. A book, *The Social Animal*, lay on the desk, and a duct tape patch covered the ripped vinyl on her chair.

"Here you go," she hid a manila folder between Paul's books, "disappear for half an hour."

"I owe you a beer. Do you want to read the file?"

"Not particularly, I'm through with newspapers, remember? But I'd check you out someday." She held Paul's arm again. "Go investigate Bernie Minerath and hurry back."

"Thanks, Annie, but everyone in Champaign calls him Bernard."

"Whoever, I love you."

Chapter Thirteen

"Why does everyone hafta shower an hour before parties kick off? The john's always so crowded."

"Who's the band tonight?"

"Pulling Department."

"Rudy, gonna get lucky?"

"How much beer you order, Jake?"

"Eight kegs, plus a tub of Ozark's premier recipe White Lightning punch. One-tenth ice, a part strawberry soda, eighty percent Everclear."

"Anybody got some shaving cream I can borrow?"

"Paul Roberts, telephone on the second floor," Tim Malito shouted from the bathroom door, "some woman."

"Probably that hot-to-trot blonde babe of yours, Robby, makin' sure you're on time pickin' her up," Stu joshed, grabbing his razor. "'Oh, Pauly, hustle your hairy ass over here to Urbana, I can't wait for you to lick me and lick me and massage my buns. Oh, Pauly, Pauly, I crave you, please come quick.'"

"That's what Roberts' wantin' too," Moose yelled, "one real fast one."

The showering, scrubbing, tooth brushing and combing KIDs, everyone sprucing up for the Christmas dance, laughed along with Stu and the Mooser. Paul, wrapped in a towel like the rest, was embarrassed but pleased by the attention— the first time in four years the brothers had joshed him about his love life.

Wondering what Sharon wanted, he picked up the hallway receiver. "Hi."

"Good evening," the unassuming voice began, "I hope this isn't a bad moment."

Summer Never Comes

Paul was confused because this wasn't his girlfriend, "Laurie Allman, nice hearing from you, how are you, where are you?"

"My dad drove me back to campus for a party at our apartment. I wanted to call before everyone arrives."

For weeks, Paul had planned to contact and update Laurie on his UNITED investigation. With studying, following leads, seeing Sharon and worrying about Lindy, he hadn't bothered. "I'm sorry, you were on my list, but I slipped."

"I understand, I've purposely stayed out of touch." She sounded as polite as two months ago. "I needed time to collect myself, longer than I expected to forget that guy in the overcoat and my poor cat. But now I think I'm over the incident."

"Wonderful." Though late to meet Sharon, he continued the conversation to amend for ignoring Laurie." With Christmas in a week, you chose a good time returning. Happy being in town? Did you see the pine tree with the ornaments in the Union? How long will you be here?"

"Only two days this trip. Lindsey's planned a dinner tonight for her boyfriend's football buddies and made certain I was invited. My dad's coming Monday to pick me up."

"And those jocks will protect you." Jeez, Paul regretted, how stupid do I sound? "Sorry, clumsy remark."

"That's all right, it shows you remember me. And yes, I feel safer, there's a second-string defensive lineman—Lindsey's boyfriend's roommate—sitting outside our door with his six pack of Stroh's. He's been on guard duty all afternoon."

"How's the farm, was the weather dry enough long enough to harvest the crops, have you stayed busy the last few months?"

"My parents saw to that. My dad enrolled me in bookkeeping courses at Lake Land College in Mattoon and my mom has me involved with our church on Sundays."

"And…" Paul thought telling her about the Thanksgiving weekend mass he attended with Sharon.

"The answer to your next question is no, my family and I haven't spotted any strangers lurking around Ashmore."

"No more run-ins with prowlers, that's fine. I've been concerned about you, even though we haven't talked."

Summer Never Comes

"Don't worry, Paul, I'm better than I was. What happened in October made me so paranoid I couldn't cope in Champaign, but I've recovered at home in the last few months. I'm registering for the spring semester and the History Department says I'll have my old TA's job back. Tell me, have you followed through with your research for the *Daily Illini?*"

"About UNITED? I'm plugging away. A few of my fraternity brothers are members and I've attended the meetings with them. Those sessions are something to see—so organized, never lasting past two hours, Bernard Minerath dealing with, and always finishing, fifteen or twenty topics." Paul nodded to a naked, trotting by on his way to the showers, Bo Balinski. "Actually, you can explain an incongruity. I've discovered Bernard is at best a part-time student. His Political Science Department transcripts show he's been enrolled at the U of I for over six and a half years but hasn't received a degree. He's totaled 107 hours of credit but earned ninety-five in his first three and a half years. In the last four semesters, including this fall, the only course he's registered in is History 298, an independent study course."

"Bernard's taken the same class for two years? Is that possible?"

"With a faculty member agreeing to act as an advisor, yes. Bernard's is Antoinette Gulley, the English history professor who piloted the balloon over Memorial Stadium on Homecoming and who I've seen at every UNITED meeting I've been to."

"It's difficult believing he never graduated. When we were together four years ago, he was a serious undergrad, researching papers and staying up late to finish assignments."

"I agree, Bernard does his work to make things happen, then expects events and people to follow his plans.'"

"Inflexible, that he was. But Bernard considered education essential, the means to enhance life. For him not finishing his degree, I'm puzzled. Something must have changed."

Paul was shivering from standing around in his towel. Over the phone, he heard a door open, and voices and laughing.

"The dinner crowd's arrived," Laurie sounded eager, "party time is approaching."

"Will you be back in Champaign soon? Next time for sure we'll meet and talk more about Bernard."

Summer Never Comes

"I'm coming to town after finals to arrange my schedule, let's plan for then."

"A date."

# # # #

Paul walked to Sharon's house wearing, at his girlfriend's request, a dress shirt, tie and sport coat. For the first few blocks he felt foolish because in the bellbottomed, flannel-shirted, parka-wearing fashions of Champaign-Urbana respectable attire stood out; and every undergrad he passed on Armory Avenue stared at him. Reaching the Quad, though, Paul's mind swung to Bernard, UNITED, his discoveries and deductions.

"Maybe he's not a student," Sharon had remarked in the Psych Building.

How astonished Paul was, when Annie Curry let him review Bernard's file, to confirm his girlfriend's intuition. Where was the justification for staying an undergrad for over six years, and enrolling in the same course with the same teacher for four straight semesters? For sure, many students stretched their University of Illinois time, but most sooner or later earned a degree, a ticket out of Champaign-Urbana. The only rationale Paul imagined was anti-war activist Bernard, whatever his age, wanting to be recognized as part of the campus community. Another deception, which Paul withheld from Laurie, was the backdating of Bernard's registration for two semesters, making it doubtful he was even in History 298 last year. Paul presumed Professor Gulley involved in this scam.

"Something must have changed," Laurie had reasoned earlier this evening. What in Bernard's life was switched from five years ago? Was his draft number, like Billy Powell's, way, way low; were there friendships he wished to maintain; did he have a local, high-paying job, an ongoing project to complete? Were principles and morals involved? The politics of their decade, the '70s, the mammoth issue of war and peace, liberals facing down right-wingers, rebellion versus acquiescence, the conviction that people in America had to do something, stand up, dissent, object and say damn it, enough of this crap, end Vietnam. Did Bernard consider himself one of the chief radicals directing this cause?

Or were he and UNITED opaque, menacing, seditious?

Summer Never Comes

Paul was ahead of himself, requiring proof before acknowledging Bernard possessed the solutions for stopping the war or indicting him a fraud. Everything about UNITED, history, accomplishments, conjectures, tomorrow's machinations, had to be studied. Their next steps, that's the worry. If up to now there are anomalies, what comes next won't be the truth. Conspiracies only widen, never, ever finish harmlessly.

And Paul wanted friends to help shape his hypotheses. Sharon was the obvious, he'd told her about the peace movement, she knew how to let him talk and her common sense was unimpeachable. What of Laurie Allman, returning next semester to campus? She's known Bernard the longest, and Paul was convinced of her sincerity. Maybe this was the moment to review his notes with Stef Tianen and Al Stojak, allow them to critique his assumptions. Stoj, comfortable as he was following Stef, would be a middling choice. But the *Daily Illini's* editor-in-chief, this was her job—double-checking, zeroing in on weaknesses, poking holes. Stef would be the pragmatic, hardheaded one. With her decidedly anti-war, pro-UNITED bias, however, would she be impartial?

A question. What if I'm mistaken? What if I've missed the innocent, obvious justifications vindicating Bernard, the ones shooting this theorizing to hell? Could I stand the embarrassment of wasting my time and demonstrating to Stef I'm a bungling reporter? Maybe I should brood over a pitcher of beer in Whitt's End before accusing the anti-war crowds and entangling my friends.

A bigger question. What if I'm right and UNITED is a danger? I'm into one hell of a scoop, demolishing the anti-war movement, disillusioning the peace trekkies, the Randy Millers, Killers, and thousands of signed-on students. The sooner I get off my ass and clue people in on the real Bernard and the bullying UNITED, the better we'll be.

The giant question. Even if I deny it, here I am, involved, like Bernard, Laurie, Randy and hundreds of fellow students. I may have stumbled into this through an offhand conversation with Stef last September, but now I'm off the sidelines, pushed to decide, an alien place for me. Will I choke; can I handle accountability, do I want this obligation? What weird problems worrying over on a Saturday night.

Paul stepped to Sharon's porch, heard Christmas carols and opened the door. Ten or twelve housemates and their dates gathered at the fireplace.

Summer Never Comes

Flickering candles, in dozens of sizes and colors, rested atop tables, stairs, the fireplace mantle and the seat of Julie's ten-speed.

"Ho, ho, ho," Mary O'Donnell smooched Paul's lips.

"What is this?" Sharon walked to his side and indignantly exclaimed.

"You weren't around, honey," Mary hugged him, "I called dibs on Mr. Roberts for the evening."

"Is this true?" Sharon feigned aggravation and Paul shrugged.

"Merry Christmas, lover," a grinning Mary whispered in her most feminine voice and released him.

"What a way to take a guy's mind off his troubles." Paul shifted toward his girlfriend and grabbed a glass of egg nog.

"And what quandaries are those?" Sharon led him to the living room.

"Who's doing the cooking?"

"Everyone pitched in this afternoon. Maureen peeled potatoes, Angie sautéed veggies and Karen baked desert. The food's baking and we'll eat in fifteen minutes." With candles and the fireplace's flames the only light, the living room was barely brighter than the dark foyer.

"You ladies host this every year?"

"Third one in a row."

"But with graduation this spring, maybe the last, an end of a splendid tradition." Mary dunked her cup in the punch bowl. "God bless us all."

"Or perhaps not." Sharon shoved a carrot between Paul's teeth. "If I stay down here next year and a few others are in grad school, there'll be other U of I Christmases."

"Have you heard from the Vet Med College?"

"Yesterday I received a courteous, bureaucratic form letter informing me the three copies of my multi-paged admissions application had been stapled, filed and processed, with interviews to be scheduled in February."

"You're confident of getting in, aren't you?"

"No doubt in my mind." Mary O'Donnell hoisted her goblet.

"And I'm not the only candidate for more of the Big U next year, right?" Sharon glanced around. "Those staying on?"

Four partiers lifted their hands, all holding liquor glasses.

"What about you, Paul;" Audrey's date asked, "you're a senior, right?"

"Accountants don't enroll in grad school. We head to the real world for forty-hour-a-week jobs, as I've been informed this semester."

"Taking the CPA exam in the spring?"

"I wouldn't miss it for all the homecomings in the world."

"True holiday humor from my boyfriend." Sharon kneaded his back.

"Is KIDs throwing a dance tonight?"

"Starting around 9:30, the band is Pulling Department. You're welcome to head over after we eat."

"To Kappa Iota Delta, a most generous fraternity."

Maureen and Sharon walked into the kitchen to check on dinner. One of the guys dropped two logs in the hearth. Sparks crackled, briefly brightening the living room.

"Anyone watch Fighting Illini basketball today?"

"We blew out Austin Peay by twenty points, same as every December. I'd like seeing us schedule tougher competition."

"What's wrong with a victory, especially this season when we may not win many Big Ten games?"

"Harv Schmidt and the 'Ohio Nicks' will bring us through."

Sharon returned and stood next to Paul. "Miss me?"

# # # #

Three tunes into Pulling Department's first set, the KIDs, their dates, and the strangers always showing for parties but who no one recognized, walked downstairs to the chapter room to dance and pack nearer the stage, with everyone way cheerier and politer than normal.

"Ozark definitely mixes a kickass punch bowl, don't you think, Jake?"

"I wish the band wouldn't take so long between songs."

"Say, Pauly, I want to introduce you to Chris White, my date for the evening." Even with Pulling Department's blasting music, for once Killer wasn't yelling. "She lives in the two-story house across Third Street."

"I've wondered about that place, it looks so small."

"Three of us live there, we couldn't squeeze in any more."

"Cousin, Ah am honored t' greet you in thes yuletide season." Kentucky bussed Sharon's cheek. "Kill-eh, Ah am convinced you have th' prettiest belle heah t'night, Ah right-leh do."

Chris was instantly enamored, and a beaming Killer rocked on his heels.

"How are you, James? Looking forward to seeing your parents next week?"

"Ah plan on leavin' Thursday, right afteh mah morn-in' classes, thank you foh in-quirin', an' drivin' right-on un-till Ah reach Lexington." He turned to Paul. "An' how ahr you-all treatin' mah fam-ly?"

"As courteously as can be, Kentucky. I wore my best paisley tie especially for her." The clique steered toward the room's center. "How's the party progressing?"

"Right fine. Th' band sounds like they-all know how t' perform, an' have all-ready played a good-leh amount of melodious music, jes' whut all these gorgeous ladies ex-pect." Kentucky bowed toward Chris and Sharon. For once he was well-attired, with a pair of Confederate gray dress pants and a polka-dot shirt. "Wall, if you-all will ex-cuse me, Ah mus' pay mah respects t' th' othehs heah t'night."

"Merry Christmas, James."

"Can you believe Scooter's terrible behavior, not telling me what my present is?" Lauren was exasperated.

"Fiancés are odder than boyfriends," Sue Aspen patted her shoulder, "men mature strangely."

"As someone married for five months, I resent that," her husband protested. "I don't think I'm at all peculiar."

"That's right, Nick, defend us," Scooter spoke up.

"If you're not, then what am I receiving?"

"Dear, when you were little did your parents let you know what your gifts were a week ahead of time?"

"That was different, Christmas is a surprise for children."

"Well, you'll have to wait." Scooter answered as Nick and he abandoned the women to refill their beer cups.

"Don't worry, acting this way keeps Scooter off guard," Lauren gossiped to Sue, "I'm fairly certain what the present is."

"Mr. Married Man, how's it goin'?" Killer flamboyantly slapped Nick's back.

"What's up? I heard you were totally soaked taking a dump this week. Must have been hilarious, pitchers and buckets pouring over the stall."

"Yep, I imagine those are the breaks." Killer looked self-important, Nick about the fortieth person joshing him about the john episode.

Summer Never Comes

"Moose couldn't quit laughing," Scooter added. The three were among the sprawling crowds surrounding the kegs.

"You guys have all the fun," Nick chugged his cup, "it would be great returning to the house for carousing like a showering."

"And leave Sue?" Scooter screamed into Nick's ear, countering the music. "The next time I'm hauled in I'll phone, but you sure as hell better quick drag your ass over here."

"Jake, you loud fart, out of the world dance."

"Appreciate the compliment, Ozark." The social chairman hung all over Kay Reising. "With a woman tonight?"

"No, you know me, drinkin' with the brothers."

Unlike Moose, Ozark and a dozen others, Dale Kinsey had a date—one of the women from the KIDs-for-Frogfeet night at the Lion. Forever upping his reputation, Dale had made certain she wore as skimpy a skirt as possible, but more lipstick than any other girl in the house. The pair loafed by the fireplace, sharing a cigarette, unbuckling the other's belt then groping asses. Dale flaunted his 'I own everything because I'm totally cool' face, and no one walked over to them to talk. After half an hour, satisfied enough KIDs had ogled his broad, Dale whispered into her ear, tongued one shoulder, and guided her through the crowd to the stairs and his room.

Six songs into the second set, Pulling Department switched from hard rock to '50s' dancing music. Kay and Jake, Killer and Chris, Stu and Joyce, Sue and Nick, Scooter and Lauren, Tim and Katy Karas, Joe and Lydia, John and Ruth, and Nemo and Debbie pushed into the dance floor.

"Party weekends are so enjoyable." Paul and Sharon bumped another couple. "My roommate should be here, these are his boogying tunes."

"They're everyone's, my dear." She moved closer and hugged him.

"Lindy's not returning to Champaign tonight. If you aren't up to driving to Urbana we can sleep here."

"A sweet offer, but we have to return, there are designs. Since this year's Christmas party is the last for us seven girls, we're cooking a champagne brunch tomorrow when everybody wakes up." Sharon raised her head and they slowly spun in a loop. "After us housemates plus boyfriends shack up in our rooms. A night of passion's desires, a Christmas love in."

Summer Never Comes

Pulling Department finished 'Silhouettes,' and the dance crowd applauded as the band tuned their instruments.

"Now a special request." The band announced.

With the first chords, the KIDs hoorayed, and Paul turned to a bemused Sharon. "Come on, let's join in."

> Lauren and Tom were lovers,
> He wanted to give her ev-er-y-thing.
> Flow-ers, pres-ents,
> But most of all, a wed-ding ring.

"Bum bum bum bum," The KIDs echoed.

A giggling Scooter and a red-faced Lauren stood among, yet apart from, the boisterous partiers.

> He saw a sign for a stock car race,
> A thousand dollar prize it read.
> He couldn't get Lauren on the phone,
> So to her mother Tommy said.

"Bum, bum, bum, bum."

Scooter snatched his fiancée and she buried her head in his neck. Everyone in the room held hands, orbiting around them. When the band came to the chorus, the crowd bellowed.

> Tell Lauren I love her,
> Ttell Lauren I need her.
> Tell Lauren I may be late,
> I've something to do that cannot wait.

Hearing the music, Ozark and Moose, each with their porcelain mugs, tramped from the living room to check out the house tradition and this evening's happy highlight. As all the KIDs, Paul had long ago memorized the words, singing the verse in a regular voice, but yelling out the chorus with his fraternity brothers.

Summer Never Comes

Tell Lauren I love her.
Tell Lauren I need her.
Tell Lauren not to cry,
My love for her will never die.

Scooter snickered and Lauren hid her face, refusing looking at anyone until the tune ended.

Tell Lauren I love her.
Tell Lauren I need her.
Tell Lauren I love her!

After an extra verse composed by Pulling Department, the crowds cheered and mobbed a delighted Scooter and blushing Lauren.

"I'm so embarrassed," she whispered to Sue Aspen.

"It will always be like this, even years from now."

Paul and Sharon climbed the stairway for a beer and to cool down. Tim Malito was there, outside the ladies' powder room, waiting for Katy. At the top, they spotted Emily by the wall. Sharon remembered the Homecoming dance, wondered if Bobby Sox were around tonight and hoped her boyfriend wouldn't wander to the kegs, stranding her with Emily.

"How are you?"

"Fine, Sharon, Merry Christmas." Emily grinned. "I'm happy seeing so many people having such a jolly time."

Never having seen her smile before, Sharon thought the response odd.

"Out for a walk tonight?" Paul noticed Emily particularly well-dressed in a woolen sweater and matching skirt.

"No," she grinned again, "I'm here for the dance."

"The band sounds professional and like another group I've heard, but can't recall," Sharon said, "Are you ready for Christmas?"

"Yes, my presents are wrapped and I hope I have enough room to bring them home." Emily looked into the chapter room and the scores of dancing couples. "I mailed out my holiday cards this morning."

"Can I get you a beer?"

"No, thank you, Paul." She sounded in high spirits.

Summer Never Comes

"Excuse me, make a hole, comin' through, man on a mission. Here you go, Emily, wine for your and a brew for me. Say, how you doin' tonight?"

Paul looked over his shoulder at the guy carrying the glasses and, totally shocked, defaulted to polite. "I don't think you two have been introduced. Sharon Taylor, this is Tommy Quarters."

Sharon sensed Paul's confusion. "Hello, did you two just arrive?"

"About ten minutes ago. With these tons of people, it took that long trekking from the front door to the steps." Tommy chugged his beer. "I've heard Pulling Department play at Chances R, they sing some good GrassRoots tunes."

"That's the band I was remembering, Emily."

"Tom treated me to dinner in the Highrise Lounge, at the top of Century Twentyone. We sat at a table next to the windows."

"Fancy place for Big U undergrads; celebrating something special?"

"Merely a merry Christmas." Emily was casual. "A shame tonight's weather is so foggy; it would be marvelous seeing the campus from that elevation."

"We can always go back on a clearer day for another meal, lunch or dinner, weekday or weekend, anytime you prefer." Tommy gazed at Emily. "How about that b-ball game today, winning by twenty points?"

"It's only Austin Peay, not Indiana or Purdue," Paul said.

"A blowout's a blowout."

"I enjoyed it also," Emily continued, smiling, "Tom bought us Section A seats, directly behind the teams' benches; we could hear the coaches talking to their players."

KIDs and their dates walked past, the juniors, seniors and Lindy's friends gaping at Tommy Quarters standing so near to Emily, his arm wrapped behind her back.

"Wanna dance, Emily? Sounds like a romantic, dreamy slow one, just what I requested." Tommy set their cups on the slate floor. "Nice making your acquaintance, Sharon. Catch you later, Paul."

"Goodbye," Emily waved.

Paul and Sharon watched them walk downstairs, Tommy opening his arms and Emily stepping into them, possessively hugging her new boyfriend.

Summer Never Comes

Katy Karas and her chortling, chuckling, crammed-with-Christmas-cheer girlfriends exited the ladies' powder room. "I have to lay off the beer, Tim's thinking he wants it five times by noon tomorrow. What a Romeo."

"Keg number six."

"I agree, Lauren, it's childish, but what can I do? KIDs are adolescents. Now can we head to my room and jump in the sack?"

# # # #

Around 2:30, Sharon and Paul left the fraternity to drive to Urbana, the fog so thick the wary Sharon braked her Camaro at every intersection. Her house was quiet, the only sounds from Angie's stereo. The pair carried off a dozen of the candles that had lighted the downstairs and set them around Sharon's bedroom.

"Can you believe we won the room raffle?" Paul rested on the bed. Sharon stepped out of her shoes and sat next to him, studying the paper he'd pulled from his pocket. "'This Gift Certificate entitles Bearer and Guest to one night's Lodging at the Century Twentyone Hotel, 302 East John, Champaign, Illinois, 61820. 384-2100.'"

"The way everybody carried on, when your name was picked I thought you'd been selected as next season's Chief Illiniwek." She unloosened a hair ribbon. "How long is the freebie good for?"

"Jake said six months, until the middle of June." Paul held Sharon's waist until both fell on the mattress.

"I hope the weather's clearer than it was tonight for Emily's dinner."

"I'm stumped about that one. You had to figure something would happen between her and Lindy—their relationship's been sliding all semester. A bust was possible, someone had to reconcile or move to cut off the other, and Emily went first." Paul sounded dejected. "But Tommy Quarters, gosh, I hope she's careful."

"What's wrong with Tommy?" Sharon looked at him. The candlelight sparkled wild, eerie shadows on the walls. "He seemed pleasant enough to me, no louder or obnoxious than anyone else tonight; and was well-mannered with Emily."

"Tommy's a despo, likely will flunk out this semester or next, been involved in disgusting stuff all year; and hangs with Kinsey and the fourth floor doper crowd, the biggest losers in the house. This is the first party I've seen him straight and not unconscious in a stairwell."

"When did my boyfriend ripen into a prude? You can't judge college students by how much they drink. This is the first KIDs dance I've attended I've seen anybody sober past eleven o'clock." She stood and unbuttoned her skirt, the dress dropping to the carpet, Paul approving of her yellow bikini panties. "How many beers did you put down tonight?"

"I'll admit any fraternity brothers of mine avoiding the bars for a whole weekend are curiosities. But Tommy's irresponsible, a not-too-mature freshman."

"Childishness is a trait describing all Champaign-Urbana students. Maybe dating Emily will better him, girlfriends sometimes do." Sharon pulled off her stockings, put her feet on the bed, and turned toward Paul. "Does Lindy know?"

"When I saw him last afternoon he was still hoping to sit down with Emily, work things through and get back together. Tommy Quarters' moving in will shock my roommate as much as it has everyone else. Too bad for Lindy, looks like his band has cost him." Paul presumed his comment would trigger their 'chance-no-chance' arguments. Sharon twisted her legs in a pretzel, the candles dimmed, and she unfastened his belt.

"Yes, poor Lindy. Maybe they'll reconcile, perhaps Emily won't care for Tommy as much as it seemed tonight. Possibly she's going out with him because she's bored waiting around for your roommate, and looking for more engaging ways to spend her time. And maybe we should climb in bed." She unzipped Paul's pants, he unclasped her bra. Shortly, they were naked and underneath the covers. Angie's stereo had stopped playing.

"Let's get this straight," Paul kissed her ear, "right now, in this house, there are seven horny couples—fondling and fooling around like we are. And everybody in the other rooms knows what everyone else is up to."

"Who can argue with college sex? Turn-ons, simultaneous stimulations, ecstasies, loving the one you're with or anyone else. Times like tonight I'm totally convinced our generation has the answers." Sharon squeezed as tight to Paul's body as she could. "A thing about the dance. What was the big deal with 'Tell Lauren I Love Her,' besides the KIDs singing the wrong words?"

Summer Never Comes

"At a party two years ago Scooter was totally inebriated. We had all kinds of booze behind the bar, and he finished off the night pouring a shot glass from every bottle into one cup and chugging it down. That evening we also played hours of old rock 'n' roll." Paul swayed on his back as Sharon mounted his stomach. "After the party, he crashed in the john, barfing his guts out. When he stopped, Stu, me and a couple others tossed him in the showers to sober up. While he was under the water, Scooter started mumbling 'Tell Laura I love her,' only substituting Lauren's name. Every party that song comes on, we sing what we did tonight."

"His fiancée wasn't pleased," Sharon whispered.

"They've known each other since their freshman year, are in love, and will be married in twelve months. Lauren tolerates the joke."

"As you said earlier, you KIDs can be kids."

"Which makes us cute." He curled his arms around Sharon's shoulders. "Speaking of questions, this evening was the third time we've danced together, the family tradition Kentucky hassled me with at the Red Lion."

Not answering, she licked Paul's shoulder.

"Well, how about it?" He exhaled, enjoying the foreplay.

"For five generations, men dancing three times with Taylor girls has been the sign for couples to become betrothed. That's what happened to my mom, our Aunt Terry, James' mother, and Granny Charlotte."

Paul looked at the curtains as Sharon kissed him again. If this was his future, he dearly prayed it come true. "What should we do with these candles?"

"Let them burn, I'm staying in bed until breakfast."

# # # #

Hauling his guitar case and duffle bag, with sixty bucks in his pocket for two nights' performances, Lindy dragged into KIDs at four in the morning, hung over, drop dead tired and absolutely needing a shower. Empty kegs were stacked in the foyer; the floor was sticky from spilt liquor; every light was on in the living room; half-filled plastic cups were piled on tables, chairs and the trophy case; and the house smelled from smoldering cigarettes. He unbuttoned his parka and plopped on the couch.

"Greetings of the seasons."

Summer Never Comes

"Killer, what's shakin'? I didn't expect anyone bein' up this late or early or whenever it is." Lindy rubbed his eyes.

"You missed the despoes by five minutes, they finally floated the last barrel and skedaddled to their rooms to smoke more grass."

"No skin off my nose, duckin' that misfit mob. What're you doin' down here?"

"Well, Lindy, if you want the facts, I just returned from escorting my date back home."

"Makin' out with the fairer sex? That's great, honest Injun." Lindy unhurriedly raised one hand and signaled the A-OK. "Where's she live?"

"Across Third Street, in that little house near the Phi Mus." Killer slouched in one of the green chairs.

"Convenience plus, hey? Nice girl?"

"Incredibly, thanks for inquirin'. Her name's Chris and we met while I was on my volunteer stint for UNITED. She has this knack of always smiling, saying the right things, and is the most considerate woman I've ever dated."

"Better late than never, that's what they pun in the funny pages." Lindy lifted his feet on the couch. "I'm glad hearin' the forecast is improvement in the ol' love life department. Treat her respectable?"

"I started out the evening as a gentleman's gentleman, wanted to be a regular guy, took a shower, smelled decent, dressed up—including fresher u-trow—purchased her a corsage and treated her to dinner. But you know me, partner, I hung around the kegs too long, got a tad heinous and figured I'd screwed up with the woman. Turns out, though, Chris wasn't bothered. On top of her straight-thinking and great manners, she's quite the party animal herself, shuffled right in there with me and we had a great time."

"You stumbled into another loose cannon to tie down with."

"Possibly, Lindy, possibly," a worn out Killer slowly answered. "Where'd Frogfeet play tonight?"

"The Lion in Bloomington again, both Friday and Saturday. The band was supposed to lay over 'til morning, but our motel reservations were jazzed around so we came back to the Big U. I swear to God, we could drive the seventy miles from that joint to Champaign in our sleep, so many times we've made the trip."

"Hey, don't knock it, steady work and pay, right?"

Summer Never Comes

"No arguments there." As wiped and aching as he felt, Lindy enjoyed this conversation with his fraternity brother, a relaxed Killer not his regular, obnoxious self. But Lindy was fantastically bushed and his mind centered to basics. "By the way, seen Robby tonight?"

"If you mean if he's upstairs in your room with his babe, the answer is negative. I'm pretty positive he bolted outta here around two a.m. Now that I reflect on it, I'm certain he's boogied."

Thank goodness, Lindy slumped on the sofa, I can head upstairs to my rack and pass out until I'm offered a richer deal. If I'm lucky, Robby'll stay with Sharon most of tomorrow, I'll fan on Sunday completely and sleep in until my Monday morning ten o'clock. How sweet.

"That's right, you've been gone tonight, so you haven't heard the latest news." As beat as Lindy, Killer sounded sympathetic. "Your old girlfriend made an appearance at the dance."

"Can't say I blame her, I've been such a horse's ass all these weeks, the way I've treated Em, she's undoubtedly lonely. Just 'cause I don't attend house functions doesn't mean Em should hide out. Bustin' away from her dorm and coming to our frat to visit her friends was a smart idea. Did she dance with Robby or Stu or anyone?"

"I'm sorry I'm the one breakin' this to you, amigo, but Emily had a date."

Unbelievably exhausted and fixating on his rack, he didn't comprehend Killer's sentence. A date, what did that mean? An appointment? A get-together? A time scheduled to do something? A meeting? No, not on Saturday night, weekends are for relaxin', kicking back, buddies and friends and dates…A date…My God, Killer's not referrin' to when, he means a who.

The door shut, locking Lindy in the heartbreak hotel.

Chapter Fourteen

A WEEK before finals, Bobby Sox hung around KIDs to study; Stu and Joyce shared an empty classroom in Gregory Hall, the ultimate in higher education isolation; Marty Marek, Moose and Ozark paid attention to Bill Wick's lesson on Bernoulli processes; Sharon, Mary O'Donnell and their housemates holed up in Urbana cramming for Monday's physiology exam; Lindy was on the road with Frogfeet; and Paul trekked to the Library, settling down in the Reference Room with his Finance 364 texts and notes.

"The Kaiser Committee assessed the country's housing situation in 1968 and found that one-eighth of the population could not afford standard housing. From 1963 to 1968 the median price of a house increased from $18,000 to $32,000. Causes were inflation, rising construction costs, and the building of larger, more luxurious homes."

Paul believed the weather and calendar helped. In dreary, chilly January students couldn't play outdoors, the ground was too muddy for chasing down frisbees and the air too frozen for football. Christmas and New Year's Eve celebrations were past and no one, not even the constantly-chugging, heinous, happy hour KIDs hosted parties. So Paul and his fraternity brothers kept inside, quit drinking and prepared for finals. The hibernation-instead-of-inebriation factor, as Lindy labeled it last year, time to keep your nose to the grindstone, your head above water.

Paul wondered if Lindy had managed any hard-core school work since the break, certain his roommate desperately needed to ace his finals for a decent grade point average. Which was possible with a serious attitude. A year ago all the KIDs were blown away when Rudy collected a B+ on the Psych 201 final, passing the course. But Lindy was out of the loop, Paul hadn't found his roommate at a desk or in the 'Brary in the last three weeks.

Summer Never Comes

The spring semester would be different, the late-May weather hot, and booking easier to blow off. Frat Park would be crowded, with everyone catching rays, dreaming of packing up and partying hard on a last Saturday night before leaving Champaign. Leaving Champaign forever.

Paul abandoned his fantasizing and focused on Fin 364, paging through a semester's worth of underlining in his textbook, reviewing the notes a second time. He'd re-check the chapters twice more ahead of the final.

"The Senate Banking Committee stated that existing federal subsidy insurance and guarantee programs functioned well to support low-and moderate-income housing, but middle-income Americans were being shut out. One of the unique results of the shortage, and high cost, of mortgage credit is the nearly 'death blow' given to housing for middle-income families. In many places, the only housing being built is high priced housing—above $30,000—which only upper income families can afford."

What was his parents' home worth, he wondered?

# # # #

The tunnel between the Undergrad and the Main Library Building was packed. Students walked up and down the sloping hallway while others relaxed in the chairs or on the formica floor, drinking coffee.

"How is your Speech 111 paper coming along?"

"Okay, I should finish my rough draft tonight, then edit the text tomorrow. I've lined up Del Hansen to type it for me."

"And your statistics course?"

"That test's at the end of finals, so I'll study next weekend. I've also got econ to cram in, which is Tuesday." Tommy Quarters set his cup on the seat's arm rest. "How about you, Emily, what're you working on?"

She noted that Tommy still used her full first name, not Will's shorter sobriquet. "My Shakespeare course. I need to review his earlier plays—the comedies and histories—this weekend."

"What is the deal with you and literature, you're always talking about those old authors, why do you appreciate them so much?"

"William Shakespeare was a playwright, not an author, and didn't write books," Emily corrected. "The fascination is the wording and composition, their balance and illusions. Reading a passage, I imagine actors in their costumes performing in front of me. Storylines are always resolved by the last act, and the plots meaningful for us today."

"But for the best? Isn't there a pile of tragedy in, in," he stumbled for examples, "*Julius Caesar* or *Romeo and Juliet*? As I remember from high school, Caesar was knifed by his friends and those lovers didn't live happily ever after."

"Why did the teenagers kill themselves, what was the implication of their suicide? Love was more important than life, they couldn't have each other, and at the end they chose nothing."

Tommy smirked, not versed enough in Shakespeare or other writers to discuss them for long, relieved his simplistic references satisfied his girlfriend. "You know, this is the first week I've sat in the Undergrad three straight nights."

"What do you think of the experience?" Emily watched the students at the vending machines, more in line for coffee than sodas.

"For certain a different setting than the rest of the semester—totally jammed and everybody's staying longer. Yesterday when we left at midnight I was amazed there were so many still hangin' around. Looks like everyone's decided booking's the thing."

"Most students comprehend this sooner or later." Emily employed a motherly tone.

"And getting out of the fraternity is helpful. KIDs isn't the ideal place to work—hell, not even close—with loud stereos, doors slamming and brothers bouncing in the hallways. The racket never quiets down until one or two in the morning."

"That's what I've heard." Emily recalled Will describing the same conundrum, how he preferred, when needing to cram or concentrate on a paper, to settle in with her in Blaisdell Hall. "But the Undergrad becomes awfully full around finals."

"Not as bad as the bars. I remember the mobs in Stan's right after the Homecoming game, stuffed wall-to-wall and stool-to-stool, everybody pushin' the bartenders for more beers, no politeness anywhere." Tommy crushed his cup. After twenty minutes' sitting in the hallway, the pair started for the Undergrad's lower level.

"What is everybody saying in the house, concerning the two of us dating?"

Summer Never Comes

"Now that I'm going out with a decent girl, the other pledges assume I'm finally leveling off, that it's a good thing I'm playing down my disgustingness, even if the makeover's only been four weeks. I've earned some respect, and my roommate, Roger Mohr, is betting I'll pull some acceptable grades."

"And the upperclassmen?"

"If you mean Lindy and his pals, I truthfully don't know. They live on different floors, have always ignored me and I've done the same. The only variable is Bobby Sox being less sociable. Up until the Christmas party he was the only one of Lindy's buddies I guessed I was friends with, the only senior I ever talked to more than saying hello. We even drank a few beers together in Whitt's End last month. But since Christmas, he won't even glance at me when we're hangin' in the living room."

"That's Bobby, emotional, loyal and forever stubborn. He most likely believes you and I have committed a great sin."

"Hell, I don't see our relationship that way. If we wanna be candid, when you and I met in the Red Lion we were both desperate, you lonely and me headin' to being the biggest, obnoxious-est turd on campus, literally falling off my last legs. In this month we've straightened each other out; you're happier and I'm mellowing. If other people—like Lindy's buddies—think we've screwed up, that's irrelevant. They're graduating in four months and'll be forgotten, we'll be in school and have each other."

"I agree, Tom, we've made a difference to each other. I'm hopeful for a bright tomorrow," she grinned, "but I don't live in KIDs."

"Does that mean you're okay with me?"

"Yes."

"Excellent." A contented Tommy dropped the smashed cup in a trash can. "Like I said, nothing's happened in the house makin' me sweat. If anyone, Bobby, Paul Roberts, or even Lindy, is pissed and has a grudge, I'm certain it'll blow over. Who gives a rat's stinking crap, that's life."

Emily was nonplussed. Will never spoke crudely when they were together.

# # # #

Summer Never Comes

"We should shove his mother-frickin' acne ass right outta the goddamned door, that's what I say, Christ-all-mighty." Bobby hammered his fist into the mattress.

"I don't think we can do that, can we?" Stu sounded levelheaded.

"Not for going out with a woman, even if she was our best friend's steady girl." Paul leaned against Bobby's bed.

"My God, I don't believe this garbage I'm hearin', especially from you, Robby. The guy's your roommate for two years, freakin' your closest pal on the whole campus, and you just sit there. What the hell ever happened to standing up for buddies?"

"Listening to you, Bobby, someone would guess Tommy Quarters hatched the whole Lindy-joining-Frogfeet episode to pry Emily away. Or maybe you think Tommy has other motives, maybe a bet with someone he could steal Emily from Lindy." Paul sipped his Old Style. "Which is not the way the deal happened. The catalyst was Lindy; he failed."

"We all know Tommy's a jerk-off, an asshole all semester, him and that limp-sticked Kinsey. I can't remember one decent thing he's done since September. Now he's with modest, down-to-earth Emily Ritter, someone deserving better than Tommy Mangy-Assed Quarters. There's gonna be major hassles, goddamn-it."

"Tommy was a total gentleman all the time Sharon and I watched him at the Christmas party."

"That's right," Stu added, "and he didn't even barf on any carpets."

The two laughed as Bobby grabbed another beer from his mini-fridge. "It still sucks and I don't know who's to blame, Lindy or Emily. How could this happen? Maybe it's our fault for not protectin' them more than we did."

"Lindy sure has gone AWOL the last few months, ever since his goofy band took off and he turned into a rock 'n' roll star. When was the last time he shot the breeze with us?" Stu finished a twelve-ouncer. "Remember a year ago, how we four munched popcorn every evening after booking at the 'Brary?"

"We were at the Undergrad," Bobby snapped, "you were hangin' around here wastin' hours watchin' the tube, waitin' around for us."

Paul chuckled.

"But we chowed popcorn every night and Lindy was in the room, that was the deal. We were buddies and aware what was going down with each other, if we were in decent shape or one of us was in trouble. Not this semester."

"You're right," Paul set his empty bottle on the carpet, "contrasted to September Lindy's another person, separated from everything he considered essential, out-of-touch with changes, including Emily. And like you, Bobby, I blame myself. Maybe I should have talked to him more than I did, warned him about what we saw and he missed."

"You're still close friends, we're his pretty good pals."

"We'll always be roommates, but the old days are over, as Stu said."

"How's he doin' grade-point-wise?"

"Don't know. We're in one class together, Phil 393, and he hooked the last hourly, a disappointment because the course is so subjective."

"He'll pull through okay," Bobby sounded assured, "old Lindy's sharp enough to recognize when the shit hits the fan it's time to hop outta the path."

"Hope you're right. Once other garbage is on your mind, you check out of studying and your grades plummet, it's tough returning." Stu was dubious. "What are Lindy's thoughts about Emily and Tommy; when did he find out about them?"

"Killer hit him with the news right after the Christmas dance." Bobby chugged a beer. "There's another numb-nutted, dimple-dicked, jack-off to blackball."

"Was he upset?"

"Startled. Until learning about Tommy Quarters, Lindy hoped Emily and he would come together and mend their relationship. His error was misjudging how far apart they'd swung. When I think back to all the days my roommate claimed he was planning to patch up their differences, but never acted… a total shame." Paul scratched his head. "And I don't think we should dump on Killer. Lindy said Killer gave him the news as decently as he could."

"Maybe Emily's going out with Tommy to prove a point, maybe she's invented a scheme to force Lindy to realize what he's doing to himself, then convince him to give in."

"Could be," Bobby speculated, "never analyzed it that way. But I don't think Emily's so devious, she's too upright to be a plotter."

"She's a woman, isn't she? They're always calculating angles."

Summer Never Comes

"That's a hell of an accusation," Bobby flipped the can opener at Stu, "because Emily's no sneak. She wouldn't play Lindy and Tommy off each other just to be a pain in the ass. If she has a plan, I'm sure her intentions are good. Lindy has to be perceptive enough to figure the game."

"Then it might work for those two." Paul picked up the can opener.

\# \# \# \#

UPI – Saigon – After analyzing Communist movements in South Vietnam since the termination of Operation Loading Dock in October, United States Army command has announced the redeployment of units in the Mekong Delta. 'These adjustments will further lessen enemy effectiveness in the region,' a spokesman stated.

\# \# \# \#

"The university community should take marked pride in UNITED's recently-concluded Food Drive for Peace," Stef Tianen's editorial read. "This admirable undertaking of forwarding food stocks to North Vietnam to atone for the Washington right-wingers' reckless aggression is a statement confirming our student body's decency. As the cargo crosses America and is shipped to Southeast Asia, it will stand as a tocsin: this nation's people have reached out to the United States government's declared enemies with a gesture of amity.

"Let us continue to assist and back UNITED. In the last few months, this organization has unfailingly championed the cause of peace. To do so in the future requires ongoing help and aid from the campus community.

"Support and join UNITED. The world is in the balance."

\# \# \# \#

The chair Maggie used is empty,
That cup of hers is filled with rain,
I sit here lookin' all over,
But what I see brings me more pain.

Summer Never Comes

Beer comes to us in glass pitchers,
We suck our suds from handled mugs.
Makes no difference how we drink it,
The thing to do is just get drunk.

Whether the tune was an Andy Arthur original, or parodying a more popular band's work, the 'Feet received the same, unexcited, never-too-loud scattered applause from the basic night-in, night-out Red Lion crowd, the inebriated undergrads at their tables, your classic groupies totally convinced Frogfeet the next Beatles—or at least another Head East, a half-dozen KIDs, Gary Anderson, Robin Ferris, who showed every night, and a second woman turning up most Wednesdays to put the moves on Woofer.

'Mad' crashed his snare to end 'Bare Trees in the Yard,' another Arthur arrangement. "Sometimes all I think we are is background noise for this mob, something a plugged-into-the-electrical-socket jukebox can handle."

"Okay, guys, good," Franky Konkel unstrapped his Fender, "but next time, Lindy, hold the tempo in 'Sweatshirt Passions,' got it?"

"No probl-lem-o, boss-man."

"Woofer, the rhythm in 'Maudlin Memories' skipped."

"I know, my right knee had a horrible itch." Donny Raasch was too engaged with his girl to offer Franky more of an answer.

"That's it for tonight, let's wrap."

"Say, Andy, when are you gonna compose a song about spring or summer or subjects besides trees with no leaves and stale beer?" Lindy swung an arm around his friend's shoulder.

"In April or May, I imagine." He strolled to the bar with Lindy. "This is a dreary time of year and people want murky, gloomy lyrics. You're a student, final are coming, what's more depressing?"

"Nailed me on that cross. But there's happiness, too," Lindy optimistically volunteered, "we just had Christmas and I collected a couple of presents from my mom."

"If you want hymns and hallelujahs, go kneel in a cathedral."

Franky, 'Mad' and Woofer worked on stage packing the band's equipment for tomorrow's gig in Mattoon. Andy and Lindy, excused because they'd set up at the evening's start, opted for a nightcap. The Jerg slid over two beers.

Summer Never Comes

"Hello."

"Hey, how you doin', sweet, sweet Robin of the Red, Red Lion, our tip-top fan, top-notch friend? What's your read on tonight's performance?"

"Magnificent," she stepped next to Lindy, "you played super sets."

"They're mostly Andy's songs. The rest of us are merely his country cousins, up there pickin', beatin' and hummin'. Right, Mister Arthur?"

"Listen to him, the boy knows what he's talking about." Andy spun away from the pair to watch a student's last attempts at mastering pinball before the Lion closed.

"What you been up to lately?" Lindy eyed Robin. She wore a green V-neck sweater along with her wide-wide bellbottoms.

"Finishing a chemistry project, booking for finals, mulling over where I should travel over semester break," she smiled again, "and listening to the cutest, blonde-haired boy on any stage in Champaign-Urbana."

"Aw, shucks," Lindy feigned embarrassment, "you probably say that to all the guitar players you know at the Big U."

"Only the certain one I wish to be my dearest companion." Robin reached for his arm.

"Crumbs from the rich woman's table. Don't you ever tire of complimenting me?"

"Never, ever, Lindy, you're worth the effort."

"Last call, guys," the Jerg yelled from his side of the bar.

"But I'm a music bum, a guy who dumps on his pals for chances to stand on a stage, hoping fans applaud. Not to sharpen too fine a point, but there's some around campus convinced I'm on the teetering edge for play-actin' like this."

"Nonsense, I'm certain you know your way. On top of that, I consider you lovable."

Lindy laughed as the house lights brightened. "Tell you what, order a couple more beers before they shut this place down. I've gotta stow my gear, and when I'm finished we'll talk some more."

"Deal."

# # # #

Summer Never Comes

Awake for five minutes, Paul heard screeching winds shaking the trees and a pebble-like tap-tap-tapping at the window. Jumping from the top bunk, he stood at the window. Heavy snow was falling, with six or seven inches on the ground, a bizarre happening in Cham-Bana.

"Close the curtains," Lindy drowsily said from under his blanket, "it's not time to get up."

"Howdy, roommate," Paul peered at the alarm, "if you've got an eight o'clock it is."

"Well, I don't." Lindy pulled the cover to his chin. "What's the scene outside?"

"A blizzard, coming down so hard I can't see the Phi Mu house across Third Street." Paul put on a pair of gym socks laying on their floor.

"Enough for canceling classes?"

"Won't happen, the weather's never that lousy."

"Today's Thursday, you don't have an eight o'clock, do you?"

"No classes until this afternoon, I'm heading to the Union for booking. Finals next week, you know; want to come along?" Paul searched for his pants.

"Not a chance, I haven't been in the rack very long."

"What time did you roll in?"

"About 4:30."

"That's a personal record, isn't it? This late night, early morning catching up with you?"

"Past tense, caught. Do you know that since autumn the only place I've managed enough shut eye is my mom's house at Thanksgiving and Christmas? There's so little time to properly rack out these days." Lindy played with the wires under Paul's mattress. "Life sucks."

"If you're dancing, pay at the door." In his closet searching for a shirt, Paul half-listened to his roommate.

"No, Robby, I'm not only raggin' about the all-hours-no-sleep trap. There's something else, the big time's comin', train's departin' the station—I've got a chance to deal dope."

Paul turned towards the bunks, and the tap-tap-taps terrifically intensified. "Talk to me about this."

"Remember the girl I told you about, Robin, the babe forever at the Lion takin' in our gigs? She was there again last night, from beginning to end, in her usual spot. After we finished playin', her and I shared a pitcher, got to talking, headed to her room in Scott Hall to fool around for a half hour, then rapped some more. Turns out she's mixed up with this gang of students distributin' the bulk of the grass and cocaine sold in Champaign, Charleston, Bloomington-Normal and other central Illinois cities. The way she describes it, the operation's fairly gigantic, with deliveries arrivin' in Cham-Bana a couple times a month and stored in two houses on north Prospect Avenue."

"What's her interest in you, besides your body?"

Lindy frowned at Paul's remark. "She's after the 'Feet to shuttle the stuff to the campuses where we play our gigs. According to Robin, right now five bands comprise the delivery service, with timetables and fixed routes for haulin' the crap to twenty-five or thirty drop-offs."

"Why do the pushers want Frogfeet?"

"Substitute personnel and extra vehicles to move the dope when demand increases. With spring break coming, February and March are busier months for supplyin' college students with weed for their vacations. Plus, if other groups break up, there'd be stand-ins for distributin' the dope. Logistically, this is a plausible arrangement. Bands are low key, we come and go, slip in, sneak out, nobody pays us attention, and with the equipment in our vans—instruments, amps, electric chords, you name it—there's no problem hidin' small packages. Hell, we always stash at least a six-pack in with 'Mad's drums."

"Where are the drugs shipped from?"

"Colorado or New Mexico, somewhere out west to here in Champaign."

"Why from that far?" Paul's newspaper instincts had him now.

"I think the pipeline deals in more than marijuana, or there's designs to expand the operation and bring in other mind-blowing, exotic, profitable drugs. And since this is the busiest campus in central Illinois, with Willard Airport, the new interstate highways and so many arriving and departing students, it's the least-hassled place to smuggle the crap into central Illinois." Lindy shook his head. "This is so wild."

"What will you do?"

"Like all of us, I've smoked my share of grass, so I hold nothing against flyin' high. A life's your own freedom. But workin' for a network dealin' the stuff scares me down to my toenails. I should forget about last night like it never happened, steer clear of something so illegal and not even phone Robin with an answer. Yet, every record has that B-side, the 'Feet could earn serious cash. So maybe I should discuss this proposition with the others, they might have more balls than me."

"I thought you guys were a rock and roll band."

"We are music, what those nighters practicin' in the basement were about. But when opportunities roll along to take home hard-core bucks, a mouse should be a man, right?"

"And possibilities for being busted don't float into our room every morning."

"Settle down, Robby. All I'm sayin' is maybe the guys in Frogfeet should have a chance at passing judgment."

"How did Robin decide on you?" A cold gust blew through the window frame, chilling Paul.

"Dale Kinsey clued her in about Frogfeet and me."

"He's involved?"

"A full-fledged, in-on-the-ground-floor pusher, like Loops, Bill Cherwinkie, K-Mow and dozens more Big U students. Doesn't nonplus me."

"Kinsey, the biggest asshole in the house, one guy that should be blackballed."

"I'll vote aye, he's bad news." Lindy tugged the drapes, looked out the window then lay back in his bunk.

"Bobby, Stu and I talked about tossing another of the brothers from KIDs."

"Who, me?" He winked at Paul. "I know lately I haven't done my share and wouldn't want to leave, but if that's what you decide, I suppose I'll drop on my sword."

"You're safe, it's Tommy Quarters. Bobby had the idea, Stu and I spent the whole evening talking him down."

"Sounds like Bobby. I don't know if he's more upset for Em or me. Bobby's protected her ever since we first started goin' out a year ago, sort of the Champaign girlfriend he's never had."

"What's your feelings?"

Summer Never Comes

"About Em and Tommy? All semester I've speculated with my luck, ignorin' her like I have, I knew something was coming. I wish I had the time to get Em to settle the problems between us, I truly do."

"Have you talked to her?"

"We met a couple days ago and covered the basics, school, our relationship, Frogfeet plus Tommy. The chat was pleasant, except for a moment when I nearly lost it, almost ignited an authentic explosion on the launch pad. If she was tired hangin' around for me, I ruminated, the street is two directions; I've had it too with not receivin' any understanding or openings to talk things out. The hell with the relationship, I rationalized, if she doesn't want me, the feelin's mutual. If she wants to date other guys, especially Tommy-turd-Quarters, go ahead, there's the exit. I was a bee's butt close to goin' ballistic, I coulda sounded like a complete horse's ass, like I dumped on you a couple of months ago. But I didn't, because it was Em."

"You've got to control your temper. One day you'll chew into a stranger, someone not allowing second chances for apologies, and land in trouble." Paul was freezing, all this time sitting on the floor without a shirt. He returned to the closet to grab a sweater. "Well, I'm hiking to the Union to study; sure you don't want to come along?"

"No, sir, I'm fallin' asleep, do some dreamin' and cut my eleven o'clock." Lindy hid underneath the covers. Sleet clattered the glass and somewhere down the hall a clock radio went off, blasting the WPGU 7:30 news report.

# # # #

His roommate walked to the john. Under the blankets, Lindy hoped to rack, but their conversation sent his mind back to the afternoon he'd seen Emily.

"I hear you and Tommy Quarters made an appearance at the Christmas dance."

"Yes." The pair sat in McDonald's again, steam rising from their hot chocolates.

"Been goin' out with him for a while?"

"We've seen each other three or four times a week for the last month."

"Which explains why I've been unsuccessful phonin' you. Was it because you were always with him or wanted to stay away from me?" Lindy avoided sarcasm.

"How long did it take to realize, Will, that I was purposely not returning your messages? Did you consider I might be dating someone else, or between your band's practices, performances and road trips, was my not calling another petty detail you forgot?"

Lindy ceded Em's allegation. Since September he'd been busy enough with Frogfeet, his schedule so hectic, that his attempts to hook up with her were half-hearted. He'd wanted to talk with Em but other stuff, either essential or trivial, came first. "Why now?"

"Even if you and I aren't going out anymore, we owe it to ourselves to be friends, and honest." A trio of students entered Mac's, bringing in a cold gust of wind.

"Is that why you two showed up at KIDs, to toss your spankin' new boyfriend in my face and embarrass me?" Instantly Lindy realized accusing Em was unfair.

"That Saturday night, Tom and I were undecided whether or not to attend the party. Neither of us cared to because we were content being a couple by ourselves, with everyone else unaware of our relationship. Yet Tom and I knew we couldn't hide forever; Champaign-Urbana is not so anonymous, sooner or later someone would see us. We concluded if we were to continue dating, we didn't wish to be sneaky and other people should know. The Christmas dance was the first opportunity to come out. We're not serious or running off to marry, only two people seeing each other and enjoying our companionship. The friendship is not a big deal."

"Except for the fact you and I don't have our relationship anymore."

"We haven't for a long, long time, not since the summer." Emily sounded frustrated. "Goodness knows, this isn't my choice, us breaking up, but you have not been around, Will, not all semester. You've ignored me."

"That's why I've phoned so often the last few weeks, to say I want to find time for you again, to pick up the threads. And I think you're being unfair, not returning my calls shut me out, I wasn't offered another chance."

"Like Homecoming?" She coldly asked.

"That was different. The band landed our first gig in front of a paying audience. Performing on such short notice showed we were a dependable group, and a main reason we've earned so much work these past months. There wasn't any alternative, I'm part of Frogfeet, the others were playin' with or without me. If I'd have blown them off, that would have been the finish of my dream, I'd never experienced the stage like I have this semester. I was right picking my music." Lindy's hand banged the tabletop.

"Oh, really, grow up, check your pride, look at the rut you're in."

Here was the fork in their conversation, Lindy's excuse to blow his temper, let everything hang out, either prudent or thoughtless and selfish, and screw the consequences. His mind struggled, summing up his life the past months, the joyful and sad, satisfying and embarrassing, accomplishments and shameful mistakes. Everyone thinks I'm a self-seeking egotist but no one analyzes my side. They think it's easy, strummin' my Gibson, singin' into the microphone. Let them try living through the work and frustrations, sacrifice the free time and weekends, miss out on our college fun. Christ, none of them could handle half the sweat and heartaches—they'd be bonkers after a week—especially my girlfriend. Screw everything, it's time someone else was slammed.

Lindy's self-analysis was encompassing but brief. First wanting to swing away, he remembered he was sitting with Em and settled himself. Decency trumped stupidity. "But I didn't want to talk about the 'Feet, Em. I want to discuss us."

"The path always circles back to that group."

"No, it doesn't; I've thought about you all semester, tried to compromise and think up answers for us. Go ask Robby."

"I'm sure you have, but you've remained with the band. They're more urgent, more valuable than me, school or your other friends. Thoughts are nice, but what you do is the most meaningful."

"You're right, I'm negotiating a bad bargain and Frogfeet's the biggest part, I can't cut loose even if I want to. I like singing for people, hearin' the applause. The balance—no sleep, no bookin' and shady scruples—is dicey, but I'll manage to stick to my guns." Lindy spoke as if defeated, knowing he wouldn't reform, not to bring up his grade point, for more rack time, his friends in KIDs, or to please Em. He was determined to see his destiny through. "Where'd you first meet Tommy?"

"At the Red Lion, the night the KIDs showed up to party for you."

"I didn't even know you were there."

Summer Never Comes

Emily wavered, seeing Will had quit fighting, her affection returning. *He's the first man I've really loved, he was so caring, candid and comical; we were so content, we could work it out, still get together as in days past. Maybe I should reconsider my pride, the missed dates, snubs and rejections, what would those matter if I took him back? I would look foolish and Tom would be offended, but he's only a freshman—so extrovert, I don't think he has trouble finding girls.*

"How're your grades gonna be this semester?"

"I should earn a 4.75 if I'm fortunate with finals. And you?"

"Okay, I suppose." Lindy focused on Emily's eyes. "Whadya say, I know I don't deserve another chance, but how about a life boat for your ol' Will?"

Once more Emily paused, glancing around Mac's, dwelling on their wonderful, intimate, blissful past, when they first met; their talks, the hours discovering and revealing each other, their year of being closest, dearest, beloved sweethearts, the kidding, musings, reflections and kindnesses. *If Will were reliable, trustable…Just like the other times?* Their earlier conversations tumbled back, the heart-to-hearts, the assurances, promises, breaches and betrayals.

"If this were two months ago, with fewer broken hopes, if you hadn't hurt me so much, maybe we could begin over. But, we can't, I cannot."

That day, returning to KIDs, and this morning in his bunk, Lindy remembered how short their meeting was—fifteen minutes. Funny, a year's friendship finished in a quarter hour. But the cause wasn't their talk, thank goodness he'd kept his cool and not blown his top. Rather the four-months' accumulation of missteps, his work with the band and compulsion to see Frogfeet through. One dream destroyed a love.

# # # #

Reuters – Hanoi – In a radio broadcast, North Vietnam's Deputy Defense Minister Muc Yuc Fo warned the United States that American troops stationed in the south face 'defeat, destruction and devastation' if they are not withdrawn within the coming year. The minister claimed that, despite the ongoing Paris peace talks, the people of North Vietnam are reaching the end of their patience with 'the ongoing occupation of our sovereign territory by Imperialist-Capitalist forces.' 'The historic epoch in the battle is approaching,' Minister Muc proclaimed.

# # # #

"The idea here is to…what?" Randy Miller asked.

"Get a count of UNITED's entire, current membership," Leander Valent demanded. "Bernard needs numbers."

Wearing his orange and black sweatshirt, Randy sat at a long, long table piled with stacks of stapled documents and mounds of rubber-banded manila folders. On the floor were five boxes overfilled with more papers. From earlier visits to UNITED's office, he knew these were a semester's worth of the recruiting squads' summary sheets and registration forms, discarded and unorganized until now.

"Of course, we want accuracy—that's central—and I apprehend the tremendous amount of material here," Leander paced by the table, "but we also must supply Bernard the most up to date, optimistic figures by tomorrow morning."

"You'd think over the last weeks someone would've recorded a running total instead of letting the information collect in this room. Where'd the numbers UNITED's been bragging over come from if nobody's examined this stuff until now?"

"The directors have reasonably tracked our progress, I will personally vouch for that. However, with the food drive, ballooning membership and Christmas vacation, record keeping lagged behind."

"So we have to tote everything up."

"Now you must count," Leander corrected.

"All right, I'll get going," again Randy surveyed the heaps, "hope I finish early enough to book for my finals."

"Excellent. If there are any more members in the office, I'll send them over." Leander walked to the door.

Alone, Randy leafed through the forms, three-ring binders, legal pads, folders and ledgers. There were students' names, addresses and phone numbers from every university dorm, sorority, frat and apartment building. UNITED had scavenged the entire campus for new members, that was certain. Randy figured there were hundreds of pages on this table with a couple thousand names. Well, somebody has to, he told himself, maybe Leander will find some help for me tonight and I can study for finals tomorrow.

# # # #

The ads were printed in the *Daily Illini* at week's end.

"Food Drive for Peace a Success!

"Forty-five tons of supplies Donated by our campus Community!

"These contributions, combined with foodstuffs collected from comrade colleges and universities, are being shipped to Vietnam.

"This effort has Demonstrated to that country, the world and the wayward Washington government, our Dedication to ending the shameful, needless, wasteful war in Southeast Asia.

"We will keep up the Struggle to stop the killing!

"UNITED to end the war!"

"UNITED was founded three months ago with the purpose of drawing together the groups opposed to the Vietnam War and aiding the cause of peace.

"These goals are being achieved!

"Over the fall semester, approximately 7300 students and faculty members enlisted to fight the war; 7300 voices collectively demanding the end of Destruction.

"As final examinations commence, UINTED will suspend recruiting activities to enable all in the campus community to concentrate on their schoolwork.

"With the new semester, however, we pledge to carry forward our Battle to halt the Murdering in Southeast Asia.

"We ask all to follow, Sacrifice and be involved!

"UNITED to end the war!"

# # # #

Good to their word, in January UNITED faded from Champaign-Urbana. Students wore orange and black shirts and the large orange flag with the black border flew from the Union's windows, but the True Believers vanished from the Quad, recruiting squads did not canvass the dorms or Greek houses, and no one hustled for money outside Second Chance, Stan's or Kam's. Whether due to Bernard's hold on the student body or undergrads tiring of the UNITED fad and more concerned with finals was the question. A conjecturing Paul and anyone else would have to wait until February for an answer.

# # # #

"How is the *DI*? I haven't visited the offices since the school year started."

"Still in Illini Hall, publishing five editions a week," Paul responded.

"Two days off, a bonus in the newspaper business." John Barrett sat behind his desk. The *Champaign News-Gazette* reporter was thirty-three, thin, with gray speckling his hair. "And the Campus Scout?"

"Evolving, every Scout's vision for the column is different. This semester a few articles have dealt with serious subjects."

"The best columnist was five or six years ago, a guy named Roger Ebert. He grew up in Urbana, but after graduation I think he relocated to Chicago."

"Mr. Barrett, about the subject I mentioned on the phone... Since autumn, you've authored several stories pertaining to UNITED's activities. I'm looking to ask some questions and for guidance with my work."

"Why come to the *News-Gazette*? We're the closed-minded, townie paper students only read when there's an article about the Fighting Illini basketball team. Do you think we care about undergrads' attitudes on the war or their peace movement?"

Paul felt uncomfortable. Antipathy between the student body and local citizens was well-known, each believing the other side owned too cozy a deal with the university. He wished to sidetrack the local feud, and was uncertain if John Barrett was facetious or straightforward.

"Relax, if you consider me a university-hater. I received my U of I degree ten years ago, and was elated to land this job and the opportunity to live around the campus. Hell, I haven't missed a home football game as an undergrad or an alum; I donate money every year and tell my friends this is a fantastic place for a top-notch education for their children. But, like you, I'm also a newspaperman, which, besides selling subscriptions, means what?"

"To investigate events and present balance to our readers."

"The anticipated answer." He grinned. "Think Harv Schmidt will ever win a Big Ten championship?"

Paul eased back in his chair, glad a cordial Mr. Barrett rapped like a student.

"What's made you so interested in the peace movement that you've researched UNITED for four months?"

"Early in the semester, Stef Tianen and I brainstormed story ideas, one being the anti-war groups. By happenstance, ten minutes later I stood next to her when the first Operation Loading Dock bulletins came over the teletype machine, and she handed me this assignment. A fluke which evolved."

"What have you found since September?"

"Incidents—some sensible and others peculiar—disconnected from the peace movement's objective and image."

"Picture or a puzzle, as a reporter I can't count the occasions I've faced that question. How about examples?"

A careful Paul hesitated. Why offer information to a stranger when he'd hid his story from Stef all semester?

"As I said, I may live on the other side, but I think of the University of Illinois as my school, I'd hate to see it taken down."

"Why that indictment, Mr. Barrett?"

"Call me John." He laid his glasses on his desk. "I've attended UNITED's meetings, questioned undergrads, took in the October rally and covered Secretary Camp's speech in Lincoln Hall. There's an asperity to the peace movement, the chain of command is too inflexible for a college crowd, decisions on how to proceed are settled at the top and passed down to members with no debates or votes. Bernard Minerath doesn't even answer questions."

Paul was relieved discovering another person with an analogous assessment. "Bernard's the key, the one who induced the old peace groups to combine into UNITED. Plus he's engineered some dramatic tactics, the

Summer Never Comes

Homecoming balloon for one. I'm convinced the group is dictatorial because of his personality—unbending and by the book."

"What else that's newsworthy?"

"The publicity from the Undersecretary Camp episode stands out."

"You've got to credit UNITED, gauging then manipulating Camp's personality. The trekkies held their signs, kept their mouths shut and let the undersecretary make an asshole out of himself."

"Strange how Bernard and his people organized so fast, especially since Camp's itinerary was unknown until three days before he flew into Savoy. But I suppose with the thirty-three thousand students on our campus, UNITED recruiting a few hundred to do the work isn't hard imagining."

"Did you talk to the picketers at the airport or Lincoln Hall, and realized where they came from? A few from our staff did. There were thirty-five hundred protesters. The majority were ignorant where any Champaign-Urbana buildings or businesses were located, didn't even recognize the names of any bars. They were obviously from out of town."

Why didn't I do that, Paul criticized himself. "Where were they from?"

"Mostly ISU and Eastern Illinois. Oddly, there were about forty claiming they drove from Rutgers." John Barrett shook his head. "A far distance to travel to hold a poster."

New Jersey, the east coast and Bernard's trips, the connection struck. "A supposition is our campus' UNITED is in contact with peace groups around the country. I wonder if it can be proved."

"Confirm there are other UNITEDs? A snap. Sit in the Newspaper Library and read through other college papers' stories, advertisements and editorials. If protesters are protesting, the schools' reporters will cover them."

"I will." Paul reached for his book bag on the floor. "Thanks for your help, John."

# # # #

"That was certainly a delicious finish to the semester," Emily lightheartedly commented.

"Good food, no meal tastier than a juicy prime rib, best we've eaten yet at the Round Barn." Tommy Quarters was baffled by Emily's insistence on returning to that restaurant, but never suggested alternates. "A few beers here at Second Chance, then we'll call it a night, okay?"

"That will be fine, Tom." Holding hands, the two skidded on John Street, unshoveled from the earlier in the week snowstorm. The pair spotted a line outside the bar's entrance stretching back thirty students.

"This is finals week, why's everybody out drinking? You don't mind waiting, do you?"

"Not at all, it will move fast." Emily's breath frosted in the chilly air.

"Positive? You feel so cold, you should wear a hat," Tommy nearly pleaded. "You know, we could drive someplace else."

"I think all the bars will be as packed with undergrads."

"You're right." The two stood by the Karmel Corn Shop. "Of course, we don't have to waste time in a tavern."

"Where would you propose we end up?" She moved closer to Tommy's side for warmth and to sidle out of the way of fellow students.

"Walking around Campustown is insane on a wintry, icy evening like this, it's smarter staying inside where there's heat and only the two of us, together, alone. Let's go back to your dorm and shack up." Uncertain of Emily's reply, he slipped his arm around her body.

"Really, now," she blushed, "but I don't think so."

As the line advanced, Tommy retreated, regretting his timing but not the proposition. "It's a wild idea, I know, I shouldn't be so impetuous. Sorry putting you on the spot."

"I don't think so," a grinning Emily repeated, "because my room's occupied. Nicole's best friend from high school is in town this weekend and sleeping on an air mattress on our floor. What if we found a place somewhere else with a bed, a hotel room perhaps, with a steamy bathtub?"

"Whoa," Tommy was thrilled, "no kiddin', you'd do it with me, not be nervous or embarrassed?"

"I'm nineteen and not a prude, Tom, I've made love before. Even stay-at-homes dig sex and fun."

"Okay, let's boogie." He hopped out of the line, pulling Emily, hurrying to his car. This was way, too super enormously simple, I never imagined she'd be this agreeing, such an easy lay. Wait'll Kinsey finds out.

# # # #

Summer Never Comes

Scooter and Lauren were inside Second Chance, sitting in a booth by the pinball machines. Both had had sack classes this semester and neither worried over finals. Though Christmas had passed, Lauren was still talking about Scooter's present, fourteen pairs of bikini panties, all bright colors with lurid, sexy patterns. "But why, oh why did you let me open the box in front of your family on Christmas morning? Both of us have to begin acting like adults."

Scooter twirled the ends of his moustache, fancying hustling back to Lauren's apartment and balling.

Despite Emily and Tommy driving to a motel, and a loafing Lauren and Scooter, many students prepared for finals this weekend.

In Room 221, Greg Hall, Joyce and Stu sat four desks away from each other with every one of their courses' texts, term papers, outlines and syllabi. The pair had been booking since 6:30, planned to stay after midnight, and return the following two nights. They only took one break, when Stu talked about the LSAT, describing it as the most arduous exam he'd experienced.

Sharon and Paul were in the Reference Room. With their late-in-the-week finals schedules, there was little pressure for the two to really hit the books, and when the Reference Room closed at ten p.m., they sat on the wide marble steps leading to the second floor.

"Do you think anybody's ever been stranded in the Stacks overnight?" Sharon stared at the murals of the hemispheres on the stairwell walls.

"Don't see why anyone would, the experience would be awfully scary."

"You're right, but you could always lock yourself in your study cage when the 'great Stacks monster' came to devour you and your books." Sharon raised her arms above her head, mimicking a scowling gargoyle, attempting to frighten a laughing Paul. The couple kissed and decided to go back to Sharon's bedroom and bed.

Lindy occupied his desk in KIDs, poring through his textbooks and notes. For a first this semester, Frogfeet had their Saturday night gig canceled and, after he loudly protested, Franky Konkel and Gary Anderson agreed not to search for substitutes. This allowed Lindy three straight nights of anxiously, earnestly-needed hard-core cramming. Unlike Robby, his finals were the first four days of the week. Lindy planned on pulling a nighter.

Without notes, outlines or papers, Dale Kinsey stepped through the Undergrad's turnstiles and roamed the upper level. After one loop, he sat in a chair, reading a magazine, watching the students at the tables in front of him. With finals week beginning, there were dozens and hundreds toiling in the place, and when one with a conspicuously high stack of textbooks left for a break, Dale pounced. He hustled towards the unguarded heap, snatched three sociology paperbacks, rushed away, and hid them on a bookshelf with the others he'd stolen this evening, hauling the cache out when the 'Brary closed. On Monday, Dale made six trips through the buyback lines at Follett's and the Illini Union book stores, exchanging the stolen merchandise for $145.

Secluded in the Undergrad's lower level, Tim Malito didn't notice the carrel's walls. All he fixated on were his statistics books and notes, breaking once in the evening to hit the john. At midnight, he hurried home to KIDs, subconsciously reviewing problems sets, oblivious to the freezing air and icy sidewalks. Entering the front door, Tim heard yelling in the living room.

"You a-hole, I don't believe it!" Bobby Sox shouted, "how could you dump it on me?"

"Sorry, pal, no diamonds, better gettin' rid of the bitch than eatin' it."

"You tell him, Killer," Shaky Jake laughed. For the third straight hand, Bobby had taken the queen of spades.

"Okay, points, listen up," Moose, the fourth in the game and scorekeeper, announced, "Jake, fifty-four, Bobby, eighty…"

"Rotten bastards."

"…Killer, sixty-nine, and Mooser, sixty-one. Who's deal?"

"Mine, goddamn-it," Bobby angrily announced.

"How long you guys been at it?" Tim unbuttoned his coat.

"Since 7:30, this is our eighth game, everybody's won once except Bobby."

"Frickin' get laid or pass."

"Yeah, yeah, yeah. What is this, left?"

Tim laid his book bag on the floor to spectate. Hearts had caught on in the fraternity before Christmas, and even during finals, two or three games were simultaneously played any time of day or night. Nobody bet money, the brothers' only intentions wasting time.

"Deuce."

Jake threw the two of clubs and Bobby's ace grabbed the first trick.

"When in doubt, bleed it out." He tossed the five of spades.

Summer Never Comes

"Thanks," Moose sweetly said, disposing his king.

"Two guys with no spades, let's be careful."

Killer took a heart and came back with diamonds, which Bobby won, plus another heart from Jake. He led the seven of clubs.

"Those are the breaks, compadre." Killer shook his head and flung the queen of spades on the table.

Jake and the Mooser slid under the card and Bobby ate the trick. All the KIDs whooped.

"Son of a bitch." He unhurriedly gathered the cards.

"Tough luck," Moose unsympathetically volunteered.

"Go to hell."

"Do Lucifer and his fellow devils play hearts in Hades?"

The hand ended and the four counted their points. Jake stood, presuming the end of the evening.

"Five," Killer said.

"One," Mooser spoke up.

"The rest." Bobby's face brightened, "Hundred bounce back."

A giggling Jake sat down and Tim went upstairs to his room. An hour later when Paul walked in, the four were still at the table playing the same game. Moose had hit a hundred, too.

# # # #

Professor Hudson promised the Phil 393 final would take sixty minutes instead of the standard three hours, a relief to the class. The fourth essay question read:

"There is a large, theoretical city in the United States. A minority of the population has been outraged by actions considered to be against its interests. This minority ceases to respect law and order. It riots, plunders and pillages its section of the city, and announces plans to march into areas of the city up to now controlled by the majority to carry out more rampaging.

"The concerns are so essential and vital, the methods of protest so extreme, that this is life or death for the city.

"You are a member of the minority.

Summer Never Comes

"Identify the issues. Should your people persist in their course? What would you do?"

Paul wrote in his blue booklet.

"Society's laws state that destruction for no reason other than violence is wrong. Insurrection, plundering and pillaging cannot be condoned.

"Yet, there are occasions, circumstances, when it is necessary to throw away the rules and utilize expedient measures, each segment of a society obviously having different criteria by which to make this judgment. If one minority is of the opinion that the established rules have broken down and laws do not lead to justice, they have the option, though not necessarily the right, to resort to extra-legal processes.

"In this particular situation, the minority has already judged the situation fundamental enough to destroy sections of its own community. If the issues are that serious, that grave enough to warrant such measures, then, as a member of the minority, I feel these violent (aggressive?) measures should be employed until the rest of the city, the majority, listens and addresses the problems facing the entire city. If some parts of our society are hurting, are in such misery, so dispossessed, it is the duty of everyone in that society to come to their aid. If those in trouble are ignored, then extra-normal channels or methods should be open for the minority to use to get their plight in front of the majority. No one should be forgotten."

Lindy gazed out the window and organized his answer.

"Throughout history minorities have broken the law for their own causes. This has been one method by which changes have occurred. The American Revolution is an example. In most cases, law-breaking has at least brought attention to the cause. This is true today with television playing such an important role in our lives. Too much or unnecessary violence detracts from the cause, or the purpose of the protest. Those outside the minority focus on the violence and not the reason for it. Television is quick to highlight this. This being the case, the minority should not continue its violent behavior into territory other than its own. It should rely on the actions it has committed thus far to be broadcast by the mass media and to demonstrate the seriousness of the particular situation. The minority should rely on its message getting out, broadcasted, to right the wrong."

# # # #

Summer Never Comes

Bernard remained on campus during finals week but did not study, instead spending his time talking to UNITED's True Believers, analyzing articles about Vietnam and exercising in the IMPE's nautilus room. With testing underway, undergrads leaving campus and a lull in the war, there was little more to occupy him. One item was an interview request from a *Daily Illini* staffer. He hadn't talked to this reporter himself, didn't know his or her name or what he or she looked like, and would handle this matter when classes re-started in February. Bernard finished twelve reps on the multi-triceps machine with eighty pounds of weight.

# # # #

Finals week ended. Students hit the bars a last night, then packed into their cars, buses or trains and bolted out of Cham-Bana. By Saturday afternoon few undergrads remained on campus—Moose couldn't find three more KIDs for a hearts game, and Sharon and Paul were the only two walking on Green Street in Campustown.

"Why do this now?" he begged.

"Because, dear, you'll be waited on quicker today than next month when everybody's back."

"I don't feel like modeling clothes, it's painful. Besides, job interviews don't start until March, so there's plenty of time for buying a suit."

"Poor baby, if you're ill, is it a tummy ache?" A teasing Sharon patted his hand. "Maybe we should check your temperature." Paul chuckled, as always tolerating his girlfriend's mocking. In the cold the two hiked past McBride's Drug Store, Paul slowing as they neared Schumacher's Men's Clothing. "Well, it's too frigid to argue."

"Common sense, Lord, that's why I love his man."

Forty-five minutes later they exited the store, Paul carrying a bag containing a new shirt and tie.

"There, all over." Sharon put on her mittens. "I like your choices, suits with vests are fashionable these days."

"The operation went faster than I expected, even with so many colors on the racks. When will the chloroform wear off?"

"The salesman said about a half hour. Will your health insurance cover the full amount or only eighty percent?"

Summer Never Comes

"Good question, we better head to McKinley Hospital to ask."

"Then you can receive a blood transfusion to pull you out of the shock." The pair hurried to Sharon's Camaro to drive to her house. All the roommates, except Maureen, had left Champaign-Urbana for the break. Paul started a fire and they lay on the pillows next to the hearth.

"When will we shop for clothes for your Vet Med College interview?"

"My wardrobe is fine, thank you. I'm wearing a blue blazer with my gray flannel skirt."

"Very conservative." Paul rubbed her leg. "When is it scheduled?"

"The third week of February."

"Think you'll be nervous?"

"A professional school is a major step, but this has been so long coming that I'm confident I'm prepared. Plus the date's nearly a month away, plenty of time for heebie jeebies." Sharon watched the burning twigs. "After three and a half years as undergrads, we're growing up; it's about tomorrow."

"And buying my first new suit since graduating from eighth grade."

"You've never been into clothes, have you. Flannel shirts and faded Levi's won't look professional at your accounting job on Michigan Avenue this summer."

"Since I like flannel, since it's my thing, if stores don't sell matching briefcases, then I can't get a job on Michigan Avenue or anywhere else in Chicago, I won't have to interview and I'm off the hook," he patted Sharon's back, "except for the suit I bought today."

"You don't want to go through with this?"

"This pending, imminent step in my life? Not willingly. Adulthood, responsibility, expectations—if I could avoid them, I would."

"A perpetually adolescent mindset isn't an option. We have to accept time is moving on and deal with the decisions." Sharon faced her boyfriend.

"There's only one for me, the tunnel away from Champaign. No substitutions or proxies, only what's pre-determined."

"Wake up, we're enrolled at the University of Illinois, with hundreds of majors and thousands of courses. You're set on accounting but if you care to, you can explore, attempt something else." Sharon meant for Paul to deliberate his future. "We're plenty young, our generation has time and potential."

Summer Never Comes

"Risk, an adventure, another crack? No, that's not prudent." Paul gazed into the fire. "Look at Lindy, forfeiting so much gambling on his band: this semester's classes, his health, friendships dating back two or three years and Emily. Where's his opportunity landing him? A grade point in the toilet, a lost girlfriend, the only times he's slept enough the last few months is vacations at his mom's house and now, hear this one, he and Frogfeet are thinking about smuggling drugs around the state. Where's the worthwhile in that? How can the dollars Lindy pockets, or any successes he believes he earns, equal the stuff he's losing?"

"Except for the dope deal, which sounds brainless, I'm certain Lindy's sacrifices have been hard for him to live with. But he's in the real world plugging away, attempting, and that's the incentive, striving for a goal. Lindy's probably not doing it for the money, he might not know why he's pushed himself as he has this semester, but he's on his stage."

"And I'm not Lindy, he's the free spirit with the passion. My psyche dictates I can't achieve anything except what will happen between now and June and after that. I'm trapped. The obvious, the meant-to-be-can't-be-stopped. And I realize I shouldn't complain about leaving school after the four great years I've had, but I can't help that, either; I'm already missing Champaign-Urbana."

"That's right, you're not your roommate, but you can challenge what's predictable."

"It's unavoidable I will graduate. You, Lindy, Kentucky, everyone's told me all semester; I should face the truth."

"Don't you think that's maudlin? Graduation is a measure of our lives, an event to embark from, not a cheerless, gloomy finale."

The fire from the kindling died down and Paul added two logs.

"Five years ago in high school I signed up for a weekend ski trip to a Wisconsin resort. Three or four bus loads, a couple hundred students, went along. Instructors taught us the basics, then sent us up the tow rope to the top of the bunny hill. It was the only time I've been on skis. I was clumsy, fell as much as everybody else and needed three or four tries to get down a hill without tumbling. But it was a blast, the most fun I ever had in high school, and I definitely wanted to go skiing again. When the weekend was over and we came home, I told my dad how exciting the trip was, about the different slopes, the thrills of zooming downhill, how some guys couldn't stop when they got to the bottom of the runs, and about the two classmates that returned with broken legs. When my dad heard about the 'broken legs' he lectured me on how dangerous skiing sounded, and told me that something so reckless wasn't worth any fun you could enjoy. He decided this was the first and last time I'd go. I was disappointed and really mad at him because the trip was such a great time. But when I went to school on Monday, I saw those guys with busted legs hopping down the hallway on their crutches. One, Mike Flannery, needed help climbing the stairs. I thought my dad was right, skiing's too hazardous, maybe it's safer for me sitting at home and watching television."

"But you lose so much, you miss seeing the hills."

"I'll experience them plenty, beginning in June, for better or worse, regardless of what I plan or manage today."

Her boyfriend's logic upset Sharon. Waiting for the inevitable was intimidating enough, while chance, risk and progress were futile. Acquiescence was okay, but inquiring and searching pointless, even if an intelligent person knew better.

"I wish," Paul fell back on the pillows, "summer would never come. If the only seasons were autumn, winter or spring, we'd always be in school and never have to graduate. Nothing would change."

"The deal with you is you love this place too much; our college bubble is too trouble-free, your reality's too uncomplicated. Life's not so trivial, we will confront questions and dilemmas, have futures to find, accomplishments to fulfill, potentials to realize. Thinking otherwise is idiocy."

"That's fine coming from you, you're heading for four more years in Champaign-Urbana, not finished in four months."

"We'll all graduate, Paul, some sooner, some later. But leaving is not an end."

The extra logs brightened the room, as expected, inevitably, he mused.

"I wish summer never comes."

Chapter Fifteen

UPI – Saigon – United States Army Headquarters reports a buildup of North Vietnamese forces in the region of Mount Atouat, Laos. Though specific numbers are unavailable, the concentration is described as 'significant.'

Reuters – Hanoi – A North Vietnamese Defense Ministry spokesman again warned the international community of imminent consequences for American forces stationed in the south if withdrawals are not accelerated. 'Responsibility for their fate rests with the Washington warmongers and murderers.'

# # # #

"She's not here." Stan stated.

"Playing in the semester's first basketball tournament at IMPE," Ollie added, "the match must've gone into overtime."

"Unlike Stef missing a meeting dealing with the paper, except when the excuse is intramurals."

"She'll be back soon, let's wait." Al Stojak led Paul into the editor-in-chief's office and sat by her desk. "We're blocking out space for the next issues of *Spectrum* and need to know when your UNITED article will be ready."

Paul squirmed. Since December he'd pretty much shunned the *Daily Illini's* offices, coming to Illini Hall to work when most staffers were out, early in the morning or on Saturdays. During Christmas vacation, finals and semester break this had been easy, everyone's schedules, including Stef's and Stoj's, jumbled. UNITED's inactivity since the food drive also helped many neglect the peace movement. But with a new semester and repeated bulletins from Vietnam, Paul knew his editor-in-chief would soon confront him. He didn't expect the showdown to be delayed by a b-ball game.

"I've started a rough draft, at least charted an outline, or thought about a framework," Paul dawdled. "The problem is I'm still following leads. You know how it is, investigations expose extra evidence to trace and substantiate."

"What exactly are you hunting, I'm missing the logic. From Stef's accounts, your writing explains the history of UNITED and the older peace groups. If you're studying the past, why are you going forward?" Stoj lit a cigarette and relaxed in his chair. "Last October should be a conclusion, your only double-checking the dates when the anti-war groups quit or the spelling of someone's name."

"Events the last four months have made the story more than a recounting. I'm not saying I'm into shocking revelations, but what I've stumbled in merits mentioning."

"For example?"

Stef's absence benefited Stoj. With her missing, *Spectrum's* editor ferreted out his own information, and Paul sensed he was not so lightweight as the *DI's* staff pigeonholed him. Was Stoj his own man? Could I count on him for advice, back up?

"There's the woman who flew the hot air balloon over Memorial Stadium during the Homecoming game, the one with the UNITED banner. Turns out she's a History Department professor teaching a class about eighteenth century England with a book on her course's reading list that's a manual for socialism and Communist coup d'état."

"Who'd care about Russia in a British history class? Sounds like someone goofed typing the reading list."

"Exactly what I was told, a mistake. But I checked deeper and found the professor herself put this book on the list."

"Happenstance at the Big U masquerading as pattern."

"Except this professor is a member of UNITED and has been Bernard Minerath's independent study instructor for more than two years. That's not coincidence."

"Instead of the puff piece Stef's depicted, are you claiming your article is front page news?" Balancing on the chair's back legs, Stoj reached behind his back for an ashtray.

Summer Never Comes

"Don't get comfortable in my office, I'm not graduating for four months." Perspiring, wearing blue Illinois sweatpants and carrying a styrofoam cup, the editor-in-chief rushed in, surprising Paul and Stoj and impelling Stoj's seat to skid, dropping him to the floor. The mood shifted in the seconds he needed to rise to his feet. Stef sat behind her desk, as ever in charge of the room and the *Daily Illini;* Stoj stood, hunting for his cigarette, re-assuming his place as Stef's subordinate; and Paul changed his mind again, opting to redact his story a while longer. "What are you discussing?"

"Paul's article for *Spectrum*. He's worked on a rough draft and we're reviewing his findings. Some are darned interesting."

"I'm sure, no one more reliable than our conscientious Mr. Roberts to provide what we're looking for." Stef dried her forehead. "But there's an adjustment, I'm choosing to run the UNITED piece next month, the middle or end of March. Word count's not critical, as long as we show the peace movement for what it is, a proactive force on campus, pulling us the hell out of the war. How's that sound?"

Because of their earlier conversation, an apprehensive Paul guessed Stoj would question the editor-in-chief. But this didn't happen. Al reached for his cigarette pack and grinned. "Okay, Stef."

"For you, Paul, I have information. Cutting through the Armory, a peace protester handed me a schedule of anti-war seminars UNITED is sponsoring next week. The topics include Vietnam's domestic politics, the Air Force's secret bombing missions and Nixon lying again about peace negotiations. Sounds like the lectures SOAP and Laurie Allman used to lob at the undergrads, only I'm certain not as boring and more relevant. Work the programs into your article."

"Okay, Stef."

# # # #

When Wednesday's mail, including report cards, was delivered to KIDs, Stu was the first in the foyer tearing open his official Big U envelope. Straight-B's, a 4.0, not lofty enough to inscribe the name Stewart C. Cummings on the Bronze Tablets, but his second best semester GPA and improvement enough to move off probation. Grinning, he strolled into the living room.

Summer Never Comes

Paul, among the hard-core bookers each semester seriously aiming for five points, pulled a 4.55. Vic Extensionelli came closest to straight A's with a 4.88. Del Hansen, Bill Wick, Nemo and the Hodster reached the mailboxes at the same time, compared report cards, and predictably discovered all earned slightly higher than a B average. Tommy Quarters did a three-point, hooks, a surprise and the minimum for active membership in the fraternity. The last two weeks with Emily in the library had helped. The living room hearts players, Moose, Killer, Jake, and Scooter, waited to finish a game before heading to the foyer. Jake had shot the moon four hands in a row and the others wanted to see if the social chairman could repeat a fifth time, the KIDs' record. Bobby Sox's report card would sit in his mail slot until he drove back to Champaign on Sunday, the day before classes.

When a weary-boned Lindy returned from Frogfeet's Charleston gig at three a.m., all he did was grab the envelope. In his room the lights were off with Paul asleep, and he hit the rack. The next morning, Lindy discovered he'd pulled a three-point and gratefully kept off probation.

# # # #

"Okay, how about some quiet?" Orion Nelson pounded his gavel. Few of the five dozen KIDs assembling in the chapter room minded their president, instead shoving and rearranging the sofas, searching for friends to sit around, giggling at jokes, grabbing empty pop cans for ash trays, or late and still walking in. The funniest were Moose and Ozark debating, from what Paul fathomed, intramural water polo or depth charging a submarine.

"Pass me a butt, will ya, Jake?"

"Where the hell's the rest of the chairs?"

"Hear what happened Thursday? After drinkin' at the Lion a pack of the brothers—'T', 'O', Plano, Rich Hynes, Bruce Lane and Donny Hepler—hiked to the Art to scope the skin flicks, all of them so drunk that on the way there they wizzed in an alley off First Street."

"How about a match?"

"Come on guys," Orion pleaded, "the sooner we start, the quicker we'll finish."

Summer Never Comes

"Halfway through the film, at the climax when eight women are gangin' up on one loser guy with a shriveled weenie, Donny is so wasted he ralphs in his seat. Everyone scatters and leaves him staring at his own puke."

"'Ralph,' a new nickname is born."

"I need two tickets for the Minnesota game."

"Got ya covered, Petey."

"Goddamn-it, now, shut up." Orion flung the gavel at the table. His outburst, habitual for a house meeting's first minutes, hushed the brothers. "Secretary will take the roll."

"I move the roll call be suspended," Bobby Sox shouted.

"Second."

"Motion carried," Orion pounded, "the meeting will come to order. The first announcement is the pledge class activation. This will take place Sunday afternoon, assuming they are all voted in." The brothers hooted as Tommy Quarters and the freshman class sunk in their seats.

Officers' reports followed, including Shaky Jake's update on Saturday night's pre-activation kegger, and House Manager Mike Nasetstein's warning that the fraternity was running short of toilet paper, with a fresh supply's delivery expected Friday. Until then, 'Stein cautioned, "crap only when ya need ta and chop 'em off short."

"New business," Orion pronounced, satisfied the meeting was cruising along.

"Yo." Wearing his orange and black sweatshirt, Randy Miller spoke loud enough to gain the mumbling room's attention. "I move that UNITED be invited to speak at a special house session next week."

"Who, where," the Mooser turned to Ozark, "what did he say?"

"Christ, so much for frickin' quick." Bobby rubbed his face as the KIDs speculated on Randy's proposal.

"Order. We have a motion on the floor. Is there a second?" Orion, anticipating his date with a physical therapy major at Murph's in twenty-five minutes, prayed for none and the meeting concluded.

"I second it, Mr. President," Killer hollered, and a dozen brothers groaned.

"Discussion," Orion declared in a tired tone. He recognized Randy again.

Summer Never Comes

"We all know what UNITED's been doing around the campus and why. Since October, this organization, to which some of us belong," he glanced toward Killer, Steve Ferris, Kenny Concord and Chuck Brunke, "has worked to keep us aware of the fighting in Vietnam. UNITED's been activists in getting us involved to end the war."

"Plus freezin' their asses off on the Quad since Thanksgiving." Bobby whispered to Paul.

"Part of their time is spent talking to students in dorms and houses, explaining the organization's goals, the war's consequences to us, and convincing students to join UNITED."

"I ain't enrollin' in nothin'," Moose boomed.

"You haven't joined the human race, yet!" Chuck Pastron yelled back.

As the brothers laughed, Ozark consoled the Mooser, patting him on the back with his one good arm, his left. Ozark had lost the other, amputated at the elbow, two years ago in a factory accident at a summer job. Since then he'd coped with an artificial prosthesis as his right.

"Order, pay attention."

"Allowing UNITED to come to KIDs doesn't mean supporting their opinions, committing ourselves or signing up. You don't even have to attend to hear their arguments. All I'm requesting is we, like most of the Greek houses, afford them the chance to talk to anybody who's concerned enough to listen." Randy glanced at Moose. "There's another point to contemplate. The way to end the war is by sticking together. If we coalesce as a group, we're stronger. If we show solidarity, the other side takes notice, when there's one voice, we cause changes. And if there ever was tragedy to rebel against, Vietnam and the right-wingers are it. Ending the war is the most important thing our generation will ever achieve."

A supportive Orion smiled at Randy then scanned the chapter room for other brothers seeking recognition. "Killer."

"Well, amigos, I think Randeroo's on the button, we should let UNITED come on in 'cause the war sucks. The more info we get telling us how big a blow job it is, the better prepared we are for the garbage coming down the pike, which for us college-age, draft-able types is nothing but totally crappy. We gotta identify what's going on. Ever since '68, the head honchos in Washington have been out to screw us university students and it's time we got back at 'em." He sat down and the room whooped, the way the brothers always down-rapped when Killer spoke at house meetings.

"Why does he get up and talk?" Stu wondered.

"Eddie McMahon." Orion eyed his watch.

"I don't think we should let those fartin' bastards inside here. Don't catch me wrong, I don't wanna pull a ROTC and ship over to 'Nam to fight, or even let that asshole Nixon nuke Hanoi, even if that's what he's gonna do anyway, and even if that would cure lots of headaches. Maybe he should atomic bomb Japan again, that came off once, finished that battle really post-haste.

"I'm for peace, man, just like Killer says, but if you ask me, these UNITED creeps are bunches of strange asses, present company excluded, naturally." Eddie tugged his pants, squinted at Randy and flicked cigarette ashes into a soda can. "All they do is stand around talkin' constitutional amendments, representative legislations and senate ad hoc subcommittees, coaxin' us to sign a piece of paper. One of 'em even came at me in the Red Lion."

"That's 'cause the Lion's the only place anyone can find you besides your rack." Moose yelled and the whole room roared.

"Order, parliamentary procedure," Orion demanded, "Brother McMahon has the floor."

"Youse guys can wrassle me and jack off with this, but I'm convinced I'm right. Let 'em on the Quad and in the Lion, then the door here into KIDs, and pretty soon they'll be all over the Big U more than they are right now, they'll goddamned take over the entire campus, including Urbana. We won't be capable to do nothin' around here without checkin' with them first and receivin' their okay. There's conceptions like the more perfect general welfare and blessings of common liberty for all for one and I don't wanna forfeit mine. Hell with 'em." Eddie sat down by a lounging Joey Panky.

"Not much logic there."

"Stu," Orion pointed the gavel toward Bobby Sox's roommate.

"I agree with Eddie-Bob. Even though I don't argue against UNITED's message, there's no reason allowing them into KIDs. There are enough spots around campus for political debates. Our fraternity should be a shelter where we can stay away from disagreements; as it's a place to disconnect from classrooms and professors. Peace is basic, but the war and the killing's not here at the Big U, it's in 'Nam and Cambodia. We shouldn't have to be involved too much. Anybody wants to rap to UNITED, let them work it out with Randy, head to the Quad or drink beers with Eddie-Bob at the Lion."

Moose and the brothers snickered and Ozark exercised his mechanical arm.

"Anyone else?" Orion studied the room. "Randy Miller again."

"I don't see the issue as remaining uninvolved. The country's been fighting for seven years. Tens of thousands have been killed, wounded or missing in action, with the MIAs the cruelest. On television every week we watch stories about Air Force bombardments, refugees fleeing their villages, and body bags and coffins. If we keep hands off, ignore these sadnesses, how many more years will we waste in Vietnam? How many more of us are gonna get drafted? When is it our turns to be killed? The point is UNITED's willing to come here and explain how to end the war. It's not too much for us to listen."

The brothers split into cliques to deliberate. Get out, stay in, escalate, hands off, be involved or indifferent, concerned or slough off. Paul couldn't figure how the vote on Randy's motion would come down.

Orion stared to his left and courteously announced, "James Patrick Cleburne."

"Wall, Ah reckon there's a pile o' disagreement heah about the wahr. Whut does th' conflict mean, por-tend? Who's right, who's wrong, who's allowed t' control South Viet-nam or permitted t' decide th' future? Who's gonna die, who will survive? Issues, questions, un-knowns. An' thet's all-right, talkin' is important, thrashin' out th' ups and downs is how we learn whut th' otheh side is up to. Nothin' wrong with a little argument, even if you Yan-kees don' know much about jaw-bonin'. When th' discussion ceases is when th' conflagrations commence." Kentucky ambled to the front. "But Ah also think thet theah has been too much debate all-readeh. Everybodeh, heah in ouh house, all oveh th' campus, an a-round th' country, has had theah say. Where has thet brung us, whut has bin accomplished? Nothin' much, ex-ceptin' dismal episodes like dear Billy Powell, ouh treasured friend, bein' made t' march oveh t' Viet-nam an' spend his days sweatin', soldierin', fightin' an' mebbe dyin'. Thet is out-rageous, an appalling, un-glorious shame. So, Ah'd say allowin' U-NITED heah would be fine. We-all'd learn somethin', we-all'd find out whut theah plans are, we-all'd know whut we can do t' help."

"And maybe we will stop this awful war."

An approving Bobby Sox nodded, a majority of the KIDs applauded, and Paul realized this was the first time he'd heard Kentucky speak a sentence minus his southern drawl.

"Question," Nemo shouted.

"Yeah, let's vote."

"The issue is: do we invite UNITED to speak in our house. All in favor, raise your right hands."

Paul was surprised as arms rose, about three quarters of the KIDs wanted UNITED at the house. In back, Moose glimpsed at his roommate, seeing Ozark's left arm—his good one—up in the air.

"You bum, Ozark, don't you understand regular procedures? This is a for-the-record, official fraternity meeting vote. Orion said for us to raise our right hands."

"Okay." Ozark dropped his left hand, pulled the artificial right arm off his elbow's stump, and lifted the now-detached mechanical limb over his head. "Happy?"

"I'm grossed out."

"Opposed." This time Orion's count was quicker. "The yeas are fifty-six, nays fifteen, and the motion carries. A notice as to a date and time will be posted. If there is no additional new business, this meeting is adjourned." He slammed the gavel and the KIDs stood and walked out.

"Not even close." Bobby Sox concluded.

# # # #

"All the little KIDs sleeping in their beds?"

"That makes us sound like a nursery."

"You have the name." Sharon and Paul sat at a Union Cafeteria table.

Paul surveyed the mid-morning crowd, chatting with friends, eating, spacing and reading the *Daily Illini*. Near the entrance, he spotted a table of True Believers wearing orange and black t-shirts. "You would've been impressed with us a few nights ago. KIDs joined the peace movement, we're allowing UNITED to speak at our house."

Summer Never Comes

"How did it happen?"

"Randy Miller proposed the idea at Monday's chapter meeting. A half-dozen guys argued for and against, with your cousin the last speaker. Kentucky was in favor, which swayed the undecideds and made the vote a landslide."

"People support them all over campus. I hear plenty of students and professors talking about activities they've volunteered for, or what they've heard others participating in. Take the way their sit-ins led off the semester." Sharon read her *DI's* front page. "'UNITED's around-the-clock, winter New Student Week peace seminars validate our campus' still-alive involvement. Thursday through Sunday in the Illini Union, for ninety-six consecutive hours, speakers and moderators explained, debated and urged undergrads to weigh the war, politics, their feelings and the next steps. With WPGU radio broadcasts and word of mouth, student interest in the teach-ins increased to the final afternoon, culminating with a speech on Sunday by the youthful William Pritchard, United States Representative from New Jersey. This newspaper actively advocates, appeals, demands,' et cetera, ad infinitum, lah-ti-dah."

"Too cold outdoors, so UNITED herds their comrades inside to remain engaged. Bernard's scripted the moves."

"Cynicism from my student cub reporter? I think you're spending too much time staking out his apartment."

"Eddie McMahon, one of the guys arguing against UNITED, hit on a theory that's been in my head." Paul peeked up from his cinnamon roll. "Eddie-Bob complained about the peace trekkies' hassling and the ways they're infiltrating our campus. He said if we aren't careful, UNITED would end up dominating Champaign-Urbana, controlling the whole peace movement, the students and the school."

"Is your fraternity brother a political science major, or has he researched UNITED as much as you have?"

"I doubt if Eddie-Bob has a major. I only see him at parties when he and his pals are high, like he was Monday night, which means there's a reasonable chance Eddie had no clue what he was saying. But he stumbled into my reasoning. There's so much evidence implicating UNITED as more than a bunch of idealistic students."

"Proof or speculation?"

Summer Never Comes

"Facts. In my room I've stockpiled dozens of old editions of the *Daily Targum*, Rutgers University's student newspaper. Their articles report the same peace movement events we've experienced in Champaign-Urbana: a group mimicking Bernard's, a moratorium in October, food drives at Christmas, a recruiting program indistinguishable from the U of I's and duplicate anti-war advertisements. Week by week matching activities, parallel stories, eight hundred miles away. Second, a friend of mine working in flight reservations at Willard Airport tells me that since September Bernard has visited Columbia, Cornell, Long Island University and Rutgers—all east coast campuses—and has showed up in New Brunswick four times in November and December."

"The guy enjoys traveling, I wish I had the time and money for vacations. Does he fly first class?"

"No, I double-checked, coach."

"Too bad, with first class you'd have a scoop, show Bernard's not a poor student, that he's got bucks behind him." Sharon paused as two True Believers stepped past. "What are you claiming, conspiracies establishing more UNITED's around the country?"

"Could be. Every time he appears on another campus something happens with that school's peace movement. Last month at Rutgers, coinciding with a Bernard visit, their UNITED held a huge rally the same day a sixteen-inch blizzard buried New Jersey. In spite of the snow, three thousand students attended with Congressman Pritchard, the same one speaking in Cham-Bana six days ago, delivering the main address."

"Your interpretation is Bernard as the ringleader, while someone else would depict his movements as coordination and sound strategy. Goodness knows the hawks and conservatives—the factions completely committed to controlling America—scheme all they can to manipulate events. Have Bernard's fellow travelers visited Champaign?"

"Not by plane, my buddy at Willard monitors passenger lists for me. If by car, I don't know. And returning to your first point, maybe these guys gather together only for dialogue. But if that's their purpose, why aren't the conferences publicized? Wherever, whenever Bernard's appeared, there have been no stories in student newspapers about 'national student peace movement leaders' talks,' 'anti-war mobilization summits' or any such crap."

"Sounds circumstantial."

Summer Never Comes

"Granted, non-facts," Paul answered, "but here's another. He journeys east of Illinois and Antoinette Gulley goes west. The professor's left Champaign five times this school year, her trips the same dates Bernard's been gone. Perhaps Illinois is a dividing line, Bernard and Gulley splitting the country into territories."

"Why don't they use the telephone? That way, my eager beaver reporter could wiretap their conversations," Sharon joked again.

"Maybe they're afraid somebody in the government, the FBI perhaps, will tape them. Espionage and surveillance are simple, remember UNITED frightening Laurie Allman off our campus."

"You mentioned she was enrolling for the spring semester, have you contacted her lately?"

"Bunches of times but I only catch her roommate, and Laurie hasn't returned my messages."

"If there's anyone she'd talk to, I'd imagine that would be you."

"Not necessarily, Laurie might think me too conspicuous because of the peace movement, and staying distant is one way for her to continue incognito. That's why I haven't visited her apartment—in case UNITED's lookouts are on duty. But I'll continue phoning, we'll hook up."

A bemused Sharon stared at Paul, wishing her boyfriend showed such initiative in the rest of his life. *Peculiar the prompts pushing people.* "What's your conclusion?"

"Perhaps Bernard travels only to compare notes with his counterparts." He picked at the cinnamon roll's crumbs. "Or maybe Eddie-Bob nailed the logic. There's a conspiracy and we're accomplices."

# # # #

Tommy Quarters and Emily shacked up twelve straight nights in twelve different motels, the Best Western on University Avenue, the Century Twentyone, both Holiday Inns, the Regal Eight, Chief Illini, Howard Johnson's, a few places twenty miles north near Rantoul and one hotel in Farmer City.

At first the screwing was a rush for both. Rolling around in clean, king-sized beds with plenty of room to straddle, spin, pivot and plunge, then sliding to the opposite side and away from your partner for five minutes, hugely outdid grappling each other's body on a worn-down dorm mattress. Emily especially enjoyed these evenings—the contentment of sharing with a man wanting her, the expectation the night would be more erotic than yesterday. On the second, a Wednesday, Tommy stripped off her clothes then knelt and licked her for what seemed like twenty minutes. She stood erect in the middle of the room, clenching Tommy's head in her palms, willing him to snort and slobber around, harder, deeper and wetter. The pair fell into bed and Tommy coached her to perform anything, everything he could concoct; carnal, kinky, abusive, utterly weird, but Emily adored these sessions and let herself go, performing whatever he extorted. Only once in the first days did she feel trapped and only twice did she fantasize Will, not Tommy, laying naked next to her.

Tommy was satisfied with Emily. She was almost as decent a lay as any of the others he'd gone through in college. Tommy dug that Emily was so yielding and wanting to be controlled. He loved it on the third night when she dutifully stood doggy-style on her hands and knees, so he could take, trash, rape her as wildly and cruelly as he could manage. Tommy inanely, irrationally reasoned that all men hormonally needed humping as much as they could, over and over and over. The more he shacked up with someone as submissive like Emily, the more he wanted to screw her—or at least any other broad on the campus—he was having such goddamned great evenings.

By the fifth or sixth days, the lovemaking switched. The two experimented less and regimented into a pattern; the timing, techniques and titillation orchestrated by Tommy. They undressed and he fondled her boobs, she plopped on her back and Tommy jammed himself inside. He massaged her neck, which really calmed her, then forced her to play with herself while he ogled and puffed a cigarette. When they woke after an hour's sleep, Tommy straddled on his knees on top of her and got her to lick him. Next, he caressed and stroked and drooled over her butt, her legs far apart, until she shuddered. A docile Emily complied, turned on by the hugging, petting, kissing, and craving.

"Oh, this has been a crazy delicious time with you." She folded her arms around Tommy's neck. This was the eighth night and they sprawled in a room in the Neil Street Holiday Inn.

Summer Never Comes

"Yeah, Emily, the week's been some trip, a total, far out, strokin' marathon." Laying on top, Tommy heavily exhaled.

"I love you, I love you, I love you." Her body shivered and she was perspiring. Emily kissed his face and grabbed Tommy tighter, hoping for him to stay on her forever. "A question, how did you think up the idea of different motels every night?"

"Why not? It's the beginning of the semester, the weather's crappy, we don't have much studying, room reservations were no problems, and the suggestion sounded like a winner when I heard about it."

"Sounded like a winner from whom?" Emily wiped her neck.

"No one in particular." Half-asleep, he rolled off her body, momentarily neglecting their conversation. "I guess a friend."

"Do you mean someone who knows what we've done this week?"

"Not in those words, not precisely, like in no one has a clue where we are tonight." Catching his slip, Tommy shifted the talk, "What a long night, what a work-out. Why don't we sleep, then get breakfast on the way back to your dorm?"

"But somebody's aware we've been with each other all week?"

"Don't any of your girlfriends think we're shacking up?"

"Nicole and a few have guessed. They're glad I've got a boyfriend again, but I haven't admitted our affair to anyone."

"That's what I mean," Tommy sighed, "especially in a place like KIDS, your buddies notice if you're gone for a few nights."

"Who's missing you?"

"The other freshmen on my floor." A wide-awake Tommy faked a laugh, mindful Emily had almost found him out. He kneaded her thighs, then her shoulders. Tommy squashed Emily to his stomach and bounced on the mattress, moving his knee up and down between her legs. Eyes closed, Emily rolled with the rhythm. She was exhausted from a week of way more physical activity than normal. But she smooched and nibbled Tommy on the neck, knowing that's what he expected. Tommy jerked his leg away from hers, which was Emily's cue to lay stock-still on her back and wait for him to straddle her, his head above her tummy.

By the ninth day everything was rote, Tommy in command, the foreplay mechanical, impersonal, heinous, like some perverted, absurd, horse's ass skin flick. All Tommy hankered after was getting his rocks off, and by the time they were finished on the twelfth night, after wheedling, deflowering her and satisfying himself, Tommy could care less about this bitch. He'd grabbed what he wanted. Like a tool, a stringed puppet, a fagged Emily obeyed, aware she didn't have to put out the ways Tommy counted on, but acquiescing because she'd somehow toppled in this web; hoping Tommy cared for her as he did when they'd met in December, but conceding she'd gone her own way and there was no one else for her now. Emily was very tired.

# # # #

Moose, Jake, Bobby Sox and Tim Malito had sat at their hearts game since lunch, one of three all-afternoon-until-dinner marathons in the living room. Other KIDs returning from two o'clock classes stopped to watch, check on who was low man and perhaps substitute for a few hands. Snubbing his fraternity brothers, Tommy Quarters slouched on a couch, reading the *Daily Illini*.

"So you did it?" Dale Kinsey strolled toward the freshman.

"Yeah, I clinched the bet." Tommy sneered.

Glancing from his cards, Bobby shook his head. Two total losers, one high, the other with his head rammed sideways through his asshole.

"Well, goddamn-it, never thought anybody'd bust my record. I hate like hell handin' over money, but that was the deal, I owe you a double saw, you son of a bitch." Kinsey flipped out a twenty dollar bill from his drug money wad. "Screwin' the same broad a dozen nights in a row ain't simple. They get too jealous, clingy. As time goes by they expect more and more, like you're s'pose t' treat her as a French whore instead of a north Champaign hooker; chat her up, play nicey-nicey, buy her some good food and fancy clothes."

"It wasn't that horrible, pretty decent, to tell the truth." Tommy bragged. "She'd probably go for another twelve with anybody else, pay her some money, she'd probably put out for a month. All that girl wants is to spread her legs. She's a sucker for the world's three oldest jokes."

Kinsey and the now-eavesdropping hearts players snickered.

"The bimbo really like layin' in the rack?"

Summer Never Comes

"No doubt. One night she worked on me for a half hour before I let 'er rip. The only crappy ass part about the twelve days was I hadda waste time teachin' her techniques. Turns out she didn't have much practice with a royal stud like me until I picked her up in the Red Lion two months ago. That was her confession, she didn't know what to do 'cause no one's ever totally used her."

"Quarters and Kinsey must be talkin' about some loser of a woman." Tim Malito opened a trick. "I gotta say I feel real sorry for whoever she was, must've gone through hell with Tommy."

Moose played the queen of diamonds. "What I wouldn't give to toss those turds out a third floor window."

"Well, for a year she was goin' out with that blonde-haired sorry has-been who didn't know how to unbuckle and yank off a bra." Kinsey slammed his head on the couch. "The nimrod didn't have the time or the nuts to unzip his pants. He walked away from a perfectly sweet lay 'cause he'd rather whack off with a guitar. Now he's lost both in the same week, just what a misfit like him deserves. Here, take your cash before I steal it back."

Abruptly, unbelievably, sadly, Bobby realized the despoes were trashing Emily. Struggling to hold his temper, he crushed the cards in his hand.

"All I can say is now she's serviced a king-sized stud," Tommy boasted again, "knows every which way to perform, appreciates 'em all, and services the way she's told."

# # # #

"I told you guys we shoulda' kicked that lousy son of a bitch outta the house. But no, you two said, you can't do that to a guy who's only datin' someone's old girlfriend. Relax, you said, everybody's smart enough to take care of themselves; calm down, chill, things work out, you said." An irate, manic Bobby stood in his room with Paul and Stu. "Frickin' Jesus Christ, what a mile-high shit pile."

"At dinner the despoes knew all about Kinsey's and Tommy Quarters' bet, how he was scamming to sleep with the same girl for more days straight than Kinsey did with one last year. They even kept a scorecard on the fourth floor, with a map taped to the wall marking where Emily and Tommy stayed every night and how many times they did it," Stu said.

"Great bunches of assholes in this fraternity," Bobby kicked the bedpost, "nothin' like exploiting other people, anything for a few chuckles, who gives a crap if they're destroyed."

"Maybe Emily won't find out. I haven't seen her around the house since the Christmas party."

"Impossible, she's got enough friends in this place and will learn how she was used. God knows what Emily'll think about us, our numb-nut brothers and herself."

A silent Paul counted record albums on Bobby's shelves.

"Is it so bad?" Stu turned toward his friends. "It's not the first time someone on this campus has had a joke played on them. This is college and crap hits the fan. Think about what we pulled on Killer in his stall in the john?"

"For God's sake, those are two opposite situations, and it's disgusting you'd think of Emily's mess and Killer equally. When we dumped the water on Killer we sent a message, a gross one for sure, but a signal we'd had enough of his obnoxiousness. He probably admitted he had it comin'. With Emily, yeah, she's not the first one slapped with the ultimate shaft of her life. But she's only searchin' for companionship, someone to care for her, as we all are. This is an unbelievably crappy trick on a sensitive, respectable girl who no way warrants such grief. That's the sin, Emily trusted Tommy Quarters and gets nailed with heartache."

Seldom had Paul heard Bobby speak with this empathy. "You're right, it's a disgrace Emily's involved with that jerk-off. Better she finds out and stops seeing him, and told the right way by someone who cares."

"Do you think Lindy will do it, inform Emily?"

"That would be a decent gesture, make up for how he's treated her this year, and reveal to Emily that Lindy caused what happened to her. If he'd paid more attention, she wouldn't have run off with the first guy to buy her a drink. Lindy should have stayed a helpful companion."

"Something's unclear." Bobby stepped to the window. "After Kinsey congratulated Tommy about the twelve nights, he ranted on about Lindy losing more than Emily, that Lindy deserved everything he got. I didn't know they were friends enough for Kinsey hating Lindy so much."

Summer Never Comes

"They're not, this year Lindy's only mentioned him once or twice." Paul answered. "Right now my roommate's a moot point, he and Frogfeet are out of town the rest of the week, over in Bloomington for their usual gig at the Lion, then Springfield for two nights. The band won't be back until Sunday morning."

"Well, one of us should talk to her real soon. If we don't, Emily'll find out from somebody else. Talk about awkward."

"I'll handle it," Bobby Sox said. "More compassionate hearing from a friend instead of being blindsided by some horse's ass."

"Poor Emily, what a crime."

# # # #

An injustice for certain, Paul decided. Emily was too gentle a person to be messed up with Tommy Quarters. Paul and his friends erred in keeping quiet and should have warned her. As should have Lindy. His roommate was Emily's boyfriend, the one she depended on and loved, with the responsibility of protecting her. At least he was until four months ago.

But Lindy was a nowhere-to-be-found, failed friend, off playing music with that stupid band. He'd dumped his old girlfriend just as he'd abandoned everyone else. Running away released Lindy from a relationship's hassles, opening more time for his goofy obsession. Worries or anxiety? Hit the road. Problems, dilemmas, tough times? Jump on stage. Conscience or accountability? Sing a song, strum your guitar, hang out in the bars. This frightened Paul. For the first time since knowing Lindy, his roommate quit caring about those dear to him.

Outside on Chalmers Street, Paul walked away from KIDs. The wind was from the north, another frigid evening, another downer.

If Frogfeet had never happened, Lindy would still be his old, considerate, steadfast self, and not an egotistical musician. At moments, the infrequent evenings when he wasn't performing, his roommate was still a good buddy. But this was rare, more a reminder of what their friendship had been. Better Lindy had stayed the same, hadn't risked, not changed. Sure, Frogfeet was working out for him, the band had gigs and made money, Lindy was chasing his dream. But the connections with his pals were torn, links split, relationships wiped away, Emily manhandled because Lindy wasn't around.

Stay as you are, sheltered and secure, that's the conclusion, play it safe, ride it out, hide. There's no harm in protecting what you had and it's okay withdrawing to your own refuge. Many, many people, Paul knew, endured their lives this way—existing, passing up chances, preserving and safeguarding instead of stumbling into traps. These hedgers seemed happy, at least content. If some deemed this retreat, too bad, not everyone enjoyed adventures. Terrible things happened if gambles failed.

Paul wanted to hike to Sharon's house, but California Avenue was a long trek on a frosty night. And he remembered she was busy, with her Vet Med College interview tomorrow morning—ironing clothes and checking with fellow candidates. Reaching the Quad, he turned to return to KIDs.

Stereos blasted, the hallways smelled like marijuana and Stu and Bobby's door was shut, the two probably at the Snack Bar for midnight munchies. In Paul's room the light was on and Lindy laid in the bottom bunk, arms hiding his head.

"I didn't expect you until Sunday."

Lindy moved his hands, uncovering a dismal, dejected face. His friend had never looked so miserable, and Paul straightaway supposed one of the brothers had told his roommate about Emily and Tommy.

"That bad?"

"It's over, the last gasp, failure with a will. Facilis descensus Averni."

Paul was puzzled, not expecting Emily's predicament to affect him this harshly. "I wouldn't go that far, there's always another chance to talk things out, to help fix this mess."

"Frogfeet was busted in Bloomington two days ago, the five of us, plus Gary Anderson and couple of the Red Lion's bartenders, arrested by state troopers for drug possession."

"Man, I'm sorry. What happened?" A stunned Paul settled in his chair.

"The cops found a couple nickel bags of cocaine stashed in 'Mad's drums. The stuff they stumbled on wasn't any larger than a fist."

"You guys went through with the deal with Robin?"

"Absolutely no way, that wasn't the case, we weren't that stupid." Lindy glanced at his roommate. "After mentioning the proposition to you last week, I talked to the guys in the band. First off, they thought it might be a lucrative sideline, as I did. Extra money for minimum work, the rush of bein' on the far side of the law and actin' like big shots. Then second thoughts set in. Andy speculated how, since Woofer and me were graduating this semester, if we did get nabbed us two could have it impossible finding jobs with drug charges on our records. To say nothing about handlin' the jail time, none of us liked the idea of windows with iron bars. And Franky turned against the deal, saying he was only interested makin' it fair and square as a rock 'n' roll band, not street hustlers. Like always, his words decided, so we passed. When I told Robin she was put out, since another of their delivery groups, Spectro Lab, just cut a demo tape and was boltin' for Los Angeles. She leaned real hard on Franky and me to change our minds, but we stood by our guns. She was so persistent, I finally flipped and told her the 'Feet's decision was final, and if movin' dope was so vital, her and I were finished as a couple. Robin was fanatically put out."

"Anyone in Frogfeet into drugs?"

"No more than a couple of joints when we jam, no acid trips or hallucinogens. Someone planted the stuff when we weren't around, then tipped off the cops. We were stunned when we got pulled over in Bloomington. The police were waitin' for us outside the bar with warrants, flashlights and handcuffs. We were set up and it's our own fault because we never worry about security. Even when the equipment van's parked on the street we don't lock it. This is the hippie '70s, right?" Lindy peered out the window. "And I made the catastrophe ten times worse. When the police stopped us to search our instruments, I asked one of the coppers to be extra careful with my guitars 'cause they were special, personal, basically one of a kind. When the officer blew me off I got totally pissed, like with you that one time last semester. I pushed right in his face, commented about what I heard he carnally performed with his mother, and the cuffs snapped on our wrists. Not my most genius idea. So, along with possession, we're charged with resisting arrest."

"Who set you up?"

"Had to be Robin and the stooges she's grifting with. We blew them off, their network was caught by the short hairs, and the goons got even."

Paul made the connections. Lindy turned down Robin, who ratted to Dale Kinsey and the Champaign dopers, who screwed Lindy and Frogfeet. "Where've you been for the last forty-eight hours?"

Summer Never Comes

"In the Bloomington slammer, all of us in one cell. It was cold in there, Robby, scared every chunk of crap right outta me. This morning Gary's girlfriend finally made our bail and we drove straight home piled in her Cutlass. Our court date's in two weeks."

"What about the band's future?"

"We're done for. The narcs impounded the van and our instruments, even my Gibson, and are holdin' everything for evidence."

Paul stepped to the bed and sat next to his roommate, wondering whether to discuss Emily. The two rapped until dawn.

# # # #

Associated Press – Washington – Responding to increasing Communist forces in Laos, the Nixon administration has declared a blockade of the port of Haiphong and the Red River delta. A Defense Department spokesman announced that 'it will be the policy of the United States Navy to halt and search any vessels presumed carrying weapons to North Vietnam.' The spokesman refused to predict what percentage of shipping moving into Haiphong would be stopped.

# # # #

Frigid, cloudless winter weather settled on Champaign-Urbana. For a week and a half, longer than any KIDs recalled, the temperature stayed below zero, north winds and snow showers gusted, sidewalks iced over, and the student body holed up indoors. Moose and Ozark quit walking to the Red Lion. 'Ralph' Hepler took to pulling the battery out of his '67 Chevy Nova and hauling it to his room each night to keep it charged. Sharon and her housemates burned every stick of firewood for extra heat. And Scooter Petersen and Lauren Rose, wanting to keep warm and be together, vanished from their friends, mixing days and nights of shacking up with hours of talking through wedding plans.

There were issues to resolve. Scooter's mother, wealthy and willful enough to always prevail, had clear-cut designs concerning the festivities for her son's marriage. These preparations included a country club setting, invitations to all the Petersen family's just-as-rich acquaintances, a five-tiered cake, a seven course dinner, and a dozen bridesmaids and groomsmen. Never the son to disagree, Scooter knew he'd have to struggle to persuade his fiancée to accept his mom's arrangements. Lauren, after spending Christmas week with Mrs. Petersen, fathomed the socially-conscious, overbearing family she was marrying into, and was tempted by her future mother-in-law's proposition to pay their wedding expenses. But she was the bride, the wedding plans her bailiwick. Though Scooter labored to convince her to yield, and even if he was really kinky in bed, Lauren wanted space—independence from Mrs. Petersen—fearing compromise at the start of the marriage would trap her for the rest of her life.

In the last week of February the flurries stopped, the sun came out, and the thermometer rose to forty degrees, balmy when compared to a month earlier. Moose and Ozark hoofed to the Lion, 'Ralph's' Nova turned over on the first crank, Sharon's housemates gladly shut the fireplace flue, and Lauren, after fifteen or sixteen straight days of balling Scooter, missed her period and told him she was pregnant.

# # # #

On the first pleasanter day, students read this advertisement in the *Daily Illini*.

"Friends, Members of UNITED!

"Blockade on the High Seas!

"The Washington pirates have proclaimed embargo, cut off the peace-loving peoples of North Vietnam from ocean-going commerce.

"The Hanoi government, in the midst of their Battle for self-determination and sovereignty over their own land, has decried our country's latest, Needless Belligerence.

"Reason and logic are forfeit. Aggression and Hostilities are Uncontrolled. Denouement approaches.

"Showing our Solidarity with those toiling and Fighting, affirming our ever-present, growing Commitment, UNITED calls on all supporters and sympathizers to assemble at one o'clock this Thursday on the Quad for a five-minute silent Vigil for Peace.

"UNITED to End the war!"

Summer Never Comes

# # # #

"The *Daily Illini* completely concurs with UNITED's appeal for this afternoon's vigil. As our allegiance to world peace grows, it is critically important to demonstrate our dissent with the bullying, warmongering posturing prevailing in Washington. We call on students, faculty and Champaign-Urbana residents to turn out on the Quad at one o'clock."

# # # #

Paul thought this one of Stef Tianen's more cogent editorials, being one of her briefest. Our country's caused a problem, maybe we can fix, let's try.

At 12:45 on Wright Street, he was one of hundreds walking toward the Quad, the mobs so big that northbound traffic jammed up to allow students to cross. Do we really care? Was there any cause crucial enough to turn out undergrads on a day's notice? Did Vietnam, war and peace, what UNITED pontificated or the *DI* printed about these issues influence us? Were the masses hiking to the Quad resolute protesters or adolescents exploiting the improving weather as an excuse to hang outside?

By the English Building, Paul guesstimated thousands of students shuffling through the slushy snow from every direction—the Library, Comm West and DKH, the frats and sororities in Urbana, the engineering campus on the far side of Green Street, the houses and apartment buildings in north Champaign, the Psych Building, Sherman Hall and Illini Tower. Leaning on a tree by the Administration Building, he surveyed the protesters, a crowd stretching halfway to the old Auditorium. They stood by themselves or in groups, purposeful, or talking and joking. Everyone faced the Union, where an enormous orange and black flag waved when the wind gusted.

The Altgeld Hall chimes clanged one o'clock, and in seconds the chattering and chuckling ended. Around him, Paul watched silent students bowing their heads, some hugging their friends or holding hands. Others concentrated on UNITED's banner, looking determined, almost proud. He looked at the Urbana side of the Quad, toward Noyes Lab and three or four roughly made signs.

"WAR is BAD!"

Summer Never Comes

"America OUT of Harm's Way!"

"PROTEST 'TIL WE DROP!"

People quieted later-arriving students, who in turn hushed the ones behind them and behind them and behind them—as if the protest's silence, starting right here, outside the Union, was spreading from the Quad, past the nearby university buildings, to the rest of the campus, over Champaign-Urbana and who knew how far. The afternoon was so still that Paul imagined all the drivers on Wright Street had shut off their cars' engines to connect with the moment.

Maybe he'd been overly cynical, perhaps his generation was concerned, thought it necessary to rally in melting snow for a country a hemisphere away. We're all together, the everyday, common people, the steadfast, die-hard organizers and the plotters orchestrating the vigil, we all want peace.

A satisfied Bernard Minerath studied the scene from the Union's second floor, the hordes on the Quad showing that four weeks' inactivity had not stifled students' support for UNITED. After the five minutes, the undergrads drifted off, leaving the Quad to attend their classes, study in the Library or return to the dorms. Bernard remained at the window and none of the True Believers in the office spoke to him until he stepped away.

# # # #

In the afternoon Paul received two quick phone calls.

"Sorry it took so long getting back to you, but I've been very occupied," Laurie Allman said.

"I can imagine, after being gone for three months, returning to campus and starting the new semester."

"I don't mean to mislead you, it's not busy due to moving back to Champaign but rather making decisions. I haven't enrolled in school."

Paul stood in the hallway, wondering if this was a long distance call. "Where are you right now?"

"At my apartment, with Lindsey, I'm here for a few days to pack my stuff. I think I'm leaving the campus for good and returning to Charleston to live on the farm with my family."

Summer Never Comes

"Hold on a minute, Laurie. You're a Champaign-Urbana lifer with six years of college. What will you do with yourself? Have you transferred to another school or quickie graduated?"

"In addition to my history courses I've earned enough education credits so I can teach. My parents found a job for me at Mattoon High School as a substitute and I begin work next week. They've even bought me a used car so I can drive myself back and forth. I guess I'm finished as a student."

"But why go? Why quit?" He was astounded. "I thought you enjoyed grad school, you liked the University of Illinois?"

"More than I can say, everything about this place—researching in the libraries, working as a TA and living on the campus. But so much has changed for me, the uncertainty and insecurity."

"UNITED," Paul jumped in, "What have they done now?"

"Not a thing, nothing's happened since last autumn with my cat. Maybe the two weeks I was their target was enough. And maybe I'm deliberating too much, or I'm not brave enough or so curious like you are investigating them. I just feel that what might happen this new semester is something I'll be unable to face. If this appears like retreat, I guess I'm guilty. But I'm at ease with my family, where I don't have to worry about strangers walking up to me to scare me. I feel safer in Charleston than here in Champaign."

"Have any troublemakers been prowling around Ashmore?"

"No, my father and brothers are guarding the farm."

"That's reassuring. But you should reconsider, not sacrifice your education. I'm sure you could feel as secure back here as at home, rely on friends and work out a schedule for your protection."

"I can't, Paul. It's a shifted environment, the university's devolving. Security versus anguish is how I put it. I've gone as far as I want and think I'll be better off at home."

Not close friends, never talking much or often, Paul did not apprehend, as he understood Lindy or Sharon, how Laurie thought. But he was let down with her choice. Quit school and not graduate? Walk away from the campus? He couldn't reckon anyone leaving Champaign-Urbana before they had to. The only sense to Laurie's decision was her suspicion of trouble coming and feeling she couldn't cope.

# # # #

"Afternoon, Paul, how's school starting?"

"Sluggish so far. I don't know why, but every year I have problems settling into the spring semester."

"It's the confusing weather, especially this year. Basic winter, a deep freeze, then nice. The only thing January and February are decent for is sleeping."

"Right." Paul chuckled. Out of school ten years, John Barrett still rationalized like a student.

"I'm calling with news concerning UNITED. I took a message from a pal working for the Illinois Central Railroad in Decatur. There's a boxcar in their dispatch yard loaded with food. The car was contracted by UNITED, the point of origin Champaign, and it was scheduled to travel to San Francisco. However, after leaving our town on Christmas Eve, the destination was switched to the railway siding where it's sat for two months. Now that the weather's warming up, the groceries inside are rotting and reeking. The foodstuffs collected before Christmas didn't reach Vietnam, never left the state. The way my buddy tells it, this boxcar wasn't intended to travel any farther than Decatur."

"UNITED's food drive was a sham?"

"Looks that way, the peace-freaks bullshitted us. A shame, such a decent idea, to aid people."

"How is the *News-Gazette* handling this scoop?"

"The particulars are yours for your article on Bernard Minerath, consider this professional courtesy. Hope it helps."

"I'm sure it will."

UNITED's food drive had been a fraud, Paul concluded, as was UNITED.

Chapter Sixteen

"How was the court appearance in Bloomington?"

"First off, Robby, it was a hearing in the judge's chambers, not a jury trial, so it was less bureaucratic than I expected. When the proceedings got goin', Gary Anderson, Tyke, the five of us and the lawyers found out that Franky, Andy, 'Mad,' Woofer and me had never been arrested before, not even for parking tickets. Imagine, Cham-Bana hippies with no priors and backgrounds as fresh as babies' bottoms. That swayed the judge, a young-at-heart himself, and he decided to ride easy on us, a six-month suspended sentence with a fine of four hundred dollars a man. Thank goodness the verdict wasn't worse and we stayed out of the slammer. The flip side is the four c-notes is all my money I've saved this winter from the 'Feet's gigs, so I'm flat broke, busted, what I call life in the raw."

"Did your side claim the marijuana the cops found was planted in your van?"

"Our attorney mentioned the possibility, but didn't stress the particulars since we didn't have any shreds of proof we were framed. Even if that pain-in-the-ass Kinsey has been boastin' over it for weeks."

Paul couldn't decipher his roommate's demeanor. Was he relieved, reconciled or glum? "Did your sassing the police during the arrest come up?"

"Turns out Tyke is buddies with two McLean County assistant state's attorneys, an authentic old-boys' network. This crowd convinced the arresting officer the possession charges shoveled us deep enough down a hole and the tirade got dismissed."

"Will the verdict appear on your record?" Paul was lying on the top bunk.

Summer Never Comes

"That's a bummer, the conviction does; I'm marked forever. This summer when I fill out job applications I'll have to disclose bein' arrested for something more than traffic violations. But I suppose it could be worse, we could've been incarcerated."

"Or not get back your instruments."

"We haven't, at least not yet. The cops won't release our van and equipment until we pay the fines. That'll happen next week when Franky and Gary make one more trip to Bloomington." Lindy peeked to the corner of their room where his guitars normally stood. "I hope they're takin' proper care of our axes."

"When will Frogfeet hit the road again?"

"Negative on that one too, I'm afraid. While we've been on this hiatus, Andy and Woofer were recruited by another band on the hunt for replacement talent. We're breakin' up, the 'Feet's last gig was this afternoon at the courthouse."

"Sounds like a quick exit. Did those two talk to the others before moving on?"

"No, just jumped through the hoop, the stern realities of glories uncertain. Hell, life spins on, even the Beatles split after ten or twelve years. I don't blame 'em, it's not like the five of us planned on headin' to California and playin' rock 'n' roll forever."

"Will you search for another group?" Paul jumped down from his bunk.

"Don't think so, Robby. In a couple days the calendar's March, too near graduation with not enough time to develop an act. Besides, who'd want a second-rate backup guitar player without his Gibson? For this semester, I'm Mr. Unobtrusive, minglin' at the back of the crowd." Lindy was pessimistic. "The year didn't work out the way I wanted. The band imploded, finals finished a near disaster, I turned my back on you guys and crashed with Em. Like my gig money goin' to pay the fine, pumped down a latrine."

"Your girlfriend, have you phoned her?"

"I don't think that conversation would total to much. Bobby said he saw Em a few days ago and she was completely ripped over the whole Tommy Quarters calamity, the nights with him in the motel rooms and the despoes' betting pool. Knowin' her as I do, what she'd want is someone to sit with and work through the whole mess, like Bobby has, a supportive friend devoting the time to cheer her up. Right now that's not me; we have too much history and I don't feel jolly."

"The days will improve, spring will be here in a few weeks," Paul wished to boost his roommate's spirits, "we can catch some rays in Frat Park, and Easter break isn't that far away."

"Really, what do I have to look forward to? Compare you and me. You've found a great girl in Sharon, a blonde no less, and after graduation you're in line for snaggin' a respectable job with a regular salary, you're ship's sailing into port. Me? My grades weren't super before last semester, now they're worse. Plus, I've got this drug arrest hangin' and I've let down my friends. I'm out on the limb." Lindy shuffled to the open window and felt the breeze warming their room. "Failure."

"What if you could go back to September and replay the last six months, aware of the consequences?"

"That's a crazy fantasy, only spacemen from *Star Trek* travel back to yesterday, and even they're scared of foolin' with the past." Lindy smiled for the first time. "Today's shrewder question is if I've learned anything. Which I have. I've discovered people shouldn't skyrocket off cliffs without computing the costs; shouldn't assume responsibilities, including homework assignments, will handle themselves; believe they can get by on three hours sleep; or suppose buddies—even close, trusty ones—will cede the benefit of the doubt without a 'thanks, I appreciate it,' once in a while. Yeah, there's basketfuls of second guessing. But, signed and sealed, if this were September and Frogfeet came knocking at our door, I'd jump, I'd balls-to-the-wall practice and play and perform again. But work like hell to prevent the heartaches for everyone."

"Sounds like common sense."

"No, wisdom's demons. Dreams are too dear."

# # # #

Associated Press – Saigon – United States Army headquarters reports that the buildup of North Vietnamese forces in the Mount Atouat territory is continuing. At present, no additional American or South Vietnamese units have been transferred to the area, but those troops stationed in the region are on alert for possible enemy attacks. In the Tonkin Gulf, the United States Navy has maneuvered closer to North Vietnamese waters. As yet, no nation's vessels sailing into Haiphong harbor have been stopped. However, 'Operation Holding Furnace,' the planned blockade of North Vietnam, is moving forward.

# # # #

On the weekend, Paul and Sharon used the Century Twentyone Hotel room they'd won in the KIDs' Christmas party raffle. As prelude to a night of shacking up in a high-class place, Sharon had purchased tickets for the Krannert Center for the Performing Arts' production of *The Playboy of the Western World*. Paul had nominal interest in theater and only seen Krannert from the outside, but his girlfriend wished to attend. As ever, her suggestion was fine with him.

"What did you think of the play, dear?" Sharon walked in and sat on the bed. The suite's window looked toward Illini Tower and the Psych Building.

"The plot was hard to follow. Who wrote it?"

"'John Millington Synge, playwright, born 1871, died 1909,'" she quoted the program, "'In 1896 Synge was befriended by fellow Irishman William Butler Yeats, who convinced him to return to Ireland to write for their countrymen. Both were among the founders of the Irish National Theater Society. Synge's works include *The Well of the Saints*, *In the Shadow of the Glen*, and the one act play, *Riders to the Sea*. His writing career is notable for its brevity, only six years.' Is Emily familiar with this guy?"

"Wouldn't doubt it, but I think Shakespeare is more her specialty, the biggies like *Macbeth* and *A Midsummer Night's Dream*." He sat next to Sharon.

"How is she?" She put an arm around Paul's waist.

"Bobby Sox talked to Emily a week ago, telling her how Tommy Quarters duped her to win his money. Turns out on top of the wager with Kinsey, the fourth floor despoes ran a betting pool with Joey Panky collecting the pot, twenty-eight dollars. Emily took being exploited awfully bad. Bobby spent an evening settling her down and helping Emily's roommate put her to sleep at three in the morning. Bobby also learned

Tommy is brutal in bed. He knows some totally sordid tricks that physically injured Emily to the point of her needing to check into McKinley Hospital. But Bobby said the damnedest part was right up until their conversation, Emily still had a thing about Tommy and thought he was a decent guy. Now she realizes she was deceived."

"I had the impression Emily would too easily move into a new relationship. Like most of our generation, maybe she's too naïve when searching for connections."

"And that's what puzzles me. Lindy dated and loved Emily for a year, understood how trusting and susceptible she is, yet abandoned her."

"You blame your roommate for what happened?"

"Lindy didn't intentionally arrange Tommy's and Emily's liaison, but if he'd shown more compassion, maybe they'd still be together and she wouldn't have gotten so screwed so many times by Tommy."

"It's not totally Lindy's fault for failing to warn her any more than it's Bobby's, Stu's or yours. I know I called Emily naïve, but she's an adult and made her own choices."

"Lindy's guiltier than us. If he'd taken the time to worry about her, Emily would have been saved."

"You mean if Lindy hadn't played with Frogfeet as much as he did."

"That's the blunder. Lindy wrapped himself so tight to the band he lost everything—Emily, his music and his money. Now what he's left with is moping in our room in KIDs, waiting for next week when his friends drive to Bloomington, pay the fine and retrieve their instruments. As Lindy said, he attempted too much."

"Took his chance."

"You beat me to the line," Paul smiled.

"I know the words by heart." Collapsing on the bed, Sharon mimicked her boyfriend, "If you dare being different you might get so beaten down you'll be worse off than if you did nothing. Ergo, a person is safer staying where she or he is. Because whatever occurs in the mundane, predetermined, everyday summation of events is the optimum you can hope for, even if it's not meaningful or inspiring. Lah-ti-dah-ti-dah, take out the trash, hold the extra pickles and maybe everyone will exist happily ever after."

"You skipped the disappearing in a crowd stanza." He studied her body.

"That's right, don't scramble from the pile or stick your neck out, never cross a bridge to a strange, faraway place, and absolutely never, not one iota, get yourself noticed. Amen."

"What happened to Lindy proves my viewpoint."

"Or is it pretext? I won't deny your roommate was supremely stiffed by hoodlums settling grudges." Sharon sat up, rubbed her neck and unzipped her skirt. "If not for that, with all their rehearsing, his band could have succeeded. The odds weren't very against him. Until the bust, Frogfeet was working steady, correct?"

"That's the message, they were arrested."

"It wasn't the group's mistake, they were unlucky to mix up with criminals."

"Reality happened, the entire idea went wrong." Paul wouldn't yield. "Lindy was thrown in jail and Emily messed up, each of them hosed by the bad guys because that's who's lurking in the real world."

"So Lindy should have sidestepped, done nothing," she was aggravated, "even when music is his passion?"

"He would've been better off."

"I've thought of something else, what's the plural of Frogfeet?" Sharon's tone softened as she stood, her dress dropping to the floor, and strolled to the bathroom." And a second detail, I wonder what size tub comes with this room."

"You want a bath right now?" A disappointed Paul eyed her slim, curved, ideal body, then stared at the bed.

"All my muscles ache." She switched on the light and batted her eyelashes. "Imagine that, big enough for both of us."

An hour later the pair were still soaking in the tub, door closed, the bathroom steamed. He caressed her round, perfect breasts, both nipples half-hidden under the soap suds, greatly desiring to take his girlfriend to bed, but the warm water was too tantalizing.

"How do you feel now?"

"Recuperating from the Vet Med interview." Sharon rested on Paul's neck, her blonde hair pulled in a bun.

"How'd the session go?"

Summer Never Comes

"It lasted forty-five minutes, with four professors on one side of the table and me on the other. They asked about my undergraduate courses, what I presumed my qualifications were, the vets I've worked for during the summers, setting up a private practice as opposed to working for the government or teaching, and how involved I intended to be in the town I settle in after graduation." Her fingers rippled the water. "I did fine except for a moment halfway through. One of them asked if I had any bad grades in high school."

"Isn't that nit-picking?"

"A query's a query. I answered I had a C in sophomore French." Sharon shoved her whole hand under the surface, creating a major wave. "The professor came back saying, 'No, Miss Taylor, you are incorrect, you received one C and one D in French.' After that, I was so miserable I wanted to hide behind my chair. But it wasn't a lie, I honestly only recalled one."

"Will the slip hurt your chances?"

"Low grades from five or six years ago are minor, I imagine Professor McNeir asked to observe how I handled myself." She stopped whisking the bathtub water and set her hand on her boyfriend's chest.

"Will you be accepted?"

"The admissions criteria include grade point average, the Veterinary Aptitude Test and the interview. My scoring will be okay."

"When will you know?"

"Middle of April. If I get in, we'll have to reserve this room for another night," she tickled Paul's arm, "or at least rent the tub."

"But no more John Millington Synge." Paul squirmed and water splashed the floor. "You win, we'll attend another play."

The two kissed and Paul ran his hand down her thigh. "Want to towel off?"

"Let's wait, my bones need more soaking." Sharon gazed at the hazy, damp tile walls.

"We'll never resolve the argument. I hope it doesn't come between us."

"Standing pat versus advancing ahead? I doubt we will. But it's not a dispute. Matters to discuss, ongoing dialogue sounds more perceptive. Don't you think someday something will happen causing you to act, make you pick sides?"

Summer Never Comes

"Most of the time I look like I've stuffed myself in a closet, wanting life to pass me by, that's how I sound to you and Lindy. But I admit responsibility has to be confronted, I can't childishly dodge the world forever. I hope I'm prepared." He brushed Sharon's hair. "Did you ever wonder about how we connected and stayed together?"

"I have, by myself and with my housemates. We spent an evening drinking two bottles of Boone's Farm wine discussing the topic, and decided you're good for me, even if we're opposites. I've been the passionate coed, you're the level-headed accountant. I've experienced college's rowdiness plus plenty of boyfriends, now with you there's time to wind down and contemplate. Am I ready for four hard-core years of grad school?"

Her response was so characteristically upfront. But Paul prayed their intimacies, the hour soaking in this bath tub for example, were off-limits to her housemates. "I sound like a time-out. Isn't there anything else?"

Sharon was silent. Our differences triggered my infatuation, but are quirks enough? Paul is intelligent, dependable, with a sense of humor when he's relaxed. But that is so ordinary, a year ago I wouldn't have thought him appealing. I enjoy our relationship and conversations, all the topics we cover, how Paul reflects then switches from negative to energetic. But he is so indecisive, inhibited. Will he eventually, beyond a doubt leap; how long do I wait? Will I continue to be happy with someone so pensive?

"In the autumn, I considered you real cute, with your brown hair curling in back of your head, someone who enjoys the Big U as much as I do. When the sweetness factor faded, I decided you were an upright person, working to get along in life. I like your scruples and see us coming together, connecting, bonding, not in a straight line or always agreeing, but by working stuff out. This makes us interesting." She rippled the water. "And your reasoning for our friendship?"

"Mostly that you've helped me assess my life, like Lindy used to."

"I've imagined I was substituting for him. Which is fine, everyone needs friends."

"But don't presume the only reason we're dating is my need for someone to take Lindy's place. I admit that was my initial rationale, but now I love you for being Sharon, not a stand-in. A girl I think of as a genuine companion, my dearest, my ideal. I'm the luckiest, most fortunate…you're the brightest, most endearing, adorable person I know."

Summer Never Comes

"Thank you," she kissed his cheek.

Eventually the two drained the tub and went to bed. They woke on Sunday morning and looked out over the campus.

# # # #

Lauren couldn't find Scooter. Every day for a week she'd telephoned the KIDs house, never catching her fiancé but leaving messages. Scooter's friends said he was gone a lot the last few days, oddly busy, bothered, with stuff on his mind, and they'd make sure he called back.

Things on his mind? Lauren expected so. She was embarrassed phoning so often, and afraid Scooter's fraternity brothers were wondering why. She knew Scooter wasn't the most reticent person, that he might confess their dilemma to anyone because he was panicked. But the shocker he'd gotten her pregnant, of all things surely her boyfriend would keep this to himself until they settled their plans. Who to tell first and when? Schedule doctor's appointments back home in Chicago or should she walk to the McKinley Hospital clinic? Keep the baby or choose something else? Should Lauren finish the semester or drop out? (And why would she be the only one to cut short her education?) Did they want to be parents when they were so, so young, in school and jobless? Did Scooter still want to marry? Should the two meet with a minister? How about their parents? Oh, my God, Lauren staggered, Mrs. Petersen, how will she treat me? How can I cope with her now that I'm having a baby—Kathie Petersen's grandchild? They had to talk, Scooter and her, Lauren anxiously wanted to, since there was little time. Because she'd spent two hours last night vomiting in the bathroom, her roommates suspected the truth but were too dear of friends to mention it. Lauren anticipated this would change, but she didn't want to confess without checking with Scooter.

Where was he?

# # # #

In the first week of March, the temperature rose to the fifties and months of snow melted, making the ground muddy. Shirtless, hot dog students in only gym trunks and tennis shoes jogged on the sidewalks, some running around Assembly Hall to the South Farms. Paul, wearing his winter coat, walked to a morning appointment with Bernard Minerath.

The Union's second floor hallway was empty, UNITED's office door open, and Bernard was seated next to a long table cluttered with piles of papers. The orange and black flag hung on the wall behind him.

"Good morning, I'm Paul Roberts from the *Daily Illini*."

"How are you?" Bernard was dressed in his normal corduroy pants and long-sleeve shirt rolled up at the elbows. Unsmiling, he stood and pumped Paul's hand. "You want to interview me."

Both sat at the table and Paul opened his notebook. "Since September, I've worked on an article about the campus anti-war movement. My starting point was the old peace groups' origins in the 1960s, their evolution over the last five years and UNITED's beginning last semester. You are in the middle of this activity."

"UNITED is the center," Bernard corrected.

"Where did the idea for UNITED originate?"

"For years, the anti-war movement has been divided, advocating many popular ideas but utilizing superfluous strategies. A telling example was the reaction to the Tet Offensive. In early 1968 the Communists attacked throughout South Vietnam, with the United States and their allies responding with excessive ferocity. In this country a people's uprising was called for to condemn the Washington government's war policies. This was the optimal opportunity for change in the last twenty years. If coordination had been achieved between citizens, liberals and the socialist bloc—if a 'peace party' had been founded—we could have withdrawn from Vietnam, with years of war avoided and thousands of soldiers' lives saved. America today would be a pacifist member of the new world order, against conflict, promoting peace, firmly opposed to belligerence, favoring accommodation and appeasement. But an error was committed, this proletariat revolt did not ignite because the country's leftist activists were insufficiently controlled. Since that year, there have been intermittent discussions focusing on better mobilization in the cause of peace. Last fall, it was the consensus of the campus' anti-war factions that, as fighting in Vietnam again intensifies, one organization—instead of multiples—would achieve the most efficient handling of our manpower."

"The logical approach," Paul volunteered.

Summer Never Comes

"The most reasonable method to battle war and thwart destruction."

Paul remembered his November conversation on the Quad with the True Believers, how they depicted the peace movement as fighting war. "Did the idea originate with a particular individual?"

"Dialogue among many activists transpired in the months before UNITED was formed. I can't precisely recall who proposed the concept or if it was the upshot of all our discussions."

"Months before, does that mean during the summer or last school year?"

"Conflict and combat take no vacation and neither should the peace movement. One difficulty we must surmount is students' and citizens' beliefs that protest is only doable at convenient places and times. We should be as steadfast to peace as the warmongers are committed to conspiracies and massacring innocent people."

"You didn't answer my question, was planning done by whichever of the peace activists were in town over the summer?"

"A small cadre was in residence and carried on in July and August. We occasionally solicited counsel from outside sources."

"Were the outsiders former and current University of Illinois students or people from other parts of the country?"

"Only those familiar with our community."

Paul picked up Bernard's aggravation over explaining specifics. "When UNITED was formed, were SOAP's, DISGUST's and RAW's members asked to join?"

"Everyone was invited, and enrollees from all the groups were assigned meaningful leadership positions. As I stated, our aim is to coalesce all anti-war elements in the greater cause of ending this government's lunacy."

Paul knew this was false. Only SCRAP's former members, likely Bernard's reliable True Believers, held authority as UNITED's directors. Others—the Randy Millers, the common people, those outside the clique—were assigned grunt work.

"How about Laurie Allman? She was SOAP's leader for five years, but had no part in UNITED's formation and since October hasn't been involved in any anti-war activities." Paul's tone was bland, hoping to mask their friendship.

Summer Never Comes

"Laurie and I might have been together in a class a few semesters ago, I am uncertain. With what little of her anti-war work I am familiar with, I was surprised when she rejected UNITED. I have no notion why. I cannot justify for individuals because the peace movement is larger than any person, requiring selfless, coordinated, lock-step efforts. All comrades and fellow travelers must be molded into the apparatus, or to quote a current author, 'a single intellectual complex.'"

"Where is that phrase from?"

Foraging through the table's piles, Bernard picked up a paperback, *Ideology and Revolution in the Soviet Union*, by Howell L. Meade. "This text is an excellent clarification of socialist and Communist movements."

Paul reached for the book. "Are there many copies around the campus?"

"Only a few, I acquired this one from Follett's close-out shelves."

Feigning curiosity in a volume he'd examined months earlier, Paul thumbed to page 46. 'Part of the effort to reach the younger generation with indoctrination materials is carried out by the educational system.... Schools perform an important part in inculcating basic attitudes like team spirit (concern for the collective) and emphasis on group approval as contrasted to personal material rewards.' He wasted an extra thirty seconds looking at a map on page 231. "I've been to your meetings, they're very structured, which is strange for anti-discipline college students. Any reason for this?"

"None I can think of," Bernard shook his head, "except the fact we have so large a membership that a solid degree of control is essential to transact business. So many undergraduates are attending the meetings, I should add, that future sessions will convene in the old Auditorium."

What is UNITED's membership?"

"Eighty-eight hundred, including three hundred faculty," Bernard answered brusquely. "We hope to keep adding to that number."

"That's half the capacity of Assembly Hall. How successful were the housing unit recruiting meetings?"

"Highly favorable. We have visited two-thirds of the dormitories and group residence houses in Champaign-Urbana, with thirty-five percent of our enlistees coming from that program. With the warming weather, however, we will be curtailing those meetings."

Summer Never Comes

Paul thought back to the KIDs' session. A majority of the fraternity had shown, giving Randy, Killer and the other UNITED representatives resolute, but KID-typical rowdy attention. Fifteen of the brothers enrolled that evening. This time Bernard told the truth. The Altgeld Hall chimes belled 8:15.

"What demonstrations will UNITED organize this spring?"

"Protests focusing on the war's blunders, dishonesties and immorality." Bernard soberly replied. "A people's march from downtown Champaign to Chanute Air Force Base in Rantoul is scheduled for May."

"Rantoul is twenty miles from here, a long trek."

"Sixteen and a half, to be exact."

"And its purpose?"

"The Air Force relentlessly bombs in Southeast Asia, not only North Vietnam but Laos, Thailand, Cambodia and China's border regions. Thousands of sorties, millions of tons of explosives, farms, entire villages and livelihoods blasted away. This daily annihilation rarely appears in newspapers or on television. Only when there are claimed statistics of success, only when pro-war, hawkish rationalization is required are the sorties and slaughters publicized. Our march will highlight this clandestine tragedy."

Paul agreed. The war, America's perverted actions in the name of aiding other countries, preserving our selfish concepts of democracy, really sucked. Why do so few Americans dissent? "What activities were most meaningful this year?"

"We have had two. The protest of Undersecretary Camp's visit last fall underscored the stupidity of our country's leaders. The non-confrontational tactics employed that day by thousands of stalwart University of Illinois students exposed the war party's shallow justifications for their conflict. I am also convinced that day was successful in terms of marketing UNITED to the campus." Bernard straightened the table's piles. "The second activity was the food drive. The coordination and enthusiasm that hundreds of students displayed was an inspiration. There was satisfaction with shipping food to the Vietnamese, realizing we have helped other peoples. It was rewarding to see effort match accomplishments."

"Did you say the Camp protest was home-grown, the work of our campus?"

Summer Never Comes

"Yes, solely planned by us, a wholly Champaign-Urbana effort."

"And how much food was collected and when did it arrive in Vietnam?"

"Forty tons were delivered to Da Nang six weeks ago, in the middle of January. We received a message of thanks from the Saigon refugee charity we dealt with. I have a copy if you'd like to quote it in your story."

"Yes," Paul took the telegram, evidence of UNITED's and Bernard's deceit. "Do you know of other campus groups around the country working as you are to end the war?"

"I'm positive there are, that is only logical. I have read newspaper stories about other movements and their activities."

"Has there been coordination with these groups?"

"Between UNITED in Champaign and activists at other locations? No."

"Any letters, phone calls, telegrams, meetings or strategy sessions?"

"Never."

"You're alone and on your own in Illinois?"

"Correct."

The chimes clanged 8:30. Paul heard footsteps in the hallway and a door being unlocked. "How did you become interested in the peace movement?"

"The Nixon-Humphrey presidential campaign was the start. We all watched the Chicago convention on television, the thousands of peace protesters marching in the streets, the rioting, and the city's police—in the name of law and order—retaliating with tear gas, beatings and arrests. After that uprising, the Democratic Party was given no chance to win the election. As the campaign progressed, however, Hubert Humphrey gained ground and the contest became a toss-up by early November. Days before the voting, I recall Lyndon Johnson announcing a halt to the bombing offensive over North Vietnam. A disparaging gambit to sway voters to elect Humphrey, a callous attempt to re-cast the Democrats as doves, the good guys, instead of unconscionable criminals responsible for four years of war and thousands of Vietnamese and American dead. This was fraud and hypocrisy, the politicians' conjurings, speeches of lies they hope the people will accept as truth. At that moment, I made up my mind to join the struggle to end the war because the country's citizens deserve integrity."

Summer Never Comes

Paul was taken with Bernard's insight, and would have been more impressed if he hadn't lied for the past half hour. "Were you a student at the University of Illinois at that time?"

"That was my second year in Champaign-Urbana. A few weeks after the election, which Nixon won by tenths of a percent, I volunteered with Students Against War and have been in other groups since then."

Paul stared at him. University records listed Bernard as twenty-four years old, but he acted and looked younger. This perception, others gauging him an undergrad, endorsed Bernard's effectiveness. As he aged, would he be replaced and leave campus?

"Will UNITED succeed?"

"Undoubtedly. Americans are repelled by the conflict's miseries. It is a short time, perhaps only months, before support completely erodes away and the people finally renounce the Washington government. At that day, the political establishment, the so-called decision makers, worried over their own self-preservation, will abandon Vietnam, regardless of whether victory is attained or lost. UNITED's role is expediting events, bringing that glorious, proletariat moment closer."

"Do you consider UNITED an inspiration or an instrument?"

"Both, we have been in the forefront of the struggle on this campus, we are the leaders." Bernard unhesitatingly, proudly answered. "The future, though, will dictate additional roles for UNITED and the rest of us. If it is necessary to conform to a different course to produce a re-order, foment revolution, overthrow our country, we shall."

The Altgeld chimes struck 8:45, time for Paul's nine o'clock.

Walking home after his classes, Paul marveled at Bernard's well-reasoned, rehearsed, concocted, devious performance. He realized how Bernard commanded UNITED and Champaign-Urbana's peace movement: experience, logic and nerve.

But, as the politicians Bernard denounced for reneging on their word, he flat-out lied. To questions about Laurie Allman, Howell Meade's book, the Camp demonstration, the food drive, contact with other campus' anti-war groups, his age, and how long he'd been at the U of I, all his answers were false. Why was he dishonest with me? Did Bernard assume I couldn't uncover the facts, that I wasn't familiar with his background before we met? Did Bernard think me so inept a newspaperman I'd swallow everything he tossed out? Paul was frustrated that someone who—before this morning—he'd never face-to-face encountered would have so negligible an opinion of his reporter's abilities.

Wait a second. Until today Bernard didn't know what I looked like, we'd never met or had a conversation. Somebody else clued him in, someone supposing me not much of a reporter or not familiar with my work investigating peace movement.

Somebody judging me irrelevant has helped confirm UNITED is a sham. Thank you, my anonymous colleague. A riddle solved, another to unravel.

# # # #

That afternoon, Paul read a copy of the *Daily Illini* in the KIDs' living room.

"Notice to Commerce College June graduates. Sign-ups for companies interviewing on campus this semester will begin this Tuesday at eight a.m. Seniors are allowed to register for a maximum of six interviews. Sequence of sign-ups to be in alphabetical order. Additional details are available in the Commerce Placement Office, 101 David Kinley Hall."

# # # #

"Kentucky,

"I haven't written for a few months because life's shifting for old Billy. I'm marching closer to the war.

"Two days before Christmas our unit got re-deployed from the base around Saigon where we were stationed for four months (the censors say I can't give you the location) to a camp out in country near the border (the censors say I can't give you the location). The officers keep us grunts busy digging foxholes and latrines, stringing booby traps, polishing our weapons and patrolling in the jungle searching for Viet Cong. We sleep on the ground, eat rations out of tin cans, don't shower for a couple weeks straight and wear the same stinking skivvies and fatigues for just as long. This is the nastiest, hellacious, most upside down, fucked-up life you can imagine. What I wouldn't give for happy hour at the White Horse!

Summer Never Comes

"One piece of luck is our sector's pretty quiet, we recon but haven't fought any meatball skirmishes. Our lieutenant says we can expect it staying this way for another month. This is fine by me because the idea of challenging Charlie scares me shitless. The old-timers say in most jungle fire fights you never see the enemy, that you're shooting blind into the brush or trying to spook them out of tunnels. Whatever happened to seeing farther ahead than forty feet? This too, not knowing what's in front of you, sounds frightening because you don't know who or what you're facing—a squad of Cong or a whole Charlie division. You don't know the odds, if it's your turn to get your own ass shot off.

"For sure somebody will ask if I've seen casualties. Yes. More than a couple times I've helped evac wounded, loading them into choppers for the flight to a safe area. And I've seen dead GIs, that's the creepiest, gruesomeest, grisliest feelings. Here in front of you is a body bag filled with someone who until two or three of hours ago was an infantryman just like yourself, doing the same things you are now, working through the days, trying to survive this shit, praying to go home. Only he didn't, his name got called and he's dead, departed, no more. Maybe he was a buddy of yours when he was alive, now he's a bag with an ID tag. You see just one (but there's always more) and you stand there and think and it drives you crazy, because you can't figure out how someone who was alive and breathing yesterday is nothing today. You want to run away from this goddamned country, their fucking war and the dip-shitted assholes who drafted us here. But you can't, you've got to handle it, don't let your buddies down, endure it until you're short, hoping you survive, that you won't end up killed and in a bag. As I said, makes you fucking nuts.

"Did I tell you Nancy Kissel writes me every week? She's working at a bank on LaSalle Street in Chicago, living with her parents to save money, and is making plans for us after I'm out of the army. Every letter has plenty of super stories about what's happening stateside, and she's always telling me to hang in and keep my head in my job. Nancy's a doll, I can't wait to see her again.

"Well, that's all for tonight. Scuttlebutt's we're heading out on patrol in the a.m., so there's gear to stow, supplies to draw and rifles to clean.

"Thanks to my old buddies for sending letters. Madj, Caker, the McNicks, Tiny, Wally, you're real decent to me. I appreciate the mail and

Summer Never Comes

have read some of the numb-nutted ones to my pals in my platoon. The guys get a rise from them.

"Billy Powell"

Chapter Seventeen

"Seems strange, hiking to a hoops game when the weather's so summer, second week of March and the temperature hit seventy-three degrees this afternoon. Frisbees are flying in Frat Park, I saw coeds sunbathing on their blankets and Bo Balinski's scheduling softball practices."

"Why so early?" Bobby Sox asked.

"Zeta Psi's Golden Boar Tournament is scheduled for the first weekend in April," Paul answered.

"Except for the fog, this would be a perfect night." Bobby and his friends climbed the stairs on Memorial Stadium's east side. Along with six or seven thousand fellow Illini, the KIDs hurried to Assembly Hall for the season's last home game. In contrast to February's parkas, ski hats and scarves, the brothers wore windbreakers and sweatshirts.

"Stu, I heard you did a number on the LSAT exam."

"Can you believe it? My roommate, Mister-Just-Escaped-Probation, maxes out."

"What was your score?"

"745. The test is graded from 200 to 800 and I'm ranked in the top ten percent."

"Congratulations, sounds like you were roughly second to none." Lindy shook his pal's hand, "And the next steps?"

"Mail applications to law schools, including the U of I."

"Isn't it tough being accepted to this place?"

"What's to lose, the worst the admissions committee can do is say no." A skateboarding undergrad careened past the four KIDs.

"Speaking of lost, anybody spotted Scooter lately?"

"A couple days ago I saw him bolt out of the house carrying a suitcase, so he and his fiancée are probably in the sack somewhere, lucky bastard."

"Don't think so, Lauren's been on the phone for a week wantin' to talk to him. She's sounded upset."

"Maybe there's anguish over the marriage thing."

"Why would Scooter cause trouble now when it's time for facing the music? For sure he's more of a milquetoast than a rebel. What do you say, Robby?"

Paul hadn't noticed his fraternity brother missing this week. But he judged the remarks relevant to himself. Decision day, time to resolve was approaching, as it had for Lindy and his band, Stu with law school, Scooter and whatever.

"How about the b-ball game tonight?" Bobby asked. "Too bad we're missing the NCAA tournament."

"I'd say our .500 season is fortunate."

"And a shocker, I'll bet even Harv Schmidt can't work out how we won six road games. Think he'll return as coach next year?"

"The pride of the Illini." Lindy pronounced.

"Don't see why not." Paul gazed upwards to Memorial Stadium's east balcony, the columns partly hidden by the fog.

"He's losing a bunch of talent from the team," Bobby hurried to keep pace with his taller buddies, "and the last two years have been bleak recruiting efforts."

"Harv'll find a way to win. We'll have to play solid defense, or bring back Greg Jackson in the middle."

"What a tank," Bobby mocked.

"Greg wasn't that huge," Stu defended the Fighting Illini's former center, "and he helped the team skate past the Slush Fund."

"I like Harv."

The KIDs paused at Florida Avenue, waiting for traffic to pass by. All four gazed across the street at Assembly Hall. The most contemporary, modern-looking building in Champaign-Urbana, "one of the two largest edge-supported domes in the world," as described by the Architecture Department, the structure was shaped like a gigantic flying saucer, a massive, shallow bowl topped by a concrete lid. Surrounded with parking lots, young, thin trees, cornfields and a cemetery, it seemed isolated from the campus, but a welcoming place to reach on an overcast evening, a port for a storm as Lindy punned. The lobby's lights beamed through the tapered, glass walls, brightening the nighttime fifteen or twenty feet out from the panes. Farther from the glass, the fog diffused the light, conjuring the illusion of a whitish cover wrapping, sheltering Assembly Hall from the darkness. The roof's wide, overhanging rim captured the blanket's top, adding to the safe, protected ambiance.

Stepping out of the misty night would be nice, Paul thought.

"Go Illini, beat the Spartans!" A Chrysler-ful of students drove by, windows rolled down, the passengers flaunting their beer bottles.

# # # #

UPI – Saigon – United States Army headquarters reports a 'massive' Communist offensive has struck the Laotian-South Vietnamese border in the Mount Atouat theater. Sources speculate the town of Bien Hien as the probable target. Defense Department officials denounced the assaults as 'counterproductive to the interests of peace.' United States and ARVN reinforcements are shifting to the area.

Reuters – Hanoi – According to Radio Hanoi, units of the United States Navy have sortied into North Vietnamese territorial waters and shelled ships at anchor in Haiphong harbor. Coastal defenses have returned the fire. 'These hostile actions against unarmed vessels underscore the brazenly belligerent intentions of Imperialist America,' a statement read, 'and will be defeated.'

# # # #

The next day, Stef Tianen wrote the *Daily Illini's* editorial.

"Hostility by any country is saddening, in the case of America, doubly so.

"In our history, our nation has prided itself on common sense, fairness and striving to accomplish right. At consequential moments time was taken, days or weeks, to evaluate alternatives, with the moral course found and followed. In Vietnam, this critical practice has been rejected. Forgotten is reassessment; mislaid the sense of integrity. Substitute is a haphazard, willy-nilly, arbitrary scheme of attacks, assaults and aggression—distressing proxies indeed.

"Granted, a belligerent North Vietnam has never retreated from imperialist, colonial powers. For decades, that country has fought against subjugation because theirs is the cause of survival, defense of their villages and farms, self-determination and reunification for a whole Vietnam with no north or south.

"Citizens of America should feel shamed by our government's misguided war, humiliated by a policy prohibiting other peoples from finding their own futures. It is time to confront the warmongers. With one voice, we must demand a re-examination of our country's ambitions, the end of this insane policy. We must call for peace."

# # # #

"ATTENTION! KIDs' chug team tryouts to be held at the Red Lion a week from Friday, starting at 3:30. Beer's on the house, spectators welcome."

One brother scribbled on the bottom: "This don't mean you, Killer."

# # # #

"I'm so happy with these invitations. Staying in your house on Tuesday nights makes handling Wednesday morning eight o'clocks simpler." A panting Paul draped the blanket over their nude bodies.

"Only natural, dear, we're closer than KIDs to the Chem Annex. What's more, weekday sex was cooked up for college undergraduates, we keep in practice." Sharon toppled off his body as the two listened to the wind from the open window. "How was your 'big interview sign up?'"

"Chaotic, Comm West's corridors were clogged with tons of confusion, akin to the Armory during registering for the semester. Only the stakes are so major, money and jobs instead of scheduling classes. Four years of college squeezed to standing in line trusting that the seniors ahead of you won't want to talk with the same companies. If you're late or your name's at the back of the queue, it's all she wrote."

Summer Never Comes

"How many did you arrange?" She snuggled to Paul's side.

"Six, all public accounting firms except for one, a cast iron foundry in Skokie searching for a pricing analyst, whatever that is. The recruiters arrive after spring break and keep coming through the middle of May."

"Is it possible you'll have a job before June?"

"That's the target. Wild, don't you think? From drinking, bellbottoms and wasting away in Champaign to haircuts, a suit, tie and brief case, every day starting at nine a.m., a paycheck and responsibility. Careers can't be simple for any person." An indifferent Paul turned toward Sharon, his girlfriend looking puzzled and pouting. "Bad form, you're sweet enough to shack up on a week night and I'm moping."

"One moment I'm relieved you're moving on in your life, two seconds later I'm confused, convinced you'll never grow up. Which alternative will win? Discover the wide world's possibilities, become, as you say, dependable, or stay stuck in the past, maybe ten years from now as a thirty-year-old somebody someday driving down for football weekends and somehow getting depressed on Sunday afternoons when it's time to depart?"

"A reason I'm detesting graduation is we'll be apart. In June, when we go home to Chicago, maybe we'll get together on weekends but not every other day like we do now. Next autumn, when you're back in Veterinary College the situation will be worse, we'll have less time."

"I agree, the routine will be strange. Of course, the trip from your parents' house to Champaign is only two hours, doable for weekends, certainly during football season."

"If I find a job in Chicago or another city close to our campus. But what if an accounting firm with branch offices across the country hires me and I'm transferred two or three states away?"

"I never considered you'd relocate." Sharon hadn't, because their months of dating had been so delightful, and her efforts over the past weeks getting into the Vet Med College were so taxing.

But now there was time for pondering, saying goodbye. Despite qualms over Paul's loner personality, she was comfortable with their frequent rendezvousing, studying in the Library, weekends hanging in the bars, sleeping together just about whenever. In a few months, though, they would leave Champaign-Urbana. For certain they'd be dear friends, but intimacy

Summer Never Comes

would vanish. Knowing the other's favorite music and munchies, Paul draping a towel in her bedroom's corner, she forgetting a pair of socks or a bra back at KIDs, when and where they'd meet on a Friday afternoon without phoning. This part of Paul's anxiety Sharon connected with because she too rued this nearing void. Reliance in another, amity, assurance, foibles no one else understood, their secluded world would slip away with the semester's end.

Sharon closed her arms around Paul's neck and humped closer to his hips, her breasts rubbing his chest, their stomachs touching. "Promise me you'll come back for Homecoming."

"If we stay in this room."

# # # #

Even with the howling exhaust fan, Randy Miller sweated while washing pots and pans in the Sigma Alpha Mu kitchen. Finishing, he drained the water, folded the towels on the sink's edge and mulled over the latest news from 'Nam.

North Vietnamese troops had advanced from their bases in Laos, encircling Bien Hien, American and ARVN units unable to stop the Viet Cong attacks. Radio Hanoi claimed the United States Navy was strafing Haiphong harbor, sinking seventeen ships in the last twenty-four hours. And an appeal had been broadcast by the Communists asking their "Socialist, Marxist, Stalinist allies to rally to support the followers of Ho Chi Minh against Imperialist assaults on freedom of the seas and the ideology of Lenin."

As Bernard predicted, escalation triggered more wounded and deaths, meaningless casualties raising the body count, pushing more Americans to condemn the war and pissing off thousands of college students. Randy was confident UNITED would organize demonstrations denouncing the Navy's attacks on Haiphong, and expected comrades at other universities to do the same. Maybe that would show Nixon and the rest of the Washington assholes it was time to quit. Done in the Sammys' kitchen, he headed to UNITED's office in the Union to check on up-to-the-minute war bulletins.

> *UPI* – Washington – After forty-eight hours of no comment, the Pentagon confirmed reports of naval activities in the Tonkin Gulf,

stating American vessels have fired on Communist ships only in self-defense and under the constraints of 'Operation Holding Furnace.' The spokesman denied Communist accusations of United States vessels violating North Vietnamese territorial waters.

# # # #

"How about this weather?" A cigarette-smoking, Coke-drinking Al Stojak stood at the counter. With the temperature outside in the seventies, the *Daily Illini's* basement offices were clammy. "Don't bother looking, she's gone again."

"We'd scheduled a meeting for 10:30. What's today's event, more racquetball, or maybe golf at Savoy?"

"Nope, an adult activity. Stef's over in Greg Hall job interviewing with a Minneapolis-St. Paul newspaper."

"I never imagined her one of the first to walk out on the Big U. Whenever we've discussed the future she's talked about grad school. Now it's find work to earn a paycheck." Paul was put out being blown off by his absent editor-in-chief but glad to again avoid a showdown. "When will Stef be back?"

"Not sure, but that's why I'm hanging around, she wants me following up on our UNITED project. Stef's newest plan is your article publishing in a week, which means you submitting a rough draft in a day or two."

Paul hesitated. One of the few *DI* staffers familiar with his story, Stoj could be Bernard's spy, the mole marking Paul as an easy-to-discount reporter.

"Right out of the blue, yesterday Stef told me your piece is running on page one instead of my weekend *Spectrum*. Which confuses the hell out of me. First, I'm in a bind because I was counting on you filling the magazine's space." Stoj rammed the 'rette in his empty pop can. "Second, remember our conversation on another day we waited for Stef? You talked about the history professor piloting the balloon at Homecoming and the book about Communism listed on her course's reading list. When Stef hit me with the page one switcheroo, I figured you'd updated her, she must have those same facts, and as a result considers your story newsworthier. I asked her if that was the reason for the shift, because your article's evolved to more, excuse me for saying so, than a boring recap of anti-war movement background. But Stef blew me off, I don't think she heard my question, she was so preoccupied with her intramurals and job interviewing."

Paul worried his undercover work was public. "Let me understand, yesterday you gave Stef the specifics about the peace movement?"

"I attempted, but our unconcerned editor-in-chief shut me down. So why she's wants it on page one is a mystery."

"Was that your first conversation with Stef about the peace movement?"

"And only. Stef's the head honcho, if she's indifferent, I wasn't insisting. What's the hang-up, have you quit working on the story?"

"Actually I've busted my butt the last few days and written three-fourths of the piece. But I want to be positive about Stef. Never in the past month did you bring it up with her?"

"Honestly, that afternoon after tipping over the chair and dropping my smoke on the floor I felt like a total fool. I forgot everything about UNITED until yesterday when Stef snatched the article away from *Spectrum*. What's the big deal?"

"Anybody else you've chatted with?"

"I told you, the story slipped my mind." Stoj was embarrassed by his lapse and perplexed with Paul's persistence. "I wouldn't discuss your piece with anyone besides Stef and you. Journalistic ethics, right?"

Paul was won over. Around the *Daily Illini* Stoj's reputation might be nonchalance, but today he was candid, diligent, rational. If someone had ratted to Bernard, the stoolie wasn't Stoj. "From what I've told you, does my article belongs on page one?"

"If it's hard news affecting what's happening right now on our campus, I say yes." He played with a match book. "What else do you have?"

# # # #

Reuters – New Brunswick – The Campus Peace Crusade, Rutgers University's student anti-war movement, announced for a school-wide general strike commencing tomorrow. 'In PROTEST against the latest American right-wing militarist belligerence in Vietnam,' a spokeswoman declared, 'our response is total disruption of ALL university activities. We anticipate dozens of campuses and THOUSANDS of comrade-students to MUSTER to our side.'

Reuters – University Park – The Nittany Radical Union of Penn State University today published their first edition of the *War Protest Times,* a journal committed to 'once and forever ending America's criminal conflict in Vietnam.' The initial issue declared for nationwide civil disobedience of 'whatever required scope to wreck the war.'

# # # #

Toting his book bag and grooving the springtime, Lindy sauntered through the Quad to the Undergraduate Library. Around him, hundreds of fellow students enjoyed the almost-August temperatures, shirtless and sunbathing on blankets, licking ice cream cones, chatting with buddies or sitting alone by a tree. One couple strolled toward Lindy, she squeezing his hip, the boyfriend jamming his fingers down the girl's bellbottoms. In the middle of the Quad, opposite Davenport Hall, a newly-planted flagpole flew UNITED's banner at half-staff. A decent-sized squad of orange and black shirted students had gathered at the pole's base, Lindy thought he spotted Randy Miller and Killer, orating and handing flyers to bystanders. Determined to be on time for his date, Lindy avoided the protesters, hurried past the old Auditorium and saw Emily standing on the Undergrad's patio.

"Thanks for coming. Can you dig this climate, cut-offs for this many days at the Ides of March? Basically a life of Riley." He leaned on the railing.

"The weather is too warm, especially evenings, my dorm room has been too muggy for sleeping." Emily's soft voice was duller than normal, her head sagging as she examined the sunken courtyard.

"Semester goin' okay?"

"Passable, at least the last weeks since things have settled down." The south wind blew from behind them, swirling Emily's hair over her face. "But you know how it is when pleasant weather arrives, so difficult to study."

"You've tapped the nail on the head. The ol' KIDs house is the craziest I've seen in months, stereos bangin', frisbees soarin', water fights breakin' out in every hallway." Lindy grinned again. "You can't even make a stab at booking. And when you boogie into the 'Brary you find out the heat's still on and the place is a for-real raisin-in-the-sun sweatbox."

Unlike their old days, Em did not laugh at his clichés, and Lindy couldn't determine if she was genuinely depressed or acting. Whatever her disposition, it was time to face the music.

"I'd say you've got a pretty decent friend in Bobby Sox."

"A savior. The first night, when Bobby came to tell me how I had been, let me know what happened to…he was so protective and practical. Bobby made certain I was aware of the whole disaster and wanted me prepared if I met any of the people in on the scheme. Bobby was so considerate, doing everything he could for Nicole and me."

"I apologize I wasn't around." He sounded repentant. "If I'd have known what was takin' place, Em, I'd have helped out."

"It's so sad living alone." Emily watched a student sitting on a bench in the courtyard. "After learning about Tom's deception, I sat at my desk in my room for days, convalescing, and didn't leave the dorm. Nicole carried my meals up to our room. I didn't study, watch television or use the telephone. My English literature professor allowed me to take an hourly exam on a Saturday morning instead of during the week. And Bobby came to Blaisdell Hall six straight days to check on me, drove Nicole and I to Neil Street in Champaign to shop, and even stayed in town one weekend to watch over me. He's driving me home for Easter."

"How you doin' now?"

"My mind is hard to work out. I'm sleeping enough, more than when I was seeing Tom, so I'm not as exhausted. And Nicole accompanied me to McKinley Hospital for a physical to ensure I hadn't picked up an infection or gotten pregnant. I'm neither, which is a great relief. But emotionally, I can't say. To focus so intensely and be wrapped up with a person, discard everything else for him, expect a future, yearn for so much pleasure… And crash. To trust, then discover how worthless hope can be, how people are cruel, there is no cure for a reversal like that."

Lindy's ears tweaked with his old girlfriend using an undergrad idiom. *Which of her former boyfriends, however, was she describing?*

Poor kid, what she went through. Em was damaged by her affair with Tommy Quarters, her mind somewhere else. Lindy was curious about what had gone down between the two. Was it true, the gossip about Tommy's manipulation and humiliations? Had that pervert really coerced her to turn those kinky tricks in bed when Lindy was positive Em wasn't at all into weird? Was Tommy such a bastard to make her a whore, and Em so innocent to become one? Lindy didn't fancy the seamy details, he always mocked the voyeurism his fraternity brothers dealt in. His intent was finding how to lend a hand. But there was a hang-up. Way beyond late, Lindy didn't suppose himself close enough to Em to coax her to open up. If she wanted to self-examine, fine, as he told Robby a week ago that was the therapy Em preferred, but he didn't wish to pry.

Now in March, Lindy realized how far he'd hurtled, his ego's consequences and Frogfeet's costs, to him and others. He'd misspoken to his roommate when claiming the band was a worthwhile, not-to-miss experience. He'd been too careless with other's feelings. His buddies in KIDs, excepting Kentucky, Bobby and Stu, were mostly oblivious, and Robby had grudgingly accepted his going AWOL. But steadfast Em, the dearest, devoted companion he'd had in Champaign, was woefully injured.

"I've been no help," Lindy sighed.

If I've been such an awful friend and don't think it right inquiring about Em's life the last few months, am I sincere enough to support her now? I've hurt her so much by blowin' her off, how can I rationalize assisting today? Why did I set up this date, anyway? Conceit—that I could make up six months in one afternoon? Apology—to settle the books then bid goodbye? For my conscience's sake? Why don't I ignore my motives and myself and attend to Em; she's the one convalescing. For once this school year, Lindy, focus on someone else.

"You know, with time on my hands, we could date again, not like the former hot 'n' heavy days, just to chat and rap like we're doin' this afternoon, search for some common ground and aid each other."

"Bobby mentioned your band is finished. I'm sorry you were arrested, but glad the sentence wasn't worse. Are you joining another?"

"Graduation is too close to re-start in Cham-Bana. I'll wait to see where I put down roots this summer, wherever that maps out being, then hook up with some musicians to jam with. For the present, I'm out of the music business, a lot freer between today and June."

Summer Never Comes

"And searching for a job? What are your plans when you leave the Big U?"

More slang, Em's coastin' to other stuff. *Now if only I can check my ego, there's an opening.*

"I'll interview, like the vast, silent majority of Commerce College seniors. I've already signed up for four, and'll probably return to Chicago to toil on the basic nine to five treadmill. Naturally, you know what's always swirled through my brain, the west coast, Los Angeles, music studios and recording sessions." *Crap, why'd I foul up again?*

On the patio, eight or ten students hustled toward the Quad, laughing and anticipating a few hours' goofing off in the sun, one pair hauling an ice chest. Likely packed with brewskies, Lindy conjectured. When they'd passed, Emily stepped away from the railing.

"Your graduation isn't far off," she sounded remote, "and spring goes quickly, particularly now that you're preparing to move away. Really, we won't see much of each other."

"I just said I'm not busy the rest of the semester, I can make time now." Lindy lamented the many, many occasions he'd retreated on that line.

"How can I believe that? I've been so disappointed—by you last autumn, then Tom last month. What words can you say or guarantees can you claim that will convince me you're honest? Why should I take another chance, Will?"

Lindy never imagined he'd be so pleased hearing his nickname. *This might be a last hurrah, but there's hope.*

"You're correct, I've no leg or right to stand on, not a prayer, except the bet I placed asking you to meet today and the payoff when you accepted. Due to my behavior, I admit I don't deserve any consideration from you. Selfish, childish, so closed-minded I'm forever embarrassed. And how Tommy Quarters treated you was infinitely worse. I see how I'm to blame, I was stupid and you were hurt. But before this went down, when we were best friends, we had it going, Em, we truly did. Whatever the happenings or adventures last year, we enjoyed our friendship, accepted each other. We can go back and use last year as a plus, catch the good parts. We can't overlook the heartaches but can bury them, not remember too often. Longo intervallo, knit with the better threads."

Okay, that's enough, my finest, sweetest and sincere, the next move's hers.

Summer Never Comes

Emily was more beat down than a semester ago, experienced with life in ways she couldn't visualize last September, now knew people were not what they seemed on the surface, they were caught with themselves, on the prowl, callous, stealing rewards. Was Will like that, only mouthing words, or has he learned and come back?

What to do? Stay or walk away? Trust, or doubt and deny? One last opportunity, or continue suspicious? As Will acknowledged, he didn't merit second chances and Emily wasn't obligated to offer any. But her boyfriend mentioned last year, when times were comfortable, enjoyable, blissful, when they'd been in love. The dozens of dates and days together, stories and jokes shared, plans discussed, dreams and delights, our wonderful yesterday. At his best, there was so much good in him.

But no one can return, all that's left is the insecure, uneasy future.

If I say yes, am I ridiculous. If no, am I a fool? I'm still so tired and wish I could avoid these choices.

# # # #

"Anyone think the demonstrating's turnin' intense this time?" Nemo yanked the grass.

"I'll betcha it's the same set up like other springs." 'Ralph' Hepler rested on his back, looking at the clear sky. "A hundred colleges go berserk, the *Daily Illini* writes more hate-the-horrible-war-editorials, some numb-nut makes a fanatical speech, bunches of us students march through Campustown, a couple windows are smashed to show we're really, totally concerned, then it's softball season."

Frat Park was packed with the most undergrads since last September's New Student Week, but minus intramural practices, coed volleyball or other exercising. Spring activities were lazier, catching rays, lobbing frisbees, and spectating the whooping Phi Sigs, equipped with cups, hoses and tubs, battling through a water fight in their front yard. Bunches of KIDs—Ozark, Orion, Stu, Bobby, Paul on his blanket, Shaky Jake, Ron Dudzik, Beebo and 'Stein—lounged under the trees chugging beers.

"Too bad we can't skip protesting and slide right to sixteen-inch."

"The ground's not hard enough for practice, smarter rallying on the streets where it's drier and nearer to the bars."

Summer Never Comes

"I don't see how you guys can joke." Randy Miller spoke up. "Everywhere in America conscientious citizens are opposing the war, we should follow their examples. That's what the country's about, making a difference, especially with a tragedy as atrocious as Vietnam or any other war."

"There's more than one goin' down?" Ozark asked.

"We're kidding, Randy." Tim O'Toole leaned on his ice chest. "We're not saying the peace movement's only for screwing off. I hate the silly-assed war as much as other draft-age students, it stinks, reeks, we should pull out and lock in jail the turds that started it. Wanna a beer?"

"That's right," Orion stretched his arms, "students are against Vietnam, at least ninety-seven or ninety-eight percent of us. The difference is you guys, the activists, are more zealous than the majority."

"Protest is commitment, without dissent, nothing's improved, without revolution the status quo, agreeable or awful, is always in place."

"Precisely. But for some of us, saying we're against Vietnam is our limit. Could be our parents ordered us to play it safe. Maybe we're slackers dealing with our own problems, don't understand the political stuff, or think someone else—like you, Randy—will handle the whole deal."

"But the war is criminal and has to be put right. If Vietnam's not stopped, our generation's the ones in trouble, we'll be swallowed up."

"Billy Powell."

The KIDs thought of their old fraternity brother and their own draft numbers. Bobby Sox sat by a tree, recalling last spring when Billy, nearing graduation and his induction date, moved from the house into Frat Park, camped in a tent, barbecued Polish sausage, drank PBRs, smoked weed and made out with Nancy.

Dale Kinsey exited the fraternity accompanied by a short, overweight woman yawning and drooping her head on his shoulder. Her jeans zipper was opened and she carried a paisley bra in one hand. The KIDs ignored them.

"The frickin' war's a freakin' blow job," Bobby condemned, "all the thousands of our buddies forced into the army and shipped to 'Nam."

"And how many returned in coffins?"

"How many of us will still make the round trip?"

Summer Never Comes

The goofing off continued around Frat Park, but these KIDS turned sober, the real world puncturing Champaign-Urbana.

"Aren't we hypocrites? Loafing under these trees on a beautiful day, with beers and bags of pretzels, enrolled in college and innocent to everything ahead of us, bum-rapping the war because we don't want to go over and fight. We're doves on the sidelines only for saving our asses." Orion drained his brew.

"What's wrong with that? I don't know about the rest of you guys but my ass is essential to me." The KIDs chuckled at Nemo's argument and reached for the fire-brewed Stroh's.

"You make a point," Jake glanced toward Frat Park, "but what about the other side, the right-wingers propping up the government's policy? After all these years and at what cost, why are they still backing Vietnam? Shouldn't we ask if anything with the war is worthwhile?"

"Right, like the domino theory the hawks lecture about. Fight in Asia or somewhere else, if we don't, sooner or later ours is the only independent country left. How about the benefit of the doubt for them?"

Randy looked at his friends, welcoming their questioning, ready with his own rationale. But Dudz spoke first.

"Hell, no, there's nothing reasonable about it. The only ones thinking that way are the generals ordering soldiers killed, the corporations swindling money selling the guns and bombs to both sides. The whole war's a goddamned, titanic, grandmother-loving disaster, it stunk when LBJ took America in and sucks today with President-Head-Glued-to-His-Gonads Nixon."

Screams from the Phi Sigs house grabbed the KIDs' attention. Paul spotted three undergrads on the roof aiming a fire hose, showering their brothers on the porch.

"'Ralph,' pass me another cool, tall one, will ya?"

# # # #

Groping her flabby ass then kissing goodbye, Dale Kinsey dumped the chubby broad off at the Snack Bar. Buying a soda and abruptly forgetting the afternoon's balling, was her name Sally or Sarah, already he couldn't remember, Dale walked to the Krannert Art Museum for his next rendezvous. He waited in the empty basement gallery, not a bit attracted to the 'Early Twentieth Century American Painters' exhibit hanging on the partitions.

"Been here long?"

"About ten minutes," Dale answered. This coed was way cuter than the whore he'd shacked up with an hour ago. "Why are you late?"

"I played and won a handball match at IMPE, then needed a shower. The girls' locker room was too crowded, so I had to clean up at my dorm."

"Yeah, you live in Scott Hall," Dale snickered. "That's one trick I'd love experiencing. Right at a hectic time, like before nine o'clock classes, sneak into the girls' john and check out those women prancin' in their panties. I could dress up as a broad in a house coat and wrap a towel around my head, even wear a bra and stuff paper in the cups to fake a pair of tits, anything for a peek at that juicy inner thigh. I could scam away with it."

"What perversion. Can't you find your jollies some other way?" Robin Ferris sat on the bench. "Let's discuss business."

"Why the rush? There's a couple hours before supper, we could massage some pleasure in with our work." His palm patted Robin's knees.

"Please, I'm glad I warned all my friends about you." She slapped Dale's hand. "Next Monday a plane is flying into Willard Airport from St. Louis. Our buddy, K-Mow, is traveling on board with five kilos of hash, primo merchandise. Besides Carbondale, the whole state's over-supplied, so the load's reserved for Champaign. Loops has spoken for half and we need to contact our network to distribute the rest."

"Don't sound so worried, we've moved that much before." Dale petted Robin's black hair. "Students are developin' such a huge drug addiction we're in a growth industry, a businessman's dream and a wet one at that. Hell, in a few years, right in time for graduation, our shares of the profits will add up to a sweet nest egg."

"And while we're earning our riches, we're smart to continue low-key and keep a step ahead of problems."

"Honey, the organization's tight, our pushers manhandle their territories, we've got spies in both towns' police departments, and the users are okay with the product." He rubbed her left shoulder.

"We can't be complacent or commit stupid mistakes."

Summer Never Comes

"We're not. There haven't been any problems since we framed that pansy-ass band in Bloomington." Irritated by Robin's arguments, Dale moved away.

"Which included one of your fraternity brothers. Don't you feel remorse for causing Frogfeet's and Bill Lindner's arrest?"

"Why should I? We offered them chances to come in with us, not my fault they refused. I regret losin' the couple of bags of grass we stashed in their van and I wasn't excited paying such a hefty bribe to the cops for the bust, especially since Lindy and his jerk-off friends weren't sentenced to jail time. But the set up sent the message. The rest of our stooge musicians are toein' the line, no one's complainin' anymore."

"Everyone's afraid they're next."

"That's right, because that's how big shots muscle to the top in the real world. Read the *Wall Street Journal*, business is done by havin' a bigger set of balls than the other dirtbags, findin' out how to extort and destroy the competition. Besides, we take care of our dopers, they definitely receive more than a fair share."

A lone art patron, a foreign student wearing a turban, strolled by, paused at each picture and was gone in five minutes.

"And what the hell kind of crap are you talkin'? As I recall, you were the one hittin' on Frogfeet in the Red Lion, offering Lindy the opportunity to come in with us." Dale tickled Robin's neck.

"I feel guilty because Lindy wasn't the misfit you claimed. He and his band were real sweeties I assumed would want to earn extra cash. I was shocked when they turned us down."

"There you go," he kissed the hair hiding her ear, "five foolish musicians not smart enough to grab for easy bucks.

"But you flaunt it so much, you're proud of screwing friends then tossing them away." She turned to face Dale.

"You just said the magic word, honey." Licking Robin's lips, he plunged in for a French kiss.

"Remember to meet the plane at the airport." She winced, then pushed her hands underneath Dale's arms, deciding an afternoon in the sack was an okay deal.

"Monday. What time?" He rose from the bench, lifting Robin with him.

"Eleven in the morning." The two hugged and Dale unzipped her bellbottoms.

# # # #

"I'm so sorry, Lauren, leaving the campus without you, but I thought going by myself the wisest."

"Where?

"Home to my mom and dad, to tell them we're having a baby."

"Behind my back, Scooter, how could you? Shouldn't we have faced them together when they learned we were, that I'm…?" A nauseous Lauren rested on the couch. *Please, stomach, not now when we're finally talking,* let me get through this without throwing up.

"I understand my parents and this was the best way. You haven't spent much time with them, only the few days around Christmas. After that visit, my mom said you were a nice person, even called you darling, and looked forward to having you for a daughter-in-law. She repeated that sentiment two days ago, how she's anticipating being friends."

"Was that before or after you announced I was pregnant? God, what must she think of us?" Discouraged, she answered her own question. "A pair of brainless adolescents landing in trouble. Whatever goodwill I had with her has vanished."

"At first, my mom chewed me out with the typical parental lectures about decency, how sneaking around bedrooms wasn't the way they raised their son. She said I was a smarter man than to go off and screw up a life. Her next reaction was crediting me for coming clean and not doing anything else so stupid."

"Did your parents wonder why I wasn't with you?"

"I accepted the blame for coming alone, that you were unaware of my trip. And my mom's feelings were the same as yours, I should have brought you along."

Lauren calmed down, relieved someone agreed with her. Maybe their mess wasn't so dire. "What kinds of senselessness did your mom think we'd do?"

"Elope without phoning our parents, then shack up in some hotel until graduation."

Summer Never Comes

She giggled at the scenario. A Champaign County Courthouse wedding with only her roommates and Scooter's fraternity brothers attending, followed by partying at the Lion, was an enticing way to go out. Imagining drinking a glass of beer, though, turned her stomach queasy.

"Or a harder choice, we'd decide against having the baby and arrange for an abortion."

Their reality's misgivings returned. Lauren confessed to being an immature twenty-one, childishly carefree and untested. Until three weeks ago there were other distractions for her life, spring break, wrapping up the semester, job hunting, merrily planning their wedding, honeymooning, finding a place for them to live, spending money. Before this month, Lauren had never contemplated motherhood, not until five or six years in the future, after their share of fun. Everything about babies were day-to-day routines, responsibilities for grown-ups. Cribs, strollers, high chairs, formula, feedings, burpings, teething, doctor visits, lining up babysitters, washing clothes, dirty diapers, nights with no sleep. *Why did this happen? Why now?*

"What do we do?" Lauren moved closer to Scooter.

"My mom has a proposal. First, my parents want to say you're completely, gladly welcomed into our family. They were pleased with our engagement last fall and accept our predicament today. Like you and I, they realize how awkward this is, but intend to completely support us and wish the best for everyone, especially the baby. They're prepared to pay for our wedding, which naturally must be soon, help us with an apartment, and my dad's certain he can line up a job for me at the bank he works for. Under the circumstances, we'll be as set as we could hope."

"All things considered." She fathomed her shifting life. "Tell me, Scooter, are we going get married and become parents?"

"Have the baby? Dear, there never was a doubt. I'm sorry my bizarreness frightened you, but I needed time to accept the shocker of fatherhood and work out what's practical for my…family."

Seeing their dilemma had solutions, Lauren was sorry she'd doubted her fiancé.

"My mom has another proposition." Scooter had reached the harshest measure. "There's so much to deal with—doctor appointments for you and the baby; wedding preparations; a new apartment; furniture, dishes and infant things to buy. Because we haven't handled this before, since being new parents is overwhelming, my mom thinks the simplest course is for you quit school right away and move in with them in Chicago so she can lend a hand."

"Not finish the semester, not graduate? Why me?"

"Because you're carrying our baby. Think for a minute. If you stay on campus, the only times for going to my parents' home are weekends." Scooter sounded logical. "Figuring the Champaign to Chicago drive time, there aren't many hours you're back there to tackle problems."

"If our wedding is small, only families and a dozen or so college friends, we'd have plenty of time over spring break to plan."

"Which is the week my mom decided would be easiest for us to move you out of your apartment and into her house."

"And leave school forever, you're down here with your buddies while I'm alone in Chicago. Isn't staying together wiser?"

"Definitely this is a sacrifice and I'll miss you greatly. But our life needs to change, besides you and me, we have a baby to care for. It's the choice we must make."

Lauren was miserable. Along with enduring embarrassment, discomfort and insecurity, here was the risk of forfeiting her freedom for two, four, six months or longer and acceding to someone else's control, someone she barely knew. At Christmas, she sensed a strong-willed, shrewd Mrs. Petersen always decided for the family. Back then, Lauren had resolved to remain her own person—not to be aloof, a troublemaker, or a snot, simply an individual—and hoped her future mother-in-law would respect her feelings. Independence was a non-starter now. No doubt Kathie Petersen meant well, and their baby's well-being was the overriding concern. But what of the trade offs? Being your own person or fewer worries? Naïveté or pragmatism? Play the hooligan college kid or reason as an adult? Working harder scraping by or security? My ego or the baby's health? Brainless or smart?

This is my first mommy-to-be lesson, Lauren thought.

# # # #

Summer Never Comes

Sharon studied the Whitt's End happy hour crowds. Students were dressed for the premature summer weather in cut-offs, sandals and sunglasses, a few were barefoot, many women wore low-slung halters, and guys stood around shirtless, showing off so-so tans. 'Help Me, Rhonda' blasted from the speakers with scores of partying, hooting undergrads screaming the chorus. She turned to her boyfriend, the moody Paul, peering at the wooden bar and his cup.

"Time for one more?"

"I shouldn't, I'll miss dinner at KIDs, but, yeah, beer feels like the thing to do."

Sharon poured refills. "Job interviews have you down?"

"They don't start for a couple of weeks so I've forgotten about them, except for remembering to wash a dress shirt to wear." One Whitt's customer fed a coin into the jukebox and selected 'Surfer Girl,' another super song for the hot afternoon. "Today's dilemma's my story for the *Daily Illini.*"

"Stef and you have another meeting?"

"She never showed, but I spent a half hour talking with Al Stojak, the weekend magazine's editor. He updated me about the plan for my article, which is printing it on page one real soon. Stoj was someone I suspected having passed Bernard the low opinion of my reporting talents. Turns out he's not a mole, the more Stoj learns about what I've uncovered, the more he wants to help."

The pair were jostled by a coed shoving her way to the bar to snatch a pitcher of Stroh's.

"Two pluses, more readers for your story and an ally on the *DI's* staff."

"What if I don't want that, what if I'm over my head, want the story forgotten? At some point this assignment switched from insignificant to newsworthy, from double-checking details to investigating issues, some of which are disturbing. Take Laurie Allman. For years she was in her oblique world, working on her private peace movement, writing and warning against the war; her only distinction having been a campus activist longer than anyone else except for old friend Bernard. Then, in two weeks last autumn, thugs terrify Laurie off campus and her college education is over. I wonder if there were other incidents, what's the regime's blueprint, what's next in the future? If the demonstrations blow up, I don't want the blame for causing trouble for Laurie, Stoj and hundreds of other undergrads."

Sharon lightheartedly bumped into Paul's hip, but sounded sensible. "Who are you worrying over, our fellow students or yourself? Why not report the facts and let the outcomes handle themselves?"

"That's the straightforward way, argue UNITED's operatives aren't the idealists they claim, expose the stalkers who hounded Laurie, say outsiders comprised the majority of the Camp protesters, and Champaign-Urbana was conned by the food drive. Accuse Bernard Minerath of masquerading as an undergrad. Write there's anecdotal proof he and Professor Gulley are conspiring with other campuses, and when I interviewed Bernard he lied about everything." He glanced at Sharon. "I put this in a story and what do I have?"

"The truth," she answered. Another Whitt's customer played 'Don't Worry Baby.'

"But no summary. What's their motive? Why were the old peace groups disbanded? Where is UNITED leading? If Bernard and other schools' anti-war groups are corresponding, that's not a crime. In a manner it's clever. With worsening news from Vietnam, protesters organizing could be vital over the next weeks." Paul chugged his beer, then, as habitual when undecided, set an elbow on the bar, resting his chin on his fist. "Bernard's lied; so what, who hasn't? But UNITED has never broken the law, which is a plus, and the students support them."

"Have you written the story?"

"Interviewing Bernard was my last research. Since then I've typed the piece into decent shape, even before discovering I'll be featured on the *DI's* front page. The body of the article—names, dates and relationships—is completed. But I haven't formulated an ending."

"Do you have evidence to support a conclusion or are you honestly uncertain? Is the question UNITED's next step or yours?"

"I can't make up my mind. This is a tricky decision because I have to consider more than myself. By a fluke I'm responsible for the whole campus, leastways everyone caught up in peace protesting. How I act, or don't, could affect all of us." An aggravated Paul waved his hand at the mobs. "Which isn't my thing since I'm no wiser than the next woman or guy in this bar. Who am I pronouncing make or break judgments, why am I accountable?"

"Because you're the one to validate UNITED as a bunch of peace-loving hippies or discrediting them as a gang of street-wise, cut-throat radicals. Call it destiny, providence or anything else, you're answerable and must do your best."

As many times this year, his girlfriend's intuition impressed Paul. For whatsoever reasons, reporter's ethics, no nerve, protecting her, wishing to conceal his investigation, Paul had shielded Sharon from many specifics and, sensing his wariness, she'd rarely pried. Despite their dual discretion, though, Sharon pieced together his story and now argued with him to decide. *Gosh, my girlfriend's fantastic.*

"I've thought about conspiracies. If that's Bernard's objective, he and UNITED enjoy advantages. Enthusiastic students as followers, the momentous cause of ending a war and an opponent, the Washington government, who's despised but has to play by the rules. The ingredients are there, except one. Conspiracy for what?"

'Little Deuce Coupe' played, bunches of couples danced between the tables, and two more coeds with empty pitchers shoved to the bar.

"There are other problems."

"Those are?"

"For one, Stoj isn't the mole for UNITED, someone else is; the spy is still out there, I can still be undercut. The second is how I collected information; I was less than honest researching the issues."

"Was Bernard truthful all year?"

"My principles are the drawback, not his. If you're conniving, there's not much left."

"Most of your work was above-board," Sharon shifted toward Paul after the coeds bought their Stroh's, "wasn't it?"

"I lied to Brad at Prairie Winds Ballooning, conned the History Department's secretaries, and feigned curiosity in Professor Gulley's classes. I violated university policy when I persuaded Annie Curry to filch Bernard's folder. Hell, she could be disciplined, too." A moping Paul heard clip-clopping sandals on the wooden floor. 'Do You Wanna Dance' finished, and for the fourth time this afternoon 'Surfer Girl' dropped on the jukebox's spindle. "Cripes, I'm just looking for more excuses."

Summer Never Comes

Admiring his decency but frustrated with vacillation, Sharon wrapped an arm around Paul's waist.

> We could ride the surf together
> While our love would grow,
> In my Woody I would take you
> Everywhere I go.

# # # #

Associated Press – New Brunswick – The student general strike at Rutgers University became violent this afternoon as protest marches turned into a riot. At the start of the day, an estimated 6000 students and faculty assembled in Buccleugh Park, planning to cross the Raritan River to the Busch campus. They were confronted by New Jersey state troopers near Rutgers Stadium. Advancing through police barricades, the protesters were joined by additional anti-war groups converging from different directions, ambushing the troopers. 'Blatantly and brutally overreacting,' in the words of an observer, the police fought their way out, arresting 250 marchers in two hours. 60 protesters and 18 troopers were hospitalized. Leaders of the Campus Peace Crusade proclaimed this protest 'a triumph.'

Associated Press – University Park – After refusing to disband, a 'Rump People's Commissariat Peace Assembly' of 380 undergraduates and faculty were detained and jailed on the Penn State University campus. The arrests commenced when a crowd of 7000 protesters challenged Pennsylvania National Guardsmen and bombarded them with stones. One Molotov cocktail was reportedly ignited on the fringe of the riot. 25 protesters and 93 guardsmen were injured. The Nittany Radical Union denounced the arrests as 'a despicable usurpation of the Constitution and vile violations of free speech and assembly.'

Summer Never Comes

NBC News today reported rioting on 86 college campuses. All the incidents ended with arrests and casualties. As of this evening, martial law has been declared at 45 schools.

# # # #

"We resolutely denounce the imposition of a curfew over the Champaign-Urbana campus." Stef Tianen wrote in the *Daily Illini*. "This seditious, big-brother course of action by university and local civil authorities mocks our country's Bill of Rights and calls into question their lawful, moral authority.

"Granted, scores of schools have been arenas of confrontation, injuries and anarchy, with more on the rim of unrest. But as of this edition's press time, no lawlessness has occurred at the University of Illinois or in the Twin Cities. Restricting the movements of this campus' citizenry can only inflame ill will already harbored by the students—the consequences being not calm, but turmoil; not goodwill, but mistrust.

"This publication urges its readers to examine their consciences, deciding on their individual course to oppose this contemptible breach of our liberties."

# # # #

"The *News-Gazette's* editorial board has debated the rationale for a nighttime curfew in our cities. Limitations, though nominal, placed on citizens' freedoms are in the least dubious, at most dictatorial.

"It can be argued, however, that a nine o'clock curfew is a prudent precaution. In past years many college campuses, including the University of Illinois, have devolved into needless violence injurious to the community. By clearing Champaign-Urbana's streets by early evening, security will hopefully prevail. On this basis, we support the curfew's imposition.

"Further, it should be stressed that freedom of speech has not been banned nor right of assembly wholly outlawed. These liberties of a free society are available and unrestricted. We urge campus residents to exercise them in adult, intelligent ways, focusing on actual injustices, using their energies to correct these wrongs."

Summer Never Comes

# # # #

The old Auditorium was designed by alumnus Clarence H. Blackall and dedicated in 1907. During the university's early decades, it served as the main site for convocations, but the school's increasing enrollment eventually made the structure obsolete. These days most undergrads knew it as a weekend theater for the raucously popular midnight skin flicks. On Wednesday afternoon, as Bernard had informed Paul, the building would be the venue for UNITED's rally.

By 3:30, all 1936 seats were filled and students still jammed in, crowding the stage and packing the lobby. The overflow sat outside on the stone steps and the Quad's grass, listening to the rally via the public address speakers sited near the doorways. Replacing the stars and stripes, UNITED's orange and black banner flew from the old Auditorium's flagstaff.

Inside, Paul stood by the back rows and spotted the largest-yet UNITED flag draped over the movie screen behind the stage. Most undergrads wore orange and black and many waved tiny UNITED pennants. As at other anti-war rallies, Paul watched Randy Miller wiring the lectern's microphones. Precisely at four o'clock, similar to a film's start, the house lights dimmed, the would-be protesters in the audience clapped, and Leander Valent walked to the podium.

"Students, comrades in our community, combatants in the battle." He pronounced and the crowds applauded. "We meet today to confront our country's failing affairs of state. The Washington government, the cabal of evil, right-wing warmongers, has again escalated the combat in Southeast Asia, a needless struggle regarded lost many years ago, yet once more inflaming world tensions. These seditious felons do not learn from history, nor recognize the hazards their irresponsible, precipitate conflict risks. But we, the people, know; we are aware of the burdens, tragedies and brutality of Vietnam. This is why other universities have acted and reacted, other student bodies today revolt and riot. We, too, in Champaign-Urbana are near the tipping point. It is our turn, up to us in this Auditorium, on this campus, to validate with our lives, our solidarity with our comrades. We, members of UNITED, must lead our fellow students to battle the war."

Summer Never Comes

The ovation grew louder with many in the audience standing. Leander Valent nodded his head.

"END THE WAR!" The chant boomed in the Auditorium. "END WAR! END THE WAR!"

"All of you know of the rally on the Quad in two days' time."

Those inside heard the cheers from the students outdoors, and applauded in response.

"We trust and expect this greatest-ever demonstration, in step with insurgencies at other universities, will impel the finish of the war. March, participate, picket, protest, disagree, say no. Get and stay involved."

"END THE WAR! END THE WAR! END THE WAR!"

"It is my duty," Leander Valent declared after the bellowing subsided, "my pleasure to introduce our campus' foremost protest activist, the student who has diligently worked this entire school year to establish the anti-war movement that we are ready to exploit in the coming days. Comrades, the leader of UNITED, Bernard Minerath."

The crowds erupted again as Bernard stepped from the stage's wing. Paul watched Randy Miller offer to shake Bernard's hand and, as usual, Bernard ignored the gesture. Just as typical, Randy smiled and applauded.

As the clapping continued, a motionless Bernard stood at the podium. Even with humid summer temperatures, he wore his habitual corduroy pants and long-sleeve shirt. He peered at the crowd, neither turning his head nor acknowledging the ovation. Bernard pushed his hand through his straight hair as the cheering quieted.

"These are hard, wearing times, difficulties and misfortunes are forced on us. We stand in peril, a place not of our choice, but of other's designs. Once more, the Washington conspirators plunder and blunder as they resort to fixated, bigot-minded, hopeless schemes for Vietnam, plots and scenarios which have always, pathetically, fatally failed. The sorties into Haiphong harbor, the raids on North Vietnam's border, are this week's proofs of a worn out, deprecated foreign policy—years of shame, years of loss. The Washington chieftains, whoever they are and regardless of political party, have consistently lacked the vision to alter what has become the predictable path of war. Their response to any situation is the same; agony and misfortune instigated by themselves, but borne by others."

Summer Never Comes

"You tell 'em," someone in the audience howled, "crazy bastards the whole frickin' bunch."

"Now that is going to change." Bernard's fist hit the lectern and the crowds clapped. "Today we will beat back the tide of suffering and quash the cruelty which so long has been Washington's agenda. Today it is time to confront the war which is so terrible."

"END THE WAR! END THE WAR! END THE WAR!" Led by the True Believers, the students in the Auditorium shouted.

"END THE WAR! END THE WAR! END THE WAR!" The students outside answered.

"We, in UNITED," Bernard intoned, "call on the entire campus to demonstrate their anger, to protest the Vietnam conflict. Too long has the government been allowed to have their own way, to maim and kill, to play with the politics of wrong. Too long has the country been indifferent and uncaring. Too long have the powers in charge prolonged the slaughter. Too long have the people acquiesced, submitted and looked away. This senseless national policy must end. This capitalist dictatorship and their carnage must be stopped. We, the people, must rise up in revolution."

Everyone by their seats, in the aisles, on the stage, herded in back, were on their feet. The hundreds of miniature orange and black pennants fluttered in the air.

"UNITED to end the war!" Bernard shouted.

"UNITED TO END THE WAR!" The crowd in the Auditorium screamed.

"UNITED TO END THE WAR!" The protesters outside roared.

Bernard left the podium, his inspired, perspiring, psyched up followers rooting and hurrahing. Again he avoided Randy's outstretched hand.

Paul followed the scene from the old Auditorium's rear. None of the students, protesters, revelers, hangers-on or the True Believers cared to leave, everybody waiting for an encore. Like an Assembly Hall concert or a band performance at Chances R, the mobs yelled in unison. Amidst the fanatical hordes, Paul was shoved and jostled as he reviewed his notes on Bernard's speech, the rhetoric about the war's terribleness, ending the conflict and insurrection. Not once had Leander Valent or Bernard spoken the word "peace."

"END THE WAR! END THE WAR! END THE WAR!"

Summer Never Comes

\# \# \# \#

UPI – Hong Kong – Credible sources in this city report vessels of the Soviet Union's navy are steaming through the Hainan Straight and into the Gulf of Tonkin.

\# \# \# \#

An hour after curfew, another warm, windy evening, fifty or sixty KIDs killed time outside their house, milling on the grass, the front patio and the sidewalks. Technically the brothers were violating the law, but no one much cared. As college undergraduates, they childishly dreamed a warning, even an emergency curfew enforced by the towns' police and Illinois State Troopers, didn't apply to them. It was a regulation meant to be broken, the students' own gripe against authority. Besides, across Third Street, a few dozen Phi Mus clustered close to their front door; three coeds stood on the porch of the two-story frame house, Killer's girlfriend's home, neighboring the sorority; and at the corner of Third and Armory a tribe of Sammys, about the same in numbers as the KIDs, congregated on their lawn. The night took on a party atmosphere, with the undergrads rapping and laughing, a stereo blasting Kenny Loggins' 'Please Come to Boston,' and the whole crowd meandering toward the intersection. How could cops control two or three hundred students, anyway?

"Afraid of the dark? Go back to mommy!" The KIDS, led by the Mooser and 'Ralph,' mocked the Sammys.

"Go inside and shave your asses!" Their Jewish neighbors barked back, glad for some rowdiness.

"Sammys dates the ugliest broads on campus!"

"KIDs eat out rag dolls!"

"At least we screw women, not key holes!"

The hollering grew noisier, with Moose standing by the railing, shouting through an orange and blue megaphone, cheerleading the brothers. The fraternities traded rudenesses, with one side howling and waiting for a response, the other coming back with a grosser, crappier slur. Shaky Jake, Bat, Vic Extensionelli, Nemo, Paul, Lindy, 'Ragman,' Sleezy Parisi, Bobby Sox, Stu, along with Dave Kallman, Dudz, Gary Chlapaty, Mark Daniels,

Summer Never Comes

O'D, Haus, Ron Golden, Bernie Wysocki and Jerry Dudek, all roared, digging the hot night, the break from studying, the crowds' jovial vibes, and the high of law breaking. Two coeds from the frame house stepped off their porch to the curb for a better view; Paul thinking one was Chris White, Killer's Christmas party date. A stereo boomed 'Questions 67 and 68.'

"One, two, three, four! Who do we want to ball some more?"

"Who's your favorite bagel hole? Sammys!"

"Your mammy, your pappy, your greasy, greasy gran'daddy. I say loop th' loop, she's a prostitute! I say loop, up-side the head, I say loop up-side the head! Ooga-booga-booga."

"Eat me, then whack off!"

"It'd be the juiciest piece you ever licked!"

"Let's eat out the Phi Mus!"

"Go stick those slimy rubbers on your ears."

Once or twice the hell-raisers heard revving car engines from a block or two away, unnerving some because the police could be patrolling, enforcing the curfew, which would be a bad scene. But the dangers didn't materialize, and by the sixth or seventh scare the whooping, bellowing, having-a-maniac-time undergrads ignored the noises.

"Who's your favorite chocolate bar?"

"KIDs fondles moldy dogs!"

"Sammys munches dead rats!"

"Two, four, six, eight," the Phi Mus howled at the guys, "go lay down and masturbate!"

Around 10:15, after forty-five minutes of childishness, ridiculousness and disgustingness, with the Supremes and Thunderclap Newman blaring from the stereos, a Ford Fairlane slowly cruised through the mobs and parked on Third Street, two car lengths north of KIDs, near the frame house. The brothers noticed the passengers were students, then disregarded the newcomers as the Sammys shrieked.

"De roof, de roof, de roof is on fire! De roof, de roof, de roof is on fire! We don't need no water let that ugly mother burn!"

And hell cut loose.

Catastrophe's harbinger was the Sammys wildly abandoning the sidewalks and herding to their house. Next, the Phi Mus panicked, fleeing through their front gate, every girl jockeying to squeeze in ahead of her sorority sisters. Then Moose and 'Ralph', spotting the Sammys' and the Mus' retreats, dropped from the railing and scrambled for the door with the nearest KIDs trailing behind.

"HOLY SHIT, THE COPS!"

Red lights flashing, horns blaring, six or seven squad cars caromed around the corner, slamming on the brakes in front of KIDs, a dozen policemen jumping out to storm the fraternity. The brothers stampeded for the doors, some laughing but most comprehending how screwed they suddenly were. Inside, still feeling defenseless, they sprinted upstairs to the supposed safety their second, third and fourth floor rooms allowed from arrest and jail. The last into the house, Orion, Jake and Tim Malito, locked the heavy oak doors a moment before the officers rushed the entrance. The only KIDs in the living room, these three heard the cops' night sticks beating outside, making a harder-than-half attempt to break through.

"What if they get in?" Orion bawled, his whole body trembling.

Upstairs, Paul and his frightened, crapping-on-the-carpet pals peered out of their darkened rooms as the police marched away from the fraternity and towards the street. All the other students that had surrounded the intersection escaped to their houses at the same time as the KIDs, all except one of Chris' friends from the little frame house. Instead of bolting she held her place, no one grasped why, ragging the officers.

"Thugs! Fascists! Who the hell do you think you are, pissing on us! Capitalists' Stooges! Brown Shirts! We've got our rights! Nazi pigs! Go back to the fucking jailhouse and lock yourselves up! Gestapo turd heads!"

As Paul and the freaking out KIDs watched, one policeman reacted. He lunged at the girl, gained momentum and raised a riot stick above his head, ready to smash downward. The coed, in the nick of time realizing the risk, fled to her house. As she ran, blinking lights, Paul thought they were flashbulbs, popped from the parked Ford Fairlane. As he looked back toward the frame house, the girl slipped in the mud with the policeman, club raised, closing on her. In an instant she was up, jumped for the porch and tumbled inside, Chris slamming the door shut. The cop lowered his stick and trooped back to the street.

"Jesus Christ."

Summer Never Comes

"They mean business tonight." Lindy hid behind the drape. As his buddies looked from the window, the Fairlane's engine turned over and the car drove away before the police could investigate.

> Call out the instigators,
> Because there's something in the air.
> We've got to get together sooner or later,
> Because the revolution's here.
> And you know that it's right.

# # # #

Nothing much happened around Assembly Hall this sultry evening. Due to the curfew, even the normally light nighttime traffic on Florida Avenue was missing and, surrounded by empty parking lots, the building stood alone, the lobby lights shining out, but not grabbing the misty, white, protecting blanket Paul imagined a week earlier. It looked forgotten, and a student would assume any disorderliness would surely occur somewhere else on the campus.

Without warning, the structure's isolation ended. A dozen rusty, clunking cars, their rear axles riding low to the road, motored through the parking lot's Fourth Street entrance. Unlike the screeching squads at KIDs, these autos unhurriedly stopped close to Assembly Hall before stopping. The passengers, a majority wearing orange and black shirts, leisurely stepped from the cars, as if owning reserved Section A concert tickets instead of trespassing on university property after curfew. These juveniles were on their own with the building, satisfied the police were upholding the law and hounding rowdy undergrads elsewhere in Champaign-Urbana.

The group gathered around a thin fellow wearing corduroys and a long sleeve shirt, instructing and pointing to Assembly Hall. Disbanding, his comrades trooped to their cars and opened the trunks, which were jam-packed with fist-sized stones. Each grabbed an armful, marched away from the caravan and circled the building. As Bernard watched, the True Believers hurled their rocks at the glass walls, breaking scores and hundreds of windows above and below the walkway. For twenty minutes, as the stones crashed the glass, the huge, shattering panes exploded in tons of noise. Any

Summer Never Comes

anarchists who hurled all their ammunition heaved extra rocks from the handy supplies piled on the ground around the shade trees. When the eight hundred-odd panes were demolished, the vandals strolled back to Bernard and the cars and drove off.

After midnight, the Ford Fairlane cruised through Champaign, parking next to the *News-Gazette's* property on Market Street. The driver, having visited a few days ago and familiar with this location, walked straight to the service door. In ten minutes, he exited the building and sped away. A quarter hour later, a fire ignited in the *News-Gazette's* lot, burning through a garbage dumpster. After scorching a delivery truck always parked in the same spot, the flames died down.

The next morning, Wally Byam and fellow *News-Gazette* employees were stunned the damage wasn't worse. A Champaign Fire Department inspector set them straight. Whoever lit the blaze wanted to do only so much damage, he reported, the arsonist knew his trade.

Chapter Eighteen

"Wall, 'if'n it isn't Mist-eh Roberts, might-eh early foh yohr kind t'be out of th' rack."

"Too warm upstairs for sleep, I thought it might be cooler down here. How about you?" Paul and his friend were the only KIDs in the living room.

"T' tell th' truth, Ah was jus' settin' heah thinkin' foh a spell, before th' broth-ehs disturb th' peace."

"Seems that's a common topic these days."

"Ex-cuse me?"

"Breaking the peace, as in the riot last night." He grabbed one of a half-dozen *Daily Illini's* lying on the table.

"Mah feel-in's ahr there's a whole lot mohr a-comin'."

Reading the lead story, Paul didn't answer.

"In the largest-ever act of vandalism in Champaign-Urbana history, Assembly Hall was the site of a massive stone throwing attack Wednesday night, with an estimated 95% of the building's lobby windows broken. No unusual activity was detected in the area until a two a. m. telephone message to the campus police reported the rampage. The anonymous caller claimed responsibility, pronouncing Assembly Hall's destruction 'a demonstration of the wasteful carnage and plundering plaguing the Vietnamese people.'"

"Have you seen this?"

"Ah did, Robbeh, a true shame." Kentucky sounded gloomy. "Our geneh-ra-shun is not turnin' out as ex-pected. Seems thet we have forgotten why we-all ahr heah in school."

"For sure." As glum as his fraternity brother, Paul flipped through the paper, stunned when he found UNITED's advertisement on page three.

"BRUTALITY ON CAMPUS!

Summer Never Comes

"THE VIOLENCE of Vietnam SPREADS!

"THE BATTLES come to Champaign-Urbana!

"STUDENTS!

"WE MUST NOT allow the establishment's LAWLESSNESS to beat us, BATTER us, grind us into the ground! FACISM must be RESISTED!

"ON FRIDAY NIGHT, join your COMRADES on the Quad to MOBILIZE AGAINST authority's ANARCHY!

"UNITED TO END THE WAR!"

Accompanying the ad was a photo of last night's scene at the little frame house on Third Street. The picture showed the girl lying on the grass, gazing toward her porch, and the state trooper in mid-stride, his night stick raised. With the camera angle, the rabble-rousing tenor of UNITED's copy and a reader's imagination, in the next instant the club would slam into the coed's head.

Paul couldn't comprehend how UNITED worked so fast to fabricate a controversy from a happening not twelve hours old. Sitting on the couch, he remembered the squad cars' revving engines, the parked Fairlane and the flashbulbs, someone snapping pictures. Fluke, chance, could the peace protesters be so lucky? Impossible, Bernard and his hoodlums were ready, the night was a setup. UNITED schemed to have the girl waiting for the cops to show, just as they'd alerted the police to the KIDs-Sammys-Phi Mus yelling match.

"Hello, Paul," Scooter rushed by carrying his notebooks, "first time this semester I've seen you awake so early."

"Too hot, couldn't rack," he replied.

"The benefit of springtime eight o'clocks, beating the heat." Scooter hurried towards the dining room and Thursday's morning's regular breakfast, cold cereal, juice and coffee. More brothers followed and Paul glanced around the living room, finding Kentucky gone without a goodbye.

"There you are, Robby," Lindy semi-tumbled down the stairway, "how about headin' to the Union for bacon and eggs, the breakfast of champions?"

"Good idea."

The closer the pair hiked to the Quad the more orange and black they spotted. Paul guessed half the students wore 'UNITED to END the WAR!' t-shirts, the Wright Street sororities plus the YMCA draped orange and

Summer Never Comes

black flags above their front doors, and motivated undergrads had glued jumbo, black letters in six of Lincoln Hall's second floor windows, spelling 'U-N-T-I-E-D.'

"There's an oops."

"Do you suppose the school colors have been replaced?"

"Could be, but I thought a student referendum was required."

"There's other ways to vote than paper ballots, all kinds of means to influence an outcome." Lindy sounded serious, then switched to astonished. "Whoa, check it out! This is what I call a student body!"

Hundreds and hundreds of undergrads trooped around the Quad's sidewalks, so many that the parade looked like a solid, but moving barricade concealing the lawn. Passing the English Building, Greg Hall and the old Auditorium, near Foreign Languages and Davenport, in front of the Union and the Administration Building, the procession orbited in a counterclockwise direction at the cadence of a funeral. Some marchers spoke in whispers, scores held hands, most wore orange and black or carried posters.

"UNITED FOREVER!"

"STOP THE WAR!"

"END VIETNAM!"

"SHUT DOWN AMERICA!"

Like Paul and Lindy, new arrivals confronting the blockade, sympathetic with the protesters or reluctant to travel solo across the Quad, joined in for at least a partial lap.

"How long have you been out here?" Paul inquired.

"About forty-five minutes, better than sitting in my nine o'clock physics lab." A nearby few laughed and one marcher hurrahed. "Anyway, this is real world, we're makin' a difference."

"Think on it, by afternoon the whole campus could be trampin' around the old Quad." This student wore the basic t-shirt, cut-offs and sandals. "I hear UNITED has runners headin' to the dorms to get everyone turnin' out for our circle. They want it to last all night, until tomorrow's rally."

"We can do it, the weather's supposed to stay toasty and there's enough campus crazies to demonstrate another thirty-six hours."

"Bernard'll figure out how to fetch people here if he wants to."

"Yeah, yeah, yeah."

Summer Never Comes

When the loop reached the Union's south steps, Paul and Lindy pulled out of line, their places snagged by five coeds.

"Come on back!" a True Believer yelled.

"You know it," Lindy agreed. Compared to the crowded Quad the Union was deserted, with hardly any students walking the hallways or snoozing in the lounges. "Impressive, Robby, don't you think? Who'd ever come up with a bolt from the blue like that, continuously protesting by constantly circling? I never thought I'd see that many Big U students so wide-awake this early in the morning. What a gem."

"It was okay, I guess," Paul was noncommittal as they stepped downstairs to the Cafeteria.

"That's your only comment, ho hum, lah-ti-dah? For a guy who's researched this peace movement thing all year you don't seem overly thrilled with what's suddenly goin' down this week. I'd of figured you'd be in your element, all over Cham-Bana interviewing, investigatin' and interrogating."

"I'm excited, but also scared as hell, right down to my sandals. What if there's a problem? What if this deal on the Quad, a mob of undergrads appearing from thin air, isn't so spontaneous as it appears? What if someone's pushing buttons and following a written script? What if it's fake, a fraud, the stuff about the peace movement, the protesters, UNITED," Paul followed his logic, "the war?"

"As in phony?" Lindy looked confused. "The student bodies we just saw outside? Hocus pocus? The fightin' and crap we watch on the tube, the politician's bullshit? We're smokin' some bad grass, Billy Powell isn't trapped in the army?"

"No, we're not hallucinating, Vietnam's casualties and dying exist, and Billy's stuck in the jungle. I'm saying the peace movement's rationale is a sham. They're not the idealists we think and their primary concern is not stopping the war, it's their purpose to keep it going."

"Hold your horses. Everything we've been through since '65 shows the war's a senseless abomination and the idiots prolonging it, our government, are pretty much criminal. Hundreds of millions of dollars wasted, destroyed villages, people burned out of their homes, thousands of dead American soldiers, riots here in the US of A, the Chi-Town convention and the assassinations. For anyone to purchase a carte blanche for more is warped."

Summer Never Comes

The two entered the serving line, each grabbing a tray, napkin and silverware. "Who'd be mindless enough not to need peace?"

"Instead of wanting the war ended, perhaps their objectives are more sinister. Chaos, anarchy, disorder."

"Seems we're practiced at keepin' the pot boilin' by ourselves, without anyone else's help."

"Maybe some of us are some of them."

"Of what, Robby, who? I'm not glimpsin' any daylight in this conversation."

"Dissidents hating America, radicals who need to see us taken down and destroyed. Subversives who detest our country. Communists."

"A bunch of Reds, like Khrushchev and Mao, on the campus? Revolution in the land of Lincoln? That'd be a real scoop for any newspaperman. Can you prove this?"

"Think back to the picture of the girl and the policeman in this morning's *Daily Illini*. She accidentally happened to be in her yard when by chance the cops were in the street and someone in a parked car with a camera just managed to take a photo. How did each of them know where to be at exactly the same time?"

"Coincidence?"

"Absolutely not, more a conspiracy with someone at the controls." Paul was unequivocal as the two sat at a table with their breakfasts. "And the Assembly Hall attack. Before last night riots around here were college pranks, impulsive, one hothead, too much beer and a few stones, like the Campustown looting the last couple of years. Shattering all of Assembly Hall's windows is the reverse. Finding the people, supplying rocks, loading however many cars were used and navigating a route to avoid the police. Organization, manipulation—traits your basic undergrad's inept at but constants describing to the max a particular Champaign-Urbana ringleader. On top of the radicals' feats the last few days, have you noticed changes in their language? Bernard Minerath and UNITED have abandoned the talk about 'peace,' and now preach 'fighting the war,' 'redirecting cruelty.' Strange phrases for hippies, I'd say. How many world problems can be solved with a militant attitude like that?"

"Are you claimin' UNITED's behind this stuff, they're the Commies?"

"The protests and lawlessness meld into a plan, to decoy students into their web. What we watched out our windows last night, the damage at Assembly Hall and this morning's *DI* convinces me. UNITED's objective is not ending the war and bringing peace. They're exploiting us as pawns to destroy our campus and other schools around the country. The anti-war faction wants disaster."

"This story I've seen you working on, is that what you're gonna explain; there's problems with the peace movement and we better double-check to see who's right?"

"The article's finished, detailing everything I've uncovered about UNITED for the whole school year—conferences and relationships between the militants, their responsibilities, who was hurt, the liars and deceivers, what wasn't the truth. Reworking the piece to add the last two days won't take long, I'd wrap it up in an hour at most. But I'm hesitant."

"Of what?"

"Whether I should submit it to my editor. I'm not sure I want to interfere."

"That makes no sense, Robby. What good are written words on sheets of paper if you won't let anybody read them? If you're convinced you're right, shouldn't you speak out?"

"Maybe acting isn't so simple. Think about last night's shouting match with the Sammys. We were out for jollies but our goofing off, along with the photograph, boomeranged into the *Daily Illini*. What else is UNITED plotting? Should I hand them the pretext for whatever's coming next? If my story's published, everybody's outraged, the peace movement's discredited and possibly the whole campus explodes. Maybe that's what the subversives want, excuses for their revolution." Paul toyed with his breakfast. "Besides, in a week this may blow over."

"And perhaps what's required is the coin's other side, an extra voice saying, 'whoa partners, hold your horses, let's not jump ship just yet, let's reconsider.' And that's you. With your snoopin' and research, the facts and figures, that's the different perspective."

"What if I'm wrong?"

"You didn't sound off the mark two minutes ago; you were convinced you had the answers. If you've nailed the evidence for a reasonable, logical conclusion, that's the ballgame."

Summer Never Comes

"It's mostly circumstantial."

"Enough, Robby. Christ, I don't understand!" Lindy's tone swung from supportive to irritated. "You accuse the peaceniks of bein' conspiracy-plotting Communists, jerkin' us around to overthrow the campus along with the country. And you've uncovered hard, fast proof. But that's not good enough because you, Paul Roberts, execute your u-turn and claim the evidence is insufficient and you don't want to make trouble. What crap. You've pored over this for six months, so like it or not, you're in this thing; this is your time to take a stand."

Lindy was worked up, and Paul worried his roommate's temper would ignite right in front of the students in the Cafeteria. God, that would be disastrous.

"Remember last fall's New Student Week, when we walked on the Quad and our conversation about our generation making things better? One of us concocted a line about savin' the world with my guitar. With everything that's gone down for me since then I haven't thought over it too much, except now, with you and your story. I'm not claiming this is the biggest-ever make-or-break time for you or our campus, and I'll wager you'll have more tight spots to face in your future, but this is a herald for what's to come. I admit the soapbox I'm sermonizing from is rickey-tickey; my track record for decisions has been awful, with my mistakes hurting more people than just me. But one thing I'm clear on is doing nothing resolves nothing. It's wrong thinkin' you can hide, especially when you're withholding information that makes a difference. Walking away from what you're convinced is true is a mistake. Rationalizing may be the easy exit today, but tomorrow, next month, someday when you're sittin' with Sharon in Second Chance sipping a beer, you'll have a clearer perception, your scruples will kick in and you'll regret sitting on your hands. It comes down to responsibility, what's right, honesty or deceiving yourself."

"Maybe…I don't want to get involved."

A student at the next table walked away, leaving a copy of the *Champaign News-Gazette*. Paul read the headline.

"ARSONIST SETS FIRE AT PAPER'S OFFICE."

# # # #

Summer Never Comes

Associated Press – Washington – The Defense Department reports that the blockade of Haiphong is tightening. Air sorties from the carriers *Kitty Hawk* and *Coral Sea* have bombed harbor, docking facilities and petroleum storage areas. Naval spokesmen now confirm reports that vessels of the Soviet Far Eastern fleet have been tracked steaming toward North Vietnam.

Reuters – Hanoi – The North Vietnamese Defense Ministry claims 27 merchant vessels have been damaged or sunk in Haiphong harbor in the last 72 hours. A spokesman again denounced these 'contemptible naval atrocities. Revenge for these piratical acts will be harshly meted out.'

# # # #

No breeze, a cloudless sky and by two o'clock the temperature rose to the mid-eighties—a record high for the day. Despite this super weather, hardly any students played in Frat Park, most having gone to circle the Quad with the protesters or, as Ozark nicknamed it at lunch, "scoop the U."

Moose was the only KID on the patio. With two cases of Old Style and a table and chair from the living room, he prepared for the chug team tryouts, gulping down twelve-ouncers as near to contest conditions as he could recollect. (As in previous springs, Moose was the all-house choice for swing man.)

"Hey, pal, whatcha up to?"

"Practicing." Moose frowned when he discovered who the voice was. "How 'bout you?"

"Not much, just figured I'd soak-up some rays this afternoon." A smirking Dale Kinsey strolled toward his fraternity brother and the beer cases.

"Suppose there's no law against that." Ignoring the interruption, Moose hunched over the table with two full beer cups close to his mouth.

"How's your time?" Dale faked his cordial-est, kissy-ass voice and counted thirty-two unopened bottles.

"A little slow," Moose peered at the table, much preferring his brews to Kinsey, "but there's a couple weeks to improve."

Summer Never Comes

"For sure, the chug contest isn't 'til next month." He kicked the cases. "Gonna drink these by yourself?"

"It's what I'm planning, since nobody else is out here."

"Don't you think the bottles'll warm up?"

"Nope." Moose wrapped his hands around both glasses and licked his lips. With a quick wrist snap, one cup jerked to his face, instantly slamming back to the table's surface. As Dale watched, the second went up and down just as swift.

"All right."

"That was more like it." The Mooser slumped in the chair, waiting to burp.

"I'll say." Dale stooped over to reach into a case.

"Get your goddamned paws away from my Old Styles."

"C'mon, I'll pay you back this weekend at the Lion."

"Like hell you will, Kinsey. I ain't never seen you buy a beer for anyone yet, 'cept for passin' around the freebies the Jerg sneaks us."

"How about only one?"

"Get bit."

"Okay, okay," Dale theatrically preached, "some friend you are."

Moose belched and decided this was as decent a moment as any to protect his cases. "You don't know jack about what the word means, you frickin' swine."

"Be that way, asshole, but I can get even with nimrods like you, I've done it before. You're not so tough you can't get taken down. I own all the tricks."

"Don't think so. Everybody's aware you screwed Lindy's band, just like all of us know the disgusting way that rat-turd toady Tommy Quarters manhandled Emily Ritter. The house is on to you, even the fourth floor despoes, and you're not scrapin' through any more shit. You've had it, Kinsey, at the end, finished. If you don't cause no more trouble, stay in your room and only play with your stereo and yourself, you may not be blackballed outta the fraternity. But if you jerk around anymore, or dump on any of our buddies, or hassle any pals of our pals, it's all she wrote—you're out on the street." He reached for two bottles. "If you survive the toss."

Dale left the patio, retreating into KIDs, resolving revenge.

Summer Never Comes

# # # #

In the afternoon, Paul cut his classes and wandered the campus.

"Maybe I don't want to get involved," he'd claimed in the Cafeteria, nearly expecting his roommate to spin somersaults.

To Lindy, plowing ahead, acting, choosing a fork in any road was clear-cut. If you chart your course, sail ahead—don't debate or mimic a stick in the mud. Focus on black and white, not grays; make up your mind, decide; don't hesitate and keep at it; any setbacks you stumble into, work 'em out, if you fail, try something new. Paul rejected that thinking. A pipedream, foolish decisions—one rash judgment could lead to hassles, problems, unknowns. Reels unraveling, Lindy might opine, ropes fraying. And his roommate would know. His stubbornness jamming with Frogfeet all those months caused him to screw up his grade point, get busted and terribly wound Emily. A pitiable record, tough envisioning in September, but written history by March.

Sometimes the dependable path was none at all. Mull it over, dawdle, deliberate a bit more, withdraw. Sure, hiding wasn't exciting and maybe you missed opportunities, but at least inaction was a safe play. Roll with the punch, turn your head, close your eyes, hold your breath when the wave washes in and you won't sink.

At the edge of the Quad, Paul sat under a tree, one of scores of loitering students taking in the protest. There were more walkers and True Believers in the circle now, followers trailing the students in front of them, everybody keeping in place, sticking to the course, adherents accepting where they were heading, no problem figuring out a direction to go. Bernard is probably pleased.

What would be the big deal if I keep quiet about UNITED? No one else knows the stuff I do, at least not the details. Al Stojak, Sharon and Lindy are the only ones I've told. They can't splice the story together, just complain I surrendered. So what? I can manage the bitching my friends toss at me. Are they so perfect, particularly my roommate? And the protest will work out. This is the University of Illinois, the middle-of-the-road Midwest, not left-wing Columbia, radical Berkley or sorrowing Kent State. There won't be any problems if my mouth stays shut. That's what I'll do, cop out, rewrite the story to give Stef what she expects for the *Daily Illini*. Sheltered, secluded, secure.

But what of honesty?

# # # #

"Hi."

"Paul, my dear, a sweet surprise, long time between visits," Sharon greeted him. "I missed our Wednesday morning wake-up yesterday. I'm getting so I don't enjoy sleeping alone through a whole week."

"Three days since our last, I want it, too."

"If we're both horny, there's a fix." She smiled as the pair walked into the living room. "Have you listened to the radio? Sorry to say, the curfew's moved up—switched from nine to eight."

"Which is a glitch for our romancing and tomorrow's rally, its starting time is scheduled for 7:30. Could be why the police revised the hour."

"I don't think they worry over when we jump into bed," Sharon good naturedly misdirected and massaged her boyfriend's arm. "Are the Commerce College job interviews on schedule?"

"No hang-up with that, there are events even UNITED can't manipulate. Mine are next Tuesday and Wednesday." Paul rubbed his eyes, daydreaming of a matinee lay with his girlfriend but reckoning there was too little time this afternoon. "Lindy and I had a talk. I explained my UNITED story to him."

"Your roommate find the narrative interesting?"

"Sure did, especially after last night's attack on Assembly Hall and this morning's phony picture in the *Daily Illini*."

"You mean the girl and the policeman? The snapshot looked genuine to me."

"That happened across the street from KIDs. Ten minutes before the skirmishing, a car drove up and parked next to our house. When the state trooper hounded the girl back to her porch, someone in the auto was ready with a camera and took the pictures. Undoubtedly a setup and more proof of the conspiracy." Paul stared at the cold fireplace. "I wonder how far it's stretched?"

"What did Lindy recommend?"

"I should see my article printed to bring the facts into the open."

"Sounds right to me. Will you take his advice?"

"No," He thoughtfully answered. "I know what you're going to say, a mistake. But I've reasoned this out and think there'll be fewer headaches if no one learns about the actual UNITED."

"Is that your criterion, the easiest course is the best?" Sharon tapped her fingers on the sofa. "You can't decide that way."

"Why not? It works for a lot of people."

"Who hedge and never accomplish a thing." She was mad. "You're always the same—sloughing the tough calls, hoping they'll vanish. It hasn't made much difference so far, since you've only been concerned with your own, lonely, solitary life. But right now, in this instant, on our campus, the circumstances are critical. With your reporting for the *DI* you've earned a chance—no, that's inaccurate—you're responsible for countless fellow students. Your actions will affect events, and persuade others—many of them your friends."

"Which is the reason I'll embargo the story. I shouldn't be accountable; let them make up their own minds."

"They're not privy to the facts you possess. You're concealing information, in a manner allowing students to go with the allegedly on-the-right-side, so-called sincere UNITED," she again spoke in a blunt tone, "since Bernard's gang is their sole choice."

"I disagree; we're all grown-ups here, at least eighteen or twenty years' worth. Individuals decide for themselves; that's what college is for, isn't it, doing your own thing?"

"If you were a lowly freshman only reading the *Daily Illini* and rapping with other students in the dorms, would you be out on the Quad right now?"

Paul peered straight ahead, arms folded across his chest.

Sharon shook her head. "Okay, another approach. With your information about UNITED and Bernard, are you attending the rally tomorrow night and breaking the curfew?"

"No, because Bernard is in the wrong. He's not interested seeing the war ended with peace taking its place."

"Progress, first-rate. Now, how do you expect other students on our campus to arrive at the same rationale?"

Summer Never Comes

"That's their problem."

"No, it's yours." Her voice was loud; Paul never having known her so angry. "Months ago you started researching this story and stumbled on incongruities—evidence that bad guys are stirring up trouble for our campus. The next step, the responsible course and your obligation, is to do something about it. Search your conscience, you can't concede to the criminals. You know too much; you're too tangled in events."

"I'm not caught; I would be if I printed the article, but I won't. I don't want to get involved." Paul realized this was the second time today he'd retreated.

"All right, have it your way. I only hope you can live with yourself."

Paul glanced at his girlfriend. Fuming, she had moved away from him and sat on the couch's opposite side. He stood to leave.

"See you later."

# # # #

As ever in life, decisions fall to individuals.

Paul drifted from Sharon's house, not knowing where to go. He shied away from KIDs, afraid of meeting Lindy or someone else who'd scold him and argue to reconsider. Wishing to hide, he wandered in Urbana, avoiding the Quad, the protesters and his friends, eventually turning toward Memorial Stadium. Walking east on Pennsylvania Avenue, Paul passed Mount Hope Cemetery and, above the leafless branches, observed the empty Memorial Stadium. As it was March, with football season six months away, the game-day pennants that flew on the balcony's flagpoles weren't out, a tiny detail leaving the stadium less colorful.

Why were Sharon and Lindy upset? It was his option, not theirs, to print or suppress his story. Paul understood Sharon's mind, she was with him at the beginning of his investigation, knew many particulars and had guessed their consequences. Now, a semester later, he was wasting his work. That was the crux of Sharon's anger.

His roommate was curious-er, unaware of the time Paul had devoted the last months, and unacquainted with Bernard until this morning. What gives? When Lindy discussed Vietnam, his attitude always was how wasteful the thousands and thousands deaths; how he hated thinking of Billy Powell in the jungles; that we knew who to blame for this stupidity and who wanted to stop it. Why did his roommate insist a report contradicting his own feelings be published?

Paul reached Fourth Street. The stadium was in front of him, the sun dropping behind the balcony. He headed south, looked at the cemetery and smiled, wondering if Bob Zuppke was buried in line with the field's fifty-yard marker, need to check that out before graduation. Paul peered ahead and saw the wrecked Assembly Hall. Flatbeds, delivery vans, scaffolding and two cranes surrounded the structure, with a repair crew cutting, hauling and bolting plywood over the broken panes. Before last night, the glass glared in the sun, so blinding Paul and his buddies couldn't stare directly at the walls. Today, with panels covering the holes where windows should be, Assembly Hall was another dull building, like Memorial Stadium without the flags. Destroying something so excellent was senseless. How could this crime happen? Why were people so malicious, why should they get away with it?

This is his friends' message.

When the question is good or evil, every person should side with truth. A no brainer. But not all thought this way, as he'd uncovered these past months.

Paul neared Assembly Hall. One police car guarded the workers and the building.

Resolving comes back to the individual. A person can solicit advice, listen to arguments, debate pluses and minuses. Yet, finally, in the end, no one else chooses. Whatever happens, whichever way you search, you have to make up your own mind. You must act.

Paul turned before reaching the squad car. This wasn't the day to walk into trouble.

# # # #

On the Quad, a spectator sitting under the tree where Paul had relaxed would not find uncertainty. Since morning, hundreds and hundreds more students had joined the protest circle. The sidewalks were crammed with undergraduates, grad students and faculty. In some spots, too many marchers overlapped the concrete and people tramped on the grass, clots in the oval. The True Believers, even instructors and professors, wore

Summer Never Comes

UNITED's orange and black shirts, and the morning's few signs and posters had multiplied into neatly-printed placards, with identical messages.

"DOWN WITH THE WAR!"
"DOWN WITH THE COUNTRY!"
"DOWN WITH SOCIETY!"
"GET DOWN TO THE END!"

For all the students parading around the perimeter, the Quad's middle was abandoned. On ordinary spring afternoons the grass would be filled with frisbees, guitars, marijuana and lovemaking. But today not a single strummed chord, no emptied beer cans, burning joints or couples humping under blankets were out there. The lawn and sunshine were off-limits. The only way to cross the Quad, say from the Administration Building to Davenport Hall, was joining UNITED's oval, which is what everyone did. No student wished to oppose this crowd, today's irresistible majority on campus.

Another particular a spectator would notice was the mood. Early on the marchers were impulsive, friendly, shouting at passersby to 'scoop a loop,' and there was, as Paul and Lindy had joined into, much spontaneous, cheerful conversation. By mid-afternoon, this party humor faded. As UNITED's shirts and placards took charge, the circle turned sullen—the real reason for being here understood. Friends still chatted amongst themselves and a few couples held hands, but not many. Protest was resolute work and the marchers accepted this.

As sunset approached, hungry undergrads left for supper and the circle thinned. By 6:30, more demonstrators departed and only True Believers wanted to stay to test the police curfew. The hard-cores, the Randy Millers, kept at it.

At 7:45, the Campus Police trooped from the walkway between the Union and Altgeld Hall. The officers spread in a picket line across the Quad, steadily shoving the protesters off the sidewalks, yard by yard herding them south past the English Building, retaking the campus for law and order.

As the oval cracked, the remaining True Believers booed the police. The students scattered to Champaign and Urbana, most hiking to their dorms but some sneaking over to Kam's, Whitt's End and Treno's, hoping the eight o'clock curfew excluded the bars.

Chapter Nineteen

Reuters – Saigon – United States and South Vietnamese troops today counterattacked in the Bien Hien theater. 'This is our primary military effort against the Communist forces which have been on the offensive for the last two weeks,' a Defense Department spokesman stated. Initial reports from the battle area describe the fighting as 'unrelenting and vicious, with mounting casualties on both sides.'

Associated Press – Washington – Naval air reconnaissance confirms vessels of the Soviet Union's Far Eastern Fleet steaming off Haiphong harbor. The Russian ships remain out of visual contact of American surface units, are not maneuvering to enter the port or initiating any actions to interfere with the Seventh Fleet's blockade of North Vietnam.

# # # #

"POLICE SMASH PEACEFUL PROTEST ON THE QUAD!

"Fellow Students! Once more Our Rights are TRAMPLED! Again, the Police-State, which previously was Our Campus, has USURPED Our Freedoms!

"Last night, the Pigs in Uniforms maliciously SHATTERED the Cadres of Our Comrade Students wishing to carry on the Circle of Protest so Nobly begun on Thursday morning!

"These Gestapo Tactics cannot be permitted to ESCALATE in Our Community!

"Come together, TODAY, on the Quad to PROTEST this BLATANT Fascist Coup!

Summer Never Comes

"JOIN the Rally tonight!
"UNITED TO END THE WAR!"

# # # #

"Robby, you up?" Lindy shook his roommate's bunk. "God, the heat, absolutely another toaster!"

"For sure." Paul watched the curtains sway with the wind. "Going to any classes?"

"Think so. I've been on a roll lately, no sense screwin' up." Lindy had become a model student the last few weeks, attending classes, booking nightly and cramming for his hourlies. "What's your program today?"

"Don't know, because of the protesting I'm fairly positive my nine o'clock's canceled, that's all I've got on Fridays. Maybe I'll stay in the rack."

"Too tropical for that, buddy. Besides, the big rally's tonight, you wouldn't want to plug in the fan and miss the action, keep in your character, so to speak?" Lindy grabbed both bedposts. "Sorry, I didn't intend to resurrect yesterday's face-off."

"Sharon and I discussed my predicament, too. We finished the same way you and I did."

"The love of your life couldn't unpadlock your mind, hey?"

"No, but after leaving her house I walked the long way back to Champaign, past the cemetery and Memorial Stadium, to Assembly Hall. What a depressing sight, cranes and dumpsters, plywood covering the windows, a hell of a disaster. The police need to catch those criminals."

"Expressly Bobby Sox's sentiments. He drove by the place last afternoon and was totally disgusted, said the setting reminded him of a giant, round lumberyard after a thunderstorm, with trash and sheathing scattered over the parking lots. Pissed him off, people turning into such total a-holes."

"That's why I'm submitting my story. Whoever wrecked Assembly Hall ought to be prosecuted. What happened two days ago can't be allowed, our generation is wiser. The issue isn't someone like me sidestepping, but doing what's right and honest." Paul spoke with moderate, partial, semi-conviction, but sounded resolute enough to his roommate. He sat at his desk in his u-trow.

Summer Never Comes

"So Assembly Hall closed the bargain, not yours truly or even your Sharon."

"The University of Illinois's my weak spot; forever a sucker for Champaign-Urbana. As students we benefit from the school's assets, our responsibility is to protect, not ruin this place, and ensure higher education is around for the generations after us."

"'To thy happy children of the future, those of the past send greetings.' Far out, I'm proud of you." Lindy stepped over to his roommate and rubbed Paul's head. "When will the *Daily Illini* print your article?'"

"Hopefully tomorrow, if I hustle and talk to Stef this morning."

"You're sayin' you haven't handed it in, and no one sees it before today's rally?"

"I didn't decide until last night. Besides, my work's not earth-shattering; on paper the story reads boring, five months of details, possibly a yawner."

"Your countering arguments will warn the students. That piece needs to be seen." Lindy grabbed his towel and soap from the closet. "Shake your ass outta that chair, suddenly this is a huge day."

# # # #

Burning sun, sizzling temperatures, miserable humidity—and year-round Cham-Bana residents described Friday's weather "like shadeless soybean fields in July." Only a breeze made the morning endurable, a strong southwest wind lobbing the KIDs' drapes away from windows, tossing in dust. For the fifth or sixth straight day, guys went shirtless and shoeless, the women walked the campus braless and, with the university's air conditioning systems offline this early in the spring, a majority of undergrads sensibly kept cool by cutting classes.

With summertime in March and excitement mushrooming for tonight's rally, sweating students collected on the Quad, the circle of protest again rotating around the perimeter, moving, no one knew why, opposite yesterday's direction. Undergrads sat on the grass and the spontaneous, singing, laughing party atmosphere returned with six packs, MD 20/20 in paper bags, joints, barbecue grills, and a half-dozen rocking blankets hiding humping couples. On the Quad's south edge, in front of the old Auditorium, the rally's stage went up. Spectating students cheered as sections of scaffolding were erected or a joist manhandled by workers dropped to the ground.

And at the northern end, opposite the old Auditorium, the day's first signs of confrontation marched into place. Fifty Illinois State Troopers, equipped with helmets, flak vests, night sticks, walkie-talkies and holstered side arms, advanced from the Union's doors and stationed themselves behind the patio's concrete railing bordering the Quad. There these establishment's sentries remained as morning moved into afternoon, not alarming anyone or issuing orders, simply holding a position where the thousands of students could not miss observing them.

By one o'clock the stage's last girders were bolted together. Randy Miller and his fellow gofers hopped on the planks, wiring the sound equipment. As at last autumn's Moratorium and the meeting in the old Auditorium forty-eight hours ago, for an instant he held the podium.

"Testing, one, two, three." The loafing Illini applauded as Randy dreamed of addressing tonight's crowds.

"Hey, loser," a partier from in front cried, "get the hell off the stage and bring on the frickin' tunes."

# # # #

"Come in, sit down." The editor-in-chief was blunt as Paul noticed—for the first time all year—no balls, gloves, racquets, tees or other sundry sports equipment cluttering her desk. "Stoj and I were worried, we've been searching for you for two days. Did you bring the article?"

He placed a manila folder in front of Stef. "A caution, this narrative may not be what you expect."

"Unforeseen is a facet of journalism." With few staffers in the *Daily Illini's* offices the rooms were quiet; mid-summer temperatures and the rally disrupting the paper as much as the rest of the campus.

Opening the envelope, Stef read about the smashed-up furniture in SOAP's, DISGUST's and RAW's offices. Paul's meetings with Laurie Allman, her years of work with the peace movement and the treachery against her. Professor Antoinette Gulley, the Homecoming balloon, her assignments with UNITED west of Illinois and Howell L. Meade's *Ideology and Revolution in the Soviet Union* on the reading list for her seventeenth century English history course. Paul outlined the Camp rally with protesters bussed into Champaign-Urbana from seven separate schools. The Christmas food drive, the loaded boxcar leaving the campus three months ago then abandoned in Decatur, Bernard Minerath's claim of receiving a thank you telegram from a Saigon relief society that allegedly accepted the foodstuffs, and Paul's failure to confirm this agency's existence. Bernard's trips and connections east of Illinois, his falsified student status and suspect age. The methodical, meticulous membership campaign. The shift in UNITED's rhetoric—from last autumn's always-peace-and-forever-love, to winter's somber tone, and this spring's in-your-face sedition and manifestos. Paul detailed his interview with Bernard, and UNITED's leader concealing and lying. He cited the coincidences between the *News-Gazette's* moderate law-and-order editorials and the fires on their property. The story finished with the Third Street incident two nights ago—the coed barely avoiding being clubbed by the policeman, and the photo appearing in yesterday's *Daily Illini*.

Straightening the pages, Stef absentmindedly tipped an empty styrofoam cup, the only thing on her desk, and Paul realized he hadn't heard a teletype or any voices since entering the editor-in-chief's office. "You're right, not what I presumed. Appointments, dates, locations and names; logical, undeniable links. How the hell did you accumulate this?"

"UNITED's first meetings started me speculating. Why our campus' acquiescence to mega-regimentation? We're flocks of free spirits—hippies with more independence than any previous generations—tolerating manipulation is too contradictory. Second, the hot air balloon led to Professor Gulley, her promoting then covering up Meade's book, and association with Bernard. The plot unraveled, tangled, or aligned, whichever verb's inserted."

"I confess, I should have been more inquisitive last semester." She stared at her duffle bag by the wall. "Is Al Stojak current on this?"

Paul was wary. Should he tie Stoj to his story or shield him? Had Stef already spoken to him, or was she now genuinely, belatedly, curious? "We once or twice discussed my research. But Stoj is such a riddle, lounging in the office, Mr. Detached, puffing his cigs; who guesses what he remembers or blows off?"

Stef was silent and Paul wondered if his explanation was plausible. Would she hassle him for conning her for five months or live up to her editor-in-chief obligations?

"You describe Bernard Minerath as a sinister, practically scary personality."

"I think so. Since last fall he's undoubtedly masterminded the entire U of I peace movement. He was behind frightening Laurie Allman off the campus, collaborated with Gulley, and handled contacts with other schools. I'd wager if we checked university records back to the '60s, Bernard's been involved in countless past protests."

"How did you come across the food drive shipment stalling in Decatur?"

"A source at the *News-Gazette* passed me the information, which I double-checked with that town's Illinois Central dispatch office."

"You should have driven there and inspected the freight car with your own eyes."

"I did, Stef." Paul was glad he'd borrowed Moose's Skylark instead of asking Sharon to escort him.

"This is credible, incredible reporting." She sounded flattering. "You've worked in the wrong department these last three years."

"I'll admit, investigating UNITED, collecting evidence and parsing the logic has produced two exciting semesters. But this was my single shot, I'm not interested in these assignments as a full-time job." Paul relaxed for the first time this morning.

"Have you considered how UNITED affords this stuff? Gulley's balloon ride, the boxcar, t-shirts, banners and flags, bussing three thousand students to our campus the day Camp was humiliated. These stunts cost serious bucks, your story doesn't clarify their funding."

"Finances are mysterious. Contributions, a dollar from an undergrad, maybe five or ten from a professor, raise some money. But whatever UNITED collects from the student body is a fraction of their expenses. I undoubtedly missed their major sources."

"Back to Bernard. You accuse him of lying during last month's interview. Are you positive, or could his phrasing, inflections and body language be interpreted in any, various ways listeners want—nothing more than propaganda perhaps?"

"Bernard definitely lied. If there was one lapse, maybe he forgot, but there were multiple mistakes, six or seven according to my notes. Bernard's too smart to slip so many times."

"You're convinced of your allegations." The editor-in-chief's tone was decided, not questioning.

"I have confirmed sources and backups."

"I'm certain you have, the entire story's factual, all seven pages read well. The puzzle is the missing conclusion. You detail a case, but leave the narrative dangling with the girl running into her house. You allude, but fail to complete."

"My concern was with documenting the record. My idea is running the story verbatim, an accounting of UNITED's cabal, with you writing an editorial arguing that Bernard and his henchmen are not candid or upfront; do not want the war ended," Paul rested his elbows on the desk and strongly emphasized his words, "but plot the opposite, intimidation and lawlessness for our campus."

"Conspiracy."

"That's my theory, our generation rejecting the society that's raised us to adulthood. A depressing thought, resorting to sedition."

"Though not unique. Throughout history, people have run away, ours isn't the first generation to punt responsibility or dribble out a clock. As pretext, I'd theorize we're too distracted—too much partying and television, we're not forced to mature until we're twenty-two or twenty-three years old. I remember my parents telling stories from the old days, when they were younger than us, working fifty-hour weeks in factories for peanut wages. Today, most of us are excused from accountability until we leave college, whenever that happens. And with graduation we're assured decent, white-collar jobs. Our life's too soft." Stef slid the papers into the envelope. "What's more, bear in mind the chaos the country's trapped in—the war, riots and assassinations. It's not the baby boomers' fault, we didn't vote for troop escalations in Vietnam, neither did Congress. And who's got the Navy staring down the Russians in the China Sea? That goofy clown in the White House. If what's going down this week sets off a revolution, it's not our sin."

"I agree, Stef, if only the world could come together to talk through solutions." Relieved by his editor's amicable mind, Paul rambled. "We're so young, with years ahead of us; supposedly the good guys in college learning the answers. When we recognize our responsibilities, then we head out to improve the world, not tear everything up. Odd, what my roommate claimed a long time ago, I've just figured out."

"And you're not the first person concocting conspiracy theories. I'm no poli sci major but I've read about other reporters imagining treason. A shadow in the wrong place, an unlocked window, a document dropped on the floor." Stef clapped her hands. "Poof! Call out the Marines, get the jails ready."

"What's happening today is more threatening than silhouettes."

"But how damaging? Beyond the fact Bernard's a liar, much of your evidence can be rationalized. I'm not contending you've wasted a semester, these facts are disturbing, especially the Laurie Allman episode. But what's your article's place in a bigger scheme?"

"This is UNITED's record for the last six months, the anti-war fanatics' deceits. Printing my article exposes the truth."

"Per your interpretation." Stef switched from assuring to nebulous.

A spasm tweaked Paul, something's strange here. "You're writing an editorial for my story, aren't you?"

"I'm unsure. Going on record would involve the paper in issues we shouldn't deal with. Instead of reporting, the *Daily Illini* would make news." The editor-in-chief peered inside the styrafoam cup. "The paper should remain neutral."

"Not involved? The one thing students know about our newspaper is we're against Vietnam. All year, in every editorial, you've denounced the government, arguing the country should withdraw. Today, with half the campus across the street on the Quad, preparing for God knows what, how can you stay neutral?"

"There's a difference. Anti-war columns are nothing more than commenting on national affairs which have been judged wrong by the majority of this country's population. There's no way I or the *DI* can influence established opinions." She glanced out the doorway, checking for staffers. "Your story is a contrary perspective, believable but opposing evidence, debate that will arouse our campus."

"Journalism's intent," Paul sharply retorted, "gather and report the facts, with logic determining meaning. For objectivity, we can allow Bernard the same amount of space right next to your editorial to defend, if he's able, what he's done this year."

"Which is still steering the *Daily Illini* into an area where I, as editor-in-chief," Stef spoke in her most egotistical voice, "as a matter of policy do not feel we should trespass."

"All right, don't write the goddamned editorial, you said my article lacks a conclusion, hand it back and I'll compose one right now. Print it under my byline and you stay out." Paul was angry, an astounding emotion for him.

Stef stood, closed her office door and gripped a golf club. "Can't do that, either."

"Christ, this is unbelievable. Why the hell not?"

"Same arguments, the *DI* shouldn't interfere with events, merely chronicle them."

"Which didn't prevent you from reporting Wednesday's vandalism at Assembly Hall," Paul shouted, "seems to me that's pretty provocative!"

"And extraordinary, Assembly Hall can't be hidden."

"Are you afraid of Bernard and UNITED?"

"I am not," Stef brusquely replied.

"Then here's the evidence censuring them, let's move ahead." Paul waved his folder.

"I'm not frightened of UNITED," she was obstinate, "but neither do I want the printed words in the *Daily Illini* to be the organ and basis for manipulating a political culture for the benefit of the dominant institutions of the state. Exploiting opinions is more expedient when throttled."

What did she say; quote word for word? I've read that passage before. Is she the mole? With the door shut, the office was hot. Paul peered into Stef's blue eyes, should I challenge her?

"You've read Meade's book, know about newspaper's functions. You're more than a sympathizer, you're in on the conspiracy, have been all along. How deep, Stef, what are your connections with UNITED?"

"I'm only the *DI's* editor, executing my task as I construe." She tapped the floor with the club.

"But you won't print my story."

"No."

"Then I'll carry it to the *News-Gazette*." Paul was furious.

Summer Never Comes

"Which will be pointless. UNITED's reputation, using by and large reliable facts, has been pumped up for six months; the student body is programmed only to accept biases lauding their peace objectives. Print what you've got in the local, townie paper, an improbable source for our cynical generation, and undergrads won't believe you. Moreover, to protect themselves the *News-Gazette* may refuse your article. Remember the arsonists; why should that newspaper pursue an issue potentially harmful to their properties and profits?"

"I think you're mistaken, and at least I can try."

"If you have the nerve. In the big world—in our society—people only care for themselves; we grab what we can from the system—accommodation, pragmatism, expediency. Whether a cause is worthy or corrupt isn't the question, scruples are secondary. For you to expose UNITED is admirable but foolish, because today in Champaign-Urbana you're on the outside—in the wrong, unwanted faction. You'll be hammered, like more resolute individuals before you. I say this as a comrade, Paul, don't chase trouble."

He sat in the chair, weighing Stef's advice, holding his story with both hands. "I guess we're done talking."

# # # #

UPI – University Park – Students set fire this morning to two Penn State University buildings. Classes and normal school activities have been suspended.

Associated Press – Washington – The Navy Department reports the *USS Jim J. Sobel*, a Gearing class destroyer, collided with a submerged Soviet submarine approximately twelve miles east-southeast of Haiphong harbor. At this time, casualties and damage to both vessels are unknown.

# # # #

All day scores, hundreds, then thousands of students on a bogus holiday jammed the Quad, half toting blankets, munchies and coolers. For the rest, a UNITED hot dog stand, 'Wienies Against War,' operated next to

Summer Never Comes

Lincoln Hall, handing out freebie sandwiches, chips and Cokes. The lines were long, but the hungry, happy undergrads waited uncomplainingly. On stage, local rock 'n' roll bands performed, holding the crowd's attention and keeping them cheerful. One group, Cast Well Division, featured Woofer Raasch and Andy Arthur. Between sets, UNITED's 'directors' grabbed the microphone.

"Take it to the end! TAKE it to the END! TAKE IT TO THE END!"

Opposite the Auditorium behind the mobs, the state troopers, reinforced to one hundred thirty, held formation on the Union's patio, walkie-talkies cackling, helmets buckled, night sticks drawn. For added defense, sandbag barricades had been stacked by the doorways. The implacable troopers took the congregating undergraduates' jeers, protecting the building.

Not all Fighting Illini crammed the Quad. Dozens sat in Second Chance, celebrating their classes' unsanctioned suspension with drinking and inebriation. KIDs' contingent, Orion, Shaky Jake, Tim Malito, Scooter, Ronny Gimbel, Ozark, Stu, John Sada, Bobby Sox and Moose, sat at an oversized table near the back bar.

"My fellow brothers," Orion wobbled and stood, "I'm pleased to announce that in ten minutes time supper will be served in the Kappa Iota Delta dining room….And you know what that means."

"Yeah, Mary Lou's gonna be totally pissed when no one except Lance, Quinn and the other wimps are the only ones chowin' down her food," Jake chugged his beer, "just like other Friday afternoons."

"Who the hell gives a frickin' flyin' crap. I propose we stay put," Moose belched, "and keep on drinkin' 'til this bar shuts down."

"Second that e-motion." Bobby rose.

"Sit down, you short shit." He yanked Bobby's shoulders, plopping him back in his chair.

"Drink up," Stu raised his glass, "we don't wanna be thirsty radicals."

"Go to hell yourself."

"Come on, Mooser, chill, be joyful, it's the weekend, the weather's gorgeous and you made the frat's chug team again, third year in a row, right?"

"There was never a doubt."

Summer Never Comes

"Guys, this joint's air conditioning ain't doin' a great blow job. Let's boogie over to the Quad, check out the peace freaks, and see if the revolution's still on schedule."

"Chug, then bolt." Ozark exercised his mechanical arm, the brothers stared at their empty glasses, and Jake pushed off from the table.

"Hold on, stick for one more round." Scooter refilled his mug with complete concentration because he, more than his pals, was exceedingly, extremely high. "I've got a tale you'll wanna hear."

# # # #

"Now who's this?" Again Lindy stood at the second floor pay phone.

"Sharon Taylor, Paul's girlfriend."

"Well, haven't seen you since last December. I'm glad we get to talk, even if not person-to-person. How's life treatin' you?"

"Fine, thank you. I feel we're close friends, I've learned so much about you from Paul."

"Likewise. Hope you don't accept as wholly factual my roommate's narrative."

"Only the true parts, which are plentiful."

Hot damn, Lindy mused, she is a decent-sounding babe, Robby's so fortunate. "You know, I just had a call from another girl, my old sweetheart, Emily Ritter. A couple days ago we met for the first time in weeks. As before, Em poured out her disappointments, in me for walking off to chase my music, as well as in the disaster with Tommy Quarters. I didn't solicit any specifics about those two's dates and she only volunteered a few; one upshot now her inability to trust people. Em was definitely letdown, adrift and not as I remembered her. For my part, I talked about Frogfeet's demise, how I was finished with bands this semester and am finding myself, even after bookin' and job hunting, with plenty of free time. The longer we chatted, the more I came to comprehend my selfishness; ego instead of my buddies, what I was convinced was cool instead of what's upright. I ignored Robby when my roomie could've used another pal to bounce ideas off; I left Em, and the worst happened. I screwed up. Even if I was undeserving, I asked Em for one more opportunity to amend and restart our relationship. That afternoon when we said goodbye, I was unsure I'd persuaded her. This morning, thank my lucky stars, Em phoned to say she'd slept on my proposition and decided yes, we'll be girlfriend and boyfriend again."

Lindy's candor charmed Sharon. "I'm happy hearing this."

"Thanks. Instead of rallying on the Quad, this afternoon I'm headin' over to her dorm to keep her company. This merry-go-round, no more stupid stuff. Starting today, I'm bottling up my derelict character; do what I can to help Em back on her feet and demonstrate I've learned my lessons."

"Very good, Lindy, a recovering Emily is worthwhile. Have you told Paul, is he around the fraternity?"

"I haven't seen Robby since we woke up, which was before Em phoned. Don't know where that boy is at the moment."

"Too bad, we argued yesterday and hadn't made up before he left my house. I want to square things with him."

"Yeah, Robby mentioned the squabble, you two love birds couldn't see eye to eye to eye. He and I had the same brand of tête a tête."

"I know, seems he's done plenty of talking," the two laughed over their parallel.

"Poor guy's got a pile on his mind these last days, hesitations, reservations and tribulations. But with this quandary, I think Robby's succeeded. He told me he was submittin' his article to the *Daily Illini*."

"Wonderful." Sharon was relieved. "I can't understand his holding back, he is so indecisive."

"That's our Robby, calculates the right and wrong sides of equations, but is scared as hell to yank the chain."

"An apt depiction, as if you've known him all your life."

"Best buddies, peas in a proverbial pod, until you appeared."

"And remain so, Paul values you."

"But you're his main squeeze, which is a whole 'nother skillet of fish."

"We're each his friend." Sharon chuckled, again taken with Lindy's openness, aware why Paul appreciated his roommate and was so depressed when he was deserted. "You mentioned Paul was walking to the *DI*?"

"He left KIDs at 9:30. But remember our Robby and this investigation he's invested a half-year of time in. After the meeting he probably scooted for the Quad to check out UNITED and the protest."

"I agree. When Paul shows up, could you tell him I phoned?"

"Willco. Maybe we'll see you around."

Summer Never Comes

"Yes, Lindy, I'd like to link up for more clichés. My best to Emily."

"Ditto, I'm for sure."

# # # #

When the sun went behind Lincoln Hall, the temperature dipped to the high-seventies. The evening would be muggy because the wind, steady since morning from the southwest, had calmed. Too uncomfortable indoors, students from everywhere in Champaign-Urbana flocked to the Quad and the big rally. On the floodlit stage, an emcee addressed the crowd.

"We've had a pretty decent day out here, sunny weather, tons of comradeship, frisbees, tunes, eats, scads of you have hustled in brewskies, a little loving, typical of our spell at the Big U. Face it, friends, we're set, made, relaxing in strawberry fields with no cares; which is excellent, decent, far out, power to the people." The front rows of True Believers cheered, with the racket echoing northward to the Union. "But we know that's just one of the story's sides. Because for every one of us enrolled in college—drawing learning from these libraries, labs and lectures, the professors and instructors, for each of us eighteen-, nineteen- and twenty-year-old students with scarcely any troubles, there's thousands around the earth that don't have it so comfortable or cozy, millions with nowhere near the privileges and pleasures we accept for granted, tens of millions with a lot less, or nothing—even less than nothing—and thieves stealing that.

"You know the message coming on the road, what I'm going to say next.

"Some of the unfortunates with the awful-est, dreadful-est deals are the down-in-the-dumps folks of Vietnam. In their huts and rice paddies in the jungles they just want to exist through a day, eke by, make whatever they can of whatever little they've got. But now, in the present, every week and month, the Vietnamese are trapped in this war, the fight started by America. No kicking back or unwinding under the trees like us here today; no liquor, no music, no honey to hug, kiss and love. Their plight is what they've endured for six cruel, crappy years. Attacks and ambushes any time of day or night, their villages bombed and blasted. Corruption and treachery, friends and family murdered right in front of them, wives with no husbands, children who've lost parents. Havoc, devastation, no hopes or likelihoods of gladder, securer futures.

"And we brewed this tragedy, our country started it, not you or me or the students lounging next to you, but this government, our nation, we, the people. And since it's the people that are responsible, all of us better do something about this."

The crowds applauded, enthusiastic, ardent but not fanatic—True Believers to die-hards to concerned citizens to passersby understanding the evening's consequences.

# # # #

Leaving Stef's office, Paul telephoned the *News-Gazette* and John Barrett, but his colleague was gone and none of the paper's staffers knew where to reach him. The likeliest place he'd be was where every conscientious reporter would head tonight, the rally. Paul thought to make for the Quad to hunt down Mr. Barrett, but reconsidered. No way would he find one person in those thousands, that's too tough, too challenging, too dangerous. Why even try?

Instead, sadly, shamefully, Paul walked to Men's Old Gym to hide his book bag and story in one of MOG's lockers.

This was the sum of his commitment, the reach of the anger he flashed at Stef, how far he was willing to stretch. Paul retreated and wandered Champaign's streets, ignorant of the vibes on the Quad, unaware his girlfriend and roommate chatted about him, not knowing both his friends' relief when he'd told Lindy he was deciding. A dejected Paul, shielding his eyes from the low sun and blowing dust, turned his back, reneged again, couldn't follow through.

Paul had guessed when he'd accused his editor-in-chief of complicity with UNITED; Stef's paraphrasing from *Ideology and Revolution in the Soviet Union* the tipoff, and her non-denial evidence enough of collusion with Bernard. This was so plain he should have reasoned the connection earlier in the school year. Movements, social, political or military, must brainwash populations, and newspapers are one media to utilize. Control of the masses managed with collaboration from the elite, pulled off in other countries, today achieved in ours. Suppose I'll have to write a few more paragraphs, Paul mused.

He'd assumed Stef too experienced and clever a journalist to deal in intrigues, thinking the editor-in-chief's peace editorials her honest judgments on the war. But principles were irrelevant; the *Daily Illini* was in on the conspiracy. That was how Bernard and his henchmen skewered publicity and reaped favorable stories—not owing to their cause's merit but to bias, connections. Paul thought of the photo of the girl and the state trooper. Fairness forfeited to manipulation, from a paper students purchased, read, and accepted as factual, five editions a week.

Paul's roaming ended in an unnamed park at Church and Davidson streets in Champaign. He slouched by a tree, gazing at picnic tables and a swing set. The grounds were shaped like a bullet, Church Street the blunt end, with wood-framed homes surrounding the field.

How established was the conspiracy? If the DI was one cell, what about the faculty and school administrators? That would explain lectures, discussion sections and labs unofficially canceled these last few days and on other occasions when support for the peace movement was beneficial. The police? The squad cars speeding to Third Street and Assembly Hall unguarded until too late? Not all the officers, but one or two lieutenants and a dispatch sergeant. Was it possible, with a few thousand quislings, that the entire country could blow up, riots like those in years' past erupting to knock off America? The 'end' Bernard and UNITED encouraged these past weeks, the conspiracy's final, ultimate scene, might be what I stumbled on then let go because I didn't want to get involved. And here I am, Paul scoffed, under a tree, moping, feeling miserable, calling myself an asshole. What a wonderful life.

At least I had a little luck. Because a distracted Stef assumed I was holding to the limited assignment she handed me last September, she neglected my story. If the editor-in-chief hadn't played every single intramural sport this school year and depended on Al Stojak to babysit, she might have halted my research weeks before I uncovered the plots I did. What of the converse? Perhaps Stef understands me deeper than I imagine, and all winter took for granted I lacked courage and would fold.

With sunset the wind dropped and the dust quit blowing. Paul stood away from the trees and turned toward campus. *What should I do, even if it's so very late?* Some acquittal, an exoneration, anything to warn the students, salvage the situation and myself. He was uncertain whether to return to KIDs, the Quad or find Sharon. That's my problem, always unsure. Paul walked east on Springfield, under the Illinois Central tracks. Maybe I'll get a break, perhaps I'm selling the baby boomers short. We're intelligent, in college booking our buns off, and shouldn't be fooled by a jerk like Bernard who wears corduroys and long-sleeve shirts even in baking, broiling weather. They—we, my generation—will unravel the truth. This mess will work out.

# # # #

Reinforced with a third battalion, two hundred state troopers occupied the south patio, deploying west toward Altgeld Hall, surveilling the swarming, massing mobs. By six o'clock, the Union, their designated command post, was closed off to students and the public, with only police permitted inside.

At 7:30, Andy and Woofer's band finished a fourth set, an evening encore after their afternoon gig. The students in front applauded, anticipating the rally's much-waited for start, and farther from the stage the thousands gathering near the Administration Building, under the trees, queuing at UNITED's hot dog stand, barbecuing by the Chem Annex, and jamming the Senior Bench of the Class of 1912, joined in. But no one cheered and "TAKE IT TO THE END" wasn't yelled. The True Believers hadn't been cued.

Cast Well Division's exit left the stage empty. The floodlights shined and Randy Miller, as-ever waiting, wanting, wishing to contribute, stood to the side. Squadrons of gnats buzzed in the haze around the spotlights and a restless Randy spied a clique advancing from Greg Hall toward the scaffolding. As Bernard and the directors marched to the platform, there was no rise in the monotonous applause. Instead, the nearest students quit clapping and the thousands followed. The director Randy recognized as this afternoon's emcee stepped to the lectern.

"So it's our country. What do we do with it, how do we, the people act? As I calculate, two options. The one is patience, adjustment, revision, reform from inside. The slow, conservative approach, the way things have operated until now—negotiation, compromise, conciliation, small steps. The other route is the activist. Militant. Confrontation. Resistance. Rebellion. The Revolution. Cataclysm. Out with the old, rip it down, start over. And that's the one I like. How come, why advocate sacrificing our security? Wouldn't amendment be preferred to anarchy and correcting favored over upheaval?"

The True Believers applauded and a close-by undergrad yelled, "You tell 'em!"

"If reorganization promised results, and reform produced progress, yes. But it doesn't. The system's a fraud, a failure, corrupted. The way our country's controlled, it can't deal with mistakes and it's preserved for insiders. The power brokers, the so-called leaders, have made the government their exclusive, restricted sphere, with only the elites in the orbit permitted to profit. For decades, the influence peddlers have manipulated for themselves—ignoring the honest concerns, the desperate needs, the sufferings, hardships and poverty of others; the unfortunates and unlucky, the ones with not enough to offer as bribes and tribute, the ones that don't count. Over the last decades, this discrimination has worsened so that now we're faced with two countries, two social orders, two castes, the haves and have-nots, a hierarchy daily more established and inflexible, a system that cannot be reformed through discussion, reshaped by debate, or altered with half-measures. They, the intolerant bureaucracy, the chauvinist oligarchs, the string pullers of our democracy, will not listen.

"That's why I say our generation, we, the people, can't waste time, our youth, our lives, on pointless attempts at irrelevant reforms, on things of insignificant substance and not even meager results. Because once we decide to take the easy way, the deliberate approach, resign and submit, we'll waste our chance, surrender our integrity, we'll become them. Whether we have thirty, twenty, ten or only a few years remaining, we should use our time on noveler approaches, to get things done, make it better, to save ourselves.

"Fellow students, comrades: the situation is perilous, the odds are long, and we need audacity to act. But act we must, to stop the war, save the country, to make our lives and our generation count."

The True Believers applauded, and the now-passionate crowd, not needing prompting, followed.

Summer Never Comes

# # # #

"This is the sweetest seat in the house." Orion pitched his empty beer bottle on the floor."

"Yeah, Jake, decent idea spectating from here," Tim Malito handed him another brew, "better than upper deck seats at Wrigley Field."

"Down the third base line," Bobby Sox added.

The KIDs, along with dozens more inebriates from Second Chance, had staggered to Lincoln Hall to watch the rally from a third floor classroom, hauling their coolers and the party atmosphere with them into the aged building.

"Sure are lots of bodies down there tonight. How many do you think?"

"At least ten or fifteen thousand, half the student body."

"Bunch of crazies, sitting there listenin' to those speeches." Ozark chugged his beer.

"What does that make us?"

"The weirdest." The Mooser uncapped an Old Style.

With no breeze from the windows, the KIDs' room was roasting. Stu gazed up, noticing an overcast hiding the stars.

"I don't know what's more mind-blowing, those thousands on the Quad, us here watching the action, or the stunner Scooter laid on us when we were at the bar drinking. Imagine, Lauren's pregnant, he's gonna be a daddy, and they're gettin' hitched in June."

"Think it's the truth? He was pretty drunk when he told us." John Sada stepped toward the window ledge.

"Stupid ass!" Bobby Sox exploded. "Who'd admit to news like that if it wasn't? There's some things college students don't bullshit about, stuff too serious even for us."

# # # #

Walking east in Campustown, Paul chose checking the Quad rather than returning to KIDs or finding Sharon. Near Wright Street, he spotted dozens of blinking, flashing, red and amber lights from the squad cars and wagons parked on barricaded Green Street. Paul saw the paddy wagons' rears pointed toward the Union, their back doors open, a scene reminding him of groceries delivered to a supermarket or truck drivers waiting for loads of cargo. Or arrested college students.

My God, that's the scenario going down tonight!

He rushed toward the Quad but didn't run, since cops patrolled the sidewalks on Wright and Green. Paul peered across the street at the overwhelming contingent of state troopers west of the Union, hidden from the Quad. Wearing riot helmets and armed with night sticks, the officers pounded the clubs into their gloves. Frightening, hundreds of uniforms on my campus.

A hustling Paul sneaked between Altgeld Hall and the Administration Building. On the left was the Union with the police, the authority and muscle; to his right the backs of the crowds with a few students roaming the rear. Farther away, through the hazy night, toward the direction the undergrads stared, Paul made out the lighted stage. Sweating from his hike, Paul kept close to the buildings, out of the troopers' line of attack and away from danger. *Lord, what a catastrophe, please keep the peace tonight, please keep everyone sensible and calm so nothing foolish will happen.*

"Fellow students," the recognizable voice echoed from the sound system, "we all must listen..."

And Paul's prayers crashed.

"...Listen, then heed our conscience," Bernard continued. "The times we move in are perilous, with powers on our planet which mean us misery and distress. As we speak, these forces of suffering are succeeding in the faraway fields of Vietnam."

"Yeah, destroy the government, throw 'em out!" the True Believers yelled. On cue, as expected, the scream was repeated by the masses behind them.

"This Friday was so, so typical of the destruction weighing on that misbegotten nation," Bernard berated. "On land, the armies of our so-called democracy fight the North Vietnamese forces of liberation, subjugating territory for the corrupt Saigon dictatorship."

The crowd booed, this time without the True Believers' prompting.

"On water, the Navy lawlessly blockades the North's harbors, flaunting the freedom of the seas and isolating that small, struggling state."

Spontaneous booing crescendoed. Some in the crowds raised their fists, agreeing with Bernard's words.

Summer Never Comes

"Yes, it seems the United States of America, our sorry, sad, lost country, is only concerned with causing the sufferings and sorrows of other peoples. It delights in humbling nations, takes satisfaction in despoiling sovereign lands. Yes, it revels in the mission of spreading hate and animosity."

Provoked by Bernard's irate voice, the mobs erupted. Hundreds stood, hoisting banners, hollering and barking. Any still-sitting students glanced around and then rose, wanting to stick with their neighbors.

"Our failed nation, a country beyond morality's limits, must be stopped." As the crowds bawled, Bernard lifted one arm over his head. Standing under the stage lights, his long sleeves were soaked from sweat, his black, very wet hair matted on his forehead. "America must be defeated, deposed, shown the bankruptcy of its course these past years. A lesson must be taught, and this is our place tonight. History hurries towards us, we cannot sidestep or stay away. We must be comrades courageous enough to meet the obligation."

Thousands of students were up, celebrating, hurrahing, jeering, yelling, insulting, slapping their neighbors' backs, hooting, catcalling, stomping their feet and tossing t-shirts, caps and half-full beer cans in the air. Nearer Paul, behind the mobs, a cadre of twenty or thirty huddled, a knot of whatevers, undergrads, UNITED supporters, troublemakers, ignoring the stage but listening to their leader instructing, motioning like a coach calling a play. As the undergrad masses howled, this squad spread out in a picket line at the rear of the students still facing the stage. Paul glanced behind him, double-checking his line of retreat toward Wright Street. He felt the perspiration in his armpits.

"This is the duty of our time, our generation's task. We must explain, show, provoke, demonstrate to our countrymen and comrades the suffering we allow in Asia, expose the pain we are permitting. We must bring the wretchedness down for the nation to see!" Bernard shrieked and stretched his dripping arm over the crowd, pointing at the Union and the state troopers. "Bring our nation down!"

For an instant, the mobs and gangs and rabbles stared at Bernard's hand in the spotlight, then as one pivoted to follow his direction.

"Bring our nation down!" Bernard demanded.

Summer Never Comes

"Bring our nation down! BRING our nation down!" The True Believers in front of the stage chanted. "BRING our nation DOWN!"

Paul watched the thousands of students turn north to the Union. The troopers tensed and the throngs scowled. The cheerleaders harangued the crowds, flailing their arms. A dispirited Paul pictured the next scene.

"BRING OUR NATION DOWN!"

"Do it for 'Nam!"

"Let's start our own WAR!"

"KILL THE PIGS!"

"BRING OUR NATION DOWN!"

The students closest to the Union, now the lead edge, were shoveled toward the building by the thousands pushing from behind. The picket line agitators, between the state troopers and the crowds, teased both sides, manipulating and funneling the students at the police. The multitudes reacted, not with one, quick rush, but a certain, inescapable creeping and shuffling forward.

"Yeah, yeah, yeah! LET'S GET 'EM THIS TIME! Yesterday Assembly Hall! Today the Union and these SWINE!"

"BRING OUR NATION DOWN!"

From the Union's flanks, the state troopers' reserve regiments advanced to support their fellow officers, the maneuver stopping the demonstrators for a few seconds but no longer. There were too many thousands cramming, impelling and shoving northward.

"Sweet Jesus Christ, this looks bad." Moose for once was rational.

"Think we're safe up here?"

"As long as there aren't more police outside plannin' on sweeping through Lincoln Hall and arresting us." Jake gripped the sill.

"Crap, it's past the curfew. We leave, we're busted, like every student on the Quad's gonna be in a half hour."

"Lord help me, I don't wanna do time in jail."

The mobs pressed closer, the orange and black banners over their heads tilted in the direction the student body was inching, at the Union and the troopers. The cheerleading, taunting rabble-rousers jumped and danced, inciting the students and unnerving the police.

"BRING DOWN THE NATION! BRING DOWN THE USA! BRING DOWN THE NATION! BRING DOWN THE USA!"

Summer Never Comes

Wiping the sweat off his forehead, Paul wanted to run but couldn't, compelled to watch his story's conclusion. God, it was hot, those police in their riot helmets must be frying.

"ANOTHER TEN MINUTES AND IT'S OVER!"

"KILL 'EM! BLAST 'EM AWAY! BUTCHER ALL THOSE SHIT-ASS PIGS!"

"THIS IS THE NIGHT, IT'S ALL FINISHED!"

"IT'S WHAT WE GOTTA DO!"

"Bring down the war!" a high-pitched, female voice squeaked. "Get to them."

Paul looked around.

"Come on, let's go, don't mope there like a tree trunk." A very adolescent, pigtailed coed tugged his t-shirt. "Leap into the action, get involved, right?"

"In that?" Paul pointed toward the Quad, to the narrowing gap between the students and the troopers. "It looks ugly."

"Let's go, haven't you heard the speeches? We're supposed to do our thing, follow, tag along, fill in the middle with everyone else. It's the age of Aquarius, right?"

"Are you sure?" Though standing close to each other, Paul shouted to make himself heard. "I don't think so."

"That's what Bernard Minerath says. He's so right, he knows what our assignment is."

"Are you positive?"

"Absolutely. I'm only a freshman, but I know that's all there is, the only course, right?" She studied the surging, swelling, heaving undergrad hordes, pennants and banners waving, the rabble-rousers swearing and goading. "It's what the *Daily Illini's* printing. Support UNITED, be involved, help out. You're a student, you know that too, right? It's the only way."

"There could be alternatives."

"I doubt it. If there were, somebody around campus would've patched together another argument, explained the other side, right? But no one did." Grinning at Paul, she flashed a 'V' with two fingers and twirled toward the crowds. "Hey, peace."

"Wait!" Paul grabbed her arm, reckoning he had little time. "It sounds bizarre, but I'm telling you this scene's wrong, tonight's a mistake. I'm a reporter for the *Daily Illini*, I've researched the peace movement and I'm convinced it's a fraud. UNITED's not for peace but wants to exploit the students; UNITED's not looking to end the war but wants anarchy, to wipe out, wreck our lives, our campus, along with the rest of the country. Proof? I'm certain Bernard Minerath's not a student, he's twenty-six years old, hasn't enrolled in a class for five semesters and a professor has covered for him all that time. Trust me, please."

Hesitating, the girl leaned in his direction. "How do you know his age?"

"I checked his transcripts, I have photocopies hidden in a gym locker, along with plenty more evidence proving he's a phony. Don't go with the crowd tonight, stay safe. There'll be another time, a better day." Paul prayed he was believable. "What's your name?"

"Haley Hunt."

"Mine's Paul Roberts. Examine the problems, consider your choices."

She surveyed the stage, the thousands of undergrads, the hopping, maniac agitators reaching for the Union's patio, the hard-boiled, case-hardened, set-for-a-fight state troopers, then moved back from the Quad and closer to Paul. "Okay, I'll sit this one out. Life means tomorrow, right?"

Haley spun and hurried toward Wright Street, her pigtails bouncing. Paul had succeeded.

Now the crowds were thirty feet from the Union, with the rabble rousers nearer. The psyched undergrads whooped, their arms and fists swinging, their flags tilting.

"BRING DOWN THE NATION! BRING DOWN THE USA!"

A detached Bernard followed the pandemonium from the stage, safely behind his directors, with no intention of jumping in with the crowds and battling the police. He'd completed his job, shown the students the path. In a few minutes, the mayhem and notoriety, the riots and headlines he'd schemed for would detonate the campus. Smirking, he stood by the lectern, arms folded on his chest, not yelling or pointing, awfully satisfied by these results.

"BRING DOWN THE NATION! BRING DOWN THE USA! BRING DOWN NATION!"

In the fog and the lamp poles' dim lights, Paul, frightened and sweating like everyone else, watched the crowds' deliberate crawl, the thousands of bodies adding their own heat to the muggy night's miserableness. The police held their ground, bracing for the clash, assuming a stance with one leg set behind their bodies. The troopers near Altgeld Hall waited for their captain's command, ready to charge the students.

A regretful Paul wished he'd behaved differently, prayed he'd decided three or four days or a week ago to publish his story. It wouldn't have been tough, all he needed was resolution to act. But Paul did nothing. Unlike Bernard, his work was unfinished. Paul sickened with the thought of the next minutes and tragedy.

"BRING DOWN THE USA!"

Insulting the troopers and the crowds, the cussing, sneering rabble-rousers hopped and pirouetted, hurrying the confrontation. Dozens of police pointed their billy clubs at the mobs, taunting the students. Behind the lines, commanders lifted their walkie-talkies, prepared to order in reinforcements the instant the melee started.

"BLAST 'EM! BLAST 'EM! BLAST 'EM!"

Two students, then a third, rushed from the packs, hurtling into the police. A squad surrounded the rioters, knocked the trio to the concrete, handcuffed their wrists and manhandled the bodies over the patio's railing to waiting officers. Expecting more attacks, the police quickly re-formed their line.

"BUTCHER ALL THE PIGS!"

Paul was trembling. Fear, honest-to-goodness, alarmingly afraid, terrified-for-what's-next panic. *Should I run away to the Church Street park or hide in my room? No, stay to witness this disaster my responsibility, my fault, my guilt, because I didn't act. That's the lesson, don't vanish into a hole, grow up, behave like an adult, have purpose. What Lindy and Sharon said was true, you had to move on, deal with what you're handed, go forward. Don't engineer excuses, take care of your life. Next time, I'll handle it better, right?*

Goosebumps covered his arms. Paul was shaking, but shivering because he was cold. *What's changed?* He looked at the tossing branches blown by winds gusting from the Union, the north. The temperature was dropping. Paul turned to the crowds and the dozens also watching the sky. Not sweating, he squeezed both hands into his armpits for warmth. Suddenly the night wasn't cut-offs and t-shirt weather, not summer. Long pants and windbreakers would be welcome. One humongous raindrop splatted the sidewalk, a second, a third, then a steady shower doused Paul and the Quad.

Summer Never Comes

The crowds' yelling died, flags fell, fists lowered, and the students' attention shifted from the troopers on the patio to their abruptly chilly, uncomfortable comrades. Behind the stage, Woofer, Andy and Cast Well Division hurried to pack away their instruments before the rain crudded them. Students hustled past Paul, abandoning the Quad, scurrying to get out of the downpour and indoors near some heat. He thought of Sharon's house and the fireplace.

The mobs' edges halted fifteen feet from the Union. The rabble-rousers bullied, but couldn't herd the undergrads closer. One True Believer charged the patio, but skidded on the slippery sidewalk. In front of the snickering students he crawled up, rubbing his buns. Lowering their clubs, the troopers stood at ease.

Scores, then hundreds, of undergrads rushed away to escape the storms. The prized objectives, concern, commitment, revolution, mobocracy, make a difference and change the world, washed away in the showers. A wasted moment. Quivering, Paul turned from the Union to hurry home to KIDs. One shoeless, shirtless student covered his girlfriend and himself with a soggy blanket, another flung her orange and black pennant into the shrubs as she shuffled through a puddle, a fourth substituted his hand-colored poster board for an umbrella. The sticky, muggy night turned frosty. Before long, only drenched True Believers milled around the Quad, the police allowing these soaked, now-not-at-all-treacherous radicals to loiter.

CHAPTER TWENTY

"WE'RE HERE, the finals," Bobby Sox slammed the balcony's railing, "I'm so frickin' psyched."

"Chill out," Stu settled his roommate. "The way you're acting you'd think the Fighting Illini made it to the Rose Bowl."

"This is the big time, we win one more heat and we're campus chug champions four years in a row." Bobby was only a bit subdued.

"That may not be easy," Scooter Petersen stood behind them, "those Delts look awful tough."

On Saturday afternoon, the Chances R's balconies were jammed with hundreds of U of I undergrads, including most of the KIDs, their girlfriends and a dozen alums, spectating the drinking contest. The event, sponsored by Champaign County's Miller beer distributor, started three hours ago with sixteen teams facing off against each other. Now the competition came to the last chug, Delta Tau Delta versus Kappa Iota Delta.

"The Mooser doesn't look too keyed."

"He's the best swing man in the Big U, he'll be fine." The hyper Bobby urged on the brothers, "Let's go you KIDs."

"Will the same guys chug this round?" Lauren asked. Pregnant two months and worn out, she was one of the few fans sitting.

"Yes, dear." Scooter absentmindedly answered. The finals were seconds away and her fiancé wanted to concentrate on the action. "'Ralph' Hepler, Del Hansen, Shaky Jake and Moose, the same four all afternoon. And, except for 'Ralph', last year's team."

"Who'd he replace?"

"Billy Powell," Bobby interrupted. "Uncle Sam in his twisted, freakin' wisdom had other squads for ol' Billy to enlist in."

Summer Never Comes

"I'll bet he's puttin' down plenty of brewskies, even if he's in the army in 'Nam."

"One more question. Each contestant has two beers apiece?"

"Right. 'Ralph,' Del and Jake drink in succession, Moose gulps his two, then the others guzzle their second glasses, one after another. The team wolfing them down quickest wins the trophy."

The jovial Illini in the bar whooped. Compared to their fans, the two teams kept cool. For the finals, the four KIDs wore the green, and for the moment dry, house jerseys. In purple, the Delts huddled up, with only the holy Lord divining their dialogue.

"Look at those puppies, what wusses," Bobby snickered, "afraid to come out."

"Let's go Delts! Let's go Delts!" their supporters roared.

The Delts stepped to their table, with eight plastic cups of beer sitting in pairs. 'Ralph,' Del, Jake and the Mooser, looking smugly confident, waited for their opponents.

"No problem, we've got 'em." Stu clapped.

"Are you ready?" The timer, a Sigma Nu, eyed both teams. "On your mark…get set…GO!"

'Ralph' instantly chugged KIDs' first beer, followed by Jake, Del and Moose, one-two-ing his in classic Champaign double-handed style with no spillage. His teammates sucked down their second cups, 'Ralph' dropping his glass on the table before Delts' anchorman lifted his last beer. The KIDs won in a runaway.

"I told you, I told you!" a shouting Stu kissed Joyce.

"Way to go KIDs!" Bobby whacked the railing again. "Right on!"

"We're number one, we're number one!"

On stage, the Mooser solemnly shook hands with each of his teammates. "Hell, yes."

"Goddamn-it, lost the bet, three bucks blown out my butt." In the crowds near the stage, Dale Kinsey gulped his beer.

"So much for loyalty, betting against your fraternity. You are a nimrod." Stef Tianen stood by him, as usual on defense to stop Dale from shoving his hand under her softball jersey.

"Screw them, I got a tip this morning the chug contest was rigged and figured I'd cash in. Except the son of a bitch that ratted to me was wrong, his ass is grass." He stroked Stef's stomach. "Speaking of pains in the rear, any word about Paul Roberts and his article?"

"Paul hasn't stopped by the *Daily Illini's* office for two weeks, and won't return my phone calls." The editor-in-chief watched the undergrads exiting Chances R. "How about you, any luck snooping around your house?"

"Practically every KID is still pissed at Tommy Quarters and me over the Emily Ritter caper. The only buddies I've got left are the fourth floor despoes, who are so wasted every day of the week they can't chase squat."

"Too successful pushing your dope. Must be rugged, running a booming, profitable business." She set her empty mug on the stage.

"It ain't funny. If that pansy-ass Roberts draws the connection between the campus peace freaks, the drug trade and the tons of money UNITED earns off their investment with sellin' the crap, we're screwed. Just like you'd be on the carpet if he or the university ever found out about your *DI* providin' them free advertising." Standing close, Dale squeezed his hand in Stef's pants. "I'd have to blow Champaign to escape the narcs and Bernard Minerath. And you'd lose that sweet newspaper job you landed in Minneapolis."

"Yes, I'm amazed Paul hasn't uncovered more. He either overlooked the links between UNITED, your pushers and the school, or our conversation the day of the rally shook him up. How should we handle it?"

"Take him out, destroy him, like we terrified the crap out of Laurie Allman and trashed his twerpy roommate's band of loser musicians. If we get Bernard's okay, I got more ways than a whorehouse to screw someone. By the first of May, Roberts can be so humiliated no one will listen to him, so scared he won't take a dump without a bodyguard."

"You'd do it again, to someone else you know?"

"If it's him or us and what we've built, you're goddamned right. You and the political science honchos can manipulate the peace movement, and Minerath can jerk off at his game, whatever in hell it is. Me? I'll grab the bucks then dodge gettin' humped in the ass." With his free hand Dale hugged the editor-in-chief. "Since we're on that subject, your apartment's close by, right?'

Ignoring the Chances R crowds, she nibbled her boyfriend's ear. A minute later, choosing conscience, finally getting what a bastard Dale was, understanding how badly she'd treated Paul, Stef shoved away.

Summer Never Comes

Finished celebrating, the KIDS left the balcony, an unsteady Lauren protected from the mobs by Scooter, Bobby and Stu. Nauseous this morning, she'd considered avoiding the chug contest, then realized this was her last chance to play a careless college student. On the rest of the school year's weekends she'd travel between Champaign and the Petersen family's house in Chicago, preparing for a June marriage, their baby's birth in October, and falling under the control of her future mother-in-law. This was the deal she'd negotiated: completing the semester in return for Saturdays and Sundays spent with Scooter's mom, plus Mrs. Petersen's total say-so over their wedding arrangements. This compromise was testing, Lauren dreaded driving the hundreds of miles and Kathie Petersen's domination, but she would graduate from the University of Illinois. Holding Bobby's arm, Lauren glanced around Chances R, at the casualness, innocence and carousing. She'd miss the spring weekends, their friends, the fun, freedom, college's wackiness, but she and Scooter had to do the realistic thing, become adults, turn responsible. Our lives will never be like this again.

# # # #

"Did I tell you what happened? Wednesday in parasitology lab, old Professor Candy instructed us to spend the class dissecting frogs for whatever we could discover on the host organisms, then he disappeared."

"That's what the class deals with, right?" Not a science guy, Paul interrupted.

"Correct. Well, old softie Sharon couldn't handle that scene," she impishly said, "I mean a cute, green, defenseless froggy, no way. When Professor Candy-Ass toddled out of the room, I snatched two of the toads and boogied myself."

"You ripped off university property." He chuckled.

"One way to dramatize." The pair lay in bed, Sharon's head on his shoulder, Paul massaging her back. Even with the drapes drawn, a shining moon brightened their motel room. "Being a beautiful afternoon, I carried the croakers to the Boneyard Creek and let them swim away."

"That was humanitarian, but what kind of veterinary career will you have if you can't stomach slicing open animals?"

Summer Never Comes

"I didn't say I couldn't perform dissections, only with the professor absent, the semester nearly over and super spring weather, killing 'Huff' and 'Puff' was inhumane." She lifted her head off Paul's chest. "Besides, I'm accepted into the Vet Med College and the deans won't toss me for stealing frogs."

He ran one finger along Sharon's neck. "How do you feel being in the college?"

"Satisfied, rewarded, my studying's accomplished something significant. I know I've barely spent any time in that building and there's another four years' work ahead, but this is a fresh start, the beginning of my career."

"I completely understand. Instead of shacking up back at your house, tonight we had an excuse for grabbing this motel room."

"That's not my meaning. I'm philosophical and you talk about love," Sharon jabbed his waist, "and lovemaking."

"No offense intended, honest." Paul hugged her, delaying the tickle attack. "I only wish we could afford the Century Twentyone as we planned and not settled for the Chief Illini Inn."

"True, but we can't run out of money with six weeks in the school year."

"Which wouldn't be smart, how could we have any more jollies?" Paul and Sharon's faces were two inches apart. He glanced at his girlfriend's suntanned breasts, as brown as the rest of her body. "Where will you live next year?"

"Same place. The Vet Med College also accepted Mary O'Donnell, and Angie and Karen Gasper will be in grad school. We figure we'll dig up three undergrads to split the rent. Next autumn's accommodations won't change."

"The good times on California Street, Urbana, Illinois."

"When the fall semester begins, though, there'll be a soberer attitude in Sharon Taylor's study habits. No more 'free the froggies' crusades."

"Did you hear the university is altering the school calendar? We'll start the third week of August instead of mid-September and the spring semester will end before Memorial Day instead of June."

"Does the new schedule begin this autumn?" Sharon mounted her boyfriend and wrapped her arms around Paul.

"One more year before the switch."

Sharon kissed Paul's lips, "Again, dear?"

"Why right now? We've got the rest of tonight, this semester," he mumbled, "and next year, too."

"Say what? Is my boyfriend dreaming?"

"I've sorted out a plan, and decided not to graduate."

"Hold on, explain yourself."

"I'll receive my bachelor's degree, then enroll in grad school to study for a master's in accounting." Paul deeply exhaled, startling Sharon.

"There's not many weeks left before June. Unless graduate business programs are different than the rest of the university, isn't it too late to apply?"

"I need to hustle filling out admissions applications and take the Graduate Record Exam, but the deadlines haven't passed. With my grade point I'll be accepted, and the advisor I talked to said I'd even have a chance at a teaching assistant's position."

Sharon scrutinized her smirking boyfriend.

"You're happy we'll be together this fall, aren't you?"

She unraveled her arms from Paul's neck and fell off his body. "Why this reversal?"

"My article that should have been printed in the *Daily Illini*, the rally practically a riot three weeks ago, the obligations I threw away." Paul laid on his side, looking at her. "The thousands of students running around that night, especially the girl who ran out from the Administration Building, none of them knowing anything, so easily influenced, listening to UNITED but not to alternatives, I'm convinced the only ones with the entire story were Bernard, Stef and me. The chaos affected me, so many clueless students following someone else's lead. Randy Miller's an example."

"One of your fraternity brothers?"

"Yes, a guy who attended every UNITED meeting, worked in their membership drives, volunteered as a stagehand at the rallies, believed in the issues, and was one of the three arrested that evening for charging the state troopers. Now the university is convening disciplinary hearings to decide if Randy and the others will be expelled."

"I didn't hear that." Sharon propped her head on a pillow.

"The announcement will be published Monday. But at least Randy was involved in UNITED long enough to realize—if he'd asked questions—what was happening. Haley Hunt, the coed on the Quad, is a scarier case. So naïve, not comprehending how the activists manipulated her and the student body, a metaphor for our generation."

"Errors and regrets," She said dryly, "seems we've discussed this before."

"You're right, I blame myself. If I'd pushed to print my article rather than let it sit in a locker in Men's Old Gym, maybe the story would have ended on the upbeat. I could've used the truth to switch more minds than Haley's, and maybe Randy wouldn't be in such heavy trouble. That's why, when I'm a TA in grad school, I'll show our fellow students there's more to care about than ourselves, other people matter."

"Sounds noble, but I don't believe you." Sharon hopped away from Paul and tugged the blanket, separating her body from his. "This is another cop-out. You don't want to leave college or face life. The only idea in your mind is to hide in school, isolated from the world."

"That's unfair. I admit I'm liable the anti-war movement's so solid on our campus, nowhere near as guilty as Bernard Minerath and his True Believers—but at fault. I should have acted responsibly earlier, understood Stef was involved in UNITED's plot, and contacted the *News-Gazette* instead of sitting alone in a park. And, yes, I enjoy my time in Champaign, who doesn't? I don't see your packed bags sitting at the curb on California Street."

"My studying veterinary medicine is altogether different, a dream since high school, what I've prepared for in four years at the University of Illinois. As for you, you're tricking yourself with willy-nilly scruples. Talk of aiding others when you're a TA sounds virtuous, but I question your sincerity."

"This tears me apart. The whole school year, Lindy and you have demanded I take a stand. Now I act, and you're mad."

"Don't you get it this isn't a decision, only more equivocation? The time for conscience was last month when everybody protested the war in the streets. Maybe we've been deceived, but the cause is worthy, the student body's intentions honest. We are on the right side. And Paul Roberts? You had evidence to affect the outcome but waffled. Today you're vacillating again, ignoring reality, supposing with a little reflection, confession, and an extra one or two years of Champaign-Urbana, you'll remedy your life."

Paul laid on his ribs, facing Sharon. He thought he'd reached a conclusion and knew his future. Optimistic when he'd told his girlfriend, her

Summer Never Comes

so negative judgment staggered him. Always logical, where was the mistake she perceived but Paul missed?

His girlfriend's eyes were shut. He listened to her breathing, wanted to touch Sharon's arm or play with her hair, but hesitated. Paul rolled to the other side of the mattress.

# # # #

Lindy took Andy Arthur's call in the early afternoon.

A record producer from California, some dude named Floater, had latched onto a tape of the music Andy had written for their old band, Frogfeet. Mr. Floater phoned, said he liked the melodies, and invited Andy to a meeting next month when he was in the Midwest. Nothing definite, no promises, but at least his buddy was catching a break. So Lindy, Andy and a bunch of Cham-Bana musicians celebrated the songwriter's good fortune, partying hard at the Red Lion, running the Jerg nuts behind the bar, dancing with dozens of women and shutting the place down.

After breakfast at Uncle John's Pancake House, a wiped-out Lindy staggered into KIDs around three a.m. He remembered his roommate, Robby, was in some motel room in a double bed laying and loving Sharon. Lucky bastard. Floundering in the foyer, Lindy spotted a single envelope in his mailbox. Stumbling, he grabbed for it. Postmarked 'Chicago, Illinois,' the return address was 4522 N. Oketo Avenue, Billy Powell's house. He collapsed on the stairs and ripped the letter open, focusing on the words as best he could in his totally inebriated condition.

Mrs. Powell, Billy's mom, wrote her son was reported missing in action in Vietnam. She wanted Lindy and all the KIDs to know.

Made in the USA
Charleston, SC
01 February 2014